Prisoners be damned. Stupidity that profound carried the death penalty.

Time.

She unlatched the door and slammed it outward, using all her strength and what mass she could bring to bear while still seated. Her tremendous strength hadn't been affected at all by the body nanotech transformation, and while the few extra kilos that had been added might slow her down a bit—though not much—they also added a little mass to the equation.

The edge of the door caught the robber in the middle of his face. The impact crushed his nose, shattered his jaw, knocked out most of his teeth, broke his skull and neck in the doing and sent his body flying for several meters. The corpse almost completed a back flip before it hit the surface of the street.

One of the robbers started firing almost at once. Thandi was impressed by his alertness and readiness.

His marksmanship, on the other hand, was execrable. All the darts sailed way too high, some of them not hitting the cab at all. Even the ones that did would have gone over Thandi's head.

If she'd been dumb enough to leave her head there in the first place, which of course she didn't. As soon as she felt the impact of the door on the robber she'd thrown herself out of the cab.

She immediately rolled under her lorry when she hit the surface—there was just enough clearance—came to a prone firing position and started shooting with her pistol. Which *was* military grade, thank you very much.

Her marksmanship was...

Almost perfect.

In the HONORVERSE by DAVID WEBER

Honor Harrington series:
On Basilisk Station • *The Honor of the Queen*
• *The Short Victorious War* • *Field of Dishonor* •
Flag in Exile • *Honor Among Enemies* • *In Enemy
Hands* • *Echoes of Honor* • *Ashes of Victory* •
War of Honor • *At All Costs* • *Mission of Honor*
• *A Rising Thunder* • *Shadow of Freedom*

Crown of Slaves series (with Eric Flint):
Crown of Slaves • *Torch of Freedom*
• *Cauldron of Ghosts*

Star Kingdom series:
A Beautiful Friendship • *Fire Season* (with Jane
Lindskold) • *Treecat Wars* (with Jane Lindskold)

Manticore Ascendant series (with Timothy Zahn):
A Call to Duty • *A Call to Arms*

Other Honorverse novels:
The Shadow of Saganami
Storm from the Shadows

House of Steel (with BuNine)

Anthologies, edited by David Weber:
More than Honor • *Worlds of Honor* •
Changer of Worlds • *The Service of the Sword*
• *In Fire Forged* • *Beginnings*

Also by DAVID WEBER and ERIC FLINT:
1633 • *1634: The Baltic War*

For a complete listing of Baen titles by David Weber
and by Eric Flint, please go to www.baen.com.

CAULDRON OF GHOSTS

An Honorverse Novel

DAVID WEBER & ERIC FLINT

BAEN

CAULDRON OF GHOSTS

This is a work of fiction. All the characters and events portrayed in this book are fictional, and any resemblance to real people or incidents is purely coincidental.

A Baen Books Original

Baen Publishing Enterprises
P.O. Box 1403
Riverdale, NY 10471
www.baen.com

ISBN: 978-1-4767-8100-6

Cover art by David Mattingly

First Baen mass market paperback printing, November 2015

Distributed by Simon & Schuster
1230 Avenue of the Americas
New York, NY 10020

Pages by Joy Freeman (www.pagesbyjoy.com)
Printed in the United States of America

To Jim Baen, who gave writers chances.
We miss you.

May 1922 Post Diaspora

"Lot of help that is too. Victor can turn almost anything into splinters."

—Yana Tretiakovna, Torch secret agent

CHAPTER 1

"So now what?" asked Yana Tretiakovna. She leaned back in her comfortable armchair, her arms crossed over her chest, and bestowed an impressive glower upon Anton Zilwicki and Victor Cachat. The first of whom was perched on a seat as he scrutinized a comp screen; the other of whom was slouched in an armchair and looking almost as disgruntled as Yana.

"I don't know," said Cachat, almost muttering the words. "I've been trying to get an answer to that very question from"—his finger pointed to the ceiling—"unnamable but no doubt exalted figures on high."

Taken literally, the gesture might have led to the conclusion that the hard-bitten atheist Victor Cachat had suddenly become a believer, since there was nothing beyond the ceiling other than the heavens. The large suite the three people were sharing was on the top floor of a former luxury hotel in Haven's capital that had been been sequestered for its own purposes decades earlier by the Legislaturalist secret police. After the revolution—the most recent one, that is—the new regime had tried but failed to find the rightful owners, since they'd all died or vanished. So, not knowing what else to do, they'd turned it into a combination safe house and luxury resort for guests of the government.

Clearly, though, Cachat was oblivious to the irony involved. Still half-muttering with disgust, he went on. "So far, I might as well have been putting the question to a streetlight. Except a lamp post would at least shed some light."

Anton's mouth quirked wryly. "I'm pretty sure the question you should be asking is 'where,' not 'what.'" He pointed to something on the screen. "See that?"

Ennui was shoved aside by interest, as Victor and Yana both rose from their chairs and came over to look at the screen.

"And what the hell is *that*?" demanded Tretiakovna. "It looks like scrambled eggs on steroids."

"It's an astrogational display showing traffic to and from the planet," said Cachat. "And that exhausts my knowledge of the matter. I can't really interpret it."

Yana stared at the screen again. The ex-Scrag looked rather alarmed.

"Do you mean to tell me that this is how orbital controllers guide spacecraft to a supposedly—ha, ha, I'm dying of laughter here—safe orbit or landing? If so, I'm never flying again. Not even a kite."

"Relax, Yana," said Anton. "They don't use this sort of condensed display at all—leaving aside the fact that all orbital routes are selected and monitored by computers. No, I slapped this together just to see if my guess was right, which is that traffic is being shifted around to allow for some sudden and unscheduled departures."

He pointed to . . . this and that and the other, all of which looked like nothing much of anything to his two companions. "Think of these as boltholes, if you will."

Victor and Yana looked at each other, then down at Anton.

"So who's bolting?" asked Yana.

Zilwicki heaved his massive shoulders. For someone built along normal human rather than dwarf lord lines, that would have been a shrug.

"How should I know?" he said. "Victor will have to find out from his unnamable but no doubt exalted figures on high."

Yana said something in a Slavic-sounding language that was almost certainly unprintable. Victor, a bit of a prude when it came to coarse language, kept his response to: "Well, hell." And a second or two later: "Hell's bells."

❖   ❖   ❖

Luckily for the dispositions of Cachat and Tretia-kovna, relief from uncertainty came a few minutes later, in the persons of Kevin Usher and Wilhelm Trajan. Usher was the head of the Federal Investigation Agency, Haven's top domestic police force; Trajan, the head of the Republic's foreign intelligence agency, the Foreign Intelligence Service.

Yana let them into the room, in response to the buzzer. As soon as they entered, Cachat rose to his feet.

"Kevin," he said, in a neutral tone. Then, nodding to Trajan: "Boss."

"Not anymore," said Wilhelm. He glanced around, spotted an empty chair, and slid into it. Once seated, he molded himself into the chair's contours, as someone does who is finally able to relax after a long period of tension.

"You're being reassigned to the foreign office," he elaborated. "No longer part of the FIS."

He did not seem dismayed at losing the services of the man whom knowledgeable people, including himself, thought to be Haven's most brilliantly capable intelligence agent. When President Pritchart had notified him of her decision to transfer Cachat, Wilhelm's reaction had been: *You mean I can go back to running a spy outfit, instead of being a lion tamer?*

Usher took a seat some distance away from Trajan. "It's one hell of a promotion, Victor. If you, ah, look at it in the right light."

Victor gave him a dark look. "Under very dim lighting, you mean."

Kevin's expression, in response, was exasperated. "Oh, for God's sake, Victor! No, I don't mean using night goggles. I mean bright—really, really, really bright— floodlights. Your days of creeping around in the shadows are over. *Over*—with a bang and a boom. O-V-E-R."

Trajan's tone was milder. "Be realistic, Victor. Your exploits in launching Torch almost blew your cover completely as it was. They left it pretty tattered. Now, after Mesa? You—and Anton, and Yana"—he nodded in their direction—"just brought back the biggest intelligence coup in galactic history for...oh, hell, who knows how many centuries? Do you really think there's any chance you can stay in your old line of work? Even using nanotech facial and body transformations won't help you, since they don't disguise DNA. Sure, that'd probably be enough for a modest, barely known sort of spy. But you? Anybody who thinks you might be coming their way will have DNA swabs taken of anybody who might *remotely* be you."

"StateSec destroyed all my DNA records except theirs the day I graduated from the Academy," said Victor. "Those are still closely guarded and I've been very careful not to scatter my DNA traces about." His tone of voice was perhaps a bit peevish.

"True enough," said Anton. "You won't find Special Officer Cachat carelessly discarding a cup after he's taken a drink from it, I will grant you that. But come on, Victor—you know the realities perfectly well. As long as you were obscure and nobody was *looking* for your DNA, those precautions were probably good enough. But *today*?"

"Exactly," said Trajan. He nodded toward the window overlooking Nouveau Paris. "Word's already leaked out to the press. Within a couple of days—a week, at the outside—your name and likeness will be known to every person on Haven above the age of five and with any interest at all in the news. As well as—more to the point—every intelligence service in the galaxy, each and every one of which will be trying to get their hands on your DNA traces. Sooner or later, at least some of them are bound to succeed. So give it up. And don't bother arguing with me or Kevin about it, either. President Pritchart made the decision. If you want it overturned, you'll have to figure out a way to get her out of office."

Usher wiped his face with a large hand. "Wilhelm, he gets enough ideas on his own without you making suggestions."

Trajan looked startled. "What? I wasn't—" Then he looked alarmed. "Officer Cachat . . ."

"I wasn't planning to organize a coup d'état," Victor said sarcastically. "I *am* a patriot, you know. Besides, I don't blame the President for the decision."

The dark look came back. "Clearly, she was misled by evil advisers."

Anton started laughing softly. "Ganny warned you, Victor. It'll be your turn now for the video treatment! I'd have some sympathy except I don't recall you ever showing any for me because *my* cover got blown."

Zilwicki looked over at Tretiakovna. "What's your guess, Yana? Ganny thought the news services would go for either 'Cachat, Slaver's Bane' or 'Black Victor.'"

"'Black Victor,'" she replied instantly. "Give Cachat his due, he isn't prone to histrionics. 'Slaver's Bane' is just too...too...not Victor. Besides, look at him."

Cachat's expression was now very dark indeed.

"'Black Victor,' it is," announced Zilwicki. "Victor, you need to buy some new clothes. All leather, neck to ankles. Black leather, it goes without saying."

For a moment, it looked as if Cachat might explode. At the very least, spout some heavy-duty profanity. But...

He didn't. Anton wasn't surprised. Victor's deeds were so flamboyant that it was easy to forget that the man behind them was not flamboyant at all. In fact, he was rather modest—and extraordinarily self-disciplined.

So, all that finally came out, in a very even and flat tone of voice, was: "Where am I being assigned, then? I'll warn you, if it's someplace that has an active cocktail circuit, I won't be any good at it. I don't drink much. Ever."

"S'true," said Yana. "He's boring, boring, boring. Well, except when he's overturning regimes and stuff like that." She actually giggled, something Anton had never heard her do before. "Cocktail circuit! Diplomatic small talk! I can see it already!"

Victor now looked long-suffering. For his part, Usher looked exasperated again.

"We are not morons," he said. "Victor, you—and you and you"—his forefinger swiveled like a turret gun, coming to bear on Anton and Yana—"are all going to Manticore. Tomorrow, so get packed."

Anton had been planning to get to Manticore anyway, and as soon as possible. He hadn't seen his lover Cathy Montaigne in more than a year. He hadn't yet come up with a way to do so that the many and manifold powers-that-be were likely to approve, though, and now it had been unexpectedly dropped in his lap.

He saw Victor glance at him and smile. There was real warmth in that smile, too, something you didn't often get from the man. Not for the first time, Anton was struck by the unlikely friendship that had grown up between him and the Havenite agent. Unlikely—yet all the stronger, perhaps, because of that very fact.

There were people in the world whom Anton liked more than he did Victor. But there were very, very few whom he trusted as much.

"And in what capacity am I going?" he asked Usher. "Somehow, even with all this new-found cordiality, I doubt that I've been assigned to Haven's foreign service."

Usher gave him a grin. "By all accounts—I was on Old Earth, remember, when the Manpower Incident went down—no star system in its right mind would assign you to its diplomatic corps."

"Yes, I remember."

It was hardly something Anton would forget. Nothing official had ever been said, and to this day Victor refused to cross any t's and dot any i's. Nonetheless, Anton was quite certain that Kevin Usher had engineered the entire episode. He'd stayed in the background, letting Cachat and the Audubon Ballroom do the rough work, but his had been the guiding hand.

Zilwicki's daughter Helen—no, all three of his children, since he'd adopted Berry and Lars afterward— were still alive because of Victor and Kevin. It was a reminder, if he needed one, that just because he didn't share someone's ideology didn't mean they didn't take it seriously themselves. Haven's political ideals were not Anton's—well, some of them were—but it had been those ideals that had shielded his family.

Suddenly, he was in a very good mood. No one in Manticore might yet know it, but the information he and Victor had brought back from Mesa was going to have an enormous impact. If things worked out the way he strongly suspected Eloise Pritchart had in mind, it would not only have ended the galaxy's longest and most savagely fought war but actually turned two bitter enemies into allies. Uneasy and hesitant allies, perhaps, but allies nonetheless. That information had also turned a friendship right side up. All the wariness and reservations he'd had to maintain about Victor Cachat were now draining away. Rapidly, too.

Something in Victor's expression made it clear that he understood that also. But all he said was: "True enough. I may be a problem child for the diplomatically inclined, but Anton gives them nightmares."

"You still haven't answered my question, Kevin," said Anton.

Usher shrugged. "How the hell should I know? All I was told by Eloise was to round up all three of you—and Herlander Simões, of course—and take you to Manticore. Victor, you're not exactly reassigned to the foreign service." He gave Trajan a reproving glance. "Wilhelm was overstating things a bit. For one thing, Leslie Montreau was in the room along with Tom Theisman when Eloise made the decision to yank you out of the FIS. She nodded quite vigorously when Tom said that maybe she didn't want—his words, not mine—'that lunatic bull in a china shop' in her department."

"What's a china shop?" asked Yana.

"It's an antique phrase," Anton explained. "'China' was a name for a fancy kind of what they called . . . porcelain, if I remember right."

"Lot of help that is. So what's porcelain?"

"Stuff that Victor could turn into splinters easily."

"Lot of help that is too. Victor can turn almost anything into splinters."

Victor waved them down impatiently. "So to whom *am* I assigned, then?"

Usher scratched his scalp. "Well . . . no one, really. Eloise just thinks having you on Manticore will be essential to firming up the new alliance."

"Why? Anton knows as much as I do—and he's Manticoran to begin with."

Usher was starting to look exasperated again. Zilwicki interjected himself into the discussion.

"That's sort of the whole point, Victor. I'm a known quantity, in the Star Kingdom. I've even had a personal audience with the Empress. You, on the other hand, are a complete *un*known. Well, almost. I think Duchess Harrington has a good sense of you. But no one else does, in Manticore."

Cachat was staring at him, obviously in complete incomprehension. It was odd, the way such a supremely capable man could be so oblivious to his own stature. That was a feature of Victor that Anton found simultaneously attractive and rather scary. In the right (or wrong) circumstances, people with little in the way of egos—more precisely, little concern for their egos—could do . . .

Pretty much anything.

"Just take my word for it, will you? They'll want to see you, and talk to you, before they'll settle down with any information you bring to them."

"What he said." Usher rose from his chair. "Oh seven hundred, tomorrow morning. Be down in the lobby, packed and ready to go."

Trajan rose also, and went to the door. "Have a nice trip," was what he said. What he meant, of course, was "have a nice *long* trip." And there seemed to be a little spring in his step, as if a great weight had finally been lifted from his shoulders.

CHAPTER 2

"Well, it would have been nice if they'd given us another week or so to complete our preparations, but I guess you can't expect too much from slavers." Colonel Nancy Anderson tapped her bottom teeth a few times with a thumbnail, in an unconscious mannerism that her subordinates had labeled *grief-unto-others*.

The "others" not being them, however, they were not perturbed by the gesture. Anderson was something of a martinet compared to most officers in Beowulf's Biological Survey Corps, but that wasn't saying much. The BSC was an intensely disciplined organization, but that was scarcely evident to those more familiar with other military services. Despite the innocuous sounding name, the BSC *was* a military outfit—one of the galaxy's elite special forces, in fact—but it had precious little time for the spit-and-polish formality so near and dear to conventional military minds. The BSC was quite capable of performing military theater with the best of them; when it came to doing its actual *job*, however, its personnel were much more of the roll-up-your-sleeves-and-get-on-with-it persuasion.

"How do you want to handle it, Nancy?" asked her XO, Commander Loren Damewood. He was lounging back in a seat at one of the com stations, studying the data on the screen more intently than his relaxed posture and lazy tone of voice would indicate. "Their transponder's showing one of the flagged Jessyk Line codes. They've used it before—though maybe not this particular ship—when they did business here."

Colonel Anderson understood his point. Slavers didn't randomly show up at stations whose control was unknown to them. And just to make sure nothing had changed since they or another ship in their company last showed up, they'd use seemingly innocuous transponder codes. Knocking at the door, as it were, with a special rhythm.

"They've got a cargo on board, then."

Damewood nodded. "And that's a two-million-ton ship, according to the sensors, so it's probably a pretty big one."

That precluded the simple and straightforward measure of disintegrating the oncoming slaver ship with Parmley Station's disguised but very powerful grasers once it got close enough. "Cargo" was a euphemism, dealing with slavers. The term meant human beings, alive and . . . certainly not well, given the realities of their situation, but still very far from dead.

"Plan C?" suggested a third officer in the command station. That was Ayibongwinkosi Kabweza, the commander of the Torch army's assault troops aboard Parmley Station.

Colonel Anderson took a moment to consider the question. She had no previous experience working with Torch military units and wanted to be sure she didn't handle the issue improperly.

The Biological Survey Corps had asked the government of Torch to provide them with a battalion for service on Parmley Station once it became clear that their plans for the station simply needed more forces than the BSC itself could provide. For all its wealth and power, Beowulf was still a one-star system and a member of the Solarian League. While the Beowulf System Defense Force was unusually large and powerful for a League member system, thanks to the existence of the Beowulf Terminus of the Manticoran Wormhole Junction, it had never needed—or maintained—a large army. Instead, it had concentrated on maintaining one whose quality was excellent, and its modest size had allowed it to be picky about the personnel it recruited and then equip them with the very best. Given the heightened political tensions of recent years, Beowulf had increased its military spending considerably, but the priority was to fully modernize its naval forces first. At least for the time being, Beowulf's available ground and marine forces remained sparse.

They'd made the request for assistance from Torch a little reluctantly. The training, methods and tactics of Torch's army units had been shaped by Thandi Palane and were based on those of the Solarian Marines, which were in many respects quite different from those of Beowulf's military, especially the BSC. Not only that, but the Royal Torch Army was still very much a work in progress, feeling its way towards its own sense of identity and organic traditions.

With no real experience to go on, it was hard to assess how well the two forces would work together. To make things still trickier, like many newly formed units, Torch's assault troops were likely to have a chip on their shoulder when dealing with forces that had been long-established. They would detect patronizing attitudes in every careless or misspoken phrase.

If Colonel Anderson chose to employ Plan C, it would be Lieutenant Colonel Kabweza and her soldiers who would carry it out. Plan C had the nickname among her BSC agents of Plan Biggest Hammer Around. If the Torch battalion she commanded shared any of the traditions and attitudes of Solarian Marines—which they were bound to, since both Palane and Kabweza came out of that military force—they would apply ferocious shock tactics in a boarding operation. The Beowulfan military, like that of Manticore, was highly skeptical of the Solarian Navy's reputation, especially that of Battle Fleet. Not so, however, of the Solarian Marines. Unlike Battle Fleet officers and crews, who could easily go through an entire career without seeing any combat at all, the Marines were a real fighting force.

It was tempting. Slaver crews, no matter how vigilant and well-armed, had no more chance of resisting a full-bore close assault by Torch units trained to Solarian Marine standards than vigilant and toothy mice had of resisting bobcats. There wasn't even much chance that the cargo would get harmed, so swiftly and savagely would the attack be driven through.

Still, there was some chance. All it would take would be for one of the slaver ship's officers on the bridge to trigger the slave evacuation procedures. The cargo would be forced out of their compartments by poison gas and expelled into vacuum. There would be no logic to doing so, since under the circumstances there was no way the slaver crew could pretend they hadn't been carrying slaves. Some of the corpses would even be drifting in sight of the Station. But the slavers might figure that they were doomed anyway—not without some reason, being honest—and choose to commit an act of mass murder as a twisted form of reprisal. God knew the slave trade attracted enough sadists and sociopaths! Indeed, one might say that those were two of the trade's more essential qualities.

But even if no harm came to the cargo, there was no chance that Torch assault troops would leave any of the crew alive. Their tactics, like those of Solarian Marines, would lean entirely toward *eliminate the threat*, not taking prisoners. Not to mention that the majority of Torch's assault troops had once been slaves themselves, and somewhere around one-third were former members of the Audubon Ballroom. Their hatred for slavers would be personal and deep. No matter how well disciplined they were, their tendency would always be to give no quarter.

Anderson shook her head. "No, Ayi, I don't think so. This will be our first operation since we transformed Parmley Station into a fortress. If possible, I want to get some intelligence out of it."

The skepticism on the lieutenant colonel's face was obvious, but Kabweza didn't say anything. However prickly they might be in some respects, Torch assault troops had been trained by Thandi Palane. Unlike some Beowulfan units, they would not be inclined to debate orders they disagreed with.

"We'll try Plan F," said Anderson. "We may as well find out now just how effective our new countersensor techniques are." Seeing the expression on Kabweza's face, Anderson smiled and said: "Oh, fine, Ayi. If it'll make you happy, we'll use your people as backup instead of Loren's usual crew."

She cocked an eye at Damewood. "If that's all right with you, XO."

"Huh." Damewood gave Kabweza a look from lowered brows. "A *small* number, Ayi. And nobody trigger-happy."

"None of my people are 'trigger-happy,'" said the lieutenant colonel. "We just don't suffer from the BSC's habitual slackness when it comes to smiting evildoers."

That got a laugh from everyone on the bridge. Kabweza waved her hand in what might have been called a conciliatory gesture. "I'll head up the section myself, just to keep you from getting nervous."

The ship's captain and executive officer bestowed upon her the sort of look naval officers might give to a lieutenant commander who'd just announced she was going to assign some perfunctory duty to herself instead of an ensign.

"I need the exercise," Kabweza issued by way of explanation.

That elicited another laugh. The lieutenant colonel looked to be as much out of shape as a lioness hunting on the savannah. She wasn't nearly as big as Thandi Palane, but she'd passed through the same rigorous regimen in the Solarian Marines.

"It's true," she insisted.

Damewood rose from his chair. Unfolded from his seat, it might be better to say. The XO seemed to have a skeleton with considerably more bones than any member of the human species had a right to. There were rumors that he was the product of dark experiments done in complete violation of Beowulf's code of biological ethics.

No one really believed the rumors. Still, they never quite died away.

"I'll get my gear." He glanced at a different com screen which showed another ship already docked to the station. "How about the *Hali Sowle*? They could make a useful diversion if Ganny's willing to stick her neck out a little itsy-bitsy teeny tiny bit."

"I heard that, smart-ass." Elfriede Margarete Butry— the "Ganny" in question—was slouched in a seat next to the bridge's entrance in a manner that seemed even more boneless than the one Damewood had assumed. In her defense, despite looking like a woman in her late thirties or early forties, she was better than twice the XO's age.

The matriarch of the clan that had once owned Parmley Station rose to her feet and planted hands on her hips. "Just what did you have in mind, Loren?" she demanded. She was rather formidable-looking, despite being less than one hundred and fifty centimeters tall. "*Exactly* in mind, I'm talking about. None of your damn BSC hand-waving bullshit."

Damewood smiled. "Nothing fancy, Ganny. It'd just be nice to have you pulling away from the station right as this new ship is arriving and cursing a blue streak on an open frequency. You could even directly warn the incoming people that they're about to be fleeced by the greediest and most unscrupulous bastards this side of Betelgeuse."

He paused, his eyebrows rising as if he'd been struck by a sudden thought. "You *do* know how to curse, don't you?"

Her reply put to rest any doubts he might have had—or anyone this side of Betelgeuse, for that matter.

✧   ✧   ✧

"Will you listen to this?" Ondøej Montoya, the *Ramathibodi*'s com officer was grinning widely. "This kind of talent shouldn't be hidden under a bushel."

He pushed a button and the transmission he'd been receiving was broadcast into the bridge.

The ship's captain frowned slightly. She found Montoya's habit of using archaic references rather annoying. What the hell was a bushel? But the frown faded quickly enough, as she listened to the broadcast. Before long, she was grinning herself.

"—*une vraie salope!* And as for you, dickless, I wouldn't wish you on a Melbourne humpmonkey! Although you'd probably do okay with my second cousin Odom—that's short for Sodom; his family dropped the 's' after his third conviction for fumbled rape, on account of he'd become an embarrassment to them—when he gets out of prison in maybe fifty or sixty years. I'll make sure to tell him to look you up although I doubt you'll still be alive by then, the way you swindle people."

Captain Tsang chuckled. "What's she so riled up about?"

Montoya shrugged. "Hard to tell, exactly. Near as I can make out, she thinks they overcharged her for everything and didn't give her anywhere near a fair price for her own goods."

Marième Tsang studied the image of the ship slowly receding from the huge bulk of Parmley Station. "She doesn't look to be carrying our sort of cargo, although you never know. What's the name of that ship?"

"The *Hali Sowle*." The com officer shook his head. "I couldn't find her registered in our data banks. But..." He shrugged again.

That didn't mean anything. Vessels plying the slave trade—even those which weren't carrying slaves themselves—did their best to stay off registries. From the look of the ship, she was just a tramp freighter who'd probably arrived at the Station more by accident than design. But as Captain Tsang had said, it was impossible to be sure without examining the vessel's interior.

Captain Tsang wasn't too worried about being swindled herself. Parmley Station was a known if unofficial transit hub for the slave trade, and the *Ramathibodi* was *not* a tramp. She was owned—not formally, of course—by the Jessyk Combine, one of Manpower's many subsidiaries. The people running Parmley would no doubt drive a hard bargain, but they'd keep it within limits or run the risk of losing most of their business over time.

Which brought to mind...

"Who *is* running Parmley these days, Ondøej? We haven't come through here in...what's it been now? Two T-years?"

"More like two and a half." Montoya worked at the console for a moment, pulling up another screen and scanning it for a few seconds. "According to this, the station is currently held by Orion Transit Enterprises. It says here that that's a subsidiary of an outfit based in Sheba's Junction named Andalaman Exports. For whatever any of that's worth."

"Not much," grunted Tsang. Sheba's Junction was hundreds of light-years away, almost on the other side

of human-occupied space. She didn't know anything
about the system beyond the name, and the only reason
she knew that was because it was unusual.

By now, the *Hali Sowle* had moved far enough away
from Parmley Station to no longer pose a traffic hazard.

"Get us a docking approach, Lieutenant Montoya,"
Tsang ordered, shifting for the moment into formalities.

"Yes, Ma'am," replied Montoya. One of the things
the captain liked about the ship's com officer, despite
some of his annoying habits, was the fact that he
didn't abuse the slackness that characterized relations
between officers and crew members on a slave ship.

The inevitable slackness, given the self-indulgence
of slaver ship companies' that was one of the perks
of the business. "Running a tight ship" was simply
impossible, under those circumstances. All a captain
could aim for was to maintain the necessary compe-
tence at the work itself.

Montoya was competent. So was the *Ramathibodi's*
pilot. Docking would take at least half an hour and
Tsang wasn't needed for any of it. So, she slouched
back in the seat at her command station and pulled
up her financial records. Studying them—basking in
them, rather; gloating over them—was her favorite
form of relaxation.

CHAPTER 3

Loren Damewood finished keying in the sequence he was using from his specialized software. Through his fingertips, he could feel the vibration of the locks opening. The sensations were very slight, of course, since he was wearing a skinsuit and gauntlets. If he'd been inside the ship instead of in the vacuum outside, that would have made an audible noise. Not a loud one, so it wouldn't be noticed by anyone aboard the *Ramathibodi* unless they were standing nearby. That was unlikely, though. Damewood had deliberately picked a cargo bay personnel hatch, and cargo bays tended to be big, empty, boring spaces unfrequented by crew people unless there was actual cargo to be transferred. And the only sort of "cargo" which would be transshipped at someplace like Parmley Station was highly unlikely to come from a standard bay like this one.

Still, he was miffed. There shouldn't have been *any* noise, if proper maintenance had been done.

But he wasn't surprised. "Proper maintenance" and "slave ship" were not terms that went together very often. There wasn't much difference between the sort

23

of people who served on the crews of pirate ships and those who worked on slavers. A few pirate captains managed to maintain tight discipline on their ship, but most didn't even try. Neither did slaver captains.

And there was a bright side. Cruddy maintenance usually went along with cruddy security, at least for anything except critical systems.

The hatch that he and his companions were gathered around began to slide open. Damewood's program wasn't doing that directly. If it had, telltales would be showing on the bridge that someone was almost certain to spot. Instead, his specialized software had insinuated itself into the ship's own operating programs. The *Ramathibodi* was opening that hatch itself, with the added modification that it was doing so without triggering any telltales or alarms.

"In we go," he murmured. To himself only, of course—all coms were silenced.

He didn't lead the way into the ship. That would have been silly, with Ayibongwinkosi Kabweza and her people present. He was the tech expert in charge of disabling security, not one of the assault troop gorillas.

The lieutenant colonel slipped through the hatch as soon as it had opened far enough to make that possible. The three members of her section had finished passing through before the hatch had time to fully open.

Loren waited until the hatch finished moving before he entered the airlock behind them. "Trigger-happy gorillas," he murmured. To himself only, of course.

Once they were in the airlock, they had to wait while Damewood's program cycled it through the process. It had been a vacuum when they entered; by the time they exited, the atmosphere would match that of the ship.

❖   ❖   ❖

In Parmley Station's number one cargo bay, Nancy Anderson and two members of her team faced the captain of the *Ramathibodi*. She'd brought five members of her own crew to the parley.

The cargo bay was a big one for a station which had not originally been intended as a freight transfer point. Designed to accommodate the sometimes large equipment items required by a space-going amusement park, it was slightly over thirty meters in its longest dimension. The slavers had advanced a third of the way in before coming to a stop. They were now separated from the BSC trio by a distance of about seven meters.

"What's your pleasure?" Anderson asked. "Full transshipment, partial—or are you just looking for supplies and R and R?"

"What R and R?" That came from one of the slaver crewmen standing a little behind Captain Tsang. It was a sarcastic remark, not a question.

"This *is* the biggest amusement park within fifty light-years." Nancy's lips twisted into a little smile. "Even if most of the rides don't work."

"Shut up, Grosvenor," said the *Ramathibodi*'s captain. To Anderson she said: "Partial transshipment. We've got more labor techs than we can sell, where we're going. May as well drop them off here."

The fact that the *Ramathibodi* only wanted a partial transshipment set the tactical parameters of the situation. If they'd been looking for a full transshipment, the BSC team could have simply waited until all the slaves were off the ship before launching their attack. Instead, it would be more complicated.

Anderson nodded. "Anything you want to pick up?"

"Pleasure units, if you have any. Those are always easy to sell. Heavy labor units, too."

"Heavy labor units, we've got. Pleasure units..." She paused, before smiling nastily. "That depends on what you're willing to pay."

"I'd want to see 'em first."

"Well, sure." Anderson gestured toward the heavy battle steel box attached to one of the compartment's bulkheads by a maglock. "But why don't we start with the labor tech transaction?"

Tsang shrugged. "Whatever suits you."

Anderson wanted to give Loren Damewood and Ayibongwinkosi Kabweza as much time as possible to get into position and prepare their attack. The dickering and exchanges needed to complete the first transaction should provide them with plenty.

She and the *Ramathibodi*'s captain moved forward to stand beside the steel box. For obvious reasons, the sort of electronic transfers that were the normal method of paying for goods and services were unsuitable for the slave trade, except in very secure locations like Mesa itself. Instead, recourse was made to more ancient forms of payment, involving the modern equivalent of cash transfers.

Such transfers were sometimes needed in perfectly legitimate businesses, so a well-developed and secure method for conducting them had been worked out centuries earlier. The method relied on the use of credit chips issued by one or another recognized major bank, usually though not always a bank headquartered on Old Earth itself.

Anderson keyed in the combination to unlock the battle steel box, and its lid slid smoothly upward.

Inside was a large number of credit chips, issued by the Banco de Madrid of Old Earth. Each of those chips was a wafer of molecular circuitry embedded inside a matrix of virtually indestructible plastic. That wafer contained a bank validation code, a numerical value, and a security key whose security was probably better protected than the Solarian League Navy's central computer command codes. Any attempt to change the value programmed into it when it was originally issued would trigger the security code and turn it into a useless, fused lump. Those chips were recognized as legal tender anywhere in the explored galaxy, but there was no way for anyone to track where they'd gone, or—best of all from the slavers' perspective—whose hands they'd passed through, since the day they'd been issued by the Banco de Madrid.

Captain Tsang leaned over far enough to examine the chips, but she didn't touch them. In fact, she was careful to keep her hands well away from the box. Any attempt to take the chips before the transaction was complete would result in a missing hand or two.

She took out a small portable device and aimed it in the direction of the chips, still being careful not to let either her hand or the unit come any nearer to the box than was necessary for the immediate purpose. She spent a few moments studying the readout; not long, just enough to verify that the chips were legitimate and that there were enough of them to cover any transactions they'd be carrying out that day.

That done, she turned to one of her subordinates and said, "Start bringing 'em out."

She then glanced around, looking for the needed exit from the compartment.

Anderson pointed to a hatch just to her left. "We'll file them through there."

As each slave passed through the hatch, Tsang's hand unit would record the amount owed until enough was reached to remove one of the chips from the box. There shouldn't be any dickering needed, not for labor techs.

Just to be on the safe side, though, she said: "We'll want standard Verge price."

"Not a problem," said Anderson, nodding.

Tsang took a couple of steps back from the box. The damn things made her nervous, even though she'd never heard of one malfunctioning.

That done, she relaxed. This looked to be a simple, straightforward matter, now that the preliminaries were done.

⋄　　　⋄　　　⋄

Trigger-happy gorillas or not, once they were inside the ship the small unit of assault troops waited for Loren to bring out more of his specialized equipment and scan the area.

"That way," he said softly. His pointing finger steered the section down the corridor branching off to the right.

The progress that followed was odd. The four assault troops moved forward quickly, leapfrogging down the corridor, one person providing cover while the others took more advanced positions. Meanwhile, in the rear—sometimes quite far to the rear—Damewood came up much more slowly. He wasn't precisely "moseying along," but an uncharitable observer might have used the term anyway.

Neither Kabweza nor any of her subordinates would

have done so, however. Indeed, the thought never crossed their minds. The XO had a reputation for being something of a wizard with his sensor gear. That ability could make a world of difference to the outcome of their mission. Torch assault troops might be the modern analog of Viking berserks, but analogy was not identity. More than three thousand years of civilization had elapsed, after all, since the legendary Ragnarr Loðbrók led his longships across the North Sea to plunder France and the British Isles.

"Two hatches up, on the left," Loren said. "That'll let us into the slave quarters through a storage compartment. It's unoccupied."

✧   ✧   ✧

It also turned out to be very full, almost to the point of being impassable without hauling supplies into the corridor, which would have been too time-consuming.

Not quite. It helped that the battle armor worn by the assault troops made it quite easy to crush whatever cartons, containers and cans needed to be crushed to clear a path.

One of those containers, as it happened, contained some sort of bright purple fruit juice. So it was on a garish note that they emerged into the slave quarters, as if they had camouflaged themselves to blend into a psychedelic landscape.

The compartment they entered was packed almost as full of people as the one they were exiting had been packed with supplies and equipment. The people were plastered against the walls, staring at them with wide-eyed alarm.

Kabweza had been expecting that, so she'd had Sergeant Supakrit X lead the way. As soon as he entered the slave quarters the sergeant opened the faceplate of his armor and stuck his tongue out.

Supakrit X was an escaped slave. His tongue displayed the genetic marker used by Manpower to identify their products. The marker was unique and difficult to duplicate—impossible, really, if it was examined at close quarters.

Which his marker was, almost immediately. A small young female slave came up to him, quite fearlessly, and pried his mouth further open with her fingers. Supakrit, who was much bigger than she was, leaned over to help her in the project. She gave the marker on his tongue a short but intense examination and then stepped back.

"It's real," she announced. "But they're not Ballroom, I'm pretty sure."

Supakrit straightened up and grinned. "Bunch of maniacs. No, girl, we're from the Royal Torch Army." He hooked a thumb at Commander Damewood. "We're working with the Biological Survey Corps."

Hearing that, one of the older male slaves grinned even more widely than the sergeant. Very few slaves had yet heard of the new former slaves' planet of Torch. But some slaves knew the truth—some of it, anyway—about the BSC. Apparently he was one.

The young woman was scowling, however. "Don't call me 'girl.'"

Kabweza moved forward. "Give us a name, then."

"Takahashi Ayako. You can call me Ayako."

The fact that she had a full name and was willing to use it publicly was significant. Manpower did not give names to its slaves. They were raised with the last three or four digits of their slave number serving the purpose. Over time, though, slaves managed to create a society of their own, with adoptive parents who took most youngsters into their shelter. Manpower's managers tolerated the practice, because it served their own purposes. It was simpler and cheaper to have slaves raise the youngsters who came out of the breeding vats instead of Manpower having to do it directly.

But while they tolerated the custom of slave families—and even made an effort not to break them up if possible—they did *not* tolerate the slaves doing so openly. A first name could be used publicly, including one chosen by the slave herself. After all, even animal pets had names. But a slave who used the surname of their parents in public was considered to be a borderline rebel and was likely to be punished.

Apparently, Ayako was such a borderline rebel—or someone acute enough to have realized almost instantly that Manpower's authority was about to be abrogated.

Despite the Japanese name and the placement of the surname first, Takahashi didn't look the least bit Oriental. Her eyes were hazel, her hair was a sort of redbrick color, and her skin was several shades darker than that of most people from East Asia.

But that wasn't atypical of human beings two thousand years after the diaspora from Earth began— even leaving aside the way Manpower's gengineers scrambled genetic lineages for their own purposes. One of Kabweza's trainers when she'd been in a Solarian Marines boot camp had been named Bjørn Haraldsson, despite to all outward appearances being of purely African descent.

"Are you here to free us?" asked the man who'd grinned in response to Supakrit X's announcement.

"Yes. But for the moment, we need you to just stay put," said Kabweza. After a very brief pause, she added: "Except for one of you who should come with us. That'll speed up the introduction."

"Me," Takahashi said immediately. "I know everybody. It's because I'm so friendly"—she gave Supakrit a sharp glance—"except when people call me 'girl.' Well, and other stuff."

She was an attractive young woman. She'd probably drawn the unwelcome attention of some of the slaver crew if there hadn't been enough pleasure slaves aboard.

Judging from the skeptical expressions on the faces of several of the slaves in the compartment, Takahashi's claim to superb friendliness was not universally shared. But if nothing else, the woman wasn't shy. That ought to be enough. Heavily-armed and very dangerous-looking people who arrive to free people from bondage don't really need much in the way of a friendly introduction, after all.

"Come with us, then." Ayibongwinkosi moved toward the hatch at the opposite end of the compartment. "The rest of you, like I said, just relax. This will all be over pretty soon."

❖   ❖   ❖

Kabweza's progress was slow. Not only was the compartment packed with people, but the same armor that had made it so easy to plow through containers required her to move carefully here. It would be easy to crush flesh and even break bones without hardly noticing.

Once at the hatch, she waited for Damewood to come up. Loren fiddled with his equipment for a few seconds. What exactly was he doing? Ayibongwinkosi didn't know and wasn't about to ask.

Click. The sound of the locks drawing back was quite audible.

"Slobs," muttered Damewood.

The likelihood that the slight sound had alerted anyone on the other side of the hatch was low. Still, Kabweza passed through the hatch by rolling and coming to a crouch, her flechette gun covering the area.

Clear. Still in a crouch, she swiveled the other way. The corridor was clear there also.

She gestured, waving the rest forward.

Takahashi was the last one to emerge. "Which way to the crew quarters?" the lieutenant colonel asked her softly. "Do you know?"

Ayako nodded and pointed in the direction Kabweza had first covered. "That way."

"Are you sure?"

The young woman got a pinched look on her face. "Yes," she said curtly. "I'm sure."

Ayibongwinkosi didn't inquire further. She nodded to Supakrit X and he took point.

CHAPTER 4

The labor tech units started arriving in ten minutes. The slaves shuffled into the compartment, their heads down and their eyes on the floor. Two of the slave ship's crew members herded them along with deactivated—for the moment—neural whips. The slavers were rather lackadaisical about it, though; clearly they weren't expecting any sort of trouble. The people being channeled through the compartment were genetic slaves who'd been born, bred and shaped by bondage. They had learned long ago that resistance simply led to suffering.

The expressions on their faces weren't so much despairing as simply blank. Despair was an emotion, after all—and Manpower's slaves discovered as children that emotions were dangerous to such as they. Those looks made Nancy furious, but she let no sign of her anger show on her own face.

After the first batch of slaves passed through the compartment, a green light on the box started flashing. While they'd been waiting for the slaves to arrive, Anderson and Tsang had programmed the box to record the right number of slaves for one chip.

"Go ahead," said Nancy. Gingerly, the *Ramathibodi's* captain reached into the box and removed one of the chips.

One chip only—and she was careful to lift that one out with just her thumb and forefinger. If the box sensed that more chips were being removed than had been properly accounted for, the lid would slam down and make sure the chips stayed inside—along with the hand that held them.

❖   ❖   ❖

When the slaves arrived at the open hatch that led into the rest of the Station, the two guards from the *Ramathibodi* relinquished control to three people from Parmley Station's contingent. Two of them were equipped with the same neural whips; the third was outfitted as a medical technician. She was there to give each arriving slave an examination to make sure no defectives were being pawned off on them.

She went about the business in a quick, almost perfunctory manner, giving each slave a scan with the medical detection device in her hand before they passed into the personnel tube beyond. The device would catch anything obvious, like a contagious disease or late-stage cancer.

It wouldn't spot more subtle problems, but those weren't of much concern. The sort of medical chicanery involved in passing off immediately defective units as healthy slaves was avoided in the slave trade as bad business. Contrary to the popular saw *there is no honor among thieves,* illegal or extra-legal transactions actually required a more punctilious attention to dealing in good faith—for the good and simple reason that no recourse to the courts was possible in the event of a dispute. That meant that such disputes were usually settled violently, which made everyone involved stay away from petty chiseling.

The other reason the medical technician didn't pay much attention was even simpler. Given the nature of Manpower's production methods, it was a given that a high percentage of their slaves would have some long-term medical problems. The sort of radical genetic engineering that created such slaves often produced unwanted side effects. A slave bred for great strength might have a severe blood pressure problem, for instance, or be prone to renal failure.

As a rule the lifespan of genetic slaves was shorter than that of most humans, even leaving aside the fact that such slaves were almost never given prolong to extend their lifespan. According to the Bible, *The days of our years are threescore years and ten*. Manpower, Inc., perhaps not wishing to seem presumptuously equal to the Lord, figured fifty or sixty years was plenty good enough for their products.

Once the medtech nodded her approval, each slave passed through the hatch into the personnel tube leading to their new quarters aboard Parmley Station. The two guards waiting inside shepherded them along. More precisely, lounged against the walls and occasionally waved them along in as perfunctory a manner as the medtech did her duties. They weren't worried about rebellion. The slaves knew perfectly well that a station like this one would have the same forced evacuation mechanisms that all slave ships did. If they rebelled successfully here in the compartments and corridors, someone in the inaccessible control room would just push a button and they'd all be expelled into vacuum.

✧   ✧   ✧

Lieutenant Colonel Ayibongwinkosi Kabweza and her team passed a total of eight hatches along the way before they finally arrived at a hatch that Ayako told them led into the crew's quarters. According to Ayako, at least six of the compartments they'd passed held slaves.

If she was disturbed by the fact that Kabweza made no effort to open those hatches and free the slaves therein, she gave no sign of it. She seemed quite intelligent; enough, probably, to realize that freeing slaves for the sake of it before the ship was secured would be counterproductive.

"This is it," she whispered, touching the hatch with a forefinger. "It'll be locked."

Damewood sneered—an expression which was wasted, because of the faceplate.

His fingers worked at his device. Less than five seconds later, he stepped back from the hatch.

"At least *this* one got some maintenance." He motioned Kabweza and her team forward with a hand gesture at the same time as the hatch started opening.

It was gorilla time now. A hatch sliding aside couldn't be broken off its hinges, of course, but the lieutenant colonel did as good an imitation of smashing down a door as was possible under the circumstances.

The compartment she found herself in was small; empty; not more than five meters long—just an entry tube. There were open hatches to the right and left at the end opposite the one she'd entered. Through the auditory-enhancement that was built into her armored skinsuit, she could hear the sound of voices coming from the hatch on the left.

Two seconds later she was passing through that hatch, her flechette gun at the ready.

Three members of the slave ship's crew were sitting at a table in a small mess hall, playing cards. Shocked by her sudden appearance, the two who were facing her—one male; one female—stared at her openmouthed. The man sitting with his back toward her was starting to turn in his seat.

Colonel Anderson had made it clear she wanted live slavers for questioning. One of the Torch soldiers in the section, Private Mary Kyllonen, was armed with an old-fashioned stun gun for precisely that reason. But since Kabweza hadn't known what they would be facing when they broke into the crew's quarters, she'd left Kyllonen in the rear—and there was no time now to bring her forward before the slavers sounded the alarm.

A bit disgruntled by the silly business of taking prisoners but obedient to orders, Kabweza fired at the lower legs of the man sitting in front of her. The shot shredded the limbs below the knees so badly that they'd have to be amputated. But with quick care he'd survive and he didn't need legs to talk.

She strode forward two paces and drove the table into the wall behind it with a powerful thrust of her foot, crushing the female crew member between them. That broke a number of the woman's ribs, one or more of which were almost certainly driven into her lungs. She gasped but made no other sound. Quick care, again; she'd survive; and she could talk in a whisper for a while.

Almost simultaneously, the lieutenant colonel slammed the butt of her weapon into the forehead of the third and final crew member. She tried to keep the impact light enough to simply stun the man, but...

That was hard to do, wearing an armored skinsuit in combat. She was pretty sure she'd broken his skull. He might survive, he might not—but Colonel Anderson seemed like a sensible commander, even if she was occasionally given to foolish whimsy. She had enough experience to understand the realities of close quarters assault.

The whole thing hadn't taken more than a few seconds. Best of all, it had been done fairly quietly. The flechette gun's knife-edged projectiles moved at high subsonic velocities, without the betraying cracking sound of a pulse rifle's supersonic darts. The man she'd shot in the legs had screamed in agony, but not for more than two seconds. Private Kyllonen had come in right behind Kabweza and silenced him with the stun gun. Neither of the other crew members had been able to call out a warning and the rest of the noises were muffled enough that there was a good chance they hadn't alerted anyone else in the ship. Even that one short scream probably hadn't done more than cause someone in the bridge to be puzzled. A brief sound, no matter how loud, tends to be dismissed if it isn't followed by anything else.

Kabweza didn't care much anyway. She was already passing through a hatch at the far end of the mess, with her section closely following. This really wasn't going to take long.

❖   ❖   ❖

Nancy Anderson's com unit buzzed softly. She held up a finger, indicating to the *Ramathibodi*'s captain that she needed a moment to take the call.

"Yes, what is it?" Her tone was mildly annoyed.

"*Sorry to bother you, Chief, but I thought you should know that the* Hali Sowle *seems to be returning to the Station.*"

Nancy had the unit on loudspeaker, so Captain Tsang could hear both sides of the exchange.

"Oh, good grief. What does that maniac want now?"

"*I have no idea, Chief. They haven't sent any messages yet. And I may have misread their change of course, although I can't think of anything else they'd be doing except coming back here.*"

"All right. She probably just wants to yell at us some more, but just to be on the safe side get the point defense units ready. The laser clusters'll be more than enough to deal with that piece of crap."

She thumbed off the com. "That's probably over-kill," she said to Tsang. "I doubt if that tub has any military hardware worth talking about. Still, we may as well play it safe. The *Hali Sowle*'s skipper really isn't playing with a full deck."

Tsang grinned. "Better she's your headache than mine." She glanced down at the device in her hand. "Unless you've come up with a different reading than I have, all the labor techs we're selling have been accounted for. You're paid up, except for one more chip."

"I concur." Anderson nodded toward the open box, which was again showing the green light. "Go ahead and take it out."

Tsang did so. "All right, that business is done. What do you want to do next? Dicker over the the pleasure units or deal with the heavy labor ones?"

The message about the *Hali Sowle*'s return had been a code. Parmley Station's control center had gotten a very brief encrypted signal from Loren Damewood, notifying them that Kabweza's team was inside the slave ship and had started their assault. Things would start moving very quickly now.

"Let's handle the pleasure units first," said Anderson. The moment they brought out the BSC people posing as Manpower pleasure slaves, Tsang and her people would get distracted and let their guard down a little further.

"Okay with me."

✧   ✧   ✧

One of the members of the section stayed behind in the mess hall to tend to the prisoners. Kabweza didn't really need the whole unit for the assault itself. There wasn't room for them anyway, in the cramped quarters they were passing through. She'd rather keep the XO and his special gear and skills with her than leave him behind to carry out simple medical tasks.

And they *were* simple. All that was needed was to keep the three prisoners alive. In good health was a moot point, and consciousness would have been a nuisance.

Corporal Bohuslav Hernandez started by applying automatic tourniquets to the mangled legs of the man Kabweza had shot, since he was the one whose injuries most needed immediate attention. He then examined the woman with the half-crushed chest and the man who'd been struck on the head.

He decided the woman would be able to breathe well enough if she were sedated. He injected her with a drug that wouldn't paralyze her or render her completely unconscious but would leave her unable to act or think coherently, much less call out any warnings to anyone else.

He was tempted to do the same with the unconscious

man, but he wasn't sure of the extent of the damage done to his brain. From the feel of it, he thought the man's skull was broken.

Hernandez decided it was best to leave well enough alone. There was no chance the man would regain consciousness before the action was all over and any warning he might make would be a moot point.

✧   ✧   ✧

Takahashi Ayako had stayed with the section, since they were still in a part of the ship she was familiar with. When they got to the next closed hatch, the freed slave made agitated motions with her hands.

That's the crew quarters, she mouthed silently.

Kabweza nodded. Like Loren's earlier sneer, the gesture was not really visible because of the shielded faceplate. But it didn't matter. Damewood had read Ayako's lips also, and was already working at his special equipment.

Overriding the security on internal hatches was child's play for someone like Loren. After a few seconds, he held up a hand, all his fingers open. Then, quickly, closed his fist and opened them again. The signal indicated that he was about to open the hatch.

Kabweza took half a step back. Behind her, so did the other remaining members of her section. Takahashi scuttled aside.

The hatch started sliding open. Kabweza went in and—

Nothing. The corridor was empty. To the left, three hatches—all of them open—led into sleeping compartments. None of them were occupied. All of them were unkept and messy.

When Ayako came into the corridor, she looked at

one of the compartments and the pinched look came back to her face. Quickly, she looked away.

"Where to now?" Ayibongwinkosi asked softly, the volume on her helmet speaker turned down very low.

Takahashi looked uncertain and made a little shrug. "I'm not really sure," she whispered. "This..." She paused and took a little breath. "This is as far as I ever...that they took me."

She pointed to a closed hatch at the very end of the corridor. "But from things they said, I think that leads into their headquarters. The 'bridge,' is that right?"

"Okay. You stay here. The rest of you, follow me."

Takahashi shuddered slightly. "I don't want to stay here. I really don't."

Ayibongwinkosi hesitated a moment. Then: "Come with us, then. But stay behind and don't get in the way."

Five seconds later, she and her section were ready at the hatch. The XO started working his magic again.

❖   ❖   ❖

Hearing some small noises behind her, Nancy turned her head and saw that two of her people were at the hatch on her side of the cargo bay. One of them said: "We've got 'em here, boss."

Anderson turned back to the *Ramathibodi*'s captain. "Okay, we're ready to start negotiating over the pleasure units. You can transfer the credit chips, if you're so inclined."

Tsang gestured at one of her subordinates to take the small bag of credit chips they'd already acquired for the labor techs onto their own ship.

"Not that we don't trust you or anything," Tsang said to Nancy. "Still, it's like the old song goes: 'better safe than sorry.'"

"An ancient saw on Old Earth said it better. 'Good fences make good neighbors.'"

Anderson and Tsang exchanged slightly derisive smiles. The derision wasn't aimed at each other so much as at the universe in general. Slave traders have an outlook on life that a fanciful poet—or literary critic, more like—might call expansively ironic.

This sort of dickering in stages was common in their business. Indeed, it was considered politesse for the purchasing party to allow the seller to periodically move their newly acquired funds to a safe place before proceeding.

Once the *Ramathibodi*'s crewman with the bag of credit chips had left, Anderson made a motion to her own people to bring the pleasure units onto the cargo bay.

There were three of them, one female and two males. All three, as one would expect, were exceedingly attractive. Unlike most slaves, they didn't keep their eyes down and their gaze on the floor. Their gazes were level, just...vacant.

Tsang smiled and rubbed her hands together. "Well, now!"

❖   ❖   ❖

When the crewman carrying the bag of credit chips arrived on the bridge—sauntered onto the bridge, it would be better to say—his first words were:

"Hey, guys, look at this! We did better than... *what the fuck?*".

❖   ❖   ❖

Showing a surprisingly limited lexicon for people whom a literary critic might call expansively ironic, Captain Tsang used the same words when Anderson and her two people suddenly drew their sidearms. Simultaneously, the tribarrel mounted on a bulkhead in the cargo bay swiveled to bring its deadly muzzles to bear on the *Ramathibodi's* contingent. And—a final insult—the three pleasure units drew tiny pistols from who-knows-where on their scantily clad persons.

"*What the fuck?*"

❖   ❖   ❖

In the end, they captured all but two of the slavers alive.

The man whose skull had been bashed by Kabweza died eighteen hours later without ever regaining consciousness. Anderson made no criticism, though. Given the difficulty of the task and the training of Torch assault troops, having only one fatality was a minor miracle.

The lieutenant colonel was less philosophical about the matter. "I'll never live this down," she predicted.

"Don't be so hard on yourself, Ayi," said Anderson soothingly. "One fatality isn't bad."

"It's better than nothing," Kabweza replied. "But I'm still going to be the butt of everyone's jokes when the rest of our people find out. Kindergarten playgrounds have more dangerous so-called 'assault troops' than we turned out to be."

❖   ❖   ❖

The death of the second slaver could not be placed at the feet of the assault troops, unless you wanted to accuse them of negligent homicide—which Anderson didn't even consider, once the circumstances were explained to her.

When the section left the mess hall, Takahashi Ayako picked up a kitchen knife that was lying on a counter. It was just a paring knife, having a blade no more than nine centimeters long. One of the assault troops spotted her doing it, but his only reaction was amusement.

"Hey, look, I just thought she was cute," Sergeant Supakrit X later explained to the battalion commander. "There she was, surrounded by apes armed to the teeth and armored to boot, but she still insisted on getting a weapon herself. If you can call a glorified toothpick a weapon."

"Cute," said Kabweza, looking disgusted.

Supakrit X made a face. "Look, Chief, I'm sorry. I misjudged."

"Cute," Kabweza repeated. "Glorified toothpick."

❖   ❖   ❖

The four slavers on the bridge had surrendered as soon as Kabweza and her soldiers burst in. None of them had been armed except the com officer, Ondøej Montoya, whom Captain Tsang had left in charge while she went aboard Parmley Station. And Montoya's sidearm—in a holster with the flap closed—would have been useless against the heavily armed assault troops' armor.

After they surrendered, Kabweza ordered all four slavers to stand against one of the bulkheads, leaning far forward and forced to support their weight on their hands. That rendered them not quite as helpless as if they'd been handcuffed, but Torch assault troops didn't carry restraining gear because they weren't usually given sappy, sentimental orders to take prisoners.

Still, they were pretty helpless. Takahashi obviously thought so. No sooner had the four slavers assumed the position than the freed slave screeched pure fury, raced forward and stabbed one of them in the kidney with her little paring knife.

The wound was not fatal. Given modern medicine, it wasn't even very serious. But the shock and pain was enough to cause the slaver to jerk back, whereupon he tripped over Takahashi and the two of them went down—the large slaver on top of the small slave.

Ironically, he'd have done better if their positions had been reversed. If Ayako had been on top, she would have stabbed him with full force; very dramatically, her hand rising above her head before she drove down the blade. She would have cut him up quite nicely, but the assault troops would probably have hauled her off before she could have done any lethal damage.

As it was, with her underneath, Kabweza and her people couldn't get to her. And since she was now driven by necessity she eschewed any dramatic stabbing and just pushed the blade as far as she could into the closest target, which happened to be the man's left eyeball.

Nine centimeters is not very long—but the skull of a human male isn't much more than twenty centimeters across in the long axis from front to back. Driven by the sort of rage possessed by Takahashi Ayako, the blade went almost halfway into the slaver's brain. And then, shrieking and cursing, she twisted and drove the blade back and forth and up and down.

It took the Torch soldiers no more than four or five seconds to get the slaver rolled over and haul Takahashi off him, but by then she'd pretty well transformed a third of his frontal lobes into hash. The autopsy 'bot later reported that she'd carved up part of the limbic system as well.

Modern medicine is not actually miraculous, although

the term is often used. For all practical purposes, the man was gone before any aid could be given him.

Or as now-corporal Supakrit X put it with great satisfaction over the troops' evening meal, "I'm telling you, that fucker was dead-dead-dead."

He wasn't especially upset by his lowly new rank. For one thing, he knew his demotion had been mostly done as a matter of principle, rather than because Kabweza was really mad at him. He figured he'd get his rank back soon enough.

Besides, the way he looked at it, he'd been busted in a good cause. It wasn't like getting demoted for being drunk and disorderly.

"And I still say she's cute," he added. "Although you'd really want to be on your best behavior on a date."

CHAPTER 5

"I'd miss Steph," Andrew Artlett protested. "Just for starters. Then there's the lousy pay."

Princess Ruth Winton frowned. "Lousy pay? You're being offered almost half again what you're making here on Torch—and you're getting top rate for starship mechanics." After a brief pause—very brief; Ruth hated admitting to a lack of complete expertise on any subject—she added: "So I'm told, anyway."

"Well, yeah. But going back to Parmley Station to work on *this* project is risky as all hell." Stoutly: "I should be getting hazard pay. That's generally figured as a hundred percent pay increase. Double-time, that is."

There were so many fallacies and lapses of logic in those statements that the Manticoran princess was rendered almost speechless.

Almost. Speechlessness was a state of affairs that was probably impossible for Ruth Winton.

"*What?* That's insane! Every single sentence you just said is blithering nonsense."

She began counting off her fingers. "First off, there's

nothing at all risky for *you* in this deal. Your aunt Elfriede, maybe—"

"Don't call her that to her face," Andrew cautioned. "She answers to Ganny. Or Ganny El, if she likes you."

"I *have* met the woman. I was just being formal. Seeing as how this is supposed to be an employment interview." Ruth looked simultaneously cross and a bit embarrassed. "Of sorts," she added.

"'Employment interview'!" Artlett said mockingly. "Oh, yeah. I can see it in the want ads now." He mimicked holding up a reading tablet. "'Wanted. Damn fool mechanic for desperado duties aiding and abetting Audubon Ballroom sociopaths—"

He glanced at the huge figure of Hugh Arai, who was lounging in a nearby armchair in the princess' suite. (Ruth called it a working office, but that was the obliviousness to luxury of someone born and raised in Mount Royal Palace in Manticore's capital city of Landing. It was a no-fooling suite, on the top floor of the finest hotel in Beacon.)

"Meaning no offense, Hugh, I'm just saying it like it is." Arai smiled at him.

Andrew resumed pretending to read a want ad: "—and Beowulfan cold-blooded killers masquerading as biologists—"

Again he glanced at Arai. "Meaning no offense. Just telling it like it is." The smile became a grin.

Back to the imaginary want ad: "—for the purpose of hunting down any and all practitioners of the slave trade, which individuals are noted—no, notorious— throughout the inhabited portions of the galaxy for their cruelty and depraved indifference to human life, including that of starship mechanics."

Triumphantly, he set down the imaginary tablet. "Ha!"

Ruth had waited for him to finish. Impatiently, because she was impatient with silliness by nature. But she'd still waited. She knew Artlett well enough by now to know there was no point in trying to derail him when he was hell-bent on riding his broad (broad? say better, oceanically expansive) sense of humor to the end of the track.

"If we might return to reality for a moment," she said, "*your* duties will keep you on Parmley Station most of the time. A construct that is not only one of the largest space-going installations within light-years of its solar system but is by now almost as heavily armed as an orbital fortress."

Hugh shook his head. "Bit of an exaggeration, Ruth. The defenses and armaments on Parmley Station aren't designed to fight off a battle fleet."

Andrew started to say something, probably along the lines of claiming that Arai was supporting him, but Hugh's deep voice rode over him easily. "But they'll squash any pirates or slavers who show up as easily as swatting an insect."

He gave Artlett a beady gaze: "As you know perfectly well, since you were paid to be a consultant when we designed those defenses."

"Still." Andrew was nothing if not stubborn. He waved his hand in a gesture that might mean . . . pretty much anything. "Pirates. Slavers. Dangerous people, no matter how you slice it."

He decided to fall back onto more sensible grounds. "And like I said, I'd miss Steph."

Ruth pounced. "Why is that? I just talked to her

this morning and she seemed quite amenable to relocating to Parmley Station."

Andrew stared at her. "She . . . But—she told me—it was just a few weeks ago!"

Ruth waved her hand airily. "That was then, this is now. She's had time since to gauge the real possibilities at either place. Here, on Torch, it seems like everybody and their grandmother is setting up a restaurant. The competition is brutal. The hours, long; the income . . ." The princess made a face, as if she had any idea of the harsh realities of trying to run a small restaurant.

Which, of course, she didn't. But Ruth Winton never let petty details like her own ignorance get in the way of a good argument. She pressed on.

"Whereas on Parmley Station—" The royal expression became positively beatific, as she contemplated the commercial advantages of opening a restaurant there.

"It's a busted enterprise," jeered Artlett. "A pipe dream on the part of my great-uncle Michael Parmley—a screwball if there ever was one—who poured a fortune into building the galaxy's most derelict orbital amusement park."

"That was then, this is now," interjected Hugh Arai. "As you know perfectly well, Andrew." He leaned forward. "Today, it's on the verge of becoming Beowulf's central hub for covert operations against Mesa and Manpower."

"The best clientele you could ask for!" Ruth said enthusiastically. "Beefy commando types. They eat like horses and tip like the upper crust."

Most of that was pretty accurate. Not all covert operations people were beefy; but they did tend to eat a lot. That was a combination of a usually high-powered metabolism with near-constant physical training.

The analogy to the tipping habits of upper crust gamblers was wide of the mark, though. Wealthy people actually tended to be on the cheapskate side when it came to things like tipping. And charity, for that matter. It had been a constant for millennia that people of average means gave a higher percentage of their income to charitable causes than rich people—especially when you factored into the equation the end beneficiaries. Average people gave to those poorer than they. Rich people usually donated their money to cultural institutions—museums, universities and opera houses, for instance—of which they or their children were major personal beneficiaries. And then named them after themselves.

There were exceptions, of course, and those individuals could be spectacular in their largesse. The Winton dynasty had a long tradition of being very generous, especially for medical causes. Ruth's misapprehension was the understandable product of her own personal experience.

But while the analogy was off, the reality remained. Covert ops people *did* tend to tip generously—and Andrew knew it, from having spent a lot of time in their company over the past period.

He ran fingers through his hair, in a gesture of exasperation. "Damn it, *she* was the one who insisted on coming here in the first place. *I* would have been perfectly happy to stay on Parmley Station. Women!"

Ruth had her own opinion—well-formed; cured; tempered; hardened; sharp on all edges and corners—as to which of the two human genders was actually prone to flightiness, inconstancy and indecision. Shakespeare's greatest play wasn't about a *princess* of Denmark, now was it?

But she saw no reason to squabble over the matter, since Artlett was now clearly on the verge of capitulating to logic and reason.

"All right, then," he said. "I'll go. If it's okay with Steph."

✧   ✧   ✧

After Andrew left the suite, Hugh cleared his throat. "I noticed that you left out some particulars."

"I wouldn't call them 'particulars.' Speculative possibilities is closer to the mark."

Arai shook his head. "You're quibbling and you know it. What you're calling 'speculative possibilities' are part of the established plans for using the *Hali Sowle*."

"Established by whom?" Ruth countered. "Ganny El still hasn't agreed—and if she doesn't, the whole deal collapses."

"I *know* you didn't learn to lie, cheat and steal at Mount Royal Palace. So where does it come from, this brazen shamelessness? This cunning deftness at misdirection and maneuver? This dazzling expertise at deceit and deception?"

"You might be surprised at what goes on in the corridors and back rooms of Mount Royal Palace, Hugh. But, no, I didn't learn the skills there. No more than the rudiments, anyway."

She sniffed. "Where do you think? I've been studying for the past three years at Zilwicki and Cachat University."

Hugh chuckled. "Point. Speaking of which, do you think they're really responsible for the slaughter on Mesa?"

"I assume you're referring to the claim being spread by Manpower through the Solarian media that they set off the nuclear explosion at Green Pines. If so, the answer is 'no.' It's clear they didn't do it. We'll get the full story from them when they arrive here."

Word had come from Sharon Justice, one of Haven's representatives on Erewhon, that Zilwicki and Cachat had arrived at Parmley Station a few weeks earlier. But her message had contained no other information beyond the bare fact that they were alive.

Arai leaned back in his chair and clasped his fingers over his belly. "Explain your reasoning." His tone wasn't argumentative, just interested.

"Hell, Hugh, it's obvious." She leaned forward in her own chair, sliding almost to the edge of it. Ruth was not capable of thinking or expounding anything in a relaxed position. Within less than a minute, Hugh knew from experience, she'd have risen from the chair and started pacing.

"For starters, if they were going to set off that large an explosion, why pick that target?"

"Well, according to the news reports—"

"Oh, please!" Ruth got to her feet. Hugh glanced at his watch. Seven seconds.

"That silly business about Green Pines being a residential center for the Mesan elite? Every other apartment in the complex inhabited by a Manpower bigshot? That's why it was targeted?"

By the time she finished, she'd taken five steps one way and was now reversing direction. Long steps, too; Ruth was a strider.

"I don't doubt that a lot of important managerial people lived there. But you know how incredibly tough

modern construction can make buildings, Hugh—
especially when they're intended for the use of the
powerful and wealthy."

She threw up her hands, without breaking stride.
"Are we supposed to believe that Anton Zilwicki was
incompetent as well as murderous? For Pete's sake, the
man used to be in charge of building entire orbital
stations. If there was anyone in the galaxy who'd know
in precise detail just how ineffective such a bomb
would be on such a target, planted in such a way—"

She finally stopped, leaning forward with her hands
on her hands. "Whoever did it set that thing off in
the *open*." She threw up her hands again. "In a stupid
park. Most of the force of the blast would have been
completely wasted! Unless your goal was to vaporize
kiddies and puppies and—and—whatever else they
had there. Miniature sailboats in the miniature lake,
whatever."

Hugh winced. Ruth could sometimes get so swallowed up in her calculations that she'd blurt out
the most insensitive and callous things without even
thinking about it.

She pulled out her minicomp. "Let me show you
something."

At that moment, the door to the suite opened and
two young women came in. The one in front, much
smaller than the one following her, immediately made
a beeline toward Hugh and, with no ceremony of
any kind, plumped herself on his lap.

The woman in the rear smiled and closed the door.
Ruth frowned at the lap-sitter. "In the long,
illustrious—and very well-recorded—annals of royalty throughout the galaxy, Berry, no ruling queen

I know of has *ever* just plopped herself on her consort's lap in public."

Berry Zilwicki curled her lip. The gesture was rather ineffective, since sneering did not come naturally to her.

"He's not my 'consort,' first of all. He's my boyfriend. And how is this 'in public'? You and Thandi are my two best friends, even leaving aside her formal status as head of the armed forces and yours as assistant chief spook."

Ruth was not fazed. "There are four people in this room. That defines 'in public' whenever royalty is engaged in pre-fornication. Which you so obviously are."

Berry kissed Hugh in a manner that left little doubt that Ruth's assessment was accurate. When she was finished, she gave the Manticoran princess as regal a look as she could manage. Which wasn't much; Berry looked down her nose about as poorly as she sneered.

Hugh cleared his throat again. "Speaking of which, Ruth and I were just discussing the chief spook when you walked in."

Torch's "chief spook" was Anton Zilwicki, Berry's adoptive father. Her expression immediately sobered.

So did Thandi Palane's, although the big woman's expression was usually pretty stern. Being born and raised on one of the Mfecane worlds didn't lead to carefree and happy-go-lucky personalities.

"Specifically," said Ruth, "I was explaining to him—since he pretended to be an ignoramus on matters of interstellar politics, which he most certainly isn't even if he does look like a Sasquatch—that there was no way—"

"Hey!" Berry protested. "Don't call my boyfriend a Bigfoot!"

She and Ruth both studied the appendages in question for a moment, which was easy to do since Hugh had one of them propped up on a small ottoman.

"I rest my case," said Ruth.

"Well... Okay, he has big feet. That doesn't mean he's abominable."

Arai made a shooing gesture with his hand. "Just keep going, Ruth."

"Yeah, I'd like to hear it myself," said Thandi, who perched herself on the armrest of a nearby divan. The piece of furniture was sturdily built, fortunately. Palane wasn't built along the purely massive lines of Arai, who'd been bred by Manpower to be a heavy labor slave, but she was tall, muscular, and weighed well over a hundred kilos.

"As I was saying to Hugh when you walked in"—Ruth began pacing again—"or about to show him, rather..."

She fiddled with her minicomp until she found what she wanted, glanced around the room for the location of the wallscreen, and brought the image up on what had seemed until the instant before to be a huge landscape called *Bernese Alps* by an ancient painter named... Ambrose Bierce, maybe. She couldn't remember. Ruth wasn't much interested in primitive art.

The wallscreen didn't really fill an entire wall—not even close, given the size of the suite—but it still measured about three meters across by a little over half that in height. The image now displayed on it was pretty spectacular—and far more grim.

"That is what the immediate surrounding area of Nouveau Paris looked like after Oscar Saint-Just set off the nuclear explosion that ended McQueen's rebellion. Notice that all of the surrounding towers are still intact? Battered pretty badly, sure—but they're still there. That's how hard it is to take down a modern ceramacrete tower."

"What's your point?" asked Berry.

"The *point* is that neither your father nor Victor Cachat are so incompetent that they'd use a bomb that way. If they did decide to strike that kind of blow at the Mesan elite, they'd do it differently. My guess is that they'd figure out a way to smuggle the bomb into the building with the highest number of bigshots and set it off inside. The ceramacrete shell would then *contain* the force of the blast and concentrate its effectiveness. And while that would still kill a lot of bystanders, it would have a much better bigshot-to-kiddies-and-puppies kill ratio."

Hugh winced again. Berry scowled. "My father would *not* do that."

Ruth shook her head. "No, he wouldn't. I was just trying to show that *even if* you leave personal psychology out of the equation, that bomb was not set off by your father and Victor."

"Victor wouldn't agree to it, either," said Thandi mildly.

"I agree," said Ruth. She paused for a moment. "It took me a long time to get over the cold-blooded way Victor let my security team get gunned down. But eventually I realized...I don't know how to put it, exactly..."

"He can be completely ruthless toward anyone he considers a combatant," Thandi said, "and Victor's definition of 'combatant' can be pretty wide. That's how he would have seen your people, especially since at the time they *were* at war with Haven. But there's no way he'd ever put children in that category. And in the end, Victor's ruthlessness always has a purpose—to defend those whom he sees as weak and helpless against those who are mighty."

She shrugged. "Like any soldier he'll accept the fact that in war there's bound to be collateral damage. Except he wouldn't use that term because he despises it. He'd call them innocent victims. And there's no way he'd deliberately use innocent victims as the mechanism for striking down his enemies—which is what they'd be, in that scenario."

Ruth studied the image on the wallscreen for a few more seconds before she switched it off. Oscar Saint-Just had been the man who trained Victor, sure enough, and the two men had a lot in common. But that commonality ended at a certain point. If anyone ever put together a visual track record of Cachat's life, there'd never be a scene like that in it.

The wallscreen reverted back to resembling a painting again. Not the same one, though. The program automatically switched the image every twelve hours and whenever someone overrode it manually. Ruth hadn't bothered to change the program because it was all pretty much the same to her. If she remembered right, this new image was another ancient painting called *Water Lilies* by . . . Claude Money. Something like that.

There was silence in the room, for a few seconds. Then Berry sighed and said softly, "I just want to see him again. And Victor too. They should be here any day. I was so happy to find out they were still alive."

There had been a time, less than two years ago, when Ruth would have been delighted to discover that Victor Cachat had shuffled off this mortal coil. But it seemed like ancient history now.

"So am I," she said. "So am I."

There was a buzz at the door. "Open," said Ruth.

One of Torch's intelligence officers came in, a man in his fifties by the name of Shai-gwun Metterling. Unlike most immigrants, he had no genetic connection to Manpower at all, neither personally nor anywhere in his heritage. He'd come to Torch because of his political convictions.

In and of itself, that wasn't all that unusual. By Ruth's rough count, there were at least twenty thousand people who'd immigrated and taken Torch citizenship since the new star nation was created who'd done so purely out of idealism. What was unusual, and had immediately caught Ruth's attention, was Metterling's background. Most such immigrants tended to have skills and training that weren't all that immediately useful. There were two hundred philosophers in the mix, twice that many poets, well over a thousand musicians—and a sad dearth of engineers and doctors.

Metterling, on the other hand, had been a colonel in the Andermani Navy's intelligence service. A well-regarded and decorated one, too, not someone who'd been cashiered. Ruth had checked, very carefully, worried that he might be a double agent. But Metterling had come through her scrutiny with flying colors.

"What's up, Shai-gwun?" she asked.

Metterling gave Thandi a glance that seemed a bit apprehensive. "We just got word from Cachat and Zilw—ah, your father, Your Majesty." That last was said to Berry.

Who practically sprang off of Hugh's lap. "They're here!"

Again, that quick glance at Palane—and it was no

longer a "bit" apprehensive. "Ah. Well, no. It seems they decided to go straight to Haven."

Thandi rose from the arm rest and stood straight up. "And aren't going to—didn't—stop here on the way?" she demanded.

"Ah. Well, General Palane... Ah. No."

"I'll kill him," Thandi predicted.

CHAPTER 6

"We haven't done that in a while," said Yuri Radamacher. His voice was barely louder than a murmur, with complex undertones that conveyed satiety, exhaustion, smug self-satisfaction, bemused wonder at capabilities thought lost forever, and, most of all—the saving grace that would keep him from ridicule or possible bodily harm—full of affection for the person lying next to him.

Who, for her part, slapped him playfully on his bare midriff. That produced a meaty sound. Yuri was not exactly fat, but he was in no danger of being blown away by a gust of wind, either.

"Don't sound so pleased with yourself," she said. "Of course we haven't done that in a while. We haven't seen each other in . . . what's it been, now? More than a T-year."

"Three hundred and ninety-six standard days. God, I've missed you."

Sharon Justice rolled onto her side and propped her head up on one hand. "I missed you too. But look at the bright side—for the first time in years, it looks like we'll be able to see each other regularly and for . . . oh, hell, it could be a long time."

Yuri hesitated, tempted to raise the subject of marriage. Even the Republic of Haven's stringent rules concerning assignments for its officials were subject to relaxation and modification when married couples were involved. But after a moment, he decided to let it slide.

He knew that Sharon was twitchy on the subject. That was not unusual, of course. The whole subject of marriage had gotten very complicated and thorny since the development of prolong. That was especially true for a society like Haven's, which tended to be conservative on social issues despite the often radical character of its politics.

The traditional concept of marriage was that of a union between two people which was expected to last a lifetime. Many did not, of course. Still, even people who got divorced generally viewed the divorce as a failure; an unfortunate and in some sense unnatural outcome.

But the same institution now had to be stretched across lifetimes that were measured in centuries, not decades. And to make things still more complicated, that greatly extended lifespan was characterized through at least eighty percent of its duration as the lifespan of a *young* person. Only toward the very end of the life of someone on prolong did the aging process and eventual decrepitude start manifesting itself. That stood in stark contrast to the ancient realities of human life, in which the period of vigorous youth was a fairly brief interlude between childhood and middle age.

The traditional institution of marriage was simply not well suited for these new conditions. Much of its stability had been provided by the "natural" aging process. As a couple grew old together, they came to rely on each other for succor and support as much as intimacy. Prosaic as it might be, sharing aches and pains did a great deal to solidify a marriage; and, on the flip side, worked against any tendencies toward infidelity.

None of that was true any longer. Even the needs and demands of child-raising, traditionally the strongest bond in a marriage, was far less important. People on prolong could bear children throughout most of their now-very-long lives, but very few did so. Most couples would devote a few decades to having and nurturing children, but no more than that. Depending on the specific star nation and its customs, they might do their child-raising early in life or they might—this was the normal practice in Manticore, Beowulf and the Andermani Empire—postpone having children until they were well established in their careers and in a more solid financial position. But whatever stretch in their long lifespans they chose to devote to child-raising, once that was done they did not usually repeat the process. And in the doing they had only devoted ten percent or less of their lives—as opposed to the one-third or even one-half of a lifetime that child-bearing and rearing had traditionally occupied.

Under that pressure—it might be more accurate to say, sudden removal of pressure—the institution of marriage was undergoing profound and manifold transformations throughout the human-inhabited portions of the galaxy. Those changes had already been underway as a result of medical and technological advances, and prolong drove them even faster. In some adventurous societies—Beowulf being a prime example—a dizzying number of variations on marriage had emerged and were being experimented with. But in other, more staid societies, the reaction tended the other way. The lifelong nature of marriage was insisted upon even more firmly—with the inevitable consequence that fewer and fewer people entered into marriage. Instead, serial cohabitation without formal marriage was becoming the norm; or, at least, the most common pattern.

Even child-bearing and raising was adapting. As had always been the case in matrilineal societies, prolong society had effectively done away with the concept of bastardy. The reasons were different, but the end result was much the same: people in advanced societies who would live for centuries usually had such a deep and widespread safety net—some of it public, some of it private—that a single parent or a couple simply didn't require marriage as a practical economic matter. The laws of most star nations did require an official recognition of parenthood, but that was separate from the legal requirements for marriage. That was to protect the children. You might not be formally married to the mother or father of your child, but you were still legally responsible for the children themselves.

All of which was well and good, and Yuri understood the dynamic on an intellectual level. The fact remained that he was a Havenite, not a Beowulfer, and like most people from Haven his basic emotional attitudes were conservative and old-fashioned. The years he'd spent as a State Security officer during the Pierre and Saint-Just period compounded the problem. Early on, he'd developed sharp differences with their policies. Given the nature of their regime, he'd had to hide his real opinions and keep an emotional distance from everybody. The end result had been a man who was innately friendly and sociable transformed into a lonely soul.

Dammit, he wanted to get *married*.

But he was almost certain that Sharon would refuse and he'd learned long ago that if you thought the answer to a question was going to be "no," it was better not to ask the question at all. Once stated openly, "no" tended to get locked in place.

So, partly out of frustration and partly out of a sense of duty, he rose from the bed, put on some clothes and headed for the kitchen. "Want some coffee?"

"Akh!" Sharon rose hurriedly from the bed and grabbed a robe. "Yes—but *I'll* make it, thank you very much. You'll break the coffeemaker."

"Don't be silly."

She brushed past him, putting on the robe and moving quickly. "Fine. You'll break the coffee."

"That's ridiculous. You can't—"

"*You* can." Sharon started working at the controls of a machine that, to Radamacher's way of thinking, bore a closer resemblance to a computer terminal than a simple device to brew a drink that the human race had been enjoying for millennia. "I love you dearly, Yuri, but you make the worst coffee this side of a Navy mess hall."

"That's where I learned to make coffee in the first place."

"I know." She pushed buttons that did mysterious things. "For years, I had a secret belief that the reason we had such a hard time fighting the Manticorans was because of the Navy's coffee. The deterioration that crap must have produced in the brains of our officers and ratings didn't bear thinking about."

The button-pushing ended with a triumphant glissando of flying fingers. Yuri had no idea what she was doing. Programming the heat death of the universe? It was a *coffee maker*, for God's sake. What was wrong with letting the gadget's own computer handle the business?

"And since I got here," she continued, "my suspicion has been confirmed. I've talked to any number of Erewhonese who've had Manticoran Navy coffee, and they all swear it's terrific."

Her ritual apparently done, Sharon finished tying up her robe and sat down at the kitchen table. "Oh, stop pouting—and have a seat, will you? The coffee will take a few minutes."

Yuri was tempted to respond *my coffee gets done in no time at all* but wisely restrained himself. As a friend who shared his own insouciant attitude toward making coffee had once said, "Gourmets are subtle and quick to anger."

He pulled up a chair and changed the subject. "Speaking of the Erewhonese, I suppose you should bring me up to date. Seeing as how I'm Haven's ambassador to Torch and—hold your breath, this takes a while—'high commissioner and envoy extraordinary' to Erewhon. In the moments I can spare from being your sex toy."

Sharon smiled. "'Sex toy,' is it? I'll remember that." The smile was replaced by a slight frown. "I assume the reason you didn't replace Guthrie as the ambassador to Erewhon also is because the Erewhonese made it clear they were not too happy with us."

"Yeah, they're still mad that Haven restarted the

war with Manticore before the ink on our mutual defense treaty had barely dried." He shrugged. "On the other hand, because we made no effort to get them to join the hostilities, they aren't *that* mad. Certainly not enough to take the risks involved in producing a major rupture with us. So, everyone agreed to one of the time-honored diplomatic code messages. 'You don't get an ambassador, you louses. Just a high commissioner etc., etc. So there.' I think that's aimed more at the Star Kingdom than us."

"Star *Empire*," Sharon corrected him. She ran fingers through her hair. Short hair, these days. She'd dyed it a nice auburn color since he'd seen her last and cut it back quite a bit. Truth be told, he preferred her hair longer. But that was an age-old tug of war between men and women that men invariably lost once a relationship congealed. Yuri might not be the sharpest pencil in the box when it came to romantic relationships, but he wasn't obtuse enough to venture into *that* mine field.

"I think you're probably right about Manticore," she said. "The Erewhonese love their subtle ploys and gestures. 'See? We made it real clear to Haven that they're in the dog house, the rotters.' I'm not sure how much good it'll do them, though."

"Might be quite a bit. The Star Empire's current prime minister is as sophisticated as they come and he's probably familiar with Erewhon's somewhat peculiar *mores*. And for sure and certain the Winton dynasty will pay attention. They're no slouches themselves when it comes to hints and veiled messages. You wouldn't think a royal lineage would have that much in common with a long line of gangsters, but there it is."

"Ha! If Victor were here, he'd say they were cut from exactly the same cloth—so why shouldn't they speak the same patois?"

That brought a few seconds' worth of silence. Then Yuri sighed and leaned back in his chair. "I still don't like the basta—man, but I have to admit I was glad to find out he was still alive. It's like the old saying: 'Yeah, he's a ruthless son of a bitch, but he's *our* ruthless son of a bitch.'"

"Are you *still* holding a grudge, Yuri? La Martine was years ago."

"He told them to break my *nose*. On purpose!"

"He sure did. That made you a bloody mess—and may very well have kept you alive."

Impatiently, Yuri shook his head. "I understand the logic, Sharon. I still don't like the man. He gave you a beating, too. I was madder about that than I was about my nose. Still am."

"Are you aware that he's been a consistent influence— no small one, either—boosting your career? Mine, too. Ever since La Martine. I'm pretty sure he's the main reason you got this posting. Kevin Usher listens to him. So does Wilhelm Trajan, although"—she grinned, here—"I don't think he does so nearly as cheerfully as Kevin does."

Yuri looked a bit guilty. "Well . . . Yeah, I sort of figured that out a while ago. Look, I'm not saying my attitude toward Cachat is rational. It's probably not. Okay, for sure it's not." Stubbornly: "I still don't like him."

The com unit on the wall chimed, indicating someone desired a connection.

Sharon punched the acceptance key. The screen came to life.

Seeing the familiar face on the screen, Sharon said: "Walter. I assume you called to talk to Haven's new ambassa—ah, high commissioner and—"

"—and envoy extraordinary and whatever other twaddle terms we need to keep up appearances." Walter Imbesi gave Radamacher a quick, almost perfunctory smile. "Actually, no. I'd been planning to give you a day or so to—ah, renew acquaintance—before bothering you with business. But something's come up that we think is pressing. As in *really* pressing."

Both Sharon and Yuri sat up straight. "Which is . . . ?" said Yuri.

"It seems Victor Cachat is back from the dead. Presumed dead, rather. Anton Zilwicki also. I have been asked to convey to you the government's displeasure at not being informed of Cachat's survival. Given that we are formally allied, they feel they should have been notified. If not at once, certainly in less time than two months."

"The ship they used to carry the message to me was an Erewhonese vessel," said Sharon. "Are you seriously going to claim you didn't get the news as soon as I did?"

"I grant you we learned the fact of their survival as soon as you did. The government's displeasure stems from your failure to formally notify them and provide any further details."

Yuri decided to let Sharon keep handling things, even though it would normally be his job as ambassador. (Fine. Envoy extra-crispy etc., etc., but in practice it came to the same thing.) But he'd just arrived and hadn't been fully briefed. More precisely, he hadn't been briefed at all. Well, leaving aside carnal matters that were none of anyone else's damn business.

Sharon obviously agreed, since she spoke without hesitation or so much as a glance in his direction. "Let's translate that statement out of diplomatese, shall we? The triumvirate that runs the show—we'll skip all the silly stuff about 'the government'—is ticked off but since they're probably not *that* ticked off—yet, anyway—they sent you as their spokesman since you don't officially have any political position or power—we'll all agree not to collapse in riotous laughter here—and so they figure coming from you it'll have less of an edge to it."

Sharon shrugged. "It was Victor's order not to divulge anything, and he's my boss."

Imbesi pursed his lips. "The conclusion I come to is that Cachat thought gaining a few weeks of secrecy was important enough to risk irritating an ally. Fine. The few weeks have now gone by—so we can move to the critical question, which is *what did he and Zilwicki discover that warrants these extreme measures?*"

He waved his hand again in a gesture which, though dismissive, was not small at all. "And please spare me the usual drivel about 'the needs of security,' Sharon. I've gotten to know Victor Cachat rather well over the past couple of years. Perhaps unusually for someone in his line of work, he's not obsessive about secrecy."

"Generally, no. You're right. But in this instance"— Sharon spread her hands in a gesture that simultaneously conveyed *I speak the solemn truth* and *it's out of my hands anyway*—"he told me nothing in the first place."

Imbesi was silent for a few seconds. Then, pursed his lips. "You're not lying, are you?"

He looked at Yuri. "I know what happened on La

Martine, High Commissioner Radamacher. We compiled an extensive file on the affair—on anything involving Victor Cachat's history, once it became clear how large a presence he was going to have for us. One of the conclusions I drew from the affair was that Cachat has an almost eerie sense for selecting his subordinates. The two of you—others—and then he gives them lots of leeway and doesn't micromanage. Some people might even accuse him of recklessness, in that regard. But I don't know of any instance where his judgment has proven faulty."

Yuri had to fight a little to keep an expressionless face. He really *didn't* like Victor Cachat. But as much as any person alive he knew just how capable the man was. Fiendishly capable, even. But Yuri didn't doubt at all whose fiend he was: Haven's, as sure as any law of thermodynamics.

So he was just as surprised as Imbesi to learn that Cachat hadn't told Sharon what he'd learned and where he was going with it. They hadn't talked about it, simply because... Well, more pressing matters arose. But he'd assumed that would be part of the briefing Sharon would give him afterward.

The Erewhonese politician's assessment was quite correct. Cachat was supremely confident in his ability to select his assistants, and then he didn't second-guess himself.

He hadn't even told *Sharon*?

Imbesi said it for him. "So all hell's about to break loose." He nodded, more to himself than anyone else. "I'll let the triumvirate know. Sharon, High Commissioner Radamacher—"

"Call me Yuri, please."

"One moment, Walter." Sharon leaned forward a little. "As long as we're on the subjects of secrecy and all hell breaking loose, when can we expect a briefing from you regarding the new relationship you've forged with Maya Sector? Congratulations, by the way. You've come up in the galaxy. You used to launder money and now you're laundering superdreadnoughts."

She smiled sweetly. "Seeing as how we're allies, as you just pointed out."

There was no reaction at all on Imbesi's face in response to those comments. Which were obviously something *else* Yuri needed to be briefed on.

After a moment, Imbesi just said: "I'll have to get back to you on that. Have a pleasant day."

The screen went dark.

"I can't remember feeling like such a complete ignoramus since I was twelve," Yuri complained. "When I got called on in class to enumerate the noble gases and I didn't have a clue what the teacher was talking about. Since when did chemical elements have an aristocracy?"

CHAPTER 7

The alley below was vacant, except for the usual piles of debris. Cary Condor removed her finger and let the curtain covering the window fall back in place. It was an old-style material curtain—a piece of decorated fabric—rather than a modern electronic screen. There was a screen in place also, and Cary flipped the switch to turn it back on.

"Are you really sure this is necessary?" she asked, as she turned away from the window. "It seems... pretty unsanitary."

"The curtain?" Stephanie Moriarty looked up from the table where she was working at a portable computer. "You'd be surprised how effective a simple material block is to a lot of surveillance techniques. There's more to the world than electrons. Besides, how is it any more unsanitary than everything else in this dump?"

Cary didn't have a good answer for that, beyond *I'm used to crappy clothes and bedding.* So she shifted her objection to the curtain onto other grounds. "If somebody comes in here on a raid it'll be a dead giveaway that we're trying to hide something. Nobody in this day and age, not even in Mesa's seccy quarters, uses antiques like this."

"Oh, for—" Moriarty took a deep breath. "Cary, if 'somebody'—and, gee whiz, who might that be other than security goons?—comes busting in here on a raid, explaining a curtain will be the least of our problems."

There came a hoarse chuckle from the figure lying on a bed in one of the corners of the room. "Probably won't be any kind of problem at all. On account of we'll be in little bitty pieces two seconds after they come in. Both of you and what's left of me."

Karen Steve Williams raised her head from the pillow enough to gaze down at her legs. Her nonexistent legs, below the knees. "I try to look on the bright side. At least my damn feet would stop itching."

Moriarty's mouth twisted into a wry smile. "Be careful what you wish for. If your no-longer-there feet can still itch, how do you know that your no-longer-there body won't itch too, once you're dead?"

Karen chuckled again. "Talk about a fix! Spend all of eternity trying to scratch a nonexistent itch with nonexistent hands."

Cary gave her two companions an exasperated look. She did not share their amusement with silly whimsies. "Once you're dead, you're dead. Not there. Your body isn't nonexistent, *you* are. Itching is irrelevant. It's like saying the color yellow won't be in harmony any longer."

"Spoilsport." That came from Karen, whose head was back on the pillow and whose eyes were closed again. She didn't have much energy these days. Cary didn't think she'd live for many more weeks. The injuries the young woman had sustained making her escape—her hair-breadth, hair-raising, barely-in-the-nick-of-time escape—from Mesa's security forces after the nuclear detonation at Green Pines had been horrible.

The amputated legs weren't even the worst of it. Karen was also missing her spleen as well as one of her kidneys and most of her liver. And there'd been some damage to her brain, too. She sometimes had trouble talking and her vision was impaired.

More to get her mind off the depressing subject of Karen's medical condition than out of any real interest, Cary moved toward the table where Stephanie was sitting. "Any news?" she asked.

Moriarty jabbed an accusatory finger at the computer screen. "This is official Mesan news, remember? Better known as the Fantasy Channel."

Cary ignored the sarcastic remark and leaned over her comrade's shoulder to get a better look at the screen. The portable computer was another antique. Its virtual screen expansion had collapsed a few weeks earlier so their view was limited to the screen's physical dimensions. Which were all of twenty-five by fifteen centimeters. It was almost like looking through a keyhole.

Cary now knew what a keyhole was, because the small apartment they'd rented actually had one as a supplement to the usual security devices. There was no key, though, which didn't matter since the lock was broken anyway. Their landlord, as shrewd and grasping as such people usually were in slums, had quickly gauged their level of desperation, divided it by his equally quick gauge of their resources, and provided them with the smallest and most rundown unit in his building for a price they could just barely afford.

At that, they'd been lucky. There'd been rumors of a robbery gone badly wrong in a nearby district just a day before they'd approached the landlord, and he'd assumed they were what was left of the criminal gang. It hadn't occurred to him that their battered appearance and the two badly injured members of their party had anything to do with the Green Pines incident.

The one male in their four-person group, Firouz Howt, had died two days later. Since disposing of the body themselves would be very dangerous, they'd decided the landlord was the lesser risk. That assessment had proven correct. He'd disposed of the body for the value of the organs and tissues, and charged them nothing.

So, he'd seen the wounds that had finally taken Firouz's life, and had had no trouble recognizing them as injuries sustained in a gunfight. The landlord had a couple of visible scars himself that showed he was no stranger to violence. But that had simply confirmed his supposition that they were criminals. And not very competent ones, so he wasn't too nervous at having them around.

That had been just about the only good luck they'd had since Green Pines, but it had been enough to keep them alive. If they could somehow come up with the money, they might even be able to get Karen the medical treatments she needed to stay alive.

The landlord had offered to be of assistance there also, as what he called their "manager" but what he meant was their pimp. Cary and Stephanie had turned him down. Partly because the idea of becoming prostitutes was repellent, partly because it would be dangerous, but mostly—being honest—because they couldn't possibly raise the sums necessary in that manner.

The news being carried on the channel Stephanie had turned to was the usual fare these days. Fifty percent, a relentless drumbeat on the ever-present danger of Audubon Ballroom terrorist activity; twenty percent, a relentless drumbeat on the also ever-present if not quite as fearsome danger of criminal activity; ten percent, bits and pieces involving official Mesan politics; ten percent, bits and pieces of galactic news. The remaining ten percent was distributed fairly evenly between quirky human interest stories, natural disasters—those were mostly of human origin given Mesa's very mild climate; fires and such—and fashions.

Yes, fashions. Most of which could only be afforded by a tiny number of seccies.

Calling it "the Fantasy Channel," therefore, was an exaggeration. If you set aside the barrages on so-called "terrorism," anyway. Most of that was made up out of whole cloth. But the other half of the news wasn't fabricated—although the Mesa authorities censored quite a bit of it. The problem wasn't so much was what said as what was *not* said. You might be told, for instance—with perfect accuracy—that a given town had been subjected to flooding or an earthquake or some other natural disaster. What wouldn't be mentioned was that the flood/earthquake/whatever had struck the seccy part of the town and due to substandard construction/corrupt business practices/overcrowding/whatever there had been considerable loss of life.

Again, like looking through a keyhole. The problem wasn't so much the distortion in what you could see.

Some distortion was there, certainly, but you could adjust for it. The big problem were all the things you couldn't see because your field of vision was too limited.

Much better and less censored news was available on subscription channels. But those were quite expensive and restricted to full citizens.

What were they *not* being told by the news media? There was no way to know. Not, at least, without access to information coming from outside the Mesan loop—and that was simply not available to seccies such as themselves.

"They're planning something, the bastards," Stephanie half-muttered as she watched the newscasters. "They're spending more time than usual hollering and screaming about the Ballroom. Way more time, in fact. It's practically all they're talking about lately."

Cary frowned. She knew what Stephanie was getting at. Provocation was probably the oldest trick in the counterrevolutionary book—and, unfortunately, was often very effective. If the Mesan media outlets were bombarding the populace with warnings about the imminent threat of terrorist outrages, those outrages were sure to come—carried out not by the so-called terrorists but by agencies of the Mesan government.

It was an effective tactic in large part because it was so hard to argue against, especially when you had no access yourself to any mass media. Fine to say "people aren't that dumb; they'll see through it." The historical record said otherwise. Over and again, throughout history, a lot of people *had* been that dumb.

"Nothing we can do about it," she said, straightening up. "Except... Do you think we ought to suspend our regular check-ins for a while? Maybe a week?"

"No, don't." That came from Karen, lying bed. Cary hadn't realized she was still awake.

"Why not?" asked Stephanie. "The odds against our check-ins turning up anything are close to astronomical anyway. So what's the harm in suspending them for a while?"

Once a day, either Cary or Stephanie ventured outside the apartment to check one of the six dead drops they maintained in various places in the city. Four of them were in the seccy quarters. The other two were in heavily trafficked areas frequented by seccies on their way to work as servants in the citizen districts.

The drop locations had been set up by the Manticoran agent who'd called himself Angus Levigne when he'd been active on Mesa. Months had gone by since he and his odd-looking partner had left the planet—or gotten killed, they didn't know which. The odds against Levigne or someone else using the sites to get in touch with them again were low, of course. Maybe not astronomically low, but pretty close. Still, since they had no other means of reestablishing contact with anyone from off-planet, they continued to maintain the routine checks.

Painfully, Karen levered herself up on one elbow. "I don't care about the drop boxes—although we may as well check them while we're out."

"I ask again: why? We can get food and supplies a lot closer than the nearest of the drop sites, so why take the risk?"

Karen shook her head. "You're not thinking far enough ahead. How much money do we have left?"

Cary was their treasurer, insofar as the term "treasure" wasn't laughable. Official Keeper of the Piggy Bank would be a more accurate way of putting it.

"Not a lot."

"Enough to pay the rent and buy food and supplies to keep us going for six more months?"

Cary took in a breath and puffed it out, swelling her cheeks. "Well. No. I figure we can go another two months for sure. Maybe up to three, if we ration really tightly."

"About what I thought. We need to face facts squarely, folks." Karen made as little waving motion with her hand, indicating her body. "I'm most likely going to be dead within three months."

Stephanie started to protest but Karen talked over her. "Cut it out, Moriarty! Optimism and keeping our spirits up is one thing. Dumber'n a box of rocks is another. You know as well as I do that I'm not going to last much longer unless we can get me some pretty major medical treatment—and how are we going to pay for *that* when we're as strapped as we are?"

Slowly, just as painfully as she'd raised herself up, Karen put her head back on the pillow and stared at the ceiling.

"When I die, two things happen. Or rather, one thing happens for sure and the other happens if we plan for it ahead of time. The thing that happens for sure is that the money we've got left will stretch further because you'll only have to feed two people instead of three. The thing that *might* happen—*if* we make our preparations ahead of time—is that you two come into a lot more money. Well . . . a fair amount more, anyway. Enough to keep you going for half a year at least."

Stephanie's expression was skeptical, bordering on sarcastic. "And just how in God's name do you think that'll— Oh."

The conclusion it had taken her half a sentence to reach had come to Cary almost immediately.

"Jesus, Karen," she said.

"When did you get religion?" Karen said. "Although I guess I should aim that more at Stephanie, seeing as how she's the one who claims to be the atheist here and you still cling to some shreds of your childhood faith. But I remind you that faith doesn't think anything but the soul is eternal, so what does it matter what happens to my body after I'm gone? I don't give a damn, myself."

She raised her head again, just enough to give her two companions a ferocious glare. "What I *do* give a damn about is that I don't want that chiseling scumbag landlord pocketing the money—which is what he did with Farouz's remains. So when I die, keep it a secret from the shithead. Cut me up yourselves—the bathtub's one of the few things in this dump that works—and freeze the parts. Then sell what you can."

She sagged back down. Her voice was getting weaker. "But you have to plan for it. Go out there and find the market. You've got weeks to do it. You ought to turn up something."

She was silent for a while. Then she said, very softly: "I'm so tired." She was asleep within seconds.

Cary and Stephanie looked at each other. Neither of them said anything for perhaps a minute.

"I don't think I can do it," Stephanie finally said. Her eyes were tearing up. "I really don't."

Cary had known that already. Stephanie had her strengths—plenty of them—but despite the airs she sometimes put on she just wasn't what you'd call "hard-boiled." She was tough enough when dealing with enemies. But butcher a dead friend? She'd make a mess of the business before she gave up altogether.

"I'll do it," Cary said. "But only if we've found a buyer."

There was silence again, for another minute. Then Stephanie sighed and got to her feet. "I guess that means I check the drop box today. And then..."

She raised her hands in a gesture that was half-despairing and half-aggravated. "Where the hell do I go to find a buyer for body parts? The only person we know who'd know is the shithead himself. And we can't ask him."

"We'll figure out something," Cary said. Trying her best to believe it.

CHAPTER 8

Looking around the office of his new boss, Lajos Irvine started counting the ways.

The ways his new boss was so much worse than his old one, Jack McBryde.

True, his old boss had turned out to be a traitor. But if you left that one flaw aside, he'd been a real pleasure to work for. Lajos hadn't appreciated how much so until he'd had some months to fully explore the depth and breadth of his new boss's qualities.

Using the term "qualities" loosely and understanding that the term was neutral. A fetid odor was also a "quality."

To start with, there was the fact that Lajos had been waiting for twenty minutes for George Vickers to make his appearance. Why had the man bothered to set the meeting at this hour in his own office if he hadn't planned to be there himself?

If this had been a one-time event, Lajos would have assumed that Vickers had been delayed unexpectedly or had simply been absentminded and forgot the time. But it wasn't a one-time occurrence, it was an every-time occurrence. Vickers was wasting the time of his subordinate for the sole purpose of showing him who was the boss.

Not that there would have ever been any doubt about it, which made the whole exercise purposeless as well as annoying.

As a genetically engineered specialist developed to infiltrate the societies of genetic slaves, Lajos Irvine was officially the equal of any other specialty line produced by the Alignment. Unlike the agents produced for the External Bureau, who were indistinguishable from general utility slave lines except for their special slave numbers, Lajos was a full member of the Alignment. Not the very innermost circles of the onion, true—although that was not precluded for him in the future—but he was still a genetic slave in form only. He'd been given prolong treatments, for instance.

Formalities aside, though, there was still a deep-seated prejudice against people like him that permeated the Alignment. Not all people shared it—McBryde hadn't, for one—but many did. And even leaving the bias aside, the fact remained that Lajos was a specialty line and George Vickers was an alpha line.

There was no chance, no matter what his accomplishments might be, that he'd ever wind up replacing Vickers in this office—so what was the point of this rigmarole?

Everything about the office reminded Lajos of what a jackass his new boss was. His eyes fell on the wall behind Vickers' desk. The equivalent of that wall in Jack McBryde's office had been decorated with a few paintings and some simple images of the McBryde family. Jack himself had been in a couple of the images, but no more than that.

That wall had vanished, destroyed with the rest of

Gamma Center. This wall, in contrast, was solid Vickers' territory. Every single thing on the wall was about him. His images—fancy holograms, these, and expensive ones at that—and his awards and certificates and decorations. The only other people in the holograms on the wall were those of Vickers' associates whom he obviously felt enhanced his own prestige. Some were his immediate superiors; others were images of people who were apparently very high up in the Alignment.

Then there was the desk. Jack McBryde's desk had been a beehive of activity. There would have been three or four virtual screens up and running, and half the desk would have been covered with slips and sheets of papic. Jack had been fond of the old-fashioned way of taking notes.

"I don't know why but I think better when I'm chewing on an idea I've written down myself." He'd given Lajos a grin and added: "Would you believe I've even been to the paper exhibit in the Museum of Science and Technology?"

"What's 'paper'?" Lajos had asked.

Jack had picked up a sheet of papic. "It's what they used to use instead of this. Looks just like it—they let me pick one up—but it feels a little different. Coarser. They made it out of pulped wood, you know."

Lajos had made a face. "Sounds awfully unsanitary."

"Oh, the paper was safe enough. The manufacturing process was destructive, though. Poisoned the environment like you wouldn't believe. Once they figured out a way to make plastic biodegradable they got rid of paper."

Vickers' desk looked like it ought to be in a museum itself. The expanse was completely empty except for one virtual screen which simply displayed the agency's logo—as if anyone who had the security clearance to get in here in the first place wouldn't know where they were.

Other than that, there was simply a nameplate perched on the corner of the desk. A big nameplate, reading:

George Vickers
Assistant Director
Central Security Agency

Perhaps most telling of all, the nameplate didn't face the visitor. It faced Vickers—or would, whenever the Great Man finally made his entrance.

Vickers *had* to have some genuine ability or he'd never have been given this post. The Alignment gave short shrift to bosses who were incompetent. But, so far at least, Lajos hadn't seen any evidence of it.

The door to the office swung open and Vickers came in.

"Ah, there you are," he said, as if Lajos hadn't been sitting there for the better part of half an hour and Vickers had been looking for him.

Damn, he missed Jack.

A thought, needless to say, that he kept entirely to himself.

❖   ❖   ❖

After George Vickers finished his explanation of Lajos Irvine's new assignment, there was silence in the room for at least half a minute.

From the self-satisfied look on his face, Vickers assumed that the silence was due to Lajos striving mightily to absorb the subtleties and profundities of the strategic thinking involved.

Instead of, as was actually the case, Lajos striving mightily not to burst out with sentences that would be:

a) True.

b) Emotionally satisfying.

c) Useless.

d) Damaging to his career.

He knew that much from the beginning, but he couldn't relinquish the sentences for half a minute.

That is the stupidest— Most of the sentences began with that clause.

What imbecile came up with this idea? Variations on that theme constituted a good two-thirds of the sentences.

What is the fucking point—

He finally managed to bring himself under control enough to utter his first words aloud.

"Uh, George, in my experience criminals make it a point to know as little as possible about anything that might be dangerous and brings them no income. As informers—on political activity, that is—they're about as useful as—as—" He tried to come up with an analogy. *Sewer rats* and *alley cats* wouldn't do because such animals might actually provide a modicum of useful information. The absence of either one in an area might indicate the presence of a terrorist cell, for instance.

Or a big, mean dog, more likely. But there was still the *possibility* of usefulness.

Criminals? One of whose characteristics was the inclination to lie as a first reaction to any question and another of which was that most of them were damn good at it.

And another of whose characteristics was that they were prone to violence.

"That raises another issue," he said. "I'm not trained—"

"Relax, Lajos," said Vickers, waving his hand in a genial manner. Or what he took to be one, anyway. "We're going to be providing you with some assistance. Nobody expects you to match muscle with hooligans."

Great. I'll be saddled with brainless goons. Which meant his already slim chances of turning up any information by infiltrating the Mesa seccy underworld just went on a starvation diet.

"But what—"

Vickers waved his hand again. The gesture, this time, was firm; decisive; not genial at all.

"It's been decided, Lajos. Just do it. We haven't gotten anywhere in weeks following the usual methods, so the powers-that-be upstairs"—he pointed at the ceiling, in blithe disregard of the fact that CSA headquarters was two miles to the west and there was nothing on the floors above them except a lot of computers and clerical workers—"have decided to try a flanking approach. It's obvious that our firm and decisive measures have driven the terrorists to bay. They're huddling in their shelters, now. If they want to do anything, they have to use criminals as their intermediaries. So—"

His chest swelled a little. "Operation Capone." He bestowed a sly smile on Irvine. "I came up with the name. Capone was a notorious Roman gangster in ancient times. The orator and philosopher Cicero even talked about him."

Operation Capone. Lajos had never heard of anyone by that name. What he did know was that all you had to do was lop the "e" off the end of the name and you had a castrated rooster. A near-mindless critter that made a lot of noise and couldn't accomplish a damn thing.

❖   ❖   ❖

After he left Vickers, Lajos went down to the mess hall in the basement. He did have his own office in the building but he didn't like to use it. The room they'd given him was more like a cubicle with delusions of grandeur than anything he'd call an "office," and Lajos didn't like feeling cramped whenever he had to do any serious thinking.

And serious thinking was called for here. Whatever he thought of them, orders were orders, and the basic law of hierarchies applied just as much to the Alignment as to any other institution in human history.

Shit rolls downhill. If this idiot scheme came apart at the seams, or just came to nothing at all, Lajos would be the one blamed. Not George Vickers. Not whoever on high gave Vickers his orders. Certainly not any of the Detweilers.

Poor put-upon Lajos Irvine, that's who'd get the fault laid at his feet.

The first thing he had to figure out was his cover identity. None of the ones he had already established would work well in this assignment.

Thankfully, the powers-that-were hadn't been stingy as well as stupid. The budget Vickers had given him was enough for Lajos to set himself up in whatever identity was most likely to be successful.

Forget being a robber, contract killer, any of that business. Lajos had neither the skills nor the temperament to pull off such identities successfully. Not long enough, anyway. Even Vickers was willing to allow that this maneuver was going to take a fair amount of time before it produced any results.

A fence, then. And he'd have to be selling something fairly exotic, in order to explain why no one in the criminal underworld in the capital's seccy quarters had run across him before.

So . . . sell what? Drugs were out. Sure, there was always some sort of new design pharmaceutical coming on line, but that was a very well-established market with well-established suppliers. Well-established suppliers with a long and well-deserved reputation for violent retaliation against newcomers and interlopers, to boot.

No, it'd have to be something less obvious. Stolen art was a possibility. But the problem there was the market was too upscale to be likely to prove very helpful in tracking down Ballroom terrorists in hiding.

Lajos didn't think there were nearly as many such terrorists as his superiors seemed to be believe, anyway. Not ever—and certainly not now, after the savage reprisals carried out in the seccy areas following Green Pines. Anyone even remotely suspected of having ties to the Ballroom had been targeted, and the authorities had been indiscriminate in their application of violence. The way they looked at it, "collateral damage" was just another term for a job well done.

Lajos estimated that somewhere around two thousand people had been killed, and at least twice that many badly injured. He was quite sure that most of the casualties had had no connection to the Ballroom, but some of them would have. The point being that he didn't think there were really that many terrorists still at large, and they'd be deep in hiding and . . .

Casualties. Fatalities. Desperate need for money...

Body parts and tissues. That was the market he'd aim for. There was a small trade in such goods in seccy areas. More modern medical methods were available and not even that expensive, but there were always some people who wanted to stay off the official grid for one reason or another. For such people, going to an established hospital for regeneration treatments posed too much of a risk, even compared to the risks of undergoing primitive organ-replacement surgery in unlicensed clinics.

The market was too erratic and marginal to have a well-established network of fences in place. There'd be some, sure, but they'd be freelancers. What the underworld called gypsies. Savage, often, but they'd be individuals or very small groups, not large gangs. The goons Vickers had promised to provide Lajos should be able to handle any problems of that nature that came up.

And he'd certainly not have any problem coming up with a supply of goods to sell. Not with the resources of the entire Mesan penal system at his disposal. Mesan authorities had no hesitation when it came to using the death penalty as a means of disciplining the population. Lajos wasn't sure of the exact number, but there'd be at least half a dozen people being executed every month. Their bodies were normally cremated, since the body parts and tissues market was too small to be of interest to the giant corporations that dominated the planet—and the wealthy individuals who ran those corporations had other and better means to provide for their medical needs.

Just a little change in methods, for a while. Cut

up the executed corpses to provide Lajos with the supplies he needed, cremate what was left and hand those remains over to the grieving relatives when there were any. Would anyone bother to weigh the ashes and try to calculate if everything was accounted for? Not likely. Not that class of people. And if they did, so what? Nobody cared what they thought anyway.

His spirits were picking up now. This...

Was still a stupid idea. But at least it'd be workable, wouldn't pose too many risks—and, who could say? Maybe he'd even turn up something.

Hearing a slight noise behind him, he turned in his seat and saw that two men had just entered the mess hall and were headed his way.

Large men. The muscle, obviously.

When they reached the table, one of them said: "Vickers sent us."

"We're supposed to give you whatever help you need," said the other. "I'm Borisav Stanković," he said. "Call me Bora." He pointed a thumb at his partner. "This is Freddie Martinez."

Martinez nodded.

Lajos rose from the table he'd been sitting at and stuck out his hand. "Pleased to meet you."

"What's the job?" asked Stanković, once the handshakes were done.

"Sit down and I'll explain it to you."

❖   ❖   ❖

After he finished, Stanković and Martinez looked at each other.

"Piece of cake," said Stanković. Martinez nodded.

A promising start, Lajos decided.

CHAPTER 9

"So I finally get to meet you, Special Officer Cachat. You made yourself impossible to find when I visited Torch for Berry's coronation." Despite the reproving words, Cathy Montaigne's tone was friendly and she was smiling. She strode forward and extended her hand.

Victor shook her hand and then executed a flourishing bow; the sort of gesture that had once been part of Haven's social protocol during the Legislaturalist era and was still part of Manticoran protocol—although you rarely saw it done outside of some formal royal occasions. And then it was done only by some members of the aristocracy and usually done badly. Cachat's performance, on the other hand, had been flawless.

Startled, Cathy looked at Anton Zilwicki. "You told me he was a rabid republican."

"I said no such thing. 'Rabid' means raving; slavering with fury; downright witless. Victor neither raves nor slavers and he certainly isn't witless. Setting that aside, yes, he's a republican. Sort of the way polonium is radioactive."

She turned back to Victor. "But he did that perfectly."

She waggled her fingers. "Maybe just a shade too flamboyantly."

"I figured it was better to err in that direction than the other," said Cachat. "Given the nature of the exercise."

"But . . . you're too young. From what Anton tells me. You wouldn't have been more than a boy during the Legislaturalist era."

"And born and raised in a Dolist slum to boot," added Anton.

"Then how would you have learned—?"

Anton made a loud snorting noise. The sound conveyed an odd cross of derision and grudging admiration. "He would have practiced it in a simulator on the way here," he said. "You wouldn't *believe* how much faith Victor has in the gadgets. He never travels without one if he can manage it—he even squeezed one into the courier ship—and he spends at least an hour a day in there practicing whatever. I'd accuse him of idolatry and worshipping golden calves except he's as much of an atheist as he is a republican."

"Oscar Saint-Just was a monster," said Victor. "Doesn't mean he wasn't smart. He believed in the value of simulator training and I learned it from him."

Cathy started to make a flippant remark but stopped. A thought had just crossed her mind. She'd never met Victor Cachat before this moment but she had seen him before, in a manner of speaking. One of Jeremy X's people had made a video recording of the gun fight in the bowels of Old Chicago between Cachat—later joined by Jeremy himself—and a group of Havenite soldiers and their Scrag allies. That had happened during the so-called Manpower Incident.

The quality of the recording had been quite poor; what you'd expect to get from a cheap handheld device in bad lighting conditions. But even so, two things had struck her powerfully when she'd watched afterward. Jeremy hadn't wanted to show it to her but she'd insisted and he owed her too much to refuse.

The first was the sheer brutality involved. "Gun fight" was far too antiseptic a term for the slaughter produced when people shot each other at literally point blank range and the person doing most of the shooting had been armed with a flechette gun.

He'd known how to use it, too, and that had been the second thing Cathy had been struck by. Once the fight began, Cachat had been nothing but a blur. Partly that was the poor quality of the recording, but mostly it had been Cachat himself. He'd moved quickly, surely, spinning, shifting aside—while every shot he fired went true. He hadn't seemed like a man so much as a killing machine.

He would have been what, at the time? Twenty-one years old? Twenty-two? Certainly not more than twenty-five.

"The fight in Old Chicago," she blurted out before she could stop herself. "When you saved Helen. You practiced that in a simulator."

Victor frowned and glanced at Zilwicki. Who, for his part, spread his hands.

"Don't look at me. I kept my description vague. Really vague. And it was all over before I got there anyway."

"Jeremy," Victor muttered. "Damn him. He told me—I asked, later—that there hadn't been any recordings made."

"He's been known to lie." That came from Anton.

Cachat's frown faded into a mildly irritated expression. "Sort of like plutonium is radioactive."

He looked back at Cathy. "Yes, I trained for it in a simulator. A much bigger and more sophisticated simulator than the portable one I take with me, of course. How else could I have managed it?"

She felt like she was being extremely rude, all of sudden. Whatever might be Victor Cachat's exotic history and peculiar attitudes, he was the man who had saved the lives of all three of her adopted children. And done so at incredibly great risk to his own.

So she extended both her hands this time and took both of his, in a gesture that was not formal in the least. "Please. Be welcome in this home. Now and always."

Cachat's poise faltered for an instant. "Well...thank you," he said awkwardly, seeming to shed a decade and two inches of psychic armor in the process. Cathy now understood the truth of something Anton had once said to her about his Havenite partner: that somewhere deep underneath Cachat's ferocious skills and adamantine willpower there remained a shy and lonely boy from the slums. Only a handful of people in the universe were ever made privy to that inner core, he'd told her—and Anton himself wasn't really one of them. Or only partly so, at any rate.

"I'm not sure if he lets anyone into that sanctum, except Thandi Palane and Ginny Usher," he'd told her. "Probably Kevin Usher, too."

Cathy decided then and there that she'd add herself to that small list. First, because she owed the man that much. Second, because she enjoyed a challenge. And finally—

She couldn't keep herself from giggling. At her age! "What's so funny?" asked Anton.

"Never mind." She didn't think even Anton would understand, not really. He thought—she was sure almost everyone did, except Jeremy X and Web Du Havel and maybe Empress Elizabeth, who'd been a close childhood friend—that Cathy's rebellious history stemmed from her deep political principles. And...

That was indeed true enough. But she couldn't deny that at least a part of the reason for her notorious past was simply a juvenile glee in thumbing her nose at the establishment. *Any* establishment.

As Countess of the Tor, Cathy's coat of arms carried the family motto *I cannot*, which according to family legend referred to the heroic stance taken by an early politician who refused to sign on to a popular but unwise law. Cathy had her doubts about the legend, but the motto suited her well enough. In the interests of full disclosure, though, she'd sometimes thought she should add to the motto *Épater la bourgeoisie*—or use it altogether as a substitute.

She'd already scandalized Manticoran polite society with her longstanding association with the terrorist madman Jeremy X—now, sadly for polite society's amour-propre, reborn as a respectable cabinet member of Torch's government. Now she could add the scandal of a friendship with the man who was rapidly becoming the Republic of Haven's most notorious secret agent.

How delightful.

She led the way through the foyer and into the rooms beyond. The first of which had the official title of "the salon" but which Anton insisted on calling "the extravagansory." Or, sometimes, "the playing field."

Cachat looked around, his expression one of mild interest.

Anton grinned. "Didn't miss a beat. Congratulations, Victor. The first time I came into this room I said 'holy shit!' It took me four hours in here before I worked up the nerve to ask where the bathroom was. Were, as it happens. There are eight of them. Would you believe she calls this a 'town house'?"

"Are you quite done?" said Cathy. This was an old jape of Anton's. Most people would have let it go by now, but he was from the Gryphon highlands. One had to make allowances.

"By certain values of 'town' and 'house,' the label is perfectly appropriate," said Cachat. His tone was as relaxed and casual as his expression. "To be sure, the values are ones that should be lined up against a wall and shot."

That was said just as mildly. Cathy wasn't fooled. She was quite certain that if—no, more likely to have been when—the Havenite agent ever lined someone against a wall and shot them, he'd do so in the same relaxed and casual manner.

Oh, this was going to be *so* delightful. She'd have to make sure she had a doctor in attendance, though, when she trotted Cachat out for his first public appearance at one of her *soirees*. He was bound to say something that would cause one or two of the more rigid members of Manticore's upper crust to suffer cardiac arrest.

❖   ❖   ❖

"He's a little unsettling, isn't he?" was Empress Elizabeth's first comment after Haven's delegation withdrew from the conference room. She looked at

Honor Alexander-Harrington, who was sitting to her left a little way down the large table in the middle of the room. "Special Officer Cachat, I mean."

Honor chuckled and reached over to scratch the ears of the cream-and-gray treecat perched on the back of the chair beside hers. "At least this time he wasn't carrying a suicide device. I don't think he was, anyway."

Captain Spencer Hawke, her personal armsman, was standing just behind her. His already-stiff stance became rigid. "I assure you, My Lady, he carried no such device...this time. We checked him over *thoroughly*." A bit grudgingly, the Grayson added: "So did the Queen's Own, of course."

"Not to mention that we had a trio of treecats keeping a beady eye on him," added Hamish Alexander-Harrington, who was seated across from Honor with Samantha, Nimitz's mate, curled up neatly in his lap. She made a very pleased with herself sound, and Nimitz and Ariel, the somewhat younger male treecat on the back of Elizabeth's chair, bleeked with laughter. Samantha deigned to open one grass-green eye and look at each of them with a predator's thoughtfulness, then closed the eye once more.

Honor shook her head. "I'm afraid neither of you really understands Victor Cachat. First of all"—she looked at Elizabeth—"to answer your question, yes, he's a little unsettling. But he's not a monster or a maniac. He's more like the closest thing a human can come to a treecat."

Nimitz issued a sound that was halfway between a purr and a growl. Ariel echoed the sound an instant later, but Samantha merely flipped the tip of her tail.

"The point being," Honor continued, "any suicide device he'd carry—anywhere, not just here—wouldn't be a bomb, or anything that would wreak indiscriminate damage. It'd be very selective, with just himself as the target."

She glanced back at Captain Hawke and then over at the two members of the Queen's Own Regiment standing guard against the wall behind Elizabeth. "We analyzed the one he brought aboard *Imperator* when he and Zilwicki paid me that little visit. If he'd activated it, it would have injected him with a chemical compound which would trigger a previously implanted chemical compound that was inert in the absence of the right catalyst...at which point it would have sent his heart into severe ventricular fibrillation while simultaneously triggering both brain and pulmonary embolisms."

The Empress grimaced. So did Hamish. For that matter—Honor glanced around the room—so did all the other people seated at the table. Those consisted of William Alexander, Baron Grantville and Prime Minister of the Star Empire of Manticore; Sir Anthony Langtry, the Star Empire's Foreign Secretary; and two admirals: Sir Thomas Caparelli, First Space Lord, and Admiral Pat Givens.

"So don't be too sure what Cachat might or might not have been carrying," Honor continued. "If he thought it was called for, he's perfectly capable of having a biological mechanism designed so that we could only detect it if we gave him a complete somatic screening. Which we didn't, of course. That would have been undiplomatic, to say the least."

Prime Minister Alexander looked alarmed. "If I'd

known he was capable of that, I think we *should* have insisted on a somatic screen."

Honor started to answer, but the treecats beat her to it. This time, *all* of them issued sounds that were pretty much pure growls, and Nimitz followed up by pressing one true-hand's palm to his mouth, then swinging it in a throwing away motion before touching the outermost finger of the same true-hand to his forehead. None of the humans in the room had any problem translating the sign for "bad idea," and Hamish barked a laugh.

"It seems none of the six-limbed participants in this little discussion agree with you," he observed, then looked at Honor for a few seconds. "But I see what you're getting at. The issue isn't what Cachat *could* do but what he *would* do."

Honor nodded. "Yes." She turned back to Elizabeth. "You already knew what Anton Zilwicki's capable of. Well, now you've gotten a feel for how far *Cachat* will go for something he thinks is really important, which is why you asked for him to come to Manticore. As partnerships go, I think the two of them are the most capable pair of spies the galaxy's produced in a long, long time. Which is the reason they've turned out to be such a nightmare for our *real* enemies—ours and Haven's—and a blessing for us. Men like them don't give their loyalty lightly, but once they do, it's stronger than battle steel."

The last phrase came out flat, certain, final.

"In other words, you're telling me it's time to quit shilly-shallying," said Elizabeth.

"If you dress that up a little, yes. It's time to decide whether you're on the floor or sitting out the dance."

The Empress chuckled. So did Hamish. Both admirals just smiled.

For his part, Foreign Secretary Langtry looked unhappy, but didn't seem inclined to say anything. Prime Minister Grantville sighed and ran his fingers through his hair.

"If I can put this into more formal language," he said, "what Honor is saying is that while it's possible Zilwicki and Cachat are wrong, it's unlikely. And it's not possible at all that either man's loyalties are in doubt. Which means our course of action should be based on those presumptions."

"Spoken like a true statesman, Willie," said Honor. Nimitz issued a noise that seemed approving. So did Ariel.

Samantha just nodded once, in the gesture the 'cats had learned from humans centuries ago.

✧   ✧   ✧

"The meeting with the Empress went pretty well, I think," said Victor later that night over dinner, in response to a question from Cathy. "Hard to be sure, of course. Nobody in that room got where they are by being easy to read."

Cathy cocked her head. "Then . . . why do you seem a bit apprehensive?"

Startled, Cachat looked up from his plate. "I do?"

"Tense as a drum," said Anton. "It's pretty hard to miss, especially coming from you."

"Oh. That." Victor had barely touched his food. Now, he laid down his utensils. Much as a medieval knight on a battlefield might lay down his sword and shield as he conceded defeat.

"I wasn't actually thinking about that at all," he

said. He glanced at his watch. "We sent the courier to Torch five days ago, right after we arrived here. It should have arrived at Beacon by now."

Anton sucked his teeth. "Carrying your message to Thandi letting her know that, hey guess what, you're now on Manticore. Having not stopped at Torch on your way to Haven."

Cathy looked back and forth between the two men. "Do you think she'll be upset with you, Victor?"

"Is Uranium 235 fissile material?" mused Anton.

"She's going to kill me," foresaw Victor.

CHAPTER 10

Thandi Palane glowered at the figures on the computer screen. She was trying to fit a round peg into a square hole: make a too-skeletal logistics network support the number of combat units she wanted for Torch's military. Palane believed in a teeth-to-tail ratio that belonged to a tiger rather than a tadpole, but the tadpole was fighting back pretty fiercely.

Her mood wasn't helped by the fact that the person sitting next to her, Captain Anton Petersen, had told her so. Several times, in fact, albeit politely. He had far more experience than Thandi did with these sorts of problems. Her own experience as a company grade Solarian Marine officer had been heavily concentrated in combat operations. Logistics on the level with which she was now trying to grapple had been something she left to others.

Her experience was short in other areas, as well. So, very soon after Torch was founded, Thandi had put in a request to both Manticore and Haven for training missions to be sent to provide her with advice and assistance.

Both star nations had agreed, although it had taken Haven a while to put their own mission together. Petersen and his aides, on the other hand, had arrived within two months. He was an officer in the Royal Manticoran Navy who'd compiled an impressive record in command of two destroyers and the light cruiser HMS *Impulse* before he'd been badly wounded. During his regeneration and physical rehab he'd moved over to the staff side and discovered he was even better at that than at commanding a Queen's ship. His superiors had thought so, as well, and he'd been working directly for its First Space Lord, Sir Thomas Caparelli, before his sudden transfer to Torch.

Anton had now been with her for more than a year, and he'd been invaluable. Although he was still technically nothing more than an "adviser," he was one of Palane's handful of chief subordinates and for all practical purposes he was in charge of Torch's navy. Even the Havenites got along well with him, after they arrived.

None of which improved her disposition at the moment, however. *I-told-you-so* may be a fine fellow but he's still not likely to be welcomed with open arms when he tells you so.

There was a buzz at the door to Thandi Palane's office. "Open," she said.

Colonel Shai-gwun Metterling came in. "A courier just arrived from Manticore. It seems—ah..."

Hearing the hesitation and trace of trepidation in her aide's voice—Shai-gwun was normally a sanguine fellow—Thandi looked up immediately. "What is it?"

"Well. It turns out Special Officer Cachat and Anton Zilwicki went to Manticore from Haven instead of, ah, as we thought they would—Cachat would, anyway—returning here."

Thandi stared at him for a couple of seconds. Then said: "He's a dead man walking."

Metterling opened his mouth; closed it. Advising his commanding officer on matters of the heart went farther outside his military occupation specialty than—than—

He couldn't think of an appropriate comparison. Composing an opera, maybe?

"Dead," Thandi repeated. Abruptly she rose from her seat. "Don't let that courier ship so much as shift a kilometer out of its orbit. I'll be taking it to Manticore. Anton, hold down the fort for me."

"Yes, General Palane. When do you expect to return?"

But she was already brushing past him and out the door. Moving like one of the four horsemen of the Apocalypse.

Death, to be specific. Famine, Pestilence and War would be straggling far behind.

◆   ◆   ◆

Although he wasn't willing to insert himself into a domestic quarrel between Palane and Cachat— talk about Scylla and Charybdis!—Captain Petersen didn't feel he could in good conscience say nothing to anyone about his superior officer's plans. She was so riled up she seemed oblivious to the fact that she was about to go AWOL. That was bad enough if you were a rating. If you were the commanding officer of the entire military...

He put in a call to Hugh Arai. In doing so, he was going completely out of channels, since Arai had no official position in either Torch's military or government.

Torch had never gotten around to adopting a formal definition of a monarch's consort.

In the real world, however, he was the right person to contact. Arai was privy to all the plans and discussions of the "inner circle," people listened to him, and Petersen had a great deal of confidence in his judgment.

In the event, the captain's concerns proved overblown. As furious as she was, by the time Thandi got to her apartment—that took fifteen minutes—and packed her bag—that took three minutes—she'd calmed down enough to realize she couldn't simply commandeer a courier vessel and head off to Manticore.

So, she put in a call to Petersen. "Sorry, Anton. I . . . sort of lost my temper, there. Cancel the hold on the courier. I'll be back within the hour."

But by then, Petersen had already alerted Arai and the consort-in-fact-if-not-in-name had informed his monarch and bed partner. He'd also given her his advice and, as she usually did, Berry accepted it.

She called Thandi at her apartment—not more than thirty seconds after Palane had broken off her call to Captain Petersen. The conversation that ensued was the last thing Thandi had expected.

"What can I do for you, Your Majesty?"

"Since when do you call me 'Your Majesty'? I've got great news, Thandi! It turns out that Daddy and Victor wound up on Manticore. Imagine that! So I've decided to kill two birds with one stone. Well, I guess that's a silly way to put it, but the point is that I want to combine seeing Daddy again with an official state visit to the Star Empire. I started to give the orders myself but then I realized that was probably inappropriate and you should do it instead.

So tell the captain of the *Pottawatomie Creek* to get ready to leave for Manticore as soon as possible. Oh, and you need to pack a bag. I want you to come with me. Captain Petersen can manage things and you'll want to see Victor anyway. I'm bringing Web and Jeremy too. Hugh will stay here and hold the fort while we're gone."

Thandi stared at the image of the young woman on the screen. Her brain seemed to have taken flight like a startled bird and was flapping around aimlessly.

She heard someone's voice behind Berry but couldn't make out the words. Then, another voice, but she couldn't understand what it was saying either.

"What do you mean you can't do that?" said Berry, looking over her shoulder.

Voices-talking-but-the-words-were-not-comprehensible.

"Oh, that's ridiculous, Hugh!" said Berry. "God, I detest stupid formalities."

Voices-talking-but-the-words-were-not-comprehensible.

"The so-called 'integrity of government' can kiss my sweet royal ass. Call Web. Tell him to make you a member of the Cabinet."

Voices-talking-but-the-words-were-not-comprehensible.

"How should I know which cabinet post, Jeremy? Who cares, anyway?" She looked back at Thandi, her expression that of someone sharing the absurdity of the world's workings with a close friend. "Can you believe this crap?"

Berry looked back over her shoulder and said: "Make him the cabinet member in charge when the queen and prime minister are out of the system. Call it the... Hell, I don't know. The Department of the Posterior."

Voices-talking-but-the-words-were-not-comprehensible.

Berry's lips tightened. "Is that so?" She looked back at Thandi. "Time to take off the royal gloves." Then, looked back over her shoulder again.

"The law says I can order one person exiled every year, right? Totally at my discretion? No appeals, no arguments, no ifs, ands or buts. I am correct, am I not?"

Voices-talking-but-the-words-were-not-comprehensible. But given the brevity of the speech it had to have been a three word response: *Yes, Your Majesty.*

Berry looked triumphant. "Fine. Spread the word far and wide—have it announced on all the news stations; hire people to shout it from the rooftops—that the first jackass who questions Hugh's right to run the show while we're gone is immediately exiled. How's that? Are we satisfied now, Mister Galaxy's-Worst-Terrorist-Turned-OCD-Protocol-Fussbudget? How about you, Doctor Anal-Retentive-Former-Coldblooded-Commando?"

She turned back to Thandi. "How soon can you get here?"

Thandi's brain came to roost where it belonged. "About half an hour."

❖   ❖   ❖

By the time Thandi got there, Ruth Winton had decided to come along also.

More precisely, the princess had announced her decision to join the party headed for Manticore but various objections were raised, centered on the fact that with Anton Zilwicki gone the princess was needed to oversee Torch's intelligence community. Said objections were overruled by Berry in a peremptory manner on the grounds that a traveling monarch needed a companion and if anybody didn't like it see aforementioned provisions for summary exile and since when was intelligence a community anyway?

"*L'état, c'est toi,*" Hugh muttered.

"What was that wisecrack?" demanded Berry.

"'Twasn't a wisecrack but the now-revealed godawful truth," said Jeremy X. He started singing the verses of *La Marseillaise*.

Under his breath.

CHAPTER 11

"Does she *ever* stop griping and grousing?" asked Colonel Donald Toussaint. His tone of voice was relaxed, though, and he was smiling rather than frowning. Apparently, he'd already been briefed on the ... distinctive personality and behavior of the *Hali Sowle*'s captain.

"Ganny?" Commander Loren Damewood shook his head but didn't look up from the console he was monitoring. "Not that I've ever noticed. But I might have missed a stretch where she was quiet, here or there, if I was preoccupied with something. After a while you just tune it out. It's like living by the ocean—before too long, you don't hear the surf unless you think about it."

Another burst came over the com. "*—the fuck designed this stupid software, anyway? For Christ's sake, I could chew some raw silicon—don't think I couldn't!—and spit out a better program than this miserable misbegotten—*"

Donald tuned it out and swiveled his seat in order to bring his three immediate subordinates into sight.

He had to fight down a grin. *This must be what the historical novels mean by "a motley crew."*

On the left, looking like a misplaced piece of heavy equipment that someone as a prank had made to resemble a human being was Major Arkaitz Ali bin Muhammad. He was even bigger and squatter than Donald himself.

The major had formerly gone by the monicker of Arkaitz X. When he joined the Torch military he dropped the "X" and, as was the usual custom, adopted as a new surname the identity of some historical leader of anti-slavery revolts or protests. In his case, the name of the man who'd led the great Zanj Rebellion against the Abbasid Caliphate more than two millennia earlier.

On the right stood a woman whose membership in the human race was evident at a glance. That was Lieutenant Colonel Ayibongwinkosi Kabweza, Donald's second-in-command. Insofar as this motley crew had a normal human member, it was Kabweza. She was the descendant in the matrilineal line of a slave freed a century earlier by a Beowulfan cruiser, but the ensuing four generations had brought the usual genetic blending. There were still traces of her maternal ancestor's largely Mfecane heritage, but she looked more like a native of Terra's great archipelago in southeast Asia than anything else.

Then, there was the person in the middle. Major Anichka Sydorenko. As was the case with Kabweza, Major Sydorenko's membership in the human race was self-evident, as was her gender. As was true of almost all former Scrag females, she was tall, blonde, blue-eyed, erect of posture and generally majestic in appearance.

Although it was encouraged, it was not a legal requirement that former Ballroom members or former

Scrags who joined the military had to abandon the "X" appellation or the Scrag habit of having no surname at all. But Torch's Secretary of War insisted that anyone who desired to rise above the rank of noncommissioned officer did have to do so. When it was pointed out (by zealous news commentators as well as disgruntled comrades) that the Secretary of War himself had not followed suit, Jeremy X argued that maintaining his established identity was essential to demonstrating civilian control of the military.

And if that argument didn't make any sense, so be it. Jeremy X he remained. Most people were pretty sure that the real reason was to quietly reassure the Ballroom that while he had formally resigned his membership he hadn't abandoned them. Not in the least.

Donald gave the two majors no more than a passing glance, however. He was mostly concerned with Lieutenant Colonel Kabweza. Until he'd arrived there a week earlier, Kabweza had been the commander of the Torch forces at Parmley Station. Furthermore, she had a real military background.

The fact that Donald had enlisted in the military was mostly a legal formality. What he really was, official rank be damned, was the Torch analog of the ancient position of *commissar* and its modern equivalent, the post of People's Commissioner favored by the former Havenite regime of Rob Pierre and Oscar Saint-Just.

The analogy was only a rough one. The original post of commissar had been created during the Russian Revolution because the Bolshevik regime didn't trust many of the former Tsarist officers who formed the backbone of its military cadre during the civil war that followed. The task of the commissars was to oversee the political reliability of the officers who directly led the armed forces in combat.

Reliability wasn't the issue here. Nobody thought that Torch's military was in any way politically suspect. A high percentage of the soldiers and officers were former members of the Audubon Ballroom, for one thing. For another, whatever political disagreements and policy disputes might exist among the military cadre, none of the officers—commissioned or noncommissioned—had their origins in the overthrown Manpower regime. And finally, there was not the proverbial cold chance in hell that any member of Torch's armed forces— officer, noncom, green private just joined yesterday, *anybody*—would defect and switch sides, which the Bolsheviks and Havenites had had to worry about.

There were some real advantages to having an enemy as blatantly committed to chattel slavery as Mesa and Manpower. *Why don't you come over to our side so we can put you in shackles and keep you there for the rest of your life—oh, and that of all your descendants too—*is about the worst recruiting pitch ever devised.

In a sense, the problem Torch faced was the exact opposite. The reason that Jeremy X had decided he needed a layer of officers like Donald (X-now-Toussaint) was not to ride herd on the officers. They were not so much overseers in the traditional manner of commissars as they were negotiators and facilitators whose main job was to ensure that the *enlisted* ranks didn't rupture military discipline and protocol.

Depending on the armed service in question, former members of the Ballroom constituted anywhere between twenty percent and forty percent of the enlisted personnel. And at least that high a percentage was made up of people who were heavily influenced by the Ballroom and its attitudes.

But the Ballroom had provided less than half that percentage of the officers.

The reason was obvious and nobody thought it was due to political discrimination. Not with Jeremy X himself as the Secretary of War! The problem was simply that the training and experience of Ballroom activists, while it had certainly exposed them to combat, had little in common with the skills and experience needed by officers of a regular military force.

The potential for clashes between officers and the ranks was clear, therefore. Jeremy had decided the best way to deal with it—forestall it where possible; diffuse it where necessary; squash it outright as a last resort—was to place some of the Ballroom's most prominent and respected leaders in the top ranks of the field grade officers.

So, in the here and now that Donald was dealing with, he was officially in charge of all Torch forces assigned to Parmley Station and whatever missions might be dispatched from there. But he knew and she knew and anyone except outright dimwits knew perfectly well that Lieutenant Colonel Kabweza would be leading any of the ground forces that actually went into combat. Just as everyone knew that Lieutenant Commander Jerome Llewellyn was the person who'd really be in charge of the two frigates which had been assigned to the Parmley Station task force whenever they went into action.

Frigates were simply too small and fragile to have any significant role in modern naval combat. The roles the frigate had once filled were now filled by destroyers in any navy which aspired to be anything more than a system-defense force, and even destroyers were experiencing a steady upward creep in size and tonnage. There was still a role for small warships—indeed, a larger one than they had played in the better part of a century—but that role was played by LACs, not frigates, thanks to the revolution in warship technology which had come out of the Havenite Wars, especially where LACs were concerned. Unlike true starships, which were required to sacrifice considerable amounts of their internal mass to the hyper generator and alpha nodes which made hyper-flight practical, LACs were pure sub-light vessels. They could use all of that mass for the additional weapons, better armor, more point defense, and *much* stronger sidewalls which were now possible, and that made them far more effective in combat. They were also more survivable and, assuming equivalent levels of technology in their construction, cost less than a frigate.

But the LAC did have one great weakness, because it *was* a sub-light warship, unable to deploy across interstellar distances on its own. It was well suited to system defense, but to project power, it required a LAC carrier, and *CLAC*s were very, very expensive.

Up until very recently, Torch's tiny navy consisted entirely of the fifteen frigates built for it by the Hauptman Cartel: seven of the *John Brown* class and eight of the newer *Nat Turner* class. The *John Brown* class were modernized conventional frigates while the *Nat Turner* class were the more fancy hyper-capable *Shrike* equivalents.

That situation had changed radically when Luiz

Rozsak handed Torch the heavy cruiser *Spartacus* and all the other captured warships which had surrendered to him after the Battle of Torch, but that gift—magnificent though it had been—was something of a problem in its own right. The primary reasons the Royal Torch Navy had consisted solely of frigates prior to the battle were fairly straightforward. First, they were the cheapest hyper-capable ships Torch could afford, and even that had been possible only because of the Hauptman Cartel's generosity. Second, (and even more importantly), they made ideal training platforms.

Because of the nature of Manpower's genetic slavery, there were very few ex-slaves who had any experience with the complex requirements of operating starships—of any kind, much less warships. There were no more than a handful who had any experience with operating the sort of huge warships—battlecruisers, dreadnoughts and superdreadnoughts—which completely dominated modern warfare. And none of those had any experience in command positions. The few ex-slaves who did have naval experience had mostly been marines. And those who hadn't been marines had almost all been simple ratings. Volunteers from Beowulf and Manticore, where liberated slaves and the children of liberated slaves had enlisted in the military with ferocious patriotism, had supplied a small core of highly experienced and highly proficient officers, but that supply could be stretched only so far. It could have been exhausted very quickly, indeed, in manning heavy hyper-capable combatants, so what would be the point of equipping Torch's navy with capital ships? Even if they could have afforded such craft, they didn't have the personnel to staff and operate them.

Most poor one-planet star nations, faced with the same reality, abandoned any idea of having a navy at all. At least, beyond whatever token force the existing regime decided was necessary for its own self-esteem. That varied quite a bit. The general pattern was that nations with a reasonably democratic political structure only maintained what pre-space travel people would have called a "coast guard." Nations which labored under autocratic regimes, on the other hand, sometimes devoted a preposterous share of the public wealth to supporting naval forces that were still much too puny to do any good in an actual war, but made the local despots feel good about themselves. These were the sort of despots who invariably paraded around in fancy military uniforms festooned with a chestful of medals and decorations.

As it happened, though, Torch's immense pharmaceutical potential gave its new government good reason to believe that it wouldn't take more than a few years before it *could* afford a real navy. Still a rather small one, granted, but a navy that would be powerful enough to deal with the sort of recent raiding expedition that would have destroyed Torch had not Luiz Rozsak and his Mayan forces stood in the way. And, thanks to Rozsak, they had a very substantial core around which that sort of navy could be built. But before they could make proper use of those ships, they had to train not simply the officers to command them but the crews to *man* them, and for that the *Nat Turner*-class frigates were ideal. Too small and feeble to survive a modern space battle, frigates were still big enough and had the FTL capability to provide Torch's fledgling navy with the experience it needed to train its officers and ratings.

And, truth be told, there were frigates . . . and then there were *frigates,* and the *Nat Turners* were significantly more dangerous than most people might have expected. Effectively, they were hyper-capable versions of the Royal Manticoran Navy's *Shrike*-class LAC but with about twice the missile capacity and a *pair* of spinal-mounted grasers, with the second energy weapon bearing aft. Their electronics were a downgraded "export version" of the RMN's (which was hardly surprising, given the fact that they'd been going to be operating in an area where the Republic of Haven's intelligence services had ready access and no one in the galaxy had dreamed Haven and Manticore might end up *allies*), but the *Turners* were probably at least as dangerous as the vast majority of the galaxy's destroyers. They were, in fact, considerably more modern and up-to-date fighting ships than the ex-State Security ships which had been handed over to Torch, and they would have eaten most navies' destroyers for lunch in a stand-up fight. The new ships were earmarked for substantial upgrading courtesy of Haven, but until that process had been completed, the *Turners* were much better training platforms *and* combat units in almost every respect.

On the other hand, training could only go so far against simulated enemies. At some point, the frigates and their crews had to be tempered in real combat.

The trick, obviously, was to pick the right enemy— and for *that* purpose, Manpower's far-flung slave-trading empire was ideal. There were any number of outposts and depots scattered throughout the human-occupied galaxy that would provide Torch's adolescent navy with opponents tough enough to test it but weak enough to be defeated if the navy handled itself properly.

Hence, also, the *Hali Sowle*. The one big problem with using frigates against the slave trade—at least, against outposts and depots if not other spacecraft—was that the ships were hard to disguise. Nothing else really looked much like a frigate. By now only the most ignorant slave traders didn't know that a slave revolt on the planet once called Verdant Vista had produced a nation of ex-slaves; that the new nation called itself Torch, a name which itself had obvious implications; that Torch had declared war on Mesa; and . . . had a small navy that mostly consisted of frigates. Granted, it wasn't the only star nation that used frigates, but the rest were either single-star systems that generally stayed out of everyone's way or the now-collapsed and ramshackle Silesian Confederacy.

So here you are, staffing a slave trading depot, and a frigate arrives in your star system. Gosh, who is it most likely to be?

There would be no such suspicion attached to the *Hali Sowle*, on the other hand. Tramp freighters were an integral part of the slave trade. Some were slave transports themselves; others provided the slave trade with the supplies it needed. No slaver would think twice at the appearance of such a craft in their star system, even if that particular freighter had never come there before.

And a *Nat Turner* could be handily fitted into many tramp merchantmen's cargo holds, which had suggested all sorts of devious possibility to the RTN's operational planners.

The *Hali Sowle*'s owner and operator had to agree to the whole project, of course. But Ganny El was nothing if not a haggler, and she had a whole clan of people she was responsible for on whose behalf to haggle.

So, haggle she did. She'd already gotten Beowulf to absorb the cost of providing prolong treatments for all clan members still young enough to benefit from them. She figured it was time to provide those same now-long-lived youngsters with the galaxy's best education, all expenses paid. By others.

Three others qualified, when it came to the galaxy's best educational systems. Manticore, Beowulf, and most of the the Solarian League's other Core worlds.

For obvious reasons, the other Core worlds were ruled out. So Ganny started chewing on the flanks of Beowulf and Manticore. Both of whom, as it happened, were patrons of the new star nation of Torch.

❖   ❖   ❖

But now, unfortunately, a hitch had developed. The *Hali Sowle*, it turned out, did not have an internal topology that leant itself to carrying the frigates inside its hull. Furthermore, being a merchant ship—and an old one, at that—it did not have the capability to operate the long-range drone sensor platforms that were critical to its mission. The compromise that had been decided upon was that the *Hali Sowle* would carry a support and communications module in its cargo hold that did have that capability. Both of the frigates would be tractored to the hull of the *Hali Sowle*, riding the racks which had been built to transport external cargo canisters back when the freighter's designers had thought they were building an honest merchantman.

That wasn't likely to be a problem, though. Unless Ganny maneuvered the freighter like an idiot once they neared a target—and nobody thought for one moment there was anything wrong with the old lady's brains—there was no real chance that frigates tractored to the ship's hull would be spotted by anyone. All she had to do was keep the roof or belly of the *Hali Sowle*'s wedge toward enemy sensors and they wouldn't be able to see a thing.

The problem lay elsewhere. Trying to integrate the new, state-of-the-art systems of the comm module with the aged and obsolescent systems of the *Hali Sowle* was proving to be trickier than anyone had foreseen.

✧ ✧ ✧

There came another string of blistering phrases over the intercom. Louder than usual, even.

"—*ever catch the worthless pedophile who foisted this piece of crap so-called software on innocent babes in the woods I swear to God I'll cut*—"

Donald Toussaint couldn't keep from wincing. Having taken a momentary break from his work at the nearby console, Loren Damewood spotted the grimace.

He laughed. "You think the grousing and griping is bad? Try negotiating with her sometime."

Donald stared at him, wide-eyed. "Did *you* have to—"

"Not personally, no. 'Course not. Way over my pay grade. Thank God." Damewood shook his head. "But the stories you hear . . . Scare children to sleep with 'em."

"—*be any razor, neither. Screw the quality of mercy. I'm going medieval. Chain saw, that's what I'll use. Never heard of a chain saw? Well, gather 'round, kiddies*—"

June 1922 Post Diaspora

"When I killed people retail, I was a terrorist. Now that I kill 'em wholesale, I'm a stalwart soldier. Get medals for it and everything."
—Sergeant Supakrit X, Royal Torch Marines

CHAPTER 12

Anton Zilwicki thought that Jacques Benton-Ramirez y Chou was restraining himself from throwing his hands up in frustration. Or, at least, the Benton-Ramirez y Chou equivalent of such a gesture. That might be no more than an eye-twitch. Jacques served Beowulf as its unofficial—and well-hidden—liaison with the Audubon Ballroom. Beyond that, he was a "director at large," a Beowulfan title that corresponded to what most star nations would have called a minister without portfolio.

Beowulfan political customs were sometimes odd, to people not used to them. This was a star system, after all, which named its elite commando unit the "Biological Survey Corps." What made that disorienting to non-Beowulfers—not to mention a little scary—was that the name wasn't simply a disguise. There were historical origins for the name; centuries earlier, it *had* been a surveying outfit. But in some way comprehended only by Beowulfers, they seemed to think that the work done by such people as Hugh Arai still did have something to do with biology.

How so? Anton had no idea. He was a simple high-lander from Gryphon. To his way of thinking, the only connection between the work of the BSC and biology was that the activity involved the rupturing—not to mention maiming, obliterating, rending, terminating; oh, it was a long list—of organisms and their various organs.

"If only you'd been able to bring back McBryde," said Jacques. He did, however, have the good grace to give Anton and Victor a wry little smile, making it clear that he was not criticizing. Simply...lamenting something that was indeed lamentable.

"Agreed," said Victor. "For our purposes, Herlander Simões is something of an idiot savant. Oh, he's got a huge amount of info about Mesa's 'open' society, but outside of his technical specialties, he's generally obtuse about anything else to do with this 'Alignment' of his. His superiors undoubtedly preferred things that way, and I'm sure McBryde told him as little as possible prior to their decision to defect. True, they were friends. But the formal relationship between the two men was that of a top level security officer handling a known security risk. Out of old habit, if nothing else, McBryde would have kept most things from him."

Eloise Pritchart shifted slightly in her chair. That wasn't due to discomfort. As you'd expect of something made for Manticoran royalty, the chair was state-of-the-art furniture, adjusting instantly to the anatomy and posture of the person sitting in it.

No, it was just that, like the representative from Beowulf at this meeting, she was also frustrated. But, also like Jacques, she had more than enough sense and experience than to suggest there was any blame to be laid at the feet of Zilwicki and Cachat. They'd done astonishingly well in their mission to Mesa. It was hardly their fault that they hadn't been able to produce everything you might possibly desire.

Jack McBryde, the man who could have told them so much, was dead. Dead at his own hand, when he destroyed the Mesan Alignment's Gamma Center as security agents were closing in on him.

The Mesan defector whom Zilwicki and Cachat had managed to bring back, Herlander Simões, was a scientist. He was proving invaluable when it came to uncovering many of Mesa's technical secrets, but he knew very little beyond that.

It might be better to say, he knew very few details. He had, on the other hand, verified enough of what McBryde had passed on to Anton and Victor to provide a general picture of the situation. Three critical points were established:

One. Lurking somewhere within Mesa's government and the corporate hierarchy that dominated the planet—Manpower's top officials, almost certainly, and there were bound to be other firms involved—was a shadowy organization known as the Mesan Alignment.

Two. The Alignment was ancient, dating all the way back to the founders of Mesa six centuries earlier. Those people, led by Leonard Detweiler, had been a political faction on Beowulf which had objected to Beowulf's stringent policies concerning manipulation of the human genome. Everyone had thought their disagreement had been satisfied by the creation of Manpower, Inc., and the selective improvement of their own citizens after they emigrated from Beowulf to Mesa.

No one had suspected just how much "improvement" they'd incorporated into their own genomes, however, and it now turned out that their purpose had been far broader and deeper than originally thought—and they had managed to keep it a secret from anyone outside their circle.

Three. The goal of the Mesan Alignment was nothing less than the conquest of the human-occupied galaxy. The conquest might at times manifest itself in more subtle ways than outright and open force, but the end remained the same regardless of the means employed. The Mesan Alignment intended to politically dominate humanity and impose its own views on the proper way to guide and shape the species.

Beyond that, several other points seemed well established also. First, the Mesan Alignment had developed at least one and probably two space propulsion systems based on new and revolutionary principles. Second, they had used those space drives to launch the savage sneak attack on Manticore known as the Yawata Strike. Third, they had been responsible for a number of assassinations and assassination attempts using some as-yet-unknown method of nanotech-based quasi-mind control, including the murders of Yves Grosclaude, Lieutenant Timothy Meares, Admiral James Webster, Lara Novakhovskaya and almost three hundred other people in the failed assassination attempt on Berry Zilwicki, and Jwei-shwan Anderman, Emperor Gustav Anderman's nephew and second in line for the Andermani throne. There'd almost certainly been others no one yet knew about... and then there was the one spectacular *failure* they all knew about: Honor Alexander-Harrington.

And, fourth, they had been largely responsible for instigating the war between the Republic of Haven and Manticore and keeping it going. It now seemed clear, for instance, that Haven's former Secretary of State Arnold Giancola had been an agent for the Mesan Alignment, given the fact that Yves Grosclaude had been the only man who could have proven that Giancola was responsible for the forged diplomatic correspondence which had sent the two star nations back to war with one another.

These last four points were perhaps not quite as well established as the first three, but you'd need a sharp knife or a razor blade to split the difference. As far as Anton was concerned, it was the difference between a 99.9 percent probability and a 99.8 percent one—of academic interest even to statisticians.

The silence in the conference room following Victor's statement went on long enough to start becoming uncomfortable. Finally, Empress Elizabeth planted her hands on the large table around which they were all sitting and said:

"Look, there's no point crying over spilt defectors. We just have to make do with what we have. The question now is, what's our next step?"

Anton started to answer that question but Victor spoke first.

"Anton and I need to go back to Mesa and fill in the missing holes."

Which was exactly what Anton had been planning to say. He sat back and waited for the inevitable outburst.

Outbursts, rather. Just about everyone spoke simultaneously.

"That's insane." (President Pritchart)

"Are you insane?" (Empress Elizabeth)

"That seems extraordinarily foolish." (Benjamin Mayhew, Protector of Grayson)

"You've gone mad." (Prime Minister Alexander)

"That's the craziest idea I've heard in ... hell, who knows?" (Admiral Givens)

"That's sheer suicide." (First Space Lord Caparelli.)

"Why not just shoot yourself?" (Foreign Secretary Langtry)

Haven's Secretary of War Tom Theisman settled for: "You're nuts."

Interestingly, Hamish Alexander-Harrington started to say something but closed his mouth when he noticed that *Honor* Alexander-Harrington was keeping silent. In fact, she looked as if she were actually considering the idea.

And—still more interesting—Anton saw that Jacques Benton-Ramirez y Chou had his lips pursed and was glancing around the room in a manner that was almost shifty-eyed.

He knew something. What? Anton had no idea. But it was sure to be ... interesting.

Once the hubbub settled down, Anton said: "Victor's right. It needs to be done and we're obviously the best people to do it. And, no, it's not a crazy idea. It'll be dangerous, for sure. Very dangerous. But not suicidal."

"Please explain why you think it wouldn't be," said Harrington. "Disguises won't be enough, not even nanotech body transformations. Not for the two of you. They're bound to obtain samples of your DNA sooner or later. They might even have them already, if you left traces on Mesa."

"I doubt that very much," said Victor. "Even if they picked up some traces of our DNA—which wouldn't be easy at all, since we weren't careless—I still don't think there's more than a one-in-ten chance they have any usable records."

"Why is that?" asked Hamish Alexander-Harrington. Like his wife's, his tone was more one of interest and assessment than outright skepticism.

"Because of Jack McBryde," said Anton. He and Victor had discussed this already. More than once. "The blast he set off that destroyed Gamma Center had to have been a shaped nuclear charge. There's no other way to explain the total destruction of the center *and* the relatively minor damage to everything around it. Which means—"

Victor picked it up: "That the charge was prepared long beforehand. And since no one person could jury-rig something like that, it had to have been set in place by the Mesan Alignment itself. Which means—"

"That they've created what amounts to an intelligence bolthole," said Anton. "They've known for some time that they couldn't be sure someone wouldn't attack and overrun Mesa. It's only a one-planet star system and it doesn't have much of a real naval force. So they made sure that, if worse came to worst, they could obliterate any evidence of their own existence."

"And go back to hiding as mere run-of-the-mill corporate monsters," finished Victor.

"The conclusion from that is obvious," said Anton.

There was silence in the room again. Finally, Empress Elizabeth rolled her eyes to the ceiling and said: "Why do I feel like a dimwit?" She brought her gaze back down and bestowed it upon Anton and Victor. It bore more resemblance—a lot more—to the gaze of a basilisk than a dimwit, though.

"Explain," she commanded. "The rest of us here are not super-spies. *What* conclusion is obvious?"

Anton and Victor looked at each other. From subtleties in Victor's expression that Anton was sure no one else in the room could have interpreted, he knew that the Havenite's attitude was: *She's your empress, dammit. YOU try to explain it without pissing her off any further.*

Anton cleared his throat. "Your Majesty, we learned enough from Jack McBryde to know that he was a key figure in Gamma Center. So key a figure, in fact, that he was able to trigger off the self-destruct mechanism without a partner."

There came simultaneous grunts from Hamish Alexander, Thomas Theisman and First Space Lord Caparelli. Harrington's eyes widened.

"Jesus H. Christ," said Caparelli. "How did we miss that?"

Seeing that the Empress' gaze was now entering *you-are-all-about-to-be-turned-into-stone* territory, Caparelli hurriedly added: "No massive self-destruct program is ever set up to be operable by just one individual, Your Majesty, unless that individual is specifically empowered to do so—and on his own initiative."

Stone, so help me God. Crumbling year-by-year under the pitiless elements.

Harrington laughed. "Elizabeth, either McBryde had that sort of authority—which is certainly possible, given this Gamma Center's obvious importance—or else he'd managed to hack the system in order to steal it for himself. If he did have the authority, he was even more senior than we'd assumed he was, and that almost certainly means he had access to the 'Alignment's' central security systems. Maybe not command authority outside the Gamma Center, but access enough to dump something of his own into them. And if he *didn't* have that authority and . . . acquired it for himself, he probably had the ability to use whatever access he did have to hack into complete command of their security protocols in general. Well . . . maybe not complete command, but awfully close."

The basilisk gaze didn't soften, exactly, but the threat level receded a bit. Limestone instead of basalt. "All right. I get that. And what follows is . . . ?"

"What *else* did he do besides blow up the center?" said Harrington. "What *other* measures did he take that would have damaged the Alignment's security protocols? If the man was prepared to defect in the first place—and to kill himself if the defection plan went south—he was *furious*. He had to have been. Not boiling over, no. Someone like McBryde would have been cold and controlled. But he was an angry, angry man. Don't think he wasn't. He wouldn't have left this life without hammering the Alignment as hard as he could."

Petrified wood territory. And ebbing fast. Elizabeth settled back in her chair, her own eyes now starting to widen.

Theisman apparently decided the royal ire had lowered enough for it to be safe for a Havenite to chime in. "He would have struck at a lot of things, Your Majesty. One that we know of for sure was Mesa's orbital traffic control. That's why the *Hali Sowle* was able to leave with no problems. We'll never know everything he did, but it's almost inconceivable—given the nature of the man's occupation—that he didn't try to shred the Mesan Alignment's records of its *enemies*."

"We don't have to guess about that, actually," said Victor. "Herlander told us 'Eggshell' was a code word that indicated McBryde planned to wreak havoc on the Alignment's security, over and above the damage done by destroying Gamma Center." He shrugged. "We don't know—probably never will—exactly how much damage he was able to do, and in which specific areas. He'd have been concentrating mostly on their records of the Ballroom, of course. But it'd be far easier to just—well..." He looked at Zilwicki. "Anton's the expert on these things. Let him explain."

"He wouldn't have tried to isolate out the Alignment's records on the Ballroom, Your Majesty. Why bother with something that complex and finicky? He would have simply targeted *all* security protocols designed to track enemies. Which, of course—"

"Would include us," said Victor. "That's why I said I don't think it's likely our DNA records still exist on Mesa. If they ever did at all, which I also doubt."

There was silence again. Then Benjamin Mayhew said, "But you can't be sure about any of this."

"No. We can't." Victor shrugged. "Our line of work has its risks, Your Grace. But the truth is, these odds are better than ones we've faced before."

The Empress' gaze was now merely skeptical.

"On occasion," Victor qualified.

"*Which* occasion?" asked Langtry.

"Victor faced worse odds during the Manpower Incident," said Anton. "Way worse. Of course, he was young and stupid then and didn't understand the difference between risky, dangerous and sheer lunacy."

Anton smiled crookedly. "Even as a youngster, I stayed farther away from that edge than he did. But I *do* know the difference between risky, dangerous and sheer lunacy, and our proposal is not lunatic. It's just risky."

"Risky as all hell, you mean," said Theisman.

"If you prefer, yes. Most of the risk, though, just comes from the intrinsic nature of the project. Penetrating the Mesan Alignment's security right on Mesa itself is a dangerous proposition whether or not they have our DNA records. But I agree with Victor. I don't think they do."

Throughout the discussion, Jacques Benton-Ramirez y Chou had remained silent. His expression had seemed a bit detached, in fact, as if he was only paying attention with part of his mind while he mostly considered something else. Now, finally, the Beowulfer spoke.

"It doesn't matter. Even if the Alignment does have Zilwicki and Cachat's DNA records—anyone's records, for that matter—there's a way to get around it. Theoretically, at least. It's never been tested under field conditions."

The Empress' lips tightened. "And, what, exactly, is 'it'?" Her gaze was reentering dangerous territory. Soapstone, at least. Maybe pumice. "Is there some reason nobody at this table except me can resist being cryptic?"

Jacques looked a bit rueful. "I wasn't trying to be mysterious, Your Majesty. It's just . . . this is something Beowulf has had under wraps for almost a year. As in deep, dark secret 'under wraps.' As Special Officer Cachat says, old habits die hard. For me to talk about something like this openly and in plain language is about as unnatural as—as—" He puffed out his cheeks, as if he couldn't find a suitable analogy.

The Empress gave him a thin smile. "Try real hard."

That produced a little chuckle around the table, shared by Benton-Ramirez y Chou himself. He gave a little shrug, as if were shedding a weight from his shoulders, and started speaking.

"The gist of it is that we've developed—"

There was a knock on the door to the conference. A real knock, too, not a buzzer or a ringer. Anton guessed that meetings held in this royal inner sanctum were so rarely interrupted that no one had ever bothered to arrange for a way to signal that someone wanted to enter.

Elizabeth frowned. "Come in," she said.

The door opened and a woman came in. Anton recognized her as one of the Empress' personal assistants, although he didn't know her name. The woman practically exuded diffidence and hesitation.

"I'm very sorry to interrupt, Your Majesty. But this is a rather unusual—"

The Empress waved her hand impatiently. "Just sum it up quickly, Beatriz."

"There's a delegation here from Torch, Your Majesty. Ah, actually, 'delegation' is probably not the right term. It seems like most of the government is here."

Elizabeth's frown vanished, replaced by a look of surprise. "Who, exactly?"

"Queen Berry. Prime Minister Du Havel. Secretary of War—ah—X. The commander of the armed forces, General Palane. And your niece, Princess Ruth."

"Dear Lord. Well, show them in, then." The Empress examined the conference table and then turned to one of her bodyguards. "We'll need to stretch this a bit. See to it, would you, Lieutenant Tengku?"

The lieutenant pushed a button so discreetly positioned on the wall that Anton hadn't noticed it before. A small control panel slid out and he began working at it. A few seconds later, the conference table began to lengthen—or rather, the entire space surrounding the table began to lengthen. Anton was eerily reminded of the standard depiction of the expansion of the universe: objects didn't spread through space; rather, space itself expanded.

The room itself didn't seem to be getting any bigger. The floor was somehow expanding without pushing against the walls; and, along with it, the table was expanding and all the chairs (and people) sitting at it were being repositioned to make room for more people. There was almost no sensation of movement involved.

He glanced at Victor to see how he was reacting to Thandi Palane's imminent arrival. The Havenite agent's eyes looked out of focus. Anton had to fight not to burst into laughter.

Being fair to Victor, he was probably looking forward to seeing her more than anything else. Anticipation—eager anticipation—would be his dominant emotion, overlying the others.

Fear. Anxiety. Dread. Trepidation. Oh, it was another long list.

CHAPTER 13

"Some introductions are in order," said Empress
Elizabeth, after the delegation from Torch had taken
seats at the table. "The young lady sitting at the far
end of the table from me is Queen Berry, Anton
Zilwicki's daughter. You all know Prime Minister Du
Havel, who is sitting next to her—and my niece Ruth,
of course. On the Queen's other side is the commander
of Torch's armed forces, General Thandi Palane."

Victor was rather impressed. The Queen of Manticore had never met Thandi before. She must have
taken the time to memorize what she looked like
from images and videos. There were plenty of mon-
archs and heads of state in the galaxy who didn't
think much beyond breakfast. Manticore's was not
one of them.

He wondered if she'd also memorized—but there
were very few images available and even fewer good
ones—

Apparently she had. Or she was just guessing right.
Elizabeth was now looking at the last member of
Torch's delegation.

As was everyone else in the room, and some of them with eyes that were very wide indeed.

"And of course none of us prior to this moment have ever met Torch's Secretary of War. I'm a bit uncertain as to the proper etiquette here. Should we call you 'Mr. X'?"

Jeremy's smile was cheerful. "Oh, goodness! No, no, Your Majesty, a simple 'Jeremy' will do fine."

Everyone continued to stare at him. *Him* being the galaxy's most notorious terrorist. Or freedom fighter, depending on how you looked at things. But either way, the pronoun was *him!*

The cheerful smile remained. "Please, everyone, relax. I left my horns and cloven hooves at home. True, I did bring the tail—but it's only vestigial, I assure you."

That brought a few answering smiles and an outright laugh from Benjamin Mayhew. Grayson's Protector looked around the room, with eyes that were shrewd as well as good-humored.

"If you'll all take the expert testimony of a Grayson," he said, "I'd say Jeremy X falls a long way short of Creation's genuine devils." More softly he added: "There are enough of those to go around—in places like Mesa, for example—but there are none of them here. Not today. Not in this room."

Nimitz yawned, then bestowed a benign gaze on Jeremy. Then, bleeked his amusement.

Between them, the devout statesman and the insouciant treecat brought relaxation back to the room.

Except on the part of the two Grayson armsmen and the two members of the Queen's Own standing against the walls, needless to say. Those worthies had never once taken their eyes off Jeremy X since he entered the room—and there seemed no chance they would until he left it.

Other than a quick, amused glance when he'd first sat down, however, Jeremy himself paid them no mind at all.

Once things had settled down, Elizabeth nodded toward Benton-Ramirez y Chou. "Jacques here was just beginning to explain to us a secret project by Beowulf that—oh."

Honor Alexander-Harrington smiled. "We should perhaps preface that by explaining to our friends from Torch the new proposal advanced by Mr. Zilwicki and Special Officer Cachat."

All eyes swiveled to them. Thandi Palane's face seemed completely blank, as it had since she entered the room. You wouldn't realize she and Victor had ever met before, if you didn't know better. Whatever emotions might be roiling under the surface, she was far too much the professional soldier to let any of it show.

"If you would do the honors, Special Officer Cachat?" Harrington continued.

Quickly, Victor sketched the proposal. He didn't delve into any of the arguments for or against, he just summarized it in a few concise sentences.

When he finished, another (if smaller) outburst filled the room.

"Daddy, you can't!" (Queen Berry)

"You're daft." (Secretary of War Jeremy X)

"That's ridiculous. You wouldn't stand a chance." (Prime Minister Du Havel)

"Are you out of your minds?" (Princess Ruth Winton)

The only contrary note came from Thandi Palane.

She said nothing at all. However, one of her eyebrows was now slightly cocked, as if she was mildly intrigued by the idea but was reserving judgment for the moment.

Quick moment.

Berry turned to her and said: "Tell them they can't do it, Thandi. Victor will listen to you even if Daddy doesn't, and Daddy won't go without him."

Palane's eyebrow cocked a little further. "Judging from recent evidence," she said, "Special Officer Cachat pays me no mind at all."

That was said without any heat, just as a simple statement of fact. So might an entomologist describe the behavior of a beetle.

Anton thought Victor might almost have winced, there. Hard to know. When he was of a mind, the Havenite agent had a stone face that put statues to shame.

"Furthermore," Palane continued, still in that same level tone of voice, "I have no authority over either one of them. And finally—"

For the first time, some emotion crept into her voice. A slightly apologetic tone. "It's probably a good idea, Berry. The truth is, neither your father nor Victor is crazy at all. Or if they are, they're crazy like a fox."

"Thandi!"

"Why don't you hear us out, girl?" said Anton to his daughter, a bit gruffly. "This is not a harebrained scheme we came up with in an idle moment. Victor and I have talked this through a lot—and now it seems the Beowulfers might be able to tip the odds still further in our favor."

Berry crossed her arms over her chest. For a

moment, she looked like a stubborn twelve-year-old. Then, perhaps reminding herself of her new august stature and her still-more-august company and surroundings, she took a deep breath and said: "Fine. Go ahead."

✧   ✧   ✧

Anton took a few minutes to explain the proposal in much greater detail than Victor had done. Along the way, various people chimed in to provide their own insights and opinions. When he was finished, he looked at Benton-Ramirez y Chou.

"As you were saying..."

Jacques nodded, and started in. "We've developed a technique to—I'm using these terms loosely, you understand—sheathe someone in a coating of fake DNA. 'Fake' in the sense that it's not the DNA of the person being sheathed. It's real DNA, just taken from someone else."

Everyone stared at him. After a moment, Foreign Secretary Langtry tugged his ear and said: "How can you possibly change someone's DNA? I would think that would—would—"

"She or he would no longer be the same person," said Eloise Pritchart. "At least, I don't think so, although I suppose that might pose an interesting philosophical question."

Jacques shook his head. "No philosophical subtleties are involved. The person's DNA doesn't get altered. What we do is..."

His face got an expression somewhere between a grimace and a rueful smile. "This really isn't as gross as it's going to sound—doesn't hurt at the time, although it's an uncomfortable adjustment afterward.

Essentially, we flay the person's skin and grow another one, using someone's else's DNA."

Berry's expression was pure grimace. "Oh, that's disgusting!"

Anton shrugged. "It's not all that different from what happens in a regeneration of destroyed skin tissue—although as far as I know there's always enough surviving skin that the injured person's own skin is used."

Jacques nodded. "The tricky part is suppressing autoimmune responses to foreign bodies. That's easy enough to do for most transplants, but the skin is the body's largest organ and the way it interacts with the rest of the body gets awfully complex. There's really no medical use for the technique, since anyone who suffers one hundred percent destruction of their skin tissue is bound to be dead anyway. But eventually it occurred to us that the intelligence uses of the technique might be tremendous if we could perfect it."

Victor's face hadn't been marked by a grimace, as you'd expect. The Havenite agent was perfectly capable of accepting even grotesque consequences if he thought they were warranted. His expression showed only keen interest.

"Correct me if I'm wrong, here," he said. "The gist of what you're saying is that we'd be protected from routine DNA sampling—hair, flakes of skin, traces of sweat, body oils, that sort of thing. So if someone tried to find out who we were from testing the residues we left on a door button or a railing, they'd be misled. But we wouldn't be protected from targeted examination. If someone tested our blood or swabbed the insides of our mouths, for instance, we'd be exposed."

"That's a pretty accurate summation. I feel obliged to point out that if your supposition that the Alignment has lost your genetic records because of McBryde's actions is correct, you might be worse off if you went to Mesa with this genetic sheath I'm describing."

"Yes, I understand that," said Victor. "If we got seriously tested after they'd already picked up routine samples, we'd show two different DNA results. That would set off alarm bells even if they didn't suspect anything beforehand."

He looked at Anton. "I still think it'd be worth it."

Anton nodded. "So do I. The only reason they'd take mouth swabs or blood samples is if they were already suspicious. Mesa isn't exactly a dictatorship—not, at least, for its own citizens—but it's a far cry from a state that respects legal procedures if they think anything important is at stake. If we're that far in the hole, they'll be trampling right over us anyway."

"What's most important about the sheath," Victor said, "isn't the fact that it hides our true identities. If we're right, they don't have those anyway. The real advantage is that it would enable us to assume *false* identities—entirely false ones, I mean. Am I right about that?"

Jacques looked puzzled. "I'm not sure— Oh." His face cleared up. "I see what you're getting at. Even if Mesa doesn't have *your* DNA records—as individuals, that is—they do know your personal history. Enough of it, anyway."

"Which means," said Anton, "that they'd be on high alert for any routine samples that showed the individuals were from either Haven—more specifically, Nouveau Paris—or Gryphon's highlands. Neither of those genetic strains is as distinct as something like"—he nodded toward Princess Ruth—"Masadan origin or"—now he glanced at Thandi—"Mfecane origin. But it's distinctive enough that they'd probably be able to spot it even from routine sampling."

"There's no 'probably' about it," said Benton-Ramirez y Chou. "The Alignment's biological skills are as good as those of us Beowulfers, for the most part, and better in some areas. They'd spot someone from Haven or Gryphon, you can be sure of it. Especially someone from Nouveau Paris or the highlands, because their methods are more than good enough for that sort of detail."

Victor's smile had little humor in it. "Precisely. So we go in sheathed as"—he looked at Zilwicki—"what strikes your fancy, Anton?"

"I've always had a yen to be a filthy-rich oligarch from one of the Verge territories, unrestrained by any code or scruple."

Jeremy grinned. "Perhaps from Hakim?"

"Just the thing." The Hakim System was notorious even by Verge standards for the behavior of its upper classes. And it was very far away from either Manticore or Haven. "And how about you, Victor? An effete snot from one of the Core planets, do you think?"

Across the table, Thandi Palane smiled—with no more humor than Victor had. "A dilettante news reporter, too rich to actually have to work at it but with delusions of journalistic grandeur. From the Hirochi system, perhaps. That was mostly settled by people from east Asia, so you'd be fairly removed from the usual Havenite genome."

Berry stared at her, aghast. "You're encouraging them!"

Palane's smile became gentler. "It's a good idea, Berry. We *do* need to find out more about the Alignment—and it's a simple fact that Victor and Anton are the best people to do the job."

Victor's gaze seemed slightly out of focus. "We could...use some help, though."

Anton understood what he meant immediately. Well...within a second, anyway. It was a little disturbing, the way his mind seemed able to track Cachat's so well.

But it *was* a great idea. "That'd be just about perfect!" He smiled broadly at Thandi. "Our very own one-person wrecking crew."

"You have got to be kidding," said Thandi.

"No, actually, I'm not," said Anton. He nodded toward Cachat. "And for sure and certain he isn't."

Honor Alexander-Harrington spoke up for the first time since the Torch delegation entered the room. "If I'm not mistaken, they're proposing that General Palane accompany the mission to Mesa. Special Officer Cachat and Mr. Zilwicki are proposing it, at least. The general herself seems to have some reservations, of course."

Berry stared at her, mouth open. Then, stared at her father. Her mouth still open.

"I can see several advantages to the idea myself," Alexander-Harrington went on. "On the other hand, I also see one big drawback—the fact that General Palane is in command of Torch's armed forces. It'd be like sending Admiral Caparelli here on an intelligence mission."

"That analogy is a bit forced, Duchess Harrington," said Jeremy X. "For two reasons. The first is that the so-called 'armed forces' of Torch bear a lot more resemblance to a work-in-progress—small work in progress—than they do to anything either you or the Republic of Haven would call a real military. General Palane has set underway a training program for ground troops that's going quite well, I think, but she has good subordinates and they could do without her for a time. That's especially true for the navy, for which her background and experience really aren't of much use."

He gave Thandi an apologetic little smile. "Meaning no offense."

She shrugged. "None taken. The truth is, Duchess Harrington, I let Captain Petersen do pretty much what he wants. He knows far more than I do about how to put together a navy from what amounts to scratch."

Harrington nodded. "Yes, I know Anton. He's a superb officer. It depends mostly on how long you'd be gone. A few months wouldn't be any particular problem. Your armed forces need that much time for training before you'd be able to launch any major operations anyway. But once you do start to engage the enemy..."

"For that, you need a real commander-in-chief," said Thandi. "On the spot and taking responsibility. Yes, I understand."

She now looked at Victor and Anton. "So, what's your estimate?"

"Three months," said Victor. "Maybe four. No more than five."

Anton pursed his lips. "Always the cheerful optimist. I agree we'll need at least three months. But I'd extend the outer limit to six."

"No longer?" asked Theisman.

"The situation is too fluid, and moving rapidly," said Anton.

"If we can't find what we need within half a year," added Victor, "it'll most likely be a moot point anyway. Which is part of the reason we'd like General Palane to come on the mission. Things are likely to get...ah, hectic."

Theisman now looked at Palane. "And exactly how would you make such a big difference, if I might ask?"

Palane looked uncomfortable. "This is a little awkward. Ah..."

"What the general is having a hard time coming right out with," said Victor, "is that there are no more than a few dozen people in the universe who are her equals when it comes to hands-on personal violence, and no more than a handful who surpass her." His tone was flat, almost harsh. "I can testify to that personally. Having her come along would be roughly equivalent to bringing a squad of Marines with us. Anybody's Marines, take your pick."

"Half a platoon, more like," said Anton. "There's a reason that Luiz Rozsak—who is nobody's fool, believe me—personally selected her for his staff despite her total lack of the usual connections. The same reason that lots of people on Torch call her *Great Kaja*. That nickname originated with former Scrags and it translates more or less as 'the Galaxy's scariest she-wolf.'"

He glanced at Caparelli. "Meaning no offense, but however capable your First Space Lord is at his normal line of work, I wouldn't trade a hundred of him for Palane where we'll be going."

Caparelli chuckled. "No offense taken." He gave Thandi a look that was a lot more interested than the casual one he'd given her when she first came in. "Are they right, General Palane? And to hell with false modesty."

"Yes," she said tersely. "They are."

While this exchange had been going on, Alexander-Harrington had been studying Palane. There was something very intense about that scrutiny, Anton thought. He wasn't sure what it was, exactly, but he suspected the duchess was beginning to shape some sort of plan.

For what? He could only guess—and his first guess was that Harrington had been struck by the same notion that had already come to him and Victor.

A war with the Mesan Alignment was now inevitable—in fact, it had already started. Sooner or later, Mesa was going to have to be conquered and occupied. Who, then, should be the occupying troops? Of a planet shaped by centuries of harsh slavery, and with a population more than two-thirds of which was made up of slaves or their disenfranchised descendants?

Torch didn't begin to have the military force needed for such an occupation, of course. But most of the occupation troops could be provided by other star nations. What Torch could provide would be a cadre of specialists, in essence—people who would understand the attitudes of the majority of Mesa's population and could serve as trusted liaisons between them and the occupying forces.

Having a Torch commander-in-chief who was familiar with the situation on the ground in Mesa due to a personal reconnaissance might prove to be invaluable, in that event. And if the seccies and slaves of a liberated Torch later learned that that same commander-in-chief had personally risked her life scouting their homeworld in preparation for its liberation . . .

Anton's own scrutiny of Harrington must have been intense also. Intense enough that she turned to look at him directly, almost as if she possessed some sort of telepathic ability.

Which was absurd. She wasn't a treecat, after all.

"I can think of some other reasons it would be a good idea for General Palane to go along on the expedition," Alexander-Harrington said. "Especially... Let's just say I'd like to have an assessment of Mesa—from being there on the ground herself, not from reports—coming from someone with her experience and abilities. That could prove very useful, down the road a bit."

She *couldn't* be telepathic, damnation. It just wasn't in the human genome.

Was it?

The personal com on Harrington's wrist must have given her a vibration, because she suddenly looked at it.

"A reminder from my staff," she said. The slight smile on her face indicated that she hadn't really needed the reminder but was appreciative of having attentive subordinates.

Turning to the Empress of Manticore, she said: "It's time Admiral Theisman and I were getting out to *Imperator*. It's always remotely possible Admiral Filareta will actually get here on schedule, after all."

CHAPTER 14

After the delegation from Torch had all entered the suite assigned to them in Mount Royal Palace, Berry turned to Thandi.

"But..." Her voice was very small. "If you go too, what'll...I mean..."

Palane put an arm around her. "You'll be fine, girlfriend. Your father will need me a lot more than you will. Jeremy isn't really planning any coup d'état, as it turns out."

"Lord, no," said Jeremy, sprawling onto a couch in the suite's central chamber. "I'd be a lamb among lions. The only woman on Torch scarier than the Great Kaja is the damn Queen herself."

Berry gave him a reproving glance. "Am not."

"Are too. The veritable reincarnation of that Russia czarina. Catherine the Great, wasn't it? Except her husband was a squishy fellow—she had him deposed, if I recall correctly—whereas our Queen's consort is one of those Beowulfan knee-breakers. Ogres flee at his approach."

In a more serious tone, he added: "I'm really quite

satisfied with the way our government's turning out, Berry. Especially you." He cast a colder eye on Du Havel, standing nearby. "I'm not even too disgruntled with our Prime Minister. Wishy-washy though he be, and given to far too many compromises with the establishment."

"We *are* the establishment, Jeremy," Web said mildly.

"Pah! Only on our own itty-bitty planet. I was speaking of the great behemoths of the galactic establishment."

Du Havel eased himself into a couch at right angles to the one Jeremy was occupying. "In any event, whether or not I am indeed guilty of compromisitis, I think it's all becoming a moot point. Or am I the only one who thinks we're about to be tasked with providing the new anti-Manpower alliance with an occupation force for Mesa? Not all of it, of course. Not even most of it."

Berry stared at him. "Huh?"

Jeremy smiled, very thinly. "I'm reading the tea leaves—say better, the entrails—about the same way as you, Web."

Berry now stared at him. "Huh?"

"Same here," chimed in Thandi. She was still on her feet, close to the door, in a parade rest stance. "In fact, I think it's pretty much a done deal."

Berry turned to stare at her. "Huh?"

The door buzzed. Thandi glanced at her watch. "About what I figured." Leaning over slightly, she opened the door.

Victor Cachat came in, followed closely by Anton Zilwicki. A little behind them was Jacques Benton-Ramirez y Chou.

Thandi and Victor looked at each other, both very stiff-faced. Anton's mouth quirked a little and he said: "You can blame me, Thandi. Victor was all for stopping at Torch first, but—"

"He's lying," said Victor.

"You're lying," said Thandi. Neither one of them looked away from each other.

"—I insisted that, oh, the hell with it. If the two of you won't accept that perfectly workable attempt to provide everyone with a way to save face, drop it anyway. We're got a mission to organize, not to mention laying plans for an occupation force for Mesa."

Berry scowled. "I hate feeling like the dunce in a crowd. What are you all talking about?"

"If it makes you feel any better, Your Majesty, I'm scrambling to catch up myself," said Jacques, closing the door behind him.

Berry was still grumpy enough to say: "Don't call me 'Your Majesty.' I hate that title." A bit belatedly, she added: "Please."

"You're not at home, Your Majesty," Web said. "He has to and you have to let him."

"What he said," chipped in Jeremy. "Although now that we're here on Manticore we're going to run into a bit of a problem. There's one too many majesties about. So we have to start adding modifiers. That's how they used to do it back in the old days. 'Your Most Christian Majesty,' 'Your Most Catholic Majesty,' that sort of thing."

He looked around the room. "What say you, gentle folk? I propose Her Most Modest Majesty."

Berry sniffed. "Wasn't three minutes ago you said I was the reincarnation of Catherine the Great."

"I was hoping you'd forgotten. All right, then. Her Most Fearsome Majesty."

Whether by conscious intent or not—and with Jeremy X you never knew; there was usually a method to his whimsy—his banter had eased some of the personal tension in the room.

Quite a bit, as it turned out. Thandi took three steps over to Victor, seized the back of his head and planted a quick, fierce kiss on his lips. "I forgive you," she said. "Don't do it again."

Then, taking him by the hand, she led him over to another couch where they both sat down. This couch was the third leg of a U-shaped furniture arrangement in the center of the room. They faced Jeremy across a table that had presumably begun life as a coffee table but had long since mutated into a low-slung version of something that belonged in a banquet hall. Web Du Havel sat to their right, on the couch that formed the connecting link to the U.

Berry sat next to Web. He slid over to allow her room in the middle of the couch so that Anton could take a seat on her other side. Jeremy did the same so that Jacques and Ruth could share his couch. The Beowulfer leaned back in a very relaxed manner, something which the high-tech and expensive piece of furniture made easy to do. Ruth, as was her habit, perched on the edge of the seat. The couch put up a fight but she mastered the beast easily enough.

Once everyone was seated—or half-seated, in the case of Ruth—Jacques said: "I wasn't actually trying to reassure Her Majesty. I really *am* trying to catch up. Am I correct in thinking that at least some of you are seriously contemplating using Torch troops as part of an occupying force for Mesa? If so, I suspect my niece is of a like mind."

"And what do you think?" asked Victor.

"I don't know. The idea hadn't even occurred to me before this."

The Havenite agent nodded at Zilwicki. "Anton and I spent a fair amount of time discussing the idea. Since we had plenty of time to spare, while we were drifting around in space. The logic is quite robust."

"Sure is," said Ruth. She started counting off on her fingers. "First, we've got to occupy Mesa. I leave aside for the moment the precise definition of 'we,' but at the very least it'll include the Star Empire, the Republic of Haven, the Kingdom of Torch, and—this is a bit of a guess, but the odds are long in favor—Beowulf."

"You can take that as a given also," said Benton-Ramirez y Chou.

"Add to that Erewhon and Maya Sector," said Victor. "Not immediately, but sooner or later it's bound to happen."

Jacques cocked his head at him. "Erewhon, I concur. But are you sure about Maya Sector? Barregos and Rozsak are about as devoted to *realpolitik* as the Andermani."

"If 'rayal politique' means what I think it means," said Berry, "I think you're misjudging them a little. Luiz Rozsak, anyway. I don't know Oravil Barregos."

"It doesn't matter," said Anton. "Cold-blooded self-interest will drive them toward us just as quickly as whatever shreds of idealism they still possess." A bit grudgingly, he added: "Which are some pretty big shreds, at least in the case of Rozsak."

"To get back to the point," said Ruth, "once everybody

figures out that we have to occupy Mesa sooner or later"—she held up another finger—"it won't take them long to realize that sooner is way better than later. That's because—"

Another finger came up. "A big part of this war is the propaganda front. Most people in the Solarian League still don't believe our version of what's happening. The single biggest step we could take to start turning that around is to overrun Mesa. Fast and hard. That way we can—hopefully—get access to their own records."

Anton grunted skeptically. "I wouldn't count on that. The very fact that McBryde could do the damage he did indicates the Alignment has contingencies in place to destroy any critical records if they need to."

Ruth looked stubborn, an expression that came rather naturally to her. "Okay, maybe. But there'll still be people who can be interrogated."

"Unless they murder all of them," said Jeremy, "which I wouldn't put past the bastards for a minute."

"All the more reason for a quick and decisive intervention," said Victor. "And, to come back to where we started, all the more reason for an occupying army that can't be bamboozled by the local authorities. Most of the troops will have to be provided by others, since Torch's army doesn't begin to be large enough. But if Torch provides . . . what should we call them?"

"Reconnaissance and liaison units," said Thandi.

"Yes, that. We'd be a long ways toward gaining the unstinting allegiance and trust of about two-thirds of the population."

"It's more than that," said Ruth. "Full citizens don't make up more than thirty percent of Mesa's population. About sixty percent are outright slaves, and the remainder are the descendants of slaves who were freed centuries ago when Mesa still allowed manumission."

Jacques pursed his lips. "How many occupying armies in history have ever enjoyed that advantage?"

"None that I know of," said Du Havel. "The closest analog I can think of was the occupation of the southern areas of the United States of America after their civil war. But slaves only constituted a minority of that population."

"The logic is pretty irresistible, I admit—at least in theory. But in practice . . ."

"Does Torch have an army that could take on that task?" said Thandi. "That's what you're wondering."

"Yes."

She shrugged. "Right now, no. But we're not all that far away, between the training programs we've got up and running and the fact that people keep volunteering for the military."

"You haven't imposed conscription, I take it?"

"No," said Du Havel.

"Not *yet*," said Jeremy. He gave the Prime Minister a sharp glance. "But we will if we need to."

Thandi raised her hand. "Let's not reopen that argument, guys. There's no point it in anyway. If we got a much bigger influx than we're getting already, our training programs would start to collapse. Our cadre is still awfully slender."

"If you're pretty close to having the forces we'd need for that purpose, then Beowulf could make up the difference," said Jacques. "Whatever that might take. The way I see this war shaping up—".

He broke off. "But we're getting way ahead of ourselves. Let's wait and see what happens with Filareta. And then, whatever the outcome, we need to have a full discussion with all the parties involved. Manticore and Haven, especially."

Thandi leaned back. "I agree."

"So do I," said Victor. "So let's move on to the subject that's immediately to hand. What's involved with this new genetic treatment you told us about? And how long would it take?"

"And how many people can you do it for?" asked Anton. "If it's this new, it's still going to be fiendishly expensive."

"Very big and fierce fiends at that," said Jacques, smiling. "But then again, Beowulf is a very big and fiercely rich planet. We can afford as many treatments as are needed, short of an entire battalion. The real question is, how many people do you want for the mission? And who?"

Victor and Anton looked at each other, then at Thandi.

"The three of us, obviously," said Zilwicki.

"Yana should come too," said Victor, "if she's willing. She just spent months on Mesa, so she knows the territory."

"She's willing," said Thandi.

"Speaking of Parmley Station..." Anton frowned. "Do you think Steph Turner would be willing to go back to Mesa? None of us know the planet the way she does."

Victor looked skeptical. "I don't know, Anton. I agree she'd be ideal, but..." He shook his head. "I can't see why she'd be willing to take the risk. She's a civilian, push comes to shove."

Jacques looked back and forth between them. "I'm not familiar with the person."

"Steph was the owner of the restaurant on Mesa that I worked at," said Anton. "We made contact with her through the Ballroom. She's not a member of it but she owed them a favor. The reason she came back with us is because the whole thing blew open right in her restaurant. She didn't have any choice. Brought her daughter out, too."

"Pay her," said Jeremy. He smiled and pointed at Benton-Ramirez y Chou with a thumb. "Out of Beowulf's treasury. They can afford whatever she wants."

Jacques didn't object. He didn't seem in the least bit concerned about the matter, in fact. "Would money do it?"

Anton and Victor looked at each other again.

"Abstractly...probably not," said Victor. "But if we tied it to something she'd really want..."

"Maybe," finished Zilwicki. "We need to figure out what that might be, though. She's already got enough to set up the restaurant she wants."

"Nancy," said Ruth. "Nancy's the key."

Jacques cocked his head. "Nancy is...?"

"Steph's daughter. She's on Beowulf at the moment, undergoing prolong treatments. She's fifteen years old. Maybe sixteen, now. In other words—"

"On the eve of all her higher education." Jacques nodded. "And if her mother is a refugee from Mesa with just enough to set up a restaurant... I assume the prolong was paid for by Beowulf, yes?"

Ruth nodded. "So there won't be anything left over. If Steph wants her to go to the best academies..."

She spread her hands. "You know how it is."

Highly advanced planets like Beowulf and Manticore had extensive and well-funded programs to enable students from lower class backgrounds to attend the finest institutions of higher education. Even so, it helped a great deal if the student's family could also provide them with assistance. In the nature of things, bureaucrats assigned to manage finances invariably found reasons that Assiduous Student's Need Alpha was really Lackadaisical Student's Whim Beta, and either refused to pay for it or didn't pay enough. Or simply took months to decide, by which time the need (or whim, if such it was) had passed by.

"It's worth a try," said Victor. "If we want Yana, we'll need to send a courier to Parmley Station anyway. We can ask Steph to come back with her. For reasons unspecified, of course—"

"Dear God, yes," said Jacques, grimacing. "This new technique isn't 'top secret.' It's . . . Let's just say it's to 'top secret' what a supernova is to 'dynamic.' We *have* to keep knowledge of it limited to the smallest circle possible."

"Steph'll come, without questioning the reason," said Anton: "She knows we wouldn't ask her if it wasn't important."

"Which brings us back to my original questions," said Victor. "How long does it take and what's involved?"

Jacques looked at him for a moment. "You understand that this new treatment isn't in place of a nanotech physiological transformation? It's added on top of it."

"Yes, obviously. It wouldn't do us much good to have our DNA disguised if we could be recognized from a visual image."

"Oh!" That came from Ruth. "Yukh. I've been through *that* process. It takes days and it's miserable."

"Really, really miserable," said Berry.

Victor shrugged. "I'm sure it's not that bad."

Berry and Ruth stared at him the way people might stare at a lunatic. Anton couldn't help but laugh.

"Girls, you need to remember the source. Black Victor, remember? Sometime, have him describe to you what StateSec Academy was like under Saint-Just."

"Oh, double-yukh," said Berry. "I remember now. Victor once told me that he had the fourth highest pain threshold ever recorded at that academy. Which begs the question—which I didn't ask then and I'm sure as hell not asking now—of how they test that in the first place."

Jacques looked interested. "I'm curious. How *do* they test that, Mr. Cachat."

"Well, mainly—"

"Enough," said Thandi. "I don't want to know either. Leaving aside how bad the nanotech treatment is, what's the new one like? And how fast is it?"

"Quicker than you'd think. It's counterintuitive, but since we're replacing the *entire* skin we don't need to allow for the usual time lapse for growth. The main thing, really, is just leaving enough time to make sure there aren't any rejections issues. The discomfort's not too bad, either."

"I assume it'll need to be done on Beowulf," said Anton.

"Oh, yes. In fact, there's only one facility in the universe that can do it. At the University of Grendel."

Thandi's expression was close to a scowl. "You let *academics* be in charge of something that requires this level of security?"

Anton chuckled. He knew Beowulf a lot better than Thandi did. The planet was...unique, in many respects.

"Well, they're Beowulfan academics," said Jacques. "From the Department of Chaotics, to be specific."

"Department of *what*?"

"It's a field of study which I believe is only found on Beowulf," Jacques explained.

"Are we gonna have fun or what?" said Anton.

CHAPTER 15

Well, what have we here? Yuri thought to himself, as he and Sharon were ushered into a suite on one of the top floors of the Suds Emporium. The room they entered was probably listed in the hotel's data bank as the living room of a suite; if so, proving yet again that the Erewhonese had a wry sense of humor. A fabled despot of the ancient Orient would have turned green with envy if he'd seen the place. All that was lacking were scantily clad slaves fanning the inhabitants with palm leaves.

And probably the only reason *that* was lacking was that the rulers of Erewhon had a very well developed sense of security. Slaves could talk—or scribble, if you cut out their tongues. The gangsters who'd originally settled Erewhon might have solved that problem by simply killing their slaves, but their descendants weren't quite that ruthless.

Not *quite*. It helped that they had excellent air conditioning.

When they got the summons from Walter Imbesi, Yuri and Sharon had presumed that they'd be meeting with him alone. Instead, the room's inhabitants included the triumvirate who semi-officially ran Erewhon—Tomas Hall, Alessandra Havlicek and Jack Fuentes—as well as Imbesi. Walter himself had no even semi-official position in Erewhon's power structure, but for all practical purposes the triumvirate was really a quadrumvirate.

Erewhon's government was not perhaps unique in the galaxy, but it came pretty close. It had a formal government apparatus, complete with a tripartite separation of powers between the executive, legislative and judicial branches, a written constitution, and a citizens' bill of rights to match the finest democracies anywhere. Then, paralleling all that, was the real fount of authority: an elaborate network of informal—it might be better to say, semi-formal—protocols and customs that bound all of the great families of Erewhon into a complex web of alliances and understandings that kept disputes within reasonable bounds.

You wouldn't think such a contradictory-seeming system would work at all, much less be a stable one. But Erewhon had been ruled that way for a long time now, without ever suffering internal strife much worse than scuffles since the conclusion of the bloody civil war between the Nationalists and Conventionalists that had taken place more than three and a half centuries earlier. On two occasions since the victory of the Nationalists in that civil war, the scuffles had begun erupting into deadly violence but they'd been squelched very quickly by the combined power of the rest of the planet's great families.

The setup might have been oppressive for most of the planet's population, except for the fact that all the great families had long ago established the practice of absorbing through adoption anyone showing real talent and promise. One of the effects of that practice, of course, was that the power and influence of the great families themselves was tremendously enhanced. Today, there was almost no one on Erewhon who couldn't consider themselves part of one of the great families, indirectly if not directly. In a very real sense, the entire population had become vested in customs that originated in the social mores of criminals, but had by now acquired a veneer of respectability so hard that no one in the galaxy challenged Erewhon's legitimacy.

Over the centuries, the practice had become a social custom so deeply ingrained that Erewhon was one of the very few star nations whose culture had no trace of xenophobia or social exclusivism. That was one of the reasons that Erewhon had been receptive from the beginning to the emergence of a star nation of former genetic slaves right next door to it. (So to speak. Torch was actually about twenty-seven light-years from Erewhon. But by the standards of modern space travel, that made them close neighbors.)

The presence of the triumvirate along with Walter Imbesi in the suite was not the most interesting factor, though. What Yuri found most significant was the presence of Luiz Rozsak, the commanding officer of Maya Sector's fleet-in-all-but-name and the man who'd defeated the armada sent to destroy Torch. By parties unknown, in the official record, but everyone knew perfectly well the mercenary armada had been hired by Manpower—or some other and still more inimical forces on Mesa.

There was a man accompanying Rozsak who was also wearing the uniform of the Solarian League Navy.

Yuri didn't know him. He'd had no contact yet with Mayan officials. The only reason he recognized Rozsak was because he'd studied Sharon's reports on the man while en route to Erewhon, which had included holopics of him.

Sharon leaned over and whispered in his ear: "That's Lieutenant Commander Jiri Watanapongse, Rozsak's intelligence specialist. He's very good."

The Erewhonese and Mayans in the suite waited politely for Yuri and Sharon to finish their hurried exchange. Then Alessandra Havlicek rose from her seat and went over to a side table laden with bottles.

"A drink?" she asked, pouring herself one. "This is Turnerian whiskey, which for my money is the best in the galaxy. But if you're not partial to whiskey..."

She finished pouring her drink and now had a free hand. She gestured with the hand to the rest of the very long and very well-laden side table. "We have pretty much anything you might enjoy."

Sharon leaned over again, whispering, "Stay away from the booze, unless you've taken an anti-alcohol—"

Yuri held up his hand. "Please, I wasn't born yesterday." He knew perfectly well that the Erewhonese—for a certainty—had all taken anti-alcohol preventatives, and the Mayan had likely done the same. He hadn't bothered to do so himself before coming here because he wasn't fond of alcoholic beverages to begin with. He'd always found that abstention worked better than any chemical measures.

He didn't bother to whisper, either. Seeing that he was following that tactical route—*we're all adults here, with no reason to play silly games*—Sharon shrugged and headed for the side table.

She *had* taken anti-alcohol preventatives. Unlike Yuri, Sharon enjoyed her liquor. Enjoyed it enough, in fact, that she used a semi-permanent subcutaneous delivery system instead of the usual pills. That enabled her to fine tune the dosage to allow her to get a slight buzz—without which she claimed booze wasn't booze—but nothing strong enough to affect her reasoning powers.

"I've never had Turnerian whiskey, but I've heard about it for years," she said to Havlicek. "How do you recommend it? Neat? On the rocks?"

"Oh, you *can't* dilute it with ice. If you really insist on chilling your liquor, then at least use—"

"Neat it is, then. Would you do me the honors?"

She and Havlicek exchanged smiles. The sort that had been exchanged between conspirators from time immemorial. Fellow spies, fellow sports fans, fellow drug addicts . . .

While Havlicek poured Sharon a glass of the whiskey, Yuri took a seat next to Watanapongse. "What are you having?" he asked, looking at the small but expensive-looking metal pot on the low table in front of the captain. There was a diminutive cup next to the pot holding some sort of very dark liquid.

"It's a type of coffee we make on Maya. If you trace it back far enough it'd have been called 'Turkish coffee,' but I don't know how much it resembles its ancestor. I've visited Terra twice, but never got a chance to try the real stuff."

It looked very strong and very bitter. Yuri decided it was just what he needed for the upcoming ordeal.

"I'll have one, then. Where—"

"I'll get it for you. It'll just take a bit." Watanapongse

rose smoothly from his armchair and headed toward a different side table. This one, Yuri saw, had what looking like coffee-making equipment on it. Or at least equipment whose ancestors had once made coffee. From what he could tell at the distance, this equipment might also be able to navigate through hyperspace.

Ordeal . . . wasn't quite the right word. Everyone would be exceedingly pleasant, he was sure of that. However battered the Republic of Haven might have been in the last stretch of the war with Manticore, it was still one of the galaxy's great military powers—far, far more powerful than either Erewhon or Maya, or even both combined. Erewhon was now an ally of the Republic, however strained that alliance might be in some respects, and he was almost certain that Maya was seeking to join that alliance. Or, at least, develop an informal relationship with Haven that came very close.

The big problem with this upcoming discussion, from Yuri's point of view, was that he knew damn good and well that within five minutes he'd be out of his pay grade; within fifteen minutes, he'd be *way* out of his pay grade; and within half an hour his pay grade would be an invisible microbe whimpering in the dust somewhere far, far below.

What was worse—oh, so very, very worse—was that he probably wouldn't be able to wriggle out of the situation by pointing to that selfsame oh-so-very-very-modest pay grade. The Erewhonese didn't think in those terms. The Mayans probably did, as a rule, but Yuri was pretty sure they were going to be pitching the rules here.

And what was absolutely certain was that Yuri and

Sharon weren't going to be able to claim that their superiors kept them on too tight of a leash for them to be able to say or agree to much of anything.

Alas, their immediate superior—for Sharon, officially; and if not Yuri, it amounted to much the same in practice—was a certain Victor Cachat. That is to say, the person who more than any other human alive today paid no attention whatsoever to pay grades. His own, least of all.

The first and most ancient law for all government officials like Yuri Radamacher—bureaucrats, to call them by their right name—was *Cover Your Ass.*

But how do you cover your ass when you're trying to cover it from the likes of Victor Cachat? The only way to do it was to satisfy him that you did your best—that is to say, your very very *very* best—to take advantage of every opportunity that came your way.

Such as the opportunity to expand an alliance against the galaxy's largest and most powerful star nation and its most vicious and cunning cabal—respectively, the Solarian League and the Mesan Alignment—by bringing in Erewhon and Maya Sector.

If Cachat were sitting in this very seat at this very moment, waiting for Captain Watanapongse to return with a pot of coffee—and the Mayan officer was even now headed back this way—would he be whining and pissing and moaning to himself that he was way above his pay grade?

Ha. The murderous brutal sociopathic reptilian callous son of a bitch would be licking his chops, that's what. Because he was dead sure and certain that he was a supremely *competent* murderous brutal sociopathic etc., etc., etc.

Watanapongse set down the pot and cup. Yuri poured the one into the other and took a careful sip.

Then, sighed.

"Good, isn't it?" asked the Mayan intelligence officer.

Yuri sighed again. That seemed easier, simpler and safer than saying anything. And within five minutes—

Jack Fuentes cleared his throat. "Thank you both for coming. The reason we asked for this meeting—"

No, two minutes. *Easier* and *simpler* and *safer* were terms that would be as foreign to Yuri Radamacher as words written in ancient Sumerian.

He wondered if the ancient Sumerians had had a term for "pay grade."

Probably. He knew they'd had executioners.

✧   ✧   ✧

"Oh, come on, Yuri. That wasn't so bad." Sharon climbed into the capsule whose hatch Yuri was holding open for her. The system of mass transport the Erewhonese had chosen for their capital city was a variant of the vacuum transport method. It was fast and efficient, but it required the use of smaller vehicles than either of them were used to. Climbing into the capsules was easier if someone gave you a bit of assistance.

Once Sharon was in place, Yuri slid into the seat behind her, spoke their destination and pressed the button indicating that the coupling was finished. The capsules could be linked in a chain as long as sixty capsules, but they were so small in diameter that two people could not sit next to each other unless one of them was an infant.

Sffffttttt. The joined capsules sped off. The arrangement made conversations a bit difficult, though.

"Admit it!" Sharon said. She started to turn her head until she remembered that she could pull up a virtual screen that would allow her to look at Yuri directly.

"Admit it," she repeated, after the screen came up.

For a moment, Yuri was tempted to claim that the awkward seating arrangement made it hard for him to get his thoughts in order. But the moment—

Sttttfffff. A chime announced they'd arrived.

—was brief. It really was a fast and efficient system.

"Okay," he said, after they climbed out. "It wasn't as bad as I thought it'd be. Mind you!" He held up a cautionary finger. "That's not saying a lot. I'm told that root canals weren't as bad as they were thought to be. But they were still pretty bad."

Sharon rolled her eyes. "Nobody's had a root canal in . . . hell, what is it? Two millennia? Outside of planets that were lost and cast back into medievalism, anyway." She took Yuri by the arm and led him toward the exit. "You're just being grumpy because you think it's an art form at which you're a maestro."

Her tone was cheerful. "And speaking of maestros, I think you did damn well today, myself. For a measly high commissioner and envoy extraordinary."

They passed out into the open. The sunlight was bright—and also quite cheering, even if the color was a little off to them. Erewhon's star was a K5, smaller and dimmer than Haven's or La Martine's, which were both G stars. To Yuri and Sharon, everything seemed to have a slightly orange cast.

There was a bit of a breeze, too, to make the day still more enjoyable. Despite his grim determination to find wrack and ruin all about, Yuri couldn't help but feel his spirits picking up.

Sharon, who knew him well, jumped onto the moment with heavy boots.

"Look at all the bright spots," she said. "First—there's no doubt about this—the Erewhonese and the Mayans have finally decided they can trust each other."

"Sure. Gangsters and traitors are natural bosom buddies."

"Second, it's just as obvious—they didn't come right out and say it, of course—that they're going to be integrating their military forces all the way down the line, not just having Erewhon serve as Maya's workshop. That has the potential to turn two third-rate powers into one that swings some real weight."

"Just what the galaxy needs. Another Machiavelli in the game."

"Stop it, Yuri. You know just as well as I do how important that could wind up being, if the Solarian League collapses—which we both think it will, and not even that far in the future."

Yuri made a face. He didn't disagree with anything Sharon was saying. It was just that . . .

They'd reached the entrance to their apartment building. He gave Sharon a warning look. As long as they'd been moving and talking out in the open, the scrambling equipment they both carried would have made it impossible for anyone to overhear their conversation or even read their lips. And once they entered their apartment, the much more powerful and sophisticated equipment there made it possible for them to speak openly again. The danger was in this transition zone. Someone could have planted surveillance gear in the vicinity which their portable scramblers couldn't handle, and they were still too far

away for the stationary equipment in their apartment
to protect them.

Of course, it was a warning that Sharon didn't
need at all, as her answering glare made clear. It was
admittedly a little silly for him to caution a former
StateSec officer on security issues.

Neither of them said anything further until they'd
reached the apartment and the door had closed behind
them. Then, after a quick glance at the monitors to
make sure the scramblers were operating, Sharon
crossed her arms and gave Yuri a level stare.

"Okay, get it out of your system. 'It was just that . . .
'. What, Yuri?"

He took a deep breath. "Why me? Why do I have
to be the one trying to thread the needle between
encouraging them—yes, I agree; of course I agree; if
they can pull off this alliance we'll all be in a better
position—and not coming right out and committing
Haven to anything because I don't have the goddam
authority to do it in the first place."

She smiled and patted his cheek. "Because you're
so good at it. That's why Victor made sure you got
the assignment."

CHAPTER 16

"I think you're all insane, of course," Honor Alexander-Harrington said with one of her crooked smiles as she sat back in her chair with her wineglass and looked at her mostly rather-less-than-reputable dinner guests. Neither of her spouses had been able to join them, and the nature of those guests—and their plans— had restricted her potential invitation list in rather draconian fashion. The table before them bore the remnants of a generous meal, and James MacGuiness made the circuit refreshing coffee cups for the coffee drinkers who had not yet transitioned to something stronger. Those coffee drinkers included Victor Cachat (not surprisingly for those who knew him) and Yana Tretiakovna, who claimed to prefer a caffeine buzz to alcohol.

"If you thought it was a bad idea, you should've said so at the time," her Uncle Jacques replied. "And if we're going to talk about insane ideas, I could think of a few of yours over the years which were even better qualified for that particular adjective."

"Well, of course you can! You don't think I'd venture

an opinion like that without having a meterstick of my own to base it on, do you? Besides, I do come by my genome honestly, you know, and if memory serves there's been a...less than fully rational action plan from both sides of the family tree upon occasion. I remember stories Daddy told me about one of my uncles, for example. Back when he was a captain in the BSC, I believe."

"If you'll pardon my saying so, Your Grace," Thandi Palane said a bit dryly, "I doubt most of your uncle's follies could outshine the one *you* pulled at a place called Cerberus."

"Or the one at a dinner party I can call to mind," Benjamin Mayhew said even more dryly. The Protector of Grayson and his wives were the only members of the dinner party which kept her guest list from being totally disreputable, in Honor's opinion.

"Details. Details!" Honor waved her wineglass dismissively. "Besides, I already admitted I needed a meterstick of my own. And I never said it was a *bad* idea, either. I just said that the whole lot of our fearless agents"—the wineglass gestured at Thandi, Victor Cachat, Anton Zilwicki, and Yana Tretiakovna—"have fairly tangential contact with rationality." Her smile faded. "And probably a little more in the way of guts than is good for them."

"While I hate to disabuse you of your obviously inflated notion of my bravery quotient, Your Grace," Zilwicki said, "I intend to emulate an Old Earth mouse to the very best of my ability once we're on-planet."

"Of course you do," Catherine Montaigne said sarcastically. "I've noticed what a shy and retiring type you are."

"Actually," Jacques Benton-Ramirez y Chou said rather more seriously, "he's not that far wrong." Montaigne looked at her old friend incredulously, and the Beowulfer shrugged. "There are lots of different ways to be as unobtrusive as possible, Catherine. One of the most effective is to be something else entirely as obtrusively as you possibly can. Which is exactly what our friends here are proposing to be, when you come down to it."

"Doesn't mean we won't have to be careful when we go about our nefarious activities," Zilwicki agreed. "But the principle's one every stage magician understands perfectly. We'll be so busy waving our public personas under everyone's noses that no one's going to be wondering what we might have hidden behind the curtain."

"That's all well and good," Honor said in a much more serious tone. "And, for what it's worth, I agree with you. But something nobody's been talking about very much is that for this Alignment to have operated so long without anyone's spotting it, even on Beowulf, it has to be very, very good at covert operations of its own . . . including penetration of other people's security. That 'sleeper agent' your people found on Torch is one example of how far they're prepared to go, and if McBryde was right about their having buried genetic 'sleepers' all over the galaxy, how confident can we really be that they haven't penetrated the BSC itself?"

"Much as it pains me to admit it, we can't be," Benton-Ramirez y Chou replied, more than a bit sourly. "Obviously, we've had to rethink everything we thought we knew about Mesa in light of the information Victor and Anton—and Yana—brought home. I have a few ideas about how we might look for those 'genetic sleepers' of yours using gene scans, but nobody's worried much about that particular form of security screening in the past. On the other hand, we've always been pretty fanatical about compartmentalizing information and operating on a 'need to know' basis. To be honest, that's one reason I was so uncomfortable bringing this new genetic sheathing technology into the light of day even under these circumstances. It's certainly not impossible that the Alignment's caught a hint of the R and D on it, or even—although I think it's very unlikely—infiltrated some of its 'sleepers' into the R and D program itself. But I guarantee you that anyone who's involved with it is going to find himself under the most intense scrutiny of his entire life as soon as we get home. And I don't see how they could have prepared a cover that's going to stand up to our newest counterintelligence types."

He took a stalk of celery from the plate in front of him and offered it to the cream and gray treecat in the high chair beside him. Bark Chewer's Bane accepted it with a pleased "Bleek!" and began chewing happily. The Blue Mountain Dancing Clan scout was Benton-Ramirez y Chou's newly assigned bodyguard, and he and Honor's uncle were settling into a comfortable working relationship. It wasn't the same as an adoption bond, as Bark Chewer's Bane's retention of his treecat name indicated, but it was the sort of relationship which was going to become increasingly common as the 'cats integrated themselves more and more thoroughly into human society.

"As soon as BCB and I get home," Benton-Ramirez y Chou went on, his expression amused as Honor rolled her eyes at the acronym he'd adopted for his new partner, "he and some of his friends and I will be personally interviewing every member of the team working on this project. Between us, I'm pretty sure we'll be able to uncover anyone with divided loyalties. After that, we'll be working our way through as much of our entire security structure as we can." He grimaced. "Obviously, we're going to be limited by time constraints and the number of 'cats available to us, so we're not going to get very far beyond the 'management' echelons for quite some time, but we'll pay special attention to plugging any leaks in our more sensitive programs. Especially this one. And if we find one"—the last amusement faded from his expression and his eyes were grim—"we'll plug it very, very thoroughly indeed."

"That sounds like a good idea to me," Cachat observed.

"And to me," Yana agreed even more firmly. The ex-Scrag had hit it off surprisingly well with their hostess. Personally, Benton-Ramirez y Chou thought that was at least partly because of how much she had in common with Nimitz. However "reformed" she and her fellow Amazons might have become since falling under Thandi Palane's influence, there was still a lot of predator in them, and especially in Yana.

"I hope this won't seem too dreadfully ignorant of me," Katherine Mayhew said, "and I know that the . . . enmity between Beowulf and Mesa's been around a long, long time, but it seems even deeper and more, well, *personal* than I'd thought it was. I haven't had the opportunity to sit in on all the intelligence briefings Benjamin has, and unlike him, no one was sending any mere women off to Old Earth for their college educations when it would've done me any good. But why in Tester's name could anyone be so filled with determination or hatred or whatever it is as to spend *six hundred years* planning something like this?" She shook her head. "I'm not questioning any of the information Mr. Zilwicki and Mr. Cachat brought back from Mesa. I'm just trying to wrap my mind around it and understand."

"That's going to be a big part of the problem when we start trying to prove any of this to the Sollies, Cat," Honor said soberly. "The League would be prepared enough to see this as more anti-Mesan panic mongering on the part of Manticore and Haven, based on our obvious, corrupt imperialism—now that we've taken our masks off, that's clearly the only reason we've been so fanatical about enforcing the Cherwell Conventions for so long!—but including Beowulf's going to make it even easier for their propagandists to attack the entire idea. *Everybody* knows Beowulfers've been lunatics on anything to do with Mesa for centuries, after all. And on the face of it, it *does* sound pretty absurd."

"I didn't mean to say that," Katherine began, but Benton-Ramirez y Chou interrupted her.

"Honor didn't mean to suggest that you had," he said. "But she's right, and so are you. It does sound absurd. For that matter, there are people back home on Beowulf who're going to find it hard to accept all of this. Of course, in their case it's not going to be because they won't believe Mesans are despicable enough for something like this; it's going to be that they can't believe we could have *missed* it for so long. And, much as I hate to admit it, one of the reasons they're going to think that way is that we've become so accustomed to thinking of all Mesans in terms of Manpower and their transstellar partners."

"Personally," Catherine Montaigne said, "I've come to the conclusion that one reason the bastards have been so busy propping Manpower up has a lot to do with setting up an obvious stalking horse. Web Du Havel and I have argued for years over why Mesa's stood so foursquare behind genetic slavery for so long given the economics of the institution and the potential social powder keg all those seccies and slaves create on Mesa itself. Now that we know about this Alignment, it makes a lot more sense. Just thinking about the hooks it can get into people by involving them in the filth of the slave trade puts an entirely new perspective on it, but when you add in the façade it sets up—the way it colors all of our thinking where Mesa as a whole is concerned—it makes even more sense."

"Exactly." Benton-Ramirez y Chou nodded. "The idea that someone might set themselves up as proponents of the galaxy's vilest form of commerce so that we'd concentrate on *that* view of their villainy and not notice an even deeper one is going to take a little getting used to. And the truth is that Beowulfers have become so set in their ways of hating and despising everything about Mesa and Manpower that it's going to take time for a lot of us to start taking this threat as seriously as we ought to."

"That's just it," Katherine Mayhew admitted. "I've always wondered exactly why the hatred between your people and the Mesans cuts so deep. I don't have any problem understanding that it *could*, you understand. After all, we have our own relationship with Masada as an example. I just don't understand the . . . the *mechanism* for it, I guess you'd say."

"I think that's because—like the original Manticoran colonists—your ancestors missed the Final War, Cat," Honor said. "By the time the first Manties debarked from *Jason*, that war had been over for a long time, but it's even further removed for you Graysons. Or *us* Graysons, I suppose I should say." She smiled again, briefly. "You didn't find out about it until you reestablished contact with the rest of the galaxy, and to be honest, you had a lot more pressing worries at the time, given Grayson's planetary environment and the Masadans, when you did find out."

"Honor's right," Benton-Ramirez y Chou agreed. "And I have to admit that as terrible as the Final War was, it has a lot more ongoing immediacy for Beowulf and Mesa than for anybody else in the League. More even than for people living in the Sol System today, for that matter. I know our Final War Museum in Grendel is the best and biggest in the entire League, but that war only gets a single wing in the Solarian Military Museum in Old Chicago."

"I don't know as much about the Final War—stupid damned name, when I think about it—as I wish I did," Cachat said. He smiled faintly. "Like the Graysons, I've had more pressing worries until very recently."

"It probably wouldn't hurt for you to spend a little time in the Museum while you're on Beowulf," Benton-Ramirez y Chou said thoughtfully. "Assuming you've got the time for it, anyway. There are some really good VR programs covering it in the System Database, though, and you're going to be spending at least a while recuperating from the mods."

"Oh, goody!" Yana snorted. "Educational VRs to distract us from all the things you're going to be doing to us. I can hardly wait."

A general chuckle ran around the table, but then Benton-Ramirez y Chou sobered and returned his attention to Katherine Mayhew.

"Despite Victor's well-taken observation on the stupidity of calling *any* war the 'final' one, Old Earth's version of it came entirely too close to being just that, at least where the Sol System was concerned," he said much more somberly. "The Ukrainian Supremacists may have started it when they turned the super soldiers loose," he glanced semi-apologetically at Yana, who snorted in amusement at his expression, "but they weren't the only lunatics running asylums. And let's be honest, the super soldiers weren't really all that much more heavily genetically modified than Honor here is. Enhanced strength, better reflexes, they heal faster, and enhanced intelligence—although that one's still a rather . . . nebulous concept—but that was small beer compared to the other crap that got turned loose. For example, there were the Asian Confederacy's version of super soldiers. Now, *those* were scary. Implanted and natural weaponry, a metabolism that was so enhanced they 'burned out' in less than twenty years and their combat gear had to include intravenous concentrated nourishment just to keep them running *that* long, and enough other genetic tinkering to make them all sterile—thank God! In terms of effectiveness in sustained combat, the mods didn't do a lot for them, given the sophistication of the weaponry available even to us poor old 'pure strain' models. Doesn't really matter all that much how strong someone is or how good his reflexes are when he's up against a main battle tank. But it turned them into god-awful special operations troops, and the 'intelligence' mods on *them* pushed them over the edge into the outright megalomania that proved Old Earth's undoing. It was when they turned on the Confederacy's political leadership in the Beijing Coup that the Final War really turned into the ultimate nightmare."

"Why *did* they stage the coup?" Cachat asked. Benton-Ramirez y Chou arched an eyebrow at him, and the Havenite shrugged. "The Confederacy was winning against the Ukrainians, from what little I know about the history involved, but that all turned around shortly after the coup. So why did they do it? And why *did* it turn around?"

"They staged the coup because they were sterile," Honor said before her uncle could reply. "They'd decided their obvious superiority to the pure strain humans who were giving them orders proved *they* should be in charge, and they'd decided they were clearly the next step in human evolution. But the Confederacy's leadership controlled the cloning farms where they were created, and the Confederacy refused to allow them unlimited reproduction." She shrugged. "So they staged their own revolt in order to take over the cloning facilities and produce more of their own kind."

"And the reason the war in Europe started turning against them," Benton-Ramirez y Chou said, nodding in agreement, "was because their mods had turned them into predators, not herd animals. Among other things, they were so full of contempt for their 'obsolescent' pure strain opponents that they tended to downplay the need to unite against their outside foes while they engaged in internal warfare with one another for control of the Confederacy."

"And while all that was going on," Catherine Montaigne put in sourly, "the idiots in Western Europe had pulled the stopper out of their own bottle of lunacy." Montaigne had spent longer on Old Earth than anyone else gathered around the table. She'd spent quite a bit of that time learning about the womb in which Mesa and genetic slavery had been conceived, and her expression was bitter. "The Ukrainian Supremacists had taken all of them by surprise by the *timing* of their attack, but everyone on the planet—hell, everyone in the entire *star system*—had seen it coming for a long, long time. The Western Europeans weren't interested in genetically modifying human beings. Instead, they decided to genetically modify *diseases* like anthrax, botulism, bubonic plague, meningitis, typhus, cholera, and something called Ebola."

"I've never even heard of most of those," Yana said plaintively.

"That's because most of them have been effectively stamped out." Montaigne's expression was grim, "and thank God for it! In fact, *most* of them had been stamped out on Old Earth before the Final War, too. Until the idiots dusted them off and sent them off to war, at least."

"How could they have expected that to *work*?" Elaine Mayhew demanded, eyes dark with the horror the mere thought of such a weapon evoked in someone who'd been raised in Grayson's hermetically sealed environments.

"They thought they'd designed firewalls into their

pet monstrosities." Benton-Ramirez y Chou's voice was even grimmer than Montaigne's. "They'd integrated 'kill switches' and stockpiled disease-specific vaccines. But once they were out into a real-world environment, their firewalls evolved right out from under them a hell of a lot faster than they'd expected. Oh, *initially*, their weapons had almost exactly the desired effect when they deployed them. That lasted as long as three years, and the Confederacy's super soldiers' hyper-active metabolisms seem to have made them even more vulnerable than pure-strain humans. But once the pathogens got loose in the civilian population of Asia, the law of unintended consequences came into play with a vengeance. By the time the same diseases started bleeding back across the frontier into Europe, they'd developed effective immunity to the vaccines which were supposed to protect *Europeans* against them."

Katherine and Elaine looked at their husband, as if they hoped he'd tell them Benton-Ramirez y Chou was exaggerating, but Benjamin shook his head.

"There's a reason they managed to kill off damned near the entire Old Earth branch of the human race," he told his wives. "And don't think it was all Europe and Asia, either. The western hemisphere made its own contribution to the holocaust."

"True," Honor agreed. "On the other hand, at least they weren't crazy enough to turn genetically engineered diseases loose on their opposition."

"Oh, no!" Benton-Ramirez y Chou showed his teeth in something which approximated a smile in much the same way a hexapuma's bared teeth approximated a pleasant greeting. "They were lots smarter than that. *They* decided to deploy weaponized *nanotech*!"

"Sweet Tester," Katherine Mayhew murmured.

"Rather than further disturb the digestion of Mac's meal," Honor said after a moment, "I propose we not go a lot deeper into the specifics of the Final War, Uncle Jacques. I don't think we really need to in order to answer Cat's original question about the... ill feeling between you noble Beowulfers and those despicable Mesans."

"No. No, we don't," Benton-Ramirez y Chou agreed. "But that 'ill feeling' owes a lot to how Beowulf and the rest of the colony systems which responded to Old Earth's attempted suicide viewed what had happened there."

He sipped from his own wineglass, then set it down very precisely.

"My own ancestors—and Honor's, of course" he nodded at his niece "—ended up in command of the Rescue Fleet. In a way, since the League grew out of the relief effort and the kick in the pants that gave to interstellar commerce and travel in general, you could say the present day Sollies are at least partly our family's fault, I suppose. On the other hand, there's more than enough blame to go around where that minor problem's concerned, so I don't intend to dwell on it. But the lesson Beowulf and most of the rest of the human race took away from the Final War was that they never—*ever*—wanted to face that sort of nightmare again. And the 'super soldiers' and, possibly even more, the mindset of the Ukrainian supremacists, was almost worse than the genengineered diseases."

Several of the others looked a bit surprised by his last sentence and he snorted.

"I know. Compared to the Asian Confederacy's

nightmares, the Scrags were actually almost benign, weren't they?" He gestured at Yana. "I mean, look at her. Then look at Honor. Not a lot to choose between them, is there?"

Yana and his niece looked at each other for a moment. Then Honor smiled slowly and shook her head.

"No, not a lot at all," she murmured.

"But the *idea* behind the Ukrainians was even worse," Benton-Ramirez y Chou said softly. "The Confederacy had seen *its* super soldiers as weapons systems, tools that wouldn't be allowed to reproduce and certainly weren't any sort of pattern for the future of humanity. But the Ukrainians had intended all along to force the evolution of the next step, of Homo superior, and that was what had initiated the entire conflict. All of the carnage, all of the destruction and the billions of lives which had been lost, *started* in the Ukrainian ideal of designed genetic uplift. The further weaponization of biotechnology, and of nanotechnology, made the devastation immeasurably worse, but the people trying to dig the human race's homeworld out of what had become a mass grave were determined that it wasn't going to happen again. The Beowulf Biosciences Code evolved directly out of the Final War. That's why it unequivocally outlaws *any* weaponization of biotech in general... and why it places such stringent limits on acceptable genetic modification of humans."

"And Mesa doesn't agree with that, obviously," Victor said.

"No, it doesn't." Benton-Ramirez y Chou agreed. "Leonard Detweiler thought it was a hysterical over-reaction to a disaster, an isolated incident which, for all its horror, had after all been limited to a single star system. Mind you, the bio weapons had jumped the fire breaks between Old Earth, Luna, and Mars, but even at their worst, they'd never gotten beyond Sol's oort cloud, and the human race had *lots* of star systems by then. And even if that hadn't been the case, then surely humanity had learned its lesson. Besides, he didn't have any real objection to outlawing weaponized biotech—or he said he didn't, at any rate. It was the Code's decision to turn its back on targeted improvement of the human genotype, to renounce the right to take our genetic destiny into our own hands, that infuriated him. 'Small minds are always terrified by great opportunities,' he said. He simply couldn't believe any *rational* species would turn its back on the opportunity to become all that it could possibly be."

He paused for a long moment, then sighed deeply.

"And the truth is, in a lot of ways, Detweiler was right," he admitted. "Again, look at Honor and Yana. Nothing horrible there, is there? Or in any of a dozen—*two* dozen—specific planetary environment genetic mods I could rattle off. Even you Graysons." He smiled at the Mayhews and shook his head. "Without the genetic mods your founders put into place so secretly, you wouldn't have survived. But what Detweiler never understood—or accepted, anyway—was that what the mainstream Beowulfan perspective rejected was the intentional *design* of a genotype which was intended from the beginning to produce a superior human, a *better* human . . . what lunatics from Adolph Hitler to the Ukrainian supremacists to the Malsathan unbeatables have all sought—a *master* race. For all intents and purposes, a separate species which, by virtue of its obvious and designed superiority to all other varieties of human being must inevitably *exercise* that superiority.

"Detweiler never understood that. He never understood that his fellow Beowulfers were repelled by the reemergence of what had once been called racism which was inherent in his proposals."

Several members of his audience looked puzzled, and he snorted and looked at Catherine Montaigne.

"I'm sure your friend Du Havel could explain the concept," he said.

"And he's done it often enough," Montagne agreed just a bit sourly, and glanced around at the other table guests. "What Jacques is talking about is the belief that certain genetic characteristics—silly things like skin color, hair color, eye color—denoted inherent superiority or inferiority. As Web is fond of pointing out, once upon a time Empress Elizabeth would have been considered naturally inferior because of her complexion and relegated by her inferiority to slave status."

"That's ridiculous!" Elaine Mayhew said sharply, and Benton-Ramirez y Chou chuckled with very little humor.

"Of course it is. It's the sort of concept that belongs to primitive history. But the problem, Elaine, is that what Detweiler was proposing would have reanimated the concept of inherent inferiority *because it would have been true*. It would have been something which could have been *demonstrated*, measured, placed on a sliding scale. Of course, exactly what constituted 'superiority' might have been open to competing interpretations, which could only have made the situation even worse. We Beowulfers are fiercely meritocratic, but we're also fanatically devoted to the concepts of social and legal equality, and what Detweiler and his clique wanted struck at the very heart of those concepts.

"So we told him no. Rather emphatically, in fact. *So* emphatically that if he had attempted to put his theories into practice on Beowulf, he would have been stripped of his license to practice medicine and imprisoned."

Benton-Ramirez y Chou shrugged. "I suppose it's possible our ancestors overreacted, although I'd argue they had good reason to. On the other hand, Detweiler was damned arrogant about his own position. He was deeply and profoundly pissed off by how . . . firmly his arguments were rejected, and it would appear the present-day members of this 'Mesan Alignment' have taken his own overreaction to truly awesome heights. When he shook the dust of Beowulf from his sandals and emigrated to Mesa, he took with him a sizable chunk of the Beowulfan medical establishment. A larger one, really, than the rest of Beowulf ever anticipated would follow him into exile, although it was still only a tiny minority of the total planetary population. And that, Katherine," he smiled wryly at Katherine Mayhew, "is exactly why the enmity between Mesa and Beowulf has been so intense for so long. You could say that Mesa is Beowulf's equivalent of Masada's Faithful, and you wouldn't be far wrong. In fact, you'd be even closer to correct than most of us have imagined over the last five or six centuries."

"That's . . . a bit of an understatement, if you don't mind my saying so," Zilwicki observed, and Benton-Ramirez y Chou nodded.

"Absolutely. I've been thinking about it a lot since you dropped McBryde's bombshell on us, and I've come to the conclusion that what's really behind this entire master plan of theirs—assuming McBryde got it right, of course—is more than simply finally accomplishing Leonard Detweiler's dream of creating a genetically superior species. That's obviously *part* of it, but looking at what we did already know about Mesa and Mesans, I'd say an equally big part of it is *proving* they were right all along. It's been a long, long time since the Final War. The feelings of revulsion and horror it generated have largely faded, and the prejudice against 'genies' is far weaker than it used to be. In fact, I would argue that if it weren't for the existence of genetic slavery, that prejudice probably would have completely ceased to exist by now. If this Alignment had been willing to take even a fraction of the resources it must have invested in its conspiracies and its infiltration and the development of the technology that made the Yawata Strike possible and spend it on propaganda—on *education*, for God's sake—it almost certainly could have convinced a large minority, possibly even a majority, of the rest of the human race to go along with it. To embark, even if more gradually and more cautiously than the Alignment might prefer, on the deliberate improvement of the human genome. For that matter, in the existence of people like Honor and Yana we've *already* deliberately improved on that genome! But I don't think it ever really occurred to them to take that approach. I think they locked themselves into the idea that their vision had to be *imposed* on the rest of us and that as the people whose ancestors had seen that division so clearly so much sooner than anyone else, it's their destiny to do just that. Which is one reason I compared them to the Faithful, Katherine. Their whole purpose—or the way they've chosen to go about achieving it, at least—is fundamentally irrational, and only someone as fanatical as the people who built 'doomsday bombs' to destroy their entire planet in order to 'save it' from Benjamin the Great and the rest of the moderates could possibly have invested so much in that irrationality."

"I agree," Honor said softly, her eyes dark. "I agree entirely. And that's what truly scares me when I think about this. Because if they really are religious fanatics in some sort of Church of Genetic Superiority, then God only knows how far they are truly prepared to go to drag us all kicking and screaming into their version of Zion."

CHAPTER 17

The first thing Thandi Palane noticed when she came into the suite was that the central salon's furniture had been rearranged so that all the couches and chairs had a good view of the HD wallscreen. The paintings which normally filled the screen had been replaced by a talk program.

"—know *anything* about this man," said one of the people sitting around the table that was pictured in the center of the screen. She was a red-haired woman with sharp features that matched her sharp tone of voice.

"I wouldn't go so far as that," said the man sitting at one end of the table. The table had an odd sort of L-shape, which led Thandi to think the man in question was the talk show's host or moderator.

The man glanced at a small screen recessed into the table. "We know, for instance, that he was the governor of La Martine province for a short time."

"Short time!" That came from the same red-haired woman. The barked laugh that followed had the same edge to it that Thandi was already coming to associate with the woman—for whom she was also already developing a dislike.

"That's what I believe is called a 'euphemism,'" the woman continued. "He was relieved from his post almost as soon as he got it—and I can't help but notice that that came *after* he spent time under arrest. You can't help but wonder—"

"Cut it out, Charlene," said a woman sitting at the other end of the table from the man Thandi presumed to be the moderator. "None of this even qualifies as 'established fact' in the first place, much less any interpretation of it. The events both you and Yael are referring to took place during the revolution that overthrew Saint-Just—and in a Havenite province that's far distant from our own borders and about which we know precious little to begin with. Everything about that revolution is still murky, especially at the edges. So I think it behooves us—"

Thandi turned to Ruth Winton, who was sitting on one of the couches next to Victor. "What's this?"

"It's a show called *The Star Empire Today*," said Ruth. "The moderator is Yael Underwood."

"He's the slimeball with the long blond hair and weaselly expression sitting on the far right," said Anton Zilwicki, who was seated on another couch in between Jacques Benton-Ramirez y Chou and Catherine Montaigne.

Cathy laughed. "God, I swear! Nobody can hold a grudge like a Gryphon highlander."

"What grudge?" asked Thandi.

Berry had come in right behind her and provided the answer—after laughing herself. "Underwood's the one who outed Daddy. That happened before we met you at the funeral ceremony for Hieronymus Stein on Erewhon."

"—*do you refuse to admit that everything about him*—"

"—*why am I the only one here who seems to remember, Florence, that this man was our sworn enemy until yesterday*—"

"—*go so far as Charlene, but what does seem fairly well established is that his role in the Manpower Incident was hardly*—"

Thandi tuned out the yabber-jabber. "What do you mean by 'outed'?"

"Underwood did a whole show devoted to Anton," explained Cathy. "He let the Talking Heads blather for a while before he trotted out somebody who actually knew something and that guy—Mr. Wright they called him, didn't they, Anton?—really spilled the beans."

"I found out later his real name's Guillermo Thatcher," said Anton. "He'd recently retired from SIS—that stands for Special Intelligence Service, if you didn't know already, which is the Manticoran civilian spook agency—and someday I hope to catch him in a dark alley with no witnesses around."

Thandi smiled. The smile widened when she saw the gloomy expression on Victor's face.

"—*Special Officer Cachat,*" the Charlene woman was saying, "*and you really have to wonder exactly what the 'Special' part of that entails, don't you? If you ask me*—"

"And now they're outing Victor, I take it?"

"Trying to," said Anton. "It's pretty flimsy stuff so far, and"—he jabbed a thick finger at the HD screen—"I don't think there's any Mr. Damn-the-bastard Wright equivalent on this panel. It's mostly been a pillow fight between Shrill Charlene and the other woman.

Her name's Florence Hu and she's more or less the
Liberal Party voice on the panel."

Cathy sniffed. "Emphasis on the 'less,' if you please."

"They're swinging at each other plenty fiercely,"
Anton continued, "but how much damage can you do
with a pillow? The simple truth is that none of them
know very much about Victor to begin with. That
includes Yael Underwood whom I also have daydreams
about meeting in a dark alley someday."

Thandi slid onto the couch next to Victor and patted his hand. "Don't let it bother you so much, dear.
It'll be over soon enough."

Victor's expression, amazingly, got more gloomy still.
"I'm afraid not," he said.

"Oh, come on. These so-called 'news talk shows'
have the attention span of a gerbil. By next week—"

"Victor is all they'll be talking about," said Anton.
"Well...might take a bit more time than that, depending on this and that and the other. There are some
ways, Thandi, in which you don't know Victor that
well. The reason for that sourpuss expression on his
face isn't because of what's on the HD screen now.
It's because he knows what he ought to do next and
he really, really, really doesn't want to do it."

Victor grunted. "The reason for the sourpuss expression, as Anton puts it, is because I find his ability
to figure out what I'm thinking distressful as well as
disturbing. He's getting better at it, too, to make it
still worse."

Thandi frowned. "What are you talking about?"

Berry, now standing next to her, looked back and
forth between the two men. "Look at 'em. It's like
they belong to some sort of weird club. You know,

the sort of goofy super-exclusive fellowship that's got stupid secret handshakes."

Ruth suddenly sat up straight and clapped her hands. "Oh, my God! That's brilliant, Anton and Victor! It's absolutely *brilliant*!"

She jumped to her feet and began pacing back and forth, gesticulating in a manner so vigorous it was almost wild. She came within a centimeter of knocking over a very expensive-looking vase perched on a side table. "You'll have to get approval, of course. Might even have to go all the way to President Pritchart. But she's an ex-spook herself so she's bound to understand why it's such a great idea."

Striding back, she passed by Benton-Ramirez y Chou and waved her hand at him. "He'll have to sign on, too, obviously. But I can't imagine that'll be a big problem."

Jacques looked up at Thandi and Berry. "What are they all talking about?"

Thandi shrugged. "Got no idea. Spook-think doesn't come naturally to me. Victor, would you care to enlighten us?"

She pursed her lips thoughtfully. "Perhaps I should rephrase that. If you don't explain yourself I'm going to take up a new aerobic exercise. It's called the Cachat Curl."

"Can I watch?" asked Berry.

Victor raised his hands in a gesture that combined exasperation and surrender. "Given that there's clearly no way to avoid publicity about..." (A deep breath, here.) "...me, we should run with it. Turn it to our advantage."

"Pile it on with a shovel," chimed in Anton. "As thick

and treacly as we can. Make sure the news outlets are obsessed with the story and for as long as possible."

He looked at Jacques. "You'll have to help. To make the scheme work right, we'll need to create a double for Victor. Um. Me, too, I guess."

"No 'guess' about it," said Victor. "Yes, you, too."

Anton chuckled but didn't look away from Jacques. "They'll have to be sheathed with our DNA, I'm thinking, not just nanotech body-transformed. Just in case someone manages to pick up trace residues. We won't expose them to the media directly, of course, since that would require them to be able to act like we do as well as looking like we do."

"God help the universe," muttered Thandi.

"That would get . . . tricky," Anton went on. "But it doesn't matter. Once we leak Victor's entire history to the press—and we *do* know where all the bones are buried—"

"Oh, so many many bones," chortled Ruth, still striding. "God, the media will go wild!"

"Especially when we leak the Ballroom footage of the Old Town gunfight," said Anton.

Victor made a noise that sounded like a vehement protest strangled before it took actual form in words. Anton gave him a sideways look. "*Of course* we have to release that, too. It'll be the icing on the cake, Victor. You know it as well as I do."

The Havenite agent's expression had passed beyond gloomy by now and had entered the territory shared by *sullen rancor* and *spread the misery*. "I've never seen that footage, but it's got to include Jeremy as well as me." He gave Cathy a sharp look. "Yes?"

"Well . . . yes, it does. Right at the end."

"He gunned down at least four of the bastards, as I recall. So let the damned media get their first actual look at what the expression 'galaxy's most deadly terrorist' actually *means*."

"That's . . . probably a good idea on its merits, now that I think about," said Anton.

As they'd been talking, Jacques' head had gone back and forth between them. Now he raised his hands.

"You're making me dizzy. I don't understand—" He broke off sharply, his eyes widening. "Oh, dear God in Heaven. That's . . . *brilliant*."

Thandi started whistling tunelessly. "If anybody thinks I can't turn the Cachat Curl into a general-purpose workout routine, you'd best start thinking again. What the hell are you all talking about?"

Jacques pointed at Victor and Anton, moving his finger between them. "First, we start creating doubles for them at the same time as we're putting them through the body-transformation and sheathing. Second—oh, somewhere around next week, as soon as everyone's off to Beowulf, we start feeding little tidbits to the media. But we don't stretch it out too long, because we want a big splash. A *really* big splash. Then we dump everything. Give Underwood as much material as he got when he did the Zilwicki exposé—what was it? two years ago?"

"Three," replied Anton.

"Hey!" said Berry. "It wasn't an 'exposé.' It was pretty positive, actually."

"Positive, negative—it doesn't matter," said Jacques. "It's just got to be explosive and exciting." He now looked at Montaigne. "I haven't seen this footage you're talking about. Is it . . . ?"

"Explosive and exciting?" She looked as if she didn't know whether to laugh or cry. "Let's put it this way. Victor gunned down at least a dozen State Sec goons and Scrags. Jeremy did for the rest. There was one badly wounded survivor. Donald X—no, I guess he's Donald Toussaint now—shot him dead. That's on the footage too."

"We can probably cut that part," said Anton.

"Why?" asked Victor. "Donald won't care. Who's going to charge him—or me, or Jeremy—with anything? The people with legal jurisdiction are the authorities on Terra. Given the current situation, they've got enough on their plates. I don't think they're going to be dredging up the Manpower Incident and sending out extradition notices."

Anton grunted. "True. Keep going, Jacques."

By now, Benton-Ramirez y Chou was on his feet along with Ruth, although he wasn't pacing. "It's brilliant. The media will go wild. I'm just starting to grasp at all the ramifications. For one thing..."

He looked down at Anton, and then at Cathy. "I know the basic facts about the Manpower Incident. Correct me if I'm wrong, but I think it's fair to say that Victor saved the lives of your children."

"There's no doubt about it," said Anton.

"Yes," said Berry. "I was there myself, although I didn't see the actual shooting."

Jacques nodded. "You're all probably too close to it to see it for what it's worth in propaganda terms. Right at the point where the leaders of Manticore and Haven are trying to convince their own populations that it's time to end the galaxy's bloodiest and bitterest war—and meeting a lot of resistance—we get a story splashed all over the media—first here in the Star Empire, then in the Republic of Haven—that tells how a young Havenite StateSec agent saved the lives of three Manticoran children—one of whom is now an officer in the fleet and another of whom is the newly crowned queen of the new star nation of Torch—and began a friendship and later a partnership with the father of those children—who's himself a well-known figure in the Star Empire—"

Ruth snickered. "Captain Zilwicki, Scourge of the Spaceways."

"—that led eventually to the uncovering of the evil masterplan of the Mesan Alignment. Who, among their many other crimes, are the ones responsible for instigating the war between Manticore and Haven and keeping it going."

He started rubbing his hands. "Not to mention that Victor was part of the underground opposition that eventually overthrew the Saint-Just regime. Oh, God, it's *brilliant*. The media will slobber over it for *weeks*. And by the time they finally start tiring of it..."

He lowered his hands and grinned. "The doubles will be ready to go to work. We trot them out from time to time in front of the media—never too close and not too often, just enough—to give the impression that Cachat and Zilwicki are both neck-deep in whatever oh-very-hush-hush scheming is being done by the authorities— the authorities *here,* you understand, and later on Haven and maybe Beowulf—while they're *actually* almost eight hundred light-years away...On Mesa, which is the last place *anybody* would think they'd gone to."

Thandi rubbed a hand over her face. "Okay, now I get it. What you're proposing is basically a diversion. A whopping big diversion." The hand came away. "You're right. It's brilliant. But we'll need a double for me also. I'm too prominent a figure to just vanish. If people see my double engaging in what looks like discussions with my Manticoran counterparts, they won't think anything of it. That's exactly what they'd expect to see."

Anton and Victor looked at each other. "She's right," said Victor. Anton nodded.

So did Jacques. "We'll include you in the mix, then." He thought for a moment. "Anyone else? This Yana person, perhaps..."

"No," that came from Victor and Thandi simultaneously.

"Nobody will notice if Yana just disappears," Thandi elaborated. "We need to give her a body transformation and a genetic sheath since she was on Mesa with Victor and Anton. But she doesn't need a double."

"The same's true of Steph Turner," Victor added. "That's assuming she agrees to come at all."

Jacques pulled out his com. "Okay. So who makes the call? And who do we start with?"

Victor and Anton exchanged looks again.

"There's something a little scary about that," mused Cathy.

"You think?" That came from Berry. But she was smiling when she said it.

"We need to start with President Pritchart," said Anton. He pointed at Victor. "*He* is actually very disciplined, believe it or not. He won't—can't—agree to this without the approval of his superiors. And given that they're bouncing his official status around, there's no one except Pritchart who could sign off on it. As for who should make the call..."

Victor pulled out his com. "I'll do it. I'd rather Jacques did, but...a special officer beards his own commander-in-chief."

"Eloise Pritchart does *not* have a beard," said Cathy.

Victor's gloomy expression was back. "Stick around," he said, as he keyed in some numbers. "By tomorrow she may have."

His face got the slightly vacant look of someone who's talking to someone far away. "This is Special Officer Cachat. Would you please pass on to President Pritchart that I need to speak with her as soon as possible."

After a moment, he continued: "Yes, I know she's very busy. This is important."

Another moment passed. Victor rolled his eyes. "Yes, thank you." He turned off the com. "Wasn't it Shakespeare who said, 'first thing we do, we kill all the bureaucrats'?"

Cathy shook her head. "No. It was lawyers."

"He got it wrong, then." He put the com away. "I wouldn't hold out great hopes that I'll be able to see her anytime soon. The president's gofer—excuse me, assistant executive director—made it pretty clear that I was a nuisance with delusions of grandeur."

"Is that so?" Jacques took his com back out. "Let me try, then." He entered some numbers and within a short time got the same slightly vacant expression.

"This is Jacques Benton-Ramirez y Chou, Third Director at Large of the Planetary Board of Directors of Beowulf. What is your name, please?"

A few seconds passed. "Well then, Assistant Executive Director Hancock. I need to speak to President Pritchart."

A few seconds passed. "I didn't say I needed an appointment, Ms. Hancock, I said I needed to speak to President Pritchart. If you require an explanation of the word 'now' I can have it provided for you by my cousin. That would be Chyang Benton-Ramirez. He's the Chairman of Beowulf's Board of Directors."

A few seconds passed. "Thank you, Assistant Executive Director Hancock."

To the people around him he said: "She's getting her."

A couple of minutes passed. "Eloise? Jacques here. Something very important has come up. I need to meet with you as soon as possible. I'll be bringing your Special Officer Cachat with me. Captain Zilwicki as well. And General Palane."

A few seconds passed. "Splendid. Fifteen-thirty it is."

He put away the com and glanced at his timepiece. "Okay, we've got a little over two hours. We'd best get moving."

❖   ❖   ❖

After they left, Ruth sat back down at looked at the HD. The talking heads were still at it.

"*—unfortunate, I agree, but there it is.*" Yael Underwood was saying. "*We just don't know very much about Cachat and what little we do know is half-speculation.*"

"Boy, are you in for a wild ride," said Ruth.

CHAPTER 18

When Steph Turner and Andrew Artlett were ushered into the conference room, they were surprised to find Queen Berry and Princess Ruth waiting for them. There was another person in the room whom they didn't recognize. That was hardly surprising, since they'd only been in the Beowulfan capital city of Columbia for a short time. Their ship had arrived the previous evening.

"Where's Victor?" Steph asked. "And Anton? They were the ones who sent me the message to come here right away."

Andrew pulled out a chair for her and helped her get seated at the table in the center of the room, facing Berry and Ruth and the unknown man. He wasn't usually given to such gallantries, but he was trying to evade the gazes coming his way. The ones that indicated *and what is he doing here?*

Recognizing the gazes, Steph said a bit awkwardly: "Andrew, uh, decided to come with me."

Having sat down by then, Andrew got a little belligerent. "I know I wasn't invited but I also know

Cachat and Zilwicki. They're up to something. Involving Steph. Which means 'up to no good,' most likely. They got a history. So I came along to make sure Steph doesn't get hustled."

Berry and Ruth looked at each other, and then at the man Steph and Andrew didn't know.

"I guess it's your call," Berry said to him.

The man chuckled. "Who knows? This whole project is scrambling everybody's preexisting notions of proper jurisdiction. But I'll kick it off."

He swiveled in his seat to face Andrew. "I assume you're Andrew Artlett, right? The now-famous—in some circles, anyway—starship mechanic who jury-rigged the repairs on the *Hali Sowle* that enabled Cachat and Zilwicki to bring back their galaxy-shaking—that's almost literally true—intelligence from Mesa."

"What of it?" Andrew demanded, leaning his weight on forearms planted on the table.

Steph put a hand on his arm. "Hon, I think he's being complimentary. Ease up on the testosterone, will you?"

"Um." Andrew settled back. The expression on his face was that of a man who was embarrassed but was valiantly refusing to acknowledge the fact. "Um," he repeated.

"I'm Henry Kham," the man said. "I'm with . . . Well, for the moment let's just call it the Inter-Agency Development Team."

"'Inter' between what agencies and developing what and who's on the team?" Andrew demanded.

Steph gave him an exasperated glance. "I think we'll find out soon enough. Now will you puh-lease let Mr. Kham finish what he's saying."

"Um."

Kham smiled. "The interaction is between a number of organizations representing—so far—four star nations. Beowulf, Manticore and Torch being three of them, which is why we're here. The Republic of Haven is also involved but they didn't have a representative available to come to this meeting."

"Where's Victor?" asked Steph.

"He's tied up at the moment."

A little choking sound came from Berry, followed almost immediately by the same sort of noise from Ruth. Kham gave them an inquisitive glance. "A poor choice of words?" he asked.

"Ah . . ." Ruth shook her head. "No, no. That's fine."

Berry murmured something that sounded like *except he usually does the tying* although Steph wasn't sure. The young queen's face was a little puffy, as if she was doing her best to stifle laughter.

Ruth flipped her hand in a shooing motion. "Keep going, Henry. Don't mind us."

Kham turned back to Steph and Andrew. "As for the project we're developing, it's basically simple. As invaluable as the information Cachat and Zilwicki brought back was, we need more. So we're planning to insert another intelligence team on Mesa." He now looked directly at Steph. "And we want to ask you to accompany them."

Andrew looked like he was about to object but Kham held up his hand. "Hear me out, please. We wouldn't be expecting Ms. Turner to play a direct role in the intelligence-gathering. What we'd want her to do is set up a safe house and provide the actual operatives with guidance and advice."

"No," said Artlett. He stood up and extended his hand to his companion. "Let's go, Steph."

"Andrew, sit down," she said.

He stared at her, half-gaping.

"Sit. Down," she repeated. "First, it's my decision, not yours. Second, you're being rude. Keep talking, Mr. Kham. What sort of safe house and with what—and how much—money?"

Kham shrugged. "We hoped you'd tell us what would work best as a safe house. Money's not an issue. We'll provide it, and as much as you need."

Steph pursed her lips and her eyes got a little unfocused.

Artlett sat back down. "Steph, you can't be seriously—"

"Be quiet. I'm thinking."

He rolled his eyes. But he kept quiet.

After half a minute or so, Steph's gaze came back in focus. "A restaurant's probably out, even though it'd be the easiest for me and ideal for a safe house."

"Agreed," said Kham. "We already thought of that, but . . ." He shook his head. "The problem is that we just don't know how much data the Mesans still have on everything connected with Cachat and Zilwicki's expedition. But you might still be in their records. We can disguise you, but part of those records are that you owned and operated a restaurant. That might be enough to get flagged if a new one opened up in the seccy quarters."

Ruth spoke up. "I suggested a flophouse. From what I've read, there are a lot of cheap boarding houses in the area."

Steph nodded. "Yeah, there are. A lot of seccies— men, mostly—are itinerant laborers. And the houses go in and out of business regularly, since they're usually just someone's home being turned to commercial use when need be. There aren't any regulations governing boardinghouses except the same fire and sanitation regs that apply to everybody. But those don't even get inspected for that often."

"That's what I figured. And it'd be pretty close to what you used to do, since—correct me if I'm wrong—part of what a boardinghouse provides are regular meals for the renters. Kind of like a small private restaurant."

"No, you're right." Steph's eyes got out of focus for a moment. Kham took the moment to interject himself.

"That was the objection, though, raised by—ah, one of the development team members," he said. "That a boardinghouse is close enough to what you used to do that it might get flagged for attention also."

"Could be," Steph said. "But that's not what makes me twitchy about the idea." She gave Ruth a sharp glance. "Did your reading indicate the other services usually provided by flophouses?"

Ruth frowned. "I'm not sure what you mean."

"Laundry's one of them. But like I said, the clientele is mostly male. So most flophouses provide prostitutes also. Sometimes that service is done directly by the woman—they're almost always women—who own the house. But it's usually contracted out."

Berry made a face. "Steph, nobody would expect you—"

Steph laughed, quite cheerfully. "You'd better not! But that's not the problem." She gave Kham a look that was not quite condemnatory but came awfully close. "Am I right in thinking that your so-called 'development team' could come up with a whore or two, if need be?"

"Well . . . they wouldn't be whores, no. They'd actually be trained intelligence operatives. But with that caveat, yes. We could." He shrugged. "Spying and sexual favors go back together a very long ways."

"Could you provide the pimp, too?" She waved her hand. "Never mind. Hypothetical question. I'm sure you could. Just like I'm sure that the reason Victor isn't here is because you're putting him through some kind of body modification process because there's no way he wouldn't insist on being part of this. Make him the official pimp and no other pimp would dare come near the place. Not, at least, after the first couple of 'em got filleted."

Steph shook her head. "But that's still not the problem. Where were you planning to set up this safe house? Neue Rostock? That'd be the best district from the standpoint of avoiding the police. Either that or Lower Radomsko. But if you set it up in Neue Rostock you'd have to deal with Dusek's organization, since they don't let . . ." Her eyes got unfocused again. "Huh. Actually, that's a possibility worth thinking about. Lower Radomsko would be a mess. Victor could handle any one of those crazy little gangs—wouldn't even work up a sweat, knowing him—but there are just so many of them and they really can get pretty crazy. Let me think."

Again, the unfocused look. After about a minute, she said: "The flophouse is a possibility. The other one is a boutique of some kind. There are a jillion of them in the seccy quarters. They open and close like flowers and most of them have the lifespan of mayflies. Nobody in authority pays any attention to them at all, except for those few in the better-off seccy districts that can get a credit line. They'll get occasional inspections from credit rating services, which are private but have connections with police and regulatory agencies. But as long as you don't try to buy on credit, you're all but invisible to anyone except your clientele."

"And those are...who?" Kham asked.

"Women, mostly. Looking for deals and..." She sighed. "Men make fun of us about it, but the truth is that a little fashion—even the cheap stuff within the reach of poor seccies—makes life a little brighter."

"Amen," said Ruth. When everyone looked at her she flushed a little. "Hey, it's true even for royalty. Main difference is just that they—well, okay, we—can afford the expensive stuff. About the only woman of any class I know who's completely indifferent to fashion"—her thumb went sideways—"is Her Mousety here and she's just plain unnatural."

"Clothes are clothes," Berry said. "What's the big deal? I never understood it. Might as well get all excited about different kinds of breakfast food."

"Like I said, unnatural." Ruth looked back at Steph. "I can see the advantages."

"How about combining the two?" suggested Kham. "A small flophouse with a small boutique attached?"

"I can't see the benefit. I think you'd be more likely to combine the disadvantages of both. But it's my turn to ask questions. What—exactly—did you want this safe house for? Or for who, I guess I should say?"

"The truth is, we don't know yet. The 'who,' I mean. The other function of the safe house—which might wind up being its only function, for all we know at the moment—is to serve as a permanent drop box. That means a place where information can be passed on. Or along."

"Or along . . ." Steph nodded. "In other words, your—should I call it the 'now-developed team'?—will actually be at least two teams. Maybe more. And you need them to be able to stay in touch without actually being in touch."

"Ah . . . well, yes."

A voice came into the room, from a hidden speaker somewhere.

"This is cumbersome," the voice said. "Ms. Turner, are you in or out?"

"Who are you?"

"Who the hell are you?"

The first question came from Steph; the other from Andrew. Both of them were looking around the conference room, trying to spot the source of the voice.

"That doesn't matter right now," the voice said.

"Do you recognize that voice?" Steph asked Andrew quietly.

He shook his head. "Nobody I know. But it's someone from the Traccora system, I'm pretty sure. We had a slaver crew come through Parmley Station from there once. The accent's pretty distinctive."

"In or out, Ms. Turner?" the voice repeated. "There are security issues involved. If the answer is 'in,' we'll continue. If it's 'out,' we thank you for your assistance—it's really been quite helpful—and bid you farewell with our good wishes."

"That's it, then," said Andrew, sounding relieved. He rose to his feet again. "Let's go, Steph."

But she made no move to rise. "If I go, what happens to Nancy?"

Both Kham and the unseen voice started to speak but Berry interrupted.

"Shut up, both of you." She gave Steph a very direct gaze. "I will take care of her until you get back. Or if you don't come back at all. Whatever Nancy needs and for however long those needs might last."

She didn't add *I swear* or *I promise* or any other such phrase. She didn't need to.

Kham now spoke. "Beowulf will assume all costs of your daughter's education, Ms. Turner. I assure you—"

"Hush. I knew that the moment you advanced the proposal. The one thing you people aren't is stingy. But that's not what I needed to know. If I get killed on this mission—and don't waste time telling me it can't happen, because it's Mesa we're talking about— then Nancy's lost the only family she has. She needs people more than money."

She and Berry looked at each other for a bit longer. Then Steph nodded. "Okay, I'm in."

"Steph!"

She turned to Andrew. "I hate those people, Andrew. You have no understanding of how deep that hate runs. You just don't. You and your folk had it rough on Parmley—rougher than I did, in some ways—but you were always you. You always had pride. You weren't defined by other people. People who despised you and made sure you knew it for as far back as you could remember and who rubbed your face in it every chance they got and if you protested or argued—even looked at them cross-eyed—they'd beat you or kill you. And do it with impunity."

She took another deep breath. "They just lost that impunity. I didn't realize it at first, when we got off Mesa. Not at all, those months we drifted in space in the *Hali Sowle*. But after we got to Torch and I saw that new world being created..."

Andrew opened his mouth; then, closed it. Then, rubbed his face.

"I guess I'm a little old to discover patriotism," Steph said. "Or maybe that's just giving myself airs and this is really nothing more than a primitive desire for vengeance. I don't care. The stinking bastards finally lost their impunity. And now somebody is getting ready to drive in the blade and I want my hand on the hilt, too."

She looked away from him and up at the wall. "That's you, isn't it, Victor? And Anton's with you?"

"In or out, Ms. Turner?" the voice said. "You understand that if the answer is 'in' and you later change your mind we'll have to sequester you until the mission is completed?"

"I thought you'd say, 'We'll have to cut your throat.'"

"Why would we do that?" The voice sounded genuinely puzzled. "No point in it."

Steph laughed. "I knew it! It's Victor. Yes, I'm in."

Andrew puffed out his cheeks. "Well. Me too, then." He pointed an accusing finger at the wall. "Don't argue with me, Victor! I'm coming too, it's settled. And how the hell did you get rid of that godawful Nouveau Paris accent?"

"Why would I argue with you? I can think of at least two ways you could be very useful, just off the top of my head. Yes, it's Victor. Berry, Ruth, Henry— show them in, please. Anton finally woke up. Thandi and Yana are climbing the walls. They don't handle tedium well."

There was a brief pause, perhaps two seconds, and the voice continued. "Yana says she votes for the boutique. Thandi won't come right out and say it but she obviously does too. I have almost no idea what you're talking about and Anton's already looking bored but I think it's probably a brilliant idea. Come on in and we'll pursue it further."

Berry and Ruth rose from the table. Kham followed them after pulling out his com and keying in some instructions.

One of the walls of the conference room began sliding aside. Beyond, Steph and Andrew could see a corridor. It looked like a hospital corridor, for whatever undefinable reason.

✧   ✧   ✧

"It's quite cunning, actually," Victor said, sticking a finger against his throat. "It's a nanotech method. They do something to my vocal cords and fiddle with the laryngeal nerve. Don't ask me the details because I don't have a clue. And, *voila,* my Nouveau Paris accent that I could never get rid of—it was always my one big weakness as a spy—is transformed into a Traccoran accent."

"I hate it," said Thandi, who was lying on a bed next to him. "I don't mind his new body. But that new voice of his..."

Victor's physique hadn't changed much. There'd been no reason to change it since it had been quite normal. But his face was completely different. He was a very handsome man, now, in a slightly androgynous way. Dark eyes were now a bright, pale green; dark coarse hair cut short was now a fancy blond hair style. Combine that with the new voice and there wasn't a trace left of Victor Cachat.

Anton...looked pretty much as he had before. Oh, his face had been completely changed, but he still had the same short, squat and extremely powerful physique.

Andrew Artlett frowned. "I don't get it. What's the point of leaving your body the same? No offense, but there aren't too many people who're built like that."

Zilwicki got a sour expression on his face and pointed at Victor. "Blame him. I was *supposed* to get redesigned as a Hakim grandee, but—"

"That idea was a nonstarter," said Victor, "once we realized that the only way to disguise him would be to make him so fat he'd look like a beach ball. So fat, in fact, that he'd face real health issues. What was far more important than that—"

"Minor issues of my life span and morbidity, that is," said Anton. Sourly.

"—was that he'd be so corpulent he'd have a hard time moving quickly in case he needed to. Which, on this mission, is not unlikely. So..."

Victor crossed one hand over the other. "The original plan was for Anton to go in as a Hakim grandee with Yana as his servant. I suggested we swap the roles. Now *Yana* is the rich bigwig and squatty here"—a thumb indicated Anton—"is the menial servant. Hakim's got a big mining industry so they use a lot of modified heavy labor slaves. Look just like him, in fact."

"He doesn't have a slave marker on his tongue," objected Steph.

"That's not really necessary," said Anton. "Hakim— this is about its only saving grace—is pretty easy-going about manumission. By now, there are quite a few descendants of ex-slaves around."

Cachat turned his head toward an open door to the side. "Yana, stop sulking in there. You've got to show yourself sooner or later."

"Screw you. This was *your* idea. I plan to hold that grudge the rest of my life."

Yana Tretiakovna came into the room. She moved with a somewhat mincing gait, quite unlike her usual athletic stride.

The reason was . . . obvious. Steph smiled. Artlett grimed.

"Don't. Say. Anything," warned Yana. She glared down at her new bosom. Her very, very impressive new bosom.

"Mind you, it's likely to be a short life," she said. "I'm bound to topple over and kill myself the moment I get distracted."

"It's a status symbol in a number of Verge cultures," Kham elaborated. "And the wealthier you are, the—ah—more voluptuous you are."

Steph and Andrew studied Yana a bit longer.

"So what do we call you now?" Andrew asked. "Midas?"

CHAPTER 19

"*What* did you say?"

Albrecht Detweiler stared at his oldest son, and the consternation in his expression would have shocked any of the relatively small number of people who'd ever met him.

"I said our analysis of what happened at Green Pines seems to have been a little in error," Benjamin Detweiler said flatly. "That bastard McBryde wasn't the only one trying to defect." Benjamin had had at least a little time to digest the information during his flight from the planetary capital of Mendel, and if there was less consternation in his expression, it was also grimmer and far more frightening than his father's. "And the way the Manties are telling it, the son of a bitch sure as hell wasn't trying to *stop* Cachat and Zilwicki. They haven't said so, but he must've deliberately suicided to cover up what he'd done!"

Albrecht stared at him for several more seconds. Then he shook himself and inhaled deeply.

"Go on," he grated. "I'm sure there's more and better yet to come."

"Zilwicki and Cachat are still alive," Benjamin told him. "I'm not sure where the hell they've been. We don't have anything like the whole story yet, but apparently they spent most of the last few months getting home. The bastards aren't letting out any more operational details than they have to, but I wouldn't be surprised if McBryde's cyber attack is the only reason they managed to get out in the first place.

"According to the best info we've got, though, they headed toward Haven, not Manticore, when they left, which probably helps explain why they were off the grid so long. I'm not sure about the reasoning behind that, either. But whatever they were thinking, what they accomplished was to get Eloise Pritchart—in person!—to Manticore, and she's apparently negotiated some kind of damned *peace treaty* with Elizabeth."

"With *Elizabeth*?"

"We've always known she's not really crazy, whatever we may've sold the Sollies," Benjamin pointed out. "Inflexible as hell sometimes, sure, but she's way too pragmatic to turn down something like that. For that matter, she'd sent Harrington to Haven to do exactly the same thing before Oyster Bay! And Pritchart brought along an argument to sweeten the deal, too, in the form of one Herlander Simões. *Dr.* Herlander Simões . . . who once upon a time worked in the Gamma Center on the streak drive."

"Oh, *shit*," Albrecht said with quiet, heartfelt intensity.

"Oh, it gets better, Father," Benjamin said harshly. "I don't know how much information McBryde actually handed Zilwicki and Cachat, or how much substantiation they've got for it, but they got one hell of a lot more than *we'd* want them to have! They're talking about virus-based nanotech assassinations, the streak drive, *and* the spider drive, and they're naming names about something called 'the Mesan Alignment.' In fact, they're busy telling the Manty Parliament—and, I'm sure, the Havenite Congress and all the *rest* of the fucking galaxy!—all about the Mesan plan to conquer the known universe. In fact, you'll be astonished to know that Secretary of State Arnold Giancola was in the nefarious Alignment's pay when he deliberately maneuvered Haven back into shooting at the Manties!"

"What?" Albrecht blinked in surprise. "We didn't have anything to do with that!"

"Of course not. But fair's fair; we did know he was fiddling the correspondence. Only after the fact, maybe, when he enlisted Nesbitt to help cover his tracks, but we did know. And apparently giving Nesbitt the nanotech to get rid of Grosclaude was a tactical error. It sounds like Usher got at least a sniff of it, and even if he hadn't, the similarities between Grosclaude's suicide and the Webster assassination—and the attempt on Harrington—are pretty obvious once someone starts looking. So the theory is that if we're the only ones with the nanotech, and if Giancola used nanotech to get rid of Grosclaude, he must've been working for us all along. At least they don't seem to have put Nesbitt into the middle of it all—yet, anyway—but their reconstruction actually makes sense, given what they think they know at this point."

"Wonderful," Albrecht said bitterly.

"Well, it isn't going to get any better, Father, and that's a fact. Apparently, it's all over the Manties' news services and sites, and even some of the Solly newsies are starting to pick up on it. It hasn't had time to actually hit Old Terra yet, but it's going to be there in the next day or so. There's no telling what's going to happen when it does, either, but it's already all over *Beowulf,* and I'll just let you imagine for yourself how *they're* responding to it."

Albrecht's mouth tightened as he contemplated the full, horrendous extent of the security breach. Just discovering Zilwicki and Cachat were still alive to dispute the Alignment's version of Green Pines would have been bad enough. The rest...!

"Thank you," he said after a moment, his tone poison-dry. "I think my imagination's up to the task of visualizing how *those* bastards will eat this up." He twitched a savage smile. "I suppose the best we can hope for is that finding out how completely we've played their so-called intelligence agencies for the last several centuries will shake their confidence. I'd *love* to see that bastard Benton Ramirez y Chou's reaction, for instance. Unfortunately, whatever we may hope for, what we can *count* on is for them to line up behind the Manties. For that matter, I wouldn't be surprised to see them actively sign up with the Manticoran Alliance...especially if Haven's already on board with it."

"Despite the Manties' confrontation with the League?" The words were a question, but Benjamin's tone made it clear he was following his father's logic only too well.

"Hell, we're the ones who've been setting things up so the League came unglued in the first place, Ben! You really think someone like *Beowulf* gives a single good goddamn about those fucking apparatchiks in Old Chicago?" Albrecht snorted contemptuously.

"I may hate the bastards, and I'll do my damnedest to cut their throats, but whatever else they may be, they're not stupid or gutless enough to let Kolokoltsov and his miserable crew browbeat them into doing one damned thing they don't *want* to do."

"You're probably right about that," Benjamin agreed glumly, then shook his head. "No, you *are* right about that."

"Unfortunately, it's not going to stop there," Albrecht went on. "Just having Haven stop shooting at Manticore's going to be bad enough, but Gold Peak is entirely too close to us for my peace of mind. She thinks too much, and she's too damned good at her job. She probably hasn't heard about any of this yet, given transit times, but she's going to soon enough. And if she's feeling adventurous—or if Elizabeth is—we could have a frigging Manty fleet right here in Mesa in a handful of T-weeks. One that'll run over anything Mesa has without even noticing it. And then there's the delightful possibility that Haven could come after us right along with Gold Peak, if they end up signing on as active military allies!"

"The same thought had occurred to me," Benjamin said grimly. As the commander of the Alignment's navy, he was only too well aware of what the only navies with operational pod-laying ships-of-the-wall and multidrive missiles could do if they were *allied* instead of shooting at one another.

"What do you think the Andies are going to do?" he asked after a moment, and his father grated a laugh.

"Isabel was always against using that nanotech anywhere we didn't have to. It looks like I should've listened." He shook his head. "I still think all the arguments for getting rid of Huang were valid, even if we didn't get him in the end, but if the Manties know about the nanotech and share that with Gustav, I think his usual 'realpolitik' will go right out the airlock. We didn't just go after his family, Benjamin—we went after the *succession*, too, and the Anderman dynasty hasn't lasted this long putting up with that kind of crap. Trust me. If he thinks the Manties are telling the truth, he's likely to come after us himself! For that matter, the Manties might deliberately strip him off from their Alliance. In fact, if they're smart, that's what they ought to do. Get Gustav out of the Sollies' line of fire and let him take care of us. It's not like they're going to need his pod-layers to kick the SLN's ass! And we just happen to have left the Andies' support structure completely intact, haven't we? That means they've got plenty of MDMs, and if Gustav comes after us while staying out of the confrontation with the League, do you really think any of our 'friends' in Old Chicago'll do one damned thing to stop him? Especially when they finally figure out what the Manties are really in a position to do to them?"

"No," Benjamin agreed bitterly. "Not in a million years."

There was silence for several seconds as father and son contemplated the shattering upheaval in the Mesan Alignment's carefully laid plans.

"All right," Albrecht said finally. "None of this is anyone's fault. Or, at least, if it *is* anyone's fault, it's mine and not anyone else's. You and Collin gave me your best estimate of what really went down at Green Pines, and I agreed with your assessment. For that matter, the fact that Cachat and Zilwicki didn't surface before this pretty much seemed to confirm it. And given the fact that none of our internal reports mentioned this 'Simões' by name—or if they did, I certainly don't remember it, anyway—I imagine I should take it all our investigators assumed he was one of the people killed by the Green Pines bombs?"

"Yes." Benjamin grimaced. "As a matter of fact, the Gamma Center records which 'mysteriously' survived McBryde's cyberbomb showed Simões as on-site when the suicide charge went off." He sighed. "I should've wondered why those records managed to survive when so much of the rest of our secure files got wiped."

"You weren't the only one who didn't think about that," his father pointed out harshly. "It did disappear him pretty neatly, though, didn't it? And no wonder we were willing to assume he'd just been vaporized! God knows enough other people were." He shook his head. "And I still think we did the right thing to use the whole mess to undercut Manticore with the League, given what we knew. But that's sort of the point, I suppose. What's that old saying? 'It's not what you don't know that hurts you; it's what you *think* you know that isn't so.' It's sure as hell true in *this* case, anyway!"

"I think we could safely agree on that, Father."

They sat silent once more for several moments. Then Albrecht shrugged.

"Well, it's not the end of the universe. And at least we've had time to get Houdini up and running."

"But we're not far enough along with it," Benjamin pointed out. "Not if the Manties—or the Andies—move as quickly as they could. And if the *Sollies* believe this, the time window's going to get even tighter."

"Tell me something I don't know." His father's tone was decidedly testy this time, but then he shook his head and raised one hand in an apologetic gesture. "Sorry, Ben. No point taking out my pissed-offedness on you. And you're right, of course. But it's not as if we never had a plan in place to deal with something like this." He paused and barked a harsh laugh. "Well, not something like *this*, so much, since we never saw this coming in our worst nightmares, but you know what I mean."

Benjamin nodded, and Albrecht tipped back in his chair, fingers drumming on its arms.

"I think we have to assume McBryde and this Simões between them have managed to compromise us almost completely, insofar as anything either of them had access to is concerned," he said after a moment. "Frankly, I doubt they have, but I'm not about to make any optimistic—any *more* optimistic—assumptions at this point. On the other hand, we're too heavily com-partmentalized for even someone like McBryde to've known about anything close to *all* the irons we have in the fire. And if Simões was in the Gamma Center, he doesn't know crap about the operational side. You and Collin—and Isabel—saw to that. In particular, nobody in the Gamma Center, including McBryde, had been briefed about Houdini before Oyster Bay. So unless we want to assume Zilwicki and Cachat have added mind reading to their repertoire, that's still secure."

"Probably," Benjamin agreed.

"Even so, we're going to have to accelerate the process. Worse, we never figured we'd have to execute Houdini under this kind of time pressure. We're going to have to figure out how to hide a hell of a lot of disappearances in a really tight time window, and that's going to be a pain in the ass." Albrecht frowned, his expression thoughtful as he regained his mental balance. "There's a limit to how many convenient air-car accidents we can arrange. On the other hand, we can probably bury a good many of them in the Green Pines casualty total. Not the really visible ones, of course, but a good percentage of the second tier live in Green Pines. We can probably get away with adding a lot of them to the casualty lists, at least as long as we're not leaving any immediate family or close friends behind."

"Collin and I will get on that as soon as he gets here," Benjamin agreed. "You've probably just put your finger on why we won't be able to hide as many of them that way as we'd like, though. A lot of those family and friends *are* going to be left behind under Houdini, and if we start expanding the Houdini lists all of a sudden . . ."

"Point taken." Albrecht nodded. "Look into it, though. Anyone we can hide that way will help. For the rest, we're just going to have to be more inventive."

He rocked his chair from side to side, thinking hard. Then he smiled suddenly, and there was actually some genuine amusement in the expression. Bitter, biting amusement, perhaps, but amusement.

"What?" Benjamin asked.

"I think it's time to make use of the Ballroom again."

"I'm not sure I'm following you."

"I don't care who the Manties are able to trot out to the newsies," Albrecht replied. "Unless they physically invade Mesa and get their hands on a solid chunk of the onion core, a bunch of Sollies—most of them, maybe—are still going to think they're lying. Especially where the Ballroom's concerned. God knows we've spent enough time, effort, and money convincing the League at large that the entire Ballroom consists of nothing but homicidal maniacs! For that matter, they've done a lot of the convincing for us, because they *are* homicidal maniacs! So I think it's time, now that these preposterous rumors about some deeply hidden, centuries-long Mesan conspiracy have been aired, for the Ballroom to decide to take vengeance. The reports are a complete fabrication, of course. At best, they're a gross, self-serving misrepresentation, anyway, so any murderous response they provoke out of the Ballroom will be entirely the Manties' fault, not that they'll ever admit their culpability. And, alas, our security here is going to turn out to be more porous than we thought it was."

Benjamin looked at him for another moment, then began to smile himself.

"Do you think we can get away with its having been 'porous' enough for them to have gotten their hands on additional nukes?"

"Well, we know from our own interrogation of that seccy bastard who was working with Zilwicki and Cachat that it was the *seccies* who brought them the nuke that went off in the park," Albrecht pointed out. "Assuming anyone on their side's concerned with telling the truth—which, admittedly, *I* wouldn't be, in their place—that little fact may just become public knowledge. In fact, now that I think about it, if Cachat and Zilwicki are telling their side of what happened, they'll probably want to stress that they certainly didn't bring any nukes to Mesa with them. So, yes,

I think it's possible some of those deeply embittered fanatics, driven to new heights of violence by the Manties' vicious lies, will inflict yet more terroristic nuclear attacks upon us. And if they're going to do that, it's only reasonable—if I can apply that term to such sociopathic butchers—that they'd be going after the upper echelons of Mesan society."

"That could very well work," Benjamin said, eyes distant as he nodded thoughtfully. Then those eyes refocused on his father, and his own smile disappeared. "If we go that way, though, it's going to push the collateral damage way up. Houdini never visualized *that*, Father."

"I know it didn't." Albrecht's expression matched his son's. "And I don't like it, either. For that matter, a lot of the people on the Houdini list aren't going to like it. But messy as it's going to be, I don't think we have any choice but to look at this option closely, Ben. We can't afford to leave any kind of breadcrumb trail.

"McBryde had to know a lot about our military R and D, given his position, but he was never briefed in on Darius, and he was at least officially outside any of the compartments that knew anything about Mannerheim or the other members of the Factor. It's possible he'd gotten some hint about the Factor, though, and he was obviously smart enough to've figured out we had to have something like Darius. For that matter, there are a hell of a lot of Manties who're smart enough to realize we'd never have been able to build the units for Oyster Bay without it. So it's going to be painfully evident to anyone inclined to believe the Manties' claims that the Mesan Alignment *they're* talking about would have to have a bolt-hole hidden away somewhere." He shook his head. "We can't afford to leave any evidence that might corroborate the notion that we simply dived down a convenient rabbit hole. If we have to inflict some 'collateral damage' to avoid that, then I'm afraid we're just going to have to inflict the damage."

Benjamin looked at him for several seconds, then nodded unhappily.

"All right," Albrecht said again. "Obviously, we're both responding off the cuff at the moment. Frankly, it's going to take a while for me, at least, to get past the simple shock quotient and be sure my mind's really working, and the last thing we need is to commit ourselves to anything we haven't thought through as carefully as possible. We need to assume time's limited, but I'm not about to start making panicked decisions that only make the situation worse. So we're not making *any* decisions until we've had a chance to actually look at this. You say Collin's on his way?"

"Yes, Sir."

"Then as soon as he gets here, the three of us need to go through everything we've got at this stage on a point-by-point basis. Should I assume that, with your usual efficiency, you've brought the actual dispatches about all of this with you?"

"I figured you'd want to see them yourself," Benjamin said with a nod, and reached into his tunic to extract a chip folio.

"One of the joys of having competent subordinates," Albrecht said in something closer to a normal tone. "In that case," he went on, holding out one hand for the folio while his other hand activated his terminal, "let's get started reviewing the damage now."

CHAPTER 20

Corporal Supakrit X set one of the two cups he was holding in front of Takahashi Ayako, then pulled out a chair and sat down at the table across from her. He blew on the coffee in his own cup while studying her. The young woman looked awfully gloomy for someone who'd recently been freed from slavery.

He thought he knew the reason, though. Uncertainty about the future—more precisely, uncertainty about one's proper course of action with regard to that future—always trumped satisfaction about the past. And while he didn't know Ayako all that well, yet—a situation he had every intention of changing as rapidly and as extensively as possible—he was pretty sure she was one of those people who defended themselves against the risk of having a bad outcome by assuming the worst was bound to happen anyway.

It was a syndrome he recognized quite easily. He'd had it himself back in the days he'd been one of Manpower's slaves. Optimism was not a wise sentiment for chattel.

"You could join the Ballroom," he said.

Ayako made a face. "And do what? Just because I killed that one shithead—the guy *raped* me; it was *personal*—doesn't mean I'm a homicidal maniac."

Supakrit placed his hand over his heart. "I'm hurt! Hurt! I was one of those homicidal maniacs myself, you know." He took a sip from the cup. "Pretty damn good at it, too."

Ayako gave him a derisive look. "Was? And just what do you think you are now, Corporal Mayhem? A philanthropist?"

He smiled. "But now I do mayhem in a uniform. Makes all the difference in the world. When I killed people retail, I was a terrorist. Now that I kill 'em wholesale, I'm a stalwart soldier. Get medals for it and everything."

"You have a medal?" Ayako's tone was skeptical.

"Well, no. General Palane's an old school Marine. She doesn't believe in handing out medals like candy the way the Solarian Navy does. I was coming up for a Good Conduct Medal but . . ." He grinned at her. "I figure you're to blame for that."

"Ha!"

"The point is, now that I'm an of-fi-cial soldier, I *can* get a medal. As a Ballroom guy, the only thing I qualified for was a wanted poster."

"They haven't made wanted posters in over a millennia."

"Fine. Wanted e-poster. I *did* get one of those."

"For what?" She waved the question away. "Never mind, I don't want to know. I'm still trying to hold onto my image of you as a nice guy even if it's getting pretty tattered."

For the first time, she drank from her cup.

"This stuff is crap," she pronounced.

"It's Marine coffee. There are rules, you know. *Navy* coffee has to be good but Marine coffee has to be terrible. Anybody who brews good coffee gets busted a rank. Two offenses in a year puts you in the brig."

There was a companionable silence for a moment. Then, Ayako sighed and shook her head. "I don't think I want to join the Ballroom."

"I don't recommend it myself, as a matter of fact." He made a gesture, indicating his uniform. "There's a reason I quit and joined the Marines. The Ballroom... Well, let's just say they're going through an identity crisis. It ain't pretty to watch, believe me."

"Really?"

"Well, yeah, sure. The Ballroom's whole purpose pretty much got the legs cut out from under it once Torch was created. It didn't help any that Jeremy quit also, of course. But even if he'd stayed in charge I think the Ballroom would be having a rough time."

He drained the coffee out of his cup. "What do they do now? Keep shooting slavers one at a time? Or in small batches, at best? Even with explosives they can't do as much damage as a warship or a Marine battalion."

"They could with nuclear weapons."

"Jeremy always ruled that out. Chemical and biological weapons too." Supakrit shook his head. "Logically, it might not make a lot of sense. What the hell, dead is dead, right? But people just don't react the same way when you use weapons that are completely indiscriminate. Jeremy never even let us use conventional explosives on anything but legitimate targets."

"Legitimate to *who*?"

The corporal chuckled. "Always a point in dispute, granted. But we blew up Manpower offices and head-quarters, we didn't blow up restaurants and apartment buildings just because there might be some scorpions caught in the mix."

"So what will they do now?" she asked.

"Don't know. And since I didn't want to stick around long enough to find out, I joined the Marines as soon as they started recruiting." Supakrit paused for a moment, thinking. "I figure they'll wind up doing one of two things. The dumb thing to do would be to keep up the terror campaign. The smart thing would be to dissolve the Ballroom and reconstitute it as a political party."

"*Political* party? I thought Torch didn't have any."

The corporal clucked his tongue. "Boy, are you a babe in the woods. Officially, no. We have what's called a 'grand coalition' in charge. But that won't—can't—last forever. I don't give it more than two or three years, myself. Sooner or later, formal factions will crystallize. That's what parties are, you know? Just a fancy way of saying 'we agree with each other and you guys are full of crap.'"

"How many?"

"I figure at least three. The Ballroom types—especially if they have enough sense to get rid of the Ballroom altogether. The people who generally agree with Du Havel. And I'd be surprised if a third party doesn't emerge also. There're always some people in any society who are just naturally conservative and they'll eventually want their own spokespeople."

"I thought Du Havel was the conservative on Torch."

Supakrit laughed. "Only by a Ballroom definition of 'conservative'—and not even most of my former comrades really think of Web that way. I'm sure Jeremy doesn't any longer, if he ever did." He made a wagging motion with his hand. "On Torch, Du Havel ranks as what you might call a centrist. Anywhere else in the galaxy except maybe Haven he'd be considered a flaming radical. Well, maybe not flaming. But radical, yes."

He paused and gave her a sideways look. "You interested in politics?"

"Not especially."

"Well, that's out too, then. So. No Ballroom for you. No smoke-filled back room either."

"Why would a back room—any room—be full of smoke? And if it was, why wouldn't everyone get out?"

"And your possible budding career as a historian gets cut short, too."

She squinted at him. "Are you making fun of me?"

"Actually, no. I'm not. I'm just trying to help you figure out what to do with your life." He held up his empty cup. "More coffee?"

"I don't think I can even finish this one. Supakrit . . ."

"Yes?"

She was silent for a few seconds, staring down at the table top. Then said, in a much softer tone than usual: "I don't know what I want to do with my life. Before the last few weeks—you were a slave; you know how it is—I didn't think about the future at all."

"Yeah, I know."

"I stayed away from getting close to anyone, too. You know."

Supakrit nodded. He knew what she was talking about very well. Better than he wished he did. As a teenager he'd made the mistake of falling in love with another slave. There'd been a few wonderful

months and then... She was taken away. He had no
idea where. Not then, not now. He'd never seen her
again. Had no idea if she was still alive—and knew
he almost certainly never would know.

He'd always understood the limits Jeremy X placed
on the Ballroom's tactics. Understood—and agreed.
But that was just tactics. Emotionally...

If Supakrit X could round up everyone in the galaxy associated with Manpower—okay, leave out the
janitors and such—and throw them into a black hole,
he'd do it without blinking. And then spend eternity
listening to them scream. (Or was it the other way
around? For them, it would be eternity. For him, just
a few seconds. He could never remember.)

Of course, people didn't live that long, not even
ones who'd gotten prolong. Speaking of which...

"You're what, Ayako? Twenty-two? Twenty-three?"

"Twenty-two."

"You've still got a few years, then. Have you started
thinking about prolong?"

She shrugged. "Can't afford it."

"Yeah. It's not cheap."

"How about you? Or are you already too old?"

Supakrit got up and went over to the coffee maker.
After pouring himself another cup, he came back to
the table. He used the time to make a decision.

A very easy decision to make, as it turned out.

After he sat down, he said: "That's one of the reasons I enlisted in the Marines. Prolong's expensive for
an individual, but governments..." He smiled at her.
"The magic of taxes, you understand. Actually, Torch
probably gets as much money from export tariffs as it
does from taxes, but the principle's the same."

"What principle?"

"The principle—one of the first ones they set up, in fact—that if you enlist in the armed forces the government of Torch will pick up the tab for your prolong treatments. I did it just in the nick of time." He blew on the coffee. "I'm thirty, if you're wondering."

Ayako scowled. "Supakrit, I really don't think I'd do well in the military."

"Neither do I," he said, still smiling. "Issues of impulse control."

"Hey! The guy had it coming!"

"I'm not denying it. As impulses go, that one was understandable. Even admirable, if you look it from the right angle. Which I did and do, by the way. But you're still probably not self-disciplined enough to like the military. Maybe the Navy, but sure as hell not the Marines."

He drank some of the coffee. Half the cup, actually. Bracing himself. The decision had come easily but implementing it was . . .

Hard. He'd been a slave for two-thirds of his life.

"There's a family provision to that principle, Ayako. Spouses and children are also covered if you enlist. And the coverage lasts as long as you're in the service, so if you get married afterward . . ."

He couldn't quite finish that thought, so he went off on a tangent. "You can petition to have parents and siblings covered too. I'm told they usually grant the petition but . . ." His expression hardened. "How many ex-slaves have parents and siblings? Or know where they are, if they do."

Ayako stared at him. Then said abruptly: "Are you proposing to me?"

"Yes. I am." Supakrit held up his hand. "Look, it can just be a formality. Nobody's going to stick their nose into our sex life."

"Shut up. What a jerk. But I'm not. Yes."

Now it was the corporal's turn to stare. "Yes... what?"

She rolled her eyes. "I'm marrying a moron. Yes, I will marry you. What the hell did you think 'yes' meant?"

She rose and held out her hand. "Come on. We'll settle the rest of it right now. I've got a private room and you don't, so we'll use mine. I'm not getting laid in a barracks. Forget that stupid coffee. I guarantee you I taste way better than it does."

But they'd only taken two steps toward the door when the com in the mess room started blaring.

All personnel assigned to Operation Serket Breach, report immediately to Launch Bay Sigma Nine. The mission will depart Parmley Station at sixteen hundred hours.

Simultaneously, Supakrit and Ayako looked at their watches.

"Hell's bells," he said.

"There ain't no justice at all," she agreed. "You better go. Just make sure you come back in one piece, okay?"

They did have time for a kiss, at least.

❖   ❖   ❖

After he left, not knowing what else to do with herself, Ayako wound up making her way into Parmley Station's control center. She didn't have any official clearance to be there, but she'd already learned that BSC personnel were willing to bend the rules if they thought there was a good reason to do so.

She figured her reason was as good as it got. So she didn't wait for anyone to challenge her. As soon as she entered she made her way toward the big tactical plot in the middle of the chamber. She'd never been inside the control center, but the tactical plot was obviously what she wanted. She'd had it described to her before. It was very similar, apparently, to the ones used by starships.

"I just got married—well, agreed to, anyway—and then you—you"—she managed enough impulse control to choke down the pejorative that had been about to emerge—"bad people yanked my fiancé off to go play Marine somewhere."

Plaintively, she added, "I don't even know where he's going because you—you—obsessive-compulsive motherfu—really bad people are maniacs about so-called security and who would I tell anyway? It's just stupid."

The five people in the center stared at her. Two of them were obviously Torches and two were just as obviously Beowulfers. She wasn't sure about the guy doing something at a console against the far wall. (Or what that called a bulkhead? Ayako wasn't sure.)

"Who are you?" one of the Beowulfers asked. He was one of the three people monitoring the tactical plot.

"And what are you doing here?" asked the man standing next to him. He was one of the Torches, as was the third person working at the tactical plot. She was the only one Ayako recognized, although she wasn't sure of the woman's name. Alexia...something.

"I told you. I just got married and my brand-new husband—okay, fine, be anal-retentive about it; my to-be-husband—is on that ship." She pointed at the tactical plot, which to her just looked like an immense kaleidoscope. "Whichever one it is. In that thing."

"The *Hali Sowle*?" That was asked by the other Beowulfer, a woman sitting at a console nearby.

"Yeah, that's it."

The male Torch at the tactical plot was now looking belligerent. "You can't just—"

"Ease up, Liam," said the Beowulfer next to him. "This might be quite charming—and the universe needs as much charm as it can get, these days."

To Ayako he said, "I take it your husband—past, present or future, we'll worry about that later—is one of the Marines or naval personnel aboard the *Hali Sowle*. What's his name?"

"Supakrit. Corporal Supakrit X. Royal Marines."

"Check that, would you, Magda?"

The Beowulfer female at the console worked the board for a few seconds and then studied the screen.

"Yeah, he's there. One of the Marines assigned to the mission."

"Hey!" protested the Torch named Liam. "Security!"

"Give it a rest, will you?" Magda was still examining the screen. "What's she going to do? Grow Warshawski sails and fly herself to give warning to whoever you might notice I didn't actually specify?"

She tapped the screen and looked up at Ayako. "What's really interesting is that Corporal Supakrit is listed in the rolls as being single."

Liam glared at Ayako. "So she's lying."

"Fuck you. Me and Supakrit just got married. Well, decided to. About two seconds before you assho—bad people—told him he had to report to launch bay whatzit."

"That order was actually given by Colonel Anderson, not us," said the woman Ayako thought was named Alexia. Her tone was mild, and seemed a bit amused. "We're just in charge of traffic and such."

The Beowulfer at the tactical plot grinned. "Like I said, charming. Just got hitched, huh? Well, come over here and I'll show you where your future husband is. I'm Bill Jokela. What's your name?"

"Takahashi Ayako. Call me Ayako." Ignoring the glare still coming from Liam, Ayako came up to stand beside Jokela. Up close, the tactical plot looked more like a kaleidoscope than ever.

Jokela pointed to one of the symbols in the plot. It was colored a bright green. "This is the *Hali Sowle*. They've already left Parmley, but they're still a good fifteen light-minutes from the hyper limit. So they won't be making their alpha translation for another—"

"Their *what*?"

Jokela paused and gave her a considering look. Then he gave the same look to the movements in the tactical plot.

"What the hell, we've got time," he said. "An introduction to basic astrogation. Pay attention, Takahashi Ayako. Who knows? You might want to make a career out of it."

CHAPTER 21

"Zachariah McBryde?"

Zachariah turned around to face the speaker, being careful not to spill his coffee. He had a bad habit of over-filling the mug, which could make walking back to his laboratory an exercise in finicky precision that almost matched the demands of his actual job.

Two men stood there, he discovered. Both were wearing severely utilitarian jumpsuits with nameplates over the left pockets—the one on the left was A. Zhilov; the one on the right, S. Arpino—and both had the elaborate security badges given to visitors draped over their chests with lanyards.

"Yes?" he said.

The one named Zhilov nodded stiffly. "Come with us, McBryde." He turned over the badge in order to show the identification on the other side, which was a hologram depicting himself and the legend *Agent, GAUL*.

Zachariah tried not to let his sudden apprehension show on his face. The Genetic Advancement and Uplift League—the "Gauls," to use the nickname

243

that was sometimes used (though never in front of them)—served the inner layers of the onion as a special security force.

Which explained Zachariah's tension. The most common use the Alignment leadership had for the Gauls was as what you might call enforcers.

"The preferred term for that is 'internal disciplinarians,' you understand," Zachariah's brother Jack had once told him. Jack had been smiling when he made the quip, but there been very little humor in the smile. Like most of the Alignment's professional security people, he hadn't had much use for the Gauls.

The tension shifted into anger. "How many times do we have to go through this rigmarole?" he demanded. "I've told you everything I know about my brother already—at least five times over. There isn't anything else. Trust me. Nothing. Nada. Zip. Zero. I have no idea why Jack did what he did."

If he did it at all, which I don't believe for a minute.

Zhilov frowned. "I have no knowledge of what you are talking about. Your family affairs do not concern us."

He turned his head to give the man next to him a quizzical look. "Do they?"

His partner Arpino was consulting a small tablet. "There is mention here of a brother by the name of Jack McBryde, who is deceased. But that has no bearing on our mission, so far as I can see."

"As I thought." Zhilov turned back to Zachariah. "Come with us, please."

Now puzzled, Zachariah felt his anger fading—but only to be replaced by annoyance. *Come with us!* As if he was some sort of servant.

He took a sip of his coffee. Partly to stall; partly

because if he did wind up having to go with them somewhere, he wanted to keep the coffee-spilling to a minimum. The janitor 'bots wouldn't complain, of course, but it was good coffee.

His brother Jack had once referred to the Gauls as *goons*. He'd gotten close-mouthed right afterward. Zachariah had gotten the impression that Jack had let that slip inadvertently.

He hadn't pressed Jack on the matter. He and his brother were both very far inside the onion, but they had different specialties. In some respects, Jack had had a higher security clearance than Zachariah did; in other respects, the situation was reversed. They were very close, probably more than most brothers were, but they were also careful not to intrude on each other's preserves.

He was tempted to try stonewalling the Gauls, but he knew that sooner or later he'd have to give in. They wouldn't have come looking for him if they hadn't had the authority to do so. They also had a reputation for rigidly following orders. They weren't stupid, certainly. No one that far into the onion lacked intelligence. But they didn't seem to have much in the way of imagination—and even less in the way of empathy.

"Fine. We'll go. Where are you taking me?"

No answer came. The Gauls just turned and headed down the corridor, with Zachariah in their wake.

◇   ◇   ◇

When the two Gauls ushered him into a room buried in one of the wings of the Science Center's labyrinthine administration building, the first person Zachariah saw was Lisa Charteris. She was sitting at the end of a conference table in the middle of the room.

Zachariah was relieved to see her. For all his outward

nonchalance dealing with the two Gauls, he'd been worried—and had grown more so when they left the science labs and headed for the admin building. He hardly ever went over there and couldn't imagine a reason the Gauls would be taking him to it unless...

Unless *what*? The fact that Zhilov and Arpino had denied knowing anything about Jack would lead to the conclusion that at least he wasn't facing another inquisition over his brother's purported treason. But why *else* would...

Zachariah didn't like uncertainty, other than the frisson of awaiting the results of a lab experiment.

Now, seeing Charteris, he relaxed a bit. The uncertainty was still there, because he had no more idea why she'd be present than he was himself. But he and Lisa got along well and always had. They weren't exactly close friends, since she maintained a certain distance. But their personal interactions had always been pleasant and they respected each other professionally.

The point being that Zachariah couldn't imagine she'd have agreed to participate in yet another interrogation of him by security people on the subject of his brother Jack. Why would she? She'd have nothing to contribute and would find the whole business distasteful at the very least. Unlike Zachariah himself, he didn't think Lisa questioned the official line that Jack had committed treason. But he was sure that she didn't think Zachariah had been involved, in whatever had really happened.

"Hi, Lisa. Fancy meeting you here."

She gave him a quick, almost fleeting smile, then motioned to a chair at the end of the table she was sitting at. "Have a seat."

He did so. He was now sitting at a right angle to

her. Glancing over his shoulder, he saw that Zhilov and
Arpino had taken positions on either side of the door
he'd just come through. They weren't exactly standing
at attention, but they came pretty close. Zachariah had
a feeling the Gauls came pretty close to standing at
attention even in a shower. The Genetic Advancement
and Uplift League was nothing if not rigid.

"What are we—"

Charteris held up a cautioning hand. "Just wait a
bit, Zachariah. She should be coming—"

The door behind her swung open and a woman
came through. Zachariah recognized her although
they'd never spoken to each other. She was high up
in the inner onion and most likely in security.

Well . . . not "security" in the same sense his brother
Jack had been. Zachariah didn't know anything specific
about his brother's work. He and Jack had been very
careful to steer clear of that subject—just as they'd
avoided discussing the exact nature of Zachariah's job.
But from various things Jack had let slip, Zachariah knew
the essential nature of his work had been what you might
call "defensive." To put it another way, Jack McBryde
had been one of the Mesan Alignment's top guardians.

The person he'd reported to, though, Isobel Bardasano, had been . . .

Different. If his brother Jack had been the human
analog of a watchdog, Bardasano had been a wolf. Of
that, Zachariah had been quite sure.

He'd only met Bardasano twice, and on both occasions the contact was brief. He remembered her quite
vividly, though. She was a striking person in her
appearance. Intense in demeanor—and covered with
flashy tattoos and body piercings.

This woman had the same casually arrogant, predatory air about her, although she had nothing visible in the way of tattoos or body piercings. Not even earrings.

He wondered if she was Bardasano's replacement. After the destruction of Gamma Center, Bardasano had disappeared. Zachariah had no idea what had become of her. It was conceivable that she'd even been executed. The Alignment didn't use the death penalty very often; not, at least, with people in the inner layers of the onion. And when it was used, it was kept very quiet. But it wasn't inconceivable that even someone as high up as Bardasano might have suffered the ultimate penalty in punishment for the disaster at Gamma Center. Zachariah was sure that the now-almost-universal belief within the Alignment's innermost core that the explosion had been caused by his brother was nonsense. But whatever had really happened, Bardasano had to have been involved in it up to her neck.

Which is where she might have finally ended up—to her neck, and no further.

The woman pulled out a chair across from Zachariah and sat down. "I'm Janice Marinescu. Nice to meet you and all that, but let's not waste time. You're familiar with the plans for Operation Houdini."

That was a statement, not a question. But Marinescu paused and gave Zachariah a level stare. Apparently, for whatever reason, she wanted him to affirm that he was familiar with Houdini.

Cautiously, he nodded. "Yes, I am. Why?"

"Because it's being implemented. The political situation is unfolding rapidly now and we don't want to take the chance that someone might take advantage of the situation—"

Someone might take advantage... Zachariah was tempted to say "Why don't you come right out and use the name Manticore, which is what you know and I know we're talking about?"

But, he didn't. The tension was back in full force. Something...

Had gone pear-shaped. Or, at least, the powers-that-were in the very innermost circles were worried that it might be going pear-shaped soon.

"—so you'll be in the third departure division. You and"—Marinescu nodded at Lisa—"Chief Scientist Charteris. Although you might not be evacuated via the same route."

Zachariah took a deep breath. That explained the presence of the Gauls. Houdini was going to tear a lot of families apart. Including his own. The authorities were seeing to it that anyone slated for Houdini who got cold feet or second thoughts would have...

Chaperones.

He decided to think of them that way. And never mind that the chaperones undoubtedly had orders to permanently silence anyone who got too recalcitrant.

Being completely cold-blooded about it, Zachariah understood the logic. The whole purpose of Houdini was to remove anyone from Mesa who could reveal anything about the onion's inner layers and inner workings. They either left the planet by evacuation or they left it by shuffling off their mortal coil.

There was no third alternative. Houdini had always been just a possibility, and one he'd never spent much time dwelling on. Now it was here. For real. As serious as the proverbial heart attack.

Zachariah felt a sharp, almost agonizing, pain in his chest, as if he were actually having a heart attack.

He wasn't. He was just facing the prospect—the now certain prospect—that within a short time he'd lose his entire family. Part of the reason he'd never dwelt on Houdini in the past was that his brother Jack had also been slated for evacuation. So whatever happened, he'd still have one sibling.

Now...nothing. No one.

He'd be leaving his girlfriend Veronica behind too, but that wasn't cause for more than regret. The relationship wasn't really all that serious.

The worst of it, in some ways, was that he couldn't even say anything to his family. The seriousness with which the Alignment took Houdini had been emphasized again and again and again. *Nobody* could be left behind on Mesa who knew anything important.

Which meant that if Zachariah did mention anything to his family—any member of it, just one—and the authorities found out, his whole family would be destroyed.

He took a deep, shuddering breath. Lisa reached out and put her hand on his, then gave it a gentle squeeze.

She'd be leaving people behind, too. He wasn't sure who, exactly. But her husband was probably one of them. Jules Charteris had a responsible position in Mesa's government, even a rather prestigious one. But no one in Mesa's formal government—well, very few people, at least—were anywhere close to the inner layers of the onion.

"How soon?" he asked Marinescu. Her only response was that same flat-eyed level stare.

CHAPTER 22

Ruth Winton barked a sarcastic laugh. "Will you look at that? The only time in recorded history—we're talking a good two thousand years—when the Talking Heads on a vid news program had their tongues tied."

It was true enough. The panel of guests on tonight's special edition of Yael Underwood's *The Star Empire Today* were all staring at the huge screen behind them. They'd just spent the last few minutes swiveled in their seats, watching the recorded footage of the gunfight in the subterranean depths of Chicago's Old Quarter that had triggered off the Manpower Incident years earlier.

It hadn't, actually. The conflict that ended with the killing by Manpower-hired mercenaries of General Raphael Durkheim, Haven's StateSec chief in the Solarian League's capital, and the subsequent destruction of Manpower Inc.'s headquarters in the same city by a retaliatory force sent by the Audubon Ballroom had actually been months in the making. But the general public—anywhere; on Haven as well as Terra, or Manticore—had never known more than the basic facts involved. And not all of those, and especially not the names of the key players who'd never been identified by the media, which was most of them.

First and foremost among those previously unidentified key players was the man sitting next to Ruth at that moment. Victor Cachat, who'd wreaked most of the havoc in the scene that had just been played out on a screen for the Talking Heads of Underwood's show. A screen, of course, that had also been watched by...

"What's the count now, Ruth?" asked Anton Zilwicki. He was seated next to Cathy Montaigne on another couch in the salon of the genetic treatment center.

Ruth glanced down at the com in her hand. "Two hundred and seventy-three million viewers as of this moment, but..." She paused for a few seconds. "It's climbing fast. Word's spreading, obviously. By the time the replays are counted, we'll be looking at somewhere between one and two billion people. That's just here in the Manticore System itself. Once the recording gets shipped to the rest of the Star Empire, Haven, Beowulf, and who knows where else, the number will start getting called 'astronomical.'"

She tapped the com screen a couple of times. "Yeah, what I figured. They're already calling it the third-most-watched news show in a decade. We're in territory that's usually only inhabited by championship sporting events."

The stunned silence of the Talking Heads had been brief, of course. They were already jabbering away again.

"—*why Captain Zilwicki trusts him so much, which has always been a mystery. What's still unclear—*"

"—*think it's now blindingly obvious—*"

"—can't say it too many times. We have no reason—none, at, all—to suddenly place our trust in Cachat. If anything, his now-proven extraordinary savagery—"

"—was dealing with the worst sort of StateSec killers and sociopathic so-called 'super-soldiers' left over from the Final War. Of course he was savage! What do you propose he should have done, Charlene? Give them a lecture? Or do you—"

✧   ✧   ✧

Sitting on the other side of Victor from Ruth, Thandi tuned it all out. She was still trying to process the experience herself. She'd known of the gunfight in the Old Quarter, but this was the first time she'd seen the recording of the event.

It wasn't the brutality of the killing that she found startling. Nor was it even Victor's ruthlessness and the skill he'd shown at killing so many people in such a short time.

Being completely objective about it, Thandi knew that if she'd been in Victor's place in that half-crumbling cavern in the ancient catacombs of Chicago, the killings would have happened even faster and more surely.

Victor probably would have died there, except that Jeremy X intervened at the end. The surviving Scrags—there'd been three of them completely unwounded and another three injured but not out of action, had all been bringing their weapons to bear on Victor when Jeremy's pistol fusillade started taking them down.

Thandi wouldn't have needed Jeremy. She was bigger than Victor, stronger than Victor, faster than Victor, a better shot with any kind of projectile weapon than Victor—there was no comparison at all between their respective skills fighting unarmed or with hand weapons—and she'd spent her whole adult life training constantly for exactly this sort of combat.

But...*at that age?* With no combat experience at all and only the rudimentary training Victor would have received at the StateSec academy and what he'd taught himself later in simulators?

Impossible. If Thandi Palane had been in Victor's position at such a young age and with his level of actual combat experience—which was to say, none at all...

There and then...

The only reason Victor had survived—no, had triumphed—was because of the man's nature. His psychology, so to speak. Even then, as raw as any newly minted young officer and only in his early twenties, he'd been a natural killer. And a superb one, an outlier at the very edge of human potential. If that had been Thandi herself down in that cavern, she'd have been dead after taking down one or two—maybe three—of her opponents.

She knew of no one that wouldn't be true of. Not one person.

Except the man she slept with every night, whenever they could.

She felt a warm glow in her heart, then, and reached out to take Victor's hand. That was probably not the reaction most lovers would have had, but they hadn't been born and raised on Ndebele.

She gave the hand a squeeze, and when he glanced at her, she gave him a warm smile.

Buster, you are so getting laid tonight.

◇　　　◇　　　◇

Anton Zilwicki's thoughts were elsewhere. He'd been associated with Victor for so long that he took the man's somewhat peculiar nature as a matter of course. Watching the recording hadn't bothered him in the least. He'd seen it before, for one thing. For another, although he hadn't been there when the killings took place, he'd arrived immediately thereafter—soon enough that when his daughter Helen burst out of the shadows where she'd been hiding and raced toward him, she'd had to practically dance to get through the carpet of bodies littering the cavern floor. She'd stepped directly on two of the bodies and had gotten so much blood on her shoes that they'd thrown them away afterward.

She'd just turned fourteen at the time. And just a short time earlier, had herself...

"Oh, hell and damnation," Anton said. "I made sure the news reporters couldn't get to Helen—the Navy was very cooperative about that—and we've got Berry trained to a T, of course. But since Lars never met Victor and never saw the mayhem, I didn't think we needed to do much preparation with him. I completely forgot—"

Underwood had shifted the focus of *The Star Empire Today*. Again, the Talking Heads were swiveled in the chairs, watching the footage recorded earlier of an interview with Lars Zilwicki. The campus grounds of the New University of Landing formed the backdrop. Lars had just started his third year there.

"—never saw it, not even the...leftovers, I guess you'd say. They made sure to take me and Berry out by a different route. I heard a lot about it later, of course. But I didn't meet Victor Cachat then, and I've never met him since."

The young man on the screen shrugged. "Being honest, it didn't have much of an impact on me. I was still way too shaken up by what Helen did the day before to think much about what happened in the cavern next to the ruins of the Artinstute where me and Berry were hiding."

Lars made a face. "Well, I guess not so much what Helen did as what I did to the bodies afterward. Those bastards had...hurt Berry. Really badly. I sort of lost it."

The image shifted to the interviewer, who was frowning slightly. "Ah...exactly what are you referring to, Mr. Zilwicki?"

Shut up, Lars, Anton silently willed at the figure on the screen. *Shut up, shut up, shut...*

"Oh, hell and damnation," he repeated aloud.

Cathy smiled. "We're talking about Lars. Being interviewed by a very attractive and sophisticated-looking young woman. You really think he's not going to keep talking?"

"She's ten years older than he is," Anton growled. "At least."

Across from him, Berry smiled also. "And that has stopped my brother...when, exactly?"

"—thought you already knew about that," Lars was saying. "After Helen made her escape from the Scrags working for Durkheim—well, indirectly, I guess; you *do* know about that, right?—she ran across three thugs in the underground passageways. They attacked her, figuring...well, we'll never know but I'm guessing they were planning to do the same...that, Berry—never mind all that."

A little apprehensively, Anton glanced at Berry. But his daughter was watching with what seemed to be a very serene expression. Knowing her, it probably was.

The incident Lars was fumbling around had been a hideous one for her, but between her innate sanity and the best therapists Cathy could hire—which meant the best therapists anywhere in the galaxy—Berry had put it all behind her quite some time ago.

"—same three who'd imprisoned me and Berry. What the shi—ah, bad men—didn't know was that even though Helen was only fourteen at the time—she was small for her age then, too, which isn't true these days, heh—she'd been training for years in martial arts by Robert Tye. Yeah, *that* Robert Tye, if you're at all familiar with martial arts."

"So she was able to successfully defend herself?" said the interviewer.

Lars grinned, a lot more coldly that any young man his age should have been able to. "That's one way to put it, I guess. She killed all three of the bastards."

The interview was cut short there. Underwood had other fish to fry. He swiveled in his chair, which took less time than it took his panel guests because he'd been half-facing the wall screen, and gave the audience a meaningful look.

Underwood was a something of a genius at his trade. He was a master of the *meaningful look* that . . . actually had no clear meaning at all but imparted the sort of gravitas to him that was invaluable for successful talk show hosts.

He broke off *the look* when he saw that his Talking Heads had resumed their normal position and turned to face them.

"Interesting, that last item, wouldn't you say? Charlene?"

Charlene Soulliere, the female guest who represented

the Progressive Party—unofficially, not in any formal sense—had a sour expression on her face, as she'd had from the beginning of the show. For reasons that made no sense in ideological terms—in the past, if anything, they'd tended in the direction of being Havenite apologists—the Progressives were now taking a stance of sharp opposition to the rapprochement between Manticore and Haven.

Why? Nobody outside the Progressives' own leadership really knew, but theories abounded.

One school of thought believed that the PP was on the Mesan Alignment's payroll. Anton thought that was unlikely, although he didn't rule it out completely. He leaned more toward the second school of thought, which was that—

The Progressives were a pack of fumble-witted loons whose incompetence at politics seemed to have no bottom.

Cathy Montaigne didn't rule that out entirely—which she did with the Mesan-Alignment-stooges theory, on the grounds that the Mesan Alignment would have to be incompetent themselves to pay good money for Progressive Party stoogery, and there was no evidence that was true—but was more inclined toward the third school of thought, which contended that—

The Progressives were angling to get back into power as part of a coalition government with the Conservative Association. That was a truly ridiculous proposition in any sane and sensible programmatic terms but couldn't be ruled out since the only difference between the Conservative Association and the PP when it came to political scruples was that the Conservative Association *did* have one fixed and invariant principle—*what's ours is ours and don't you even THINK about mucking around with it in any way whatsoever*—and the Progressives had none at all beyond the craving for political power.

"Any comment, Charlene?"

Soulliere sniffed. "One has to wonder if there is *anyone* in that crowd whose first recourse when faced with a problem isn't to resort to violence—and the most brutal sort of violence at that. Do I need to remind the panel that the father of this fourteen-year-old homicidal maniac is the man who littered the grounds of the Tor estate with corpses not all that long ago?"

Cathy almost sprang out of her seat with excitement. "Yes! Go for it, Mack! Gut the fucking asshole!"

Cathy proceeded to issue several more sentences which, though grammatically impeccable, transgressed the bounds of propriety. Pretty much the way piranhas transgress the bounds of dining etiquette.

The "Mack" in question was Macauley Sinclair, the panelist sitting just to the left of the moderator. He was a short fellow with a round, cheery face, who represented the Liberal Party on the panel in the same informal way that Soulliere spoke for the Progressives.

He'd taken the place of Florence Hu on the panel. Cathy had pulled a lot of strings to make sure of that. For *this* show, she wanted a Liberal voice that didn't quaver and whine. There was a reason politicians and (especially) their staffs called Sinclair "Mack the Knife" in private.

Yael Underwood, being an expert at the business, immediately saw to it that Sinclair got the floor.

"Homicidal maniac, is it?" he jeered. Then, he

broke the normal rules of Talking Headship and looked directly at the viewing audience. "For reasons that are understandable, Lars Zilwicki didn't go into the details of the incident. I happen to know them, however—as should Ms. Sanctimonious over here, if she'd done her homework."

He gave her a skeptical glance. "At least, one has to *hope* that Soulliere's comment was the product of ignorance."

She tried to angrily interrupt but Sinclair drove right over her. Looking back at the viewing audience he continued.

"Here are the details—the very grim details. The three men in question—rightly called 'thugs' by Lars Zilwicki—had kidnapped the boy and his sister Berry and were holding them captive in Chicago's infamous underground warrens. Lars was eleven years old at the time; Berry, thirteen. Both of them were badly beaten, especially the girl—who was also repeatedly gang-raped. These were the three unfortunate gentlemen whom the small fourteen-year-old girl that—"

He had a truly magnificent sneer. "—Sanctimonious Soulliere calls a 'homicidal maniac' killed in self-defense when they tried to visit the same atrocities upon her."

The whole panel erupted. But Mack the Knife's voice rose above the babble—largely because he kept speaking directly at the viewers.

"—no mistake what this is really all about. The same Progressives who proved themselves completely incapable of leading a war against the Republic of Haven when such a war was *needed,* are now trying to sabotage a peace treaty with the Republic when *that* is needed and finally available. And they're doing so for no better reason—assuming there's any coherent thought at all involved—than political maneuvering."

A subscriber to Theory #3, clearly, although he was leaving the door open for Theory #2. In line with Cathy's own position, in other words.

That was hardly surprising, since he more or less worked for her. Informally, true, and without remuneration. But there was a reason that Sinclair's other nickname was Montaigne's Mugger.

Anton brought his attention back to the talk show. Sinclair was still going strong. For all that he was barely over five feet tall and was wearing a very expensive suit, it wasn't hard at all to imagine him wielding a claymore like his ancestors had.

Whack. "—ignore what she says. The real reason for Soulliere's hostility to Cachat is purely because the man is walking, breathing, living, tried and tested proof—tried and tested three times over—that there is no better ally for us in a fight than the same Havenites we've been fighting for what sometimes seems like a lifetime. I ask you—"

Babble, babble, babble. Soulliere was trying desperately to make herself heard, but the panel was now clearly swinging in Sinclair's direction. Who was back to looking straight at the audience.

"—really simple question, as simple as it gets. You're attacked by thugs in a dark alley. Who do you want coming to your defense?"

A *truly* magnificent sneer.

Whack. "Soulliere and her back room cronies? Or Victor Cachat and Anton Zilwicki? Or—better yet, because we're talking a *war* here, folks, one that's going to make our fight with Haven look like a playground spat—would you prefer a bunch of young homicidal maniacs in uniform? Such as—"

He turned to Underwood. Something indefinable in the talk show host's posture made Anton realize that Underwood and Sinclair had set this up in advance.

"I believe you have some relevant footage, Yael, am I correct?"

"Well...yes. As it happens, we do."

The back screen lit up with an image of Anton's daughter Helen. She was wearing her dress uniform and posed somewhat formally with four other young naval officers. Anton recognized all but one of them. They were friends of Helen's as well as comrades; people she'd gone through the naval academy with at Saganami Island.

She looked...

Good. Really good. She would never be a beauty, but—thank God—she took after her mother more than her father in that department. And while she might be a tad on the stocky, well-muscled side, she stood with the obvious grace of more than ten years training in Neue-Stil Handgemenge, one of the most lethal martial arts in galactic history. But what she looked like most of all was a young woman proud of her uniform, committed to her star nation, confident in herself, and prepared to spit in the entire galaxy's eye if that was what duty and that uniform demanded of her.

Sinclair spoke again. "That's the young woman Soulliere called a 'homicidal maniac.' Not just the *girl* who escaped her Manpower kidnappers on Old Earth when she was only fourteen T-years old, but also the young woman who served as Sir Aivars Terekov's assistant tactical officer throughout the Battle of Monica. And never mind that when the wolves come baying at our door again, Soulliere and her Progressive pack of curs will be the first ones screaming for exactly *this* young homicidal maniac—and her friends—to come to their rescue.

"Again."

Soulliere went ballistic at that point. Anton thought that "pack of curs" was probably over the top for what was, after all, an evening talk show program.

Not that he gave a damn. He started softly singing a tune.

> *"Oh, the shark has pretty teeth, dear*
> *And he shows 'em, pearly white..."*

He was pretty sure the same lyrics were being sung by people all over the Star Empire, at that moment. It was a very old song, after all.

"This is going *splendidly!*" Cathy exclaimed. She took Anton's hand and gave it a squeeze.

I am so getting laid tonight.

He managed to keep a solemn face, though.

July 1922 Post Diaspora

"You're all under arrest. It turns out I have a long-suppressed megalomaniacal personality. Who knew?"

—Hugh Arai, consort to Queen Berry of Torch

CHAPTER 23

"Talk about a stroke of genius," Ruth said, shaking her head with admiration as she studied the data on her tablet. "Which one of you wants to take the credit? Or are you willing to split it, in the spirit of"—she waved her hand airily—"whatever. Take your pick. Collectivism, cooperation, humility, whatever rings your bell."

Victor looked disgusted. "Let Anton have it—or better yet, Yana." Who, for her part, was looking at her own body in the same wall mirror Victor was using—and didn't look any happier than he did.

"I look like a cow. What possible use are udders this size? I've got enough production capacity for quadruplets—but there are still only two nipples. So what's the point?"

She glared at Victor. "Do men really like this nonsense?"

Victor didn't look at her. He was still examining his own body and looking no happier than she did. "Ask someone else," he said. "I was socially deprived as a youth. My opinion on these matters is not to be trusted."

Thandi Palane had left off examining her new body ten minutes earlier and was now relaxing in an armchair. Her cheerful equanimity concerning her new physique was due to the simple fact that it wasn't much different from her old one. Given that Thandi's ability to commit mayhem was a large part of the reason she'd been included in the mission, it would have been counterproductive to change her body so much that all of her muscle memory would have gotten skewed. So, the gengineers had settled for adding a little weight and height.

The main change had been to her face. They'd eliminated the distinctive Ndebele facial features. They'd left her very pale skin tone as it was, but she now looked like someone from a heavy gravity planet whose ancestry had been mostly northern European instead of African. She was also a lot less good-looking.

Yana, on the other hand, now had a physique that looked like a teenage boy's notion of the perfect female figure. A particularly callow boy, at that.

The engineers had given her a face to go with it, too. The former attractive blonde was now a gorgeous brunette whose ancestry seemed to be East Asian rather than Slavic. About the only thing they hadn't changed very much was her height. Nanobots could do a lot, but the only way to drastically shorten someone was to remove bone or cartilage, both of which carried health risks if taken too far. So, they'd shortened her, but only by two centimeters. That would be enough to throw off any automatic body gauge software that Mesa's security forces might be using.

The precaution was probably unnecessary, but changing a person's height by a few centimeters was not significantly risky—so why not do it? Anton, Victor and Thandi had all had their heights changed as well, but in their cases they'd been made a little taller.

"Take credit for what, Ruth?" asked Andrew Artlett. He was sitting next to Steph Turner on a sofa against the wall opposite the big mirror. His physical appearance had been modified only slightly, because there was no need to do more than that. The one time Mesan inspectors had come aboard the *Hali Sowle*, Andrew had stayed in his cabin. The Mesans might still have his genetic record—or rather, that of the Parmley clan members to whom he was closely related—but they hadn't made any physical images of him. The only reason nanobots had been used on him at all—his nose and brow ridge had been thickened, his cheekbones made more prominent and his eye and hair color changed—was to protect against the remote chance that the Mesans had somehow gotten their hands on old holopics of him. That chance was so remote it was well-nigh astronomical, but since a minor body adaptation was easy they'd decided to do it.

More precisely, Anton and Victor had decided to have it done—over Andrew's protests. He'd accused them of being motivated by nothing more than a determination to spread the misery around.

There was . . . possibly a bit of truth to the charge. Nanobot body engineering was a thoroughly unpleasant experience.

"Take a look at this," Ruth said. She keyed in some commands and her virtual screen was enlarged tenfold and projected far enough away so Andrew and Steph could see it easily.

"You see this and this? And this?" She manipulated

the cursor to highlight three figures on the screen. The figures were labeled *Perspective Density*, *Adjustment Velocity* and *Reversal Prospect*.

Andrew's frown was enhanced by his modified brow ridge. Steph's frown looked about the same as it always did, because her features had been modified to make her face a bit more slender. As with Andrew, her body modification had been minimal and mostly confined to her face. The likelihood that Mesa had good holopics of someone who'd owned a small restaurant in the seccy quarters was small. They might have a few images, but they wouldn't be precise enough for body identification software.

The real danger for her was that the Mesans certainly had her DNA on record, for the good and simple reason that Mesa obtained DNA samples at birth from every resident of the planet. And even if Victor and Anton's hypothesis that Jack McBryde had badly damaged Mesa's security files was correct, it was unlikely that McBryde had gone so far as to destroy *all* DNA records. He would have targeted the records of Mesa's enemies—which, ironically, would not have included Steph Turner at the time.

So, she'd gotten a genetic sheath, as had Andrew. Steph's was more subtle than that given to everyone else, though. There was no need to disguise her origins as a Mesa seccy. To the contrary, that would be an integral part of her cover. They'd only needed to put a few changes in the sheath that would obscure her individual identity.

"Ruth, I haven't got the faintest idea what any of those numbers mean," said Steph.

"Same here," said Andrew. "And I'll add to that—hey,

I'm a dummy, okay?—that I don't even understand what the terms mean. I know what each one of those words means, taken by itself. But what the hell is the 'density' of a perspective?"

Berry piped up. "I'm a dummy, too." She was perched on the edge of her seat and leaning over in order to get a better view of the screen. "How about an explanation?"

Ruth looked at each of them in turn, her expression a mix of puzzlement, mild consternation, and uncertainty. Those sentiments could be translated—quite easily, by her best friend Berry—into the following phrases:

How can anyone be this ignorant of basic sociometric attitude assessments?

Am I supposed to explain *what this all means?*

I'm really not the best person to do that since my explanation is likely to be harder to understand by people who don't know anything to begin with.

Anton came to her rescue. "Translated a bit roughly, the terms mean the following. 'Perspective density' refers to the sureness of the opinion. They call it density because—"

"—they're a pack of cone-headed sociometricians and they'd rather die than use clear terminology," said Victor.

"Well, yes, that too. But as I was saying before I was interrupted by Secret Agent Sourpuss, they use the term 'density' because the firmness with which someone holds an opinion is usually the product of multiple cross-associations. To give an example, a person believes a planet is a sphere because they know many things which all reinforce that opinion. Whereas if their opinion on a given subject is established by only one or two inputs, that opinion's density will be thin."

"Except the term they actually use for a thinly sustained opinion is 'disagglutinated,'" said Victor. "It's got six syllables instead of one. This is why Anton and I are spies instead of sociometrician cone-heads."

Anton shook his head sadly. "He's always had a bitter streak. Mind you, he's also right. They are a lot of cone-heads."

"What does the number mean, then?" asked Andrew. "Perspective density: 0.67."

Ruth decided she could answer that one easily enough. "It's a scale of 0 to 1, in which '0' means the perspective is so disagglutinated—and for the record, *I* think the term is quite appropriate—that it might as well not exist, and '1' is a perspective so heavily and completely buttressed by a multitude of other opinions that it is accepted as pure and simple fact."

"Give me examples," said Steph.

Ruth was back at sea again. *Examples? How do you give examples of basic—*

"'A moon is made out of green cheese,'" said Anton. "That'd get a PD rating of 0.01—or maybe 0.02 or 0.03. Nothing is ever ranked an absolute 0—or an absolute 1. On the opposite end, let's take the statement 'a moon orbits a planet.' That'd get a PD rating of .9 something."

He looked at the screen. "What that number tells us is that the perspective of the Star Empire's population as a whole—Ruth didn't point to that figure but it's on the upper left of the screen—you see it? 0.99? that means the analysis applies to the entire population within one-hundredth of a point of certainty—"

"To anybody except statisticians playing cover-your-ass that means *absolute* certainty," said Victor.

Anton continued. "—is two-thirds of the way toward being rock solid that the events and statements of fact shown in the recent *The Star Empire Today* are correct."

"That doesn't make any sense at all!" protested Andrew. "Not the two-thirds part, that's probably okay. But what's this nonsense about 0.99 certainty of the opinion of the *entire* population." Her threw up his hands. "You said the number of people who've seen the show so far isn't more than half a billion, right? That's short—way, way short—of even the Manticore System's total population. That's what? three billion?"

"Just about," Anton replied. "A bit over, as I recall."

"That's not even twenty percent, then."

Ruth was about to explode. *How can anybody be so grossly ignorant of the simplest and most—*

But this time, Berry came to her rescue. "That's a *sample* of half a billion, Andrew. That's gigantic. Most opinion samples are quite satisfied their results are accurate if they sample just one or two percent."

"Less than that," said Victor. "The number doesn't mean that 99 percent of the Star Empire's opinion was taken. It just means that there's at least a 99 percent chance—it's actually a 100 percent chance, for all practical purposes—that the opinion sample represents that of the entire population."

He scratched his jaw. "That number's not the surprise. It's the density number. I'd expected something in the 0.3 range. 0.4 if we were lucky."

"The *AV* number's even more surprising," said Cathy Montaigne. She was perched on the armrest of the couch occupied by Anton.

"AV means 'adjustment velocity,' right?" said Steph.

"The number means squat to me anyway, but why is it surprising?"

"It refers to the speed with which people's perspective is changing," Cathy explained, "and it's always closely associated with perspective density. The basic rule-of-thumb—although there are exceptions—is that the more densely someone holds an opinion, the more slowly it's likely to change. And vice versa, of course."

Andrew grunted. "Okay, I get it. To use an example, my opinion that Victor and Anton railroaded me into getting a horde of subatomic golems set loose inside my body to torture and torment me for no better motive than spite is so densely held that it will only change—if it does at all—at the speed with which a proton decays. What would that number be, by the way?"

Cathy laughed. "That number would approach infinity—or eternity, I should say. Sociometricians would give it a 'less than 0.01 percent.' That's as low as they ever go on account of"—she pointed at Victor—"what he says. Cover their ass."

"Why do they express it as a 'less than' instead of just giving it a straight number?" asked Berry.

"Because they're a bunch of cone-heads," said Victor. He nodded toward the screen. "What that number up there means—the AV figure of greater than 36 percent—is that opinions are shifting toward greater density at a rate that is thirty-six percent above the norm for perspective shifts at that density."

"Huh?" said Andrew.

Ruth tried to come back in at that point. "What they're trying to measure is how fast a perspective is shifting compared to how fast you'd normally *expect* that solidly held an opinion to shift. If the shift is in the direction of favoring the new opinion, it'll be expressed in the positive using the symbol for 'more than.' If it's shifting against, it'll be expressed as a negative."

"Huh?" Andrew repeated.

"The gist of what it means in the here and now," said Victor, "is that the impact of Yael Underwood's broadcast about—about—"

"About you, dear," said Thandi smiling broadly. "Just suck it up."

"About me," Victor said sourly, "is that the public opinion of the Star Empire is shifting in favor of our perspective on the real nature of interstellar politics a lot faster than such solidly held opinions—remember, that number was 0.67—usually shift. When they shift at all, which usually they don't—or shift in a negative direction."

There was a moment's silence. Then Steph said, "Wow. I'm right, aren't I? It's a 'wow'?"

Finally, Ruth felt back on sure ground. "It's a great big *huge* 'wow.' The only explanation I can think of is that the emotional impact of seeing a young StateSec officer risk his own life in order to save the life of an RMN officer's daughter just blew away a lot of established preconceptions. And then their continuing close friendship—which it obviously is even if both of them will probably try to make light of it—added layers of density to the new perspective."

"I think she's right," said Cathy. "The personal history between Anton and Victor makes their intelligence concerning Mesa plausible to people. Which it wouldn't be at all if someone said: 'Hey, guess what?

A couple of spies—one from Manticore, one from Haven—decided to work together and look what they discovered. Imagine that!'"

"So what does that last number mean?" asked Berry. "The one labeled 'reversal prospect'?"

"That's sociometrician gobbledygook for 'how likely is it that this perspective development will be reversed?'" said Victor. "And it's a bunch of twaddle, since all it does is say the other way around what the PD and AV numbers already established."

Anton smiled. "Leaving aside Victor's commentary, it is true that the RP number closely correlates to the other numbers."

"Closely correlates," sniffed Victor. "As in the chance for losing a game is ninety percent 'closely correlates' with the chance of winning being ten percent."

While they'd been bantering, Cathy had been monitoring her watch. "It's about time. Ruth, change to the live feed, will you?"

"Sure." The Manticoran princess tapped her tablet a few times and the image on the big virtual screen shifted to an outside view of Mount Royal Palace. A shuttle was coming in for a landing.

A minute or so went by, while the shuttle settled in and an armed security detachment took positions near the hatch through which the passengers would be disembarking.

The hatch opened and the first passenger came down the ramp. The reporter, who'd been prattling vacuities while she waited for something to happen, immediately said: "As expected, that's President Eloise Pritchart, arriving for her scheduled meeting with the Empress and the Prime Minister. Following her is Haven's Secretary of War Thomas Theisman. And now, if our private sources are accurate, we should be seeing..."

A short, very wide-shouldered man started down the ramp. "Yes, that's him. The now-famous Captain Zilwicki, formerly an intelligence officer in the Royal Manticoran Navy and now operating on his own. Or, often, in tandem with his unlikely partner..."

Another man came down the ramp. He was dressed all in black, in garments which were very closely patterned on the former uniform of Haven's now-defunct State Security.

"And that's Victor Cachat, who has become just as famous as Zilwicki." The reporter chuckled. "The more sensational news outlets have started referring to him as 'Black Victor,' we're told."

"Yes!" exclaimed Anton, pumping his fist. "Join the Notoriety Club, buddy."

Victor was back to looking disgruntled; sour; even sullen.

"When are we leaving?" he demanded. "At least on Mesa I'll be able to get some privacy."

Ruth pursed her lips. "That may be the single most deranged statement I've ever heard in my life." Then, with a grin: "But what else could you expect from..." Her voice lowered an octave and took on a pronounced tremor. "...*Black Victor?*"

CHAPTER 24

"Just what I always wanted," Yana Tretiakovna said sardonically, gazing at the detailed holograph floating before her. "My very own starship." She paused for a moment, head cocked, then frowned. "It's smaller than I thought it would be, though. Is this the compact version?"

Her appearance had changed radically, shifting from a Slavic to an East Asian template and becoming increasingly voluptuous. The process wasn't complete, but it was close enough for her to begin the necessary therapy to adjust for her...rearranged (and considerably more top-heavy) physique, and she was not pleased by the discomfort level that her new physique imposed as she grimly jogged on the gymnasium's treadmill every day. That was probably the real reason she'd been so enthusiastic about taking a break from that strenuous exercise routine, Anton Zilwicki thought.

Of course, the fact that she was thoroughly pissed off that *he'd* required so little in the way of alterations and virtually no PT or specialized exercise programs suggested it might be...unwise of him to twit her over her enthusiasm. On the other hand, he'd loyally spent his gym time right beside his new partner, since his own idea of a "mild workout" would have reduced half the galaxy's professional bodybuilders to tears.

"It's not actually *your* starship, you know," he pointed out mildly. "I'm sure the BSC would like to get her back intact at the end of the day."

"I'm not planning on breaking it," she replied a bit snippily. "And it's not like I'm really going to be the one in charge of this side of the operation, either. If memory serves, you're the senior member of this team."

"Nonsense! No Technician class worker from Hakim could *possibly* be senior to a Patrician like you. Your lightest whim is my command, Mistress. Within reason, of course."

"Oh, of *course*!" Yana's tone was sarcastic, but her eyes were thoughtful as she studied the lines of the sleek little starship's image. "And speaking of handing ships back over intact, just how was the Survey Corps able to lay its hands on this one so promptly?"

"They didn't." Anton shrugged. "That is, they didn't have to 'lay hands' on anything; they own the *Brixton's Comet* outright, and have—according to Uncle Jacques—for over thirty T-years. They just didn't get around to mentioning it to anyone."

Yana smiled at Anton's use of the we're-less-than-totally-fond-of-him-but-he's-not-all-that-bad nickname Jacques Benton-Ramirez y Chou had received from the small party of spies planning on sneaking onto the most dangerous planet in the galaxy. No one was quite certain how it had begun, although Yana suspected it stemmed from the conferences which both he and his formidable niece had attended in the Old

Star Kingdom, but it had been Victor Cachat who'd first used it—completely deadpan—to Benton-Ramirez y Chou's face. To his credit, the half-sized Beowulfer had simply gone right ahead with the abstruse point he'd been explaining at the time without so much as a blink. From his reaction and from what she knew about the BSC, Yana wouldn't have been especially surprised to discover that some of his team members during his own time in Beowulf's special forces had called him the same thing. Or something even more disrespectful, given the BSC's informality in the field and just how well he'd performed there. It was the sort of backhanded compliment elite forces routinely paid to those they most respected. Whatever the reason, he seemed perfectly comfortable with it.

And it certainly took less time to say than his surname did.

"And just how sure are they that no one *outside* the BSC knows that they've owned her outright for years and years?" she asked.

"Fairly confident." Anton shrugged again. "That's about as good as it gets in this business, you know. They bought her—had her built, really, right here in the Hidalgo Yard—through about six layers of shell companies, and they've operated her on a lease basis ever since. And according to Uncle Jacques, she's only been used twice in all that time for specific covert operations. They've actually earned back her construction costs several times over by now, all through legitimate leases, and she's been leased so many times, by so many different lessees, that she has an absolutely ironclad history, no matter how deep anyone looks from the outside. About the only way anyone could consider her suspect would be for the 'anyone' in question to have someone deep enough inside the BSC to know all about her. And if they've got anyone that deep, we're all screwed before we ever leave Beowulf, so I figure we might as well operate on the assumption that *her* identity's at least as secure as ours are going to be."

Yana considered that for a moment, then nodded. For all her often deliberately "lowbrow" public persona, the ex-Scrag was ferociously intelligent, and while her actual experience and skill set tended more towards focused mayhem than covert operations, she'd had enough experience operating with the duo of Cachat & Zilwicki to accept Anton's analysis without too many qualms.

Now he manipulated the image, expanding it until they could make out the hull's details.

"She's a nice little ship, actually," he pointed out with a connoisseur's enthusiasm. "Only about forty-five thousand tons, of course, but in most ways she's a lot like Duchess Harrington's personal yacht, the *Tankersley*. She's fitted up on a rather more luxurious scale than the duchess ever considered necessary, and she doesn't have accommodations for quite as many warm bodies, but the basic power plant and automation are virtually identical."

"That's good, considering how little *I* know about the guts of a starship," Yana observed dryly. She was a skilled small-craft pilot, at home behind the controls of anything from high-performance air-breathing atmospheric craft to heavy-lift cargo shuttles or an all-up armored assault shuttle, but all of that experience was strictly sub-light.

"Don't worry," Anton said reassuringly. "I know *my* way around a starship's innards just fine, and this design incorporates so much automation—and so many multiply redundant backup systems—that the possibility of any sort of serious malfunction's effectively nonexistent. And," he added feelingly, "she's not only one hell of a lot younger than *Hali Sowle*, but she's been properly maintained for her entire life."

"Well, *that's* a relief. I've spent long enough drifting around playing cards for one lifetime, thank you very much."

"Me, too." Anton grinned. "And while we're on the subject of reasons not to worry, the reason she's got all that automation is that she was intended from the beginning to be operated by a two-person crew. It's not like I'm going to need a lot of assistant engineers, and I'll probably be able to find time in my arduous schedule to do any astrogating we need, as well."

"You get us there in one piece, and I'll be happy," Yana told him. *Brixton's Comet's* normal-space controls were essentially little more than an upgraded and fancified version of a regular cargo shuttle. In fact, they were a bit simpler even than that, since the yacht had never been intended for atmospheric flight. Of course, there was the minor matter of the Visigoth Wormhole to consider. Which reminded her . . .

"You do realize that getting us there in one piece includes getting us through the damned wormhole, don't you?" she asked.

"Between Visigoth's traffic control, the ship's computers, and my own odd few decades of naval service, I'm sure we'll be able to limp through it somehow," he assured her.

"Yeah, sure," she agreed, eyes fixed on the holograph.

"Don't worry about it," he said in a rather more reassuring tone. "We'll be fine at least as far as the transportation's involved. And we'll be a lot more comfortable than the others will."

"Well, than Andrew and Steph will be, anyway," Yana corrected him with a smile, and he chuckled.

"Actually, I think *they're* probably going to be more comfortable than Victor is," he said. "Working crew berths aboard liners like the *Pygmalion* may not be luxury suites, but they aren't exactly dungeon cells, either. Their quarters will actually be more comfortable—and probably more spacious—than anything Andrew had growing up on Parmley Station, and they'll be a hell of a lot better than anything Steph had as a seccy growing up in Mendel. But poor Victor! Can you even imagine how badly his revolutionary's instincts are going to revolt against a first-class suite on one of the fanciest luxury liners in space?" Anton shook his head, his sad expression belied by the twinkle in his deep eyes. "I foresee great angst on his part!"

"Bull." Yana laughed. "You know exactly how he and the kaja will be spending their time in that first-class suite of theirs!"

"I have no idea what you could possibly be talking about," Anton said virtuously, and Yana laughed again.

She had a point, Anton conceded, and even if she hadn't had one, Victor Cachat was nothing if not adaptable. And the fact that Mesa was one of *Pygmalion*'s regular stops (and that her captain owed Jacques Benton-Ramirez y Chou several very sizable personal favors) was going to prove very useful. The ship, one of the Tobias Lines' elite vessels, had exactly zero connection with anything Beowulfan and the line's owners had been among the Solarian League's most vociferous critics of "Manticoran mercantile imperialism" for the last forty or fifty T-years. They deeply resented Manticoran penetration of what they considered to be rightfully "their" markets, especially as that penetration pushed them further and further out of the bulk freight carrying trade and into the passenger traffic. They couldn't complain about their profit margin on the fast, sleek liners they continued to operate, but a very high profit margin on a couple of dozen vessels came in a poor second compared to a moderate profit margin on several score vessels.

What mattered at the moment was that there was absolutely nothing to make even a member of the Mesan Alignment suspicious of *Pygmalion*'s pedigree, and she'd plied the same route—which included both Beowulf and Mesa—for the last seven T-years. She was a thoroughly known quantity, and her owners didn't need to know that Captain Vandor's daughter-in-law owed her life and the lives of her three then-unborn children to a BSC covert team under the command of one Major Jacques Benton-Ramirez y Chou. In fact, Captain Vandor and his family had been very careful about seeing to it that that particular bit of knowledge did not become public. There were several reasons for that, but the most important one was that Vandor was a man who believed in paying his debts, which included keeping secret the identity of the unknown criminals who'd raided the offices of a highly respected Solarian shipping line—the one, in fact, which had employed (and *continued* to employ) one Sebastián Vandor—and in the process "kidnapped" a secretarial worker who had subsequently managed to escape from her abductors and was now the mother of Sebastián's grandchildren.

The Tobias Lines would have looked with disfavor upon any efforts to publicize the fact that its current CEO's (sadly deceased) brother had been using the company's assets to cover Manpower shipments of genetic slaves *inside* the League. Of course, that had been back in the good old days when Tobias had still boasted a sizable freighter fleet. Times had changed...but memories were long, and there was no statute of limitations on the League's anti-slavery laws. But that once-upon-a-time relationship was one reason *Pygmalion* served the Mesan run and enjoyed a certain coziness with the Mesa System's government and its various agencies.

All of which only helped make the liner one of the least likely to be suspected means whereby desperate and cunning spies might be inserted into the very heart of darkness.

Brixton's Comet wasn't quite as speedy as *Pygmalion*. The passenger liner had military grade particle screening and a military grade hyper generator, as did most of the galaxy's relatively small number of really fast passenger liners and specialty freighters. *Brixton's Comet*, although she was obviously the sort of plaything only the fabulously wealthy might possess, did *not* have military grade particle screening. She could go as high in hyper-space as *Pygmalion* could, but her sustained velocity there was barely seventy percent as great. The passenger liner could make the trip from Beowulf to Mesa via the Visigoth System and its wormhole junction in little more than twelve

T-days; *Brixton's Comet* would require eighteen. On the other hand, the yacht wasn't dependent upon the passenger liner's schedule and Yana and Anton ought to be able to leave at least a full T-week and a half before *Pygmalion* did. That meant they ought to arrive in Mesa a good four T-days sooner than the rest of their team did, which would give them that additional time to establish their own covers... and that much more separation from the insertion of the others.

Victor and Thandi would enter Mesa openly, relying upon their thoroughly legal (albeit rather less than legally *obtained*) visas, which would subject them to the full rigor of Mesan Customs. That was fine, since the Mesans were supposed to figure out—eventually—that Victor's ostensible reason for visiting their fine planet was not precisely what he had declared upon arrival. Mesa being Mesa, the authorities ought to be quite satisfied with that discovery and pat themselves on the back for it without spending much thought worrying over the possibility that the dark little secret they'd discovered about their guest was there specifically to *be* discovered and provide the sort of answer which would keep them from looking any deeper.

Andrew Artlett and Steph Turner would enter Mesa in less visible fashion. It wasn't at all uncommon for ships like *Pygmalion* to sign on temporary crew, and it wasn't much less common for that temporary crew to jump ship. It was an acknowledged way for the big lines, especially, to find the hands they needed in a short-term arrangement with the understanding that they could pay dirt poor wages because what the short-term hands in question had in mind was finding cheap transportation to where they really wanted to go. "Gypsies" was the most commonly used polite term for people like that, and nobody worried his head too much over their comings and goings. Admittedly, Mesa was likely to keep a much closer eye on any gypsies who decided to stay on in someplace like Mendel, but Victor had come up with an extremely Victor-like plan to let them drop entirely off the grid once they were on-planet.

As a general rule, Anton Zilwicki disliked plans which had too many moving parts. The Demon Murphy was the unceasing foe of those who became too enamored of their own cleverness, and Zilwicki had adopted the KISS Principle as his guiding light long, long ago. In this instance, however, he'd considered every aspect of the insertion plan, and assuming they were going to actually continue with what Duchess Harrington had so aptly described as their insanity, he was satisfied this was the best way to go about it.

Besides, he thought, looking down at the hologram, *she really is a sweet little ship. I'm going to enjoy playing with her. And this time I'm not going to spend T-weeks on end playing cards and listening to Andrew whistle. What's a little possibility of mayhem and disaster compared to* that?

CHAPTER 25

Cary Condor took off her hat and hung it on a peg next to the door. Like everything else in their apartment, the peg was an antique. It was a piece of actual wood, made from one of the trees called nackels that covered much of Mesa's lowlands. Nackelwood had no interesting grain; no aromatic odor; nothing. Its sole virtues were that it was readily available, easy to work and cheap.

It was a fairly common material used for furniture in seccy areas—but even in seccy areas most small items like clothing pegs were made of modern extrusile memory foams. As the hat drew near, the foam's embedded sensorium would cause it to extrude as a peg shape, which it would withdraw once the object was removed. Using a wood peg, on the other hand...

The thing was rigid, fixed, immovable, an actual *safety hazard*. What if you slipped? You could lose an eye on the damn thing.

But that was admittedly far down the list of dangers they faced. So Cary didn't give the peg more than a perfunctory scowl before hanging up her hat and turning to her companions.

Just one companion, as it turned out. Karen was still asleep.

"How is she?"

Stephanie was sitting at the small kitchen table. "No better—but no worse, either, from what I can tell. I think her condition may have stabilized, at least a little."

Sighing, Cary pulled out a chair and joined Stephanie at the table. "What makes the whole thing so horrible is that if we could just get her some decent medical care..."

"We could heal her. Completely. New legs, new organs, the works. With modern medicine, it wouldn't be that hard and not even too expensive." She shrugged. "For all the good that does. We might as well wish for our own spacecraft and no-questions-asked orbit clearance, while we're at it."

Cary laughed. "And a pilot, don't forget! Neither one of us knows a thing about operating spaceships."

"Or even flyers, in your case," said Stephanie. "Hell, I can barely manage to handle a simple flyer myself."

Cary winced. She'd flown with Stephanie, once, with Stephanie at the controls.

Once. It was an experience she'd sworn never to repeat. Most seccies—Cary and Stephanie were no exception—had little experience operating equipment beyond whatever they might learn on a job. Most seccies who knew how to fly learned the skills as cabbies, personal valets or lorry drivers. Stephanie's experience had come entirely from a few months she'd spent working for a restaurant as a parking attendant.

Cary *hated* Mesa's overlords. Manpower, Inc., the Jessyk Combine, any and all of them. She knew that David Pritchard's detonation of the nuclear device at Green Pines had been tactically insane—not to mention suicidal for himself. But she'd never had any trouble understanding the emotions that had driven him to do it.

More than half of Mesa's population was kept in conditions of chattel slavery, without even the hope of manumission. The descendants of slaves who'd been freed centuries earlier when manumission had still been legal, seccies like Cary herself, lived in conditions that were better but only marginally so. Worse, actually, in material terms, more often than not. But unlike an outright slave, a seccy had a certain degree of personal freedom. Very circumscribed freedom, granted, but at least someone like Cary didn't have to account to a master or mistress for everything they did or every step they took.

Her angry musings were interrupted by Stephanie. "Look, there's no point chewing on ourselves over Karen's situation. The truth is, we're lucky any of us are still alive. Once David—and damn him again—set off that bomb, something like this was bound to happen."

Cary couldn't help but shiver. The weeks following the detonation at Green Pines had been . . .

Hideous. Mesa's security forces had gone berserk. They'd ripped through the seccy quarters like weasels set loose in a chicken coop. Their official rationale had been "rooting out terrorists," but that had been an excuse—and one they didn't care at all if anyone believed. They'd simply been wreaking vengeance.

Ironically, that very savagery was probably all that

had kept Cary and Karen and Stephanie from being captured. The security forces had been so engrossed in random slaughter that they'd actually been a little lax in punishing real enemies.

So, keeping just half a step ahead of their pursuers, Cary and her two companions had managed to escape, although Karen had been terribly injured in the process. But the security forces had captured most of their former confederates.

They'd caught the leader of their group, Carl Hansen, within a few hours after Green Pines. His corpse, rather. Carl had committed suicide when he realized he had no chance of escape. If he hadn't, the security thugs would have caught everyone. But Carl's suicide bought the rest of them a little breathing space.

Cary didn't know who else might have also escaped. Unfortunately, they couldn't use the drop boxes to reestablish contact with any of them who'd done so. Angus Levigne had set up those locations, and he'd been insistent on keeping knowledge of them restricted to a small circle. The only ones in that circle who were still alive were the three women in that apartment.

A finger poked her shoulder. "Hey, snap out of it," said Stephanie. "Whatever place you're at right now, it's not doing you any good. Let's concentrate on the moment. Did you find out anything today?"

Cary realized that she had wandered off mentally. That happened to her a lot, just as the nightmares came to her almost every night. She knew she was suffering from a bad case of PTSD—which, like Karen's injuries, was a medical condition that could be easily cured if she had access to the right treatment.

Sure. All she and Moriarty had to do was steal

a flyer, hope that Stephanie wouldn't kill them in a crash along the way, steal a shuttle at the spaceport that neither of them knew how to operate so they could reach orbit where they could steal a spacecraft neither of them knew how to operate so they could travel to a planet neither of them knew how to navigate to where they could get the medical assistance they needed from nobody they knew which they'd pay for with money they didn't have.

The tough problem, of course, would be evading Mesa's orbital defenses.

She couldn't help but break into laughter. Genuine laughter, too, even if it was probably a bit hysterical.

"Well, the drop box had nothing, as usual. But I did meet that person you were told to look for."

Stephanie's lips tightened. "So, at least that . . ." She took a breath. "Wasn't wasted."

Stephanie had been the one who'd made the initial contact with the district's criminal gang. Since they didn't have any money to spare, she'd paid for the information they needed a different way.

It had been unpleasant, certainly, but no worse than anything they'd already been through. Both of them had spent time in the custody of the security forces, in the past, being interrogated. "Interrogation," in the parlance of Mesa's security thugs, routinely included rape. That was almost invariably true for young women, usually true for young men, as likely as not for middle-aged people and not unheard of even in the case of the elderly.

Cary had gone through it twice. The worst of it, in a way, had been the bizarrely impersonal nature of the brutality. Her rapists had seemed to be acting out some sort of routine, as if what they were engaged in was just part of a job. It wasn't simply that they treated her as slab of meat; so far as she could tell, they really didn't see her as anything else. They might as well have been butchers working at their trade.

She shook her head, shaking away the memories at the same time. She could do it with those, because she'd been able to get psychological treatment afterward that had prevented the trauma from getting fixed into PTSD.

"Anyway, what you learned turned out to be true. I went to that bar he told you about."

"The Rhodesian Rendezvous."

"Yeah. Talk about a dive! That place is a little scary. Well, more than a little. The only people who seem to hang out there are roughnecks to a man—and I do mean *man*. I was the only woman in the place."

She chuckled, very dryly. "For once, I was glad I don't look like you." Cary wasn't unattractive. But she wasn't nearly as good-looking as Moriarty.

For her part, Stephanie made a face. "Trust me, girl. Looking like me is as much of a curse as a blessing. Anyway, what happened then?"

"That guy was there, all right. The one that—what was his name? I can't remember—told you to ask for."

"Jake. Something. I don't remember his last name. For that matter, I'm not sure he ever gave it to me."

"Well, for whatever it's worth, at least Jake didn't cheat you. Triêu Chuanli was there, all right. In one of the back rooms, not in the main area of the bar. I had to do some fast talking to get to see him, but they finally let me."

Stephanie's lips quirked. "Bet they made it like some sort of royal audience."

"Actually, no. Well, *they* did—the two goons who ushered me back there, I mean—but Chuanli himself was pretty low key. He was even polite. Asked me to sit, if I wanted any sort of refreshment. Ha!" She smiled. "Just as if I was a proper lady and he was a proper gentleman offering tea and crumpets. Whatever crumpets are."

"They're a goofy type of pancake. The ancient Angleterrans used to eat them, whoever they were." Moriarty made an impatient shooing motion with her hand. "Keep going."

Cary decided to cut the small talk that had followed for a few minutes. Triêu—he'd insisted on being on a first name basis—really had been quite pleasant, even cordial. If she hadn't known he was some sort of higher-up in a criminal cabal, Cary would have thought he was a professional of some sort. Maybe even a university professor.

Good-looking guy, too. But again, she shook her head.

"The long and the short of it is that, yes, he'd be interested in our merchandise whenever we see fit to present him with it. He was obviously curious as to why we didn't have it right now—or even have a date in mind. But he didn't push that at all."

"Is that the long or the short? And whichever it is, what's the kicker? There's got to be one."

Cary smiled. "Bad expression. I should have said, 'the short and the short of it.' What it came down to was, yes, he'd be willing to buy. No, he wasn't slobbering all over himself with eagerness. This sort of merchandise, it seems, does have a market but it's a pretty erratic one and if it takes too long maintaining the merchandise in good condition can cost enough to eat up any profits he might make. You can't just stuff it into a freezer. So—this is the kicker—the price isn't that great. He'll give us a deal. We either take a straight-up payment—"

"For how much?"

Cary gave her the amount, in all three currencies Chuanli had offered to deal in. Moriarty grimaced.

"That's not much," she said. "Wouldn't keep us going for more than another three months, tops."

"Or we can share part of the risk with him. We could wind up with quite a bit more, if he can turn the merchandise around quickly. Or we might end up with even less than the straight-up price, if it takes too long. In whatever case, though, we don't get paid until he makes the sale. Or sales—which is more likely—if he winds up having more than one customer."

Stephanie grimaced again. "That means we have to trust him, too."

Cary and pursed her lips. "I don't think that's actually a problem, Stephanie. It's hard to explain, but... I get the sense that when you deal with someone like Chuanli, it's taken for granted that everyone is acting in good faith. Honor among thieves, I'd guess you'd say. That's probably because since nobody can appeal a dispute to the courts, nobody wants to take a risk that the swindled party comes back at you with bloodshed in mind."

Stephanie rolled her eyes. "Oh, right." She spread out her hands, indicating the cramped apartment. "We're practically awash in hit men. Oh, wait. I guess that'd have to be hit girls, since there are no actual men here."

"Hey, look. Nobody ever promised us a rose garden."

"Yeah, but is it too much to ask for a *cactus* garden? This is pushing it." Stephanie chewed on her lower lip for a few seconds. "So what do you think? Go for the better but riskier deal?"

"Yeah."

She chewed on her lip for a few more seconds. "Okay. What the hell. We may as well keep living dangerously, given our track record."

CHAPTER 26

Lajos Irvine's boss George Vickers had done one thing right, at least. The two assistants he'd provided Lajos looked to be a lot more capable than the numbskulls he'd been provided the last time his superiors decided he needed support.

That had been Isabel Bardasano's doing. The now-deceased former head of Alignment Security had normally been as sharp as they come. But that time, the fieldcraft of the meatheads she'd handed Lajos had been so bad they'd given themselves away to the targets as soon as they encountered them. Being fair to Bardasano, she'd been in a hurry and the only forces she had immediately at hand were some of Mesa's security people. They hadn't been part of even the outermost layers of the Alignment and were accustomed to dealing with seccies. They'd also had the vicious nature and the overconfidence that normally infected a "security force" whose brutality and violence was unchecked by anything remotely like "legal rights" on the part of their victims. A very little bit of that was enough to turn even once-intelligent human beings into arrogant, head-breaking thugs, and Lajos' hastily assigned "backup" had been at their trade entirely too long.

To make things worse—not to mention terrifying—the targets in question had been the deadliest bastards Lajos had ever run across in his entire career. One of them, especially. That maniac had gunned down all three goons in that many seconds—no, probably less. Lajos didn't remember too well because he'd been so frightened.

He'd been even more frightened a short time later when the two targets dragged him into a tunnel and had a short discussion over whether or not to kill him. That they'd do so without hesitation had been manifestly obvious. Lajos still woke up sometimes with nightmares of the cold gaze of the gunman. Those black eyes had been as merciless as a spider's. He'd never forget them.

This time around, though, the higher-ups seemed to have had their heads screwed on straight. These two agents were part of the Alignment and had the earmarks of people with experience in the field against serious opponents. They were the police equivalent of elite special forces, not uniformed goons. Lajos didn't have any doubt that the men would handle themselves just fine if it came down to rough stuff. Which, hopefully, it wouldn't. Lajos had no romantic notions concerning violence. If all went as planned, his transactions and dealings with Mesa's seccy underworld would be as banal and unexciting as grocery shopping.

Lajos finished reading through his notes and turned away from the monitor. "I'm thinking our best bet is to approach either Jurgen Dusek in Neue Rostock or go the other way and see if we can get someone in Lower Radomsko interested."

Neue Rostock was at the center of the seccy districts in the capital. It was a heavily crime-ridden area and Dusek was the district's acknowledged crime boss. Not the only one, but what ancient gangsters would have called the *capo di tutti capi*.

Lower Radomsko presented a different picture. It was also well into the central areas inhabited by seccies and was, if anything, even more crime-ridden than Neue Rostock. But its underworld was disorganized, dominated by a multitude of small gangs none of whom recognized any master.

"I'd go for Neue Rostock," advised Stanković. "Dealing with Dusek will be a lot easier than trying to deal with that mob of crazies in Lower Radomsko."

Martinez issued a little grunt, which seemed to indicate his agreement.

Lajos leaned the same way as Stanković, but for the moment he decided to play the devil's advocate. "Yeah, that's true—but so is the corollary. If things go wrong, dealing with Dusek will be a lot *less* easy. I've never dealt with the man before, but I know a lot about him. By all accounts, once you scratch that gangster-politesse veneer of his you're dealing with Attila the Hun's first cousin. He's the mean one in the family, by the way."

Stanković chuckled. "Yeah, I've heard the same thing. But . . ." He turned his head sideways a little, to give Lajos a slanted gaze. "Don't take this the wrong way, boss, but I don't think you've had much experience in Lower Radomsko."

"None at all," Lajos agreed. "Personally, that is. I

know a fair amount about it, though, just from—" He waved his hand. "Stuff."

"Yeah, that's what I thought. The thing is, you really have to spend time there to get a good sense of it. Freddie and I never did ourselves but we worked with a Mesan security agent—one of the Tabbies—who'd spent years there. The stories he had to tell..." He shook his head. "The place is a shithole."

Lajos leaned back in his chair, his interest rising. "Go on," he said.

"It's..." Stanković groped for words.

"Fucking lunacy," provided Martinez.

His partner nodded. "That's about right. It's just chaos, boss. You'll think you've made a deal, gotten some sort of arrangement—this happened to the Tabby *three times*, I'm not kidding—and the next minute some other asshole has shoved his way in and you've got to start all over. One of those times he told us he wound up having to deal with four gangs. And it wasn't any big money deal, neither."

"Just looking for a runaway slave," said Martinez. "The bounty amounted to pocket change. But for the sorry-ass screwballs in Lower Radomsko"—he rubbed a thumb and two fingers together—"what you and I would call pocket change is worth killing over."

"He got the runaway, eventually," said Stanković. "But not before five people had been killed—one of whom was the runaway herself. Got her throat cut by one gang just so another one wouldn't get the bounty."

"Screw Lower Radomsko," said Martinez.

Lajos laughed and raised his hands in a mock gesture of surrender. "Okay, okay, guys. I'm convinced. Neue Rostock it'll be, then."

Lajos was pleased. More than a decision had been arrived at here, he knew. A working relationship had been moved forward, too. He'd been worried about that a little. Lajos' entire career had been as a lone wolf. He had no experience handling other agents and hadn't been sure if he had the skills or aptitude for it. Judging from the friendly expressions on the faces of Stanković and Martinez, though, it seemed he did.

❖   ❖   ❖

"What's up, boss? Did you get the results from—"

Seeing the people already sitting in Lisa Charteris's office, Zachariah McBryde abruptly stopped talking. When he got the summons to report to Charteris—which came via personal courier, which was unusual but not unheard-of—he'd assumed she wanted to discuss one of the projects they were working on.

That couldn't possibly be what she'd summoned him for, though, he now realized. Two of the four scientists in the room had no connection to the work he was doing, and he didn't recognize one of them at all.

But the icing on the cake was the presence of Janice Marinescu. He hadn't seen her since the meeting where she informed Zachariah and Lisa that Operation Houdini was being set underway.

He got a sharp, sinking feeling in his stomach. The experiments he'd been running lately had been difficult enough to keep his mind focused. As time went by with no further notice or even mention of Houdini, he'd managed to half-forget about the issue. And now here it was, back in full force. There could be no other reason for Marinescu's presence.

"Okay, we're all here," Marinescu said. "The five of you in this room are the people from this science project who've been selected for Houdini. Lisa Charteris is in overall charge of the center. Three of you"—she glanced briefly at Zachariah and the two scientists he knew—"are task force directors, and Gail Weiss is . . . let's just say she has special skills we don't want to lose.

"As you've probably already guessed, Houdini has just gone from alert status to active status. The first division is already being taken off-planet. Unfortunately, we're evacuating a lot more people in a shorter span of time than we'd foreseen. That means we're forced to use avenues of exfiltration that we hadn't planned on originally. Many of us—including all five of you in this room—will be evacuated via Manpower shipping."

One of the task force directors, Stefka Juarez, made a face. It had been an involuntary reaction and the expression left her face within two seconds, but Marinescu spotted it and gaze her a hard gaze. "Is there a problem, Ms. Juarez?"

She didn't wait for an answer before continuing. "It's a little late in the day, don't you think, to discover you have qualms about Manpower's activities. You're in the inner layers of the onion and have been since you were a teenager. You've known for years—and if you had any disagreements you certainly kept them quiet—that the Alignment's long-term goals required the development of genetic slavery. And still do—and will, for several more generations."

She stopped and gave all of them that cold gaze. "The same goes for the rest of you. So if it turns out—which it has—that you have to be exfiltrated by ships from the slave trade, deal with it. You may have been able to keep your hands clean in your scientific work, but others of us—me, for one—have not enjoyed that luxury. You'll forgive me if I don't have any sympathy for your current plight. Which, as plights go, isn't much."

She stopped to look at each one of them in turn, for a second or two. "Do any of you have anything you want to say?"

All of them were silent. Charteris and Gail Weiss shook their heads.

"Very well." Marinescu had her hands folded in her lap. Now she unclasped them and pointed at the door. "When you leave here, each of you will be escorted by a member of the Genetic Advancement and Uplift League to a briefing room. There, you'll be given the details of your evacuation route. Everything you need to know except the exact time of departure and the specific ship you'll be taking. We won't know that for a while yet. Right now, we're only halfway through scheduling the evacuation details for the second division."

The third of the task force directors, Joseph van Vleet, was frowning. "How will we know—"

"—when to leave? The same member of the Uplift League whom you'll meet when you leave here will come and notify you. They will also accompany you throughout the evacuation. Every stage of it until you reach your final destination."

Once again, Juarez grimaced. Zachariah barely knew her, since their work was in areas quite far removed from each other. He couldn't help but wonder, though, how someone who'd been made a task force director could have such abysmal social skills.

"Is that really necessary?" she asked.

Marinescu looked at her the way a predator studies

the weakest member of a herd. After a short pause, she said: "The very fact you ask that question demonstrates that it is."

She turned her eyes onto the rest of them. "Do I need to explain again—how many times has each of you been briefed on Houdini? at least three—that the whole point of the operation is to prevent our enemies from learning *anything* about the Alignment. I should say, as little as possible about the Alignment and nothing at all about the inner layers of the onion—or even the onion's existence. The only way to be sure of that is to follow two essential guidelines.

"First, no one outside the group selected for Houdini can know anything about it. That means *nobody*. That includes spouses, parents, children, siblings, cousins, friends—*nobody*. Second, nobody can be left behind who does know about Houdini. *Nobody*. Not. One. Single. Person."

She paused again, to scan all of their faces. Looking for weakness, hesitation, indecision, vacillation . . . anything that would trigger her predator's instincts. Her own gaze was pitiless.

Zachariah held his breath. The moment was . . . *dangerous*. Really, really dangerous.

"If you don't understand exactly what that means," she continued, "let me explain it to you as clearly as I can. If you tell anyone about Houdini who is not part of it, that person will be eliminated. So will any person that that person might have told. I stress *might* have told. We will bend the stick in the direction of caution, be assured of that."

She nodded toward Lisa. "If Director Charteris tells her husband or any of her three children, to give a hypothetical example, all of them will be eliminated. Including herself, of course. Violating the tenets of Houdini will be considered high treason. Do you all understand me?"

Lisa's face was drawn, but she nodded curtly. So did Zachariah and van Vleet. Weiss and Juarez just stared down at the floor.

"Just to be clear on this. 'Telling anyone' will be interpreted as broadly as possible. So don't try—don't even entertain the possibility in your dreams—to let your family and friends know you'll be leaving by some circuitous or indirect means. Do not tell them that you'll be going on a long trip soon due to your work. Do not give them unusual gifts. Do not take them on sudden vacations. Do or say absolutely *nothing* that is in any way out of the ordinary. And don't doubt for a moment that you will be under surveillance. We will know if you do."

She paused again. "I repeat: do you all understand me, in every particular?"

This time, everyone nodded.

"Good. Now, as to the second issue. It may turn out—this is not likely, but it can't be ruled out altogether—that at some point in the evacuation, through no fault of your own, you become compromised. If that happens, the member of the—the Gaul, to hell with circumlocutions, will see to it that you do not fall into enemy hands. You won't have to do anything. It will be done for you. If you need me to spell that out, I will do so."

Again, the pause. By now Zachariah just wanted to get the meeting over with. He felt like he'd been beaten on the head with a club. Beaten on his spirit, rather—or soul, if he had one.

Marinescu was not one to let anything slide, however. "I repeat. Do any of you need me to spell out what this means?"

All five of them shook their heads.

"Good. Director Charteris, if you would lead the way? You will be followed by the others at five-second intervals in alphabetical order. After Charteris, Juarez goes, followed by McBryde and van Vleet. Ms. Weiss, you go last."

Charteris was already on her feet and heading for the door. After a slight hesitation, Juarez got up and followed. After the director passed through the door, Juarez glanced at her timepiece. Five seconds later, she followed.

Zachariah did the same. When he came through the door, Lisa was no longer in sight. Juarez and her escort were already well down the corridor.

One of the three Gauls still waiting stepped up. "Task Force Director McBryde, I will be your escort. Come with me, please."

Zachariah recognized him, but he couldn't remember if this one was Zhilov or Arpino. But the man was already moving down the corridor so he didn't ask.

He didn't suppose it mattered anyway. He felt a lot like a man being led to the scaffold. Under the circumstances, would you ask the executioner his name? It seemed like a waste of time and effort. In the nature of things, your relationship with your executioner was fleeting.

CHAPTER 27

Colonel Nancy Anderson waited until the *Hali Sowle* was eight light-minutes away from the trading depot before she said anything about their mission. There was no rational reason for that. If anything they'd said or done or just blind bad luck had given them away to the Manpower personnel staffing the depot, they were as good as dead anyway. At that range, even low-powered missiles carrying small warheads would easily destroy a ship like the *Hali Sowle*.

And whether they'd been found out or not, why bother keeping silent for any length of time once the *Hali Sowle* left the depot? They were a starship, not a submarine maintaining silence under the surface of an ocean lest they be detected by their enemies. In space, as the old saw went, no one can hear you scream—or talk, or sing, or whisper, or shout at the top of your lungs.

But, rational or not, the time just passed had been very tense. All members of the BSC handled tension well; Anderson handled it particularly well or she'd never have reached the rank of colonel. Still...

Eight light-minutes was one Astronomical Unit, one of the most ancient of all measures. It was the distance between Sol and Terra back in the human race's system of origin.

Most Beowulfers might not be superstitious—but they still ate comfort food like anyone else. One AU was the astrogational equivalent. For reasons that might make no sense, star travelers just seemed to relax a little once they'd gone that distance.

"Well, I didn't spot any problems. Did anyone?"

"No," said Damewood. "The lion moved among the lambs with nary a one of the little fuzzballs sensing anything amiss." He pointed to his work station, with the special displays now up that he'd made sure were not in sight when Manpower's inspectors came through. "I was checking too, you'd better believe it."

Sitting in the captain's seat, Ganny El blew a raspberry. "'The lion moved among the lambs'! Yeah, right. Completely toothless lion—no claws, neither—and a pack of lambs that sure looked like predators to me." She held up an admonishing finger. "I'm telling you, I'm not doing this again! You hear that, Anderson? I don't care how much money you wave under my nose."

The colonel smiled but didn't say anything. She had no more intention than Ganny of repeating the somewhat hair-raising experiment. One test run, carried out at a large and well-equipped Manpower depot, was enough to determine if there was any significant chance that the identity of the *Hali Sowle* would flag any alarms. They'd decided it was better to take the risk now with a skeleton crew than find out later when the *Hali Sowle* was carrying a full complement.

But no alarms had been triggered. Neither by the name nor the characteristics of the ship itself. The *Hali Sowle* had arrived at Balcescu Station after approaching and identifying itself quite openly; had spent two days at the depot engaged in trade and simply enjoying the depot's restaurants and shops; and had then left in just as straightforward a manner. And there'd been no trouble of any kind, leaving aside the quarrel Ganny had gotten into with a shopkeeper whom she accused of trying to fleece her.

So, it now seemed clear that the *Hali Sowle* could go anywhere safely except possibly to Mesa itself. And if Zilwicki and Cachat were right in their estimate that the destruction of Gamma Center (and Jack McBryde's accompanying actions) had obliterated the Mesan records of the vessel altogether, the *Hali Sowle* could even go to Mesa.

But no one proposed to send the *Hali Sowle* to Mesa. It would be too risky to use the ship a second time to get the spies off the planet—much less onto it in the first place—and there was certainly no chance of using the *Hali Sowle* as a raider in the system. Mesa's naval forces might be on the paltry side when compared to the fleets of star nations like Manticore and Haven, but they were more than powerful enough to swat two frigates as if they were insects.

Leaving aside Mesa, though, it now seemed that the rest of the galaxy was open to the *Hali Sowle*'s new business.

Purely as an idle exercise, Anderson tried to calculate how much money it *would* take to get Ganny to withdraw her proclamation. The number would be large, certainly, but very far short of infinity. The

Parmley clan's matriarch wasn't exactly avaricious, since it was never her own wealth that concerned her. But she kept an eye out for the interests of her kin like no one Nancy had ever seen.

Now that she'd finagled a full suite of prolong treatments for every member of the clan who could benefit from them and also bargained to get excellent educations for all the youngsters—and even a few of the adults who had a mind to go to school—what fresh field could she aspire to conquer?

There had be *something*, knowing Ganny, but what?.

Loren Damewood had apparently been undertaking the same exercise. And, as was the XO's way, didn't hesitate from putting his speculations in words.

"Oh, come on, Ganny. There's got to be *some* price you'd settle for. What have you got a hankering for these days? Mansions on the shores of the Emerald Sea for each and every one of your kinfolk, down to the babes and toddlers? All-expenses-paid cruises on luxury liners through the Core worlds?"

Nancy couldn't resist joining in. "How about precious metals and jewelry? That's been a winner for going on ten thousand years."

Ganny's sneer was every bit as flamboyant as her cursing. "Even if such a price existed—which for the record, it doesn't—what difference would it make to you? Between the whole lot—scrape it up from every member of the BSC anywhere in the galaxy—you couldn't come close. Seeing as how 'BSC' really stands for 'Beggars' Succor and Care.'"

Damewood clutched his chest. "Oh, Ganny! That's cold!"

❖   ❖   ❖

Csilla Ferenc watched the departing freighter on the screen. She had no interest in the vessel itself. The receding image was just something to look at—and wasn't even real any longer, at this distance. The software used by Balcescu Station's astrogation control substituted a stylized symbol for an actual image of a ship when it was too far away to be seen clearly with optical equipment.

She was just brooding. The departure of the *Hali Soul*—no, *Sowle*—had gone with even less notice than a tramp freighter normally would have gotten. That was because traffic through Balcescu had risen sharply over the past few weeks.

What bothered Ferenc wasn't the heavy workload, so much. She didn't enjoy it, but the overtime pay was nice. No, what bothered her was that she didn't know the reason for the increase in traffic.

Sure, the extra ships that came through were all from Mesa and had impeccable papers. (Which were electronic, not molecular, of course; but the old term was still used by most traffic control services.) But maybe that was the problem. Their documentation was *too* good, in a way. In Ferenc's experience, the documentation for real shipping concerns got frayed at the edges after a while.

Not that of this additional traffic, though. Their credentials and bona fides and bills of lading looked like they'd just come out of the virtual presses at the headquarters of Manpower, the Jessyk Combine, Axelrod Transstellar, and Technodyne.

They had serious backing behind them, too. Any questions beyond the routine ones got stonewalled—and both times she'd tried to push a little, Csilla had gotten slapped down by her superiors.

Slapped down hard and fast.

It was the speed of the reprimands that had struck her the most. The management of Balcescu were rude bastards and had been as long as Ferenc had been at the station. Reprimands were always a lot harsher than they should have been.

But they never came all that quickly. The station's bosses were as lazy as they were nasty. Usually, you'd find out a tick had been placed in your records a week or two—sometimes a month or two—after the incident that triggered it.

Not now. Those two reprimands had been given to her within hours. Within less than an hour, in the case of the second one.

And all she'd asked for was identification for the three individuals listed as "supercargo; special assignments"! Normally, she would have gotten chewed out if she *hadn't* insisted on an explanation.

Something was going on. And what bothered Ferenc was that the explanation that kept coming to her made her profoundly uneasy.

At that moment, as it happened, the person sitting at the control station next to her voiced her own worries.

"Csilla, do you think there's really anything to all the Mantie hollering about a 'secret conspiracy' behind Manpower?"

Ferenc glanced around the control room quickly. The only other person within hearing range was András Kocsis, and he wasn't paying any attention because he was in the middle of directing an incoming freighter.

She wasn't worried about András anyway. He was just a working stiff like them.

Reassured, she turned to the man who'd asked

the question, Béla Harsányi. "Are you *trying* to get into trouble?"

Béla looked uncomfortable—but stubborn. "Come on, Csilla. You've got to have been wondering about it yourself." He motioned toward his own control screen. "I mean, look at the traffic we've been getting. Some of these ships we've never seen at all before, and many of the ones we have are acting...You know. Weird."

Weird. Depending on how you looked at it, that was either discretion or circumlocution. In plain language, what Harsányi meant was that the crews of the slave ships—some of them, anyway—hadn't been behaving in their usual manner when they came into the station on what was still called "shore leave."

First off, a lot fewer of them took shore leave than normal.

Second, and more tellingly, they hadn't been behaving like arrogant assholes when they did. They'd seemed a little subdued, actually—as if they knew something themselves that was making them a little nervous.

She kept her hair in a braid when she was on duty. That was an old habit from her days on a station whose artificial gravity had been erratic. One experience with being caught trying to follow traffic with her long hair flying all over and impeding her vision had been enough.

She might have given up the habit after she got to Balcescu, since there was no danger at all that *this* station was going to suffer from the same problem. Balcescu Station wasn't a flea-bitten third rate transfer point in the sticks, it was Manpower's principal depot in this whole star region. But by then she'd found that being able to fiddle with the braid was a way of calming herself down when she got a little agitated.

She was fiddling with it now. "I don't know, Béla. Yeah, sure, I've wondered myself. But..."

She let go of the braid and shrugged. "First, we'll probably never know. And second, let's *hope* we never know because the only way I can see we'd find out..."

She decided to let the sentence die a natural death. But Harsányi's lips peeled back, revealing clenched teeth.

"Yeah, right," he said. "The only way we'll find out is if the Manties decide to prove it—in which case we're dead meat anyway."

That was...something of an exaggeration, Csilla thought. Balcescu Station wasn't anywhere near the most likely avenues of approach the Mantie fleet would take if it decided to strike at Mesa. But it couldn't be ruled out.

Not with the Manties. Unlike the great majority of the population of Mesa—not to mention the morons in the Solarian League—Ferenc and Harsányi knew the realities of interstellar warfare.

Some of those realities, anyway. Enough to know that the Manties, if they decided to be, could be the scariest people in the universe for people like her and Béla.

First, the Manties hated slavers—and she and Béla were part and parcel of the slave trade even if they didn't have any personal contact with slaves themselves. Second, Csilla had just celebrated her fortieth birthday—and the Manties had been at war for more than half her lifespan. Third, going by the record, they were awfully damn good at it.

"Oh, I wouldn't go *that* far," Csilla said. "Dead meat's a little extreme, don't you think?"

But by the time she finished the sentence, she was back to fiddling with her braid.

❖   ❖   ❖

Elsewhere in Balcescu Station, in a much fancier work area, someone else was fretting over the same issue. That was the station's CO, Zoltan Somogyi, Csilla Ferenc's ultimate boss in the depot and the originator of the two reprimands that she was still smarting from.

Somogyi himself had forgotten about the reprimands—and done so within hours. He hadn't issued them because he was worried about Csilla Ferenc. He barely knew the woman. She worked for him but he was the top manager of the Station. So did almost eight hundred other people.

No, he'd issued those reprimands, along with more than a dozen similar ones, because he'd been told in no uncertain terms by people he knew even less well than he did Ferenc that they would tolerate no interference with what they were doing—about which he knew even less. The one thing—the only thing, really—he did know about the people who'd given him those instructions was that their authority was paramount. Within Manpower, Inc., as well as . . .

Beyond it. How far beyond it he didn't know. And that was what was causing him to lose sleep.

People like Ferenc and Harsányi knew nothing of the Mesan Alignment, not even of its existence. So far as they knew, they were simply employees of one of the giant corporations that effectively ruled their home planet. And if the work that corporation did was unsavory in the eyes of much of the human race, they were largely indifferent to the matter—just as, in ages past, men who went into the bowels of a planet to dig out its mineral wealth didn't think much about the fact that many people thought the work they did was crude, dirty and beneath their own dignity.

In truth, Zoltan Somogyi didn't know much more about the Mesan Alignment than his employees. The difference was that he knew it *did exist* although he thought it was nothing more than an organization dedicated to the secret uplift of the Mesan genome. He had hopes he might eventually be asked to join, in fact.

But there were less benign forces in Mesan society, who were even more secretive and a lot more dangerous. Somogyi was highly placed enough to have realized years before that someone, somewhere, was pulling the strings.

Who they were . . . he didn't know, although he suspected they were Manpower's innermost circle.

What their goals were . . . he didn't know.

What their plans were for *him* . . . he didn't know that, either.

What worried him was that he thought such plans probably existed. And whatever they were, probably weren't going to be good for him. Not because those mysterious hidden powers bore any animosity toward him but simply because he was beneath their notice.

When a behemoth makes plans to go somewhere, do those plans take into consideration the small and fragile creatures that might get underfoot along the way?

CHAPTER 28

"Well, we're back." Berry started toward Hugh but then stopped and gave him a wary look. "Any problems while we were gone?"

Hugh marked the place and set down his tablet on a side table next to the very comfortable-looking armchair he was sitting in. "Other than two insurrections—both suppressed with great bloodshed—three attempted coups d'état—you'll find the heads of the ringleaders on pikes lining Vesey Boulevard—and one disgruntled constitutional fetishist who exiled himself rather than submit to royal tyranny, no. There were no problems. I don't count the six plays, three street performances, eighteen vids and two old-fashioned pamphlets which denounced the brutal rule of the Usurper Arai. Speaking of which—"

A large forefinger swept across the group entering the salon behind Berry. "You're all under arrest. It turns out I have a long-suppressed megalomaniacal personality. Who knew?"

Berry gave him a look that combined exasperation and (some) amusement, then proceeded to squelch the usurper's scheme by the simple expedient of sitting on his lap, wrapping her arm around his neck and giving him a kiss.

Meanwhile, Jeremy took a seat facing Hugh while Princess Ruth and Web Du Havel sat on a couch at right angles to him. "Out of idle curiosity," asked Ruth, "how much of that has any truth at all to it?"

Hugh extricated himself from the royal embrace. "There *were* a couple of vids made. One of them was a spoof, the other was . . . deranged. And there really was a guy who went into exile in protest against what he called constitutional irregularities. He posted a long list of them on a public web site. It's still up, if you're curious. It's called 'The Road to Serfdom.'"

"Constitutional irregularities, it is?" Du Havel shook his head. "Interesting concept—given that Torch hasn't yet adopted a formal constitution."

"Yup. He listed that as Irregularity Number One."

Ruth frowned. "Now that I think about it, why *haven't* we adopted a constitution?"

Jeremy nodded in the direction of Du Havel. "That's the Prime Minister's doing. He's been stalling the matter with all his legendary skill and cunning. I'd accuse him of plotting against the nation except that I agree with him. The last thing we need to be doing right now is wasting time and energy wrangling over the provisions of a formal constitution."

Ruth looked at Du Havel. "Can you explain your reasoning? I'm not necessarily quarreling with you, but it seems . . . I don't know. Kind of"—she chuckled—"well. Irregular."

"I think we'd do a lot better to let things shake down for a few years before we tried to put anything in writing." Du Havel made a face. "Right now is not the time. We don't have much in the way of collective experience and most of our individual citizens have even less. Slavery's not exactly a great school for learning constitutional principles."

Web started rolling up his sleeves, which was a habitual mannerism whenever he was expounding on something. "One of the keys to a good constitution is to keep it short and sweet. The great-great-granddaddy of them all, the constitution of the ancient United States of America, was less than five thousand words long. That includes what they called the 'Bill of Rights.' Part of the reason they were able to keep their constitution that short was because they'd had years of experience trying to manage their affairs with an earlier version of it that proved to have a lot of defects. In contrast, lots of constitutionally based polities have tried to rush the process. Sometimes it works, but usually what results are hideously massive and tortuous documents that please nobody except lawyers. I'd just as soon avoid that."

"But what—" Ruth was interrupted by a chime. That came from a large screen on the wall behind her which was currently depicting a pastoral scene but doubled as the salon's com unit.

"Are we expecting to hear from anyone?" Berry asked.

Hugh scratched his chin. "Well...not exactly 'expecting.' But I'm pretty sure that'll be either Yuri Radamacher or Sharon Justice. Or both, more likely."

Berry's eyebrows went up. "They're here? On Torch?"

"Got here two days ago."

"Well, accept the call, then."

Hugh pressed the acceptance key built into the side table and the big screen came to life.

Sure enough, it was Radamacher and Justice. The high commissioner had presented his credentials to Queen Berry and Prime Minister Du Havel a couple of weeks ago. But that had been in the course of a very short visit he'd made to Torch shortly after he reached his new post. He'd spent most of his time on Erewhon.

"Hello, Your Mousety," said Radamacher.

"I love that title," Berry said, beaming.

Ruth rolled her eyes. "Ramses and Nebuchadnezzar are spinning in their graves."

Radamacher smiled and continued. "We'd like to speak to you, please."

Berry looked around. "Uh...which one of us? Or two or three?"

"All of you. Or at least, all of you that I can see in the screen. To enumerate, in addition to yourself, that would be Princess Ruth, Prime Minister Du Havel, Secretary of War Jeremy X and Secretary of the Posterior Arai."

Berry burst into laughter. "Did you really use that title?"

Hugh shrugged. "It was your idea, remember? What the hell, I thought it was sort of charming—and it helped keep tempers from rising since most people understood that my so-called 'post' was ad hoc and jury-rigged."

While he'd been talking, Berry had pressed the key which indicated to the security guards outside that the callers were to be allowed into the royal presence.

A short time later, the door opened and the two Havenites came in. Berry indicated the unoccupied couch to her left that faced Ruth and Web. The four pieces of furniture in the center of the room—two couches and two large armchairs—formed an oblong around a low and large table.

"Have a seat," she said. "What's on your mind?"

After Radamacher and Justice sat down, the high commissioner etc. etc. nodded toward his companion. "Sharon has some information she thinks we should share with you. Officially, I'm not here, by the way."

Web got up and moved toward a side table. "Something to drink? Tea? Coffee? Khava juice?"

Yuri peered suspiciously at a beaker filled with a thick-looking liquid colored somewhere between amber and terra cotta. "What's khava juice? And what does it taste like?"

"It's made from khava—that's a root, apparently, not a fruit—grown on Kapteyn 2. I have no idea what it tastes like. And I'm not about to find out, either."

Jeremy chuckled. "That's our Prime Minister. Set in his ways. Conservative through and through." Which was perhaps an odd way to describe the head of government of a nation created by a slave revolt—but the former leader of the Audubon Ballroom had his own way of looking at things.

"As for what it tastes like," Jeremy continued, "it tastes crappy. I mean, *look* at the stuff."

"Coffee, please," said Sharon.

"Unofficially, me too," said Yuri.

"Why are you not official?" asked Ruth. She waved her hand. "That's an unofficial question, of course."

"The usual. Plausible deniability. Whoever came up with that term, incidentally? Whoever she or he is, they've got to be burning in hell somewhere."

"Freezing, more like," said Hugh. "I'm willing to bet the guilty party is spending eternity in Malebolge, Dante's eighth level of hell. That's the level assigned to hypocrites, grafters, counterfeiters and counselors of fraud. As for who it was, the swindle goes back so far it's impossible to say for sure. My money's on Octavian."

"Who's Octavian?" asked Berry.

"Octavian De Brassieres," said Ruth. "Makes sense. He was the Legislaturalist who proposed the 'unfit for office' provision in Haven's new constitution back in the 1850s."

Hugh winced slightly, but said nothing. Ruth wasn't looking his way in any event, since she was still focused on Radamacher.

For his part, Yuri was smiling, but the source of his amusement might have been the general situation. "The reason I'm not official is because the government of Haven has, as yet, taken no position on the developments which Sharon is about to explain. For that matter, the government of Haven does not, as yet, officially know anything at all about these developments."

"And unofficially?"

"I'm sure Cachat has figured it out by now. Who he's told, though . . ." He waggled his hand. "Anton Zilwicki and Kevin Usher, almost certainly, and if so that means President Pritchart probably knows and so does the Countess of the Tor—and if she knows, she's very likely to have passed the information on to Empress Elizabeth."

Ruth frowned. "Everyone who matters, in other words. So why bother with the pretense?" She shook her head. "Never mind. Silly question. So what are these developments?"

Web came back with two cups of coffee and handed them to Sharon and Yuri. "I'm now filled with curiosity myself."

Sharon set down the cup without tasting it. "In a nutshell, Erewhon and Maya Sector have formed an alliance. Whether it's informal or formal, I don't know. Yet. But regardless, it's a real alliance. The heart of it so far is that Erewhon is serving Maya as its armaments developer and manufacturer."

She paused to pick up the coffee cup and blow on it, which gave everyone some time to think over what she'd said.

Yuri had been blowing on his coffee all along and now took a tentative sip from the cup. Still too hot, though. He moved the cup away but didn't set it down.

"Do you know," he mused, "that just in the last two hundred T-years and just in the Republic of Haven alone—I looked it up once when I had way too much spare time on my hands—there have been eleven separate inventions to cool coffee in a cup. Well, any kind of hot liquids, I suppose. Yet not one of them has ever been commercially successful."

He tried the coffee again. Still too hot. He set it down. "Either we're all a bunch of hopeless reactionaries—which is doubtful, given the giddiness with which fashion changes—or social conventions usually trump practicality. Blowing on a cup is such a nice way to pause a discussion without being awkward about it."

"Does he always philosophize?" demanded Jeremy.

"Pretty much," said Sharon. She finally took a sip from the cup and her eyes widened. "My, that's good. Sumatran?"

Du Havel bestowed upon her the approving look

of one connoisseur encountering another. "Allowing for some evolution, yes. The coffee beans are actually grown on Gascogne, one of the moons of a giant gas planet near Mendelschoen. But the strain originates from Terra's Indonesia."

Ruth was looking impatient. Her knowledge of coffee extended far enough to distinguish it from tea and no farther. "What sort of manufacturing?" she asked.

"Naval, mostly. Everything from SDs on down."

That caused everyone to sit back a little. "They're building *superdreadnoughts* for Maya?" asked Hugh.

"How many?" asked Ruth.

"At least a dozen. As well as a lot of lighter warships. You name it, the Erewhonese are building them. Battlecruisers—with pod capability. Multidrive missiles for the arsenal ships that Rozsak used so effectively in the Battle of Torch. Cruisers. Destroyers. No CLACs, so far I've been able to determine. Not yet, anyway."

Du Havel rubbed the top of his head. "Good Lord. I knew they were developing good relations, but I had no idea it had progressed *that* far."

"Who's building the ships?" asked Hugh. "Specifically, I mean. And how long has this been going on?"

"The work's mostly being done by the Carlucci Group. Maybe all of it, although they're bound to have subcontracted a lot. As for how long . . . I'm not sure. At least two years, though."

"And how soon will the ships start being commissioned?" That came from Jeremy.

"For the wallers, probably another two years. But they'll have functioning pod battlecruisers within a year. As for cruisers and destroyers . . . I can't swear to it, but I think those have already entered Mayan service. I'm almost certain that Rozsak has already been able to replace everything he lost at the Battle of Torch." She smiled at Berry. "Giving you the *Spartacus* and the other ships they captured at that battle was generous, no question about it. But Rozsak knew he'd be making up the loss very quickly."

"*And* with ships that didn't pose the same problems with public relations," said Jeremy. He grunted. "I'm still appreciative of the gesture."

Web finished with his scalp-rubbing. "We all are—but it now goes way beyond being appreciative." He gave Sharon and Yuri a keen look. "Why are you telling us this—when you know perfectly good and well the end result will be to pull us away from Haven?"

"Oh, I wouldn't put it that way," said Yuri. The coffee had cooled enough for him to slurp from it, cheerfully and noisily. "Here's the way I look at things—me and Sharon both. Given what happened to Filareta's fleet at Manticore, we're bound to see a full-scale war erupting between the Solarian League and the Manties—with us now allied to them. That alliance is shaky enough—well, maybe not 'shaky' but certainly full of problems and pitfalls—that both Haven and the Star Empire are going to be preoccupied with their own situations for a while." He paused to slurp from his cup again.

Sharon picked up the train of thought smoothly. "So what does that mean for Torch? Things could get pretty dicey—*unless* you solidify your relations with other protectors. Ones who are nearby, like Erewhon and Maya."

"And ones who, like Maya, have a proven and tested track record when it comes to protecting Torch," said Hugh. "But I'd still like to know why you initiated this."

Sharon set down the cup, leaned back, and crossed her arms over her chest. "It seems like the right thing to do. Speed up a process that's inevitable anyway—and one that causes Haven no harm at all. Nor the Manties, for that matter, although"—she gave Ruth a quick, semi-apologetic little tilt of the head—"that's not my main concern."

Hugh nodded. "Yeah, I get that. But..." He got an odd smile on his face. "In my experience—even with Beowulfers—envoys extraordinary with special sauce etc. etc. are not famous for their bold initiatives."

Yuri had been about to finish his coffee. Now, he paused, looking a bit disconcerted. "Well..."

"Face it, Yuri," said Sharon. "Cachat's rubbing off on you."

"Oh, God help me."

CHAPTER 29

Andrew looked around the big room on the ground floor of the building they'd just purchased. "Well, this is going to take a fair amount of work. If you're planning to set up a boutique down here, that is. How about we change the plan to running a day care center? Then all we have to do is coat the walls and put some sort of padding on the floor. As long as they're bright colors, we're fine. You know what kids are like."

Steph ignored him. She and Andrew had been a couple for less than a year, but that was enough time for her to figure out that he was the sort of person who needed to maintain a patina of silly jabber in order to steady his nerves. It could be irritating, but as faults went she could live with it easily enough. Her daughter Nancy's father had been a drunk who got violent at times.

Well, with her, only once. There were advantages to being a professional cook. Knives—big knives—were readily at hand and she was proficient in their use. She hadn't even had to cut him much. When he sobered up he contemplated the wounds and decided to search for greener pastures elsewhere. Since Nancy had only been eight months old, she had no memory of her father—which suited Steph just fine.

She'd considered running a day care center, in fact. She'd even gone so far as to broach the idea to Anton and Victor. But after discussing the matter, they'd all agreed that the risks outweighed the benefits.

The problem with kids was that they tended to have parents. And while you could explain away the comings and goings of strange people easily enough to four- and five-year-olds, that was a lot harder to do with adults. All the more so when the adults in question would initially be a bit wary of the people running a new day care center and would be watching them closely.

No, better to stick with the boutique plan. No one would think anything of people entering and leaving such a shop, especially if they were women.

All of which Andrew knew perfectly well since he'd been part of the discussion. It was odd, really, how a man who was almost astonishingly resourceful in so many ways could have such childish habits. But Steph had long since come to terms with the fact that the universe was an imperfect place. Here was just further proof—and by no means the worst she'd ever encountered. Far from it.

"It's mostly just putting up shelves," she said. "And lots of racks, of course, but we can buy those."

With the funds at their disposal, they could have easily afforded to pay contractors to do all the work of putting up the shelving as well. But from the viewpoint of spies—that was a neutral way of saying *professional paranoia*—the term "outside contractors" was synonymous with "potential informants."

There was other construction they'd be doing beyond putting up shelves, after all. They'd also be creating a hiding place for people who needed to get out of sight of the authorities. To make such a hidey-hole effective they'd need more than just clever construction, too. They'd need to include scrambling and shielding equipment, some of which was fairly bulky. There would be no way to keep all that secret with contractors trooping in and out of the building.

So, Andrew would have to do all of it, with whatever (none-too-expert) help Steph could give him. But she wasn't worried about it. This was the same man, after all, who'd jury-rigged a starship's hyper generator.

✧   ✧   ✧

The thing about Mesa's capital city of Mendel that struck Thandi the most, as she maneuvered the air lorry along the crowded primary traffic lane, was how wealthy even the poorest neighborhoods were. To be sure, compared to the districts inhabited by Mesa's full citizens, the seccy quarters were rundown—and very badly so, in some areas. They were more crowded, more cramped, much dirtier and showed signs of disrepair and even outright decay almost anywhere you looked.

Still, compared to her home planet of Ndebele and most worlds of the Verge, the seccies lived in relative luxury. Leaving aside buildings which were completely abandoned, everyone had power and climate control. The quarters might be overcrowded by Mesan standards but they were nothing like the teeming hovels she'd seen on many worlds—or the slum in which she'd grown up herself, for that matter.

It was an ancient pattern, she knew. The degree to which people were dissatisfied by their lot in life was determined by their relative position in a given society, not by some sort of absolute and external measure. From time immemorial, reactionaries had pointed out (quite correctly) that the less privileged in their own societies were veritable Midases compared to paleolithic hunters and gatherers. Never understanding—mostly because they didn't want to understand—that such comparisons were pointless.

What mattered to a seccy mother tending her sick child was not that children in ancient times or on some far-off Verge worlds often died in infancy—and she should damn well be grateful that there was little chance her own child would actually perish. No, what mattered was that if she were a full citizen she'd be able to give her child the best possible medical care instead of the very sub-standard care she could actually afford.

Even knowing all that, Thandi still found the situation a little disorienting. Subconsciously, she'd been expecting to encounter conditions in Mesa's seccy quarters that were similar to those she'd grown up in.

As she made her way through the canyonlike depths of the stacked traffic lanes between the tenement towers, though, Thandi began to realize that the differences were greater than they'd initially seemed—not just the differences with the well-to-do citizen quarters but even with those of her native Ndebele.

Victor and Anton had explained the history to her, and now she was seeing it for herself. The seccy districts of Mesa, unlike the hovels on Ndebele or many other Verge worlds, were built along recognizably modern principles. That meant building up, using the benefits of counter-grav, rather than sprawling outward.

The advantages to that sort of hyperurban planning were manifold. High density populations had a much smaller ecological footprint than ones which sprawled into huge suburbs and exurbs. They were much more energy efficient, they were more economically productive, they invariably had a higher average educational level—the list went on and on.

But Mesa's seccy districts had been built on the cheap, so to speak. The residential towers had almost all been built long after the initial colonization period and were something of an afterthought. And they'd been intended from the outset to warehouse the manumitted slaves who were growing in numbers that hadn't originally been anticipated, which explained quite a bit about *how* they'd been built.

Because they were intended for poor folks—and for people in whom the full citizens of Mesa did not want to encourage any pretenses to equality—they were deliberately designed to be far more utilitarian and to have a generally second- or third-class quality of life. At the time they were initially constructed, they had decent amenities (heat, air conditioning, grav shafts, etc.), but they were barebones. They were also shorter—never more than three hundred stories tall, less than half the height of most "proper" residential towers. That was to insure that anyone living in them would be looking up at the "high castle" of their genetic and legal betters—in essence, subject to what you might call residential sumptuary laws.

The seccy districts had originally been designed to form a widely separated "ring ghetto" around the central portion of Mendel, with its green belts, parks, etc. Over the centuries, though, the inner core of Mendel had slowly expanded outward from its original size and enveloped most of the original seccy towers. Those had been demolished and replaced with "proper" towers, pushing the ghetto farther and farther out even as the number of seccies living in it got higher and higher.

Worse, from the seccies' viewpoint, since the initial colonization the construction of those residential towers had been handed over to the local branch of one of the transstellars, Maidenstone Enterprises of Mesa. MEM hadn't wasted a whole lot of time and effort on meeting code standards. To the credit of the Mendel city government, it had at least tried to see to it that code was observed at the time of construction, but this was no longer something which was put out for bids. Maidenstone's construction had become increasingly slipshod, with serious maintenance issues which the slumlords who owned the towers didn't work very hard to put right. Accordingly, the population density per square kilometer was far lower than in the "good parts" of Mendel, but the population density per building was much higher, with people packed into very restricted space.

The population of Mendel's seccy areas was somewhere between ten and twelve million people. (The authorities made no attempt to take a rigorously accurate census. Why bother? Seccies couldn't vote.) All told it covered a little under two hundred square kilometers—but a good third of that space was taken up by industrial sections and commercial spokes. Those, while functional and modern, were considered eyesores which the full citizens didn't want in their landscaped parts of the city. Having them in the seccy areas made sense anyway because seccies provided the non-slave labor force. The managers and supervisors, at least above the level of shop foremen, were almost always full citizens.

The commercial spokes with their industrial nodes also served the purpose of dividing the seccy ghetto into distinct districts. The spokes and nodes were well lit and patrolled by private security forces as well as the city's own police, which both protected the facilities they held and discouraged seccies from taking "shortcuts" across them anywhere except at the duly authorized transit points. In effect, they served as social breakwaters, helping to prevent the seccies from organizing on a city-wide scale.

These were modern industries, though, based on modern technology. They did not produce much in the way of pollution and environmental contamination, so they had little impact on the citizenry itself. But for the seccies and slaves working in those industries and commercial zones, they were still bleak, hard areas. Hectare after hectare of stark manufacturing facilities, transportation systems—and pavement everywhere else. The trees and shrubs that adorned the citizen districts were not to be found here. The most you'd see in the way of gardens were flowerboxes suspended from the windows of cheap restaurants and diners catering to the seccy workforce.

It wasn't the smoky hell of a pre-Diaspora industrial slum, and the poverty wasn't as bad as it was on many Verge worlds. There were even a few parks, zoos and museums scattered about. But the most striking aspect of the seccy ghetto, to Thandi, was the apparent absence of law. More precisely, the absence of official authority. That had not been true on Ndebele.

Granted, the law had been corrupt and often brutal. But it had still been present.

Here . . .

True enough, the technical features seemed to be under official control—such things as traffic governors and boundaries, which were readily visible, and she presumed such things as waste disposal and power distribution, which were not. Those were the sort of things that *had* to be regulated or chaos would result and would inevitably spread to the citizen areas.

But beyond such matters, Mesa's powers-that-be didn't seem to care much how the seccies regulated their own affairs. After she'd left Zilwicki's ship with the load she was carrying and passed through the starport's entry and customs gate, she'd seen only one police vehicle—and that had been within the first kilometer of travel. Shortly thereafter she'd entered the seccy districts and from that time since, so far as she could tell, there was no police presence at all.

On Ndebele, in contrast, police had been visible everywhere. Granted, the term "police" was something of a misnomer since they'd behaved much more like an occupying army. They often ignored crimes committed against the poor and powerless—and when they didn't, invariably responded slowly—but they were nonetheless an ever-present reality.

Here . . . nothing. Thandi felt something almost like relief as she headed down the access ramp into the labyrinth of underground service ways and away from the aerial traffic lanes between the dreary canyons of seccy residential towers.

She knew what she was encountering, because Victor had described it to her. She now realized, though, that on some level she simply hadn't believed him. After all, how can you run a huge city without law enforcement? This side of the pearly gates of heaven, at least, that was simply impossible.

Of course, there *was* law enforcement—it just wasn't the formal law, and the enforcers were more or less self-appointed. When it came to this issue, at least, the seccy quarters of Mesa were as close as humanity had ever gotten to untrammeled libertarianism. And if that state of affairs was impossible to distinguish from one in which crime lords ran the show, so much the worse for libertarianism.

Being fair—so Victor had told her, anyway—in some of the seccy districts the crime bosses probably did a better job of maintaining order and dispensing justice than the authorities would. Certainly Mesan authorities. Disorder and dissatisfaction were bad for business, after all, including illegal businesses. And the cut that the crime bosses took from every legitimate business was probably no worse than taxes would have been.

More than legal scholars liked to admit, the concept of a protection racket was often hard to distinguish on the ground floor from what people got from legal authorities. To a crime boss, you turned over a portion of the proceeds of your business or profession and in return you got protection, stability, stable supplies and prices—even, in the best run areas, a measure of social welfare. To a legitimate government, you turned over a portion of the proceeds of your business and profession and in return you got...

About the same results. Superior results, to be sure, in well-run societies like Beowulf and Manticore—even much superior ones. But in many of the Verge

worlds—certainly on Thandi's native Mfecane planets—
most people would have been better off with a well-
run crime syndicate in charge than the "legitimate"
thugs and thieves they actually got.

The deeper and ultimately insoluble problem was
that even in the best-run seccy quarters, the people
who really ran things had no formally recognized
claim to that position.

"Authority" was a term that the human race had
seen abused more times than anyone could remember, but it was still not just a name. The term meant
legitimate power, not just power as such. And what
defined legitimacy was that the power so held was
formally recognized and accepted by everyone as
rightfully obtained and established.

There was no such formal legitimacy in the seccy
quarters, not even the best-run ones. True, there was
an approximation. Each district had what amounted
to an informal council of the crime bosses, overseen
by the most powerful of them. In Neue Rostock, that
top boss was Jurgen Dusek. All of the major crime
bosses maintained contact with each other through
yet another informal council. Membership in that
council was tantamount to being recognized as one
of the top circle.

The council preferred to keep conflicts under control
and as a rule, managed to do so. But should one of the
great crime lords die or simply lose their grip, with no
clear line of succession, struggle and conflict invariably
erupted. And not struggle waged by established legal
norms kept within tightly defined boundaries, either.
What usually resulted was warfare. Sometimes under the
surface, sometimes out in the open. Sometimes resolved

by a few killings, sometimes by slaughter. Sometimes of short duration, sometimes seeming to be endless.

If Neue Rostock embodied one extreme, Lower Radomsko embodied the other. Half a century earlier, the crime boss who'd controlled the district had been assassinated by a rival, who'd in turn been assassinated within two hours by another rival, who'd then been assassinated less than a day later by yet another rival—who'd died herself the next day from wounds incurred in the fighting.

Thereafter, the district had dissolved into anarchy, from which it had still not recovered. The neighboring bosses didn't like the chaos, but they preferred it to the risk of letting another boss gain even more influence and power in the region. Lower Radomsko was a byword in Mesa's seccy areas for what happened if you didn't have a capable and tough boss running the show. The district remained the most violent area on Mesa—and the poorest.

❖   ❖   ❖

She was now in the lowest traffic lane in a commercial thoroughfare, as she'd been since she descended the access ramp. Subterranean commercial thoroughfares were normal in cities the size of Mendel. The population density that resulted from modern urban construction, with its emphasis on counter-grav-supported towers, had many advantages from an economic and ecological standpoint. But it did pose huge challenges for traffic. One of the standard measures was to assign commercial traffic to special underground avenues and only allow them to join above-ground air traffic when they were ready to make a delivery—and, as much as possible, to situate the delivery entrances below the surface as well.

The thoroughfare she was in had four vertical lanes and she was in the bottom one. Another lorry suddenly emerged from an intersecting feeder lane and turned sharply, going into a sudden descent right above her. Her lorry's computer program reacted by doing an emergency landing and coming to a stop, just centimeters above the ground surface.

"Bastards," she muttered. The pejorative wasn't aimed at the other driver so much as it was at the people responsible for the situation in general. Normally, traffic control programs would have automatically prevented such an occurrence by changing the velocities or lane levels of the two vehicles as needed. She'd already noticed, however, that the control programs had seemed a little ragged for the past half-kilometer or so.

Another lorry came out of the same feeder lane, swerved into the lane set aside for traffic going the other way—luckily there was no one there—and then cut directly across in front of her. The lorry came to a stop, also at ground level, forming the crossbar of a T with Thandi's.

She glanced at the rearview screen. Not to her surprise, a third lorry had come up from behind and blocked her from going backward.

She didn't bother checking the sides of her vehicle. She was too close to the wall on her right and the vehicles ahead and behind were so close that she didn't have room to maneuver the lorry around them to the left. Instead—perhaps belatedly—she checked her position on the location screen. It took a moment to interpret what she was seeing, since the locator program didn't recognize or use the unofficial names for Mendel's seccy quarters.

Sure enough. She'd entered Lower Radomsko. Just a corner of it, which the traffic program would have taken her through in a couple of minutes. But that had been enough, it seemed.

Most likely, someone in traffic control had been bribed to steer her this way. Thandi's air lorry had been bought, not rented or leased, but in the short time since they'd arrived on Mesa she hadn't had time to fix a logo to the vehicle. She had the logo ready to be applied, even—"Komlanc Intermodal Transport, Ltd."—but it was sitting in the cargo hold along with the goods she was hauling to Steph Turner's boutique-to-be.

The absence of identification on the lorry probably didn't matter, though. A quick check, which anyone working in traffic control could have been able to do, would have turned up the fact that Komlanc Intermodal wasn't a registered freight hauler. It was a so-called "gypsy outfit"—very common in Mesa's seccy areas, but without any sort of official legitimacy. Or, more to the point, official sanction and protection.

In most seccy districts, that wouldn't have been a problem. The "worst" that would happen was that representatives of a local crime boss would have shown up soon enough and arrangements would have been made in a reasonably amicable manner. Bribes going one way; informal sanction and protection the other—which was exactly what Victor had figured on doing anyway. He'd been planning all along to infiltrate himself into the seccy areas by using the existing criminal networks.

But this was Lower Radomsko, not one of the well-run districts like Neue Rostock or Ayacucho. Someone was just planning to hijack the lorry. And, most likely, kill her in the process.

People were starting to emerge from the vehicles ahead of and behind her. Two men from the front vehicle; a man and a woman from the rear one. All of them except the woman were armed with pistols. She was carrying a small packet that probably contained explosives.

"You *stupid* bastards," she muttered, then keyed a signal on her com.

◇ ◇ ◇

Victor was four blocks away and five levels up when he got the signal. He immediately pushed the button that instructed his special program to turn control of the vehicle over to him. More precisely, that allowed him to take control of the vehicle without that fact being broadcast to a traffic control center. The air car slipped out of the level he was in, went down to the uppermost of the commercial levels and headed toward Thandi's location just behind a lorry.

Unless the lorry driver was completely inattentive he'd spot Victor in his rear viewer. With a commercial vehicle under automatic control, it was possible he wouldn't be paying attention, but that wasn't something to be counted on. It wouldn't matter anyway since Victor would be leaving his vicinity in another block and a half. The odds that a lorry driver in this area—he was almost certainly a seccy himself—would report a fleeting traffic violation to the police when he wasn't personally affected were almost nil.

The real risk was that the program that controlled traffic in the area would immediately spot the violation—two violations; in fact: entering a commercial lane with a private vehicle and taking personal control of the vehicle in an area designated for automatic traffic—and alert the authorities. But the program Victor had used to override the automatic controls had been designed by Anton, whose cybernetic skills vastly exceeded those of whoever designed the traffic program. It would fool the traffic controller into thinking Victor was still under automatic guidance. For all practical purposes, Victor had simply vanished from the grid—except the grid thought he was still there.

Anton had also given them all scrambling programs for their coms which would shield their conversations from any but the most high-powered decryption efforts. Such efforts could only be done by Mesan security agencies and *would* only be done if they were directly suspicious—in which case, they'd almost certainly be doomed anyway so there was no point worrying about it.

Thandi gave him a quick sketch of the situation. *"Biggest problem is with the lorry overhead,"* she concluded. *"There's no movement from there at all."*

"I'll handle that," Victor said. "You just deal with the ones coming at you. Speaking of which, survivors would be handy."

"Yana was right. You're no fun at all."

✧   ✧   ✧

Yana entered the central chamber of the *Brixton's Comet.* The chamber had an official title which she didn't remember. She just called it "the salon."

Anton called it "Xanadu." When she asked, he'd refused to explain what the term meant on the grounds that it would be too embarrassing. But she didn't believe him. Zilwicki was about as prone to embarrassment as a lava flow.

Anton was where he almost always was when awake—
at the computer terminal he'd set up in a corner of the
salon. Using the term "corner" loosely, since the chamber
bore only a vague resemblance to anything rectilinear.
So far as Yana could tell, the *Brixton's Comet* had been
designed by a lunatic. She could only hope the ship's
engines and controls were more coherent than its interior and furnishings.

She crossed the salon and went into the chamber
which Anton had set aside as her living quarters. He
called that chamber "Shangri-La." A term which he
also refused to explain on the same spurious grounds.

The bed in that chamber could have been used as
the playing field for at least four sports that Yana was
familiar with, except the footing would have been too
treacherous for any of those sports except the most
ancient one.

She came back out of the chamber, planted her
hands on her hips—which were now way too ample, in
her opinion, albeit not as grotesque as her bosom—and
gave Anton a disgusted look.

"You're not going to be any more fun than Victor
was, are you?"

CHAPTER 30

The man who seemed to be leading the four robbers was now close to the cab of the lorry. "In there!" he shouted. "Open up!" To give emphasis to the demand, he brandished the pistol in his hand as if it were a sword. What did he think *that* would accomplish?

For that matter, what did he think the pistol itself would accomplish? A military grade pulse rifle would certainly be able to fire projectiles into the cab. So would the most powerful sidearms, at least if the shots struck squarely. But the piece of crap he was wielding? It had no chance at all of doing so. This was a relatively modern cargo lorry she was driving, designed and built for heavy work, not a flimsy and lightly designed personal sport vehicle.

It was presumably because they understood that much that the female robber was carrying a sack with her. Thandi was pretty sure that sack held explosives of some kind with which they could breach the cab door. She could hole up in the cab for a bit, but not more than a minute. Less, if the female robber was proficient with explosives.

"I need a timetable," she said into the com.

"*Give me ten more seconds, if you can. If not, try for five.*"

Victor was without a doubt the most nerveless person Thandi had ever met. In times of stress, his demeanor was calm; his expression, impassive; his voice, level; even his pulse remained steady. Still he was human, not a robot. It was a sign of Victor's tension that he'd answered her in complete sentences instead of a few words. By the time he was done, three seconds had already passed. She figured it had taken her another three seconds to contemplate the matter.

One one thousand.

Two one thousand.

The lead robber pounded on the cab's door with the butt of his pistol. "Open up, goddam you!"

Prisoners be damned. Stupidity that profound carried the death penalty.

Time.

She unlatched the door and slammed it outward, using all her strength and what mass she could bring to bear while still seated. Her tremendous strength hadn't been affected at all by the body nanotech transformation and while the few extra kilos that had been added might slow her down a bit—though not much—they also added a little mass to the equation.

The edge of the door caught the robber in the middle of his face. The impact crushed his nose, shattered his jaw, knocked out most of his teeth, broke his skull and neck in the doing and sent his body flying for several meters. The corpse almost completed a back flip before it hit the surface of the street.

One of the robbers started firing almost at once. Thandi was impressed by his alertness and readiness.

His marksmanship, on the other hand, was execrable. All the darts sailed way too high, some of them not hitting the cab at all. Even the ones that did would have gone over Thandi's head.

If she'd been dumb enough to leave her head there in the first place, which of course she didn't. As soon as she felt the impact of the door on the robber she'd thrown herself out of the cab.

Out—and down. Essentially, except for the fact that her motions were controlled, she fell almost two meters.

But everything was controlled. She immediately rolled under her lorry when she hit the surface—there was just enough clearance—came to a prone firing position and started shooting with her pistol. Which *was* military grade, thank you very much.

Her marksmanship was...

Almost perfect. Not quite, though, because she fired as soon as the first target came to bear rather than waiting an extra split-second to aim more carefully. So, her first double-tapped shots went wild.

But that was only by Thandi Palane's values of "wild shots," which most people would have considered ridiculous. Instead of destroying the target's kneecap, the pulser darts severed the anterior tibial artery and shattered the upper fibula. The robber screeched, his lower leg was instantly soaked in blood, his pistol went flying and he collapsed.

That didn't stop Thandi from cursing herself. But it also didn't stop her from taking down the other two robbers. Both with knee shots. Perfect knee shots.

The second male robber screeched also; and, also, fell to the street surface. But unlike the first one she'd shot, this robber held on to his pistol. Thandi took care of that problem with a shot that disarmed him. It might be better to say, dis-handed him. The habit of double-tapping when she fired was too deeply ingrained to control in combat conditions. And what two pulser darts fired from a military-grade handgun will do to a human hand, with its nineteen bones and multitude of tendons, nerves and blood vessels, doesn't bear thinking about.

The female robber just stared at her, mouth agape. She remained standing, too. Thandi thought she didn't realize what had happened to her, since it had all happened so quickly.

For a moment, she was tempted to put an end to the woman's confusion, either by shooting out her other knee or putting an end to her existence altogether. But that seemed excessive, since the woman wasn't holding any weapon except the packet of explosives—which she'd obviously not armed yet. Besides, Victor wanted prisoners.

So she just rolled out from under the lorry and sprang upright. Pointing to the woman's shattered knee with her pistol, she said: "Fall down, you dimwit."

The woman, her mouth still gaping, looked down at her knee. Her lower leg was completely blood-soaked by now.

"You fucking bitch!" she screeched.

Then she finally collapsed. The explosive packet fell on the street surface a meter away from her.

Thandi strode over and kicked it out of reach. To be on the safe side, she kicked it far enough for it to fall into a stairwell leading down to what looked like the entrance to a warehouse. If it exploded at this point, unless the robbers had used an insanely powerful charge, the blast would have no effect except on the outer surface of the building.

Now, where was Victor? From the sounds coming from above, Thandi knew he'd been busy. But doing what, exactly?

She looked up and didn't know whether to laugh or snarl. *Cachat, you—you—*

❖   ❖   ❖

Victor's task had been trickier than Thandi's. Overcoming four people on the ground, for someone like her, was fairly straightforward. But overcoming one or more people behind the controls of an operating commercial lorry positioned in a lane that was ten meters in the air was a different proposition altogether.

Victor was a firm adherent to the KISS principle. So he initiated the encounter by ramming his own vehicle into the lorry. His vehicle was a personal air car and the target vehicle was a lorry massing at least seven times as much. But he wasn't trying to destroy the lorry—and on the flip side, he didn't care how much damage he did to his own vehicle. He had more than enough funds to buy another one—or another twenty, for that matter. All he needed was the element of surprise.

The impact was jarring, for him much more than for the occupant or occupants of the lorry. But he was expecting it and he, she or they weren't. The protective equipment in modern vehicles was more than adequate to keep everyone involved in the collision from being seriously injured. What such equipment *wasn't* designed for was to keep them from being confused and startled.

Then, when the lorry was driven a bit forward and

into the side of the adjacent building, very startled. Then, when a maniac emerged from the air car—literally, *emerged*: the crazy idiot was already on the vehicle's hood and—

Pointing a weapon at the lorry.

A magazine-fed grenade launcher, to be precise.

Profoundly startled.

There were two robbers in that lorry, one male and one female. The female was the driver and the male was in overall charge of the high-jacking.

High-jacking *attempt*, rather.

"Hey!" the driver yelled. "That son of a bitch has a—"

It really wasn't fair. The thirty-five-millimeter, pulser-driven grenade was designed to deal with much tougher targets than a commercial air lorry. It punched straight through the driver-side door and detonated in almost the exact center of the cab...whose windows (and a substantial portion of the supporting structure) blew abruptly outward. The detonation of thirty-two grams of highly advanced chemical explosive gutted the cab and shredded its occupants.

At that point, the lorry's automatic traffic program gave up the ghost. It analyzed the situation as one of complete vehicular disorder and gave a signal that caused all the lorry's machinery to shut down. Which it did instantly, except for the built-in delay procedures that allowed the counter-grav to bring the lorry down in a reasonably gentle manner and select a spot on the surface below that was reasonably unimpeded.

"Reasonably unimpeded," given the current condition of *that* street surface, was a very relative term. So, the descending lorry landed right on top of one of the robbers and crushed him to a pulp.

Fortunately, that was the robber who was already dead.

Meanwhile, Victor's own vehicle's traffic program had come to the same conclusion. With all systems shut off, the air car's counter-grav brought it down in reasonably controlled manner. On an empty patch of street, this time around.

Victor hopped off the air car. "Good work," he said.

"And where the hell are *your* survivors?" was Thandi's response.

He grinned at her. "I knew I could count on you. How many do we have?"

"Three. None of them are exactly in tip-top condition, you understand."

"As long as they can talk."

"Talk about *what*? And why did we need any survivors at all? The way I see it—"

She glanced around. Sure enough, there were at least a dozen onlookers that she could see. The subterranean commercial thoroughfares had slidewalks also, although they weren't as heavily trafficked as the ones in residential areas—and judging from the evidence, didn't work as well either. At least one of the slidewalks was completely out of order. She could see a couple of people walking on their own power.

Quite a bit of power, now. They weren't quite running, but they weren't wasting any time, either. Clearly, they didn't want to stay in this vicinity any longer than they needed to.

"Dead assholes tell no tales," she concluded.

"Tell tales to who? We're in Lower Radomsko, Thandi. Nobody gives a damn what happens here. Well, that's not quite right. A lot of people give a damn, but the only ones in position to do anything about it are whatever local gang is in charge. And those assholes, as you put it—"

He indicated the dead and wounded bodies lying about. "Are mostly right here. At least, I'm pretty sure they are. That's why I wanted prisoners. To find out."

"To find out . . . why?"

"So we could decide if my provisional change of plans makes sense, what else?"

And with that, Victor went over to the nearest wounded robber. This was the second one Thandi had shot, as it happened.

"Who's your boss?" he asked. "And where can we find him?"

The man, who'd been doing his best to staunch the blood flow from his knee with a mangled hand, looked up at Victor and snarled. "Fuck you!"

"The name of your boss," Victor repeated. He pulled out a small pistol. "And his or her present location."

His tone of voice was neutral in all respects. Calm, level, even—seemingly devoid of any emotion.

Thandi knew him very well by now. At times like this, Cachat was utterly lethal.

"Tell him," she said to the man on the street, moved by a vague humanitarian impulse. Very vague—in all likelihood, the robbers had been planning to kill her after they high-jacked the lorry. "Tell him right now."

"Fuck you too!"

Victor shot the man in the head. Then, moved over to the woman.

"Your turn. The name of your boss. His or her location. You have"—he glanced at his timepiece—"five seconds."

"Oh, for the love of God," said Thandi, moved by another humanitarian impulse. "Give the poor woman at least ten seconds. Look at her. She's in shock."

There was no expression on Victor's face, "If you insist." To the woman: "You have ten seconds. Starting..." He glanced again at the timepiece. "Now."

Thandi sighed. "Tell him. If you don't, he'll kill you and move on to the last guy and do the same. If he doesn't get the answer from him, he's dead too."

That had taken about seven seconds. Victor started counting off. "Three seconds left. Two. One."

"Stop!" the woman yelped. "For Chrissake, stop!" She held up a bloody hand and used it to wave Victor away. Tried to, rather. "You already killed the fucking boss! He's in that lorry you—you—what the hell did you do to it, anyway?"

Victor ignored the question. "How many are left in your gang, then? And where's your headquarters?"

"Left?" She choked down a hysterical laugh. "*Left?* There isn't anybody left, you—you— Whatever your name is. You already killed everybody. Except me and"—she glanced over at the other gang survivor. He'd finished jury-rigging a tourniquet with his belt and was staring at them.

"And Teddy, over there."

Victor nodded at the man. "Pleased to meet you, Teddy." Then, looked back at the woman. "And what's your name?"

She hesitated for a moment. Then, shrugged slightly. She could only use one shoulder to do so, because her right hand was still occupied keeping pressure on the wound in her knee. "I'm Calantha Patwary. People call me Callie."

"Pleased to meet you also, Callie. I'm Achmed Buenaventura and my partner here"—he pointed to Thandi with a thumb—"is Evelyn del Vecchio. Now that we've all become acquainted, how would the two of you like to come to work for me?"

He looked around the area. "Seeing as how the neighborhood obviously needs someone new in charge."

Callie and Teddy stared up at him. Callie's mouth was gaping again.

Thandi knew how she felt. She was almost gaping herself.

Victor Cachat and his damn improvisations. Otherwise known as the maniac's wild ride. And . . . here we go.

CHAPTER 31

"Does he *ever* stick to a plan?" groused Yana, after she read the message on the screen that Anton had just decrypted.

"Not that I can recall," said Anton. His tone of voice was mild. "Do keep in mind that the universe never seems to stick to a plan either. Relax, Yana. Victor is in a league of his own when it comes to improvising. He's something of a genius at it."

Yana looked dubious. "I thought the idea was to steer clear of Lower Radomsko altogether."

"Yes, it was. That's because if you muck around in that area, some gang is bound to jump you. But that's sort of a moot point now, isn't it? Just crossing one little itty-bitty corner of the place brought a gang down on us. Or I should say, down on Thandi Palane and Victor Cachat."

Yana chuckled. "Talk about shooting for the Darwin Award."

Anton nodded. "As acts of suicidal folly goes, that one's a real contender for the title. We didn't plan for it, but what's done is done. And now we've cleared a corner for ourselves in Lower Radomsko. So why not set up shop? There are some real advantages to working out of that area, you know, in addition to the drawbacks."

"Such as?"

"For starters, the Mesan authorities ignore Lower Radomsko almost entirely. Saburo told us they occasionally send in a few agents, but that's only for specific purposes. Tracking down runaway slaves, usually."

"Okay. What else?"

"None of the automatic surveillance equipment works in Lower Radomsko. I mean, *none*. The local gangs make it a point to trash anything that gets set up. According to Saburo, the Mesan security agencies don't even try any more except when some newly appointed big shot does the usual new-broom-sweeps-clean routine. Then they piddle around for a while installing surveillance devices, all of which get wrecked almost as soon as they're set up. After a few weeks, the new big shot has become a worn down and wiser big shot. That happens pretty fast in agencies working in the seccy districts. Either that, or the big shot just gets fired—sorry, transferred laterally—and a more sensible person comes in as their replacement."

"And . . . what else?"

"You have to fend off other Lower Radomsko gangs, but the bigger and stronger crime organizations in other districts leave you alone. It's just not worth it for them to deal with the headaches involved."

Having finally found what seemed like a flaw in the new plan, Yana pounced. "Yeah—exactly! We'll be wasting most of our time and energy defending ourselves against petty gangsters."

Anton leaned back in his chair and looked up at the tall woman. The expression on his face was simultaneously pitying and derisive.

"Which part of 'Thandi Palane and Victor Cachat' did you miss, Yana? The one thing we are *not* going to be doing is defending ourselves against petty gangsters."

Yana stared at him, then at the screen. Then, scratched her jaw. "I take it phrases like 'preemptive strike' and 'do unto others before they do unto you' are applicable here."

Anton smiled and looked back at the message. He indicated the last two sentences with a finger. "This is the real problem on our hands at the moment. Forget the gangsters. Wannabe gangsters, I should say."

Yana studied the sentences. *Lorry serviceable and cargo fine. But will need new personal transport.*

"What's the problem?" she asked. "That dealer he bought the air car from had plenty of others on his lot."

Anton clucked his tongue. "How does it happen that a former Scrag is such a neophyte—I'm tempted to say, a hopeless naif—when it comes to the basic principles of crime and wrongdoing?"

She grinned. "We're super soldiers, remember? Did Achilles and Hector know how to pick locks?"

Anton was a little surprised that Yana knew the Homeric legends. But only a little. You had to be careful with terms like "Scrags." Leaving aside the fact that it might be offensive to people like Yana— although it usually wasn't; ex-Scrags were anything but thin-skinned—the bigger problem was that it could lead you to underestimate them.

Yes, the descendants of the "super soldiers" of the Final War tended to be arrogant, narcissistic, often ignorant and way too full of themselves. But there was a reason for the term "super." That hadn't been mere propaganda on the part of the Ukrainian tyrants who created Yana's ancestors and set them loose on the world. Even as heavily outnumbered as they'd been, the super soldiers had come awfully close to winning the Final War in its opening phases. Of course, once the initial surprise attacks had been blunted and everyone had started opening up their own private arsenals of horrors, things had gone downhill for all concerned.

Quickly.

"You still haven't explained why Victor can't just go back to the same dealer," she said.

"Think it through, Yana. All the way through. What's Victor's new cover story going to be? He just blew off completely any chance that anyone with half a brain is going to believe he's really an investigative reporter. Didn't he?"

She rubbed her jaw again. "Um. Yeah. Unless he figures out a way to shift it all onto Thandi."

Anton shook his head. "That'd be stupid. Thandi looks like a big dumb laborer now. Victor will want to keep that disguise going. He'll let it slip that she helped him some, probably, but he'll take most of the credit for destroying that gang."

"I *still* don't see why he can't just buy himself another air car."

"How did he lose the one he had? The last thing he wants people in Lower Radomsko to think now is the truth—which is that Thandi got ambushed and he wrecked the car coming to her aid. No, no, no. That won't do at all for—"

His voice, already deep, dropped another octave.

"Achmed the Atrocious, new crime lord of Lower Radomsko. Soon to be *over*-lord of the dump. So it'll seem, anyway."

Comprehension dawned. "Okay, I get it. He *planned* to wreck the air car. From the moment he bought the damn thing."

"From the moment he landed on Mesa," Anton corrected her. "Hell, who knows? Maybe the fiend planned it before he even left the Core."

There was nothing wrong with Yana's brain. She had already thought through the logic. "Right. And would a criminal mastermind *buy* himself a new air car after deliberately wrecking the one he had? Not hardly. Not when he can sell the wreckage for parts and scrounge up another one by taking it from the next gang who gets the Victor treatment."

She shook her head. "He is a bad, bad man, Anton."

"They don't call him Achmed the Atrocious for nothing."

❖   ❖   ❖

"Are you sure, Victor?" Thandi asked. She gave the two wounded criminals slumped in the back of the lorry's cab a look that was free of anything resembling the gentler virtues. Mercy, compassion, empathy—not a trace. "That equipment is expensive to run, you know."

Victor's lips quirked. "We have plenty of money. And what better way to make sure it's working properly?"

For their part, neither Callie nor Teddy—a name Thandi thought was ridiculous for a thug—was paying them attention any longer. Once the effects of the adrenaline started fading, the pain of their injuries had surged up in full force. Just to keep them quiet, if nothing else, Victor had given them a powerful sedative. They were still conscious—sort of—but they were now half-reclined and pretty much oblivious to everything around them.

"Aren't you worried—"

"That if you go straight from here to Steph's boutique that'll draw attention to them?" Victor shook his head. "Who cares where we go? If the Mesan police even noticed this fracas at all, they'll have written it off as just another criminal incident in Lower Radomsko. The population density in the seccy quarters makes it impractical for the cops to maintain close surveillance. They just assume the crime bosses will keep a lid on things, and if they don't the authorities will start breathing fire on *them,* not the small fry."

He waved his hand at their surroundings. There were still some onlookers, but they were being very careful to keep a distance and a low profile. "The only gang controlling this area is the one we just took down. And I doubt they would have had the resources to follow you anyway. They certainly wouldn't have had good enough tracking equipment, which means they'd have to follow you in person. And how likely is that?"

It was . . . close to impossible. Tailing a vehicle in a modern major city by eyesight alone required a large team of surveillance experts—emphasis on *large* and *expert.* There was probably no gang in Lower Radomsko who could have managed that. Even someone like Dusek would be hard-pressed unless he had plenty of advance notice.

She ran fingers through her hair. The sensation was strange. Thandi always kept her hair cut short, as soldiers usually did. Still, she'd had *some* hair. She was rather proud of it, in fact, although she'd never have admitted that to anyone. The albinism that was typical of modern Ndebelans sometimes resulted—as it had with her—in hair that was colored a brilliant platinum as well as being tightly curled.

Now, her hair was of a piece with the rest of her. Dull, drab, dreary. The only reason it wasn't lank was because it was too short altogether. Colored a sort of icky gray-brown, it was less than two centimeters long except for an idiotic-looking pigtail that was apparently considered the height of fashion on her supposed home planet. (That was a Verge world by the name of Pezenec. Thandi had never been there—never been near it—but she'd spent hours studying the planet on their way to Mesa.)

"All right," she said. "Where and when will we meet up again?" She didn't ask him where he'd be going and what he'd be doing. That was need to know—which she didn't.

"I'm not sure. It depends on this, that and the other. Within two days, though, unless something gets really tangled up."

And with that, he opened the passenger door of the lorry and swung himself out of the cab. Once on the ground he took a few seconds to study the area nearby and then set off at a brisk pace toward one of the buildings to the rear.

Thandi didn't wait to see where he was going. She started the lorry and keyed in the directions. That took no time at all, since it was the same directions she'd been following when the ambush happened.

Was there a word for an ambush gone badly wrong? she wondered. There damn well ought to be.

She thought about for a while, as the lorry made its way through the streets.

Slambush? Scrambush? Lamebush?

Eventually she settled on *ambust.*

❖   ❖   ❖

The man was one scary son of a bitch. But Hasrul's mother was in bad shape now. He *had* to scrape up the money to get her the medicine she needed—and soon. He didn't think Mama would last much longer if he didn't.

"Oh, come on," the man said. He leaned a shoulder against the wall of the building they were standing next to. But he didn't put any real weight on it, and Hasrul was sure he could still spring into action in an split second.

"I'm almost insulted," the man continued. "Do you really think I need to steal from someone like you?"

Hasrul hated to admit it, but the man had a point. His clothing didn't qualify as rags, but give it a few more months and they might. Mama's condition was draining every source of funds the family could get its hands on. There wasn't much left for anything else except the bare necessities.

"I haven't got the tools," he protested. "Can't afford them, neither."

"I didn't think you did and I didn't think you could. So what?" The man cocked his head a little. "Are you going to tell me with a straight face that you don't know who can do the work and does have the tools? If you do, you've insulted me twice and you're getting onto thin ice."

Hasrul ignored the implied threat. Sure, this guy was scary as hell, but he wasn't the only scary son of a bitch around and Hasrul was used to threats. What did interest him was the man's use of the word "ice." Between that and the accent, Hasrul was now sure he was an offworlder. There wasn't much ice on Mesa outside of refrigerating units and the polar ice caps.

Perhaps oddly, that reassured Hasrul. The truth was, some of the people in Lower Radomsko sure as hell *would* steal the clothing from a twelve-year-old boy—and cut his throat in the bargain. But he didn't think someone who could afford the passage on a starship would bother.

"Yeah, sure, I know somebody. What do you want me to tell him? And what's in it for me?"

The man hooked a thumb over his shoulder, pointing down the street. They were standing in the mouth of the alley, so the wrecked vehicles were still in sight. "Tell him I've got what's left of one air car—pretty fancy one, too; it's a Lecuyer 80 Zed Alpha—and two lorries. He's welcome to cut them all up and sell what he can."

One of the lorries was still undamaged. But Hasrul knew that cutting it up for parts was safer than trying to sell an unregistered vehicle. The police didn't bother with checking vehicle registrations in Lower Radomsko, but if you went beyond those limits you might get into trouble. You were sure to get the registration checked if you went outside the seccy districts.

"What's the split?" he asked.

"Seventy-thirty."

"Which way?"

"He's doing all the work. Seventy for him and thirty for me."

"He'll try to cheat you."

"That's a given. As long as he doesn't get too greedy, I'll look the other way."

"And how will he know what's too greedy and what isn't?"

For the first time, a smile came to the man's face. Now, he was a *really* scary son of a bitch. "He'll know he crossed the line when he sees his brains on the ground. So you can tell him that I recommend he err on the side of caution."

Hasrul wasn't exactly sure what the word "err" meant, but the context made it clear enough.

And, again, he felt reassured. There was something completely relaxed about the way this man issued threats. They didn't even seem like threats at all. Just...foresight. Predictions of what was sure to come. Not even old Bianka the fortune-teller could make something sound that certain.

Hasrul really couldn't imagine this guy killing or hurting someone like him, who was barely more than a child. Not because he wasn't ruthless enough but just because it would be beneath his dignity.

That still left the critical issue to be resolved.

"What's in it for me?"

The man pushed back against the wall and came to a straight-up standing position. "I'll leave that up to you. You can choose between five percent of whatever I get or a favor."

"What do you mean, 'a favor'?"

"Just what it sounds like. I'll owe you a favor. Call it in whenever you like. If it's within reason, I'll do it."

"Who gets to decide if it's reasonable?"

"Me, of course." His smile came back—only this time it seemed to have some real humor in it. "Don't worry, kid. If I can't or won't do you the favor you ask for, pick another one. You won't have to look for brains on the ground. I'll just use the word 'no.'"

The sensible choice was the five percent commission, of course. But . . .

That would only get Mama medicine for a couple of weeks. And there was something about this guy.

"What's your name?"

"Achmed. Achmed Buenaventura."

"I'm Hasrul Goosens. You owe me a favor. Well, you will, anyway. In about four hours."

CHAPTER 32

"Are you fucking crazy?" Andrew hissed, when he saw the two criminals in the back of the lorry's cab.

"It's Victor's idea, not mine," Thandi said. "But there's no point fretting over it now. What's done is done."

"What's done is most certainly *not* done." He pointed an accusing finger at the objects of his wrath. The gesture was a little silly-looking, though. As cramped as they were in the cab, he had to keep his hand tucked up against his chest. "Just dump them somewhere. Far from here."

"No. We're not going to do that, Andrew, so just drop it. Help me get them inside."

"People will see us! They'll be suspicious."

"It's a service alley—with nobody in sight."

"There's a street lamp."

"It's fifty meters away and it doesn't shed any light back here."

"But somebody—"

"Andrew, shut up. Shut. Up. Just keep the door open."

She reached over the seat and pulled Callie up. Then, in as close an approximation as she could get to a fireman's carry inside the confines of the cab, she got her out of the lorry and down in the alley. From there, it was easy work to get the injured and unconscious woman inside the leased unit through a side door.

Thankfully, Artlett kept quiet and opened doors as needed. Once they were inside the unit, Thandi laid Callie down on the floor of one of the back rooms. There was no furniture in that room as yet.

Within two minutes, she'd laid Teddy down next to her.

"Okay, let's get the equipment inside."

"We'll need to use the service entrance in the back. It's got the only door big enough."

While Andrew went to get that door open, Thandi returned to the lorry and drove it around to the service entrance through two connecting tunnels. As was usually true with residential towers with commercial establishments on the lower floors, all deliveries of goods and equipment were done by way of underground arteries. She hadn't wanted to unload the two injured people at the large service entrance because there was almost bound to be someone in sight. But the area wasn't especially well lit, and unloading equipment in innocuously marked containers (using the same logo of Komlanc Intermodal Transport) didn't reveal anything significant, even if someone was watching. They were opening a business, after all. New businesses needed supplies and equipment.

After opening the rear of the lorry, the first container she brought out was the one holding the scrambling and anti-eavesdropping devices. It wasn't all that big a container—two meters long, one wide and one

deep—but it weighed quite a bit. Since she was carrying the container on a portable counter-grav generator,
however, that wasn't a problem.

Andrew directed her, and she guided the container
down a steep flight of stairs into the basement. Into
a subbasement, actually, since the entry was already
below ground.

"No elevator?"

"Not one that's operating. Which word in 'seccy
district' are you having the most trouble with?"

Thandi was amused rather than irritated. Now that
they'd gotten the wounded criminals out of public
sight, her mood was improving. Andrew Artlett could
turn grumpiness into an art form.

He waved his hand toward the ceiling. "The elevators serving the upper floors are mostly working, of
course. This building's over three hundred stories tall.
But the maintenance budget is stretched and the work
crews are stretched even worse. They don't try to keep
nonessential equipment operating. The only people who
use the basements and subbasements are shop owners
on the bottom floors. If they want working elevators,
they can damn well pay to fix them themselves."

As it turned out, the subbasement was the lowest
of five subbasements. By now, they were far underground. It was also now clear to Thandi why Andrew
and Victor hadn't been worried that the equipment
they'd soon have in operation would be detected by
anyone in Mesan security. Between the equipment's
own shielding and the meters of soil and ceramacrete
between the subbasement and the surface, nothing
would be detected. Nothing, at least, strong enough
to be analyzed. A huge and densely populated modern

city generated so much electronic noise that any given signal got degraded quickly even without shielding.

After she unloaded the container, Thandi let Andrew go to work getting the equipment up and running while she took the counter-grav generator back upstairs. There were more containers to be brought in.

She left the largest of them till the end. That contained the medical unit, which was the heaviest of the containers as well as the biggest. She wouldn't be able to fit that one down the stairs to the basement. She probably couldn't take it up the stairs to the higher floors either. They'd have to set it up in one of the back rooms of the main floor. That would pose a bit of a security risk, but there was no way around it.

Victor had insisted on bringing the medical unit. He claimed it was probably even more important than the scrambling gear. She'd been doubtful, herself, but hadn't argued the point. Anton hadn't been inclined to debate the matter either.

And now...it looked as if Victor might have been right. There were a number of ways to solidify the allegiance of people to a new criminal gang. She'd never contemplated the problem before, but it now occurred to her that being able to offer good medical care was probably very high on the list.

The unit wasn't state of the art. That would have required Beowulfan design and manufacture, which would be risky if it was spotted anywhere on Mesa. But it was fairly close, being a topline unit made on Strathmoor. It wouldn't be as versatile as the much larger stationary equipment in a hospital, but that sort of full-spectrum capability was probably not going to be needed anyway. Or, if it was needed, would be a moot point—since they'd all be facing interrogators in Mesa's equivalent of a dungeon. Who were not likely to be offering them tender loving care.

Since Andrew was still preoccupied with the scrambling gear, Steph Turner made the decision as to where she wanted the med unit.

"All the way in the back, I think. There's a really big walk-in pantry next to the kitchen. Once we place the med unit against the back wall, Andrew can build a set of shelves that swing aside and hide it if necessary." Steph made a face. "That's about as primitive as things get in the way of disguises. But it's the best we can do."

"No, it makes sense to me," said Thandi. "A full-bore search of the building by security agents won't be fooled, but if you get that kind of search you're screwed anyway. A fake wall, especially if it's got shelves on it holding food supplies, will be enough to hide the med unit from anyone who wanders back there by mistake. Or from thieves—not that there's much chance of thieves getting past that equipment Andrew's setting up in the basement."

"Or my favorite cleaver," Steph said, very matter-of-factly. "I didn't bring all my cooking stuff, since I'm not setting up a commercial diner. But I got the basics."

❖   ❖   ❖

Before long, it was done. And now it was time to give the med unit its maiden voyage.

So to speak. She didn't think there was really much chance Callie was still a maiden.

"Which one goes in first?" Steph asked.

"The woman. Her injuries are worse."

Steph frowned. "How can you tell? Those legs both look like a mess."

"I'm the one who shot them and I know where the darts hit. Callie doesn't have a knee left. Teddy does, even if the area around it is pretty chewed up."

"Whatever you say, O Dealer in Death and Destruction."

"I could have just killed them, you know."

Thandi left unsaid the fact that she damn well *would* have, too, if it hadn't been for Victor and his schemes.

❖   ❖   ❖

Since he had a few hours to spare, Victor decided he might as well use them productively. Three of the safe drops he'd set up the last time he and Anton had been on Mesa were within reach in the time he had available, unless he ran into trouble before he could get out of Lower Radomsko.

That wasn't likely, though. He'd checked the locator on his air car before ramming the lorry and knew that he was close to the outskirts of Lower Radomsko. By now, word of the killings would have spread for blocks—and he only had four or five blocks to go.

So, he set off walking. Two things were a given, here. First, the residents of an area like this could recognize at a glance someone who projected an aura that said: *Do not mess with me. Do not even think about it.* Second, Victor could project that predatory aura superbly well. He'd learned how to do it in the abstract while still at the StateSec Academy, practicing in a simulator. In the years that had gone by since, the aura had become a reality. If anyone was stupid enough to mess with him here, they would find themselves in a world of hurt.

He didn't even think about it—which, of course, just made the aura that much more intimidating. He spent the time working through the angles of his newly improvised plan.

He considered and then discarded the idea of actually taking control of Lower Radomsko. That was certainly possible. Victor couldn't have done it on his own. But with Thandi available, it was by no means out of the question. Still, even with her, the project would take too much time.

He wasn't sure why he thought that, exactly. How much time was "too much," in such a fluid situation?

But Victor trusted his instincts—which were not "instincts" at all, really. The mind involved here was that of a man who was superb at this sort of work and now had a lot of experience at it. Not as much experience as someone like Kevin Usher, but with possibly even more than Kevin in the way of raw talent.

That mind operated on many levels, not all of them fully conscious and some of them not conscious at all. Analyzing, gauging, assessing, calculating. Term after term could be added to that list, but after a while it became pointless because the thinking involved had no defined boundaries or rigid pathways. This was art, not science.

So while Victor couldn't have explained *why* he didn't think they had enough time to take over Lower Radomsko, he was sure they didn't. The interstellar political situation was coming to a boil. It probably would have done so anyway, but the complete destruction of Filareta's fleet made it certain—and raised the heat by an order of magnitude. Anybody with any sense at all could now see that the Solarian League was doomed. The only uncertainty that remained was the exact manner in which it would disintegrate.

But however that disintegration unfolded, one feature of it was now a given. Mesa was doomed also. And Victor was sure that doom wouldn't be long in the making.

So.

By the time he passed the boundary of Lower Radomsko, he'd come to a decision. They didn't need to actually take over Lower Radomsko, they just needed to make it look like they could. That would be enough to steer the plan back to its original center, which was to use Jurgen Dusek's criminal network to infiltrate Mesa. But now they'd be in a much stronger position to do so.

That was a pleasant thought. And so it was with a cheery smile that he greeted the cab driver who responded to his com signal. The driver was wary, coming this close to Lower Radomsko. (He wouldn't have gone *into* Lower Radomsko at all, under any circumstances, for any amount of money.) But Victor's good humor seemed to reassure him in the course of their bargaining. Besides, the money he was being offered for several hours easy work was at least twice as much—more like three times as much—as he would have earned that day in the normal course of business.

❖   ❖   ❖

The cabbie's name was Bertie Jaffarally. By the time he finished driving Victor around to the various locations where the dead letter boxes were set up, he was thinking of him in his own mind as "Achmed the Affable" and wondering if he could set up some sort of connection. Achmed was obviously a well-to-do off-worlder. People like that sometimes hired cabbies on a regular basis.

It never occurred to Bertie that what Achmed was really doing was checking dead drops. He had only a fuzzy understanding of what a "dead letter box" was in the first place. He'd heard the term used in a few thrillers he'd seen and read, and had a vague image of them as actual boxes. Or something like that. An old-fashioned mailbox, maybe.

✧   ✧   ✧

In the modern era, no one used actual boxes of any kind except on very rare occasions. The terms "dead drop" or "dead letter box" simply referred to any method that allowed two agents to communicate with each other or pass items back and forth without coming into direct contact.

The first dead drop was a cybercache concealed in the corner of the elevator of an office building. The cache was further protected by miniaturized scrambling equipment and could only be accessed if the elevator was sent to four floors in a specific order. (Floors 115, 38, 209, 66.) It was perhaps the safest of the dead drops Victor had set up but also the most exasperating, since the chances that the agent would be alone in the elevator for all four floors in sequence were slight. What usually had to be done was for the agent to travel to the four floors in the right sequence, mark his or her presence by touching the concealed cybercache and simultaneously keying an innocuous signal from a com, but get off the elevator whenever someone else came on and stayed long enough that suspicions might be aroused. A process that could theoretically be done in a few minutes could sometimes take more than half an hour. This time, Victor had to travel to the final (66th) floor three separate times before he was alone on the elevator and could drain the cache's data into his com.

The second dead drop was a robot fortune teller in an amusement arcade. Victor was rather proud of that one, although Anton had made wisecracks about it for days after they set it up. Which he could do, since Anton had been the one who'd had to reprogram the robot in the first place. The skills required to do that properly had been far beyond Victor's abilities. His role had just been to bribe the arcade manager to give them access to the robot. He'd explained that was needed to find out if his wife was using the robot to check on his own fidelity. And if that seemed like circular reasoning or the mindset of a man who was simultaneously duplicitous and gullible, the arcade manager had been completely indifferent. The bribe had been quite large.

In the case of this dead drop, once the agent entered the privacy of the booth, he or she entered or retrieved the data using a one-time pad. Again, the term "pad" was of antique origin. What this dead drop actually used was the text of a popular electronic cookbook that anyone might have in their com unit. The cookbook's menu items were selected in sequence of prime numbers working backward from one hundred. Victor figured the security was worth the risk that they'd eventually run out of prime numbers. There were twenty-five prime numbers between one hundred and one. The likelihood that the dead drop would be needed more times than that for separate and distinct information transfers was fairly low.

Victor didn't bother decrypting the information on the spot. For one thing, there was probably wasn't anything there. For another, it would take too long. No one spent *that* much time in a booth listening to a robot fortune-teller, no matter how gullible they were. The robot was a cheap model with only a few dozen "fortunes" to be told and none of them took more than a minute.

The third dead drop he visited that day was his favorite, although it was probably the chanciest of the three.

Like any planet with a mild climate, Mesa had oceans and the oceans were full of fish. Not "fish," precisely, but the similarity of Mesa's mobile marine life to Terran analogs was close enough that everyone used the term without thinking about it. Convergent evolution had produced sea-creatures which were torpedo-shaped, bilaterally symmetrical, had heads and tails—although the tails had horizontal flukes like those of Terran whales—and fins. A few more than most Terran fish, and predominantly lobe-finned rather than ray-finned.

Close enough for everyone to call them "fish," and never mind that the internal organs were quite a bit different.

When you combined "lots of fish" with "lots of poverty" what you invariably got were fish markets. *Big* fish markets—with lots and lots of fish being displayed on lots and lots of fish-seller's stands. Big stands, too.

The number of such stands fluctuated, but it was never less than twenty. Since the Mesan week had the same number of days as the Terran week that most humans still kept as a standard—seven days, although the names varied a lot—and Victor was partial to prime numbers, the routine was easy to remember. Place the message at whatever fish stand corresponded to the day of the week, figuring the week ran from Monday to Sunday, counting from the south and skipping the prime number of two.

The day was Thursday. That meant the eleventh stand from the south. He'd also check the seventh and fifth stands, because he couldn't assume the agent leaving the message would have done so on the same day Victor arrived. He or she might have dropped it on Wednesday or Tuesday. If they'd dropped it earlier than that it was a moot point. Fish were a perishable product as well as an edible one. Victor figured that any message more than three days old had been discarded or eaten.

Well, not "eaten," since the message would have been inserted in the flukes and nobody ate flukes except devotees to one of the Mesan versions of fish stew that used the entire fish, even the internal organs. But it didn't matter, because the message would be on a chip delicate enough that it would dissolve entirely if cooked. (Nobody, not even the poorest seccy on Mesa, ate fish flukes raw.)

The trick, obviously, was in spotting the right fish. The most commonly sold fish on Mesa was called *bacau* and could be found on any fish stand. The agent dropping the fish would insert the chip into the flukes of a *bacau* resting at the rear of the display, and select the one that had the most vivid lateral stripe. It was the commonly held belief on Mesa—seccy belief; free citizens rarely ate *bacau*—that a vivid lateral stripe indicated an excess of pollutants in the flesh.

That belief was accurate, as it happened. But Victor didn't care about that one way or another because he had no intention of eating the fish. *Bacau* had an oily flavor he didn't care for, which was the reason free citizens usually avoided it. The reason he'd chosen the stripe method was because a *bacau* with a vivid lateral stripe at the back of the stand was the one most likely to be passed over by real customers.

There was one other feature of this dead drop that Victor liked, although it also increased the risk. (Very slightly, though.) He'd have to wait before he'd find out if there'd been any messages at the first two drops. Here, he'd know right away, since no one would insert a chip into a fish fluke unless they had something to pass on.

Victor glanced around to see if any of the vendors running the stall were watching. If they were, he'd have to buy the fish. He didn't care about the cost, but hauling fish around would be a nuisance.

But no one was watching. It took only a few seconds to feel the flukes of the four *bacau* who had the brightest stripes. The chip was delicate, and not large, and to the naked eyes just looked like part of the fluke. But it was still detectable if a person knew what to look for.

Nothing. He moved on to the seventh stand. Again, no one was watching. There, he checked only three fish. None of the others in the back of the stand had a prominent stripe.

Also nothing. He moved on to the fifth stand.

And found a chip in the first fluke he touched.

And . . . one of the vendors was eyeing him. Not quite with suspicion, but teetering on the edge.

Nothing for it. He'd have to buy the blasted thing.

On a positive note, *bacau* weren't a particularly large fish. This one weighed less than a kilo.

On a negative note, *bacau* were smelly—and if he didn't get it into a refrigerator pretty soon, the fish would get downright stinky. They didn't keep very well. But Victor figured he could find a place to get rid of it without being seen before he left the fish market.

He went up to the vendor and inquired as to the price, making sure to lay on his accent as thickly as possible.

The vendor didn't quite sneer at the idiot offworlder as he charged him for a crappy *bacau* the same price he'd charge a knowledgeable customer for a delicacy. But he came close.

That was the reaction Victor wanted, of course. There was no way he'd ever be able to pass as a native Mesan. The next best option was to get typecast as a damn fool tourist who didn't know up from down. One who'd buy a *bacau* with a vivid lateral stripe for as much money as he could have spent to get a shelled *perido* or half a kilo of *kint*.

❖   ❖   ❖

On the way out, Victor dumped the fish in the most logical place—onto the pile of *bacau* displayed at the stand nearest to the exit. By then, he'd extracted the cyberchip and slid it into his pocket. He'd have preferred to hide it in his mouth, so he could have swallowed it in an emergency. But the material used to make that type of chip really was quite delicate. It didn't handle saliva any better than hot soup.

Once he was back in the cab, he gave Bertie another cheery smile. He was now in a very good mood. He hadn't expected to find anything at any of the dead drop locations. No matter what it was—he'd have to wait a while before he could decrypt it—the message was probably good news. At least one of the seccy rebels they'd dealt with on their previous mission was still alive and functioning.

Well, probably. It was also possible that they'd all been captured, had divulged too much when interrogated, and the message in the dead drop had actually been placed there by Mesan security agents with nefarious intent and evil design.

But it was a nice sunny day and Victor wasn't inclined to worry. Why should he? Hadn't the day started off with an ambush turned around in a sprightly manner? Surely that was a good omen, even if Victor didn't believe in silly superstitions.

"Where to now?" asked Bertie.

"I'm done with my errands for the day. Drop me off at the same place you picked me up." He pulled out his com. "And give me a number where I can reach you. I'll be needing cab service pretty often, I'm thinking."

❖   ❖   ❖

Hell of a nice guy, Achmed. Bertie wished all his customers were like that.

CHAPTER 33

"I'll be honest with you, Mr. Huygens. As I'm sure you know, there's something of a glut in that market at the moment—has been for a while, now—and it's not a big market to begin with. So I have to tell you the same thing I've told the other vendors who've approached me lately. Unless you're willing to share the risks with us, the price I can offer you for the items is pretty low."

Lajos Irvine frowned. "What risks are you referring to, specifically?" He was tempted to ask why the market in body parts and tissues had a glut, but refrained from do so. His cover identity as "Carlos Huygens" was that of a fence working in that market. Presumably, he'd already know the answer.

Sitting in a chair across the desk from Lajos, Triêu Chuanli leaned back, raised his arms and clasped his hands behind his neck. "The usual. It's one risk, really, with several dimensions. Human tissues and body parts—especially functional organs—degenerate quickly unless you preserve them. And doing that properly requires a lot more than just tossing them into a freezer. I'm sure I don't have to spell that out for you, since you have the same problem at your end."

Lajos had to scramble mentally to get out of the hole he'd just dug himself into. A fence should have known that already, also.

This was the problem with trying to penetrate a target using a preconceived scheme like the one Vickers had come up with. You were likely to stumble over your own cover because you'd had to fit the cover to the scheme instead of developing a plan based on a cover which you could establish solidly.

There was an old saw about authors that Lajos had heard once: *writers write what they know about.* The same principle applied to covert agents like himself.

"Yeah, sure. Just wanted to be sure we were on the same wavelength. How much of the risk do you propose I take on?"

He held his breath, hoping that wasn't also something well established in the trade.

But Chuanli didn't seem suspicious, so apparently it wasn't. "The way the market is now, we'd want you to cover thirty percent of any expenses incurred until the product is actually sold. That's the same deal we've made with our other vendors."

Lajos decided that was something he could ask about safely enough. "How many competitors am I dealing with here?"

"Just two. And they're not really competitors the way I think you're using the term. Neither party are pros. They're making what amounts to private sales. And one of them is just a possibility anyway. The agreement's been made but they still haven't come up with the goods."

The gangster who was Jurgen Dusek's top lieutenant smiled thinly. "Which means they're waiting on someone to die but don't want to do the work themselves. Most likely a family member. I didn't inquire, of course."

Lajos nodded, doing his best to give the gesture an aura of knowledge and familiarity. *Yeah, sure, I run into that all the time myself.*

In point of fact, it hadn't even occurred to him that people might be selling off the body parts and tissues of their own family members. Seccies were generally poor, compared to free citizens, but in absolute terms they weren't *that* poor. An especially indigent family might have trouble covering funeral expenses, but that could always be handled by donating the body to a university or research institute. They wouldn't get any money for it, but the tissues and body parts of someone dying of old age—or disease, although that was rare—weren't worth much anyway on the black market.

The exceptions might be someone who died accidentally or committed suicide while still young and healthy. Or was murdered, although that might involve the police too much. Lajos supposed a family in dire straits might decide to sell off the body under such circumstances. But that obviously wasn't the case here, since the suppliers involved hadn't yet produced the goods. Why wait, unless...

It suddenly dawned on Lajos that there was one scenario he could envision that would explain the matter. What if someone had a family member who was dying of injuries but, for some reason, had to keep that fact quiet?

Someone like a criminal, maybe, injured in the

course of committing a crime. A robbery gone badly wrong, for instance. Or...

A Ballroom terrorist. Or a member of one of the seccy revolutionary groups. They'd all been hammered badly in the crackdown after Green Pines. Which, now that he thought it about—belatedly, alas—was also what probably explained the glut in the market recently.

He started to get a little excited. Maybe he could turn Vickers' idiot scheme around and actually get some results from it. What was that old expression? *Make a silk purse out of a sow's ear.*

"So, are those terms acceptable to you, Mr. Huygens?"

Lajos realized he's let his mind drift. "Uh, yes, Mr. Chuanli. Thirty percent of the costs. I can handle that."

"How soon can I expect a delivery?"

"That depends on you, really. What's selling most quickly right now?" Then, realizing that was another question he should probably already know the answer to, he added hurriedly: "For your customers, I mean. I don't want to assume the general market conditions apply."

"The fastest turnover is always with juvenile body parts. The younger, the better, is the general rule."

"That's what I figured. I just wanted to be sure." Lajos rose from his chair and extended his hand across the desk. "Give me three days."

"I'll be expecting you, then." Chuanli got up as well and they shook hands.

It took a while to exit the building, since Dusek conducted his operation out of the largest edifice in Neue Rostock. In fact, it was one of the largest in the entire city of Mendel. The building was not especially tall—just under three hundred stories—because of the height restrictions in seccy areas. But it had originally been designed as a combined light manufacturing and commercial complex. It was squat and broad; almost ziggurat-shaped if a ziggurat had ever risen a kilometer high and had shallowly recessed terraces and tiers. Almost four centuries had gone by since the building was erected, and over the years it had become a gigantic labyrinth. As had Neue Rostock crime lords before him, Dusek saw to it that there were no accurate plans or blueprints of the layout in existence—and at least once every five years he had new construction and demolition carried out to make obsolete whatever extensive knowledge of the interior had fallen into hostile (or official) hands. He maintained a small army of youngsters on his payroll who had three jobs and three jobs only—learn the maze, serve as guides for those who needed them, and keep the knowledge to themselves. Anyone found blabbing to others about the building's layout—or even with written notes or sketches in their possession—would be . . .

Disappeared. There were an untold—literally, untold—number of nooks and crannies and secret chambers and passages in the enormous edifice which might serve that purpose. And then be sealed over.

Eventually, the eleven-year-old girl who'd served as his escort led Lajos out of the building onto a street. Lajos looked up at the sky. From what he could see, it'd probably start raining by late afternoon, but right now it was still a bright and sunny day. Well . . . as bright and sunny as the narrow man-made canyons between giant buildings ever got.

That matched his mood. Things were looking up.

Well . . . *might* be looking up. It never paid to get ahead of yourself.

✧   ✧   ✧

"I think he's a phony," said Triêu Chuanli.

The man looking at Chuanli in the com screen cocked his head. "Why?" asked Jurgen Dusek. The crime boss wasn't asking the question in a challenging manner. He'd just watched the recording Triêu had made of the interview and had come to the same tentative conclusion himself. But Dusek was in the habit of encouraging his subordinates to explain their reasoning. It was one of the things that made him a pleasure to work for—as long as you stayed clear of angering him, of course. Then Mr. Nice Boss became something very different, very quickly.

"He's fumbling a little," Triêu said. "I don't think he really knows the business that well. What kind of fence has to ask the questions he did?"

Dusek nodded. "Yeah, that was my sense of it also. Okay, so we're agreed he's a phony. But what kind of phony? Who is he really and what does he really want?"

"Well, he could be working for one of our rivals who's thinking of a little encroachment, or just scouting out the territory. McLeod, maybe, or Bachue the Nose."

Dusek shook his head. "Possible, but not likely. McLeod's too cautious. And while the Nose is a sure-enough witch sometimes, she just doesn't have the heft to seriously consider messing with us. Besides, why use a trafficker in this trade for the purpose? It'd make a lot more sense to go with something less flaky. You know what the body parts and tissues market is like. Up, down, up, down—sometimes I'm tempted to get out of it altogether."

Chuanli shrugged. "Just raising the possibility. I don't think it's at all likely myself. But the alternative makes even less sense to me."

Dusek knew what he was talking about. The alternative explanation was that "Mr. Huygens" was working for one or another of Mesa's security agencies. Probably one of the government ones although there was a chance he might be employed by one of the private contractors.

Normally, Dusek would have agreed with Chuanli that that was even less likely than another gang being involved. Why would a security agency bother with such an elaborate rigmarole? The agents handling Neue Rostock for the two most important official agencies—the Tableland Auditor Board and the Interservice Verification Agency—both knew how to reach Dusek if they wanted to find out anything. The TAB agent, Phuong Wilson, even had one of his private numbers.

Jurgen made it a point to stay on reasonably good terms with Mesa's security forces, especially the Tabbies. That meant keeping the Ballroom out of Neue Rostock altogether and keeping a lid on the seccy radicals. Once in a while—not often; Jurgen had no more love for Mesan authorities than any seccy—he'd even turn over one of them. (Although never a member of the Ballroom, which could be really dangerous.)

So why would anyone screw around with something this elaborate?

Triêu put into words the same conclusion Jurgen was coming to. Coming toward, it would be better to say. Everything was still tentative.

"My guess? One of two things—or more likely, both of them together. One of the security outfits has a new boss and he or she is doing the usual routine."

"New broom sweeps clean. New and improved service under new management. Blah blah blah. Okay. What's the other possibility?"

"Everything's starting to come apart at the seams, boss. Slowly, at first—but it'll speed up, you watch."

Dusek made a face. "I don't want to hear that, Triêu. Business is fine the way it is."

His lieutenant shrugged. "I don't like it either. But I think Manpower finally pissed off one too many crowds—and from the looks of it, this new crowd can hammer everyone else flat. The Sollies just lost, what? Four hundred superdreadnoughts?"

"Thereabouts." The news of the destruction of Filareta's fleet at Manticore had just reached Mesa. Just been made known to the public, at least. The powers-that-be had undoubtedly learned of it weeks earlier.

Dusek could follow the logic himself. All too easily. "And if the Manties can manage that, who's to say they can't decide to scrub Manpower out of existence?"

Chuanli nodded. "And if you and I can figure that out, so can lots of other people. Like security agents."

"That still doesn't explain this guy."

"Not specifically, no. But I'm willing to bet we're going to start seeing a lot of weird stuff happening. Everybody and their grandmother is going to be working the angles."

Chuanli's hypothesis was just that, a hypothesis. But Dusek decided he was likely right.

"Okay. Let's string this 'Mr. Huygens' along some more, then. See what happens. In the meantime, I'll give my tame Tabby a call and see if he can tell me anything."

❖   ❖   ❖

"You heard me," Lajos said. "Babies, infants and toddlers. Tissues'll do, but functioning organs are better."

The security officer on the screen kept staring at
him. Maybe she was dimwitted.

"Get over it, Officer Mendez," Lajos said. "You've
got to have some on stock."

"But . . ." Mendez looked to the side, at something
or someone—probably someone—Lajos couldn't see.
After a couple of seconds, she looked back. "We're
running a prison here, Agent Irvine, not a nursery."

Definitely a dimwit. Either that, or—being fair; you
never knew—she was laboring under dimwit orders. "I
know that. Here's what else I know. You maintain the
second largest morgue in the city. I can't believe you're
not getting spillover from other morgues, especially the
main police morgue. Their business comes in spurts,
and yours is a lot more predictable. So have somebody
check. There'll be at least some of the stuff I need."

Abruptly, she nodded. "I'll get back to you."

❖   ❖   ❖

After she cut off the contact, Officer Mendez turned
to her supervisor, Lieutenant Jernigan. She'd been
standing far enough away not to be visible on the
screen. She'd had no particular reason to do that. It
was just the ingrained habit of someone who shirked
responsibility as much as possible.

"What's the story, Lieutenant?"

"I don't think we have any. He'd be right, normally.
But things have been a little hectic lately."

Hectic. Leave it to Jernigan to be slack about
everything, including the way she described things.
It'd be better to say that the correctional center had
bordered on chaos ever since Green Pines. Supervisors

had been forced to improvise. One of their hastily made decisions had probably been to lighten the workload on the staff by jettisoning any cases that seemed cut-and-dried.

Such as cases involving babies and infants dying in accidents. Unless there were clear indications of foul play, just feed them into the incinerator and give the ashes to the grieving families. That was quick, easy—and best of all, required very little labor. The crematoriums were mostly automated.

Not being a slacker like Jernigan, Officer Mendez took the time to check. But her supervisor turned out to be right. At the moment, the correctional center's morgue had no suitable cadavers.

She then checked the city's main morgue. Same story. Apparently, things had been hectic for them also over the past few weeks.

Enough. She kicked the problem upstairs. Jernigan immediately kicked it up another level.

By the end of the day, the problem arrived back where it started. On the desk of Lajos Irvine's boss, George Vickers.

"Oh, for Pete's sake," he said. "Do I have to do everything?"

He put in a call to a friend of his who worked for the Long Range Planning Board and explained the problem.

The friend—Juan Morris was his name—scratched his jaw and gave the matter some thought,

"Well . . . We've got two probable culls coming up. The final decision hasn't been made yet, but let me see what I can do."

❖　　❖　　❖

Morris got back to him toward the end of the next day. "Sorry it took so long, George. Things have been a little crazy around here since...well, never mind the details. A missing link in the chain of command—and way high up, to make things worse. But that winds up working in your favor since Valerie's tearing her hair out and moving the culls up—she's authorized to make that decision, lucky for you—will lighten the work load some."

Vickers nodded. "Good. How soon...?"

"Oh, the culls were done immediately. How do you want the remains? Intact, dismembered, exsected—what?"

"Hell, I don't know. Leave them whole—better drain the fluids, though, and pouch them—and I'll let Irvine figure out how he wants to handle it. That's his headache."

❖   ❖   ❖

Less than a day later, the goods were delivered to Irvine's office. After he opened up the containers he spent some time staring at the contents. There were times he really hated his job.

Really hated it—and more so and more often, these last months.

Lajos had been exhilarated when he'd first been brought all the way into the onion, after Green Pines, as a reward for ferreting out McBryde's treason. But as time passed and he became more familiar with the Alignment's goals and methods, his uneasiness had grown.

Some of that uneasiness, perhaps most of it, was the skepticism of a man who'd spent his adult life testing the limits of rational planning in the trenches, so to speak. He'd never heard of the Scot poet Robert Burns. But if someone had recited to him that poet's most famous line of verse—*The best-laid schemes o' mice an' men gang aft agley*—he'd have immediately responded: "You can say that again."

He was a firm believer in the ancient Murphy's law. And he found it hard to believe that the law could be abrogated simply by planning really well and for centuries at a time.

But some of that uneasiness went beyond pragmatism. Some of it had a moral nature. As hard-bitten and tough-minded as Lajos had thought himself to be, he'd never imagined a ruthlessness as unadulterated and adamantine—as *pure*—as that of the Alignment's central leadership. He could accept—he had accepted—the brutalities visited on slaves and seccies as an unfortunate necessity for the eventual advancement of the Mesan genome. But he'd come to understand that the Detweilers and those around them simply didn't care at all. The misery and injustice that Lajos saw around him every day, and hardened himself against, was simply data to them—and not particularly important data at that.

The objects he was staring at now were the gruesome remains of what had once been human beings. Very small ones—and very defenseless ones. But he was quite sure that if he could look at those objects through the eyes of his ultimate superiors he would see nothing of the sort.

Just...objects. Being put to good use now that they turned out to be unsuitable for their original purpose.

August 1922 Post Diaspora

"Hell, I'm sorry I asked at all."

—Stephanie Moriarty, Mesan revolutionary

CHAPTER 34

Zachariah McBryde had never been able to weep for his brother Jack. He wasn't sure why, exactly. At first, he'd been too shocked—not just at Jack's death but at the manner of it. Suicide, committed by a traitor? It was unthinkable.

Eventually, the fact of his brother's death had sunk in. But to this day, Zachariah had never accepted the explanation given by the authorities.

He'd said nothing, however; made no protest.

Life inside the onion, especially for someone as far into it as Zachariah, was far removed from what most people would have considered "tyranny." The onion was not governed by democratic principles, certainly. The Detweilers had always been and still were the ultimate authority, much like the family that owned and managed a huge corporation.

But there was more to it than that. The family owners of a firm commanded the loyalty of their employees simply by paying them. The Detweilers did that as well, but the people bound to them in the onion also shared a common vision of humanity's future. They were dedicated to a cause, a purpose, that went far beyond the simple acquisition of material goods and comforts.

The human race had produced many such ideologically driven and ideologically cohered organizations in its history. Most of them had been religious, most of the rest had been political, and some had been purely social in their orientation. But almost all of them had had one thing in common: united by a determination to persevere over opposition and enmity, they tended to be tightly disciplined and hierarchical. That hierarchy might be selected by democratic methods and guided by an egalitarian ethos, but it was ultimately authoritarian. Or, at least, tended in that direction. A pope is still a pope, even if he is selected by a conclave of his peers.

The Mesan Alignment was more hierarchical and authoritarian than most, by virtue of its own defining principles. There was no more than lip service paid to democratic methods, and none at all to egalitarianism, as you'd expect from a movement based on the principles of genetic superiority and inferiority. Ultimately, the Detweilers ruled because they were the Detweilers—the alphas of the alpha lines. More like a medieval dynasty, in some ways, than anything else.

That said, it was a modern dynasty with a modern, even hyper-sophisticated, attitude toward command and obedience. Members of the onion, especially those in the inner layers, were given a great deal of latitude. Their views were actively solicited and encouraged, not simply tolerated. An outsider—the archetypical alien from another universe, for instance—who observed the interactions of members of the onion as they went about their work, would have found them impossible to distinguish from the interaction of people in a democratic polity guided entirely by legal principles.

Until the ax came down. Then, the differences became clear and stark.

One could put that as crudely as possible. It takes a long time to execute someone in a democracy ruled by law. The Detweilers or their delegated lieutenants could do it in minutes, even seconds—no longer than it took for the order to be transmitted and the where-withal of homicide assembled.

So, Zachariah had kept his mouth shut about his brother Jack's supposed treason. The sophistication of the Alignment's leadership had been demonstrated by their refusal to punish any member of Jack's family. That had been true even informally. No one had lost a job, been demoted, or been refused later advancement. But open protest—resistance of any kind to the official line—would have been exceedingly dangerous. Quite probably fatal.

For all those reasons—perhaps other reasons, too; it was certainly not something Zachariah was going to discuss with a therapist—he'd never wept for his brother.

Now, as he watched his home planet receding in the viewscreen, he could finally grieve Jack's death— because he was grieving for his entire family. The rest of them were still alive, true enough. But there was little chance that Zachariah would ever see them again. Now that the final great struggle was at hand after centuries of preparation, no one in the inner layers of the onion thought it was going to be easy—and certainly not quick.

The problem was simple and inevitable, as the leaders of the Alignment had always known it would be. The prerequisite for accomplishing their goal was the dissolution of the Solarian League. Whatever its faults and weaknesses—its many, many, many weaknesses—the League was just too great an obstacle to their purpose, by virtue of its social mass if nothing else.

Early on, the Detweilers had pondered the possibility of using the League as a vessel for the transformation of the species, but they had never found a plausible mechanism for doing so. The League had to go, therefore. But that same immensity meant that great forces needed to be assembled against the League—and very few of those forces could be allowed to understand their own purpose. They were themselves inimical to the Alignment; more so, in many ways, than the League itself.

Leonard Detweiler's great-great-great-grand-daughter Cecilia had once depicted the problem thusly: *We will bring down the great bison with a pack of wolves. The tricky part is that we don't control the wolves.*

Thankfully, there had been enough room on the slave ship for Zachariah to have a private cabin. At least he was spared the presence of his Gaul keeper. So, as he watched Mesa dwindle in the viewscreen until it was just one bright speck among a multitude, he wept, softly and steadily. What made the tears so bitter was that he had never been able to say goodbye to anyone.

He was still weeping when the ship made its alpha translation and he left the system of his birth. Probably forever. Almost certainly for many years.

❖   ❖   ❖

When she came into the living room of their apartment, Stephanie Moriarty's face was taut and drawn. So much so that her natural beauty was overwhelmed by her own expression.

Cary Condor noticed at once. "What's wrong?"

"I'm . . . not sure 'wrong' is the right word." She began slowly removing her jacket. There'd been a chill that morning when she left. As she did so, she retrieved something from one of the pockets and held it up.

"I found this in the fish."

"Oh, my God." Cary practically whispered the words. She got up hastily and came over to stare at the little chip; so flimsy it was translucent. It looked more like a fish scale than anything manufactured. That was by design, of course.

"I'll get the reader. Don't move. Well . . . I mean, don't . . ."

Moriarty's expression shifted into something more derisive. Perhaps oddly, that made her look beautiful again. "I *did* manage to get it all the way here without destroying it, you know. I think I can hold on for another few seconds."

"Okay, okay, sorry. It's just . . . *Jesus.* I never expected we'd . . ."

"It might be nothing, you know."

"Don't be ridiculous, Stephanie."

Cary rummaged around in the drawer where she kept the specialized tablet. She kept it hidden for reasons that weren't really very reasonable. To the eye, the tablet looked no different than any other. Only a close and careful examination would reveal the unusually small slot where an out-of-the-ordinary chip could be inserted. The only people who would conduct that sort of examination were Mesan security agencies and if they'd fallen into their hands the proverbial goose was cooked anyway.

Whatever a goose was. She finally found the damn thing and held it up triumphantly.

"How could it be 'nothing'?" she demanded. "Who would put a blank chip in a *bacau* fluke?"

"Oh, gee, let's see. The Tabbies, for starters. Then there are the Ivas. The Bureau of—well, no, those thugs haven't got the brains—but there's always the—"

"Shut up." Cary took the chip and carefully inserted it into the reader. "If they'd spotted us they wouldn't be fooling around with something like this."

"Sure they would. Use us as bait to reel in our confederates. All of whom are dead and missing except Karen, I grant you, but they don't know that."

By now, Cary had the necessary codes entered. "Shut. Up."

It wasn't that she didn't understand the possibility that some security agency was playing a longer game than usual. She just didn't want to think about that while there was still a chance—one hell of a good chance, in her opinion—that—

The message came up and she began reading it off. "Ambassador Jim Johnson."

Stephanie had her own tablet out. "*The Envoy* by Giacomo ibn Giovanni al-Fulan. Got it."

"Mary had a little lamb whose fleece was white as snow," said Cary, speaking slowly.

Stephanie had been counting off the words as they were spoken. "Chapter Eleven, got it." Her half-surly skepticism was gone by now. "This *has* to be from Angus."

That was a reference to the Havenite agent who'd set up this system, Angus Levigne. The cypher was an idiosyncratic one that he'd devised himself. "It's not as tight as a one-time pad," he'd explained, "but it's less limited, too. Any really good decryption expert could crack it, but not very quickly because there are so many arbitrary variables that you commit to memory."

In that matter-of-fact absolute-zero way he had, Angus added: "Be easier to just subject you to truth drugs. Speaking of which"—he'd handed them a large vial of tablets—"take one of these at least once a month. They're a composite designed to counter truth drugs."

He'd sounded quite pleased. Angus was . . . a little weird. And a lot scary.

❖   ❖   ❖

It took a while to finish. When they were done, the two women stared at each other.

"Can we trust it?" Stephanie finally asked.

"Who knows, for sure?" Cary shrugged. "But the way I look at it, somebody would have had to crack Angus himself to get all the variables that make the cypher work. And how likely is that?"

Stephanie chewed on her lower lip. After a few seconds, she said: "To be honest, I can't imagine it happening at all. I'm pretty sure he could resist torture for . . . well, a long time."

Cary chuckled. But there was no humor in the sound. "'Long time' as in . . . ?"

"Really long time. But it wouldn't matter anyway because he'd be gone way before then. He's . . . you know."

"Weird."

Stephanie's smile did have some humor in it. "Let's

just think of him as 'different,' how's that? The key
point is, yes, I think we can trust it."

"Yeah, me too. We'll both have to go, though. The
way this contact works, one person can't do it alone."

Stephanie looked to the corner where Karen was
resting. Sleeping, rather. She slept most of the time now.

"It'd just be for a few hours. And it's not until
tomorrow anyway. She'll wake up sometime before
then and we can explain it to her. So at least if she
wakes up while we're gone she won't wonder what
happened to us."

"And if we don't come back at all..."

"She's dead in a few days instead of a few weeks.
Way it is."

As was generally true of seccy revolutionaries on
Mesa, both women were awfully hard-boiled themselves. That was the baseline against which you had
to measure someone like Angus Levigne. Even by
their standards he'd been...

Weird and scary.

CHAPTER 35

"I still find it hard to believe this is the way people crossed oceans," said Malissa Vaughn. "For *centuries*."

Standing next to her at the rail of the *Magellan*'s observation deck, her husband smiled. The expression managed to combine condescension and uneasiness.

The condescension came in his reply: "Your history's creaky. Try millennia, dear. *Lots* of millennia."

The uneasiness came from the fact that Jeffrey Vaughn was now regretting he'd ever come up with this idea for a vacation in the first place. At the time, spending two weeks aboard a recreation of a vessel from ancient history had seemed charming—and the term *seasick* just a historical curiosity.

Unfortunately, he was now discovering that even aboard a huge luxury liner equipped with stabilizers there was no way to evade the fundamental facts of his current existence:

The ship he was on floated directly upon the water, supported by ancient principles of buoyancy rather than modern principles of counter-grav.

The water immediately in question was a tiny, tiny, tiny portion of a very, very, very big ocean.

The latent energy in a planetwide ocean impacted by a planetary atmosphere dwarfed even the energy production and capabilities of modern civilization.

Which meant the ship . . . *jiggled.* Went up and down and side to side and back and forth as it damn well pleased and his stomach was welcome to take the hindmost if it didn't like it.

"All you all right, dear?"

"I'm fine," he said. Thereby unconsciously exhibiting another historical phenomenon, the ingrained reluctance of the human male to admit to frailty—a trait which was almost as deep-seated as the reluctance to ask directions from strangers.

"You don't look fine. You look almost green, in f—"

That was as far as she got before the explosion that ripped a huge tear in the *Magellan*'s hull threw both of them off the deck and into the water. They fell almost thirty meters. Neither one of them was directly killed by the impact, but Jeffrey was knocked unconscious and drowned quickly. Malissa was so dazed that when she came back up to the surface she just swam in a circle. She didn't even notice that the ship was getting farther and farther away.

But it didn't get very far. Another explosion staggered the ship, this one at the bow. Within two minutes, the *Magellan* was visibly settling in the water and starting to list to starboard. By then, however, the emergency evacuation procedures were already underway.

In the ancient days when ships like this were the standard form of seagoing vessel, the training for emergency evacuation measures was usually done in a casual and slipshod manner. Typically, a cruise ship setting out on a voyage would have a single drill early on, which consisted of nothing more than lining up the passengers in their designated evacuation areas and then dismissing them almost immediately. No one actually got *into* the lifeboats; indeed, the lifeboats never so much as budged on their davits.

But the *Magellan* was a novelty on Mesa. It was one of the very few floating ships of any size on the whole planet. In fact, it was the first passenger vessel in almost four centuries—and its two predecessors had been much smaller river boats. So, the evacuation drills had been taken quite seriously. They'd had two drills on the cruise already, even though the voyage was still less than half over. And each drill concluded with the passengers and crew getting aboard the escape shuttles. The only thing that wasn't done that would be in a real emergency was lifting the shuttles out of their cradles and flying to safety. That would have been costly—and the one thing no one in that day and age was worried about was the possibility that simple counter-grav atmospheric craft would malfunction.

So, within a short time a full third of the ship's complement had been ferried off the *Magellan* and were on their way to the mainland. Another five hundred were loading into more shuttles.

The first shuttle to explode had actually not left the ship yet. It was still resting in its cradle when it disappeared in a fireball that killed everyone already aboard and still loading, as well as every exposed person on the deck for sixty meters on either side. The exact death toll would never be known.

Less than ten seconds later, two of the shuttles already in the air exploded. Five seconds after that, two more shuttles on the ship blew up. The accumulated fatalities already numbered at least a thousand.

Panic-stricken passengers and crew now sought safety inside the ship. Sinking or not, the *Magellan* had sturdy bulkheads. Almost no damage caused by the exploding shuttles had penetrated the interior. The open decks where the shuttles had been berthed, on the other hand, were places of sheer carnage.

Shortly thereafter, just as the surviving members of the crew were starting to bring some order out of the chaos, a third explosion struck the *Magellan*. As well built as she was, the liner had never been designed to handle this sort of damage. It capsized within a minute. The almost stately pace at which the ship had been settling until then turned into something much more rapid and terrifying. The bow plunged beneath the surface and the stern rose up out of the water. Four and a half minutes later, the last few meters of the stern sank below the waves.

Of the 2,744 passengers and 963 crew members aboard, only 855 survived. Three of the shuttles that had managed to lift off the *Magellan* made it to the coast unharmed. That accounted for almost six hundred of the survivors. The rest were rescued after the ship sank, pulled out of the water by rescue craft flying out from the mainland. The first of them arrived forty minutes after the alarm was sent on the heels of the initial explosion. Fortunately, the explosions had spread a lot of floatable debris into the water surrounding the ship, so people who lived long enough to get off the ship had something to hang onto. And since the ship had been sailing in Mesa's northern subtropical zone, hypothermia had not been a problem.

One of the first people pulled out of the ocean was Malissa Vaughn. Despite being addled by her impact on the water, she was a good swimmer and her natural instincts had kept her afloat. Because the ship had travelled another two hundred meters from where she'd been thrown before the second explosion finally brought it to a halt, she hadn't been struck by any of the debris produced by the exploding shuttles, either.

She didn't remember a thing. Her last memory had been of walking onto the deck with her husband. He'd wanted some fresh air.

Between the force and fire of the explosions and the number of people who drowned, very few bodies were recovered. The identities of those killed had to be reconstructed from the ship's own records—or rather, the records held by its parent company, Voyages Unlimited. The *Magellan* had sunk in ten kilometers of water, so salvaging the ship's own computers would have been very costly. Why bother, when the parent company held duplicate records in its computers on dry land?

✦   ✦   ✦

As soon as the first shuttle blew up, it became obvious to the authorities that the catastrophe which had struck—was still striking—the *Magellan* could not possibly be the result of an accident. Even the explosions on board the ship itself, especially *two* of them, were highly suspect. But given that the vessel's design and construction were hardly what anyone would have called standard, and given that very few people on Mesa—outside of the officers and crew of the *Magellan* itself—had any experience with floating ships, it was conceivable that some peculiar mishap or set of mishaps had occurred.

Counter-grav shuttles, on the other hand, were about as exotic as boots—and just as reliable. The moment the first shuttle exploded in its cradle, any thought that they might be dealing with an accident went out the window.

The Green Pines incident had occurred only one year before, after all. The possibility—no, the probability—of another terrorist outrage was well established.

Voyages Unlimited (not to mention its insurers) was entirely in favor of adopting a terrorist explanation. You might even say, ecstatically in favor. But their public spokesmen, being practiced professionals, managed to maintain their mournfully solemn expressions throughout.

✧   ✧   ✧

"Are you *listening* to this shit, boss?" Skylar Beckert, Director of Domestic Intelligence Analysis for the Mesan Internal Security Directorate, demanded as she burst into Bentley Howell 's office. Howell was the MISD's commanding officer, and as a rule, he didn't usually react well to uninvited eruptions into his office. Skylar, however, was something of an exception to that rule, even under ordinary conditions—which these assuredly were not—because of how often she and her people had ferreted out the exact information Howell required. Including information which rivals like Fran Selig or Gillian Drescher had had no intention of sharing with MISD.

"Of course I'm listening, Sky!" Howell snapped. He was glaring at the com unit on the corner of his desk. "I missed the first twenty seconds or so, though. Who the fuck is this?"

"They claim they're the Audubon Ballroom," Beckert replied. "They're delivering some kind of 'manifesto'... and taking credit—if you can call it that—for the *Magellan*."

"*Bastards!*" Howell hissed. "I *told* Selig and McGillicuddy—"

"Boss, I know that's who they *claim* to be," Beckert cautioned, "but I don't think we can necessarily take that at face value. Some other terrorist organization might be responsible and just trying to deflect the reprisals on someone else."

"Oh, *right*..." Howell's tone oozed sarcasm. "Just what terrorists are famous for, their shrewdness and sagacity."

Beckert hid an internal sigh behind an attentive expression. Commissioner Howell's contempt for all seccies and slaves—and especially for *ex*-slaves—was the one truly dangerous chink in his armor, in her opinion. There were times when it was wiser not to press a point too strongly, however, so she simply walked around the end of his desk until she could see the com image at which he had been glaring when she entered.

That image was of a person sitting at a small table and looking directly at the viewer. The gender of the person couldn't be determined, thanks to carefully baggy clothing and the fact that his or her face and voice were being electronically shielded, and a corner of her mind wondered why they'd bothered with a visual image at all. Proving the point that there was a real person behind it? The wreckage still settling on the ocean floor had already made *that* clear enough! And despite her own caution to Howell, Beckert could think of very few other organizations which might have had enough sheer gall—or enough raw hatred—to carry out an attack like this on *Mesa*, of all planets.

Whoever the hell they really are, they picked the wrong world to try this shit on, she thought grimly.

"—while millions of disenfranchised citizens live in abject poverty," the speaker was saying. "We can only hope the scavengers on the ocean floor get some sustenance from our blow for freedom. They perform a useful function, unlike the parasites who have the wealth to idle away their time on monstrously expensive and ostentatious luxuries. All such—"

❖   ❖   ❖

"—warned. Continue on your present course and—"

The same transmission was being ignored in a hotel room two kilometers away. The Solarian League newscaster was chivvying his crew to assemble their equipment—*now! now! now!*—so they could get to the scene of the disaster and start recording before any of their competitors.

Xavier Conde was not one of the League's top newscasters, but he was solidly in the second tier. He had many of the prerequisites for the job down cold. He was good-looking, telegenic, as ambitious as Satan and not burdened by an excessive number of scruples.

He was also not especially bright, which might have had something to do with his continued failure to crack into the top tier in his profession. Or perhaps the problem lay more in the fact that he was convinced he *was* extraordinarily intelligent—so he kept coming up with half-baked schemes to prove it. He might have gotten farther if he'd just accepted his limits with equanimity. After all, there were any number of well-known newscasters whom no one had ever suspected of being the sharpest edges around.

Conde and his team had arrived on Mesa a month earlier, to do a special report on the casualties suffered by the planet's so-called "seccies" in the Green Pines outrage. His thesis—which he genuinely thought to be original—was that terrorists often kill and main "their own" in the course of their fanatical crusades.

Mesa's Directorate of Culture and Information, needless to say, had been very supportive of the project.

"Come on, people! Let's *go-go-go!*"

CHAPTER 36

"So how's married life treating you?" one of his bunk-mates asked Supakrit X. But the newly (re)promoted sergeant gave no answer.

Lying on his own bunk across the narrow aisle, Corporal Bohuslav Hernandez raised his head from his pillow and looked over at the still form of the sergeant. "Treating him pretty good, I'd say. He's already asleep."

"I still think he's nuts," said the fourth member of the cabin, Corporal Ted Vlachos. He was sitting on the edge of the bunk just above Hernandez. "You wouldn't catch me sharing a bed with that woman. Tick her off a little too much—*zip*—you're for the long jump."

His fellow corporal made no reply, since he couldn't think of one that wouldn't be excessively rude. Vlachos should be so lucky. As far as Hernandez was aware, the slob hadn't had a bedmate in at least six months—even though, being bisexual, he had a wider field than most.

Vlachos was . . . unpleasant. It didn't help that he snored, bathed no more often than regulations required,

410

chewed his food with his mouth open, made invariably stupid jokes, the list went on and on. How the man had ever made it beyond private was one of the mysteries of the universe.

"Leaving in fifteen seconds," came the voice of the *Hali Sowle's* captain over the com. *"If you haven't secured yourself by then and something goes wrong, don't come whining to me."*

Bohuslav grinned. Ganny El, on the other hand... There was an old lady with ungracious manners, an abrasive personality, a well-nigh total disrespect for protocol—and a way with fools that was one of the wonders of the universe.

He checked to make sure he was strapped into the bunk, then looked over at Supakrit again. The sergeant, alas, had not secured himself before falling asleep. On the other hand, he looked so placid and boneless that Bohuslav figured he'd probably survive any mishaps that were survivable at all. The odds of that happening were microscopic, anyway.

And here we go.

❖   ❖   ❖

The personnel tubes and umbilicals detached. The battered and bedamned looking freighter (whose hyper generator had been *thoroughly* overhauled after its recent maintenance issues, thank you very much) drifted clear of Parmley Station on carefully metered bursts from her maneuvering thrusters. *Hali Sowle* was in no enormous hurry, and it took several minutes for her to gain enough clearance to go to her main fusion-powered reaction thrusters and accelerate away from the station at a sedate twenty gravities' acceleration. (Ganny El was frugal—some might even have gone so far as to use the term chintzy—with her reactor mass.) At that rate, it took her a leisurely fifty-five seconds to clear the mandatory three hundred-kilometer deep impeller-free safety zone around the station. The two *Turner*-class frigates, the *Gabriel Prosser* and the *Denmark Vesey*, kept pace with her until all three vessels crossed the perimeter and shut down thrusters. Then they rolled slightly as her heavy-lift tractors reached out, locked them up, and settled them into their jury-rigged nests on her flank.

Three more minutes passed as the frigates each locked a personnel tube to the far larger freighter and tested them for pressure and security. The frigates were fully self-contained and self-sufficient starships, of course, but why should their crews stay penned up inside their tiny hulls when much larger open spaces were available (within reason, of course) aboard *Hali Sowle*? Pressure checks satisfactorily completed, each frigate's CO gave the freighter's command deck the go ahead. Then—

"That's that, Parmley. We're out of here," Ganny El announced over the com. The *Hali Sowle*'s wedge came up and the freighter leapt instantly to one hundred and seventy gravities. Five minutes later, she was nearly eighty thousand kilometers out, headed for the hyper limit at over five hundred kilometers per second.

✧   ✧   ✧

Captain Anton Petersen keyed his control unit and a new set of figures came up on the wallscreen in the conference room. "These are my projections for assembling and training the special units. We need a name for them, by the way. Best way to tank morale I know is to assign someone to a 'special unit.'"

Hugh Arai chuckled. "No kidding. In the BSC, that's a euphemism for cleaning the toilets."

Petersen smiled. "It's got a wider application in the RMN—but none of them bring good cheer to those assigned."

"Call them the Royal Commandos," suggested Ruth.

"They're not anything of the sort!" said Jeremy X scornfully. "These lads and lasses aren't going to be storming fortresses. Their work will be more along the lines of turning over rocks to see what might be crawling around underneath."

"That's sort of what *most* people's 'commandos' do, Jeremy," Hugh pointed out mildly. "My own stalwart companions of the BSC come to mind. 'Storm fortresses'?" He shuddered. "That's what *Marines* are for! Not, mind you," he continued judiciously, "that these lads are likely to be up to BSC standards any time soon. Take some training, some good doctrine, and a *lot* of experience to get there. So I'll grant you the ancient and respected title might be just a *tad* premature at this point."

"Call them the 'Royal Mousers,' then," said Berry.

"That's preposter—" But the Secretary of War broke off, frowning.

"Kind of like it, myself," said Hugh.

Ruth sniffed. "Well, of course you do. Currying royal favor, seeing as how if you lose it the consequences are personal and immediate. But I think it's a little . . . I don't know. Disrespectful. Well, maybe not *dis*-respectful. Unrespectful?"

"Pfah." That came from Jeremy, whose frown was clearing away. "Do them good not to be fawned over. Besides, they're ex-slaves. Easily pleased by the occasional tidbit. All we need is to come up with a snazzy unit logo and they'll be purring like—"

Hugh winced. "Please don't say it."

"—cats. With fresh-caught rodents squirming in their maws."

Ruth still looked skeptical, but her always-active mind was intrigued. "How about... A snarling cat's head over... What? Crossed swords, maybe?"

"Oh, pfui!" protested Berry. "I don't want them *snarling*. Cat's head, fine—but it should be the Cheshire cat. Better yet, just its grin before it fades away entirely. Over..."

Her eyes got a little criss-crossed, as she pondered the problem. "Rodents petrified, staring up—two on each side. And over the grin... Crossed lariats, maybe?"

Classic heraldry was something of a hobby for Petersen, but he managed not to wince at the Queen's suggestion. The Cheshire cat was fine, and so were the terrified rodents. The crossed lariats, on the other hand, wouldn't do at all.

Fortunately, tradition was at hand. "For the crest, I recommend going with either a pair of lions—sejant or rampant, either'll work—or crossed keys. To avoid grumbling from the churches, though, if we opt for the latter we should use a different design than the keys of Saint Peter."

Everyone stared at him.

"What's 'sejant' and 'rampant'?" asked Berry.

"The terms aren't used in *modern* heraldry," explained Petersen. His tone of voice had a touch of acerbic disdain in it. "Haven't been used in well over a thousand T-years, in fact... except by those of us who really *understand* the importance of tradition. They're from

the classic forms and are based on ancient Norman—
that's an Old Earth language, one of Standard English's
less reputable ancestors. Not that Standard English *has*
any reputable ancestors now that I think about it." He
shrugged. "Anyway, 'sejant' means sitting on guard, and
'rampant' shows the beast upright with paws raised as
if it were entering battle."

Berry made a face. "Seems...excessive, for a Cheshire
cat. Let's go with the crossed keys."

"Done," said Hugh. "Royal Mousers it is."

Petersen cleared his throat. "I recommend using
Royal Mouser Corps instead. The troops in the unit
will start calling themselves 'mousers' immediately, but
they'll be disgruntled if they don't have the dignity
of 'corps' formally attached to the name."

Hugh looked at Berry. "Okay with me."

"Me, too," she replied. "Jeremy?"

"I rather like it. And now that the folderol is taken
care of, exactly how large a corps do you envision,
Captain Petersen? And organized how?"

"We'll start with a force of around four hundred officers and enlisted troops—the size of a small battalion—
commanded by a lieutenant colonel. They'll be divided
into four companies of one hundred people, each commanded by a captain. Each company, in turn, will be
divided into four platoons of twenty soldiers, commanded
by a lieutenant, along with a special platoon of twenty
commanded by another captain. That special platoon
will consist mostly of intelligence specialists."

"Seems a little top-heavy," said Jeremy. "In terms
of the officers-to-enlisted ratio, I mean."

"It is, measured by the standards of combat units."
Petersen shrugged. "But the mission assigned to the

Mousers is extremely complicated and will require a lot in the way of individual and small unit initiative. I think it'd be wise to have a heavy cadre of officers and noncoms."

Jeremy looked at Hugh. "Do you have a problem with that?"

Hugh scratched his jaw. "Well... I understand Anton's reasoning. We don't use the same grades, but the BSC has a similar organizational structure—and for pretty much the same reason. What bothers me is that Torch's armed forces are already strapped for officers, especially commissioned ones. This will aggravate the problem some."

The Secretary of War looked mildly exasperated. "A straight answer please. Yes or no?"

"Yes, yes. I'm just fretting out loud."

❖   ❖   ❖

Walter Imbesi looked out over Erewhon's capital city of Maytag. From his vantage point on one of the observation decks just a few floors from the very top of the Suds Emporium, he had an excellent view of Whirlpool Gulf and the harbor area. Both of which were causing him to muse on history, at the moment.

Or, more likely, he was musing on history because of the political situation. The landscape below was just a prop, you might say. Imbesi had a strong sense of irony. Once again, the present found reflection in the past.

Most visitors to Erewhon—most of the planet's own citizens, for that matter—thought Whirlpool Gulf got its name from the maelstroms that formed in its narrow expanse due to the heavy tide. In fact, the name came from the same whimsy that led those ancient gangsters to bestow the name of Maytag on their new capital and call its tallest and most prestigious edifice the Suds. They planned to launder their reputations as well as their money, but couldn't resist thumbing their nose at the galaxy while they were about it.

He turned his head slightly. "Is either of you a student of ancient history?"

"Not me," said Sharon Justice.

"Define 'ancient,'" said Yuri Radamacher.

"Anything pre-Diaspora." Walter took his eyes away from the view and swiveled to face the other occupants of the observation deck. Which was more in the way of a small and luxurious lounge, really, than what most people thought of as a "deck." The Suds had been designed with an eye in mind for informal and highly discreet conversations. The material lining the walls shielded the room from most methods of spying, and powerful electronic scramblers did for the rest. Visitors were always welcome to bring their own antidetection gear, of course.

"Specifically," he continued, "the two centuries between the discovery of atmospheric flight and the first interstellar expedition."

"Christopher Columbus discovered the moon, right?" said Sharon.

Imbesi winced. "I hope that's a joke. The moon was 'discovered' by australopithecines. Columbus' discoveries happened almost half a millennium before the development of air flight."

"Hey, *I* thought it was funny."

Yuri ignored the banter. "I know a fair amount about it. Why?"

"Our situation reminds me of one that existed in that period—and I think we can find a solution to our problem there as well. An inspiration, at least."

"Explain, please."

"After the first of the great world wars, two of Europe's major powers—Russia and Germany—found themselves ostracized by the rest for political reasons. The reasons varied between the two, and certainly aren't close to anything we face today. But the gist of their problem was quite similar. Russia was a vast country with a lot of space difficult for any foreign power to investigate. It was also a desperately poor country with a great need for technical assistance. Germany was almost the polar opposite: highly advanced, for the time, but a relatively small country with little in the way of privacy. It had also been forced to disarm itself as a result of losing the war.

"So, they cut a deal. The Russians allowed the Germans to set up secret development projects far inside its borders, which they used to build and test weapons. They also engaged in military training. In exchange, the Germans gave the Russians technical assistance and advice in creating a modern officer corps for its own army."

Yuri was frowning slightly. "I knew the bare bones of that. But as I recall, there are a lot of differences..."

Walter made a dismissive gesture with his hand. "Oh, certainly. For starters, the Germans and Russians were deeply suspicious of each other, which"—here came a gleaming smile—"I daresay is not true of any of us."

He bestowed the gleaming smile on the fourth occupant of the room, Lieutenant Commander Watanapongse. The Mayan intelligence officer who was doubling here as an informal negotiator for Governor Barregos and Admiral Rozsak had been silent so far. He now broke his silence. In a manner of speaking.

He issued a noncommittal grunt. But there was a definite trace of humor there, as well.

"Like all analogies," Imbesi continued, "you can only push it so far. For one thing, we're not proposing a formal military alliance and we're working with three parties instead of two. For another, the issue of maneuvering room for training purposes isn't really that important. The galaxy's a lot bigger than a planet. We can find an uninhabitable red giant system somewhere in which to conduct maneuvers."

Sharon had a sly smile on her face. "I have to say that I find the suggestion Haven is in any way comparable to that dirt-poor, hardscrabble—what did you say the name was—?"

"Russia."

"Is probably grounds for an affair of honor. Luckily for you, I left my dueling pistols at home."

Imbesi raised his hands in protest. "I meant to imply no such thing."

"Best not to," said Watanapongse, smiling. "The truth is, Haven surpasses us in some areas relevant to military technology. And there's no comparison at all when it comes to battle-readiness and combat experience. What we could really use from you is something short of a formal alliance—that might stir up sleeping dogs at home we'd just as soon kept slumbering—but as close to it as possible."

"You're proposing a secret defensive agreement, is what it sounds like," said Yuri. "More precisely, a secret addendum to the defensive agreement we already have."

Watanapongse and Imbesi looked at each other. "That would do it, I think," said Imbesi.

"As long as we really keep it secret," agreed the Mayan intelligence officer.

"What would the basic provisions be? In terms of what you'd want from us?"

"In essence—I'm keeping this very brief for the moment; we can draw up the specific language later— we'd want Haven to provide us with a last-resort guarantee of military support—warships, I mean, not just assistance and advice—if all hell breaks loose and the Sollies start sending battle fleets our way with blood in their eye." He nodded toward Imbesi. "Or if they come at Erewhon. But in this scenario, it's more likely Maya would be the target."

"Yes, I understand," said Yuri. "You want to maintain as long as possible your current pose as neutrals—in the case of Erewhon—or good little OFS types, in yours. But if and when the Sollies see through the façade and decide to punish you, you want Haven to come to your aid."

"It'll be 'when,' sooner or later," said Watanapongse. "We're just hoping 'if' doesn't become 'when' until the Solarian League has already crumbled or the Sollies are too weak and disorganized to do very much about it."

Yuri smiled. "You know, there's another analogy from ancient history that's more appropriate here. Did you ever hear of the Monroe Doctrine?"

The Mayan shook his head. Imbesi leaned his head back and laughed. "Of course!" he said.

Seeing Watanapongse's puzzled expression, he explained. "One of the other great powers at the time, the United States of America, dominated Terra's western hemisphere. They declared the entire hemisphere off limits to the older Eurasian states."

Turning back to Yuri, he said: "That's about right. That would allow us to remain an independent and steadily stronger power center, while you establish that you don't intend to let any outside interests intervene in the area and create any dangerous instability on your southern flanks."

"So far, so good—from your point of view," said Yuri. "But—forgive me for being blunt—what's in it for us?"

"Goodwill?" That came from the Mayan lieutenant commander.

Yuri shrugged. "I'm not one to dismiss the importance of goodwill, even between star nations. Still, if you want me to pass this along to Eloise Pritchart, a bit of icing on the cake would be helpful."

Imbesi and Watanapongse looked at each other, for a moment. "It's your call, Jiri," said the Erewhonese.

"Barregos' call, with a lot of input from Luiz," responded the Mayan officer. "But we already discussed this possibility before I left and my instructions are pretty clear. We can provide Haven with intelligence on the Solarian League that's way more extensive and deeper than anything you—or the Manties—could turn up on your own."

He plucked at the sleeve of his uniform. "Seeing as how, not to put too fine a point on it, I *am* still an intelligence officer in the Solarian Navy. Just as Luiz is an admiral and Oravil is one of the League's OFS sector governors."

"Sounds good to me, Yuri," said Sharon. "Granted, if the wheels come off the provisions of the agreement are weighted heavily in favor of Maya and Erewhon. But we're *already* at war with the Sollies and it's quite possible the wheels will never come off at all. Maya may well be able to slide through the whole crisis without ever triggering off a direct confrontation with the League. At least, one that involves massive military intervention by the Sollies."

"Yeah, that's the way it looks to me too. Not my decision, of course. I'm the lowly one in this august company, being as I am a mere high commissioner and envoy extraordinary."

Imbesi smiled. "How silly of me. I forgot to mention that the *official* reason I asked for this meeting was to present you with a formal request to take back to Nouveau Paris. Erewhon now feels that it would be best if Haven's interests here were represented by an ambassador. Specifically, an ambassador extraordinary and plenipotentiary."

In its flowery arcane language, that was diplomacy's highest ranking. The sort of ambassador whose signature on a treaty could—and had many times in history—sent armies and fleets into motion.

Yuri nodded. "I see. Do you have a specific recom—"

"Pfah. You, of course."

CHAPTER 37

Victor gazed down at the recumbent form on the narrow bed. "When was the last time she was awake?"

"It's been twenty hours," said Cary. "We're getting worried."

"Karen's condition seems to have worsened a lot recently," said Stephanie. "Starting a week ago. Before that, her deterioration was more or less steady but didn't change much from day to day."

Victor wasn't surprised. Given the young woman's injuries, she had to have a tough constitution just to have stayed alive this long.

"All right," he said. "It'll pose some risks, but we don't have any choice. We'll move her tonight."

Cary frowned. "Move her? Where?"

"And why?" added Moriarty.

"Never mind the 'where.' You don't need to know. As for the 'why,' we have access to a regeneration unit. It's not the sort of full-fledged unit a hospital would have, so we won't be able to heal all of the damage. But at least we can stabilize her condition and keep her alive."

"For how long?"

"Medically speaking, for years. The political situation is likely to pose the real hazard." Victor turned away from the bed. "I'll send people over to pick her up. They'll be here just after nightfall. Have her ready to go."

"Ready...how?"

He shrugged. "As best you can."

"Not a chance," said Stephanie firmly. "She can't even stand up."

Since Karen's legs were missing below the knees, she couldn't walk out under her own power. Victor was searching for an alternative. Simply carrying the woman out on a litter could be done, of course. There wasn't really that much risk involved. After nightfall, unless there was someone specifically spying on them—in which case, the authorities were already alerted and the hammer was probably about to fall anyway—they could only be spotted by one of the surveillance cameras that were scattered throughout most of the seccy quarters.

But the lighting in the corridors was pretty poor. Anyone monitoring the images would be able to determine that one live human body was being carried by two other people, but they wouldn't see enough detail to tell exactly what was happening. Illness, an injury of some sort, it could be a number of things. It would be easy to disguise everyone's features enough to throw off automatic face recognition software—even assuming that Mesan security had good enough images of the three women in the first place.

So, a little disguise...misdirection, rather...

"We won't carry her out on a stretcher. We'll carry

her slung by the shoulders, one person on each side. I'll have the two people who pick her up act casually, even convivially. If the incident does get picked up by a surveillance camera, anyone studying the recording is likely to think Karen just got drunk at a party and two friends came to take her home."

Stephanie and Cary looked at each other.

"That'll work," said Stephanie, with a hard little smile on her face. "Everybody knows seccies are a bunch of souses and drug addicts."

"It might be a little rough on Karen," said Cary, "but she's tough enough to take it. And she's light enough that the two of us can lift her."

Victor shook his head. "You won't be carrying her. Not both of you, anyway. I need Cary to come with me on my visit to Chuanli. She'll need to introduce me."

Both women frowned. "Why do you want to see *him*?" asked Stephanie. "I'd figure at this point—since we won't be selling him Karen's body parts after all—that we'd want to steer clear of him."

"You really want to know? You don't need to but"— he shrugged—"there's no security issues involved."

Again, Stephanie and Cary looked at each other.

"No," said Cary.

"Yes," said Stephanie. "I'm tired of groping in the dark."

"It's simple enough. I'm going to take over Lower Radomsko—or rather, convince Jurgen Dusek that I can—in order to use Dusek's criminal network to do this, that and the other." He smiled a little apologetically. "Sorry, those details you *don't* need to know."

"Hell, I'm sorry I asked at all," said Stephanie.

❖   ❖   ❖

The guy was just as freaky as Angus Levigne. And while he didn't look like him at all—he was strikingly handsome, for one thing, which you could hardly say of Angus—he had the same air about him. Hard as a diamond; ruthless; deadly. Did Manticore have a factory that stamped them out like robots?

The name he'd given Cary and Stephanie was Philip Watson. Stephanie was sure it was a pseudonym, just as she was sure "Angus Levigne" had been as well. Watson hadn't precisely identified himself in terms of who he represented. Levigne had been equally vague. But Carl Hansen had told them Levigne and the squat powerful-looking man who'd come with him on that previous mission were Manticoran agents. Stephanie had seen no reason to doubt him, even though the two agents who'd come to Mesa earlier had spoken with completely different accents.

She hadn't recognized either one of those accents. But this guy, Watson, spoke with yet a third accent, one which Stephanie did recognize. Manticorans rarely came to Mesa but Dockhorns came often because they were heavily involved in the slave trade. Stephanie had encountered several of them over the years. The accent was quite distinctive.

Why would a Dockhorn be working for Manticore? That didn't make much sense.

She'd been immediately suspicious but...

The problem was, she couldn't think of any logical reason Watson would be anything *other* than a Manticoran agent. It made even less sense that one of Mesa's security agencies would be running such an elaborate sting operation. Why bother? If they knew enough to have completely penetrated the security arrangements made by Levigne, they'd know that Stephanie and her two surviving confederates were isolated small fry. They'd just stamp them out.

She'd discuss it with Cary after she got back. There could be several explanations, after all. In the meantime, she needed to do what she could to get Karen ready.

There was that about Watson. She'd had the same sense about Levigne, too. They might be utterly ruthless but they were not disloyal. Something about them—it was there even if she couldn't put a finger on it—exuded *you don't leave a fallen comrade behind* just as surely as they did deadliness.

Stephanie's eyes teared up—something which almost never happened to her. But she and Cary and Karen had become very close over the years of struggle, especially the harrowing period since Green Pines. She'd been sure Karen was doomed and that they'd even have to dismember her.

She managed a little chuckle, then. Karen might still be doomed, of course. As Watson had intimated, the political situation remained perilous. But whatever else, at least they wouldn't have to cut her up like an animal carcass.

She managed an outright laugh, at that point. Talk about a low bar!

❖   ❖   ❖

"We used them quite a bit on Parmley Station," Andrew explained. Thandi followed his finger as he pointed to the objects positioned at intervals just under the basement's ceiling. There were ten of them, all told; four down each side and one in the center of the narrow walls that formed the ends of the sunken chamber.

"And there are more along the floor," pointing those out as well. "The gadgets were originally mining equipment."

Seeing Thandi's small frown of puzzlement, Artlett got a jeering smile on his face. "Soldiers! Talk about one-track minds. Not 'mining' as in warfare, Thandi. 'Mining' as in digging deep holes in the ground to haul out minerals."

The frown stayed in place. "Do they still do that?"

"Yeah, believe it or not. It's a rare practice nowadays, of course. It's generally much easier and more efficient—not to mention cheaper—to either use one or another type of molecular recombination or just strip away an entire asteroid. But occasionally there's a substance that's worth getting the old-fashioned way. The thing is, such mines almost always require deep penetration. So—"

He indicated the gadgets once again. "These things. They're called pressor nodes. Once they're triggered, they set up a lattice that reinforces whatever structure they're embedded in, like a mine tunnel or a cavern. We used them as safety precautions in parts of the station that were at risk of rupturing. I had to adapt them some, so they'd hold something together as well as resist external pressures and impacts."

Thandi was impressed. Artlett could be a pain in the neck, but the man was a genuine wizard when it came to tech stuff. "In other words, by setting them up here you've turned this subbasement into what amounts to a bomb shelter."

Andrew waggled his hand. "Within limits. A direct hit by a targeted penetration bomb will punch through. And it doesn't stand a chance against a kinetic energy weapon strike from orbit. But we should survive anything short of that."

She frowned. "I'd think something that effective would generate so much energy that it'd be easily detected."

"Well, sure—but we won't be using them except in an emergency. That's 'emergency' as in 'the Mesan authorities are trying to blow their way into the place'—in which case, what difference does it make if they detect the use of pressor nodes? They already know we're here or we wouldn't need to use them at all. We faced the same problem in Parmley Station. We didn't want slavers to be able to detect our locations, which they certainly would have if we'd kept the nodes powered all the time. But we didn't need to, since they were only there for emergencies."

He gave Thandi the sort of pitying look usually reserved for children having trouble with simple math problems. Then, pointed to one of the pieces of equipment in a corner of the chamber. "See that? It's a Faber-Knapp battery. I've been charging it ever since we arrived. In another day or so, there'll be enough energy stored up to give all the nodes a power surge to keep the structure intact long enough for us to make our escape."

"Escape wh—"

"And before you ask 'where,' let me show you something." He led the way around a corner in the chamber. Thandi saw what looked for all the world like a spaceship hatch recessed into the wall.

"That's an access hatch that leads to one of the sewer lines," he said.

She made a face. Seeing it, Andrew chuckled.

"Relax. I looked around a bit. That sewer doesn't look like it's been used in decades. This is a big city and it's been here for centuries. Given that much time, the subterranean passages will be a gigantic maze. After a while, no one really knows exactly what exists and where it goes."

"Are you sure there's a way out?"

He gave her the same pitying look—adjusted downward, so to speak. *Poor kid can't add two plus two.* "How am I supposed to know? It'd take days—weeks, maybe months—to explore what's probably out there. But it can't be any worse than the situation we'd be in, can it?"

She smiled. "Point taken."

When they got back into the main part of the chamber, Thandi glanced at the ceiling. "How's she doing?"

Andrew shook his head. "*She's* not in there any longer. The guy is. What's his name?"

"Teddy."

"Yeah, him. Silly name for a thug, you ask me. We swapped them out quickly to make sure his wounds got stabilized. After a couple of more hours, we'll swap them again. They'll stay in longer, the second time around."

"Where is she?"

"We've got her in a room on the second floor."

Thandi frowned. "Who's watching her? You're down here and I thought I heard Steph moving around in the front room."

"Relax. Her wounds aren't life-threatening."

"I'm not worried about that. If she escapes, we could have trouble."

"Escape!" Andrew's mouth twisted into a jeer again. "First off, she's heavily sedated. Second, she's not getting out of *that* room—I know; I made sure it was secure—with anything less than explosives, which she doesn't have. And they'd kill her if she set them off, anyway, in that small a room. It's not much more than a glorified closet."

❖   ❖   ❖

Anton frowned at the figures on the screen. "What the hell...?"

A possible explanation came to him. He was not one to jump to conclusions, though. So he spent a few minutes pondering various ways he might be able to cross-check the information. Not to make sure it was accurate—he'd already made sure of that—but to develop the needed correlations.

Correlation wasn't causality, of course, not even when it reached one hundred percent. A toddler's ability to walk is invariably preceded by feeding on milk. It does not thereby follow that milk causes pedestrianism. Still, if he could produce the same results within a reasonable margin of error using several different correlations, he'd know he had a line on something.

So. His initial results had been obtained by cross-checking disappearances with residence. An obvious correlation would be to cross-check disappearances with occupations. Another would be to cross-check disappearances with job status. A third might be...

Mesan citizens registered their DNA at birth. Cracking into those records would be tricky, but Anton was sure he could manage it. The bigger problem would be crunching the numbers involved, after he got them. But there were advantages to being Cathy Montaigne's

lover. She was always willing to place her wealth at
his disposal when he needed something for his work.
Such as a shipboard computer whose capabilities
vastly exceeded anything a pleasure yacht required.
Centillions trembled at its approach; vigintillions just
fell over dead.

That correlation would be a lot fuzzier than the
others—and they were already fuzzy—but if Anton's
surmise was correct he should be able to see regular
patterns. However Mesa might be ranking its citizens,
that should manifest itself in the genomes selected.
There'd be clusters involved.

One more correlation. Perhaps...

"That is so freaky," said Yana. "I'll never get used
to it."

Startled, Anton's eyes came back into focus. He
looked to his left and saw that Yana was sprawled on
the luxurious divan against the salon's wall. (Technically,
it was a bulkhead, but the term just didn't fit—really,
really didn't fit—the splendor of the thing. What sort
of self-respecting bulkhead is laden with original works
of art each of which cost a small fortune?)

"What's freaky?" he asked.

"You are. I've been watching you for ten minutes.
In that entire time you haven't moved except for
blinking your eyes and occasionally twitching a finger."

"I'm thinking," he said defensively.

She shook her head. "You are *not*. Thinking is
what people do for maybe fifteen seconds at a stretch.
What you're doing is even more unnatural than this
ridiculous fake body of mine."

However often Yana groused privately about her new
physique, she never broke cover when it came to her

apparel. Right now, she was wearing an outfit designed by one of Terra's top couturier which accentuate her already flamboyant figure and clung to her like mist. Literally, like mist: the material was just barely short of transparent and seemed somehow aerated. The material was something Anton had never heard of before, called vaporaise. The stuff was apparently so expensive that when gold bullion came calling it had to use the servants' entrance.

"Of course!" he exclaimed. He turned back to the computer. "Correlate disappearances with fashion purchases."

"Glad to be of help," said Yana.

⋄   ⋄   ⋄

"Are we expecting any trouble?" asked Borisav Stanković, as they neared the entrance to their destination.

Lajos Irvine shook his head. "No. And if there were any—no offense, guys, but we're on Dusek's turf—there isn't much you could do anyway."

"Yeah, we'd be toast before we knew anything was up," said Freddie Martinez.

His tone was placid. It was a sign of the high quality of Lajos' sidekicks that neither one of them felt any need to strut or swagger. Even the Alignment's gunmen were top grade.

"So why are we here?" Stanković wasn't being belligerent, he just wanted to make sure he and Freddie understood what they were supposed to do.

"You're basically window-dressing, Bora. I'm trying to pass myself off as a person of substance in the milieu."

"That being the criminal underworld," said Stanković, nodding. "It wouldn't do for such a fine and upstanding fellow to carry his own goods to an exchange. Especially without bodyguards."

He and Martinez were both carrying valises that held the body parts Lajos would be selling today. Both in their left hands, leaving the right hands free in case weapons needed to be drawn.

Not that they would be—or could be. If they were walking into an ambush, the first sign of trouble would be their sudden and near-instantaneous demise. Men like Dusek and Chuanli weren't fumblers. But it was all a moot point. The goods they were carrying weren't valuable enough—not even close—for Dusek to tarnish his reputation for straight dealing. Lajos was bringing his own bodyguards simply because of protocol. In the sometimes topsy-turvy world of organized crime, it would be considered a faux pas to do otherwise. Like wearing casual work clothes to a ball. Appearances needed to be maintained.

CHAPTER 38

"I wish every day was like this," said Bea Henderson. She leaned back in the pilot's seat and sipped appreciatively from a cup of coffee that her copilot had just brought up from the small galley behind the cockpit.

Carefully balancing his own cup, George Couch slid into his seat. He gave the landscape below no more than a passing glance—which was understandable given that the otherwise-spectacular scenery of Mesa's famous Ganymede Canyons was obscured by fog. That was not unusual this time of day. The sun had just come up over the horizon.

"Enjoy it while it lasts," he said. "Soon enough, we'll have another pack of drunken assholes to deal with."

Henderson made a face. Their job as pilots for Knight Tours paid quite well, since their employer catered to a very upper crust clientele. But that also meant they were expected to personally cater to their customers, not simply provide piloting skills. Some of those customers were friendly and pleasant people, but a fair number of them had the arrogant sense of entitlement that often came with great wealth—especially if they were born into it. They could be a real pain in the butt to deal with.

This morning, though, they'd gotten orders from their employer to deadhead into Mendel. Normally, they'd make sure to have passengers going both ways. But apparently, a very exclusive party needed to be chauffeured around this afternoon and they'd been willing to pay enough to make the expense worth it.

They'd be entering the capital's air space within a few minutes. Henderson leaned forward to contact the control tower.

"What the hell . . . ?" She saw that her copilot was staring at one of the screens. "Hey, Bea, you'd better—*oh, shit!*"

That was all the warning she got before the surface-to-air missile fired from somewhere in the broken terrain below them blew the shuttle into pieces.

❖   ❖   ❖

"—identities of the people killed haven't been released yet," the newscaster was saying. "But there were no survivors and initial reports indicate that the tour shuttle had a full complement aboard. That would mean about two dozen people lost their lives in addition to the pilot and copilot. Authorities say the accident appears to have been caused by a freakish malfunction of—"

❖   ❖   ❖

"Well, that was a complete waste of time," Xavier Conde complained.

Not to mention a complete waste of money, thought his producer, Vittoria Daramy. But she didn't say it out loud. That would have precipitated another quarrel and, at least for the moment, she was tired of bickering with her temperamental newscaster.

The problem was that although Xavier Conde was

certainly not one of the real superstars of the interstellar news media, he was well known enough and popular enough that if their mutual antagonism got heated to the point where one or the other of them had to go, she would be the one sent to the chopping block.

She knew that Conde had tried to get her fired once already, for what he called her "obsessive chit-pinching." The reason he hadn't succeeded was that he was notorious for not getting along with his staff—especially producers—and for being financially wasteful. Their mutual employer had apparently decided that if they caved in to Conde's demand they'd just have to go through it again a short time later.

Sooner or later, though . . .

Gloomily, she stared out the shuttle window at the ocean below.

The vast, featureless, looks-the-same-everywhere ocean. The same ocean which, by the time they got there to do what Conde had been certain would be a dramatic newscast on the disaster, had swallowed up every trace of the *Magellan* and all of the victims except those who had already been airlifted to the mainland.

Where *other* newscasters, who hadn't wasted their time and money leasing a private shuttle to take them out into the middle of watery nowhere, were already in place and already interviewing the survivors.

Being honest with herself, Vittoria hadn't put up a big struggle against the idea. The planet she and Conde both came from, El Hira, lacked the sort of immense oceans that existed on Mesa or Terra. Plenty of smallish seas, and more lakes that anyone had ever counted, but no body of water as deep and expansive as this one. She hadn't quite realized how long it would take to get there and how little there would be to see once they did.

Their recording tech had tried to caution them. Alex Xu *did* come from a water world—from a family of fishers, in fact. He understood much better than they did that a disaster of the magnitude of the one that had struck the *Magellan* would leave no traces behind within a very short time span. But Conde had brushed his warning aside and Vittoria had been too preoccupied trying to arrange for the lease of a shuttle on such short notice to really think about it.

So, here they were. Short of a scoop, on the short end of a large bill from a leasing company, more than a day behind on the project they were *supposed* to be working on—and saddled with an egotistical newscaster who was being even more unpleasant than usual.

There were times Vittoria regretted her long-ago choice not to accept the offer of a post as an associate professor in journalism from New Mali Central University. Not many, true. For thing, her current salary was half again what she could ever have hoped to earn even as a tenured professor. For another, students could be as aggravating as newscasters and there were a lot more of them.

❖   ❖   ❖

"It's absurd!" said Harriet Caldwell forcefully. "Absurd." She shook her tablet under her supervisor Anthony Lindstrom's nose as if she were rattling a sheaf of papic. "For God's sake, Tony—look at these figures! There is no way—no fucking way—that the Ballroom has the capacity to pull off something like this! They simply can't do it. They don't have the people, they don't have the weaponry—and for sure and certain they don't have access to the credentials they'd need to put enough people on board a luxury liner to set that many bombs. Not to mention that they'd need at least one software wizard to bypass all the alarms they would have set off even if they did."

She finally came up for air, giving Lindstrom a chance to get a word in edgewise. "We *are* talking about the same people who did Green Pines, aren't we? I really don't see how you can be so sure than a terrorist outfit that could steal a nuclear device and kill thousands of people with it aren't capable of killing quite a bit fewer people with conventional explosives."

"Tony, you're comparing apples and oranges and you know it. Sure, they killed a lot more people at Green Pines—but that's only because they managed somehow to get their hands on what was probably a construction device. We did find one that had gone missing. That's another thing entirely from—"

"'Gone missing,'" he mimicked sarcastically. "How about we translate that from minimalism? What you really *meant* to say is that they *did* have a software wizard who was capable of deactivating the device's locator beacon—something which you know damn good and well is almost impossible to do without access to the specific codes. Yet somehow—according to you—this same great sorcerer wasn't capable of bypassing the comparatively piddly security programs on board a cruise ship. Do I have this right?"

By now, she was practically hopping up and down with exasperation. "Tony, that's not a fair comparison and you know it! I never said the Audubon Ballroom were a bunch of clowns. They've got hundreds—hell, thousands—of corpses in their wake that proves otherwise. But they don't—they've never—operated on this scale before. They send in lone assassins or small teams, which is why they can be so hard to stop. Two, three—never more than five—people. To explain Green Pines, all you need to come up with is *two* people. One—okay, fine, software whiz—to deactivate the beacon. And the other willing to commit suicide taking the device to the target."

"You need more than that," Lindstrom said. "Where'd they get the device in the first place? We don't leave those things lying around anywhere, you know."

She glared at him. After a moment, through gritted teeth, she said: "Fine. They had some more confederates."

Lindstrom shook his head. "You're obsessing over this, Harriet. Just let it go."

He refrained from adding, which he could have, that Harriet Caldwell was notoriously obsessive—to the point where she'd been urged to get psychological counseling.

Urged by her friends, though, not by Lindstrom himself. As aggravating as she could be, the fact remained that Harriet's obsessiveness was part of what made her such an excellent security analyst. There was a reason that her colleagues in the Mesan Office of Investigation's Domestic Intelligence Branch, partly in jest, partly out of spite, and in good part out of admiration, called her *No-Sparrow-Shall-Fall Caldwell*.

"Just let it go," he repeated, knowing full well that she wouldn't. But at least he could buy himself some peace in the meantime.

❖   ❖   ❖

By the next day, Janice Marinescu had been informed of the activities of Xavier Conde and his team, as well as the dissenting opinion being advanced by one of the analysts in MOI DIB. None of the individuals involved including the analyst's supervisor were part of the onion, but all of them were being monitored—directly, in the case of the newscaster, indirectly in the case of the analyst.

She brought the matters up in her team's morning conference. Concluding with: "I think we can turn Conde's activities to our benefit. Is Mitchell's team available?"

"Yes," said Kevin Haas, her chief lieutenant. "They just finished with the Fischer job last night. I agree that they'd be the ideal team for that. Do you want them to handle"—he glanced down at his tablet—"the Caldwell problem as well."

Marinescu shook her head. "No, that'd be overkill. We don't have all that many Alignment teams at our disposal. Just farm it out to one of our liaisons at the OPS."

"Done," he said, making a note on his tablet.

September 1922 Post Diaspora

"I urge you to surrender immediately, but it won't exactly break our hearts if you don't."

—Colonel Donald Toussaint, RTN

CHAPTER 39

Triêu Chuanli was much as Victor remembered him. Slender, a bit on the short side; relaxed and debonair in his demeanor; a gentleman to all outward appearances. He didn't seem quite as suave as he had in Victor's earlier encounters with him, though. Perhaps Chuanli was a bit startled to find himself in a room with a man even more handsome than he was.

By now, Victor had adapted to his new appearance. Flexible as always, he'd discovered that being extremely good-looking was an excellent disguise in its own right. It was much like being extremely ugly—people didn't notice *you* because they were so dazzled or repelled by your features.

Beowulf's nanotech engineers had given him the sort of good looks found in models, not those found in vid stars. Despite their reputation for being gorgeous, most vid stars—although they were certainly attractive—had features that were far enough away from an abstract ideal to give them a definite personality that viewers could attach to their performance. Not so, for models. They were mute; ultimately, possessing no personality at all. That was not their function. They needed to possess a beauty that was so idealized and abstract that it did not detract from what *really* mattered, which was the attractiveness of the goods they were displaying.

In short, peas in a pod. And a good-looking pea in a pod is still a pea in a pod. A passerby would notice such a person, just as they would notice a particularly striking flower. But if they were asked an hour later to describe them, they would find it surprisingly difficult.

Well...Its petals were red. It had a...you know... a stalk.

Well...He had blond hair and blue eyes. His features were really...you know...regular.

The only thing really distinctive and easily described were height, hair and eye color. There wasn't much Victor could do about his height—except that it was average to begin with—but he could handle the rest. He carried with him at all times the wherewithal to change his hair and eye color within seconds. And naturally, being Victor, he'd trained himself to do so both in a simulator and in real physical practice.

❖   ❖   ❖

"The situation in Lower Radomsko is a nuisance, certainly," said Chuanli in response to Victor's opening remarks. "But it's a familiar nuisance. We've lived with it for decades, now. It's one of those problems for which the proposed remedies always seem worse than the disease itself."

Victor nodded. "Yes, I understand that. But the danger of a disease is closely tied to...the environment, let's call it."

He made it a point to thicken his Dockhorn accent

as much as possible, almost to the point of caricature. Not quite, but . . . close. His aim was for Chuanli to suspect him of being an off-worlder who was *mimicking* someone from Dockhorn.

Whether he could do so or not was unclear. The problem wasn't on Victor's end. Oddly, where in times past he'd found it well-nigh impossible to disguise his natural Nouveau Paris accent, he was finding it quite easy to manipulate his new voice.

But it didn't do any good to present a Dockhorn accent which was not quite right—if Chuanli wasn't familiar enough with the accent to know the difference. For all the man's sophistication, it was that of a gangster who'd been born and raised and spent his whole life in very constrained circumstances. A sophisticated Mesan seccy is still a Mesan seccy.

What Victor was figuring on was that Chuanli was probably recording this entire conversation—and would have a real language expert study it afterward, if he decided the matter was important enough.

"The environment," stated Chuanli. His tone of voice was flat and devoid of affect. "Meaning . . .".

"The political environment, I'm referring to. To be precise, the fact that the current setup on Mesa— specifically, in the seccy quarters—is about to become a textbook example of what will happen to a house of cards when a strong wind comes up. A hurricane-force wind, I should say."

He frowned, as if a sudden thought had occurred to him. "You *do* have hurricanes here on Mesa, don't you?"

Chuanli gave him a thin smile that had very little in the way of friendliness. "Lots of 'em, on the coasts.

But here in Mendel, we're up on the tablelands. About the worst we ever get is ... ."

He turned his head toward one of the two body-guards standing against the wall behind him. "What would you call it, Stefan? A stiff breeze?"

The bodyguard's thick lips curled into a sneer. "Breeze, my ass. A zephyr. A real man can piss right into it."

The sneer made it clear that he had his doubts as to the manhood of the visitor in the room.

Victor grinned at him. The expression was not one that came naturally to him, but hours of practice in a simulator had perfected it. The grin had even less in the way of friendliness than Chuanli's smile. It was a predator's grin. A shark's grin.

"You won't be able to piss into this wind, trust me. It's got a name. We call it 'the manticore.' When it blew through my home system it flattened everything. Well, everything that had the initials OFS or the logos of any transstellar operating out of Mesa, anyway."

The level of tension in the room went instantly from *mild* to *moderate-and-rising-fast*.

But there was no trace of that in Chuanli's tone. That remained, as it had since the interview began, calm and relaxed.

"I wasn't aware the manticore blew in Dockhorn. Unless my astrography is way off, you're five hundred light-years from the Star Empire and not connected by any direct wormholes."

"You're correct. But Dockhorn isn't actually my home system. It's just the system my associates and I find it useful to operate from at the moment."

"Your associates being..."

Victor made a dismissive hand gesture. "There's no need to get into that yet. My purpose in this meeting is not to persuade you of anything, Mr. Chuanli. I'll be doing that with practical results. I simply wanted, as a matter of courtesy, to let you know that my associates and I will be probing business possibilities in Lower Radomsko. None of our projects should conflict with any of your interests and we hope to develop good relations with you and Mr. Dusek."

He rose and gave Chuanli a polite nod, then repeated the nod to bodyguard Stefan. He ignored the other bodyguard.

"I'd appreciate an escort out of the building," he said. His smile this time was genuine. "I'm afraid I'll get quite lost otherwise."

Chuanli smiled back. "I can pretty much guarantee that." He gestured toward the door behind Victor. "You'll find the same boy out there who guided you here in the first place. He'll lead you out."

❖   ❖   ❖

The boy gave his name as Ambros. Apparently, his superb memory for three-dimensional mazes didn't extend to nomenclature. On the way in, he'd told Victor his name was Thanh.

But that might be intentional, too. If seccy sophistication had its limits, it also had its subtleties. That could be the boy's way of letting Victor know that he couldn't be bribed. More precisely, he *could* be bribed—but the bribe wouldn't do any good.

A fine and sprightly young lad, in short. Victor had been much like him, at the age of ten, when he'd supplemented his family's meager income running errands for the gangsters in his part of the Nouveau

Paris slums. You did your job, you kept your mouth shut—and if you did take a bribe you made sure the boss knew about it and didn't think you were up to no good.

It wasn't perhaps quite as easy to make someone disappear in Nouveau Paris as it was in Neue Rostock. But it was easy enough.

❖   ❖   ❖

"He neglected to mention that little detail," said Thandi sourly as she gazed down on the recumbent form of Karen Steve Williams. The *truncated* form, that is.

"Pretty hard to pretend we're just hauling our drunken friend home by supporting her on our shoulders when she doesn't have any legs below the knees," she continued. "Oh, well. You work with Vic—Philip Watson, you learn to improvise."

She looked around the room. Seeing nothing there of any use, she went into the small adjoining lavatory. Happily, the chamber's facilities were either dysfunctional or the women hiding in the apartment were trying to save money by using the antique device of towels to dry themselves off.

The things were still made, albeit not in large quantities. That was true of a surprising number of ancient objects. You could even find buggy whips. Thandi had made that discovery by accident during her recent stay on Beowulf. Given the planet's laissez-faire mores, she'd taken the occasion to expand her collection of toys at a specialty shop.

She hadn't been personally interested in the buggy whips, or any of the various whips, canes and switches on display. When she was in the mood, her sexual predilections ran somewhat outside the normal range, but they didn't include sadomasochism—and even if they had, Victor would have refused to participate.

She took down two towels and began rolling them up. "If we cover her with something," she said, coming back into the main room, "these should pass as legs. We'll need a way to attach them to her stumps, though. Push comes to shove, we could use some sort of twine, but that's likely to be uncomfortable for her."

Happily, there was one ancient product that was still widely in use. Some things were so perfectly designed for their purpose that modern substitutes weren't much needed. "We've got some duct tape," said Stephanie. She rummaged in a small chest in a corner and came up with a roll. What was left of it, rather. Duct tape had a lot of uses in an old and decrepit building like this one.

Moving slowly and carefully, so as not to arouse the badly injured woman, Thandi used the tape to secure the rolled towels and attach them to Karen's stumps. She then rolled her up in the blanket on the cot and lifted her into her arms.

"Need some help?" Cary asked. Thandi shook her head. She didn't need any help at all carrying Karen, and wouldn't have even if the woman had been whole and healthy.

"No, I've got it. Just guide me out and open whatever doors need opening."

❖   ❖   ❖

They only passed one surveillance camera on the way out of the building. It was possible there were others that had been carefully disguised, but Thandi doubted the authorities would bother with such curlicues. From the looks of the one they did pass, she didn't think it was operational anyway.

But there was no point taking chances. So, although she was careful never to look at the camera, she had a disgruntled expression on her face. And just as they passed beneath it, muttered loudly: "Next time, bitch, you can damn well haul yourself back home. I'm getting sick of this."

❖   ❖   ❖

It took less than three minutes to get out of the building. Like all residential structures in the seccy districts—anywhere in Mendel, outside of a few very wealthy enclaves—the apartment building the three women lived in was more than two hundred stories tall. But their apartment, being one of the worst, was located close to ground level. Its only view, if you could call it that, was of a service alley. The only reason it took as long as it did was because the direct route to the street had been blocked by a wall that had collapsed years earlier. Not being a load-bearing structure, the landlord had seen no reason to spend the money to fix the problem. There were at least four alternate ways to exit the building, after all. And if that was inconvenient for the tenants on the lower levels, so be it.

Thandi had a taxi waiting for her. Using the air lorry would have been a tad conspicuous for this purpose, and the taxi driver wasn't charging by the minute. His name was Bertie Jaffarally and Victor had put him on a retainer to make his services available full-time and around the clock.

To Thandi's way of thinking, that seemed rather incautious. "He's already been connected to you," she pointed out to Victor.

But he'd just shaken his head. "Yes, and so what? You and I are already connected anyway. Or have you forgotten a certain ambush gone awry? Dead and wounded bodies lying all over the street? You think we weren't spotted?"

"Well . . . by passersby. That doesn't mean the authorities . . ."

"Sure they do, Thandi. This is a seccy area on Mesa. That means poverty on the ground floor coupled with plenty of money in the hands of the powers-that-be. Don't think for a moment that the security agencies in Mendel—and there are at least nine that I know of—don't keep a jillion people on their payroll. Or at least pay them for the odd tidbit of information. I can pretty much guarantee that within an hour of that fracas the word had been brought to at least one of those agencies, and probably three or four."

"You didn't seem too concerned at the time," she said.

He shrugged. "I wasn't—then or now. That's because I'm intimately familiar with the Three Laws of Thermosecurity."

"You just made that up."

"Did not. The first law is that the desire of authorities in charge of security for information will continue in a straight line with no limits in time and space short of the heat death of the universe. The second law is that the willingness of *their* authorities to supply them with the budget they need to do that has very definite limits, both in time and space. Hence the third law, which is the one we are now operating under. The information assembled by security authorities invariably overwhelms their ability to analyze the information. They are, in effect, suffocated by their own insecurity."

By then, she was exasperated. "That's nonsense. What you're saying is that security is impossible—which isn't true and you know it as well as I do."

"Yes, but it's possible *despite* the natural inclinations of security agencies. Basically what it takes are agents who know how to triage data and aren't afraid to do so. Such agents exist, of course, but..."

He took the time to buff his nails and examine them. "We are rare as hen's teeth. Thandi, I don't tell you how to lead close quarters assaults. Perhaps you should refrain from telling me how to do spook stuff."

That was...hard to dispute.

So, she used Bertie and his taxi. It was certainly a lot more convenient than any alternative she could think of. And if—as they certainly were—someone was watching and would report the incident to one or another security agency...

She knew what Victor would say. *Who cares? Just another seccy drunk or drug addict being taken home by a friend. It's called hiding in plain sight.*

He could be aggravating, at times. It was a good thing she was in love with the man. Or the same hands that could clean and jerk two hundred and seventy kilos would have long since crushed his windpipe.

CHAPTER 40

"Are you going to stare off into space the rest of the day?" Yana demanded. She placed her hands on her hips—and then immediately snatched them away. She *hated* that newly developed mannerism. It was hard to combat, though, given her new hips.

Anton glanced up and smiled. "Actually, I wasn't staring off into space, lost in my own thoughts. I was just contemplating the wisdom of the bard."

"The 'bard'? What are you, giving names to your computers now? This'll end badly, Anton, I warn you."

"The term refers to an ancient poet and playwright by the name of Shakespeare. I was thinking of a line from one of his greatest plays. *Something is rotten in the state of Denmark.*"

He withdrew a data chip from the console, pushed the chair back and rose to his feet. "Almost literally rotten. The rats are deserting the sinking ship called Mesa. I'm now sure of it. I've run seven different correlations and they all come up with the same result. Well . . . allowing for values of 'same result' that are pretty damn generous."

Yana knew the result he was talking about. One of the enjoyable things about working with Anton and Victor was that neither one of them was prone to security-for-its-own-sake. The mathematical techniques Anton had been using to crunch his data were beyond her grasp, but she knew what he'd been looking for.

"How damn generous?" she asked.

He grimaced. "Let's put it this say. *I* can see a pattern—okay, through a glass darkly, I admit—but if I tried to present this to most analysts they'd tell me I was hallucinating. The statistical equivalent of spots in my eyes from staring at something too long. And if I tried to present the data in a court of law I'd be disbarred for incompetence. If I were a lawyer in the first place, which thank you very much I am not."

She nodded. "That's okay, Anton. My money's on you, and the other analysts can take a hike. If you say the pattern is there, I'll take your word for it. But do you have any sense for hard numbers yet?".

"Hell, I don't have any sense for *soft* numbers yet." He shook his head. "We could be looking at anything from a few thousand people to . . . a hundred thousand? Maybe even a quarter of a million."

He scowled at the data chit in his hand. "But I'd be surprised if the figures aren't actually at the small end. The best numbers I can crunch are the ones involving fatal accidents. Those are intrinsically harder to fuzz up, assuming someone's trying to, than things like job vacancies and fashion purchases. That's presuming that Mesa's authorities aren't engaged in complete fakery, but I think that's a fair presumption. This isn't a full-blown police state, and there are some real problems with outright fraud conducted on a massive scale. It's not that easy to pull off and you run the risk—which gets bigger as time passes—of corrupting your entire system."

"By 'complete fakery,' what do you mean?"

"For instance, reporting fatal accidents that never happened at all. Or, conversely, making the results of fatal accidents vanish entirely. To do the first, you need the collusion of . . . hell, tons of people. First responders, med technicians, police—not to mention news reporters. Doing the other is even harder. Unless you impose a completely totalitarian regime, which opens up its own Pandora's box, you wind up constantly stumbling over your own lies."

Yana frowned. "I . . . think I'm following you. What you're saying is that if you want to 'disappear' someone in a fatal accident you have to arrange for an *actual* accident—preferably one that does kill somebody—but which has a logical built-in explanation for the fact that there's no corpse of the person you wanted to disappear."

"Exactly. Blow up a luxury liner in mid-ocean as just happened to the *Magellan*. Blame it on Ballroom terrorists. Very few bodies recovered so the passenger list comes from computer records. Blow up a shuttle right over Ganymede Canyons, probably the most rugged and inaccessible terrain on the planet. No bodies recovered."

Yana pursed her lips. "What were the total fatalities in the *Magellan* incident? Three thousand?"

"A little less—and over a hundred bodies were recovered. Still, the total number of missing-presumed-dead-identities-reconstructed-by-computer came to more than twenty-seven hundred persons. But, of course, only a small percentage of those would have been mysterious disappearances. The great majority would have been legitimate."

"Why do you say that? I'd think... Oh. I see your point. This goes back to what you were saying earlier—unless you set up an outright police state, it's not all that easy to just make people vanish."

"No, it isn't. What you'd have to do..." He thought for a moment. "Ha. That's an idea. We need to check to see who if anybody, and I'm willing to bet it was nobody important, survived from the departments that oversee passengers and crew. I'm not sure what they're called on a luxury liner."

It didn't take Yana more than a moment to follow the logic. "Yes. Kill off anyone who could personally contradict the official roster. But... what about the shuttle accident in the Canyons? They couldn't possibly—ah."

He smiled. "Sure you could—just make sure all the people you 'disappeared with no bodies recovered' were people without any close relatives. Preferably, with no very close friends, either."

"Right. Because no one else would make a huge fuss if the hunt for the bodies was called off because... How would they put it? 'Conditions were too dangerous for further operations.'"

Then, she shook her head. "But, if you're right, even big incidents like the *Magellan* aren't enough to disappear people in even four figures, much less five. The shuttle could have only accounted for twenty or so. That's one hell of a lot of 'mysterious' shuttle accidents being called for. No way people wouldn't get suspicious quickly. Those things don't crash that often. You just can't disappear thousands of people using those sort of custom-fit retail measures."

"Exactly—and the implications of that are pretty frightening. If I'm right . . . what happens when the people behind this pattern *do* start disappearing people in large numbers?" Anton closed his fingers over the chip. "We've got to get this to Victor as soon as possible. Is that ragamuffin of his hanging around?"

"He won't be, most likely, but he'll have one of his minions out there. I still think Victor is nuts, using that pack of street kids."

Anton chuckled. "His own Baker Street Irregulars. Don't second-guess him, Yana. In his own line of work, Victor's better than anybody. If he says the connection is secure, I'll take his word for it."

"Oh, sure. I'd no more argue the point with him than I'd argue with a snake over proper slithering techniques. Even if I thought the snake was crazy."

✧   ✧   ✧

Ten minutes later, they left the ship. To all appearances, on another one of the Hakim grandee's shopping sprees. By now, they'd established that those took place on a regular basis.

Spaceport regulations required them to leave via a gate at ground level before they could use any of the air traffic lanes. In the space just beyond the gate, a crowd of seccy beggars had gathered as they always did. Most of them were youngsters, since the seccies had learned long ago that the chance of cadging money from visiting offworlders was greatly improved if the beggars were children.

Most such visitors would ignore the beggars and have their air cars aloft as soon as they passed through the gate. But the Hakim grandee seemed to take a (probably sick) pleasure in personally dispensing money to those less fortunate. So, as she did routinely, she leaned out of the window of her vehicle and placed credit chits in grubby little hands.

Oddly, she didn't just toss them in the air and let the children scrabble for her largesse. It seemed highly unsanitary, but...

She could certainly afford the best antiseptic and preventive medical care, after all. Presumably her method allowed her to think of herself as a veritable saint.

Of sorts. One of the security people monitoring the spaceport's traffic had dubbed her Angel Boobs three days after she arrived.

❖   ❖   ❖

Yana outdid herself that day. In addition to the usual jewelry, fine art and very expensive clothing, she came back with a banded coramine lizard from one of the worlds in the Astophel system. Anton thought the creature was hideously ugly—not to mention being fifty centimeters long and weighing in the vicinity of twenty kilos. But there was no denying that its hide coruscated like a rippling rainbow.

"What does the damn thing eat?" he asked, glancing back from the driver's seat.

"Dwarves, I was told. Main reason I bought it."

"You're still holding a grudge about the tits, aren't you?"

❖   ❖   ❖

The girl who took the chit with the imbedded data was named Lily Berenger. She was only nine years old but she was well-trained. As soon as she saw that she was surrounded by other kids, she dropped the chit on the ground. Screeching with anxiety, she stooped to pick it up, immediately popped it into her mouth and started fighting with another girl as if they were struggling over possession of the item.

That girl's name was Magda Yunkers and she was Lily's best friend. She was also one of Hasrul's "minions."

The fight went on for some time and, to all outward appearances, looked pretty ferocious. Lily and Magda, like all of the minions, took great pride in their craftsmanship. The crowd of kids surrounding them cheered them on, needless to say, half of them because they enjoyed watching a fight and the other half because they were also minions and were part of the act.

Eventually, Lily emerged as the apparent victor. Strutting off with two friends in tow, she headed for the nearest transport tube. She was careful, as she had been even in the heat of the "fight," to keep the chit firmly ensconced in her cheek. If she was stopped and interrogated by security officials or policemen, she'd swallow the chit. Unless the officials had a stomach pump with them and used it immediately, the material the chit was made from would be dissolved by her digestive fluids before they could detect it.

Yana thought Victor was at least half-crazy to put such trust in mere children. But he knew what he was doing. Twice, in the past, he'd used exactly such a group of slum children to serve as his auxiliaries. After the first such occasion, he'd had State Security's tech people develop the material he'd used ever since for this purpose.

The nice thing about the material was its plasticity. It could easily be molded into a multitude of shapes and forms. Credit chits, old-fashioned coins, chewing gum—once he'd even used it to make a toy air car. And no matter what its form, two minutes in a kid's stomach and it was nothing but molecules. None of them exotic, either, so even if the child's stomach contents were extracted and analyzed they'd appear to be innocent.

The reason Victor was partial to using children for such purposes was because he understood the psychology of slum street kids perfectly. He'd been one himself. They could fold under torture, of course—almost anyone could—but they tended to have an exaggerated, even a romantic, conception of personal honor. *You take the king's coin, you're the king's man* was a sentiment that came naturally to them. And they'd stick to it, as long as the "king" in question behaved toward them properly. They wouldn't tattle on you, and they wouldn't betray you. Not for money, at least.

Criminal overlords like Dusek and Chuanli understood them also, of course, which was exactly why they used such children as guides in their labyrinth. And if that suggested that patriotic secret agents and gangsters had a lot in common, well... Victor had figured that out for himself a long time ago.

⋄   ⋄   ⋄

In due time—much quicker than you might think—Lily passed the chit on to Hasrul Goosens. He, in turn, brought it directly to Victor even though normally Hasrul would have used one of the dead drops that Victor had set up for him.

He couldn't use the ones that Cachat had originally

set up for Carl Hansen and his seccy rebels because they were unsuitable for children. An obvious street kid riding elevators or wandering around a fish market would be automatically suspect, and why would such an urchin be going into an automated fortune teller booth?

This time, however, Hasrul wanted to see for himself the results of the favor he'd called in from Achmed. So he came directly to the safe house run by Steph Turner—understanding that the term "directly" was figurative. Hasrul was quite at home moving through the long-forgotten underground passageways of the seccy districts. There was no way a Mesan security agent would be able to follow him through that subterranean maze, and while there were certain dangers, they weren't excessive. There were a number of human predators who prowled those passageways, but a dirty urchin wearing clothes that weren't more than two grades above rags was not their natural target. The biggest danger was that he might run into one of the fairly large number of insane people who lived down there. But most of them were harmless, and he figured he could outrun the ones who weren't.

On this occasion, he encountered no trouble at all.

Hasrul was expecting to get a lecture from the man he knew as Achmed on the subject of needlessly violating security protocols. But Achmed said nothing when Steph led the boy into the back rooms of the boutique.

Nothing except: "Came to see your mother, huh? Relax, kid. She's doing fine."

Thereby reinforcing Hasrul's allegiance, which had been rock solid anyway. It didn't occur to the boy that perhaps that was the reason for Achmed's unexpected response. But he was only twelve, after all. Astute for his age and shrewd in the way such children often are. But not a master spy.

✧   ✧   ✧

The medical unit seemed like something out of a fable to Hasrul. He knew they existed, but he'd never seen one. For seccies, unless they were one of the few who were well-to-do, "medical care" meant seeing a doctor or a nurse who had at least a modicum of training but not much in the way of equipment and that, fairly rudimentary.

He stared down at his mother, resting in the healing compartment, through the viewscreen that Achmed turned on.

"Is she asleep?" he asked.

"Not exactly," said Achmed. "She's basically in what amounts to a coma, except that it's artificially induced and controlled."

The boy looked up at him, his normally impassive expression tight with anxiety. "But she's okay?"

Achmed placed a reassuring hand on his shoulder. "She's fine, Hasrul. She didn't have any active injuries. She was just suffering from a nasty combination of diseases—severe bronchitis, for one—that were piled onto exhaustion. That's a dangerous combination, but it's one that's easily treated."

Hearing a slight noise behind them, Hasrul looked over his shoulder and saw that a man he didn't know had entered the chamber.

Apparently, the newcomer knew of Hasrul's situation, or he'd deduced it from overhearing part of their conversation. "The thing works, kid, believe me," he said. He lifted one of his knees and gave it a slap. The motion was a bit awkward but the slap was a solid one. "This knee was so much hamburger a few weeks ago. It's still not as good as new, but it will be once—"

He nodded toward the med unit. "Your mother comes out of it and I can go back in." With a cheerful grin, he added: "We've been using it in shifts, between me and Callie and your mama and the new girl. I'm Teddy, by way."

"What happened to your knee?" Hasrul asked.

Teddy indicated Achmed with his thumb. "The boss's girlfriend shot it off."

"Why'd she do that?"

"Well, Achmed wasn't our boss then. We had, ah . . ."

"A minor altercation," said Achmed smoothly.

At that point a woman came into the chamber. Hasrul looked up at her.

And up. And up. He didn't know her but he had a feeling . . .

"And speak of the devil," said Teddy. He gave the unknown woman the same cheerful grin. "Meaning no offense, Evelyn."

"None taken," she said. But her eyes had never left Hasrul.

"You must be the boy Achmed keeps bragging about," she said. "Hasrul, right? I'm Evelyn del Vecchio."

He nodded. To allegiance and loyalty, trepidation was now added. Hasrul had never been especially scared of Achmed himself. But his girlfriend . . .

"Very pleased to meet you," he said firmly. Any other response struck him as most unwise.

✧ ✧ ✧

"Well, that tears it," Victor said later, after he'd been able to read Anton's summary of the data. He didn't try tackling the data itself. For starters, the math was way over his head. And when you had Anton on your team, why would you fiddle with stuff like this? It'd be like having a master chef on your team but insisting on cooking lunch yourself. "All hell's about to break loose."

Thandi had been reading the same summary, over his shoulder. "Why do you say that? All Anton's claiming is that the rats are deserting a sinking ship. And even he admits that the data that led him to that conclusion is fuzzy as all hell."

"If Anton says the pattern is there, I believe him, fuzzy data or not. And the thing is, we're not actually talking about rats doing something purely pragmatic like abandoning a doomed vessel. We're talking about fanatics working on a long-range plan. You don't scheme for six centuries and then just cut and run."

Victor had a peculiar expression on his face. It seemed to Thandi like a weird mix of pride—no, more like a craftsman's self-esteem and self-assurance—combined with what looked like a tinge of guilt.

"The scary thing is that I can think the way they do even if I really don't," he said. "If that makes any sense."

She could follow the convoluted logic. "So . . . you don't really think you think what?" She shook her head. "God, that's twisted. What I mean is, what do you think they're doing?"

"They can't just run and hide, Thandi. They've got to destroy any evidence they ever existed in the first place. That's been their basic tactic all along. And the pattern Anton's pointing to matches perfectly with something else that's been bothering me."

"Which is?"

"You've been following the news."

"About the *Magellan*?"

"And that shuttle that supposedly blew up over Ganymede Canyons. If you think that happened because of a freak accident you're a lot more gullible than I think you are. That was an act of sabotage as surely as what took place aboard the cruise ship. The question then becomes: who did it? The Ballroom's being blamed, but I don't believe that for a minute."

Thandi shook her head. "No, of course not. We got a thorough briefing from Saburo and Jeremy concerning the Ballroom's assets on Mesa. No names were mentioned because—"

"First, we didn't need them so there was no point in possibly compromising security. And second, because there really wasn't much anyway." Victor raised Anton's data chip. "The Ballroom certainly didn't have the assets to pull off something like the *Magellan*."

"So you think they were acts of provocation." Thandi's tone made it clear that was a statement, not a question.

"Yes, but... There's something off about it."

Thandi frowned. "Off... how? Seems like pretty standard fare to me." Her voice got a little sing-song tone to it. "'The wickett ee-vil Ballroom terrorist fiends are working night and day, plotting still greater acts of monstrous villainy against the pee-pul, deeds so foul their like has never been contemplated before... blah blah blah. How is that 'off'?"

Victor chuckled. "Up to a point, it's standard fare.

But where it's off is in the constant drumbeat about the Ballroom's *capability*. They emphasize that over and again. Which is in direct contravention to the usual tactics used against revolutionary and opposition groups. In which..." He cleared his throat. "I am something of an expert, having been trained by Oscar Saint-Just himself—who was a monster, I grant you, but was no slouch either."

Now, Thandi grinned. "I can't wait to hear this. Lessons in wrongdoing from a master of the trade."

"Very witty. The key nexus—perhaps combination is the right term—is to emphasize the opposition's villainy but also to downplay their capabilities. You don't want to build up the image of their *prowess*, for God's sake—"

"You don't believe in God."

"Very witty. Because if you do that, you're effectively serving as your enemy's recruiting agent. *Wow! If they're that good, maybe I should join them.* See what I mean?"

She frowned thoughtfully. "Now that you point it out..." She looked over at the wallscreen. "Their coverage of the Ballroom does seem almost...Well, not laudatory. But—"

"But not disparaging," Victor concluded for her. He shook his head. "It's all wrong, Thandi. The correct tactic is to *sneer*. That's why terrorists are always 'cowardly,' even though the phrase 'cowardly terrorist' is an idiotic oxymoron."

"Okay. And what follows?"

He got up and looked around the room, as if he were gauging it as a shelter or a refuge. "What follows is that I'm pretty sure we're going to be glad Andrew brought those pressor nodes with him. From now on, everybody's got to sleep in the lowest subbasement where he placed them."

She finally understood what he was getting at. "Jesus. Do you really think they're *that* ruthless?"

He gave her the cold, flat-eyed stare that Victor could do like no one else she'd ever known. "These are the same people who subjected millions upon millions of people to lives of unending slavery, brutality and horror for more than half a millennium. Of course they're that ruthless."

CHAPTER 41

Elsewhere in Mendel, in a hotel suite that was a lot less luxurious than Anton and Yana's yacht, a person who was widely considered one of the Solarian League's best investigative journalists was expressing her own suspicions.

"Everything about this is fishy," Audrey O'Hanrahan stated forcefully. "The picture you're painting for me—trying to paint—is like a...like a..." She paused, then chuckled harshly. "It's like a *manticore*, that's what it is. Bits and pieces of completely different animals stuck together with narrative glue and passed off as a real live critter. I don't buy it."

The Mesan public information officer across the suite's small desk from her looked deeply offended. Or he tried to, anyway. O'Hanrahan was quite certain—for a host of reasons—that his high dudgeon was equally false.

"Audrey," he began in a tone which fused *let's-be-reasonable-about-this* with a finely calculated dash of *I'm-being-as-patient-with-you-as-I-can* and overlaid by just a hint of *but-even-my-superbly-controlled-temper-has-its-limits*, "I *assure* you—"

She waved him down.

"Spare me, Kyle. Why are you making such a big deal about the so-called 'Ballroom threat'? And why do you think you could sell it to me for even a heartbeat? I covered the aftermath of Green Pines, remember?"

He started to argue the point. "Oh, come on. You didn't get here until—"

"I got here plenty soon enough. It's not as if your security forces had been subtle and their activities hard to document. I know *exactly* how savagely they behaved."

Her face tightened with anger.

"You have no idea how fortunate you were that my producers convinced me to leave out the most damning footage I'd recorded. But leaving all of that aside, you—you *personally*—kept assuring me of how thoroughly and completely your security forces had 'rooted out and destroyed'—that was your phrase, not mine—the Ballroom on Mesa. In fact, you claimed at the time—your phrase again, not mine—that 'not even pitiful remnants remain intact.' Which, by the way, I thought at the time was a particularly fatuous way to put it."

Kyle Fraenzl's expression was now stiff with indignation. The stiffness being required, of course, because the indignation was manufactured. O'Hanrahan wasn't going to let him get away with *that*, either.

"Come on, Kyle. There's no point pretending. Both of us know one of two things is true—either you were lying then, or you're lying now. Which is it?"

He sniffed, then looked out the window.

"There's nothing to see out there but drizzle," she told him remorselessly. "We're a thousand meters up.

So quit stalling. Lies past, lies present—I won't bother asking about lies future, because that's given—but which is it in *this* case?"

✧   ✧   ✧

Fraenzl had had the misfortune of dealing with O'Hanrahan in the past. The Directorate of Culture and Information had assigned him to her during the aftermath of the Green Pines disaster, and she'd been just as unwilling then to pretend she believed him as she was now. Other newsies understood they had to at least *pretend* they thought he was telling them the truth—wink-wink, nudge-nudge—if they wanted any sort of access. But not O'Hanrahan. And the worst of it was that he knew there was no point even trying to evade her. She wouldn't let him get away with it, and her name was far too well known outside the Mesa System for him to even contemplate freezing her out. The instant he tried to do that, she would announce to the galaxy at large that there Had To Be A Reason, and her reputation for journalistic integrity—not to mention her willingness to go for the jugular of even the most powerful vested interests—gave her far too powerful a microphone. The last thing Mesa needed at this moment in history was the sort of public relations black eye an Audrey O'Hanrahan could deliver. So he had only two options: answer questions with a reasonable degree of veracity, or get up and walk out in a huff.

Personally, he would have opted for the huffy walkout. Indeed, he yearned for it. But he'd been given his instructions by the Director for Culture and Information himself.

"Whatever you do," Director Lackland had told him, "don't walk out on her. God knows I'd've been a hell of a lot happier if she hadn't decided to poke her nose into this story in the first place, but now that she's here, we can't afford to even look like we're trying to shut her out. She'll just make a ruckus about it that's likely to do more damage than anything else. Every third word in her report will be either 'evasive,' 'dissembling,' or 'elusory.'"

So he was stuck. All he could do now was follow his instructions to the letter, however foolish that might make him appear.

"In retrospect"—he cleared his throat—"we were perhaps overly sanguine."

"'Perhaps?'"

The single word oozed sarcasm, and he clenched his jaw.

"Fine. We *were* overly sanguine."

"The word 'sanguine' derives from the same root as the word 'sanguinary'—which means 'bloodthirsty.' Which your security forces certainly were at the time. Remember—I was personally a *witness*. So now you're telling me that in addition to being a pack of rabid beasts, they were also *incompetent*?"

Fraenzl felt himself glaring at her. The woman's ability to twist words was—was—

She smiled at him. The expression was simultaneously sanguine and sanguinary.

"You might want to watch your blood pressure, Kyle," she said. "Besides, by now you ought to be used to me. And I'm still waiting for an answer."

✧　　✧　　✧

By the time Fraenzl left, O'Hanrahan had squeezed out of him an official acknowledgment that the assessments made by the planetary security agencies after

Green Pines concerning their success in destroying the Ballroom on Mesa had been—the phrase he finally settled on was "magnified by optimistic bias."

The obtuseness of government officials—or of corporate spokespeople, who were a variety of the same species—when it came to confessing their mistakes never ceased to amaze her. A simple "Hey, we were wrong" or "Yeah, we screwed up badly" would do far less damage in the long run than the sort of mealy-mouthed verbiage they insisted upon.

Magnified by optimistic bias. Was she going to have fun with that!

She pushed back from the desk and crossed to the window. As the lead reporter for *The Truth Will Out*, the most widely watched investigative news site on Old Earth itself, her producers were less tightfisted than most. So she'd been able to afford the extra expense of a room overlooking an actual landscape instead of the artificial canyons—however tastefully decorated they might be—that made up most of the modern city's interior. From her present perspective, she could see all the way to the edge of the tableland upon which Mendel was situated.

Or she could have, anyway, if it hadn't still been overcast and drizzly. But it didn't matter. She wasn't really interested in the view; she just found that staring into a distance helped concentrate her thinking.

She twisted a lock of auburn hair around one index finger, crystal blue eyes narrowed, while she contemplated her assignment here. Her *real* assignment, which was one of the trickiest she'd ever been given, and not her cover assignment.

Audrey O'Hanrahan had devoted thirty T-years

to establishing herself as one of two or three of the Solarian League's—perhaps even the whole human race's—most diligent, scrupulous, and unbiased investigative reporters. Time after time, she'd demonstrated that if Audrey O'Hanrahan said something was true or false, you could count on it. In particular, you could count on her news accounts to be *impartial*. Like anyone, she could make an occasional mistake, but any mistake of *hers* was promptly acknowledged and publicly corrected. And no one who didn't have her own ax to grind had ever seriously accused her of slanting her reports to fit some preconceived notion or allegiance.

Of course, like everyone, she reflected, there were a few private and personal facets of her personality and her life which she kept to herself. Like the minor fact that she was a Mesan alpha-line.

She smiled slightly at that thought. Her carefully designed genotype gave her certain ... advantages over the pure strain humans around her, but she'd still had to put in the long, grueling hours—years and *years* of hours—to earn her position of trust and her reputation as a muckraker. And perhaps the most ironic part of all was that she truly *was* a muckraker, that she truly did live to expose hypocrisy, deceit, corruption, and the abuse of power, position, or wealth. It might have seemed odd in someone whose entire life was dedicated to the oldest, most deeply hidden conspiracy in galactic history, yet she absolutely *hated* the personal greed, avarice, and narcissism that lay behind so much corruption and manipulation. In fact, the genuineness of that hatred, of the passion she brought to her reportage, was one of the great strengths which had allowed her to establish her well-earned—and much feared—reputation.

And then there was the other edge of the sword, the hidden reason that made her stature as a teller of truths and slayer of giants so important to the Alignment.

As usual, her instructions had been not so much vague as . . . broad. Despite the security of her communications chain, her superiors hadn't wanted to be too explicit. That, she had decided long ago, was one of the hallmarks of your true conspirator, and she supposed it made sense, even if it did occasionally make things a bit more difficult for the people in the field. Still, she was an alpha-line. She'd learned how to read between the lines around the same time she'd learned how to talk. Well, by the time she graduated from high school and been recruited as an active operative, at any rate. She knew the basic parameters of her assignment, and she found it interesting that she'd been given precise and specific instructions to rent a small suite in a moderately priced hotel named the Huntington Arms. Now why, she'd wondered, had they wanted her in that particular hotel? That sort of decision was usually left up to her.

The reason for the instruction was becoming clearer now, however. And she was beginning to suspect exactly why her superiors had given her the other instructions she'd received, as well.

O'Hanrahan had never been part of the plans for Operation Houdini. In fact, she'd never heard of Houdini, other than as the name of an obscure ancient magician and trickster. But she was one of the tiny handful of human beings who knew not only of the

Mesan Alignment's existence, but of its actual purpose, as well, and she'd realized T-months ago that the Alignment's master plan was entering a critical phase. She strongly suspected that it was happening sooner than anyone inside the onion had anticipated, and she was an astute and expert analyst of interstellar political affairs. And of military affairs, as well, since the two subjects overlapped more and more these days. It had become obvious to her that Mesa—more precisely, the political setup on Mesa that had existed for the past several centuries—was doomed. Doomed in the near future, not in some misty, far off temporal Neverland. Given that, and what she knew about the Alignment's ultimate objectives, even someone far less gifted than an alpha-line could have figured out that something *like* Houdini had to be in the offing.

She knew, as did most alpha-line operatives, that while the majority of the Alignment's core members were no longer located on Mesa—had not been for decades, in fact—there were still an awful lot of them residing on the planet.

How many? *That*, she didn't know, but the number had to be somewhere in the low to middle five figures. Until the time came to abandon the mask which had served it so well, at least some of the members of the onion—the core group, hiding behind the millions of members of the Mesan Alignment who'd never heard of the Detweiler Plan—had to remain here, on Mesa itself, to manage all the levers of power the onion had spent so long putting in place. Some of those managers would be ultimately dispensable, if that became necessary, but many—most—would not. That meant they had to be gotten off the planet, in complete secrecy, leaving not a trace behind of where they'd gone, who they'd truly been, or what had happened to them. And now, given the unexpected rapidity with which the situation had gone pear-shaped, they had to be gotten off quickly.

Much more quickly, she was sure, than any plans would have provided for when they were first laid down. And that meant . . .

Drastic measures. *Drastic* ones. She could see no other way to manage such an evacuation under the current circumstances. And that assessment fitted perfectly with her new assignment . . . and with the fact that her lodgings had been specified. Her superiors hadn't *suggested* that she stay at the Huntington Arms; they'd made it an order—a very *explicit* order. The sort of order someone gave to a very important asset who might have been at risk if she'd stayed anywhere she might choose.

They wanted her safely out of any possible target zones. So whatever evacuation plan might have been put into place was about to be—might already have *been*—set in motion, and that made her instructions to cover the official Mesan System government's posture and actions make perfect sense. They would require her to step farther than usual out of her role as reporter into her role as commentator and analyst, but this wouldn't be the first time that had been true, and she was equally comfortable in either. She knew exactly how to craft her reports to accomplish her assigned mission.

One. Harshly criticize—no, lambaste; not even that, excoriate—Mesa's authorities for their past, present, and future brutality dealing with their own slaves and the citizens those authorities disdainfully labeled "seccies."

Two. Disparage—ridicule, deride, even sneer at in every way possible (without, of course, compromising her reputation for impartiality)—the incompetence of those same authorities when it came to actually catching and suppressing real terrorists instead of terrorizing innocent people.

Three. Advance the proposition—as a conjecture, at least—that the Audubon Ballroom's presence and capacity for action on Mesa might be a lot greater than the authorities wanted to admit. That last part, her superiors had cautioned her—as if she'd needed them to!—had to be done carefully, lest suspicion arise that she was inflating the threat for the sake of sensationalism.

But, of course, that wouldn't be a problem. First, because she'd always conscientiously avoided any reputation for sensational reportage. And, second, because if she was right about the immediacy of whatever evacuation plan was in place, and if the concerns of those same superiors about where she was to stay were well placed, it would soon be all but impossible to oversensationalize the events that would actually be occurring.

It was a good thing, she reflected, that *The Truth Will Out* allowed her such a generous operating budget. She'd need it. Within two days, at the outside, she had to hire some good bodyguards. An attempt on her life was very likely, and it couldn't be obviously fumbled, either. It would have to look quite serious—the sort of murder attempt that might be made either by Ballroom killers or (take your pick) agents from one or another disgruntled official body or aggrieved transstellar who'd finally decided she'd made herself a pain in the posterior once too often.

Two such murder attempts had been made on her before. In both cases, the perpetrators' identity had never been established, although theories abounded. And in both cases, that hadn't mattered at all. One of those attempts had been completely genuine, as a matter of fact, and that hadn't mattered, either. The attempts had sent viewership through the proverbial roof—and, of course, cemented the seriousness with which her reports were seen by the public. After all, if they hadn't been accurate, why would anyone have wanted to shut her up?

Luckily for her—well, no, it had been *planned* for, generations before—her genetic line had as one of its characteristics a pronounced taste for excitement. Some people called it *adrenaline junkie*.

A crude and rather silly term, she'd always thought. Adrenaline was the effect, not the cause. The cause lay in a complex constellation of genes carefully nurtured by the Alignment's gengineers.

❖   ❖   ❖

The next morning, she began recording her first report.

"This is Audrey O'Hanrahan, reporting from Mesa, where disaster and catastrophe are in the air."

Good, she thought. *It's not just a decent intro; it'll make a good tease before the report actually runs.*

"Viewers who followed my reports on the events on Mesa after the Green Pines terrorist attack may recall that I was both skeptical of the official accounts and critical of the behavior of Mesa's security forces at the time. Their brutality—I would not and did not shy from the term bestiality—was astonishing. Coupled to that, however, was the incompetence I suggested was running in tandem. Brutal people are not necessarily stupid; but the fact remains that brutality tends to stupefy. That is just as true of the perpetrators as it is of their victims.

"It now seems my cautions were justified. A highly placed spokesman for the government admitted to me yesterday that the claims made at the time by Mesa's security agencies that they had crushed the Audubon Ballroom and its associated terrorist cells among the so-called 'seccies'—Mesa's second-class, largely disenfranchised citizens—were 'magnified by optimistic bias.'

"This is what's known in the journalist's trade as a weasel statement. What he really meant was: 'We were so besotted with vengeance that we never actually bothered to check our victims' guilt or innocence.' Which also meant, of course, that those who might *actually* have been guilty would have found it much easier to escape punishment. This is the sort of ineptitude that makes it possible for a society's enemies to evade apprehension while they lay plans for further outrages.

"Brutality married to ineptitude—Mesa's Office of Public Safety ought to use that slogan instead of the preposterous one they now have: 'Always vigilant, always prepared.'"

She looked directly into the pickup and shook her head.

"Talk about 'magnified by optimistic bias'!"

❖　　❖　　❖

Twenty minutes later, she'd finished the rough recording and replayed it, considering it this time from an editor's perspective. It was good, she thought.

Possibly a little over the top in a few places, but not bad at all for a rough cut. She could always tone those places down a bit if they really needed it, but she'd learned long ago to put at least a few hours between the actual recording and any editorial decisions.

Besides, now that she'd had a chance to appreciate it properly, she'd probably better not wait about that other little matter.

She activated her com and punched in the combination of the private security force she'd used before on Mesa. It was not an Alignment front, as such, but it had been carefully vetted—and in some cases staffed by—the onion's own security experts.

"Cerberus Security? This is Audrey O'Hanrahan. Could I speak to Lee Seagraves, please. Yes, I'll hold."

She *loved* her job.

CHAPTER 42

The down-at-the-heels freighter came over the alpha wall just over twenty-three and a half light-minutes from the F7 star which had been christened Balcescu by its ethnic Hungarian settlers. Its Warshawski sails flashed blue brilliance as they bled transit energy before reconfiguring into a standard impeller wedge. It took a moment orienting itself—even the best astrogation was usually off at least a little—then began its steady acceleration towards its destination, just over eleven light-minutes farther in-system.

✧　　✧　　✧

"We've got a hyper translation," Sophie Bordás, Balcescu Station's sensor officer, reported.

"Really?" The station's CO, Zoltan Somogyi, set his coffee cup aside and rotated his comfortable station chair towards the sensor section. "And what can you tell me about it?"

"Not much," Bordás replied, carefully not adding the word "obviously" to her response. "It's right on the hyper limit, and all I got at this point is the FTL signal from its impeller wedge. Looks to be somewhere around one million tons, give or take, from its wedge strength, and it's only hitting about one hundred and seventy-six gravities' acceleration." She shrugged. "The little I can see so far, looks like it's probably a tramp freighter. They only brought about fifteen hundred KPS across the alpha wall with them, so assuming constant acceleration, we're looking at about four hours and twelve minutes for them to reach Debrecen orbit, with turnover in just under three hours."

Somogyi tilted back in his chair, his expression thoughtful. The hardscrabble colony on Balcescu's only habitable planet of Debrecen didn't ask many questions about the goings-on aboard the installation orbiting it. Until some OG's superiors in the Jessyk Combine had stepped in to take over its management, Balcescu Station had been slowly disintegrating from lack of maintenance. And it had suffered that lack of maintenance because the entire star system didn't have a collective pot to piss in and there had been no real traffic through it for at least the last forty T-years or so. As far as the people of Debrecen were concerned, it didn't matter why Jessyk had wanted the derelict platform. What mattered was that it actually offered to lease it, repair it, and bring at least a trickle of trade into the system. If anyone on Debrecen had really thought about the economics involved—or been sufficiently aware of those economics' reality—he would quickly have realized that the in-system "trade" carried out by Jessyk's corporate partners couldn't possibly allow them to recoup even the pittance they paid the system government for their lease. It was highly probable that none of them would have cared, either, of course.

Balcescu Station was divided into two parts. The main body of the station was exactly what it appeared to be—a somewhat rundown trading depot. The slave trade was conducted entirely out of a portion of the station that was kept segregated from the rest, with only limited access from one part to the other.

As deceptions went, this one was awfully threadbare. Few if any of the people working in the legitimate area of Balcescu had any illusions about what was happening in the restricted area. But the old expression applied to them—*see no evil; hear no evil; speak no evil*—or they'd be looking for another job. And jobs on Balcescu Station paid far better than most jobs planetside.

Furthermore, the Jessyk Combine had a quite clear—and mutually lucrative—understanding with the local OFS authorities, which meant that unlike the situation in the nearby Maya Sector, the Solarian League Navy would never dream of dropping by Balcescu without warning them to get any embarrassing evidence of prohibited activities out of sight before its arrival. Nobody else was likely to have much interest in this armpit-of-the-universe star system—they were over two light-centuries from Erewhon—much less one of those busybodies like Haven or Manticore. And from the most recent news reports, Manticore had enough problems with the League already without adding another unauthorized incursion into Solly-climb space to the pot. Still...

"Keep an eye on it, Sophie. Make sure it's really alone. And let me know as soon as it squawks its transponder code."

"Sure," Bordás responded. "I already requested them to, but it's going to be another eight minutes or so before my transmission reaches them."

"Understood," Somogyi said, and reached for his coffee cup once more.

◆   ◆   ◆

"They're requesting our transponder code," *Hali Sowle*'s com officer said crisply.

"Why, that's right neighborly of them," Ganny El observed, raising her battered, silver-chased coffee mug in salute.

"Should I respond?" Lieutenant Frank Johnson looked up, his eyes settling on a point midway between Ganny El and Lieutenant Colonel Kabweza.

"Well," Kabweza smiled faintly, "I think we should leave that up to the experts. Ganny?"

"Wouldn't want to be all neat and orderly on the bastards," Ganny replied. "Last thing we need is for the misbegotten SOBs to think we might be . . . oh, *military* or something. Let 'em wait for another six or seven minutes, Frank. Then switch 'er on and let's see if they welcome us back with a big slobbery kiss."

◆   ◆   ◆

"I've got the transponder code from our visitor," Sophie Bordás said with an expression of mild surprise. "It's the *Hali Sowle*. Were we expecting them back this soon?"

Zoltan Somogyi swiveled in his chair to face her again. He was a bit surprised by the identification himself, but not so surprised that he spilled any coffee from his cup.

"No, we weren't. The impression I got from their captain—what was that harpy's name—?"

"Gamble Las Vegas." Bordás had rather enjoyed the older woman herself, although she was admittedly a bit odd. She wondered if the name meant something in Vegas' native tongue, whatever that was.

"Yeah, her. What a piece of work. Anyway, she did say they'd be coming back this way, but I got the impression they were headed for Prime next and then on to Ajay." He pursed his lips. "Although, now that I think about it, I can't recall her saying anything specific. Maybe I misunderstood her."

He leaned forward to study the sensor officer's display. "Anything look wrong to you?"

"Not really. Hold on. Let me check." Sophie tapped commands, bringing up some data, and examined it for a few seconds.

"Nope. Everything looks the same. Signature matches the database from her last visit perfectly."

Satisfied, Somogyi leaned back in his chair and lifted his cup. "Well, we'll find out soon enough."

There was nothing in sight for her to do for a while—as usual, here at bustling Balcescu Station—so Sophie brought the romance she was reading back up on her display. People could say what they wanted to about Somogyi—yeah, sure, he could be an asshole sometimes—but he wasn't given to fussing over pointless rules like the prohibition against personal entertainment on the job, even when the alternative was twiddling your thumbs.

It'd be pretty hard for him to do so, of course. Given that at that very moment he was playing solitaire on his own console.

❖   ❖   ❖

While Bordás found her bookmark and resumed reading, other members of Balcescu Station's personnel were busier. In Station Flight Control, Csilla Ferenc was discussing *Prince Sundjata*'s projected outbound vector with Tabitha Crowley, her astrogator, while

Béla Harsányi monitored the newly arrived incoming freighter and András Kocsis oversaw *Luigi Pirandello*'s final preparations for getting underway.

They weren't all that busy, though. For three controllers to oversee the same number of ships was an easy workload, especially since the incoming ship was still eleven light-minutes out. For that matter, even *Prince Sundjata* wouldn't be getting underway for over three hours yet, so there wasn't that much rush.

◇ ◇ ◇

Zachariah McBryde wasn't sorry to be leaving Balcescu Station, even if the ship on which he found himself was an antiquated slave trader instead of the luxury liner upon which he'd made the first leg of his voyage from Mesa. Or even the rather less prepossessing general utility hauler which had delivered him to Balcescu in the first place. As depressing as he found the slave ship *Prince Sundjata*, it had at least the virtue that the slaves were kept in their quarters so he didn't have to see them.

Balcescu Station had been an active depot, but not one oriented toward visitors. To make things worse, their Gaul keepers had insisted that Zachariah and the other "special passengers" had to remain at all times in the restricted area of the station—*restricted* being a euphemism for that portion devoted to the slave trade. The only thing to do, for the three days he and his companions had spent there while waiting for their further transport, was to sit at a none-too-sturdy little table in a "bistro" with delusions of grandeur and drink coffee whose claims to being "gourmet" were even more delusional.

And watch, as slaves were moved through the facility,

either being shipped onto or from slave traders or being reassigned to new quarters. It was one thing to know in the abstract about the critical role genetic slavery played in the Alignment's long-term plans. It was another to watch the concrete results parading back and forth in front of you. Try as one might, it was impossible for anyone with any imagination or empathy at all not to see those wretched creatures as one's own kin. A fair distance removed, perhaps, but still kin.

Coming on top of his depression at being separated from his entire family, the time he'd spent in Balcescu had left Zachariah in a very dark place. He was glad to be leaving.

His only real regret was that Lisa Charteris was being shipped out on a different vessel, the *Luigi Pirandello*, scheduled to leave the station soon after *Prince Sundjata*. She was the last personal contact he had with his previous life. The one other project director he'd known slightly, Joseph van Vleet, would be leaving with her.

That left him only the company of Stefka Juarez and Gail Weiss, both of whom he knew by name only. Juarez been the director of a project far removed from Zachariah's concerns—he didn't even precisely know what her field was; something to do with nanotech, he thought—and he'd met Gail Weiss for the first time when Marinescu had assembled the five of them as part of Houdini. He had no idea at all what her work had been.

The two women had to share a cabin. Thankfully, Zachariah had one to himself. He been told that the voyage to the next destination, whose identity had not been revealed, would take several weeks. He figured on spending most of that time catching up on research papers and finishing a couple of long postponed projects of personal literary advancement. He hadn't read Tolstoy's *War and Peace* since he was a university student, and he'd never been able to do more than put a small dent in Natchaya Suramongkol's eleven-volume magnum opus The *Annals of Ayutthaya.*

The one other advantage to *Prince Sundjata* was that the cabins were so tiny he no longer had to share his accommodations with his Gaul keeper, A. Zhilov.

No, two advantages. When their party of five reached Balcescu Station, three of the five Gauls who'd accompanied them had returned the next day to Mesa. From this point on, apparently, the people overseeing the Houdini evacuation had decided that only one Gaul keeper per ship was enough. So, S. Arpino would be going with Lisa and van Vleet on the *Luigi Pirandello,* while Zhilov would be hovering around Zachariah and the two women. With three of them to hover over, hopefully Zachariah would be spared the Gaul's dour company at least most of the time.

He still didn't know what the "A" stood for. Being honest, he didn't care either. Zachariah had found the Gauls to be as entertaining and convivial as so many toadstools.

"Leaving Balcescu Station in ten minutes." That terse announcement came over the cabin's com, and he recognized the ship's captain's voice. He wasn't quite sure of the woman's name—Bogdanov? Bogunov?—because he'd only heard it once. But she had a distinctive, gravelly voice.

To Zachariah's surprise, that announcement was followed by: *"If any of the passengers want to join us on the command deck, feel free to do so. Just stay out of our way."*

It took him no more than five seconds to decide that anything was better than staying in this claustrophobic small cabin. At least on the command deck he'd be able to see something. Probably not a lot, given the injunction to keep from getting underfoot, but at least there'd be displays. *Prince Sundjata* was a working vessel—a very working vessel—not a liner or a cruise ship. There weren't going to be any observation decks or viewports. Which was fair enough, he supposed, if somewhat grumpily. After all, viewports really weren't all that useful in space travel.

❖   ❖   ❖

"Looks like we may lose at least one fish." Commander Loren Damewood was monitoring *Hali Sowle*'s drone sensor platforms. The freighter had made turnover and begun decelerating towards Balcescu Station at its same steady hundred and seventy-six gravities eighteen minutes ago. She was still over eighty-two million kilometers out, her velocity up to 16,604 KPS, but it would be close to two more hours before she was in any position to . . . inconvenience the station's inhabitants. Now he looked up from his displays with a grimace.

"Bogey Two's just brought her impellers up and gotten underway. She's headed almost directly away from us, too. Looks like she's pulling around a hundred seventy gravities, so she's a little slower than we are, but she's going to have an awful big head start. If any of the others pull out in the next hour or so, were going to lose at least one of them for sure. Unless we send both frigates after them, anyway."

Major Anichka Sydorenko glanced at her Havenite advisor, Lieutenant Commander Loriane Lansiquot. "I don't like the thought of losing one of them, either," she said. "But I think I like the thought of not keeping *Geronimo* close enough to cover *Hali Sowle* and the station if any surprises turned up even less."

Lansiquot nodded ever so slightly in approval.

Damewood frowned. "Are you sure?"

Sydorenko managed not to glare at him. Just before General Palane left for Manticore, she'd picked Sydorenko as the best prospect for quick advancement into the Royal Torch Navy's command ranks. The posting had been gratifying, of course, but it also meant Anichka had to contend with what seemed like a small host of naval advisors. It wasn't just Manticorans and Havenites, either. The BSC had detached Damewood for this mission to oversee the sensor platforms since they were of Beowulfan design and manufacture.

She'd kept her army rank because the debate was still raging as to whether Torch should have a unitary military or divide into separate services. So far, the unitary position had held firm, because it had Palane's backing. But now that she was absent and apparently would be for quite some time, those favoring a division were gaining ground. Secretary of War Jeremy X was wavering, apparently.

Sydorenko agreed with Palane on the merits of the issue, but at the moment she'd have preferred a naval rank for personal reasons. Maybe the blasted foreign snots would be less patronizing if they didn't think they were dealing with an army grunt as well as a novice.

Then again, maybe she was just being overly sensitive. Even if most people would've considered the phrase "overly sensitive Scrag" a galaxy-class oxymoron.

Sydorenko decided to stick with Lansiquot's advice.

Loriane was a tac officer by training. Push come to shove, Damewood was just a tech geek.

"We'll stick with the plan," she said. "The primary mission's taking out the station, and just by the way keeping anybody with an onboard armament from taking out our ride home in the process. If a single ship gets away while we're doing that, so be it. Anyway," she showed her teeth for a moment, "it really won't hurt for Mesa's other scum suckers to know we're serious. In fact, I sort of like the thought of letting as many of them as possible sweat while they wonder if we're coming for *them* next."

◇   ◇   ◇

It took Zachariah a while to find his way to the command deck. He had to get directions from crew members on four separate occasions. The process was aggravating enough that he'd decided to complain to the captain when he reached the command deck. Would it be too much to ask them to place a few simple directional plaques at passage junctions?

Eventually, though, he realized there was a method to the madness. Rebellions aboard slave trading ships weren't unheard of, and sometimes the slaves even managed to circumvent the spacing mechanisms that usually kept them cowed. Not often, of course. Still, there was no reason to give a hand to even such a remote possibility by providing the slaves with signs telling them where to go to kill the crew and capture the ship.

By the time he came onto the command deck, he saw that his two remaining companions had arrived before him. Juarez and Weiss were standing close to one of the bulkheads, watching the proceedings with considerable interest.

A. Zhilov had arrived also, unfortunately. But by now, Zachariah was accustomed to that particular ghost at the banquet. He went over to stand beside them.

Weiss and Juarez had apparently come to the same conclusion as he had about the scarcity of viewports, because their attention was fixed on the maneuvering plot near the center of the bridge. He doubted they could make much sense of it—he certainly couldn't—but the icons and moving lights were a lot more interesting than the data being displayed on any of the control panels.

"Wedge is nominal, Captain," said one of the crew. The woman was doing something at her control panel, but Zachariah couldn't tell what it was because her back was turned toward him.

"Gravitic Two is acting up again," said the crewman sitting just to her left. His console was angled sixty degrees away, though, so Zachariah could see his control board. Most of that was given over at the moment to gravitics data, he thought, but one of the panels was a radar display. "We really need to get that entire array replaced, or at least get it a full overhaul, Ma'am."

"Tell it to management, Davenport," the captain replied with a snort. "*I've* been telling them about it long enough. Maybe you'll have more luck!"

Zachariah glanced around the command deck. In addition to the captain, the helmswoman at her station, and the two crewmembers he'd already seen, there were two more. One was obviously the com officer, but the other was working at a console in the far corner. He had rather strikingly colored hair—genuinely red, not the brick hues that normally came with the term "redhead." Zachariah didn't think it was artificially tinted, either.

At the distance, Zachariah couldn't really tell what

the man's station was. Probably something to do with the ship's internal functions. Atmosphere, temperature, humidity, gravity, artificial light quality—some UV, but not too much—liquid water supply, that sort of thing. He thought that post was called *environmental officer.*

Whatever that one control panel might be, radar or gravitics or whatever else, it was clearly monitoring *Prince Sundjata's* progress as it accelerated away from Balcescu Station. Zachariah looked back and forth between that panel and the maneuvering plot until he was sure he knew which symbols in the plot indicated the ship and which the station. The *Prince Sundjata* was the green sphere with the circumpolar yellow band and Balcescu Station was represented by a bright lavender octahedron. He presumed that the green sphere with the equatorial orange band still resting alongside the station was the *Luigi Pirandello.*

"Clearing Balcescu Station's orbital space, Captain," the first crewwoman—the astrogator, perhaps—announced. "We have onboard control."

"Put us on profile, then, Tabitha," Captain Bogunov commanded.

"Yes, Ma'am."

Bogunov watched the maneuvering plot for another moment, then turned away and gave the three visitors a smile and nod.

"And that's it, folks. We're off to—"

Zhilov cleared his throat noisily. The captain gave him a sour glance.

"To wherever we are going," she finished.

"Security must be maintained," Juarez said. There was more than a trace of sarcasm in her tone, and she waved a finger around, indicating the bulkheads.

"The gremlins who infest the reaches of interstellar space might be listening."

Zhilov glowered at her, but said nothing.

❖　❖　❖

"Definitely going to lose Bogey Two," Loren Damewood observed to no one in particular. Major Sydorenko gave him a somewhat more pointed glare—not that *any* of her glares could be considered blunt objects—and he shrugged. "Just saying," he said.

"If we do, we do," she said rather more testily than she'd actually intended to. "First the station, then making sure we don't lose our ride home again—those are the first two priorities. Everything else is a piss poor third. And speaking of priorities," she added quite unnecessarily, "I want those frigates ready to launch at a moment's notice."

"Twitchy, are we?" Colonel Donald Toussaint observed. He was all but lounging on a nearby console seat and had a smug smile on his face. The smile of a brass hat along for the ride because this was the RTN's first real engagement and he wanted a ringside seat.

Advisers, counselors, consultants—a damn commissar, even. All Anichka needed to put her completely on edge was—

"Some coffee, Ma'am?"

She turned her head to see her orderly Jeff Gomez holding out a cup for her. The liquid in it looked as black and thick as lava.

"Strong," he added, smiling. "Just the way you like it."

She managed—barely—not to snarl at him. But she declined the coffee.

CHAPTER 43

"All right, we're close enough," Ganny said. "So go charge, or whatever you call it. And the frigates can tally ho."

She'd had the com on, so her statements were heard throughout the ship. Waiting in the assault shuttles in the bays which had once housed humble cargo shuttles—but the *Hali Sowle*'s innocence was far behind her—some of the Marines frowned. Ganny's pronouncement was decidedly un-military, bordered on the disrespectful, and made light of an upcoming deed of heroism and martial glory.

Most of them smiled, though, and a few laughed out loud. By now, they were accustomed to Ganny.

For her part, Lieutenant Colonel Kabweza maintained a straight face, as befitted her dignity as the commander of the operation. She did chuckle about it later, though.

On the command deck, Major Sydorenko kept a straight face, too, even though Ganny had just grossly violated several millennia of protocol. She was the lawful commander of *Hali Sowle*, and as such still the traditional "Mistress after God," but she certainly wasn't the *military* commander of the expedition. She could give whatever orders she liked aboard her own ship, and Sydorenko's ignorance of how to run a starship was great enough that she wouldn't have attempted to overrule Ganny there even if she'd had the authority to do so. But the major *was* supposed to issue any and all military orders. Orders which included niggling little things like when to launch the attack.

Fortunately for Ganny—or maybe the other way around, given the old woman's pugnacious nature—Sydorenko was amused, not offended. Due to her own lineage, she wasn't much given to genuflecting at the altar of protocol. Scrags might have been "super" soldiers in general, but that did not run to blind obedience. In fact, they'd been notoriously insubordinate. There were drawbacks to telling someone they were a superior breed. That being so, why should they tamely accept the orders of someone who was clearly their inferior?

Besides, despite the casual nature of her comment, Ganny was a stone cold professional, and "we're close enough" translated to "we've reached the ops plan's carefully calculated and specified range." And a very tense time they'd had of it over the last couple of hours. They'd been in-system for just over five hours; *Hali Sowle*'s velocity relative to Balcescu Station was down to a mere 4,280 KPS; and the range was barely eight million kilometers. Most of them had been privately nervous that something would go wrong at the last minute, and that nervousness probably helped explain those smiles and chuckles.

Still . . .

Colonel Toussaint cleared his throat. "I believe Anichka's supposed to give that order, Ganny."

Ganny waved her hand. "Fine, fine. Give it, then."

Sadly, military propriety took another hit.

"*You heard the Old Lady,*" Sydorenko's voice came over every listening com. "*Let us now do unto others as they have wet dreams of doing unto us.*"

✧   ✧   ✧

It was sadly undramatic in many ways.

Hali Sowle was fitted with a pair of shuttle bays, one at each end of her main hull. Back in the carefree days when she'd been an innocent smuggler, spreading her wares across the galaxy with a fine disregard for customs duties and import fees, each of those bays had housed three standard heavy lift cargo shuttles. She still had one cargo shuttle, but that was mainly for show. Or, more precisely, to maintain her innocent façade by chauffeuring members of her crew and/or cargo items to and from orbital freight platforms or planetary facilities. It would never do to use her other small craft for that sort of operation. No one was likely to mistake a Manticoran Mk 19 Condor Owl heavy assault shuttle for an item on a civilian freighter's normal equipment list.

The Mk 19—actually, these were Mk 19Ts, the export version especially modified for Torch's requirements— was a bit larger than a standard cargo shuttle, but not hugely so. With the same variable wing geometry as the Royal Manticoran Navy's pinnaces, it was capable of landing up to one hundred twenty-five troops in full battle armor or up to two hundred in regular battle dress or armored skin suits on just about any imaginable surface. It was more heavily armored than a pinnace, with a pair of thirty-millimeter pulsers mounted in its bow and a dorsal turret which mounted a twenty-millimeter tribarrel. It had twice as many hardpoints for external ordinance as the standard pinnace did, and also fitted a modest internal weapons bay.

All in all, the Mk 19 Tango was well-suited to handing out mayhem, homicide, and devastation, yet there was no drama about their deployment. No sounding trumpets, no stirring music—indeed, no fuss or bother at all. Four of them simply slid out of the freighter's bays, each loaded with fifty skinsuited Marines, and began accelerating towards Balcescu Station at five hundred gravities.

The frigates' departure was no more spectacular. *Hali Sowle* simply dropped her wedge long enough for the warships to deactivate their tractors. Then the freighter's heavy cargo-handling tractors, fitted with the standard industrial tractor/pressor heads, thrust them gently away from her. She didn't really need to move them far—just enough for their maneuvering thrusters to clear their threat zone of her hull—but Ganny El wasn't taking any chances with her paint. The pressors moved them gently but firmly five hundred meters clear of her ship before they disengaged, at which point they engaged their own thrusters and went darting away. They had to get at least a hundred and fifty kilometers clear of her before any of them could bring their wedges up once more, but they were over a million kilometers out of range of any shipkiller missiles Balcescu Station might have managed to conceal from them.

As soon as they reached a safe range, one of them—*Denmark Vesey*—also went immediately to five hundred gravities of acceleration, slightly behind the assault shuttles which had required no persnickety maneuvers before bringing up their own wedges. *Her* destination, however, was not Balcescu Station but the closer of the two starships which had departed from it. Her sister ship *Gabriel Prosser*, on the other hand, remained in close company with *Hali Sowle* as both of them continued to decelerate, although at a somewhat higher rate. At 225 Gs, she and the freighter would come to a halt relative to Balcescu Station at a range of just over eight hundred thousand kilometers, rather than the zero/zero solution she'd been headed for at 176 Gs. That would be far enough to keep her out of any mischief where hidden energy weapons might be concerned, and *Gabriel Prosser*'s counter missiles and point defense should be more than sufficient to cover both of them against any missile threat the station might present.

✧   ✧   ✧

"Oh . . . *shit*." Béla Harsányi had been supervising *Hali Sowle*'s approach. That made him the first person in Balcescu Station's flight control center to see the incoming tramp freighter suddenly transform into a gargoyle. "Hey! Hey! We got trouble, people!"

András Kocsis scowled but didn't look up. In fact, he'd only half-heard Harsányi's panicky shout. He was involved at secondhand in a dispute between Balcescu Station's cargo management systems supervisor and *Luigi Pirandello*'s purser—a dispute made even more irritating because the freighter was over eight million kilometers from the station, which put the next best thing to one full minute's com lag into the acrimonious discussion.

Csilla Ferenc, on the other hand, was listlessly working her way through a stack of routine correspondence.

Prince Sundjata was fifty million kilometers downrange, the next best thing to two hours out and less than three hours from the hyper limit, and Cargo Management had found no fault in *her* purser's paperwork. That meant Csilla had had no excuse not to finally deal with her backlogged electronic mail.

Harsányi's sudden exclamation provided her with one.

"What's wrong, Béla?" she asked, rising immediately and moving to the other controller's console. She was concerned, but not unduly alarmed. Béla was a nice guy, but he was a worrywart. Truth be told, he really wasn't suited for his job. Csilla thought he'd do better if he transferred to some occupation that was less stressful for him—although, given Harsányi's jitters, that might only be something like supervising janitorial remotes.

The moment she saw his display, though, her moderate concern spiked. Within three seconds, once she'd fully grasped what was happening—the main features, anyway—she was in a state of terror. That sudden, purposeful cluster of small craft impeller signatures accelerating towards Balcescu Station couldn't be mistaken for anything but an assault. And while it was possible there was a pirate somewhere in the galaxy stupid enough to attack a Jessyk Combine base, it was far more likely that this was something much, much worse than that. It had "military" written all over it, and while she watched, the freighter's impeller signature reappeared as she brought her wedge back up.

And so did the signatures of the smaller, faster, but much-bigger-than-any-assault-shuttle vessels on either side of her. That screamed "military" even more loudly than the assault shuttles did, and she swallowed hard. This was completely outside her experience and had only been covered in her (long past) training in a perfunctory manner.

And the reason that training had been perfunctory, she had concluded at the time, was because if something like this ever happened, anyone it happened *to* would be so well and truly screwed that all the training in the galaxy would make exactly zero difference to what happened to her.

Harsányi seemed paralyzed, so Ferenc hit the headset button that gave her a direct link to the station's CO— both his personal cabin as well as the command deck.

"*Code Red! Code Red!* That freighter's launching an attack on the station!" As frightened as she was, she took a moment to double check what she saw on the display. "We have three—no, *four*—incoming shuttles, and she's launched a couple of warships! One of them's headed our way at five hundred gravities! They're maybe twenty minutes out and coming in fast!"

❖   ❖   ❖

Zoltan Somogyi heard Ferenc's screeched warning, but it was no more than another background element in his mosaic of sudden disaster. Sophie Bordás had picked up *Hali Sowle*'s abrupt transformation almost as quickly as Harsányi, and by the time Ferenc's confirmation reached the command deck, Somogyi was already listening to quite a different message.

"—Toussaint, commanding the RTNS *Bastille* and the Royal Torch Marines who will be arriving aboard your station in about nineteen minutes. I urge you to surrender immediately, but it won't exactly break our hearts if you don't. Here are our terms of engagement should you decide not to, however. If you choose to resist, we will follow the laws of war as established in the Deneb Accords . . . up to a point. Any combatant who surrenders will be taken prisoner and not harmed. If, however—*I will say this once, and once only*—you murder, or cause to be murdered, or *allow* to be murdered any slave aboard the station, your lives are forfeit. *All* of them. Any of you who are armed or in uniform will be summarily executed. Any civilians in the employ of the station or any political institution or transstellar using or connected to the station will also be executed. Again, I strongly urge you to surrender immediately. You stand no chance against us, and an immediate surrender may avoid any little . . . unpleasantness should a single slave aboard that station be killed."

When the voice identifying itself as Colonel Toussaint finished speaking, Somogyi and Sophie Bordás stared at each other. Then, as if they shared the same spinal cord, they both simultaneously swiveled their chairs and looked at a control console against the bulkhead five meters away. Then—again simultaneously—they looked at the security guard standing watch at the entrance to the command deck.

The station's CO pointed a slightly shaking finger at the console. "Corporal Laski, move over there and guard that console. Take your sidearm out of its holster. If anyone—*anyone at all*, except me—approaches you, shoot them. Immediately."

The corporal was no more than twenty T-years old. He did as he was told, but his eyes were wide and he looked to be a little shaky himself—especially when he drew his pulser. Bordás hissed in alarm. She thought the kid was just as likely to shoot one of them by accident as he was to fend off—

Fend off who? Who would be insane enough to trigger the controls that launched the automatic spacing mechanisms in every slave hold on the station and caused the death of more than two thousand slaves? Those controls were only there as a last resort in the event of a slave rebellion that spread beyond a single hold and threatened the entire station. It had never been used. It had actual *dust* on it.

But she knew the answer as soon as she asked herself the question. Not all of the people directly involved in the slave trade were... normal. Some of them were as psychologically twisted as a pretzel.

"That's not going to do any good!" she cried. "Every hold has its own set of controls!"

"I know that," Somogyi said through clenched teeth. He'd swiveled back to his console. "But it's the best I can do from here. *What the hell is happening?* Get me—who's in command of the security force this shift?"

"Binford."

"Get him."

"Yes, Sir!"

It took less than five seconds for Bordás to make the connection, and Jeremy Binford sounded insanely normal when he answered.

"Hi, Soph!" he said cheerfully. "What can I do for you?"

She started to scream at him, then swallowed hard. Of course he sounded calm. Nobody outside Flight Control and the command deck had any inkling yet of the disaster speeding towards them.

"Somogyi needs to talk to you," she said tersely, instead, and switched the connection to the CO's console.

"That you, Binford?" Somogyi said, then went straight on. "Look, I don't have much time to explain, but in about twenty minutes—"

❖ ❖ ❖

At first, the consternation on *Prince Sundjata*'s bridge wasn't nearly as great as it was on Balcescu Station. The slave ship was still well over a hundred and fifty million kilometers—and almost two and a half hours at her present acceleration rate—from the hyper limit. But she was also over 2.3 light-minutes from the station, well outside the range of anything which might happen in its immediate surroundings. Gravitic scanners were FTL, and *Prince Sundjata*'s sensors had quickly detected the shuttles' impeller signatures, but for all their combat power, the Mk 19Ts were obviously small craft, and equally obviously headed for the station, not launching any whimsical pursuit of the departing slave ship.

That changed radically about six minutes after she'd picked up the shuttles, however.

"We've got trouble coming, Ma'am," Mason Scribner, *Prince Sundjata*'s sensor officer, said as he turned away from his console. "I've got two more impeller signatures. One of them's matching decel with the freighter, but the other one's accelerating like a bat out of hell. I think that one's coming after us and the *Luigi Pirandello*."

"Not heading for the station?" Bogunov asked sharply.

"Could be," Scribner conceded. He was the closest thing the slave ship had to a tactical officer, although no one was more aware than he was of his limited qualifications for that post, but he shook his head. "If those are assault shuttles, they aren't going to need anybody else's firepower to deal with anything Somogyi could think about throwing at them. Besides, the one staying back with the freighter's better placed to support any assault. We'll know for sure in another two or three minutes, when the shuttles have to make turnover for their zero/zero with the station. If this other bastard doesn't flip with them, then he's damn sure coming after us."

"What is he, do you think?"

"From their acceleration, they've got to be warships," Scribner replied. "The lead one—I guess we should label it 'Bogey One'—is pulling right on five hundred gravities. That means a military-grade impeller. And it's small."

"A destroyer?"

"Not even that big, Ma'am."

"Well . . . fuck."

"Smaller than a destroyer" meant either frigates or LACs, Bogunov thought, and none of the military forces who regularly used such ships were going to be friendly. And if they were *frigates*, then most likely they belonged to . . .

If *Prince Sundjata* couldn't make it over the alpha wall, they were really and truly screwed. It was sometimes a death sentence if a slaver was caught by the Manties, Haven, or Beowulf, which was bad enough. But only Torch would be sending frigates here, and that was *very* bad. If their captors were actually exslaves themselves, that death sentence was probably pretty much guaranteed.

She pressed a stud on the arm of her command chair.

"Engineering," a voice untouched by the alarm coursing through her own veins replied.

"Mitch, it's the captain," she said crisply. "How good is our compensator?"

"What?" The chief engineer's voice still wasn't alarmed, but it was clearly surprised. "It's fine, Ma'am. Uh, is there some reason it *shouldn't* be?"

"Not yet," she told him a bit more grimly. "But I want you to cut the margin to zero."

There was silence for a moment, then the sound of a cleared throat.

"Are you sure about that, Ma'am? I know I said it's fine, but we're over two thirds of the way through the current maintenance cycle. If we put that kind of stress on it, we could—"

"I know," Bogunov cut him off.

And she did know. According to The Book, civilian-grade inertial compensators were never supposed to be run at more than eighty percent of their theoretical maximum. The only good thing about the failure of a compensator at high rates of acceleration was that the people aboard the ship in which it was fitted would probably be dead before they knew anything about it. A couple of hundred uncompensated gravities would turn them into anchovy paste on the bulkheads with terrifying efficiency. The *chances* of a compensator failure weren't especially high, although the curve bent upward sharply as you got closer to full power, but it seldom gave you any warning *before* it failed. That meant maxing the compensator wasn't something that gave you any margin at all for error. But—

"I know," she repeated. "But someone's attacking the station, and we've got at least two warships— probably frigates," she added, knowing he could figure out who they most likely belonged to as well as she could "—and they're pulling five hundred gravities. I *need* those extra fifty gees, Mitch."

There was another, briefer silence. Then—

"I guess you do, Ma'am. You'll have full power in twenty seconds."

"Good."

Bogunov released the stud and turned towards Tabitha Crowley, her astrogator. There was a reason she'd gone to maximum power, despite the risks involved. At a hundred seventy gravities, they *wouldn't* beat anything that could pull *five hundred* gravities to the hyper wall. Oh, it was unlikely any pursuer could actually overhaul them before they escaped into hyper, but *missiles* might be another matter entirely. She needed to get together with Matsuzawa and Scribner and figure out—

She paused as she found herself looking at the visitors she'd invited onto the command deck—and now wished she hadn't. Whether or not they really understood what was happening, they clearly understood enough to be worried as hell, and she couldn't blame them.

"I'll have to ask you all to return to your quarters."

"No." That came from the man who was their... guardian. "We all need to be in one room."

Bogunov winced. She couldn't help it. She wasn't supposed to know why the Gaul—what was his name? Zhukov? something like that—was aboard or even that he *was* a Gaul. Then again, she knew quite a few things she wasn't supposed to know, and she'd transported some unsavory and... high-risk passengers other than slaves in her day. That was why she'd used the ship's com systems to eavesdrop on *these* passengers. No names had been given to her before they departed Balcescu Station, but she'd overheard a brief snatch of conversation between the man—Zachariah—and one of the women. She didn't pretend to understand what either of them did or who they worked for, but clearly whoever it was had no intention of allowing their knowledge—whatever the hell it might be—to fall into enemy hands. It wasn't the first time someone who worked for the Jessyk Combine and Manpower had encountered a similar situation; both transstellars paid well, but were also ruthless about eliminating employees who might have compromised their operations.

And that was why she knew Zhukov—or whatever the hell his name was—wanted them all in one compartment: so he could kill all of them if they were going to be captured. She had no idea what information they possessed might be so dangerous to whoever had sent him along to kill them, and she didn't *want* to know, just as she'd been very careful to refrain from anything that even *looked* like she might be trying to find out who'd given him his orders in the first place. From their drawn expressions, however, it was obvious that the three scientists were as aware of why Zhukov—or whoever—was there as she was.

"There's an officers' lounge just down the passage," she said, pointing to the bridge hatch. "Second hatch on the left."

He nodded, then waved his charges toward the exit.

"Let's go, people."

They didn't move.

"*Now*," he said, drawing a small pulser from his jacket.

The male scientist made a face, but turned to go.

The two women fell into line behind him. Their keeper brought up the rear.

Bogunov turned back to her sensor officer.

"Any developments, Mase?"

"Not yet." Scribner's naturally pale face looked considerably paler than usual, and she wondered how much of that was due to the tactical situation and how much to what he'd just witnessed right here on the bridge. "We'll know for sure in about another—" he checked the time display "—forty-three seconds if Bogey One's going to rendezvous with the station. Even if they are, if five hundred gees is the most they can pull they're not going to be able to overhaul us. But . . ."

His voice trailed off, and Bogunov nodded. She could fill in the rest for herself. At five hundred gravities, Bogey One was already well above the maximum acceleration rate frigates of most navies could turn out. Another not-so-subtle suggestion that they were looking at the Royal Torch Navy. It was unlikely any pursuer would have still more acceleration in reserve, but it certainly wasn't impossible. And who knew what sort of missiles they might carry? Torch's frigates came from the Manties, who'd demonstrated over and over again the . . . unwisdom of underestimating their ships' acceleration rates.

And the still *greater* unwisdom of underestimating their missiles' range.

"Well . . . fuck," she repeated.

CHAPTER 44

Once they reached the officers' lounge, Zachariah
pulled out a chair from the compartment's single table
and sat down. With a hand gesture, he invited Weiss
and Juarez to join him.

He didn't bother to extend the same invitation
to Zhilov. Zachariah knew perfectly well why the
Gaul had insisted they all needed to be in the same
compartment—so he could murder the three of them
at his convenience, should their capture become imminent. If there'd been any doubt about that, the fact
that Zhilov hadn't bothered to reseal his jacket after
returning his pulser to its belt holster—and that he
made no attempt to conceal the weapon afterward—
had resolved it quite handily.

Stefka Juarez stared at that pulser for a moment
before abruptly sitting down. She then transferred the
stare to a blank stretch of the far bulkhead. Her olive
complexion was dark enough she didn't look pale, but
her expression was so tightly drawn her face looked
like a mask.

Gail Weiss seemed more relaxed. Much more, in

fact. Rather than sitting, she moved over to the beverage dispenser.

"Anybody besides me want some coffee? Stefka? Zachariah?"

"I'll have some," Zachariah said. "Black, please. And thanks."

Juarez just kept staring at the bulkhead.

Zachariah noted that Weiss hadn't bothered to extend her invitation to Zhilov, either. That was interesting. He knew nothing about the woman or her personal history, but she clearly had a spine. She would neither quaver in front of the Gaul nor make any pointless attempt at placating him.

For the first time, he noticed that she was rather nice-looking. Tall, a bit on the heavy side; hazel eyes; a rich head of auburn hair. She wasn't exactly pretty, and was certainly not beautiful, but she had the sort of open-featured face that reflected a strong and vivid personality.

This was a ridiculous time, however, to be contemplating the attractiveness of a woman he barely knew at all, and he shifted his attention back to Juarez as Weiss took her own seat at the table with both cups of coffee and slid one of them over to him.

"Stefka..." He really didn't know her well enough for that familiarity, but Juarez was so tense he wanted to crack through her brittle exterior, "relax, will you? There's really not much chance we won't make it to the hyper limit."

Juarez jerked her head around to look at him. "You're just guessing! You don't know that!"

Zachariah began to respond, then paused as Weiss tapped a command into the tabletop unit. The lounge's smart wall came to life in response, showing them a duplicate of *Prince Sundjata*'s maneuvering plot. Not the most soothing of all possible images, he thought as he surveyed the imagery. The once-amber icon which had represented the freighter approaching Balcescu Station had turned crimson...and been joined by six smaller, equally crimson icons. Four of the quintet of smaller light dots which had been accelerating towards the station had now made turnover, decelerating just as hard towards rendezvous with it.

The fifth had not, and his coffee seemed suddenly less tasty at the confirmation that at least one of the attacking warships was in pursuit of *Luigi Pirandello* and their own vessel. Juarez clearly recognized the same thing, and she jabbed a finger at it.

"See?!" she demanded. "They *are* chasing us!"

"Maybe they are," Weiss said calmly. "Doesn't mean they'll catch us, though. In fact, they won't."

"Oh, yeah? And what makes you so sure of that?" Juarez snapped back.

"The fact that astrogation is one of my specialties," the other woman replied. She leaned back in her chair and gestured with her coffee cup at the display. "Even if that's a Manty-built frigate, there's no way it has the acceleration to overhaul us short of the wall. One of their LACs might have the legs for it, but if they'd brought LACs along, then they'd have been pulling somewhere closer to seven hundred Gs on their approach to the station. I'm entirely in favor of Captain Bogunov running as fast as we can just in case, even if that does put a bit more strain on the compensator than I'm entirely happy with. Every bit of additional velocity we can tack on to our base—and as quickly as we can tack it—is a really good idea, since things can always go wrong. For example, we *could* lose an impeller node. Chances are about one in four hundred thousand of that happening, you understand, but there's something to be said for not taking any chances that it might. Unless it does, though, there's no way they can catch us."

"They don't have to catch as to kill us with missiles," Juarez pointed out. She didn't sound a lot calmer, Zachariah noted.

"No, but they'd still have to bring us into missile *range*," Weiss replied. "And, like I say, nothing this side of a LAC is going to manage that, either."

"Are you sure it's *not* a LAC?" Zachariah asked.

"Positive," Weiss said firmly. "First, Bogunov's sensor officer would have to be completely incompetent to be unable to distinguish between a light attack craft and a destroyer or a frigate. Second, like I said, if it was a LAC, it would already be showing a hell of a lot more acceleration than we're seeing." She sipped coffee, then twitched her head at the smart wall again. "And since it is a frigate, it can't have the mass or volume to mount the sorts of launchers the Manties' long-range missiles need. So, it doesn't have a LAC's legs to run us down, and it doesn't have a cruiser or battlecruiser's missile range to kill us if it can't catch us."

She took another sip from her coffee. Which was also black, Zachariah noted approvingly. Like everyone else in his family except weak-sister JoAnne, Zachariah sneered at adulterating the beverage essential to the pursuit of knowledge and wisdom.

Juarez was now staring at Weiss with the same

intensity she'd lavished upon the bulkhead earlier. But where her stare had been blank before, it now bordered on hostility.

"And what makes you such an expert on the subject?" she demanded.

"The fact that I *am* an expert on the subject. Project Mir—" Weiss began, then stopped and flicked a glance in Zhilov's direction. The Gaul clearly wasn't concerned about maintaining security about project code names at this point, however, but habits died hard, so she shrugged, then looked back at Juarez.

"The project I headed up," she continued, naming no names, "was devoted to the study of naval tactics. Which, for anyone with a brain—that excludes pretty much the entire officer corps of the Sollies' Battle Fleet, of course—means constant and careful analysis of the Manty-Haven war. If it would settle your nerves, I can lecture you into a state of utter stupor on the capabilities of any class of warships in the galaxy."

A crooked half-smile came to her face. "I'll grant you, my expertise is academic, not hands-on. But I'm not the one flying this ship. Captain Bogunov is—and I've seen nothing so far that leads me to think she's no good at it."

❖ ❖ ❖

Fourteen million kilometers astern of *Prince Sundjata*, Captain Roldão Brandt had reached a far less happy conclusion on the command deck of *Luigi Pirandello*, and he glared at *Prince Sundjata*'s icon. It was probably small souled of him to resent Caroline Bogunov's good fortune, but that didn't keep him from wishing their positions were reversed. He'd picked up Colonel Toussaint's transmission to Somogyi—his ship was eighteen million kilometers from Balcescu Station but almost directly on Toussaint's transmission path and the colonel hadn't bothered to encrypt his transmission or use a whisker laser—so there was no question at all in his mind about just who the star system's unwelcome visitors were. And looking at the numbers on his display, there was no doubt that even at his best acceleration the frigate pursuing his ship could bring her into missile range in no more than another hour or so.

Unlike *Prince Sundjata*.

He looked up from his display and glanced at Genora Hinkley, his second officer, who shook her head.

"No way, Captain," Genora said. "No way we're going to out run the bastards."

"So you think we should just go ahead and stop running?" Brandt asked, and Hinkley shrugged.

Brandt thought about it for a moment, then shook his head and answered his own question.

"So far, we're still way out of weapons' range," he said. "It's going to take them a while to change that, and in the meantime, who knows what may happen?" He removed his cap, ran his fingers through his hair, and twitched a smile. "*Their* compensator may fail. Or they may blow two or three nodes and have to reduce acceleration. Or it might turn out there's more trouble aboard the station than they counted on and they end up recalled to help deal with it."

"And just how likely are any of those to happen?" Hinkley asked with what might actually have been a tiny edge of humor. *Gallows* humor, perhaps, but still humor.

"A tad more likely than the system's primary suddenly deciding to go nova," Brandt told him. "Not a *lot* more likely, maybe, but more likely. And in the meantime, I figure it's smarter to play the hand all the way out rather than fold any earlier than we have to."

"Our compensator's more likely to fail than theirs is," Hinkley pointed out, and Brandt shrugged.

"Of course it is. If it goes, though, at least it'll be fast. And to be honest, I'd rather take my chances with compensator failure than with a shipload of ex-slaves. Half of them are probably ex-*Ballroom*, for that matter! I'd really, really rather not make their acquaintance, if it's all the same to you."

"Oh, it's *definitely* all the same to me!" Hinkley said fervently.

"Good. On the other hand, let's get some security in place. I don't want the cargo getting wind of this—the last thing we need is for them to try to break out and seize the ship—and I don't want any of our more panic-prone people on this bridge to argue with any decisions I may have to make."

"On it," Hinkley agreed laconically.

✦ ✦ ✦

"I'm *not* arguing. I'm just telling you that I'm doing the best I can," Zoltan Somogyi tried to speak as calmly as he could, although he rather suspected that the sweat streaking his face suggested he was less than happy about the situation. "Look, I'm no angel, but do you think I want to give you an *excuse* to slaughter all of us?!"

The face on his com display seemed unmoved by his plea, and he swallowed a desire to curse wildly.

He and Bordás had done their best to prevent panic, but their efforts had not been blessed by success. What he'd *wanted* to do was to sit on any news of the situation until the Torch assault shuttles had already docked and begun disgorging their troops. The sudden emergence of four shuttles' worth of armed-to-the-teeth Marines who already knew combat was probable should have gone through any attempted resistance like a graser through Swiss cheese, and with just about the same consequences the cheese would have suffered. While that would have been a bit hard on anyone who got in their way, it should also be fast enough for them to secure control of the slave holds before any of his less tightly wrapped personnel did something profoundly stupid and got all of them killed. Under the circumstances, Somogyi would have been just delighted to sustain the collateral damage involved if it kept his own personal hide intact.

Unfortunately, word had leaked almost instantly. He was pretty sure it had been someone in Flight Control, not that it really mattered. The station's personnel had been given almost fourteen minutes to go from flat-footed surprise to fullbore panic, and things had gone downhill from the moment the word broke. Now the shuttles were less than three minutes out, and things were not looking good from the perspective of Angela Somogyi's little boy Zoltan.

"The first thing we did," he told Colonel Toussaint, "was to lock out the jettison command." He didn't much care for the way the ex-slave's eyes flickered at his use of the word "jettison," but he also had no choice but to continue. "You *know* how they're set up. I've got an armed guard sitting on the master panel here on the command deck, but there are local command stations on each of the holds. For now, we've managed to lock them down, but there are some people on the station who don't trust your offer not to shoot them out of hand if we surrender. Or maybe they're just crazies—I don't know! But *somebody's* trying to hack into the local control station on Hold Number Three. I've got security people trying to fight their way in to stop them, and my people here on the command deck are trying to keep them locked out, but we're losing ground and if they cut the physical links between our systems and the local station, then there won't be anything I can—"

"It sounds to me like you have a problem then, Mr. Somogyi," Toussaint said coldly. "I'm sure you'll forgive me if I don't feel a huge amount of sympathy for you."

"I don't want your damn sympathy!" Somogyi snapped, then shoved himself physically back in his command chair. "I want to stay alive," he said frankly then, his tone flat, "and for that to happen those slaves you're so eager to rescue have to stay alive, too. So I know you hate my guts and the guts of everyone else on the station, but at this moment, you and I want the same thing, whatever our reasons for it."

Donald Toussaint felt a faint—very faint—stir of respect for the Balcescu Station CO. Not enough to make him want to do anything except put a pulser dart squarely between the man's eyes, of course. Unfortunately, Somogyi had a point. A very good point, in fact.

Donald looked at the secondary com screen by his right knee and a skinsuited Ayibongwinkosi Kabweza looked back at him from it. She'd been monitoring his communications with Somogyi while her command shuttle decelerated towards the station. Now he worked one eyebrow at her.

"I've been looking at the schematic he uploaded to us," Kabweza said, her voice audible in his earbug, although Somogyi couldn't hear it. "As nearly as we can tell, it matches everything we already knew about its layout. I think he's being straight with us—if only to save his own ass, of course—and I think we can do it. But it's not going to be pretty."

Donald pressed the stud that muted Somogyi's end of the link and shrugged.

"I can live with *plenty* of 'not pretty' where these people are concerned Ayibongwinkosi. But how confident are you about that second 'I think' of yours?"

"Confident we can take out the bastards trying to hack the system? Completely. Whether or not we can do it without spacing the slaves ourselves is something else. The odds are in our favor, though. And let's be honest here. If we *don't* get in there before the SOBs crack the security lockout, then all those people are as good as dead anyway. Nobody who wasn't all the way around the bend would even be *thinking* about spacing any slaves with my people about to reach right down their throats and rip their hearts out."

She had a point, Donald thought. And—

"They just cut the physical connection," Somogyi said harshly. "We're done from here, Colonel. And the handful of security people I've got down there only have sidearms, certainly not enough firepower to fight their way in."

The station commander's expression was haggard, his eyes desperate, and Donald released the muting stud.

"Then we'll just have to see about doing it ourselves, Mr. Somogyi," he said coldly. "You might want to suggest to your people that they stay the hell out of our way."

❖   ❖   ❖

"You heard the Colonel, Wat," Kabweza said to Lieutenant Wat Tyler, the commanding officer of the platoon assigned to her command shuttle. "Are your people clear on what we're doing?"

"Clear, Ma'am!" Tyler assured her. "We don't have enough time for any fancy planning, so I figure we go with a modification of an Alpha Breach?"

"Works," Kabweza approved. She punched a quick command into her console, and a schematic of Balcescu Station appeared on the HUDs of both her own and Tyler's skinsuit helmets. She manipulated it quickly, highlighting four points on the station's skin. "About here, I think," she said.

"Yes, Ma'am." Tyler tapped a command of his own into the data pad on his left forearm, dropping the same image to his senior noncoms. Confirmation of receipt came back almost instantly, and he nodded in satisfaction. Then he looked back at Kabweza. "I'm guessing you're not planning on staying here aboard the shuttle?"

Technically, it was a question. His tone of voice made it a statement, and Kabweza smiled at him.

"Listen up, people!" he announced over the platoon's general link. "The Old Lady's taking us in in person. That means *she's* the one who's going to be doing the post-op critique of just how well you do. You might want to bear that in mind."

❖   ❖   ❖

"*Shit!*"

Aatifa Villanueva flung herself to the deck as another burst of pulser darts sizzled past her from the twisted and ruined hatch and ricocheted madly off a bulkhead. None of the ricochets came *her* way, fortunately, but a shrill scream from somewhere behind her said someone else had been less fortunate.

"This is fucking crazy!" Alexi Grigorev shouted from beside her. "There's no *way* we're getting in there!"

Grigorev had been Villanueva's partner for almost a year now, and she'd found him considerably closer to tolerable than a lot of the people she'd worked with in her career with the Jessyk Combine. He *did* have a way of belaboring the obvious sometimes, though.

"And just what the hell do you think is going to happen if we *don't* get in there, Alyusha?" She heard the desperation in her own tone, but there wasn't much she could do about that at the moment. "We lose one of those slaves—just *one*—and we might as well cut our own throats!"

"And getting our heads blown off is better than that exactly how?" Grigorev demanded, poking his hand around the edge of the hatch and sending a burst of darts back up the passageway. He still didn't know exactly how the lunatics they were fighting had managed to blow the hatch on their way in. They shouldn't have been able to do it, but the truth was that slavers and the other sorts of outlaws who consorted with them were likely to have all sorts of things they weren't supposed to have in their pockets at any given moment. It went with the paranoia, although he hated to think which of them had been paranoid enough to carry a demo charge *that* powerful around with him.

The bad news was that it had let the lunatics in question in; the *good* news—such as it was and what there was of it—was that it meant they couldn't close the hatch behind them again. Which did him and the rest of the security personnel Jeremy Benford had managed to get down here a whole hell of a lot of good with at least two people covering the hatch with pulser fire.

"It's not going to—" Villanueva started to snap back, then cut herself off as Somogyi's voice came over their com links.

"Listen up! Just stay where you are—those people are going to take care of it themselves! Stay out of their way!"

Villanueva and Grigorev looked at each other. Neither of them was very happy about the thought of being caught between their own lunatics and the attacking lunatics—probably ex-Ballroom, and not all that ex-, given what Villanueva knew about Torch. On the other hand, it beat hell out of trying to get through that hatch themselves, and she found herself hoping the Torches hurried the hell up.

❖   ❖   ❖

The Mk 19 Tango nosed into the docking bay and opened its ventral hatch. Half a dozen skinsuited Marines floated through it, then used their suit thrusters to take up positions covering the bay's gallery with an assortment of lethal weaponry. The technicians in that gallery took note of their arrival and were very, very careful about extending the personnel tube to mate with the assault shuttle's main hatch. The operation took a little longer than usual; none of those technicians wanted any of the passengers aboard that shuttle to find any fault at all with their safety procedures. Within less than three minutes, however, the first squad of Marines came swimming out of the tube into the gallery's artificial gravity and landed as neatly as so many cats. *Big* cats, festooned with the sharp, lethal claws of pulse rifles and heavy flechette guns. They unlimbered their own weaponry, and the gallery techs smiled weakly at them.

The smiles of very small, very inoffensive, very *obe-dient* mice trying hard to placate the hunting felines who had just invaded their rathole.

❖   ❖   ❖

Ayibongwinkosi Kabweza watched approvingly as Lieutenant Tyler's platoon went to work. Their shuttle had backed off to give them working room—and to avoid any odd bits and pieces of .debris which might presently find themselves floating around for some reason—and the ring charges being sealed against the station's skin. There were some definite minuses to their hastily revised ops plan, but that was the way it went in combat. Nothing was ever neat and tidy when it came down to it, and as she'd told Toussaint, when everything else was factored in, fast and dirty gave the slaves in that hold their best chance of survival.

And however true that might be, there was at least one added incentive to doing it this way. It was unlikely any of the slavers trying to space the slaves had thought to bring along skinsuits of their own, given the lack of warning and improvisational nature of their current efforts.

Which, when you came right down to it, was about as poetic as justice got.

❖   ❖   ❖

"Will you *hurry*?!" Constance Mastroianni snapped.

The whine and sizzle of pulser darts had faded in intensity behind her, and she wished she could convince herself that was a good thing. Unfortunately, the most probable explanation was that Somogyi's stooges were lying back to clear the way for the fucking Audubon Ballroom.

"If you think you can do this better than I can,"

Liang MacHowell told her through gritted teeth, his eyes on the lines of code scrolling across his display, "then you can fucking well do it yourself!"

"All right. All right!" Mastroianni's right hand made a fluttery, vaguely soothing gesture. "It's just—"

She cut herself off with a little shrug, and MacHowell grunted.

He went on with his work, and Mastroianni turned back to the half-dozen other men and women covering the access hatch behind them. She slapped her palms together two or three times, bouncing on the balls of her feet, feeling the conflicting tides of adrenaline and terror ripsaw their way through her and swore viciously under her breath.

Royal Torch Marines—yeah, sure *they are!* she thought harshly. *I don't know what Somogyi's been smoking, but I'll be* damned *if he's going to hand* me *over to the frigging Ballroom!*

Constance Mastroianni had been in the trade too long to be taken in by that kind of crap. The Ballroom had almost gotten her once already—if she'd been ten minutes early for that appointment, the bomb that gutted the Manpower office would have gotten her, too—and they weren't getting another shot. Not unless she had an equalizer of her own in hand, anyway!

She slapped her palms together again, trying to pretend her own plans weren't the counsel of despair. After all, they could make sweet promises to her exactly the same way they'd made them to Somogyi, and sooner or later, she'd have to meet their terms. But she could at least make them wait, make them pause and talk to her, walk them back a little bit from the immediate brink of the assault. And they *would* talk to her, she thought grimly. Once she had control of the emergency jettisoning system, they'd *damned* well talk to her! And then—

She stopped herself short again. If she'd been one bit less desperate, it would have occurred to her that the reason she was stopping herself was that she didn't have a clue about where any negotiations with the Ballroom were ultimately going to end. Or if she did have any clues, she sure as hell didn't want to dwell on them! But at least she was *doing* something, not just sitting around on her ass like Somogyi.

She wheeled back toward MacHowell and stopped herself just before she asked him for yet another progress report. He was a far better hacker than she was, and she knew it. More to the point, nagging him wasn't going to make him go any faster. It was just—

Stop that, she told herself firmly. *He'll get there when he gets there, and we've isolated the controls from all the rest of the station's systems. There's no way anybody outside this compartment can know whether or not we've already cracked the access codes. They're going to have to assume we* have, *and that means—*

❖   ❖   ❖

"Beta Charge ready!" Sergeant Supakrit X announced over his com, stepping back to a safe distance from the ring charge his section had sealed in place. His team had finished before the other three, he noted with grim satisfaction, even with Vlachos dragging ass as usual.

He watched the remaining icons on his HUD switch from amber to red as the other charges came live, and smiled.

"Fire in the hole!" Lieutenant Tyler announced, and pressed the button.

❖   ❖   ❖

Constance Mastroianni's ruminations came to an abrupt end as the breaching charges blew four almost perfectly circular divots out of Balcescu Station's thick skin. A station like Balcescu contained a stupendous amount of atmosphere. All bad holovid features notwithstanding, something that size normally decompressed only slowly—unless, of course, its hull had suffered catastrophic damage.

Which, come to think of it, was exactly what had happened to Balcescu Station, locally, at least.

She had time for a single scream of terror.

❖   ❖   ❖

Aatifa Villanueva and Alexi Grigorev were outside the suddenly ruptured compartment. Unfortunately for them, the station blast doors were *behind* them, and the hatch *into* the compartment had already been wrecked. They had more time than Mastroianni—not much, but a *little* more—to realize what was happening, and it did them not one bit of good.

❖   ❖   ❖

Well, would you look at that? Supakrit X thought as the first body erupted from the sudden hole in the station's skin. The woman was still waving her arms, her face twisted in a rictus of absolute, hopeless terror, and the sergeant bared his teeth, thinking about all the slaves who'd experienced the same terror over the years.

Hers wasn't the only body to go soaring out into space, and he had no doubt they were going to find other slavers' bodies inside the compartment. According to the assault shuttle's sensors, the slaves they'd been trying to jettison were still physically unharmed, although the poor bastards were probably scared half to death. Ironically, the very hatch and heavy pressure bulkheads which sealed the slave hold off from from the station as a whole so that its sentient cargo could be expelled into space without any fuss or bother to the station's other inhabitants had protected them from the catastrophic depressurization just outside it. And they'd have hours of air inside there with them. There'd be plenty of time to slap patches over the breaches and repressurize the compartment before the Torches needed to pop the hatch and get them out.

"All right, people," Lieutenant Tyler said. "Let's get our point people in there. And remember, there could still be some bastard who'd had time to get into his skin suit before we came calling. Let's just send anyone like that along to keep his friends company, shall we?"

As orders went, that one worked just fine for Sergeant Supakrit X.

Just fine.

CHAPTER 45

Even the surprisingly good coffee of *Prince Sundjata's* officers' lounge dispenser had started tasting like acid to Zachariah McBryde as he sat with his two fellow scientists, watching the smart wall's imagery. The looming presence of their Gaul guard/executioner was impossible to ignore, but Zachariah wasn't really worried about anything that might happen to *Prince Sundjata*. It was obvious to him that Gail Weiss must have been as good at her job as he'd been at his, because every single thing she'd predicted about Bogey One had come true ... so far, at last.

But if that was good news for *Prince Sundjata*, it was very, very bad news for *Luigi Pirandello*, and his eyes were bitter as he watched the smart wall.

The Torch assault shuttles and frigates had launched seventy-seven minutes ago. For closing in on an hour and a half, he'd watched Bogey One steadily pursuing the second slave ship. For nineteen minutes, the range had continued to open, but then the frigate's superior acceleration had matched velocity with *Luigi Pirandello*. Over the fifty-eight minutes since, the almost twenty-eight million kilometers between pursuer and pursued had been pared away. *Prince Sundjata*'s velocity was still higher than Bogey One's, and the range between her and the Torch warship was still growing, albeit at a slower rate, but it was only a matter of time—and not much of it—before *Luigi Pirandello*'s desperate race would be over.

He didn't realize just how bleak his own expression was. Not till Weiss's hand came gently down on the white-knuckled fist clenched around his coffee cup. He turned his head towards her, and she smiled sadly.

✦   ✦   ✦

"We've got a signal coming in, Sir," Jürgen Acker, Roldão Brandt's com officer, said flatly.

Captain Brandt sighed and took off his cap to run his fingers through his hair yet again, then paused, looking down at it. He grimaced and tossed it onto his console, then leaned back in his command chair and crossed his legs.

"Put it through," he said resignedly.

"—is Lieutenant Commander Tunni Bayano, commanding the Royal Torch Navy ship *Denmark Vesey*," He heard. "At present acceleration rates, you will be in my missile envelope in four-point-seven minutes. If you have not agreed to surrender within the next five minutes, I will open fire. This is your first and only warning. Bayano, clear."

With the range down to ten million kilometers, the transmission lag was only a little over thirty light-seconds, so there was time for Brandt to consider his response. Not *much* time, however, and he turned his head to raise his eyebrows at Hinkley.

"Well?"

"We're fucked," Hinkley snorted. "But at least he's giving us a chance to surrender."

"Of course he is. He wants the cargo delivered safe and sound. Doesn't necessarily mean he has any warm and fuzzy feelings for *us*, though."

They looked at one another for a moment, then Brandt shrugged and glanced at the com officer.

"Put me through to them."

"Yes, Sir!" The com officer didn't even try to hide his relief. "Open mike, Sir," he said, and Brandt drew a deep breath.

"This is a slave ship," he said as calmly as he could, "and it's not unheard of for Manticoran, Havenite, and Beowulfan warships to space the crews of captured slave ships. I can only assume that your Royal Torch Navy will follow the same policy. So I don't really see where accepting your offer and surrendering would do me or my crew very much good."

The response came back almost exactly one minute later, as if his counterpart had been expecting the query/protest and had his reply ready and waiting.

"First, it is the policy of the navies you just listed to *automatically* space captured slavers only if those slavers have killed some or all of the slaves on board. Granted, it sometimes happens anyway, but I feel certain that if you surrender your ship, you won't have been stupid enough to have killed any slaves aboard it first. Second, we are not Manticorans, Havenites, or Beowulfers. Torch has declared *war* on Mesa, and we intend to press the fight until you surrender unconditionally. We intend not simply to punish those involved in the criminal enterprise of genetic slavery, but to destroy that institution completely. We will press the fight until we receive unconditional surrender, and we consider all Manpower and/or Jessyk Combine starships to be military combatants. That means we will not feel bound by any of the niceties of interstellar admiralty law when it comes to...apprehending them. We will, however, honor the provisos of the Deneb Accords where enemy combatants are concerned. As such, we will consider any who surrender to us prisoners of war and treat them accordingly. There is, however, one proviso, you understand, which is that you *have* been smart enough to do no harm to any slaves aboard your ship. If you violate that proviso, you might as well shoot yourselves right now and save us the trouble of shoving you out of the airlocks."

"Do I have your word on that, Sir?"

Bayano's voice, hitherto flat and emotionless, had taken on a distinctly sarcastic tone when it came back forty seconds later.

"I'm an ex-slave myself. Until a few months ago, when I was commissioned, I went by the name of Tunni X. I find it interesting that you now think my word is worth having in the first place."

"What can I say?" Brandt picked his cap up and put it back on again. "We're living in a new galaxy."

"You have my word," Bayano said flatly forty-seven seconds later. "And you'd better check the time, because you have exactly fifty-two seconds left in which to surrender."

"Very well," Brandt said heavily. "We surrender. What do you want us to do?"

"Continue your acceleration," Bayano instructed him. "At your acceleration rate, our velocities will equalize in approximately twenty-five minutes. At that time, the range will be just over two million kilometers. You will place your entire crew aboard your small craft and abandon ship at that point. My pinnace will then make rendezvous with your vessel and my people will board it. Any member of your crew found on board at that time will be subject to summary execution. If we determine that any of the slaves aboard your ship have been killed, I *will* open fire on your small craft, and there will be no survivors. Is that clearly understood? Do you have anything you want to tell me now about the status of the slaves aboard your vessel?"

Brandt nodded to himself in understanding. Given *Luigi Pirandello*'s present velocity, it would have been impossible for her to decelerate to zero relative to the system primary before crossing the hyper limit. Obviously, *Denmark Vesey* had no intention of allowing him to slip away into hyper. By continuing to accelerate towards the limit, however, he effectively added his own ship's maximum acceleration to the frigate's *deceleration*, allowing them to equalize velocity at such a relatively short range.

"As you said," his tone was weary when he replied, "I'm not stupid enough to have harmed any of them with a frigate on my ass. Your conditions are clearly understood. We will comply."

"Good. Bayano, clear."

Brandt sat motionless a moment longer, tipped back in his chair, then let it come upright and swiveled it to face the rest of his bridge crew.

"Anyone have anything to say?" he asked almost whimsically.

"I don't know how our people are going to react to abandoning ship," Hinkley said. She looked around the bridge uncertainly, her hands almost flapping about. "You know some of them are going to figure this is just a way for the Torches to get us far enough away from the cargo for them to burn us all out of space without risking any damage to their friends in the slave holds, don't you?"

"Tell me something I *don't* know," Brandt retorted.

"I know one thing," Acker said, his expression grim. "First thing we better do is put Voigt and Ingraham in irons."

"Or just shoot 'em," Hinkley agreed. "God, we don't want either of them running around loose once the entire crew hears about this! The holds all have individual spacing controls, and *those* two—!"

That was a mark of incipient panic. What she'd said was true...but the captain could lock down all the holds from right here on the command deck. He took three steps to his own console and began keying in the commands. Within ten seconds it was done.

Still, she and Acker had a point. Even if Voigt and Ingraham could no longer inflict any wholesale harm on the slaves, they could still start killing them one at a time, which would have exactly the same result when the Torch boarding party came aboard and found the bodies. Whether or not Bayano intended to keep his word and allow them to live as long as they complied with his surrender terms—*all* his surrender terms—Brandt had no doubt at all that he would shoot every personnel shuttle out of space if *they* failed to comply with their side of those terms.

He turned to the two security people regarding the command deck hatch.

"Go get Voigt and Ingraham. They'll both be in

Engineering. Put them in irons and drag them to the shuttle bay. If they give you any crap, you have my permission—no, I hereby *order* you—to use any level of force, including lethal force, to make them comply."

The two guards left immediately. They were hurrying, in fact. They both knew Voigt and Ingraham as well as anyone else in the crew. Brandt watched them go, then—belatedly—spotted the third figure standing at a hatch. He'd completely forgotten that the man—Arpino, his name was—had also been on the command deck. He'd come there as soon as the crisis began, and as his much as he would have liked to, Brandt hadn't ordered him to leave. The captain's superiors had made it clear that Arpino was to be given whatever latitude he wanted in carrying out his duties.

Duties which . . . had never been specified.

Brandt hadn't liked those orders then, and he didn't like them now. In fact, he'd already made up his mind that if Arpino gave him any grief over his decision to surrender, the man was going to suffer a serious accident.

"You will be surrendering the ship, then," Arpino said. It was a statement, not a question.

"We don't have any choice."

Brandt braced himself for an argument, but Arpino simply turned and left the command deck. Unsealing his jacket as he went.

❖   ❖   ❖

The two guards found Voigt and Ingraham in *Luigi Pirandello*'s engineering section. No one outside the slave ship's command deck had been privy to Brandt's conversation with Bayano, but no one needed to have been to understand what the captain's most likely options were. Voigt and Ingraham were both waving their hands around in a half-shouted "discussion" with three of their fellow engineering techs.

The guards, who had their pulsers drawn, although not raised, interrupted the noisy conversation to inform them they were under arrest. Voigt threw up his hands in disgust and sat down on the deck. Ingraham just started screeching at them instead of her fellow techs.

The senior guard, Janice Wendel, had had to put up with Ingraham for almost three years. That was more than enough, so she raised her pistol and shot Ingraham twice. Tried to, rather. Between her own anxiety, lack of experience in real combat, and habitual slackness when it came to putting in time on the firing range, she made a mess of it. The first hypersonic dart missed entirely and went ricocheting wildly around Engineering. Somehow, it failed to hit anyone else or to inflict damage on anything critical. The second was *almost* a hit, and Ingraham's right ear disintegrated in an explosion of blood and all but vaporized tissue. The damage sent her staggering back against the bulkhead with her hand clapped to the mangled side of her head—still screeching, somehow.

Wendel took three steps forward, brought the muzzle of the pulser to within five centimeters of Ingraham's head, and fired again.

At that range, she could hardly miss, and the entire top of the engineering tech's skull exploded in a cloud of red, gray brain tissue, and tiny white fragments of bone.

The woman was dead before she hit the deck.

Wendel turned to face Voigt, who was staring up at her with his mouth open. She pointed the pulser at his head. The fact that her hand was shaking just made the situation even more terrifying for him.

"I—am—not—carrying—you," she ground out. "Get up, put your hands behind you, and start moving for the shuttle bay. Or I'll shoot you dead, too."

He scrambled to his feet fast enough to have won the gold medal in that event, if any athletic competition had ever featured it, and put his hands behind him for the manacles.

❖　　　❖　　　❖

Captain Bogunov did the captives-in-all-but-name the favor of transmitting the latest news through the com and the officers' lounge. They didn't need her to tell them that *Prince Sundjata*'s escape was virtually assured now that Bogey One had begun decelerating. The icons on the smart wall had already told them that, but she was able to confirm that Roldão Brandt had agreed to surrender his ship to the frigate.

Zachariah felt a deep sadness. His last friend in the universe, Lisa Charteris, would soon be gone, too.

❖　　　❖　　　❖

In fact, she was already dead. Arpino had found her lying on her bunk and staring at the ceiling. She glanced at him when he entered the cabin and then looked back up at the ceiling. A moment later, she closed her eyes.

There was nothing to say, so nothing was. When the Gaul closed the cabin door behind him, the bunk was already soaked with blood.

The other Houdini participant on the ship, Joseph van Vleet, wasn't in his cabin. But it took Arpino only three minutes to find him. By the very nature of the slave ship's design, with the great bulk of its space sealed off, and with locks that van Vleet lacked the codes to open—there just weren't many places to hide.

The Gaul found him in the second utility cabinet he searched. Two seconds later, its contents were also becoming blood-soaked.

That job done, Arpino went to his own cabin, lay down on the bunk, and gazed up at the overhead with his hands folded behind his head.

There was nothing to do now but wait.

❖   ❖   ❖

"All right, that's it," Captain Brandt announced. *Luigi Pirandello*'s velocity was exactly that of *Denmark Vesey*, and he nodded to his astrogator. "Kill the accel, and let's get the hell down to the boat bay and find out if these...people intend to keep their word or not."

"Yes, Sir!"

The astrogator shut down the slave ship's impeller wedge and half-dashed off the command deck and down the passageway towards the boat bay. Brandt took a moment to exchange one last glance with Hinkle, and then the two of them followed somewhat more sedately. Even aboard a slave ship, there were traditions and appearances to maintain.

The first of *Luigi Pirandello*'s personnel shuttles had already departed, and the flight engineer sealed the hatch behind the captain and his exec as soon as they were aboard. The copilot was peering back from the flight deck, and Brandt waved both hands in the traditional hand signal of the order to undock. That was all the flight crew needed, and the shuttle had already detached her umbilicals and begun drifting out of the bay on maneuvering thrusters before the captain had settled into his own seat.

He watched through the viewport as the boat bay moved away from him. Then they were out, the viewport filled with a field of stars, and he closed his eyes and waited to find out just how honest Tunni Bayano had really been.

✧   ✧   ✧

Lieutenant Marcos Xiorro watched as his pinnace slid steadily closer to the waiting freighter. According to the manifest the slave ship's captain had transmitted in obedience to Lieutenant Commander Bayano, there were almost five hundred slaves in its holds, and Xiorro wondered if the captain had informed those slaves that they were about to be rescued.

Well, he thought. *It won't matter one way or the other in a few more minutes.*

In a way, he rather hoped the slaver captain *hadn't* informed his cargo. This would be the very first slave ship the Royal Torch Navy had ever intercepted, and Xiorro was rather looking forward to going down in the history books as the officer who'd led the boarding party. Of course, the Marines were along to do any grunt work that might be necessary, but that wouldn't detract one bit from the Navy's glory, and Xiorro felt his lips twitch in a faint smile of amusement at his own vanity as he silently rehearsed the words he'd chosen.

"The Navy's here!" That was what he was going to say, because for the first time in galactic history, the navy doing the rescuing belonged to an entire star nation of ex-slaves. Those ex-slaves would never forget their gratitude to all the other navies which had rescued them and others like them over the decades and centuries, but the date was special. This was the day slaves rescued their own.

✧   ✧   ✧

The Gaul named Arpino had never appeared on *Luigi Pirandello*'s crew list, and in the haste to evacuate the ship, neither of the two shuttles' flight crews realized that he wasn't aboard the other one. Even if they'd known, they probably wouldn't have worried *too* much, on the theory that anything that happened to somebody stupid enough to miss his assigned ride when the Torches found him was no more than he deserved.

But Arpino hadn't "missed" his assigned ride. He was exactly where he was supposed to be under the orders intended to ensure that *no* evidence of Lisa Charteris's or Joseph van Vleet's deaths ever came to light. After all, the mere existence of their dead bodies might cause someone to wonder how two prominent Mesan scientists who had officially perished in an air car disaster had been discovered aboard a slave ship with heads shattered by pulser darts. For that matter, he couldn't be certain that none of *Luigi Pirandello*'s crew people hadn't heard Charteris or van Vleet's names. So it would be as well to leave no loose ends, and he'd spent the half-dozen minutes since the personnel shuttles' departure on the slave ship's command deck, inputting a code no one except its captain and his executive officer was supposed to know.

Now he sat calmly, watching the screen which showed the interior of the brightly lit boat bay. He watched the Torch pinnace slide into it on skillfully metered bursts from its thrusters. It was a tricky maneuver, with no boat bay personnel ready to assist with the bay's docking tractors, but the pilot of that pinnace clearly knew what he was doing.

The pinnace came to a halt, hovering within no more than four or five centimeters of exactly the right position, and Seleven Arpino entered the last digit of the code he wasn't supposed to know.

$$\diamond \qquad \diamond \qquad \diamond$$

Zachariah McBryde lunged to his feet in disbelief. He felt Zhilov behind him, knew the Gaul had stabbed an instinctive hand towards his pulser, but he couldn't look away from the smart wall where *Luigi Pirandello* had just exploded.

For instants which felt like eons he simply couldn't process the data. His thoughts skittered like a man on slick ice, unable to grasp what had just happened. It was insane! Brandt had *surrendered* his ship—he'd taken all of his people off aboard its shuttles. Why in God's name had he done that if he'd intended to set a scuttling charge behind him?! He'd put all of his people into what amounted to a shooting gallery for the Torch frigate, and the destruction of *Denmark Vesey's* pinnace and all its personnel was guaranteed to—

Then he knew. It was the only possible answer, and he started to whirl accusingly toward Zhilov in a triumph of reflex over rationality. The last thing he needed to do was to confront Zhilov. If the Gaul decided that Zachariah's rage represented a threat to his own ability to control the situation, he wouldn't hesitate an instant before killing the scientist where he stood. But before Zachariah could turn, he froze again, eyes sick as the inevitable happened.

Roldão Brandt never had the opportunity to protest his people's innocence. It probably wouldn't have mattered if he had—not with five hundred slaves and the twenty-seven Royal Torch Navy and Marine personnel dead in a blossom of nuclear fire.

Two million kilometers was too great a range for

energy weapons, but the crimson icons of missiles streaked towards the helpless personnel shuttles. It took thirty-three seconds for them to reach their targets—thirty-three seconds in which Zachariah could not look away from the smart wall. Thirty-three seconds that ended in the obliteration of every remaining man and woman who'd been aboard *Luigi Pirandello*.

"Oh my God! Oh my God! Omigod! Omigod-omigod-*omigod!*"

It was Stefka Juarez, a corner of Zachariah's mind realized, starting to shake off its paralysis. The woman stood to his right, one fist pressed against her mouth, eyes wide with horror.

"They fired!" she blurted. "They *fired!* And now—" she turned slowly, like a woman in a nightmare, to face Zhilov "—*now they're going to fire on us!*"

Zachariah shook himself. That was ridiculous! *Prince Sundjata* was less than two and a half minutes from the hyper limit. They were that close to escaping—in fact, they'd all begun to relax with the knowledge that they were going to live after all. That was what had made the destruction of *Luigi Pirandello* so shocking, so paralyzing.

But Zachariah was a physicist. He wasn't a weapons expert like Gail Weiss, but he could solve simple intercept problems, and he'd solve this one long since. Even if *Denmark Vesey* really had mounted the multidrive missiles Weiss had assured them couldn't possibly be fitted into a frigate's hull, and even if those missiles were capable of sustaining a thousand gravities of acceleration indefinitely, it would still take them over an hour to reach *Prince Sundjata* at this range.

Whatever her field might have been, it was obvious

that Juarez was no physicist. Or, if she was, that her brain had been totally jellied by panic, because she lowered her hand from her mouth to point a shaking index finger at Zhilov.

"You *bastard!*" she hissed. "You *fucking* bastard! You killed all of us! You've—you've—!"

Words failed her, and she flung herself at the Gaul.

Whether *Luigi Pirandello*'s destruction had surprised him as much as anyone else, or whether it was the sheer insanity of Juarez's reaction, Zhilov's response was slow. His pulser cleared the holster, but before he could aim or fire, she was upon him. Most members of the onion had received at least some rudimentary martial arts training in their youth, but any training Juarez might have received was decidedly not in evidence as she went for the Gaul's eyes with daggered fingernails. He got his left forearm up barely in time to block her first, frenzied strike, and her body slammed into his, pinning his right arm—and the pulser—between them, as her other hand came up and eluded his block.

Zhilov bellowed in pain as his right eye erupted in blood. Then he got a knee up, slamming it into her belly. She bounced away from him, whooping for breath as she folded up, but she never got a chance to recover the wind which had been knocked so brutally out of her. Before she could even begin to straighten, the pulser rose. It whined and a three-dart burst hit her on the crown of her head, pulverizing her skull instantly.

It was all one mad whirl of motion and insanity, of violence and blood, and yet even as it exploded about Zachariah, it all seemed to be happening in slow

motion. He watched Juarez stagger backward, watched
that pulser rise, watched the woman's head explode . . .
and realized the pulser was still rising, still swinging.

Swinging towards *him*.

He didn't know what Zhilov was thinking. For
that matter, he didn't know *if* Zhilov was thinking,
and there wasn't time to ponder the Gaul's motives.
Maybe he was simply reacting to the suddenness of
the attack, the pain in his ruptured eye. Or perhaps
he was reacting to . . . neutralize his two remaining
charges before they took advantage of his weakened
position to escape the certainty of death he represented
if anything like this day's events should occur again.
Or maybe he was reacting to something else entirely.

It didn't matter. Zacharias saw that pulser coming,
knew he was going to die, then saw the weapon go
bouncing upward as Gail Weiss' right foot left the
deck in a powerful snap kick which landed perfectly
on the Gaul's gun hand.

The pulser went flying. Zhilov's left arm lashed out,
his forearm hammering Weiss across the side of the
head. She went down—unconscious or dead; Zachariah
didn't know—and then *he* was moving, as well.

Zhilov was badly off-center, unbalanced, half blind
as he fought to regain the center he'd lost, and Zachariah knew that if he did, he and Weiss would be as
dead as Juarez. It didn't matter what had started the
explosion of violence. What mattered was that whether
by instinct or intent, Zhilov meant to kill all of them.

Zachariah McBryde was a scientist, not a trained
security man like his brother had been. For Zachariah,
"martial arts" had been no more than an exercise form,
never something he'd intended or expected to actually

need. But as Zhilov twisted back towards him, he felt himself moving forward, driving into the Gaul. Zhilov was favoring his right hand—obviously Weiss' kick had done significant damage to it—but his *left* arm was scything inward, and his left hand flexed strangely. The organic laminate blade which emerged suddenly from the back of his left hand projected almost eight centimeters beyond the knuckles and swept toward Zachariah's throat.

The scientist's right arm thrust vertically upwards like a sword, hammering into the inside of Zhilov's left forearm, blocking the blade's strike. And then Zachariah's left hand went for the Gaul's good eye and his right knee slammed forward in a vicious strike to Zhilov's groin.

The Gaul blocked part of its force, but not all of it, and he jackknifed forward. Both of Zachariah's hands cupped Zhilov's head and he jerked downward with all the strength of his back as his knee came up again.

He was trying to drive his kneecap into the Gaul's face, but he missed his mark as Zhilov threw himself forward, trying to knock Zachariah from his feet.

Unfortunately for Zhilov, that meant Zachariah's knee caught him squarely in the throat, instead.

The Gaul went down, both hands clutching at his throat. The impact knocked Zachariah off his feet, as well, and he rolled frantically as he heard Zhilov's hacking, coughing fight to breathe. He doubted very much that he could have done enough damage to crush the other man's larynx, and if he hadn't, if the far better trained Gaul regained his breath, got back to his feet . . .

Zachariah's hand came down on something angular.

It closed instinctively, and as he slammed into a bulkhead and rolled back up onto one knee, three meters from his opponent, he discovered the angular something was Zhilov's pulser.

His hand rose as the Gaul shook himself and started to shove back upright—still hacking, still coughing—only to freeze. His gory face was expressionless, but his good eye widened in sudden awareness.

And then Zachariah McBryde's trigger finger tightened and a four-dart burst of fire blew Anthony Zhilov's chest into a steaming red mist.

CHAPTER 46

Csilla Ferenc had never been so terrified in her life. She thought she'd reached the limit of fear in those horrible moments when armored soldiers had come into the station's traffic control center and taken her prisoner along with the others. But their captors then had been no worse than vigilant. One of them had even been rather good-humored, in a rough sort of way.

Now, their captors were in a rage. Stalking up and down the line of prisoners standing still—no; rigid as ceramacrete—with their pulse rifles no longer held carefully pointed away but leveled.

Except for a few bigshots like Somogyi, they'd all been herded into the station's largest hold. Hundreds of them. At first, she'd taken some comfort in being just one person half-buried in those numbers. But then something happened. She didn't know what it was but apparently, from what their captors were saying to each other, someone had destroyed one of their ships.

She was sure they were all about to be slaughtered. Then a short woman she didn't know—some sort of officer, from her uniform—came into the hold, almost running.

"*Stand down!*" she shouted. "*God damn you—stand down!*" She slowed her pace and lowered her voice—a bit. "You're supposed to be soldiers, not a fucking mob. Stand down, I said!"

She pointed to one of the soldiers. "Sergeant Supakrit, are you in command of your unit?"

The big soldier looked meaner than just about any of them, but his expression was . . . well, not calm, exactly. But he seemed to have himself under control.

"Yes, Colonel Kabweza, I have them . . . They'll obey me."

"Good. You just got a field promotion to lieutenant. Junk the stupid 'X' and get a last name. Now bring your unit forward and stand guard over the prisoners. I want you prepared to shoot *dead*"—she turned and glared at the rest of the soldiers—"any worthless goddam so-called Marine who does not do *fucking exactly* what I tell them to do. Am I clear, Lieutenant?"

"Yes, Ma'am. Up front, people." A small group of soldiers came toward him. They had their rifles pointed upward, but it was obvious even to a civilian like Ferenc that they were ready to use them—and not against her.

A little shudder seemed to go through the mob of soldiers. One of them, a short stocky woman who looked to be about Csilla's own age, was standing a couple of meters away. She now looked at Csilla. Glared at her, rather.

"I didn't do it," Csilla said, in a small, tremulous voice. "Whatever happened, I didn't do it."

Her knees buckled. A moment later, she was sprawled on the floor, half-erect, supported on one hand. She started to cry. "I just work here. It's the only job on the planet for people like me that doesn't pay shit.

My husband can't work because he was crippled in an accident and we have three kids. My dad's sick, too."

She took a slow, shaky breath. "I just *work* here."

The female soldier took a slow breath herself, which also seemed a little shaky. Then, looked at the rifle in her hands and brought it up so that it was pointed at the ceiling of the hold.

"Ah, hell," she said.

◇   ◇   ◇

Breathing heavily and trying to regain his composure, Zachariah turned and saw Gail Weiss on her knees a few meters away. The blow she'd taken from Zhilov's forearm didn't seem to have done any major damage, so far as he could tell.

"Are you all right?" he asked.

She raised her head and looked up at him. He was relieved to see that her eyes seem to be able to focus. She might have a concussion, but he didn't think it would be a major one.

Her eyes moved to look at Zhilov's corpse. It was as if she was watching a cobra, to see if there might still be any life in the serpent. But she didn't seem to be in a panic, or confused.

"Jesus, that was close," she said, her voice husky. "I can live with being killed for a good reason—"

Abruptly, she broke off and choked down a laugh. "Talk about a phrase that makes no sense!" She took a breath, then another, calming herself. "But I'm damned if I want to get killed because two maniacs went at each other."

She rose to her feet, went over to the table and sat down. Then she drank what was left from her coffee cup and carefully placed it back on the table.

"I knew—we both knew—he was here to execute us in case of capture. But I should have realized there was more to it. You know how the Alignment's security people think. You heard Marinescu. Anybody who knows anything about Houdini either vanishes or dies. They were steel-hard on the subject."

He nodded wearily. "So they had a second string to their bow. That's what happened to the *Luigi Pirandello*. Arpino killed Charteris and van Vleet. Then he waited for the best available opportunity target and blew the ship. Thereby covering his own tracks. Now, nobody who's not in the Alignment will have any idea what happened to Charteris and van Vleet. They're not missing persons who get discovered as corpses—murdered for mysterious reasons. They're just vapor now, indistinguishable from any other interstellar gasses."

Zachariah looked around the chamber, which bore a lot more resemblance now to a slaughterhouse than an officers' lounge. There was blood everywhere.

He was surprised no one had come to see what was happening. But the hatch was closed—and it was as solid as any ship's hatch. And now that he thought back on it, the only really loud noises had been people shouting. The exact words wouldn't have been distinguishable on the command deck, if they'd been heard at all. It was certainly not something they'd come to investigate, given their wariness around Zhilov.

"So now what do we do?"

"For starters, we need a cover story that'll satisfy Captain Bogunov. I don't think she'll press too hard if we give her anything that's reasonably coherent."

She looked back and forth between the two corpses.

"What do you think? Should we put the gun in Stefka's hand and claim she—no, that won't work. How did she shoot him four times in the chest and he was *still* able to take the gun back and kill her?"

"I think we should just stick to the truth," said Zachariah. "She panicked, attacked him, he killed her—but then ran wild. You knocked the gun out of his hand and I picked it up and killed him. I think that'll be enough to satisfy Bogunov, at least until she can get us off her hands."

"And then what?"

He shrugged. "We tell the same story all the way through to the end. What the hell, it's true—that *is* what happened. I don't think the Alignment will punish us for it. There's no reason to, once we've completed Houdini."

Weiss thought about it, for a moment. "Well . . . That's true enough." Her mouth twisted into a little smile. "You've got to say this much for our security people—they're as cold-blooded and ruthless as a spider, but they're just as practical, too. They don't kill people out of spite."

❖   ❖   ❖

"What the hell happened?" Colonel Donald Toussaint demanded. He knew no one aboard *Hali Sowle* had any more information than he did, but he half-glared around the freighter's bridge anyway.

Denmark Vesey was almost six light-minutes from Balcescu Station, and both she and *Luigi Pirandello* had disappeared from the FTL gravitic sensors the moment their velocities equalized and they shut down their impeller wedges. The sensor drone *Hali Sowle* had deployed had tracked the passenger shuttles' wedges after they separated from the ship, then tracked the pinnace's wedge until *it* was shut down. Then nothing. Nothing at all... until, three hundred and eighty-three seconds later, light-speed scanners had detected the nuclear explosion which had destroyed the freighter in a blinding bubble of light.

Followed, thirty seconds after *that* by the missile detonations which had killed *Luigi Pirandello*'s shuttles.

Lieutenant Commander Bayano's report had come in one minute after that. The frigate CO's summation of the events themselves had been clear and professional, but at the end, it had become almost plaintive.

"None of it makes any *sense,* Sir," his recorded message said from Toussaint's com screen as he played it back the second time. He'd viewed it the first time by himself. Now he wanted all the different perspectives on it he could get.

"They'd already surrendered and left the ship in their personnel shuttles," Bayano continued. "They had to have known—dammit, I warned them *twice,* and I was blunt about it—that we'd take out all of them if so much as one slave was killed. So why blow their ship at that point? What the *fuck* did they think they were *doing*?" He'd been visibly shaken himself, then grimaced. "Sorry, Sir. I know you don't know either, but losing Lieutenant Xiorro and all his people when we had the situation under *control*... that hurts. That hurts a lot."

"Maybe they just wanted to get revenge by killing some of our people at the same time," Lieutenant Commander Lansiquot said now. The Havenite adviser was standing next to Major Sydorenko, close enough to the screen to view the report along with her and the colonel. Toussaint had invited him to do just that, and now he paused the recorded message's playback and raised both eyebrows at Lansiquot.

Sydorenko's expression was tight, hard, coldly furious. "Like Commander Bayano says, damn it. Bastards killed Lieutenant Xiorro and all his Marines. That's got to be why they did it."

Donald waved his hand, trying not to be impatient with people either. "Meaning no offense, but neither one of you was ever a slave. I was—so was Tunni—and what they did makes no sense. It just doesn't. These people were *slavers*, for Christ's sake, not religious or political fanatics. Any slaver crew is likely to have one or two loose screws rattling around who might be crazy enough to do something like this, but *all* of them?"

He glared back down at Bayano's frozen image in his display. Lansiquot started to say something but stopped abruptly, and Sydorenko inhaled sharply.

"Can we hear the rest of Commander Bayano's report, Sir?" she asked. *Before I shoot my mouth off again* was left unspoken.

"Of course." Toussaint gave her a humorless smile which strongly suggested that he'd heard what she'd left unspoken, and touched the screen again.

Bayano's frozen image sprang back to life, and he shook his head like a traveler pondering the Sphinx's riddles.

"I had fairly extensive contact with the ship's captain, Colonel, and he sure didn't seem like he was in a suicidal mood to me. That's the main reason I'm so frigging lost for any explanation of what he did! He actually sounded *reasonable*, like someone who wanted to at least get his own people out of it alive, and he said all the right things. He even *did* all the right things . . . right up to the last moment."

They could see him pause for a moment, and his expression become . . . not chagrinned, exactly. Rueful, perhaps.

"The truth is, Colonel, I think now I may have jumped the gun when I opened fire. Looking back on it, I don't think the people in the shuttles had any idea what was going to happen."

"Fuck 'em," Toussaint told Bayano's image bluntly, then glanced back up at Sydorenko and Lansiquot. "That's pretty much what I told Tunni when I receipted his report, and I stand by it. I think he was probably right about how much Brandt and the other people in those shuttles had to do with it, but the fact remains that they were a bunch of stinking slavers. And assuming he *was* right, they wouldn't have known anything so there'd have been no point in keeping them alive to be interrogated."

He leaned back in his chair. "I look on the bright side. We just proved to any slaver who needs it that we mean what we say. We warned them, they didn't heed us—regardless of who 'they' are, exactly—and we exacted the penalty we said we would. Let the rest of them learn from that." He swiveled to look up at Sydorenko. "Make sure we collect every scrap of recording that exists on the incident, Anichka. Our records, the *Denmark Vesey's*—the station's, if they have any. When we get back to Torch, I'll tell our intelligence people they need to squeeze that data for all it's worth so we can hopefully figure out what really happened and why. There's a mystery here somewhere, I can smell it."

❖   ❖   ❖

It was perfectly obvious to Zachariah that Captain Bogunov didn't believe much of their story. But it was just as obvious that she had no intention of trying to ferret out the truth herself.

Let the authorities—whoever the hell they might be—sort this out for themselves. The same authorities who had stressed to her that she should ask no questions of the passengers and let Zhilov do pretty much whatever he had a mind to do.

"I'm afraid I'll have to put you in confinement for the rest of the trip, though," she said apologetically. "Pick whichever of your cabins you want. It'll be a little crowded but . . . that's the way it is. I haven't got the personnel to keep a guard on more than one cabin."

❖   ❖   ❖

They settled in Gail's cabin, which she'd shared with Juarez, since it had two bunks.

After Zachariah stowed away his few possessions, he sat across from Gail at the little extruding shelf that served the cabin as a pitiful excuse for a dining table.

"Did you leave everyone behind?" she asked him.

"Yes. Lisa was the only friend I had left, and . . ."

She nodded. "I guess I was lucky. My husband and I divorced a year ago and we had no kids. And my parents are both dead. I have a brother but we've never been close. You?"

After a moment's hesitation, Zach began talking about his family. He was still doing so two hours later, as the ship vanished into the universe. By then, they were holding hands.

CHAPTER 47

From long practice and experience, Triêu Chuanli had no trouble keeping his expression impassive as he moved through the havoc that had once been the headquarters—lair, it might be better to say—of Lower Radomsko's most notorious gang. But in truth, he was a little shaken.

It wasn't so much the blood and gore, by itself. A man didn't rise to the position of Jurgen Dusek's top lieutenant if he was squeamish or faint-hearted. No, it was the...

What *was* it exactly? Chuanli tried to pin down what was bothering him so much about the ruin and destruction. Everything seemed just a bit...

"Too clean," he said.

He'd been speaking to himself, but two of the people who'd come with him were standing close enough to overhear.

Tamara Hess made a face. "You call this *clean*? I'm sure glad you're not my janitor bot."

The other person, Henry Copper, shook his head. "No, Tam, he's right. Except 'clean' is off a little. I think 'precise' is the word you're looking for, Triêu."

557

That finally brought the whole scene into focus for Chuanli. He looked around the room buried deep within one of Lower Radomsko's residential towers. This time, noting the location of the splatter and other details as if he were a forensic medical examiner investigating a crime scene.

Yes, Henry was right. Too precise. Too one-sided, also. It was a little hard to be certain because some of the bodies were badly damaged, even leaving aside the one that had been decapitated. But so far as Chuanli could tell not one of the five people in this room had had time to defend themselves—despite the plethora of weapons available. He was pretty sure that at least three of them had never even had time to get to their feet.

"Check the magazines on all the weapons," he said. "I want to know if any of them were fired. And see if any are missing, as best you can."

That last order would be largely guesswork, of course. Still, at least with sidearms, they could check the pistols against holsters. There might be some gun cases in one of the closets, too.

Between Tamara and Henry and the other people Chuanli had brought with him, the work was done within a few minutes.

"The only weapon fired in this room," Henry reported, "was that guy's." He pointed to one of the corpses lying in a corner. "And from the look of the wound and the tear in the bottom of the holster, I think he shot himself in the foot without ever getting the gun clear."

"Missing weapons?"

"No way to be sure, but none that I can see."

Tamara chimed in. "Every body has a weapon

associated with it except that of the woman over there. She had two, one of them a backup in her boot. Neither was fired."

Chuanli nodded. "And the other rooms?" They'd found a total of nine corpses in the apartment complex.

"Same story," said Henry. "One guy killed in the corridor coming out of the bathroom. Two of them killed in bed while they were—" He waved his hand. "The one in the front room..."

"We think he was on his feet and facing his killer," said Tamara. "He'd drawn his pistol, too, looks like. But it was lying on the floor a couple of meters away, never fired."

By now, Triêu had a rough picture of what must have happened. "So...One shooter comes in the front door by blowing it in with an explosive charge. They could do that because their target was too careless to keep a guard on duty in the corridor. That made one hell of a racket, which would have momentarily stunned everybody. He or she shoots the guard on duty in the front room and then moves into this room—what I'd call a living room if it weren't such a pigsty—and guns down all five people here. Meanwhile, another party or parties blows in the wall connecting the kitchen to the corridor on the other side and clears the bedrooms. He shoots the couple while they're screwing and takes down the last guy coming out of the toilet."

He looked back and forth between Henry and Tamara. "Does that match what you saw?"

Both of them nodded.

"Is there any indication there were more than two shooters?"

They looked at each other and then shook their heads.

Chuanli whistled tunelessly. "Mary. Mother. Of. God." He said the words slowly and evenly. "That means the shooter who came in the front had to move . . . really, really fast. And he—maybe she—couldn't afford to miss at all. Given the time they had."

He gave the room one last look and then headed for the door. "All right, let's go. You never know. A police squad might actually come to investigate."

Tamara snorted. "You mean, before the sun goes nova? Maybe four billion years from now?"

Chuanli didn't argue the point. She could well be right. The police didn't respond quickly anywhere in the seccy districts. In Lower Radomsko, they often didn't bother responding at all.

❖　　❖　　❖

"Our best people couldn't have done that, Jurgen. Well, a bunch of us could—but two shooters? No way. At least one of them *has* to be military." Chuanli shook his head. "And I mean with commando training and experience, or at least some sort of elite unit that does close assaults. The Marines, maybe. *Solarian* Marines, not those jackoffs calling themselves 'marines' that Mesa's got."

"Could be more than one," Dusek mused. "I'm sure Watson has some sort of background. Maybe that big woman our surveillance team spotted, too."

Neue Rostock's head boss leaned back in his large and comfortable swivel chair, propped his feet up on the desk and clasped his hands over his belly. "All right, let's think this through. The way I see it, we're looking at three possibilities. The first one is the obvious one."

"Watson's trying to intimidate us as a prelude to a power grab."

"Right. In support of that theory..." He nodded toward the large freezecube perched on the far corner of the desk. Visible in it, although the features were a little hard to make out because of the damage, was a head. Dusek had had the head identified as that of Willi the Chin, the (former) leader of the destroyed gang. The monicker had been bestowed on him because of a very prominent chin, but there was no evidence of it now. That feature had been mostly shot off the face, along with the left cheek and ear.

The freezecube had been delivered that morning by a street kid. They didn't know which one because the kid had plopped the package on the landing, whistled at the two people standing guard at the entrance to Dusek's inner sanctum some twenty meters away, and hurried off. They hadn't pursued the kid because they'd been delayed by the necessity of checking to see if the package was a bomb. All they had were a couple of recordings taken by surveillance cameras, but they weren't any help because the kid had disguised his features by some sort of shielding device that a street kid had no business being in possession of. Those things were expensive.

The package had come with a note. *With my compliments. Philip Watson.*

"But that's about the only thing supporting the theory. Tell me, Triêu—as a purely academic exercise since I'm sure this thought has never, ever, not even once crossed your mind—if you wanted to bring me down, is this how you'd start?"

Chuanli smiled. "Not unless I was an imbecile. I

wouldn't try to intimidate you at all. I'd just go for it straight. Now that I think about it—for the very very first time ever—it occurs to me that taking you out would be a risky enough enterprise without giving you advance warning to boot."

Dusek nodded. "What I figured. As a threat, this is just stupid. And I don't think Watson is stupid. So. That brings us to the second alternative. He really does intend to do what he implied he was doing—take over Lower Radomsko himself."

He paused for a moment, contemplating the mangled and severed head in the freezecube.

"What's wrong with that picture, Triêu?"

"They went after the wrong gang." Dusek wasn't surprised that the answer came instantly. Major seccy criminal organizations didn't call it by that term, but they engaged in what military forces called contingency planning. He and Chuanli and several other of his close lieutenants had once spent a whole afternoon discussing how they might take Lower Radomsko, if they ever decided to do it.

"They should have hit either the Nessie Girls or the Rukken. Taking out Willi the Chin and his loony bin doesn't get you anything. Well, a lot of good public relations with the people in the area, but that's what they call a really intangible asset. The Willies were probably the freakiest gang in Lower Radomsko, just in terms of sheer viciousness and unpredictability. Civilians were scared to death of them. But either the Nessies or the Rukken were more powerful—and a lot more successful in business terms."

"Right. And there's this, too." Dusek picked up a data chip lying on his desk. "It took a while to crack the codes, but we analyzed this after you left to check on what had happened to Willi the Chin."

The data chip had been included in the package with the severed head. "So what is it?" Chuanli asked.

"Willi the Chin's business records. All of them, so far as we can tell."

"Ah." Chuanli leaned back in his own chair and looked thoughtfully at the ceiling. "And so Theory Number 2 just got iced. Why in the world would Watson send us Willi the Chin's records if he was planning to take over his business?"

He brought his eyes back down. "Okay, you're the brains of the outfit. Why you're the boss. You said there were three alternatives."

"The third explanation is that Watson is establishing his credentials. His *bona fides*, as they say. He does in fact want to work with us, but it's got little or nothing to do with Lower Radomsko."

"What does it have to do with, then?"

"I haven't got a clue." Dusek lowered his feet to the floor and brought the seat to an upright position. "Whatever it is, though, it's bound to be pretty...what's the word? Spectacular, maybe? You don't wipe out the craziest gang in Lower Radomsko just in order to prove you can run a small-time gambling operation. "

Chuanli had his lips pursed in thought. "No, you don't. All right. What do you want to do now?"

"I don't think we need to do anything. Unless I'm badly mistaken, we'll be hearing from Watson very soon. Asking for another meeting."

"Do we agree?"

Dusek scratched behind his head. "Yes. We can always say 'no' to whatever he proposes." He held up an admonishing finger. "One thing, though, Triêu. Tell him he can bring one—that's it, one—person with him. And if it's a woman, she's got to be normal sized."

✧　　✧　　✧

When Hasrul brought back Dusek's reply to his request for a second interview, Victor chuckled and showed it to Thandi.

"Guess I've been made," she said.

"You think?" He looked at Cary, who'd come to check on Karen. "You'll be coming with me."

"If Chuanli is there, he'll recognize me," she protested.

"All the better. It'll add to our mysterious aura."

Thandi sniffed. "Is that what it's called? Aura? I thought you were just making it up as you go."

"Like I said. Mysterious aura."

CHAPTER 48

As soon as Victor saw the three men emerging from the same entrance he and Cary were approaching, he felt a thrill run down his spine. This sort of sheer blind luck happened just as rarely in his line of work as anywhere else in the universe.

"D'you see those men?" he asked. He faced her and spoke softly, as if he were engaged in a conversation, but not in a whisper. Whispering was inherently melodramatic. It tended to draw attention where simple speech didn't. The trick was knowing how to speak in a way that your lips couldn't be read. That meant the words would be slurred a bit. What actually came out was closer to: *Yuh thee ose meh?* But they'd still be perfectly understandable to anyone close by.

Cary, although she was technically an amateur, had lots of experience with clandestine activity. Her tradecraft was as good as most professionals Victor had known. Her only response was a slight nod.

"Trip and fall when you get near them. Nothing fancy. Don't get hurt."

This time, she didn't bother nodding.

As they drew near, Victor gave the approaching trio no more than a long glance. Nothing rude; just the sort of quick appraisal that a man such as he seemed to be would give people like them when they came into proximity. The same glance came back to him from two of the three men, the two obvious sidekicks. The shorter, slighter man in the middle didn't look at him at all.

He did look at Cary, though, as did his two companions. Again, nothing rude; no gawking was involved. Nothing more than presumably heterosexual males in good health being idly appreciative of an attractive woman they weren't familiar with. The gazes, if you could call them that, didn't last more than a second or two.

When they were two meters away, Cary's left foot seemed to catch on something on the floor. Happily for the subterfuge, the flooring in seccy quarters often *did* have minor imperfections. She squawked something meaningless—*urk!* more or less—made a desperate attempt to catch her stride—just as desperate as Victor's awkward attempt to grab her arm—and went sprawling down on her hands and knees.

The reaction of the trio was smooth and instantaneous. The one in the middle stopped abruptly, poised to run; the one on the left stepped back a pace, his hand moving toward his jacket; the one on the right stood still and made the same hand gesture.

Victor also stopped abruptly. Then, without making a big show of it, he was careful to move forward slowly and deliberately while keeping both of his hands in plain sight. By the time he reached Cary and bent over to help her, he could sense the relaxation in the people opposite them.

What followed was not blind luck, just a validation of Victor's quick gauge of likelihoods. It was pleasing to have one's skill demonstrated, to be sure, but there was no thrilling sensation in the spine.

If he'd been the one to trip and fall, none of the men would have come to help. A young woman, on the other hand...

The bodyguard who hadn't stepped back took Cary's other arm and assisted Victor in getting her back on her feet. Victor gave him a quick glance. "Thank you, sir." He already had Cary's right arm in his left hand. Now his free hand came around to settle on her left arm just below the other man's. The fellow smiled at Cary, gave Victor a nod, and stepped away.

Victor paid him no further mind. His concerned attention was now entirely on Cary. "Are you all right?" he asked. "That was a nasty fall."

She shook her head. "I'm fine. A little shook up is all. I'm sure it looked worse than it was."

By then, the trio had resumed their progress and were several meters away. One of the bodyguards turned back to look at them but Victor was careful to keep his eyes on Cary alone. It was essential that no suspicions be aroused by the incident.

Once they were ten meters off, he took Cary by the elbow and headed once again for the entrance to Jurgen Dusek's complex. Two people, one male and one female, emerged from what must be recessed guard posts. Both of them were holding pulse rifles. The weapons were not aimed at anyone, but could obviously be brought to bear in an instant.

"And what was that all about?" she asked—also being careful not to move her lips much, he was pleased to see. The words came out as: *An wha was zat aw a-out?*

"Tell you later," was all he said. That seemed more appropriate than *Hallelujah!*

✧　　✧　　✧

The trip through the headquarters complex wasn't as tortuous as the one that had gotten them there. They couldn't possibly have managed that at all without being guided by one of Dusek's kids—in this instance, a girl who looked to be about ten years old, although she conducted herself with a solemnity that more properly belonged to an elderly usher in an opera house.

"Not as tortuous," though, still meant a maze of passageways—a maze that, the farther they progressed through it, was clearly designed for defensive purposes. This went far beyond the complexity you'd encounter in any gigantic residential/commercial edifice that had undergone the inevitable Brownian motion that affected the internal layout of such buildings when they'd been in existence for centuries. Anton had checked the records for Victor and discovered that this particular building had been erected in 1576 PD, almost three and a half centuries earlier. ("Erected in 1576" actually meant "erected *by* 1576." Even with modern construction methods and materials, it took several years to put up an edifice this huge.)

Of course, some of the walls in ceramacrete buildings were load-bearing, and those were usually made of ceramacrete as well. Rearranging *those* walls was technically possible, but it was so difficult and required such specialized—and very expensive—equipment that it was rarely done. So, the original structural grid of the building tended to remain the same even over a period of centuries.

But the same was not true of other walls—or even floors. Ceramacrete was so strong and durable that it was actually more expensive to raze a large building made of the material than it was to erect it in the first place. As a result, such buildings once created were as permanent as any of the major geographical features of the surrounding countryside.

More permanent, in fact. It would be easier and cheaper to level hills and small mountains, or drain swamps, or change the course of rivers—or even redesign small gulfs, bays and inlets—than it would be to level the ceramacrete constructions that made up the heart of any modern city.

The end result, over a long period of time, was that the interior of such edifices underwent a constant rearrangement within the fixed structure of the load-bearing grid. Modest apartments were replaced by larger and more expensive ones, or the converse; one type of shop was replaced by another that had different space or height requirements; corridors, auditoriums and interior parks were redirected or shifted, expanded or contracted—the process was never-ending.

In most modern societies, therefore, the laws regulating such (re)construction were strict and well-enforced. You not only needed a permit to undertake such a project, you needed to file—and maintain—your plans, diagrams and blueprints. In theory, even in the largest such building in existence, police or firefighters or medical personnel could find their way anywhere using their equipment's computers to access the up-to-date data off the net.

Not so, however, in societies whose central authorities were weak or corrupt—or, as here on Mesa, simply didn't care what second-class citizens did in their own districts.

That was foolish on their part, looked at from one direction—because it meant that if a major revolt *did* take place, the military forces trying to suppress the revolt would be forced to operate on the worst conceivable terrain. Thandi had told Victor that Solarian Marines dreaded nothing so much as having to engage in inner-city—not even that; inner-*edifice*—street fighting. The advantage was entirely on the side of the defenders, no matter how lightly armed—even if the attackers had access to up-to-date and accurate records of the interior layout. If they had to operate blind . . .

On most worlds, this wasn't a huge problem. First, organized armies seldom met in pitched combat on inhabited planets because of the provisions of the Eridani Edict and the Deneb Accords. A planet was required by interstellar law to surrender when an opponent controlled orbital space around it; if it didn't, then the attackers were allowed to use kinetic energy weapons against its planet-side defenders, and very few people were stupid enough to go up against KEWs. So armies—and Marines—were unlikely to encounter one another in that sort of urbanized terrain.

Second, very few guerrilla or terrorist organizations had the manpower to mount a coordinated defense of such a large tower. They could have all sorts of positional advantages, but if the attackers had the manpower and the technology to come at them from too many directions at once, that wouldn't do them a great deal of use. That meant that even OFS police actions were unlikely to face that sort of challenge very often. As far as police organizations were concerned, they were usually quite good at taking down individual floors or even multifloor levels of towers, although the job got a lot harder if they didn't know the lay of the land. On the other hand, most criminal organizations suffered from the same relatively low manpower levels as terrorists and guerrillas: it was simply very, very difficult for such organizations to match the sort of manpower and equipment a genuine government could throw at them.

And third, cities—on most of the really poor Verge worlds, at least—tended to sprawl horizontally rather than rise vertically. For all ceramacrete's advantages as a construction material, it was by no means the cheapest. Or, rather, its *components* were (quite literally) "dirt cheap," but the technology and technicians required to pour and fuse it were not. Urban centers, and the housing of the local elites, might well be of the latest design, using ceramacrete and counter-grav to reach the heights of any Core World city, but the natural lairs of criminals, outlaws, and terrorists tended to be found among the sheltering cover of the lower class and the outright poverty stricken. And as long as there was space available, which there usually was on Verge planets, the poor population would spread by erecting flimsy and rather low buildings, usually made of local materials that were the native analog for wood, stone, brick and thatch.

Buildings, in short, that a modern mechanized military force like the Solarian Marines could tear their way through easily.

Mesa was an exception. It was a highly advanced

society whose cities—and especially the capital of Mendel—had been built along modern lines. But which, because of its peculiar social structure, had allowed a large portion of its population to ignore the law when it came to internal construction.

Why? Victor had pondered the problem when he first encountered it. Nothing he had seen or learned about the still-mysterious Alignment led him to think they were at all sloppy or haphazard in their planning or actions. So why would they have tolerated, all these centuries, such an obvious chink in their armor?

Eventually, he'd concluded that their seeming-carelessness stemmed from two factors. The first was the awkwardness—for them—of Mesa's political structure. The planet's regime was not a police state in the normal, so-called "totalitarian" sense of the term. (Victor always added *so-called* to the term because such societies were anything *but* "totalitarian" in the long run—as the Pierre-Saint-Just regime on Haven had just proven again. They rarely lasted more than one or two centuries and often collapsed in mere decades or even a few years.)

Mesa was a hybrid. For a very large minority of its population, the full citizens, it was fairly democratic, egalitarian and ruled by law. True, it had a corporate political structure rather than that of a republic like Haven or a constitutional monarchy like the Star Empire—but so did Beowulf and any number of star nations which no one considered authoritarian or repressive. Moreover, however constrained the political power of the citizenry might be, their personal liberties were generally respected.

Not so for the seccies, of course, much less the

outright slaves. The slaves could be controlled directly by their own masters. There were twice as many slaves as there were free citizens on Mesa, but that ratio was not historically unusual for slave-based societies. The ratio between Spartans and helots had been considerably worse, almost eight-to-one, and the ratio of slaves to owners and overseers on Caribbean plantations had been even more extreme. But the advantages of better organization and communication and an effective monopoly on weapons—at least, beyond the level of blades and clubs—made their rule quite secure.

There was the occasional example of successful slave revolts, like the one on ancient Haiti. But such revolts were few and far between. In their great majority, throughout history, slave revolts had been mercilessly crushed.

But what did they do with seccies, who constituted a full ten percent of the population? Seccies had no direct and immediate owners to oversee them, which meant the authorities would have to do it. Such a responsibility, however, quickly becomes impossible for normal-sized police and regulatory agencies. Law-enforcement has to be *self*-enforced to be workable, in most societies. The great majority of people obey the laws not because they fear punishment but because they acquiesce. They usually agree with the laws—most of them, anyway—and see them as being in their own interests. The first line of enforcement is their personal conscience and the second line is not a policeman's citation or an arrest, it is the social disapproval of friends, family and neighbors.

Which carried the problem back full circle. The only way to really control the seccies would have been to set up a full-blown police state—but that would have brought all the problems of such a regime. Time after time, since the rise of literate and industrial civilization, "totalitarian" states had proven themselves to be extremely brittle, however hard and impervious they might appear at any one time. Would the people who'd created the Alignment—people who were not only shrewd and intelligent but also thought in terms of *centuries*—have chosen that option?

Victor thought not. The more he chewed on the problem, the more he concluded that the Alignment had made...perhaps not the "right" choice, but certainly the best available one.

And he also thought the choice had been made easier for them because of a second factor. Anton had convinced him that the Alignment was withdrawing from Mesa. And given their track record, the obvious corollary was that they had always *planned* to abandon Mesa at some point.

Which meant...

Ultimately, they simply didn't care what grief the seccies could visit on their betters if they ever decided to rise up *en masse* and turn their all-but-unregulated gigantic dwellings into the worst fighting terrain any ground-based military force had probably ever encountered in galactic history.

By then, the Alignment would be long gone. Well... more likely, *short* gone. But gone, nonetheless.

Would an organization that had been willing to subject tens of millions of their fellow human beings to slavery over a period of centuries simply to further their long-term goals flinch for an instant at letting their Mesan dupes and stooges reap the whirlwind they'd sown?

Victor was actually laughing at the thought—softly; there was no boisterous hilarity involved—when he was finally ushered into Jurgen Dusek's innermost sanctum.

More likely, Victor thought, one of several innermost sanctums. The man who, for more than three decades, had been Neue Rostock's effective political leader in addition to his more respectable role of head gangster, would have a long-term way of thinking, too.

CHAPTER 49

As soon as the introductory pleasantries were concluded, Victor pointed to the door behind him with his thumb and said, "I don't know what he claimed to be, but that fellow who just left is a police agent. I ran into him the last time I was here on Mesa. I wasn't sure of his identity at the time, though, so I let him go. I'd say I 'unfortunately' let him go, but it was actually quite fortunate, as it turns out. I put a tracking device on him this time so I'll be able to reel him in and find out what he knows."

Jurgen Dusek and Triêu Chuanli stared at him.

Dusek was sitting behind a large desk and Chuanli had a chair positioned just to its right. One guard stood behind them and two more were positioned at the door Victor and Cary had entered through.

Cary stared at Victor too. The statements he'd just made...had not been part of the plan they'd discussed.

"You've been here on Mesa before, Mr. Watson?" asked Dusek. "I hadn't been aware of that."

"Yes. We've met, in fact. Well..." Victor nodded at

Chuanli. "I only met in person with him. On several occasions. But I assumed at the time that he was keeping you up-to-date on the progress of our negotiations and was probably showing you at least some of the recordings he would have made."

Chuanli was now frowning. "*What* negotia—I'm sorry, but I don't remember you at all."

Victor ignored that. "I'm quite sure he made a recording—and showed it to you afterward, Mr. Dusek—of that understandable if slightly ridiculous test you gave me to check my credentials. So to speak."

"*What* test?" That came from Dusek himself.

"Oh, you must remember. You sicced three goons on me at the Rhodesian Rendezvous to see if I could handle myself the way one of Oscar Saint-Just's top agents should be able to. I was with a very attractive female partner at the time—blonde, tall, went by the name of Yana. The goons hit on her as their way of getting the fight started. It didn't last long and went badly for them."

Chuanli was now wide-eyed. Cary's eyes were even wider. *None* of this had been part of their plan. Had no remote connection to their plan. Didn't bear any more resemblance to their plan than an air car did to the very startled bird that her mind had turned into. Squawking and flapping all over the place.

Cary Condor had just been initiated into the *Hey-look-Victor's-improvising* club.

After a moment, Chuanli sucked in a breath. "Chaz, Rick, Giselle—draw out your weapons. *Easy*—don't shoot him. Don't point them at him, even. But be ready to take him down instantly."

By then, all three guards had their pistols pointed

at Victor. Well, not *quite* at Victor—they were off target by maybe five centimeters.

"This guy is really, really dangerous," Chuanli added.

Throughout, Dusek's expression hadn't changed at all. He'd just studied Victor carefully, almost the way a scientist would study data.

"Everybody relax," he said firmly. "Mr.—Whozzit—is not planning any rough stuff. He wouldn't have said any of this if he was."

Victor nodded. "Quite right."

"Since the subject is on the floor," Dusek continued, "what *is* your real name? It's clearly not Philip Watson. The last time you went by . . ."

He turned his head toward Chuanli but didn't take his eyes off Victor. "What was it, Triêu?"

By now, Chuanli had regained his composure. "McRae. Daniel McRae. Said he'd been in Haven's State Security."

"The last part's true," said Victor. "My name is Victor Cachat. I was in fact one of Saint-Just's trouble-shooters, although I wasn't as close to him as I intimated at the time to Mr. Chuanli. Actually, I was part of the opposition that eventually overthrew Saint-Just. The real reason I came here last time, with my partner Anton Zilwicki—he's a Manticoran agent, by the by—was to investigate Mesa. We'd come to suspect and have since confirmed that Mesa's government, Manpower, Inc.—the whole setup in this star system—is a fake. Well, maybe not a *fake* so much as a host organisim constructed specifically to support a parasite hiding inside it. As nearly as we can tell, the system government as a whole is exactly what it appears to be, but there's a secret organization called the

Mesan Alignment that's actually been manipulating that government—and everything else in the damned system—for the last several centuries. The reason I came back—with Anton again, never mind where he is at the moment—was because Manticore and Haven are now in an alliance against the Solarian League and wanted more information about the Alignment. We have, to put it as mildly as I possibly can, got a grudge against the Alignment. Seeing as it has also now been established that the Alignment engineered the war between our two nations that has resulted in the death of millions of people, had assassinated or caused to be assassinated several of our leaders, and was responsible for the recent Yawata Strike that murdered still more millions of Manticorans."

He cleared his throat. "You have tested my mettle, and should know what it is by now. Trust me when I tell you that the havoc that will soon be visited upon Mesa will turn this planet into a large scale replica of what happened in the Rhodesian Rendezvous. You have two choices, Mr. Dusek. Either pretend none of this is happening and try to keep being a successful criminal boss, or rise to the occasion. This first option will succeed for a short time and then end disastrously. The second has a chance of ending disastrously in the very near future but, I think, an even better chance of elevating your status considerably in the long run."

"Elevate it to what?"

Victor shrugged. "The future is hard to predict. But I can with some confidence make the following...what to call them? Prognostications, let's say. First, sooner or later—more likely sooner than later—Manticore or Haven, or both, will come calling on Mesa. At a guess,

I think it'll most likely be Manticore alone, initially. The Star Empire is better positioned, in astrographic terms, and has more in the way of expedition-ready forces right now than my nation. But be assured that Haven will be coming hard on their heels. We lost about two million people in the Battle of Manticore, each and every one of those lives we are now holding the Alignment accountable for. The *Mesan* Alignment, I will remind you.

"Secondly, my Manticoran partner and I—mostly him—have established that the Alignment is withdrawing all of its people from Mesa. By now, most of them will have already gone. In order to cover that disappearance, they've been carrying out staged so-called 'Ballroom terrorist actions' which will likely culminate when they start detonating nuclear charges on Mesa."

For the first time, Dusek seemed startled. "For God's sake, *why*?"

"The detonations will serve several purposes. It will cover up those who disappeared by . . . disintegrating their memory, so to speak. Second, it will plunge the planet into chaos, which will further help cover the disappearances. Mesa's police and military forces are also being duped, and they're certain to respond by running amok in the seccy quarters. That's because the third function of the explosions will be to serve the propaganda campaign the Alignment is certain to launch—has already launched, rather—by pointing to the detonations as the dastardly work of the Audubon Ballroom and the seccy revolutionary bands to whom they are allied and who are providing them with shelter."

He pointed to Cary with a thumb. "That would be

her, and her two surviving comrades, one of whom was so badly injured that they thought they would have to sell her body parts after she died."

Dusek gave Cary a quick glance. "I take it that's no longer true?"

"No. One of the pieces of equipment I brought with me was a regeneration chamber. A portable one, of course, so it has its limits. But the woman's no longer in danger of losing her life. Well, not at least as a result of previous injuries. There is a real chance of new ones now, of course."

For her part, Cary was frozen stiff. She was now discovering that the *Hey-look-Victor's-improvising* club was *not* a fan club. At one time or another—this very moment, in her case—every member of that club had wanted to strangle the lunatic.

"Keep going," said Dusek. He now had his elbows propped on the desk and his fingers laced together in front of his chin. "This is getting interesting."

Chuanli seemed to choke a little.

"To go back a little, once the Alignment starts setting off the charges, you know as well as I do how the authorities will react. They'll start butchering people in the seccy quarters, wildly and indiscriminately. They'll claim to be combatting terrorism, of course."

He stopped, and looked back and forth between Dusek and Chuanli. "Or do you think their reaction might be more reasoned and judicious?" he asked, in a mild tone of voice.

Chuanli grimaced. Dusek sucked his teeth.

Victor waited for them to think through the logic for themselves. It took some time. Not, he was sure, because either of them was slow-witted. Probably not even—not much, anyway—because they really doubted him. But just because he was forcing them to think in very unfamiliar channels.

"You're leading up to something," Dusek finally said. "What is it?"

"As I said, rise to the occasion. Prepare ahead of time. You control this entire district and you can quickly make contact with the other main bosses in other districts." Victor spread his hands—slowly—in a gesture which indicated the surroundings. "Have you ever considered how hard it would be to reduce a tower like this one if it was being held by an armed and determined force? Especially one that has access—which I'm sure you do—to the subterranean passages of the city?"

"You said yourself they'd be using nukes."

Victor shrugged. "Yes, but the group using the nukes is the one busy pulling its people out of Mesa under cover of a *terrorist* campaign. The group which would be trying to take Neue Rostock away from you would be the established, legal government—such as it is and what there is of it—not the Alignment. Its weapons choice is unlikely to run in the same direction. Frankly, KEWs would be a lot more likely in their case, not that there's all that much difference between those and nukes from a ground-zero perspective. But even KEWs—and nukes—have their limits. I've personally *seen* the buildings in Nouveau Paris that surrounded McQueen's headquarters when Saint-Just set off the bomb he'd planted inside it. All of them were still standing. In fact, they were still standing solidly enough that *repairing* the damage—and there was a lot of it, don't misunderstand me—turned out to be far cheaper than trying to demolish them. The work's well underway, as a matter of fact. Once it's done—and once they finish decontaminating them—the plan is to put them back to use.

"If the Mesans use nukes or KEWs at all, which isn't likely to begin with, they wouldn't go beyond kiloton-range levels. But the truth is that kiloton-sized bombs won't do that much to a structure like this one, and they'd have hardly any effect on the underground areas. And if they try to escalate the size used, they'll get resistance—to say the least—from their own citizenry."

Dusek was silent for a moment, then looked at Chuanli.

"What do you think, Triêu?"

His lieutenant hesitated, glancing at Victor.

"Oh, hell, forget he's here and just talk openly," Dusek said, sounding a bit irritated—not at Chuanli, but at the universe in general. "He's either telling the truth or we'll see to it he vanishes himself."

"Well, first, we already have plans for a fighting retreat and an evacuation. We'd have to adapt them some, because we were thinking in terms of being attacked by a coalition of the other gangs, not the government. But not really all that much, I don't think."

Chuanli nodded at Victor. "He's right about what it would be like fighting in this kind of building. It's the main reason—we've talked about it—that the big bosses don't think of seriously going at each other. If the police or even the military forces attack us, we can certainly hold them off long enough to withdraw into the tunnels. From there..."

His eyes got a little vacant, as he did some estimates and calculations. "Well, they'd wipe us out in the end, probably. They could use poison gas, stuff like that, and eventually get to us. But they couldn't do it quickly, unless..."

"Unless what?"

He looked at Victor. "I'm not so sure they wouldn't just evacuate all the citizens from the city and then bring down some big kinetic strikes. I'm not saying they'd *like* the idea, but it would be one way to finish things quickly."

"Which would be in clear—rather massive, in fact—violation of the Eridani Edict," Victor pointed out.

Chuanli leaned back, a slight sneer on his face. "As if they'd care about that! For that matter, it *wouldn't* violate the Edict, as far as I can see. I'm not an experienced interstellar secret agent, and no seccy's ever served in the Mesan military, but as I understand it, the Eridani Edict only applies to *acts of war*, and this would be a 'police action' or the suppression of domestic unrest or a rebellion. Seems to me I've read more than one account of system governments doing just that, and unless they lost the civil war afterward, none of them ever got the chop for it. So there's no way in hell the Sollies would try to enforce the Edict here!"

Victor leaned forward. The expression on his face was that of the killer. The same one they'd seen on a different face that had exterminated three thugs in a saloon as if they'd been so many insects. It was hard to describe, because it was expressionless—yet somehow conveyed utter menace.

"What part of 'Manticore and Haven are holding a real grudge' do you not understand? Who cares whether or not the Sollies decide it would constitute an Eridani violation or try to enforce the Edict? *My nation will.* So will the Star Empire. If Mesa's authorities violate the Edict, each and every one of them just made themselves criminally culpable. And don't think for one moment that the Mesan government isn't sweating just that possibility. Sooner or later, they *are* going to face the Manties and us, whether they know about the Alignment or not, and they know it. Any one of them who has two brain cells to rub together will realize that if they use anything heavy enough to completely flatten targets as hard as your towers over an area this large—and kill that many people—whoever gave the order is *not* going to live to a ripe old age to endure the pangs of conscience."

He leaned back again, letting the expression fade—not away, just . . . on hold.

There was silence in the room again, for a while. Quite a while, in fact. Jurgen Dusek was not given to hasty and reckless decisions.

Finally, he said: "All right. What are those recommendations? *Specifically.* Keep it simple. I'm just a modest gangster."

Victor chuckled. "First, let me go. I need to track down that fellow and squeeze him dry. Second—before I go—we need to establish some reliable means of communication. Third, start taking the necessary steps to be ready to defend this building and evacuate your people—I recommend you define that term very broadly—into the tunnels. They'll need food and provisions for a fairly lengthy stay. First and foremost, a safe water supply."

"That's not a problem," said Chuanli, shaking his head. "This building has its own wells." Then he looked a little startled at saying it. He was discovering himself on the precipice of joining another informal club, the one called *Hey-look-Victor's-sucking-everybody-into-his-schemes-like-a-black-hole-again.*

"That's all you need to do, right now," Victor concluded. "Please notice that none of this commits you to anything yet."

"Except letting you walk out of here, free as a bird." It turned out Dusek could put on an excellent menacing expression himself. Not in Victor's league, true, but most respectable. "Free to go talk to the OPS, or whoever else might strike your fancy."

Now, Victor's face exuded nothing but good cheer. "Oh, come on, Jurgen. Do you really think *any* Mesan security agency could dream up a sting operation this outlandish?"

After a moment, Dusek laughed. "Point taken. You're either what you say you are or you're a complete lunatic. Either way . . . I guess you walk."

He looked at the guards. "Put away your weapons. Triêu, we'll need to figure out ways to stay in touch with him. We can start with the kids, but we'll need at least one backup method."

Chuanli nodded. "I'll have Noel and Truong start the other preparations. Evacuation on the scale we're talking won't be easy." He glanced at Victor and then looked back at his boss. "You need to give me some guidance here. Exactly how far do I interpret 'our people,' for this purpose?"

Dusek had kept looking at Victor. "What exactly did you mean earlier, when you referred to me elevating my status?"

"Figure it out, Jurgen," Victor said, in that same

cheery tone. "Once the Mesan powers-that-be come tumbling down—which they will, don't doubt it for a moment—who replaces them? The slaves won't be in any position to put together a new government. It'll have to be based on the seccies. Who've never been allowed even a modicum of self-government and whose religious affiliations are all over the place. There's only one really well-established and at least halfway-accepted authority among seccies, and that's the gangs."

Victor rose to his feet, indicating with a little gesture that Cary should do the same. "There's already one well-respected star nation whose founders laundered themselves out of criminal status. Who's to say it can't be done again?"

❖   ❖   ❖

As they followed a boy leading them out of the complex, Cary advanced a proposition in a tight, still-frightened whisper.

"*Watson-Levigne-Cachat-whoever the hell you are, you are fucking insane.*"

Thereby joining another Victor club. Also not a fan club.

❖   ❖   ❖

In the office behind, Triêu Chuanli waited patiently for his boss to answer his question. He knew it would take a while. But it would come eventually.

Finally, Dusek spoke. "How many people live in this building?"

"Nobody knows for sure. I'd say . . . thirty-five thousand, thereabouts."

Dusek nodded. "What I figure too. Okay, then. They're all our people. Every man, woman and child."

CHAPTER 50

"He changed the plan *again?*" Yana threw up her hands. "Why do we even bother making plans at all?"

Anton chewed his lower lip as he read the note over again. "What Victor would tell you is that plans aren't blueprints, they're simply guides that lead you to the next plan."

Satisfied that he hadn't missed any nuance, Anton removed the chip and disposed of it by the crude and simple method of chewing on it a few times and swallowing it. He thought the things were rather tasty and wondered if whichever twisted mind in Haven's now-happily-defunct State Security's tech department had designed the disposable data chips had done that deliberately.

They probably had. Say whatever else you would about the murderous bastards, SS had been thorough and systematic.

"Victor is nuts," Yana said firmly.

"Nuts or not, he's got a track record that suggests he knows what he's doing. And it's a moot point now, because he's forced the issue and we need to get the hell out of Dodge."

"Who or what is 'Dodge'?"

"Old Terran slang phrase. Dodge was a town in the middle of the western hemisphere's northern continent that was either the most dangerous place in the world or the most boring, depending on the version you hear. In this application"—he gave the yacht's salon a quick and somewhat nostalgic examination—"it means we either need to get off the planet or vacate the ship."

"Why would we have to do either one? The Mesans haven't given any sign they're suspicious of us, and we've been here for two months now."

"If Victor's right, Yana, the situation's about to explode. At that point, two things will happen. Well, one of them for sure and the other with a probability way higher than I want to risk. The for-sure thing that's going to happen is that the security agencies' suspicion meter is going to go through the ceiling. The thing that's way too likely to happen is that the spaceport is going to be targeted."

"Targeted by who?"

"And isn't that a fascinating question?" He started collecting all the data chips and portable drives and stuffing them in a briefcase. "Let's go. We need to meet with Victor right away. We're bound to be gone for at least a day so pack as much as you can fit in an overnight bag. Even if they inspect us, that'll pass muster."

Yana frowned at his briefcase. "Yeah, sure, I've stayed over at hotels in the city a couple of times before. But how are you going to explain all the software if we get stopped?"

Anton grinned at her. "Little trick I picked up from Victor. The first thing anyone will see if they look at the software is a wild and woolly collection of fetish pornography. That's if they look with the sort of portable reader security guards will carry. If we get taken in to security for a more rigorous exam it won't hold up, but Victor swears that ninety-nine guards out of a hundred will take it at face value because who'd like fetishes that weird if they weren't genuine?"

Yana's interest perked up. "Really? Like what?"

Anton sealed up the briefcase and headed for his cabin. "My favorite's toxophilia, arousal from archery. You wouldn't believe the poses people get into. Remember: one overnight bag, that's it."

❖   ❖   ❖

"You were the shooter who came through the front entrance," said Triêu Chuanli.

Since it was a statement rather than a question, Thandi decided to ignore it. She kept her attention on the man behind the desk, whom she presumed to be Jurgen Dusek.

"Mr. Cachat said you have some skills that would be useful to us," said Dusek. His hands were splayed across the desk as if he were trying to hold it down. Thandi suspected that was an unconscious reaction on his part, that of a man prepared to thrust himself out of harm's way should it prove necessary.

It seemed Victor was right, then. The destruction of the Chinnies had established their credentials with Neue Rostock's boss in a way nothing else could have.

That came as something of a relief. She'd have disliked the idea that the butchery had been pointless. The problem wasn't with her conscience, exactly. She and Victor had researched their target and if ever nine people richly deserved to be exterminated, it was Willie the Chin and his pack of sadistic thugs. But Thandi was a professional soldier. As hardboiled as she was from her background, training and experience, she disapproved of killing unless it had a clearly defined and coherent military purpose.

"I was an officer in the Solarian Marines, with both staff and combat experience."

"What's your name?"

"You can call me Evelyn del Vecchio for the moment."

Chuanli frowned. "Why are you being cagey about your identity when Cachat isn't?"

"There are reasons. Just take my word for it."

She and Victor had discussed the matter and decided on this course of action. On the one hand, they didn't want to tell outright lies to Dusek, because that could backfire on them eventually. On the other hand, it would be too risky to give them her real identity. Victor Cachat and Anton Zilwicki had notoriety, but unless you were aware of their reputations—which no one on Mesa outside the inner circles was, because those same inner circles had blacked out almost all news from Manticore and Haven—their titles didn't mean much. "Special Officer" could be anything or nothing, and Zilwicki didn't even have a formal title.

General Thandi Palane, commander of Torch's armed forces, on the other hand . . .

By now, many people on Mesa including seccies and slaves had heard of Torch. They knew very few details, as a rule, and most of them probably never heard of Thandi. But it wouldn't matter. All it would take is for one greedy underling in Dusek's gang to decide that reporting her to the authorities would be more rewarding and less risky than going along with Dusek, and Mesa's security agencies would be put on full alert.

That would probably be happening soon, anyway, at which point they'd tell Dusek the truth, but one of the few religious saws that Victor was partial to was *sufficient unto the day is the evil thereof.*

Fortunately, Dusek decided to drop the issue. "Fine. Evelyn it is. How much experience have you had defending—or attacking—a building like this one?"

"Not much. Hardly anyone does. That's because the worst nightmare a ground forces officer can imagine would be to try to take a building like this by force. Usually, you try to avoid it at all costs. If you absolutely must neutralize this sort of structure and can't take the time for a siege, you call in the navy and have them break it down with KEW penetrators dropped from orbit."

"So what's to stop Mesa from doing that to us?"

"Nothing. But Victor and I don't think they'll start that way. The problem with using KEWs in your own backyard is that while they don't leave a lot of contamination to clean up the way nukes do, they still make one hell of a mess. It's hard to contain the side effects, too, in a big city."

"Side effects?" said Chuanli. "What do you mean?"

"Power conduits. Water mains. Sewers. Transport tubes. Almost all the guts and blood and nerves of a city are subterranean. You know how you're always supposed to check with the authorities before you dig anywhere? That's so you don't accidentally cut through something you don't know is there. And in a city as old as this one, there's almost *always* something down there you don't know about. You got a map of the city?"

Dusek nodded. "Bring it up, Triêu."

His lieutenant fiddled with his com for a moment. A virtual screen appeared against one of the side walls. After a little more fiddling, a map of Mendel appeared.

Thandi started using the laser pointer feature on her own com. "Okay. Here's city center. Moving out toward the seccy ring districts, here's Neue Rostock. And then moving still further out in a straight line we find... Oh, well, what is this? Looks like a major power plant."

"It is," grunted Dusek. "That's Generator Station Number Three. Two of our people work in maintenance there."

Chuanli's lips twisted a little. "That's 'maintenance' as in they oversee janitor bots. Not 'maintenance' as in they're highly trained and skilled workers who know how to do critical stuff. Those jobs are reserved for citizens."

Thandi nodded. Virtually all residential towers in any city would have their own fusion reactors in the basement. They didn't cost that much, reactor mass was cheap, and it made sense to use a distributed power net for a city whose individual structures might house up to a quarter million people. And especially since those structures could become literal death traps if the power went *down* suddenly and unexpectedly. Connecting all the towers to a central grid gave the entire city a huge degree of redundancy, and even in an emergency that knocked out the entire grid, a tower's dedicated reactor would keep *its* vital environmental systems and grav shafts on line. But it was still cheaper to build centralized power collection ground stations stations for orbital power satellites to fill the needs of things like industrial sites, public parks, space ports, and other major infrastructure. Reactor mass might be cheap, but *sunlight* came completely free of charge. But the need for it to be collected and distributed did create its own vulnerability.

"Doesn't matter who works there," she said. "What's important at the moment isn't the plant, it's the *location*. Where do you imagine the power conduits go, from the plant to"—her pointer flickered around the central area of the metropolis—"places the powers-that-be really care about?"

She looked at Dusek and smiled. "And don't tell me you don't know, because no slum dweller worth her salt hasn't figured out how to tap into those conduits."

"That would be illegal power bootlegging," Dusek said mildly. "One of our more profitable lines, as it happens. We charge half what the utility company does. Got customers coming out of our ears. I have to keep it within limits, of course, or we'd start getting heat. Too bad. If I could charge what the market would bear I could retire."

He leaned back in his chair, now using his hands for that purpose. Clearly, thoughts of defensive reactions had slipped his mind. "I see what you're saying. I imagine one of those KEWs would punch a hell of a big hole in the ground."

Dusek started gently tapping his fingers on the desk, while looking at the map image.

"All right. So how do you think they'll start?"

He looked away and gave Thandi a very friendly smile. "But I'm forgetting my manners. Triêu, do the honors, will you. Evelyn, what'll you have? Coffee? Tea? Whiskey? Beer?"

Thandi glanced at her com. It was after noon.

"Whiskey, with a beer chaser."

Victor would have a fit, if he were here. The boy was *such* a prude about some things. But, first, Thandi was pretty sure that whiskey-and-beer would cement her credentials, especially because—point two—with her metabolism and constitution, getting drunk was a lot easier said than done. She'd only managed to do it twice in her life.

All of which Victor knew perfectly well, but he'd still have a fit. Mr. Deadly Do-Wrong Mow-'em-Down-Without-Blinking.

Go figure.

Happily, he wasn't here.

❖   ❖   ❖

Lajos Irvine recognized the man as soon as he turned away from the shop window he'd been looking into. He was the one who'd been with the woman who stumbled.

"Hey—" He started to call out a warning, but Stanković and Martinez were already drawing their guns.

But the man already had his *aimed*—no, he was *firing*. One shot each, striking Irvine's two bodyguards in the hollow of the throat. An assassin's target, right above where body armor would end. Too high to hit the aorta and kill someone instantly, but still with a good chance for a fatal wound and, no matter what, instantly incapacitating.

Both men dropped their pistols and clutched their throats, staggering back. Two more people—man on the left, woman on the right—stepped out of doorways to either side of the corridor a few meters further down. Both held flechette guns. Both fired, shooting the legs out from under Stanković and Martinez, then raced forward and shot them again at point blank range.

So Lajos surmised anyway. He didn't actually see what happened once the two moved past him. That's because he was preoccupied.

Staring at a pulser barrel aimed right between his eyes at a range of fifteen centimeters would do that.

"This is theoretically foolish on my part," the man said. "Bringing a gun this close without firing it can be risky, against the wrong opponent. There are at least two ways you could try to disarm me before I could fire."

He paused for perhaps a second. "But you're not going to do that, are you?"

Again, he paused. Lajos stared at the barrel, paralyzed.

"That was a question, if I didn't make it clear."

Perhaps the most frightening thing, oddly, was the way the man talked. Evenly, calmly—the tone seemed as level as a pool on a windless day. And just as placid.

Lajos didn't have any doubt this man could and would kill him without hesitating, if he chose to do so.

His throat felt as if he'd been shot himself. He couldn't speak. So he shook his head. Violently—until he brought it to a sudden halt.

"Good. Now, turn around and follow my associates. Callie, lead the way, if you would."

Lajos turned and . . . came close to vomiting. What flechette guns fired at close range did to a human head was . . . was . . .

Neither Bora nor Freddie really had heads any longer. Their brains were splattered all down the corridor, horrid little gray-white chunks of meat soaked in blood.

The woman stepped around the blood and opened yet another door in the corridor. This one led into another shop. Baked goods.

Where was everybody? The shopkeepers? The customers?

He glanced around furtively as they passed through the bakery, expecting to see the corpses of the proprietor, customers—*somebody*.

How could everyone just . . . be gone?

Lajos wasn't accustomed to this sort of violence, but he wasn't the least bit stupid. He knew the answer; it just took him a little while before he was able to accept it.

If the three killers hadn't killed the witnesses, they'd either bought them off or brought pressure to bear on them. Either alternative—and they were likely to be combined—was in its own way a lot scarier than if they'd just shot the bystanders.

✧   ✧   ✧

After passing through a maze of corridors, rooms, stairs, passageways of all kinds, they reached a room almost small enough to be a closet.

"We're going to blind you now. Relax, there's no permanent damage."

Something was stuck to his forehead. An instant later, a translucent sheet blocked his vision in all directions except straight down. He could see his feet and perhaps ten centimeters of floor ahead of them.

"All right, let's go."

✧   ✧   ✧

Eventually, they came to a halt. Someone touched his forehead and the translucent sheet vanished. Then they removed the device that had been stuck to his forehead. From the brief glimpse he got of the thing, it reminded Lajos of a large and very flat insect.

He looked around. The small room was a cell, about three meters by two, with one door. There was also a cot, bedding, a portable lavatory. And...

That was it.

The only other person in the room was the man. He was giving Lajos a cold, level stare that seemed somehow familiar.

"We've met before," the man said.

"We have?"

"Once. It was in a café. You came in and sat at a table. Three colleagues of yours came in a bit later and sat at another. Two men and a woman. I shot and killed all three of them. My partner dragged you out from where you were hiding under the table and we took you into an underground passageway. I considered killing you as well, but since I wasn't certain you were guilty of anything, I decided to let you go. My partner—I'm sure you remember him; short; wide as eternal damnation—punched you and knocked you unconscious."

He stopped and studied Lajos. Exactly the way Lajos remembered the man studying him once before. With those black, black eyes. Which were now blue, sure, and the guy didn't look at all the same, but Lajos didn't doubt for a moment he was exactly who he said he was.

"What—what..." He took a breath. "Do you want from me?"

"The truth. No, that's a silly way of putting it. Let's say I want *truths*, plural. You are in fact guilty of sin. I'm not sure exactly of what yet, but I intend to find out."

He pointed to the cot. "Get some rest. I don't believe in torture, partly because it would demean my dignity and partly because it's unreliable. People will babble anything to get pain to cease, and without a second source to check against, you never know whether it was the truth or not. I'm not much more partial to so-called truth drugs. First, because they're aptly called 'so-called.' Second, because they have unpredictable results. Third, because some people— me, for one—have taken antidotes ahead of time. I suspect you have as well."

He stepped back to the door. "I like to keep things simple. Here's how it will be. Every few hours I will come in here and require you to tell me something which is true and of reasonably great importance concerning your identity, work and whatever else you think might placate me. If you do so, I will leave, not to return for several more hours. If, during any of those visits, I am not satisfied, I will kill you."

And with that, he turned and began opening the door.

"Hey…Wait! How am I supposed to know if what I tell you is 'of reasonably great importance'?"

"If you see your brains lying on the ground, you'll know you fell short of your goal. I recommend you err on the side of generosity and largesse."

CHAPTER 51

For more than two centuries, the central attraction in Franklin Tower's Hugo de Vries Park had been its huge ice skating rink, the largest anywhere on Mesa. The rink was oval-shaped, three hundred meters long by two hundred meters at its widest dimension. There was a large island in the center of the rink where skaters could rest and enjoy snacks and beverages.

Surrounding the rink were various cafés and restaurants, as well as amusement attractions and rides. The tallest was a ferris wheel, which rose sixty meters above the park's floor. At the insistence of Mendel's city authorities, each gondola had its own emergency counter-grav, even though the wheel's operation—indeed, its attraction—relied on simple mechanical principles that were thousands of years old.

Most of the amusement rides in Hugo de Vries Park were of antique design. That was part of the park's attraction. There was even a merry-go-round.

This being a weekend, the ice skating rink and the park around it were full of people—somewhere between one and two thousand, by later estimates.

Only a few of those people noticed the large containers suspended from the ceiling, more than a hundred meters above the floor. None of them were part of the park's maintenance crew, so they had no way of knowing that until very recently there had only been three of those containers, not the four that were actually there on that day.

The three legitimate containers were simply air purifying mechanisms. The fourth one, which had been put in place a week earlier, was supposed to be another—so, at least, the park's maintenance director had been told. He'd thought the whole business was silly, since the three purifiers they'd had for decades did a perfectly adequate job of keeping the park's air clear. He figured someone in Mendel's city government had probably been bribed to authorize another, a form of mild corruption that was hardly unknown in the city.

Of the small number of people who'd seen the containers, only two noticed when one of them suddenly dropped from the ceiling, a couple named Mark Lewis and Sheila Dawson. They spotted the falling object because their gondola had just reached the apex of the ferris wheel's rotation.

Lewis stared at it, his mouth gaping. His wife had better reflexes. She leaned over and yelled at the people far below on the skating rink, who were directly under the falling container.

"Hey, look out!"

A cargo-handling tractor-presser device—basically, a high-tech cargo hook, a generator that could switch back and forth between tractor and pressor mode—had been placed inside the container. It now got kicked with an overload charge which ruptured the container, and the highly pressurized ethylene oxide within was explosively dispersed. That was followed, moments later, by an incendiary explosion which ignited the now-dispersed ethylene oxide.

As thermobaric weapons went, this was pretty crude. But the ingredients were readily available—despite being highly toxic as well as flammable, ethylene oxide had a multitude of industrial uses—and it served its current purpose well enough. Fuel-air bombs are highly destructive, and the effect is magnified if the explosion occurs in a confined space.

The enormous blast wave was enough to kill almost everyone in the park. Those closest to it were essentially obliterated. Those farther away were torn apart; those at the fringes remained more or less bodily intact but the internal damage killed most of them quickly.

The small number who survived because they were in some sort of shelter were the unluckiest of all. They had their lungs ruptured by the sudden vacuum produced in the aftermath of the blast as the combusting vapor cloud literally sucked the available oxgeen out of the air about them.

The force of the explosion also killed some people who were outside the park, if they were close enough to one of the entrances. In all, the death toll was later estimated as being somewhere between eighteen hundred and nineteen hundred people. There would never be a precise count. Many bodies had not only been completely shredded with no recognizable features, but the intense heat of the explosion—close to three thousand degrees Celsius—had also destroyed even the DNA traces.

❖   ❖   ❖

"—*learn that indulging yourselves in idle amuse-ment while slaves endure lives of unending toil*—"

Harriet Caldwell was paying no attention to the broadcast being played over the Risk Assessment Division's com. If it was genuine it was just more Ballroom-style drivel. But she didn't believe that to be true; and, besides, she was completely absorbed in another effort to persuade her boss to think outside the box.

"—liminary reports indicate the fuel used was ethylene oxide, Tony. *Ethylene oxide!* Do you have any idea how dangerous that stuff is?"

Her supervisor, Anthony Lindstrom, had a long-suffering look on his face. "No; in fact, I've never heard of it. But I'm sure you're about to enlighten me."

"It's a cyclic ether. It's not only flammable at room temperature, it's carcinogenic and mutagenic. The shit's *nasty*. The only reason it's available at all is because it's used in a lot of chemical reactions—but like any really dangerous substance, it's carefully monitored. You don't just waltz into a pharmacy and order up a few barrels of the stuff."

By now, Lindstrom was fed up with Caldwell's obsession. "For fuck's sake, Harriet! You don't just waltz into a pharmacy—into any-Goddam-where—and order up a nuclear device, either. But the Ballroom managed to do that at Green Pines, didn't they?"

She glared up at him. "You know what I think about that."

"Yes, I do. You have convinced yourself that the combined wisdom of every analyst at the OPS—"

"They're a bunch of stupid goons and you know it!"

"I will pretend I didn't hear that. Their combined

wisdom is completely off, according to you, and none of this—not Green Pines, not anything that's followed—is the work of Ballroom killers. Instead..."

He gave her a peering, inquisitive look that practically dripped skepticism. "Instead you think we're dealing with a hitherto-unknown band of seccy malcontents who have mysterious and presumably extra-planetary backers."

"They're hardly mysterious, Tony. Manticore and Haven have both made it crystal clear for centuries what they think of us, they are currently on a rampage, and we *know* they sent agents here a year ago."

"Correction. You *surmise* they sent agents here a year ago. That's never been confirmed or—" His com buzzer sounded and he glanced at it. "Hold on, I've got to take this."

Caldwell could only hear his side of the ensuing conversation.

"Yes, Ma'am. But—"

"Ma'am, I really think—"

"Yes, Ma'am. I'll get on it right away."

He had an exasperated expression on his face. "We'll have to continue this...discussion, later. That was Janine Riccardo. She wants us—that's me and you; she specifically named you—to go to the scene of the blast and find out what we can."

"But..." Neither Caldwell not Lindstrom really had the training for that sort of work—and none of the equipment, at least readily available. On the other hand...

Riccardo was the Director of the Mesan Office of Investigation, widely considered the planet's elite police organization. She was also their ultimate boss, since they were one of the divisions within the MOI's Domestic Intelligence Branch.

Part of the problem Harriet had been facing all along was that the MOI normally restricted its investigations to full citizens. In fact, it was prohibited by its charter from involving itself in seccy and slave affairs. Despite the charter, however, there was often not a clear line separating citizens' criminal activity from that of seccies—and, much less commonly, slaves. So, it was customary for the Domestic Intelligence Branch to liaise with the Office of Public Safety and the Mesan Internal Security Directorate when intelligence matters crossed the line between full citizens and second-class citizens.

"Liaise with" is one of those phrases that can have a lot of meanings. In this case, the relationship was uncomfortable at best. The DIB was rather disdainful of the OPS and especially the MISD. Harriet's attitude that they were "stupid goons" was widely shared in the DIB, even if most people would be more discreet about saying it out loud. For their part, the OPS considered the DIB a bunch of effete snobs who had no experience with the hard-knuckle realities of dealing with seccies.

The point being that, even if she'd been able to persuade her immediate superior that her suspicions were correct, it wouldn't really have done much good. The OPS was directly in charge of the investigation of the recent string of terrorist outrages, and they weren't likely to given any credence to DIB fairy tales.

The fact that Riccardo had specified Harriet herself to join the investigation, though, had to mean that she was aware of Harriet's assessments and had at least some sympathy with them. And Riccardo, being the Director of the MOI, *did* have a lot of clout in Mesa's power structure. If she roared loud enough, not even the stupid goons over at the OPS would be able to brush her off.

"Let's go, then," she said.

"We're just wasting our time," groused Lindstrom.

"Maybe not, boss. And, anyway, orders are orders."

"A pity I can never get you to see that when you're dealing with me."

❖   ❖   ❖

"Let's *go-go-go*, people! Dammit, get a move on! The early team gets the scoop!"

Xavier Conde was being an ass again, but his producer Vittoria Daramy had decided to go along with his latest hot-flash frenzy. From the initial reports they'd heard of the immense destruction involved in the De Vries Park explosion, she didn't think the authorities would let them get close enough for any really dramatic footage. But, on the positive side, Franklin Tower was nearby and they could use the air car they'd already leased rather than having to make special (and expensive) arrangements.

Personally, she thought they'd make better use of their time (not to mention money) by just plugging away on the documentary they were *supposed* to be making. But if she tried to put her foot down, they'd wind up wasting the day anyway because Xavier would have a hissy-fit. He did hissy-fits really well, and they always lasted for hours. Even if she did manage to get him back to work, he wouldn't do anything worthwhile.

❖   ❖   ❖

Since Lindstrom was in charge of the investigation, they took his officially assigned air car instead of

Harriet's. That was fine with her. As a DIB division head, Lindstrom rated an armored limousine. The "armor" wasn't much, really, just sheathing to protect the occupants from small arms fire. But it was still a limousine, which meant it had luxurious seating in the passenger compartment. It even had its own miniature bar, although neither she nor Lindstrom used it because they were on the job.

The only drawback was that the limo also required a chauffeur. Harriet was fond of driving herself—but Lindstrom probably wouldn't have let her do so anyway. The one time he'd ridden with her he'd complained afterward that she'd overused the manual controls (which was true enough; she *liked* to drive) and that riding with her was dangerous (which it most certainly was not; she was a *good* driver).

Even that drawback had its advantages, though. On their way to Franklin Tower, she could use her com to find out more about the availability of ethylene oxide in Mendel.

❖   ❖   ❖

Conde had wanted a private garage for their air car, but Vittoria had seen no good reason for that additional—and in her opinion, quite frivolous—expense. There was no reason they couldn't use the public garage like most people staying at the hotel.

Nor had she seen any reason to pay extra for valet parking, either. The hotel garage's slidewalks were perfectly functional and merely standing on your feet for a couple of minutes or so was hardly a great burden. The newscaster had made a fuss over that issue also, of course.

As he did again today, as the three of them made

their way toward their air car's location. The garage had been unusually crowded the evening before so they'd had to park their air car in a far corner.

"The time we're wasting here will probably cost us the scoop," Conde complained. "Just a few chits!"

"Oh, can it, Xavier," said the recording tech, Alex Xu. "First of all, I'm the one carrying all the equipment, not you, and you don't hear me bitching about it. And second, in what alternate universe that you seem to live in is valet parking faster than getting your own vehicle? Those programs are about as primitive as they come."

Vittoria thought quite highly of Alex. He didn't have to put up with any crap from the newscaster because in his own specialty, unlike Xavier, Alex *was* considered top rate. If the newscaster tried to get *him* fired, Xu's response would be "fuck you, asshole, I quit anyway"—and he'd have another gig the next day.

As they neared their air car, Conde started complaining again. "For God's sake! Is it too much to ask a hotel to maintain proper lighting in their garage?" He gave Vittoria an angry glance. "Of course, if you didn't insist on putting us in the cheapest dumps—"

"Shut up, Xavier!" That came from Alex, who'd stopped abruptly. "Something's wrong. Lighting doesn't just—"

Two figures emerged out of the gloom, coming from behind a nearby air car. A moment later, Vittoria spotted two more coming from different directions.

All of them were armed.

"'Shut up' is excellent advice," said one of the figures. "All of you would do well to follow it."

She couldn't tell the genders of any of the people, since they were all face- and voice-shielded. But the one who'd spoken was either a large man or a very large woman. Shielding couldn't disguise sheer size.

She was terrified already, and the next words the person spoke didn't help at all.

"We're from the Audubon Ballroom, and if you give us any shit, you're all dead."

The faint sound of an approaching vehicle came from behind them. A moment later, a bulky personnel van drew up alongside. As was standard for such vehicles, the windows were all shaded.

"Get in. Now."

✧   ✧   ✧

At the same moment, the limousine carrying Harriet Caldwell and Tony Lindstrom was approaching the exit of their own garage. It had taken them a while to get there because the offices of the DIB were buried deep within one of the huge towers at the center of the city. Government accountants weren't perhaps as frugal as viewcast producers, but they'd seen no reason to provide mere fellow civil servants with private parking facilities—claims of security risks be damned. The last recorded instance of a DIB agent murdered in a public garage had been a hundred and thirteen years earlier, and the killer had been his own wife, irate over the very public affair he'd been conducting with a fellow agent.

Whom the wife had also shot, but only wounded before she was taken out herself by the accused adulteress.

That long and uneventful streak of unnecessary security precautions now came to an abrupt end. The side hatch of a cargo van parked near the garage exit slid open as the limousine approached. The 10 mm heavy tribarrel pulser positioned within the cargo compartment began firing as soon as the limousine came in sight. The weapon was firing super-dense 65 gram explosive rounds with a maximum rate of fire of up to 3,000 RPM (1,000 per barrel).

The limousine's armor was designed to deflect or absorb light pulser rounds, not this sort of military-grade fire. The vehicle more or less just came apart. As did, needless to say, its three occupants.

It was all over in five seconds. The two shooters hurried out of the cargo van and disappeared around a corner of the garage. By the time the nearest witness—who'd only overheard the slaughter, not seen it—approached warily, they'd already gone up sixty floors on one elevator, crossed a short corridor to another, gone down seventeen floors, and were now on a slidewalk which would eventually take them through an aerial passageway to one of the adjoining commercial towers.

They'd been able to move quickly because they were quite unencumbered. They'd left the tribarrel behind in the van.

It didn't take the police long to identify the weapon. It was a M247 Heavy Tribarrel manufactured under license by Rensselaer Industries, whose facility had—until very recently—been located in one of the industrial modules of a space station named HMSS *Vulcan* which had once orbited a planet named Sphynx.

How the weapon had been obtained, on the other hand, remained a complete mystery. It was not available to the public even in the Star Empire of Manticore, because it was designed and made strictly for the Manticoran infantry and Marines.

❖   ❖   ❖

"—now been warned. Any and all agents of oppression, be they from the OPS or the MOI or any of Mesa's instruments of tyranny can expect the same justice at the hands—"

❖   ❖   ❖

"I don't want any more fucking excuses!" raged François McGillicuddy, Mesa's Director of Security. "I want some answers! How in hell is the Audubon Ballroom dropping their manifestos into our planetary data net?"

"They can't possibly be doing this with just their own on-planet resources," said one of his assistants, Grace Summers. "They *have* to be getting help from the Manties or the Havenites."

"Or both," added her colleague, Aidan Crowder. "Or Beowulf."

"Or—or—or! Just listen to yourselves, Goddamit." McGillicuddy slammed an open palm on his desk. "I don't want fucking possibilities—I can get those from my granddaughter. I want *answers*."

He glared at them for a moment longer, then reached out and stabbed at his desk com. "Zeno, tell those assholes running Customs they're doing a pisspoor job. From now on, I want full searches of any and all cargo being brought into Mesa. They're letting *weapons* through."

"Ah...Chief." Crowder took a little breath. "I really don't think it's likely that—"

"Shut. The. Fuck. Up. I said *answers*, not prattle."

Which was exactly why Grace had kept her own mouth shut.

CHAPTER 52

"My current estimate—my very rough estimate—is somewhere between five and twenty thousand people," said Anton. "I'm certain that it's at least three thousand, and I doubt very much if it's more than thirty."

Yana whistled softly. "That many?"

"Actually, the comment you should be making is: *that few?* Think about it, everyone."

He looked around at the people sitting at the table in a small conference room in Neue Rostock. They consisted of himself, Thandi, Victor, Yana, Jurgen Dusek and Triêu Chuanli. "If I'm right," he continued, "what's happening is that Mesa's innermost circle—what we're calling the Alignment—is pulling up its stakes and leaving the planet. Every single one of them. This is from a world that has a total population of close to six billion people. Do the math."

Yana did, and it didn't take her but a moment. Abstruse statistical theory might be beyond her, but she could do straightforward arithmetic in her head much faster than most people.

She whistled again, more loudly this time. "I see

what you mean. Even at the high end—thirty thousand, you said—we're talking about no more than one-half of one-thousandth of one percent of the population."

Anton nodded. "And it could conceivably be smaller than that by an order of magnitude. Either way, relative to the entire population, that's probably the smallest ruling class in the history of the human race. And they've been doing it, don't forget, for *six hundred years*."

Thandi shook her head. "I don't see how that small a group could manage it."

"They could if they have what you might call the right mechanism in place and they're prepared to be patient. A very small gear can run a very big machine, if it's designed properly. Each gear turns one bigger, and then bigger, and then bigger. It takes a lot of time, of course."

"Everybody looks at the big bad wolf and misses the much badder but itsy-bitsy teeny-tiny monster hiding in its ruff." Yana ran fingers through her long, glossy black hair. That mannerism she rather enjoyed. "You'd set up a huge front operation. Call it ... Manpower, Inc."

"Those fuckers." That came from Dusek.

Victor looked at him. "I take it you're not skeptical any longer?"

"I'm not sure I ever was, the minute I first heard you lay out your theory." He and Chuanli exchanged glances. "It explains a lot of things."

"That's putting it too strongly, I think," said Chuanli. "Boss," he added, almost as an afterthought. Dusek didn't seem to need having his ego stroked. His subordinates felt free to disagree with him, although they were respectful about it.

Chuanli made a waving motion with his hand. "It doesn't actually *explain* much of anything. But it sure fits, doesn't it?"

"Explain that, please," said Victor.

Chuanli gnawed on his lower lip. "I've always had this weird sense—so has Jurgen—that a lot of times when you're dealing with Mesan bigshots, you keep feeling..."

He looked to Dusek for help. "How would you put it?"

"Gears slipping. It's like you're dealing with people who just aren't bright enough for the positions they hold—and then suddenly everything's in gear again. Looking back on it, as if someone with real brains just issued everybody's marching orders."

Anton grunted softly. "That...makes sense. If you're running a conspiracy you need to make sure that your puppets aren't too capable—or if they are, either get rid of them or absorb them into the conspiracy or, at the very least, keep them at a distance. Any way you do it, though, you're always working through layers that are a little more sluggish than they ought to be."

"Especially when there aren't that many of you to begin with," added Victor. He shook his head. "But this is all speculation. What is *not* speculation is that we know—know for sure and certain—that the Ballroom is not behind this string of so-called terrorist incidents."

"How are you so sure?" asked Chuanli.

"From the best sources possible—Jeremy X and Saburo X."

Even Dusek, who had a world-class poker face, looked impressed. "Never heard of the second guy," he said.

"Not surprising," said Anton. "He was the person in charge of the Ballroom's activities on Mesa. About as black an op as there exists anywhere."

"That's not quite accurate," said Victor. "Nobody can really be 'in charge' of something at that great a distance. But there is no one off Mesa who knows more than Saburo does—and he certainly would have known if the Ballroom here had the capability to be pulling off these sorts of exploits."

"Maybe his information is out of date," suggested Chuanli. "When did you last hear from him? Or them?"

Victor had a thin smile on his face. "We—'we' being all four of us here—spent a total of six, maybe seven hours, being briefed by the two of them. That happened about three months ago. So, no, their information wasn't very far out of date."

"Oh." Dusek suddenly chuckled. "I'm curious, since I've heard about the guy for so long. What's Jeremy X like? In person, I mean?"

"Quite charming, actually," said Anton. "And maybe the best pistol shot in the galaxy." He hooked a thumb at Victor. "He owes his life to that, in fact."

Dusek and Chuanli both looked keenly interested. But Victor made a firm gesture with his hand, the gist of which was *not now*.

"It's a long story," he said. "For the moment, what matters is that if Anton's right—and I am quite sure he is—we're going to start seeing 'terrorist incidents' a lot worse than anything we've seen so far. Including the use of nukes. That'll be the magic cloak the Alignment spreads over everything to hide their own disappearance."

Dusek's expression was grim. "And if that happens—when it happens—Mesan security forces will run wild, especially the MISD."

Chuanli started to explain the acronym. "That stands for—"

"Mesan Internal Security Directorate," Victor finished. "We know. And you can be sure of this—at least one of the 'terrorist incidents' will strike hard at MISD personnel. Probably not even at them directly but at their families."

Dusek sighed. "Christ. I hadn't thought of that. They're bad enough under any conditions, but if they think they're on a personal mission of vengeance..."

The retaliatory pogroms carried out against the seccy districts following Green Pines had been largely the work of the OPS and—especially—MISD teams which targeted specific neighborhoods within specific residential towers. The MISD was ruthless about snatching seccies off the street, interrogating them however brutally they liked, and making potential troublemakers disappear without a trace. They were accustomed to the protection of their reputation and aura of terror, and their contempt for the seccies was (in some ways) even greater than their contempt for the slaves. That contempt expressed itself in a total disregard for any possible personal rights on the part of the seccies whose paths they crossed, but it also expressed itself in a sort of institutional overconfidence.

Any seccy who might think about offering the MISD resistance knew there was literally no limit to what would happen to him or those he cared about as part of the MISD policy that "we can always make it worse." The seccies as a group realized that the nail which stands highest gets hammered first and hardest. Individual seccies, faced with being dragged off by the MISD, or seeing someone they loved being dragged off, might resist (in a fatalistic, hopeless sort of way) because this was the worst thing they could visualize happening to themselves or those loved ones. However, seccies as a group fully realized that if they attempted to impede or resist OPS or MISD arrests, sweeps, etc., they would only succeed in marking themselves and their families for "special attention." However bitterly they might hate the security goons, and however bitterly they might regret what was happening to a fellow seccy and/or his family, their own families were also hostages to fortune. They dared not draw the MISD's fury down upon them, especially when centuries of experience had demonstrated to them that resistance was ultimately hopeless and futile, anyway.

Because of this, MISD troopers and the majority of the analysts working for MISD and OPS—even those who at least attempted to avoid this particular trap—tended to regard all seccies as feckless, cowardly, and subservient. They were a technically free but contemptible and easily cowed layer of society without any more rights (but allowed a few more "privileges") than the slaves who constituted the even larger layer beneath them and for whom MISD and OPS had even more contempt.

What these people failed to appreciate, however, was that once someone realizes they are extremely likely to be killed anyway, "we can always make it worse" becomes an ineffective tool. If seccies and their families—their children—were going to be subjected to mass murder, the equation changed. What Anton and Victor were calculating on—counting on—was that under those circumstance the seccies damned well *would* fight back. And they'd do so with all the ferocity of centuries worth of hatred and bitterness backing up the desperation of any cornered animal.

Judging from the expressions on their faces, Jurgen Dusek and Triêu Chuanli had already come to that conclusion themselves.

"This isn't going to be like it was after Green Pines, boss," said Chuanli. "And that was pretty horrible."

Dusek was staring at a blank spot on the wall, his expression bleak. "No, it'll be ten times worse. Hell, a *hundred* times worse." The boss of Neue Rostock transferred his gaze from the wall to Anton and Victor—and then, to Thandi.

They'd revealed Thandi's true identity to Dusek and Chuanli at the start of the meeting. They'd urged the two of them to keep it to themselves, at least for the time being, and were pretty confident they'd actually do so. The old quip *three can keep a secret, if two of them are dead* had some truth to it, but there were exceptions. Experienced and successful gangsters were likely to be one of them.

"What are our chances, if we put up a real fight?" he asked her.

"How many people do you have?"

"I've got about two hundred shooters ready to go—right this minute if I need them—and another five hundred who could back them up within a day. Beyond that..." He looked at his chief subordinate. "What do you think, Triêu?"

Chuanli shrugged. "The problem will be the number of weapons we've got available, not the number of people. There are about thirty-five thousand people living in Neue Rostock and plenty of them—men, women, children, old folks—will fight if their backs are against the wall."

"What weapons *do* you have?" asked Thandi.

"Lots of civilian grade pulsers," replied Chuanli. "All told . . . pistols, rifles, everything . . . somewhere around three thousand. That's not counting the odd pistol here and there that someone's got tucked away."

Dusek chuckled, his expression becoming almost cheerful for a moment. "There's got to be at least another three thousand of those. One of the few advantages of being a seccy is that the powers-that-be don't give a fuck what we do as long as we keep it to our own districts."

Then his face hardened again. "But there's a lot less in the way of military hardware. There, we've got maybe a hundred and fifty, hundred and seventy-five mil-spec pulse rifles—don't have a huge amount of ammo for them, I'm afraid—and eleven tribarrels. Two of those're heavy enough to give at least some anti-armor capability. And we've got half a dozen plasma rifles, although I don't know how much good they'll be inside a tower. For that matter, some of my people've read the manuals, but no one's ever actually used one of 'em. And we've got a couple of dozen light SAMs—the Banshee; it's the standard Peaceforce portable SAM—and a couple of crates of Lancer anti-armor rockets."

"Don't forget the grenade launchers, boss," Chuanli put in. Victor raised an eyebrow at him, and the gangster chuckled. "We've heard about your escapade in Lower Radomsko. We don't actually *use* them very often, you understand, but there's damned few things more impressive to someone looking into its business end than a grenade launcher. We've got a couple of dozen of them. And we've got forty or fifty flechette guns, too." He shrugged. "Doubt they'll be much use against MSID goons in armor, but what the hell? Couldn't *hurt* to add 'em to the mix!"

Thandi's eyes widened. "*That* much? That's way better than I expected. I figured you'd just have a few light tribarrels."

Again, Dusek chuckled. "One of the other charming characteristics of the OPS—hell, every security force on the planet except the Mesan Office of Investigation—is that they're corrupt as well as vicious. That's usually another burden on us, of course. But it also means it's not hard to find a goon who's greedy enough to sell us heavy weaponry."

Thandi nodded. That was a common phenomenon on Verge worlds too, but not on this scale. The difference went back to Mesa's peculiar and unique social structure. The level of oppression visited on seccies was not much different from that leveled on Verge populations, but because Mesa was a highly advanced society the seccies were simply a lot wealthier. Or, at least, weren't dirt-poor. Some of them could *afford* tribarrels and plasma guns.

"If you're that well armed," Thandi said, "you— we—can put up one hell of a fight. Trying to take a modern ceramacrete tower by frontal assault is a pure bitch. The worst terrain imaginable, from an infantry officer's perspective. And Neue Rostock will be even worse because unless I'm badly mistaken any diagrams and schematics the authorities have of the building's internal layout are useless."

Both Dusek and Chuanli grinned. The expressions were thin and savage.

"Worse than useless," said Chuanli. "We have the key passageways booby-trapped, which no schematic would show even if they did have accurate ones."

"So does Bachue the Nose in Hancock, McLeod in Wister Haven—any gang leader worth a damn in every district makes sure of that," added Dusek. "It's part of what keeps the peace between us. Of course, the booby traps we've got in place aren't aimed at stopping people in utility armor or battle armor. We were thinking more in terms of what you might call intramural spats. But I'm sure someone with your credentials—" he smiled wolfishly at Thandi "—could show us how to *upgrade* them a bit."

Thandi nodded.

"No problem. And we need to think about simple corridor denial, too. Even with the arsenal you've got, trying to hold every meter of something this big with that few shooters would be a losing proposition. But if you chop up the access routes—completely block some of them, turn others into cul-de-sacs, pre-plan fields of fire with loopholes and covered positions, lay a few minefields that *your* people know how to navigate at a run and then suck the bad guys into following them—and then use the tower's environmental and service systems against them, as long as they last, anyway . . ."

Her own smile was to Dusek's and Chuanli's grins what a sabretooth was to an ocelot.

"In that kind of fighting the advantage is entirely with the defenders. The imbalance in heavy weaponry isn't completely neutralized, of course, but forward progress is slow—and bloody as hell, for the attackers. But—"

She held up a finger. "Remember what I told you about KEW strikes. Sooner or later—and if they have a smart commander it'll be sooner, unless she gets overruled by her superiors—they'll realize they've walked into a meat grinder. At that point they'll pull back their troops and hammer us with KEWs before they resume the attack."

"And that'll be the end."

Thandi shook her head. "Not necessarily. If they settle for tactical-yield KEWs, the building will still be there. It'll be badly damaged, but if we weren't caught in the strike itself, we can keep fighting. In some ways, the terrain will be even worse for the attackers. But we *have* to evacuate the building first or the casualties will be...really, really horrible."

"Yes, I understand that." Dusek looked at Chuanli. "Triêu, I'm putting you in charge of the evacuation. We need to get everybody out of the building and into the underground passages within..."

He turned back to Thandi. "What's the time frame?"

"You've got a few days. I figure you've got at least a week, in fact. Even if the balloon goes up tomorrow, it'll take the OPS a couple of days to react—and the Peaceforce will take longer than that. I'm guessing the regular OPS troopers will come in first, and they'll come in overconfident, figuring that they can just storm their way into the districts the way they always have before. By the time they realize what a mess they've gotten themselves into, a day or two will have gone by. It'll take them another day or two before they're willing to admit it and call in the MISD to save their asses, and the Misties aren't going to have a lot better notion of what they're walking into than the Safeties. They'll get educated real quick when they hit one of the towers, though. It's hard to estimate how many people they'll be willing to lose before they admit a bunch of raggedy *seccies* kicked their asses, but they will eventually. Call it another day or two, and then..."

She made a face.

"Hard to tell with these vicious bastards, but most civilian authorities would shy away from ordering kinetic strikes on their own capital city. Even with tactical KEWs, there's going to be a lot of collateral damage, including damage to citizen districts. You're unleashing a lot of kinetic energy on a small amount of land. The debris alone will start fires all over Mendel. So..."

After pondering the matter for a few seconds, she shrugged. "Like I said, it's hard to tell what people like this might be willing to do. But I can't imagine them making the decision without spending at least a day arguing about it."

Dusek nodded. "An absolute minimum of four days—more likely six or so—is what you're saying, and maybe longer. That gives us enough time, although..."

It was his turn to grimace. "It's going to be rough as hell, that many people trying to survive underground. For a few days, sure. But after that..."

"Can you get some of the other districts to take them in. Some of them, at least?" asked Yana.

"Oh, yeah," Dusek replied. "Bachue the Nose won't agree, the damn witch. But McLeod would. So would three or four other gang bosses I'm on good terms with. But what good would that do in the long run? They're going to be attacking all the seccy districts."

Thandi exchanged glances with Victor.

"Maybe not," he said. "Look, from a strategic point of view there's no way we can win this anyway. Speaking in the long run."

"But we can drag it out in the short run—a lot—if

we deliberately draw the MISD's attention to Neue Rostock as soon as the fighting starts," added Thandi.

Dusek frowned at her. "Why in God's name would we do that?"

"Because that allows you to send your people into the other districts for safekeeping," she said. "All that's left behind is a fighting force."

"Ah." He took a deep breath and slowly blew it out. "But it also means losing Neue Rostock, which in the long run..."

"There *is* no long run, Jurgen," said Victor forcefully. "Unless..."

He nodded at Anton. "Anton and Yana take the yacht back to Manticore and get help." A thin, savage grin came onto his own face. "Since the Mesans want to play 'let's get a bigger club,' we'll go get us a really, really *big* club."

"Would the Manties agree?"

"If Anton's the one bringing the news, yes. He has...credentials."

Thandi smiled. "It doesn't hurt that his girlfriend's the leader of the Liberal Party and a close childhood friend of Empress Elizabeth." She could have added *although they've been politically estranged as adults* but saw no point to that. Besides, Cathy Montaigne and Elizabeth had been getting along pretty well lately. "Besides, he's met the Empress herself—done her a couple of really *big* favors, in fact—and he and Victor here have actually rubbed shoulders with Duchess Harrington."

"The *Salamander*?" Dusek looked impressed, and Thandi smothered a chuckle. Some reputations obviously leaked through just about *any* filters.

"I agree about sending Anton," said Yana. "But there's no reason for me to go. My only credentials are that I used to be a Scrag, and those take you exactly nowhere."

Zilwicki started to say something but Yana waved him down. "Shut up, Anton. What's even more important is that these Mesans are the same people who murdered my best friend Lara and"—her own thin grin somehow managed to be even more savage than Victor's—"the way I look at it, being a super-soldier extra-magnum genetic specimen and all, is that these *shitheads* have been taking my name in vain. So I'm staying. Don't anybody bother arguing the point."

After a moment, Chuanli smiled. "Wouldn't dream of it."

Victor had been frowning, though. "But how's Anton going to get permission to take the ship out of orbit? For that matter, how does he get away with taking the shuttle up if Yana isn't seen returning with him? They'll think he's trying to steal it or something."

That . . . was a problem.

"Don't worry about it," said Dusek. "We've been smuggling stuff—including people—off this planet for a long time. What we do is, Anton and Yana return to the ship bringing a small cargo container. When the port guards investigate the contents, they'll find it's full of Mesan gourmet foods—yeah, we have some, every planet does—"

"The vassu liver pâté's to die for," said Chuanli.

"—which you're planning to take home with you seeing as how you've decided to leave because of all the trouble. Then after you get on board, Anton—good servant that he is—takes the container back to where he leased it."

"Which happens to be one of our firms," interjected Chuanli.

"We're silent partners," said Dusek. "The face of the company's a citizen, but we actually run it. He just gets a cut."

Victor leaned back, his frown clearing away. "I see. The container is designed—and shielded, I assume—to hide a person, and the port guards probably won't give it more than a perfunctory examination anyway because they're expecting it to be coming back out. So Yana leaves that way."

"That's it. We've done it dozens of times. I might mention that the port guards are more or less on our payroll, anyhow. Informally speaking."

Anton chuckled. "And the humble bribe strikes again. Okay, that works. We'd better move as soon as possible, though."

"We can have the container full and ready to go in three hours," said Chuanli.

"Three hours it is, then."

CHAPTER 53

After they'd been bundled into the van, Vittoria and her two companions had been manacled by some sort of device she hadn't seen—and she hadn't seen them because the first thing they'd done was slap something on her forehead that immediately blinded her behind a sheet of translucent . . . something.

The one thing she had seen before that happened, though, had given her a little ray of hope. One of their abductors had taken the time to pick up Dennis's vid gear and bring it into the van. Why would they bother to do that if they were just going to murder them? The gear was valuable, but not so valuable that she could imagine terrorists running the risk of trying to sell it on the black market.

It was a pretty dim ray of hope, granted, but it was all she had.

Xavier Conde tried to say something about five minutes after they were abducted. But before he got more than half a sentence out one of their captors said: "One more word and we'll gag you. Electronic gags work by paralyzing your vocal cords, if you didn't know—and there's sometimes permanent damage."

That shut him up. Without his mellifluent voice, Xavier Conde was barely a cut above an unskilled laborer.

She couldn't tell how long the ensuing trip took. Between her blindness and fear, it seemed to last for hours.

Eventually, the van came to a stop. "Out," was the command. She had to move carefully because they still kept the blinders on and she couldn't see more than a little sliver of space just in front of her feet.

After she got out of the van, she found herself on some kind of hard, rough flooring. Like the pavement in a garage, maybe, that hadn't been maintained in years. She had a vague sense of emptiness around her, too, as if they were in some sort of large abandoned building.

"Where are—?" She broke off, since it would be idiotic to expect an answer to that question. "What are you going to do to us?"

That was probably just as idiotic a question, as one of her captors immediately made clear by slapping her on the back of the head. "Shut up."

But the voice of the head captor said: "Just relax. Soon you'll be starring in a public service message. Do exactly as we tell you and nobody gets hurt."

Public service message. That meant some sort of terrorist propaganda skit. It'd be humiliating, certainly, but . . .

Fuck it. If her employers expected Vittoria to maintain heroic silence on behalf of Mesa, which wasn't even her own star nation, they could damn well think again. She'd say—hell, she'd babble and add hosannas and hallelujahs—anything these frightening people wanted her to say.

❖   ❖   ❖

Victor accompanied Anton and Yana all the way to the entrance of Neue Rostock they'd be using to return to the port. That entrance didn't lead directly to the outside, of course. It passed through several underground passageways before a hidden door—more like a ship's hatch—would let them out in the sub-basement of an adjoining commercial tower where they'd parked their expensive air car. By the time any surveillance cameras could pick up Anton and Yana again, they'd already be halfway to their destination.

There were advantages to working with long-standing and successful crime bosses. Another one was that they wouldn't have to fumble around getting Andrew and Steph and the three seccy women they'd been hiding from the boutique to Neue Rostock. Chuanli had a team taking care of that for them. They'd even bring the regeneration unit—with Karen still in it—back to Neue Rostock.

How? Victor hadn't asked. Partly as a matter of politesse, but mostly because he was preoccupied.

Victor Cachat had known Anton Zilwicki almost his whole adult life. And while the times they'd been together were only a small portion of that adult life, they were among the most . . .

Memorable? That seemed an absurdly spartan way of putting it.

Anton was looking at him with an odd expression on his face—one that Victor suspected was mirroring his own. What did you say to a friend and colleague like that at a time like this?

Fortunately, Anton was better with words than he was. Perhaps that came from his long association with the Countess of the Tor, who gave speeches like nobody's business.

"If we never see each other again, Victor, I want you know that I have cherished you since the day I first laid eyes on you in Chicago and will continue to do so until the day I die. You've been the guardian dragon in my life, watching over those I love as well as your own. I am eternally in your debt."

Victor looked away, embarrassed. Then, forced himself to look back. He wasn't good at this—never had been and never would be—but some things had to be said.

"I think the debt runs more the other way, Anton. It's easy for—for a dragon—to lose himself in his fury. Lose himself forever, if he's not careful. You've been one of my lifelines. In some ways, I think, the most important one."

They stared at each other for a few seconds. Then Yana made an exasperated noise and said: "Since the two of you are too hung up to kiss each other, *I'll* do it for him."

She matched deed to word, sweeping Victor into an embrace and kissing him . . . *not* the way a proper woman kisses her uncle.

Then she released him and turned away. "Come on, Anton, you've got a fleet to catch."

He and Victor exchanged one last smile and he followed her. After a moment, Victor turned back into Neue Rostock.

✧   ✧   ✧

"Hey, what about me?" Anton asked plaintively a short while later. "Don't I get a kiss too?"

"Forget it. Dwarf lords don't ring my bell. Borderline

sociopaths ring my bell. Besides, your squeeze scares me more than Victor's does."

"Huh? Thandi can take a gorilla three falls out of three."

"Yeah, so? Your old lady gives speeches—and what's worse, people *listen* to them. We're into lynch mob territory now. Way scarier than gorillas."

❖   ❖   ❖

Their captors had led them into a small room somewhere in the building and sat them down on chairs. Vittoria thought it was a small room, anyway. Being blinded by that horrid translucent sheet—which was only "translucent" by the faintest margin, in these surroundings; she might as well have been wearing an old-fashioned blindfold—seemed to heighten her other senses. In some manner she couldn't exactly pin down, the place they were now located in just *seemed* small, where the place they'd first been unloaded from the van had seemed cavernous.

How long they waited there, she had no idea. She heard at least one of their captors walk away, but others stayed with them, and when Xavier—the fucking idiot!—tried to say something again, someone struck him. Pretty hard, too, from the sound of it.

"Which word in 'shut up' are you having trouble with, moron?" the terrorist demanded.

Eventually, one or more of their captors returned. "Okay, we're ready. Get up."

By that point, Vittoria was relieved to be doing anything. One of her captors lifted her out of the chair by an arm and guided her away. She sensed that she'd passed through a door, but thereafter all she could determine was that they were being moved down some sort of corridor. Then, through what she thought was another doorway. Then, she was forced down onto a chair again—not because she put up a fight, but simply because her sightless clumsiness made her captor handle her roughly.

A few seconds later, she felt a tap on her forehead and the translucent sheet vanished. She could see again!

Barely—there was a bright light shining at her, almost directly in her eyes. When she adjusted, though, she realized that there wasn't much to see anyway. They were in a room that was not very big—perhaps ten by twelve meters, with a rather low ceiling—and completely bare. So far as she could see, there were no windows and only one door. The walls were colored a sort of greenish off-white and were otherwise completely undecorated.

She wasn't sitting next to Xavier and Alex, but facing them at a distance of three meters or so. Her two companions were still standing.

The captor who'd brought the vid equipment from the garage—so she assumed, anyway; they were all face-shielded and wearing identical gray clothing, so it might have been a different one—placed it next to the recording tech. The big captor, the one who'd done most of the talking so far, pointed at it.

"Set the stuff up," he commanded. "You have three minutes."

"It takes at least five!" protested Alex.

"Fine. You have six minutes." The big captor glanced at his wrist com. "If you're not recording by then I'll kill you."

The man didn't bother to draw the pistol at his waist, and the threat was made so matter-of-factly that it didn't quite register on Vittoria for a moment. Then she couldn't help but gasp.

"What do you want me to do?" she asked. Some part of her was furious at herself for being so craven, but that part was overwhelmed by the rest of her, which was purely and simply terrified.

"For the moment, nothing." The captor pointed to Xavier. "You, get ready to read a little speech."

Thankfully, Conde had enough sense to keep his mouth shut.

❖   ❖   ❖

When Alex said he had everything ready to go, the captor glanced at his wrist com again. "Four minutes and forty seconds. You lied, but we'll let it go."

He nodded at one of the other captors, who stepped up to Xavier and moved him to stand just a meter from Vittoria, facing the vid recorder. Then he handed him three sheets of papic.

"All right. Start."

Nervously, Xavier licked his lips. But he was accustomed to reading text written by someone else smoothly and easily, so he went right into it.

"Once again, we in the Audubon Ballroom find ourselves forced to impart another lesson to Mesa's rulers."

Some manic little sliver of Vittoria's brain noted the use of the passive tense, which was particularly unfortunate in a manifesto of this nature. Her producer's training almost led her to blurt out a protest. *Hey! That should read: 'We in the Ballroom will now teach another lesson—'*

She was so distracted that the next part of the speech didn't register on her clearly.

"—all you understand are actions, we present you with another to demonstrate our resolve. Let all those who seek to undermine the faith the masses have in our cause take heed."

Two of the captors who'd been standing just behind and a little to the side of Alex as he recorded Xavier stepped forward. Vittoria saw that they'd drawn their pistols.

They were pointing them at her! Why?

The fusillade took her down, spilling her off the chair as it splattered the wall behind her with blood, brains and shredded pieces of tissue. So she didn't get to see Xavier vomit, or the beating he got from his captors that forced him to finish the manifesto.

She might have gotten a tiny bit of satisfaction out of that part, at least. It was a pretty savage beating.

❖   ❖   ❖

"First the killing in our own garage and now this!" said François McGillicuddy, half-shouting. "What the fuck is going on?"

Grace Summers managed to refrain from responding with: *I'd think it was pretty obvious.* Instead she satisfied herself with a simple declarative sentence: "The Ballroom wants to publicly demonstrate they have the capability to strike at anyone. They killed our people to show they could penetrate our security and—"

"Conde's just a fucking newscaster!" said McGillicuddy. "He had no more security than—than—my fucking grandmother."

That was perhaps not an apt comparison, since Genevieve McGillicuddy was part of Mesa's very upper crust and had quite a bit of security. But perhaps her grandson didn't realize that since he'd spent his entire life in that wealthy cocoon.

Blessedly, Grace's colleague picked up the slack. "True—but he's also quite well known," said Aidan Crowder. "And unlike the assassination of the DIB people, the murder of that poor woman and Conde's beating was recorded and dumped into the data net. Everybody and—and—their grandmother will be talking about it."

"Fuck everybody's grandmother." McGillicuddy reached out and stabbed at his desk com. "Zeno, I want an immediate doubling of security details on—on—everybody who might need it," he finished lamely.

And their grandmother, thought Grace. But she didn't say it, of course.

CHAPTER 54

"Janice, we've got a problem," said George Vickers. "Three of my agents have gone missing. Lajos Irvine, Borisav Stanković and Fred Martinez. They haven't reported back in days."

Janice Marinescu bit off a snarled *who gives a fuck?* They were right on the cusp of the whole campaign and this—jackass—insisted on pestering her with a problem like this?

"Why the hell haven't you—oh. Never mind." She'd just remembered that the three agents were engaged in undercover work. The trackers that were embedded in Alignment personnel on Mesa sometimes didn't work if they were taken behind shielding—or just too many meters of soil, if someone went underground. Given the nature of their duties, that wasn't unlikely to happen.

"Hold on a minute." She brought up her own records and gave them a quick examination. She was almost sure she already knew the answer to her question, but for something like this she felt obligated to make sure.

"Okay, what I thought. None of them were slated

for Houdini. I assume their meds have been kept up to date?"

She gave the figure on the screen a sharp look. "Yes?"

"Yeah, sure. All my people had the refresher within the last two months."

The special med implants in the trackers were good for at least a year. More to the point, if they weren't pinged periodically the suicide program would automatically be initiated.

"At this stage of the game, I think we should just forget about them," she said.

"What if they've been captured? Get interrogated?"

"By *who*? The reason we've been using long-shot schemes to catch more terrorists is because there are so few of them left. At least, in any position to do anything. But even if they are being interrogated by some unknown and mysterious parties, so what? Stanković and Martinez are in the very outer peel and don't know anything our enemies—the smartest of them, that is, which excludes any seccy I've ever heard of—can't already figure out. Irvine knows a little more, but . . ."

She shrugged. "That's exactly why his med implant includes the truth serum safety."

They'd never seen any reason to notify Lajos of that feature of his implants, either. To what purpose? If he got captured and interrogated with truth drugs, better for him as well as everybody else if he just dropped dead.

"What about torture?"

This was a waste of her time—time which was now extremely precious. "George, drop it. That's an order. And why are *you* fussing about it? You're slated for evacuation soon yourself."

She didn't need to double-check her records to make sure she remembered the details for *that* evacuation. By now, she knew them by heart.

"Yes, I know. I just..." He raised his hands in a gesture of surrender. "Fine. If you don't care, I don't care. Signing off."

A moment later, the screen reverted to standby.

She rose from her console and went over to another. Normally, that would have been staffed by one of her team members, but there were now only two of them left in the Houdini control room.

She brought up the status of her own evacuation. That one would be much more roundabout than most, because by the time *she* left the whole planet would be descending into chaos.

Good. She saw that the flyer had been brought to the underground garage. It would be fueled and ready to go.

Kevin Haas came into the room. "Get some sleep, Janice. There's nothing left to do but wait, and we won't have much chance for sleep for at least thirty-six hours after we leave."

She knew her partner was right, but...

Firmly, she told herself she was just suffering from a case of jitters. She got up and headed for the control center's small bunkroom.

❖   ❖   ❖

"I'll make it easier for you the first time around," said the man. "Just answer one question and I'll leave for another stretch. Fair warning, though. I am extremely good at detecting lies. It's part of the reason I don't use truth drugs. So if the answer is 'no,' don't try to say 'yes' in order to drag everything out. And if it's 'yes,' you'd better say so. The minute—the second—I think you're lying to me, I will kill you."

As was true of everything about the monster, what made him so frightening was his invariant understatement. The threats were simple, straightforward, as matter-of-fact as a man might say the sky was overcast. He never scowled, never snarled, never glared. Right now, he hadn't even bothered to take out his gun in order to emphasize Lajos' imminent peril.

He didn't need to. He knew that Lajos knew he'd do exactly what he said he would, when he would, and how he would.

Still, Lajos struggled to retain some personal dignity. "You've never even told me your name. Not last time either."

There was no longer any point in trying to claim he'd never been in that café. He also didn't doubt the man's claim that he was good at ferreting out lies.

"My apologies. I didn't mean to be rude. My name is Victor Cachat. I'm currently a Special Officer in the Republic of Haven's Federal Intelligence Service. Prior to that—"

But Lajos didn't listen to any of the rest. His worst fears had been confirmed. It had been foolish to even ask that question.

Lajos had been part of the extensive debriefing conducted by Collin Detweiler after the McBryde/Green Pines fiasco. He was the only surviving eyewitness who'd had contact with the two men suspected of being the foreign agents behind the whole affair. He'd been dismissed after his testimony was taken and examined, but not before he'd learned the basic facts as established by Detweiler and his team.

Cachat. *Again.* He and his Manticoran partner were supposed to be *dead.* How had the man managed to—?

But what difference did it make? Lajos didn't doubt him, any more than he doubted any of the man's threats.

Cachat finished. Then paused for a moment. Then:

"Here's the question. All I need for now is a simple 'yes' or 'no.' We know you're a member of the Alignment. More specifically, that you're working for their security forces. Don't bother trying to deny that because it's pointless."

"So what's your question?"

"Are you ready and willing to die for the Alignment? Not in the abstract, but here and now."

Cachet glanced at his timepiece. "I'll make it even easier for you. I'll give you five minutes to think about it. If the answer is 'yes,' say so at any point you choose, I'll shoot you dead and we're both done. If the answer's 'no,' you don't have to say anything. If you're still silent when the time's up, I'll just leave. When I come back, though, I'll have more questions."

He looked at the timepiece again. "Starting the count . . . now."

Lajos' brain spent the next few minutes scurrying around in his skull like a mouse trapped in a cage.

There was no way out. And . . .

He realized, finally, just how badly his faith in the Alignment—its purpose, its mission, and for sure and certain its methods—had been eroded over the past year.

How much? He didn't know yet. But he was no longer willing to die for it.

He didn't say anything, though. He just waited.

"Time's up," Cachat said. "I'll see you in a few

hours, then." He glanced around the cell. "Do you need more water? Food?"

"No, I'm fine." The moment he said it, he realized what an absurd statement that was. He was anything *but* fine. Given the parameters of his situation, though . . .

Again, he struggled to retain some dignity. "I don't suppose you could do anything about the *quality* of the food, could you?"

"No, sorry. If it makes you feel any better, I'm eating the same stuff you are. The kitchens—"

He shook his head, as if he were irritated with himself. And with that he left.

❖   ❖   ❖

As was true of modern residential towers everywhere, most people in Neue Rostock ate food that they prepared themselves in their own kitchens. Still, with this many people concentrated in a single building, there was always a large number who wanted to eat at one of the cafeterias or restaurants scattered throughout Neue Rostock.

But now, the tower's public kitchens were closing. The cooks had spent the last period making foods that could be carried easily and would keep for days without refrigeration. The foods weren't noxious, but probably the best that could be said for most of them was that they were bland.

For thousands of people undergoing an evacuation, however, it made for the most practical diet. Chuanli was finding refuge for them in other towers, but it was a slow process and priority was being given to children, the elderly and the ill. Some of Neue Rostock's people would be living underground for days, maybe weeks.

❖   ❖   ❖

The evacuation was proceeding a lot more smoothly than Thandi had expected. She'd underestimated— quite badly, in fact—the extent to which Dusek and his people wielded authority in Neue Rostock.

The problem, she now realized, was with the very term "criminal gang." Both words in that term were... off.

To begin with, while many of the activities Dusek oversaw were against Mesan law, most *seccies* had little if any problem with them. For the most part, those activities which Dusek and his people operated directly themselves involved entertainment—defining the term a bit broadly to include liquor, drugs, gambling, sex, bot fighting, all sorts of racing and sports matches. He even owned and operated a third of the district's public libraries.

Seccy social mores were perhaps coarse, by the standards of many worlds—certainly the Core worlds—but that just reflected the reality of their lives. The more unsavory of those businesses, like prostitution, were ameliorated by seccy attitudes. Many young women and men did a stint working that trade and left it after a few years with usually little in the way of permanent consequences. Very often, the way they quit was by being matched up with someone by one of the mating services—some of which were also run by Dusek.

Many of whatever social services existed in Neue Rostock were maintained by the gang. If someone needed medical treatment and couldn't afford it, their first (and usually only, and always last) recourse was to ask the gang for help. As long as you hadn't done something to put you in Dusek's bad graces, a loan would always be forthcoming. And while outright grants were never given, Dusek was willing to forgive a loan in cases of real hardship. A lot of families over the years had seen their old folks die in reasonable comfort and grace thanks to a loan from the gang—which, if they really couldn't afford to pay it back, would usually be cancelled.

In short, using the term *criminal* to describe Dusek and his people . . . wasn't inaccurate, exactly. But it was also much too limited. If he was Neue Rostock's robber baron, the *baron* part of the description was preeminent.

The term "gang" was even more misleading. To begin with, it was closer to a small army than anything usually implied by the term "gang." Dusek had hundreds of people on his own payroll, and thousands more whose income derived from him indirectly.

The reason none of the major crime lords in the seccy districts had tried to take over Lower Radomsko wasn't because they *couldn't* have done so. Dusek, for instance, could have flattened any of the Lower Radomsko gangs—or all of them put together. The real deterrent was that if any one of them tried, the other major bosses would come in also to prevent them from gaining another large territory.

The term "organization" was a lot more accurate than "gang." The seccies themselves usually called Dusek's organization "the outfit."

So, the evacuation was going quite well. The outfit had even managed to keep most signs of it from becoming evident outside of Neue Rostock. People whose jobs were such that an absence would have become quickly noticed by the authorities were allowed to keep going to work for the time being.

The situation couldn't last for very long, of course, especially with people being filtered into neighboring towers. But unless Victor and Anton's assessment was badly off, it wasn't going to anyway.

Thandi had no opinion on that subject herself. But by now, she did have a firm opinion on the subject of Cachat & Zilwicki Espionage, Ltd.

It was the best outfit of its kind in the galaxy.

October 1922 Post Diaspora

"We have, to put it as mildly as I possibly can, got a grudge against the Alignment."

—Victor Cachat, Haven agent

CHAPTER 55

"They're almost in the zone," said Kevin Haas.

Janice Marinescu was watching the progress of the commercial flyer on her own screen. On board were George Vickers and two other alpha-line high-ranking members of the Alignment.

The flyer was now coming in for a landing at the airfield just outside the city of Dobzhansky, three hundred kilometers to the southwest of Mendel. From there, Vickers and his companions were supposed to take a shuttle to one of the orbital stations, where they would board the Jessyk Combine vessel that would take them outsystem. They were starting their Houdini evacuation.

Starting... and ending. All of them had been carefully evaluated and found wanting in one important respect or another. In the case of Vickers—the only one of the three Janice knew personally—the problem was excessive narcissism and egotism, an unfortunate side effect that tended to crop up in his genetic line.

There was a tried and tested method—tested for at least ten millennia, since humans first began domesticating animals—for dealing with that problem. Cull the unwanted variants in the genetic line.

The final decision had been made by Collin Detweiler two days ago, just before he left himself.

"Okay...*now*," said Haas.

Marinescu keyed in the command. The nuclear device that had been secreted in the flyer's cargo bay detonated.

The yield of the explosion was eight kilotons, roughly half the size of the "Little Boy" bomb used on Hiroshima over two millennia earlier. The height at which the detonation occurred was a little over five hundred meters, which was just about the same height as that of the Hiroshima detonation.

Ideally, they'd have detonated the bomb at a greater altitude, but they'd waited because the flyer's course took it almost directly over a large playing field where two local schools were having a sports match. The stands were full of teenage students and their families.

The hypocenter was not quite above the playing field. It was a hundred meters to the north of what would have been the outer wall of the stadium except that the stadium was just two long rows of tiered seats on either side of the field. But the practical effect was about the same. The framework of the seats was ceramacrete but the seats themselves and the awning that shielded spectators from the sun were not. Except for twenty-six people who were inside the ceramacrete shells—nine girls, seven boys and two teachers using the toilets; three janitors playing a card game while they waited for the game to end; and five students making purchases from bots at the concession stand—everyone attending the match was killed instantly. First, incinerated by the radiant heat from the fireball. Many of the victims left only shadows on the seats behind. Then, the remains were pulverized and dispersed like so much dust by the blast wave.

The concession stand under the southern tier of seats was open at either end. The blast wave came through and battered the five students there into literal pulp. A few of the people in the toilets and two of the janitors in their small supply room survived the blast, although all of them were badly injured. All of them would soon suffer the effects of severe radiation poisoning as well. In the end, only two would survive—and one of those would never come out of a coma.

Dobzhansky had no seccy district at all. The population was made up entirely of citizens. That population also produced, per capita, more members of Mesa's police, security forces and military than any other town or city on the planet.

Marinescu, Haas and their team, assembled and overseen by Collin Detweiler, had crunched the numbers carefully. Every battalion-sized police, security or military force in Mesa had just lost one or more family members of anywhere between five and seventeen percent of its troops.

There was not a single other measure they'd been able to devise that was more certain of enraging those forces. Those who had not personally lost family members in the Dobzhansky terrorist attack would almost certainly have friends who had.

Investigation would determine that the two seccies who'd loaded the baggage onto that flyer had both disappeared. When their apartments were searched, propaganda literature from the Audubon Ballroom would be found on the personal computers of both of them.

The culprits would never be found, however. Within two hours of their disappearance, they'd been consumed in a commercial garbage disintegrator whose security program had been bypassed by one of the Alignment's top software specialists.

The software specialist would be one of the very last evacuees. The two Alignment agents who'd kidnapped the baggage handlers were not slated for Houdini. They'd both die soon when their med implants failed to receive the ping that would abort the suicide program.

One of them would die from a heart attack, the other from a stroke. The Alignment had been careful to vary the cause of death so that there would be no unusual statistical "clumps." Each program was also tailored to the individual's medical history. Or medical records, at least. Those sometimes needed to be tweaked to give a healthy person a plausible cause of death.

✧　　✧　　✧

"Ready on Target Beta," said Haas.

Marinescu monitored the input from the camera perched inside the auditorium on one of the lower floors of Saracen Tower. Today's keynote speaker had been introduced and was beginning his speech.

"Go," she said. Haas keyed in the command.

The device planted in the auditorium's utility closet was a tactical nuke, much smaller than the one used at Dobzhansky, and the tower's loadbearing walls channeled the blast. Like most towers (or, at least, those built for full citizens), Saracen was actually a honeycomb of ceramacrete tubes arranged in cells which ringed a central core. They were very *large* tubes—those in Saracen were fifty meters across—and very, *very* tough, deliberately designed to contain disasters like fires or the sorts of "natural" explosions humans were capable of accidentally producing under almost any circumstances. The tower's central cell consisted of six fifty-meter tubes arranged in a ring around a central fifty meter-wide air shaft which also gave access to small air cars. Outside that central cell was what amounted to an enormous atrium, thirty meters across, with pedestrian ways and traffic lanes for the small, electric vehicles which scurried about the tower's interior facing the kilometer and a half-tall atrium walls. Suspended pedestrian and vehicle ways crossed the atrium at regular intervals, providing a sense of airiness and space even at the heart of the vast, kilometer-wide structure. A second ring of cells, each identical to the central core, threaded around the atrium like the beads of a necklace, surrounded by yet another atrium and yet another ring of cells.

In all, there was a total of four rings of cells wrapped around the central core, which made the entire tower just under nine hundred meters in diameter and one and a half kilometers tall. The solid ceramacrete loadbearing walls of the tubes were incredibly strong, and the floor plates of each of its five hundred floors were also fused ceramacrete, substantially stronger and more resistant than thrice their own thickness of solid granite.

Still, the cells—and floor plates—were cross-connected at almost every level by doors, archways, grav shafts, emergency stairwells, and all the thousand-and-one elements of a modern building's circulatory and respiratory systems. The auditorium was in the tower's second ring, roughly six hundred meters from the tower's outer face, and the blast front was enough to blow any closed opening in its path wide open, but the overall effect was rather like setting off a small nuclear device (a very small one, in fact, barely ten percent as large as the ancient atomic bomb exploded over Hiroshima) inside a mountain cave. It hollowed out a vast chamber directly above and below itself and sent blast, heat, and fragments scything through the two adjacent loadbearing tubes on either side, and vented to both the central air shaft of its cell and the adjacent atrium, but the auditorium was on only the fortieth floor The blast front never even reached the tower's outermost cells, never so much as blew out a single exterior window.

Inside the tower was quite another matter, of course. The explosion was more than enough to kill the 1,463 people in the auditorium and every living soul on the seventy-one floors above it in the same loadbearing tube. The blast vented into the atrium directly beyond the auditorium, inflicting very heavy casualties on those hapless souls strolling along the pedestrian ways or dawdling over a cup of coffee in one of the sidewalk cafés. Rather amazingly—and in testimony to both the freakishness of blast waves and the confining effect of those ceramacrete floor plates—six people on the auditorium tube's ninth floor actually survived, as did a hundred and twelve on the eighth floor, and over two hundred on the seventh. Below the seventh, there were only non-life-threatening injuries, but there were no survivors at all between the fortieth and the hundred and eleventh floors, and casualties in the adjoining tubes and those facing the blast site across the atrium space were very heavy.

In all, nine thousand, nine hundred and forty-one people were killed outright. Another seven hundred and two would later succumb to their injuries.

The meeting had been sponsored by Bateson University. The speaker had been Mesa's Assistant Director of Scientific Research. His topic had been *Projections for research grants in 1923.*

Mesa had just lost a significant portion of its scientific establishment.

One of those slated to speak later that day had been Lisa Charteris. According to the program, she was just returning from a weeks-long stay in a research institute on McClintock Island. Her husband Jules had just entered the auditorium when the blast went off. He'd been looking forward to seeing his wife again. She'd been incommunicado, as was normal procedure for seminars held at that institute.

Jules had been personally invited by Lisa's boss, at Collin Detweiler's instruction. As always, the Alignment worked in layers. The blast would not only explain Lisa Charteris's disappearance. By killing her husband it would also eliminate the one person most likely to probe that disappearance.

Charteris herself had never been told of the plan, of course. There was no reason to upset her, especially since that would undermine her effectiveness. By the time she found out about her husband's death, if she ever did, many years would have gone by. Time would have softened her memory and the precise events of that horrible day of carnage so long ago would have been blurred by that same passage of time.

A number of other scientists were supposed to have been there that day, who, in the event, never showed up. Those were the ones who'd already left Mesa as part of Houdini.

The surviving records would, indeed, show that they'd been there. But the blast would have destroyed their physical persons along with the persons of anyone who might have been able to say otherwise.

⬧ ⬧ ⬧

"Target Gamma... now."

Marinescu keyed in yet another command and a huge shopping center in one of the towers inhabited by citizens was ground zero for another tactical nuke, this one with a yield of just over a kiloton.

The time was far from ideal, since the lunchtime crowd would have thinned and the evening crowd hadn't started arriving. But this all needed to be done in a very short span of time. Even as it was, eleven thousand six hundred and three people were killed immediately. Almost as many would die within the next few days from the effects of radiation, burns and radiation poisoning.

Among the people whose lives were spared by the timing were Zachariah McBryde's mother Christina and his younger sister Arianne. They'd been planning to shop together that evening, after dinner.

They both lived in the building, Dedrick Tower, but their apartments were far enough from the blast that they suffered no injuries. Christina's apartment was barely even rattled. Arianne's was closer, and she lost some fragile personal items tossed off their shelves by the concussion. But nothing worse.

⬧ ⬧ ⬧

"Delta ready."

"Firing... now."

Another large bomb, twelve kilotons. Set off in the middle of an outdoor amusement park located on Mendel's outskirts.

Three and a half thousand dead immediately or within a few hours. Another eleven hundred would die from the effects. One hundred and two would never really recover.

Almost all of the employees of Blue Lagoon Park and the majority of its customers came from the surrounding suburbs. These were citizen areas which, albeit not to the same extent as Dobzhansky, also provided a considerable number of Mendel's police and security forces and military personnel.

By the team's calculations, the percentage of those forces who'd now been immediately impacted by the terrorist outrages had climbed to somewhere between seven and twenty-two percent, depending on the specific unit.

◇ ◇ ◇

"Epsilon."

"Let's hope...*yes*. Misfire as planned."

Epsilon was another big device: thirteen kilotons and, literally, *big*. It was three meters long, almost two meters across in its widest lateral dimension, two meters high, and weighed just short of five thousand kilograms.

Obviously jerry-built and poorly designed to begin with, it was not surprising the bomb failed to detonate. And thankfully so. The bomb would be found in a maintenance shop in another residential tower set aside for citizens. Had the perpetrators succeeded in their plans, the death toll could have been in the tens of thousands.

The five seccy repair workers who were the only ones who used that maintenance shop had all gone missing. They would also never be found. The Alignment had seen to that.

But, of course, they'd still get the blame for it. Investigation would determine that the seccy foreman of the crew, Sepp Richter, had been taking courses in applied physics at a small college catering to seccies. Ballroom propaganda would be found on his personal computer as well as that of two other repair workers—and on the school computer assigned to the physics instructor.

Who was also missing.

✧   ✧   ✧

The driver's manifest listed the contents of the container in the cargo compartment as an aquarium being delivered to a law firm, presumably for display in their waiting room.

The driver—a seccy, like most such—had no reason to question the legitimacy of the manifest. He was not permitted to examine sealed containers anyway.

Nor did he question the legitimacy of the route he was given. The law firm was located on the 468th floor of Rasmussen Tower, one of Mendel's most luxurious and expensive residential/commercial buildings. Deliveries made to such an address allowed a commercial van to use airspace normally reserved for passenger vehicles.

He was still required to use special commercial lanes, of course.

The first sign that anything was amiss was when he suddenly found his hands, as if of their own volition, overriding the traffic program and taking direct control of the vehicle. An alarm immediately started blaring.

You are not authorized for manual operation in this area. Immediately restore the automatic program. Warning. You will be heavily fined if you—

But he was paying no attention. To his horror, his hands—*his own hands!*—were steering the van right up into the most heavily trafficked lanes. The only thing that was now preventing collisions were the van's own emergency programs. But in this sort of dense traffic they could not possibly—

⋄   ⋄   ⋄

"Zeta ready."

"Triggering . . . now."

The final blast was another tactical nuke, but a big one—about three kilotons. All vehicles in the vicinity of the van were obliterated. Those in the fireball itself ceased to exist above a molecular level; those beyond it survived only in pieces—and the passengers in still smaller pieces.

Vehicles farther away survived the radiant heat relatively intact—although the passagers usually didn't—but the blast wave hurled them in all directions, smashing into other vehicles or into the surrounding buildings. Or, often enough, both. The space between the city center's kilometer-high towers was narrower than the spacing became farther out, and the one between Rasmussen Tower and the neighboring Jarrett Tower was a narrow and very deep artificial canyon. Vehicles caught in that explosion were like small pebbles in a can. They caromed off everything until they finally just came apart altogether.

The death toll wasn't as high as in the Dobzhansky and amusement park blasts. But an astonishingly high percentage of the casualties were movers and shakers in Mesan society, and because of the nature of the disaster itself, many of the bodies would never be identified.

Indeed, many of those who died there would never be known at all. Thousands of people vanished in Mendel that day. How many of them were incinerated in the shopping mall? Turned into shadows on the walls and floors of the amusement park? Simply... vanished in that canyon of death?

No one would ever know. No one would ever be able to prove anything about those disappearances, one way or the other.

The delivery company's records would be searched and the identity of the driver determined. A search of his apartment would also uncover ties to the Audubon Ballroom.

❖   ❖   ❖

"Okay, Janice, we're out of here."

"Just a...second. There, it's set. Let's go."

❖   ❖   ❖

Six minutes later, the small personal flyer in the garage half a kilometer away took to the air. On the horizon, Marinescu and Haas could see the blast cloud above the amusement park.

They headed north to the rendezvous.

Nine minutes later, Eta detonated. Their control center vanished. So did the small town surrounding it.

Haldane was a resort town in the hills east of Mendel, a place of small houses and cottages—some of them, admittedly, not all *that* small—laid out as a deliberate escape from the urban towers in which the vast majority of Mesa's population lived. The permanent population was only two and a half thousand, but on any given day there was a transient population of at least twice that many people. And, like the population that used the traffic lanes where the van had detonated, the resort's clientele included a large number of the planet's most prominent and important people.

A large part of the reason for Haldane's popularity with the upper crust was that one of the town's specialties was anonymity. It was the sort of resort that even a celebrity could visit without much informal notice being taken—and no formal notice of any kind. The electronic ledgers of all hotels were wiped every morning, and even while they lasted a good third of the registrants had names like Smith, Johnson, Williams and Brown.

The Eta bomb was the biggest of all. Forty-five kilotons, detonated at ground level.

Grotesque overkill, for a town that size. There was literally nothing left at all.

CHAPTER 56

The best adjective for the atmosphere in the sumptuous conference room was probably "brittle," although "frightened" would have run a very close second. The men and women seated around the conference table understood the terror, consternation, and fury filling the hearts and minds of the Mesa System's citizens. Indeed, they understood it far better than most of those millions upon millions of citizens understood, because unlike them, they knew how much damage the string of nuclear explosions had actually done... and threatened to do yet.

Bryce Lackland, the Director of Culture and Information, had managed to keep a lid on the actual casualty figures from the Saracen Tower bomb and the air van bomb which had detonated equidistantly between Masten Tower and Rasmussen Tower, but the *number* of people who'd been killed was far from the worst damage they'd inflicted. The *nature* of the people who died made the appalling loss of life still worse. A painful percentage of Mesa's top-tier scientists had perished, yet even that was less ominous than the casualties which had been suffered among the families of the planetary security forces.

"I'm telling you," Brianna Pearson said emphatically into the tension-curdled atmosphere, "we do *not* want to turn OPS—or, even worse, MISD—loose. Not without bringing in people from outside the Capital District, anyway!"

"There's no time to bring in anyone else!" Regan Snyder snapped, and Pearson glared at her. "We have to act *now*, and we have to act *decisively*," the tall, raven-haired Snyder continued harshly. "We've let the damned seccies have too much free rein for too long, and this is what we get for it! It's time we *explained* reality to them in terms even they can understand!"

Pearson never took her glare off Snyder, but the corner of one eye was watching Brandon Ward, the General Board of Mesa's CEO. What she saw there wasn't encouraging.

Ward was a tall, fair-haired man with gray eyes and a strong chin. He carried himself with the grace of an athlete, maintained by the hours he put in on handball courts, and he projected the image and attitude of a decisive person with genuine power. Unfortunately, any decisiveness he might once have cherished had been leached out of him long ago, and the truth was that his actual power was an amorphous proposition, at best. Chief Executive Officer or no, he'd long since learned the true limits the General Board imposed upon him. His ability to *administer* Mesa was almost as great as someone looking in from the outside might have supposed it to be. His ability to formulate and control Mesa's *policies* was quite another matter, and Snyder—although officially "only" the Director of

Commerce—was Manpower Incorporated's representative on the Board.

And Ward knew it.

Snyder stood a hundred seventy-three centimeters tall and was almost as athletic as Ward (although her chosen sports had more to do with bedrooms than handball courts), with strikingly good looks which owed very little to biosculpt and quite a lot to the same genetic modification which had given her that midnight hair and incredibly blue eyes. Those portions of her appearance were due to her parents' choices before she'd ever been born, but the stylish tattoos and body piercings were her own addition. At the age of fifty-one, she was forty years younger than Ward, although both of them were third-generation prolong recipients. Unlike him, however, Snyder was a member of the New Lodges, the members of the Mesan social elite who chose to flaunt their status and revel in their power. In Pearson's opinion, that was stupid. The Audubon Ballroom had made a special point of picking off members of the New Lodges whenever possible, especially any of them with direct links to Manpower, and Snyder's link to Manpower was very exalted indeed. She was VP of Operations in the Mesa System, which would have put her at the very apex of any Ballroom hit list even without her arrogant, sneering lifestyle.

On the other hand, Pearson acknowledged to herself, *she is VP of Operations, so maybe she's not quite as stupid as I thought. Given her job, she couldn't paste a bigger target on her back however she chose to dress, now could she? So why not live whatever way she chooses?*

On more mature consideration, however, she *was* just as stupid as Pearson had ever thought.

"I think Brianna has a point," Jackson Chicherin put in, his courteous, academic tone contrasting sharply with Snyder's grating anger. The Commerce Director looked away from Pearson to glare at him, instead, and he shrugged. "The situation's bad enough now without our making it even worse," he pointed out. "If we turn Public Safety loose on the seccy districts and *don't* bring in units from outside the Capital District, it's going to be a bloodbath. Too many of their people have lost family or friends. All some of them will be interested in is getting payback, and if they can't get it from whoever actually set off those bombs, they'll take it from anyone they can catch."

Snyder's blue eyes hardened with disdain as they bored into the short, wiry Chicherin. Part of that was the contempt of someone who considered herself a predator among predators, cutting her way up the corporate ladder with ruthlessness and determination, for someone who was basically an academic. A highly skilled, very wealthy academic, and Vice President of Research and Development for the Mesan Genetic Consultancy, but still an academic with an academic's squeamishness for the way things worked in the real world.

"Maybe a little bloodletting's what we need," she said now, her eyes as coldly reptilian as her voice. "As far as I'm concerned, we should simply call in kinetic strikes on the bastards! Level their damned towers and be done with it once and for all!" she went on, amply confirming Pearson's estimate of her intellectual capacity. Or of her ability to pour piss out of a boot, for that matter.

"You're out of your mind," Pearson said flatly. Snyder's blue eyes flashed fire, and Pearson sneered. "If you want to destroy the entire city of Mendel, you go right ahead," she said. "*I'm* going to be moving to the country first, though! Do you have *any* idea what kind of KEW you'd need to take out a modern residential tower? Or even one of those seccy deathtraps? You can't use that kind of weapon without plenty of collateral damage, Regan! And that wouldn't be the only 'collateral damage' you'd be doing, either!"

"We've let the whole frigging seccy question fester for way too long," Snyder grated. "It was a mistake to ever allow manumission, and we've been paying for it ever since. I say it's time we finally put an end to the problem once and for all, because if we don't, I'll guarantee you we'll see more of this kind of crap! And don't think for a minute that it won't spread from the seccies to the slaves if we don't stamp on it fast and hard. Whether we use KEWs or not, I stand by my original argument. We need to spill enough blood to drive those bastards back into their holes and keep them hiding there for the next T-century!"

"What you're going to get if you turn OPS loose the way its troopers are feeling right this minute will be one hell of a lot more than 'enough blood'—whatever that is!" Pearson said sharply. "And what we don't *need* right now is a bloodbath!"

"Why not?" François McGillicuddy demanded, and Pearson managed—somehow—not to roll her eyes.

McGillicuddy was a senior board member of Atkinson, McGillicuddy, & Shivaprakash, a major transstellar investment firm with branches in many of the Solarian League's major star systems. He was also Director of

Security, a plum post which had fallen to AMS as the result of intricate negotiations with Manpower and the Jessyk Combine. Negotiations which would never have succeeded if he hadn't demonstrated his willingness to work hand-in-glove with Snyder. That meant his attitude was hardly surprising, but the post he held made that attitude even more... unfortunate.

Pearson herself was Vice President of Operations (Mesa) for Technodyne Industries, which was how she found herself on the General Board. Technodyne had suffered major losses—both financially and in terms of prestige—after the disaster of the Battle of Monica, although it had recovered much of the lost ground by providing its newly developed Cataphract long-range missile to the Solarian League Navy. Overall, its position on the General Board was still weaker than it had been, as Pearson was only too well aware. She'd gotten her start in Technodyne's public relations division, however. That gave her a somewhat different perspective from many of her colleagues, who seemed blissfully unaware of—or, even worse, dismissive of—the public relations implications of what they were discussing, and all of her instincts were ringing loud, insistent alarm bells as she listened to Snyder and McGillicuddy.

"Regan's right," McGillicuddy continued now, as if to prove how justified her fears were. "We need to send a message to the seccies. Even more important, maybe, we need to send one to the *slaves*. And we need to send it right now, before those Ballroom 'manifestoes' have time to sink in. God only knows how they're likely to react after that!"

His gray eyes were as fiery as Snyder's, but there was

more fear under that anger. Snyder, Pearson suspected, didn't yet actually feel personally threatened. She was too fundamentally arrogant—and had too much faith in her own security measures—to consider that there might be another nuclear device out there somewhere with *her* name on it. McGillicuddy, on the other hand, had been growing increasingly anxious about the potential for seccy or even slave violence—or perhaps it would have been more accurate to say *additional* seccy or slave violence—ever since Green Pines. Recent events would suggest his anxiety had been entirely justified, and he was clearly terrified of where the next round of terrorist attacks might go. There might be one person on Mesa—Regan Snyder, for example—the seccies hated more than the system's Director of Security, but it was unlikely there were two of them. And blowing up the head of the forces responsible for preventing acts of terror would have to sound very attractive to the terrorists bent on committing them.

"Look," Pearson said, making herself sit back and pitch her voice as reasonably as possible, "I'm not saying measures don't have to be taken. I'm not even saying that 'sending a message' to the seccies is necessarily a terrible idea. I'm simply saying there's enough trouble already headed our way without adding this kind of interstellar public relations black eye to the mix."

"Oh, give me a *break*, Brianna!" Snyder sneered. "We're *Mesa*, remember? Every do-gooder and moral crusader in the explored galaxy's spent the last four or five T-centuries telling everyone what moral lepers we are. You really think that breaking a few heads— hell, breaking a few *necks!*—is going to make us even more leprous?"

"What I'm saying," Pearson's tone was just a bit over controlled, "is that the Manties and the Havenites are screaming nonsense about our being behind the attacks on Manticore. They're telling everyone who'll listen that we've been manipulating the League into attacking Manticore, as well. It's ridiculous, and only a fool would believe we would—or *could*—do something like that! But if we respond to these attacks with wholesale bloodshed, we'll hand them a golden opportunity to hammer us for it. It's going to be bad enough whatever we do, but if we pile up some sort of massive body count, you can be damned sure their propagandists'll use it for all it's worth! Give them enough opportunities to paint us as the galaxy's bogeyman, and their claims will start gaining traction. If nothing else, it would make it a hell of a lot harder for our friends in the League to scare up any support for us if they decided to come after Mesa directly! With them already blowing away Solly battle fleets right and left, do you really want to hand them that sort of hammer in addition? And don't forget, that muckraking bitch O'Hanrahan is right here in-system at this very moment. She'd be right on top of any 'excesses' our security forces might commit, and don't think for an instant that she wouldn't be shouting about them at the top of her lungs to all her League audience! You have no *idea* how much influence that woman has, and she'll pull out all the stops on this one."

Chicherin leaned back in his chair, watching the other members of the General Board, and tried to keep his dismay from showing. He was an alpha-line whose family had been part of the Alignment for generations, and like the vast majority of the Alignment's membership he'd always hated Manpower and the institution of genetic slavery.

From a cold-blooded business perspective, Mesa's position as the galaxy's foremost genetic slaver was a continual stumbling block for Mesan Genetic Consultancy. MGC was what some people mockingly described as "the kinder, gentler face of Mesa," a firm which provided many of the same services as those provided by Beowulfan geneticists. It was known to push the limits of the Beowulf Biosciences Code hard—even to ignore them, upon occasion—but partly because of that, it had produced some of the most successful genetic modifications for colonists whose planets demanded that sort of alteration. Unfortunately, quite a lot of people who would have dealt with MGC under other circumstances had been scared off by a combination of moral repugnance for the slave trade and fear that the genetic mods *they* wanted would be "contaminated" by Manpower's. And however much Chicherin hated to admit it, quite a lot of the basic R&D which underlay MGC's accomplishments really had originated in Manpower's labs. There were times he felt dirtied by that knowledge, but research was research. Even though he would never have condoned the programs which had produced that data, he could hardly justify not making use of it.

From a personal moral perspective, he loathed the institutionalization of an entire subset of the human race which was automatically considered inferior—indeed, *sub*human—and denied the dignity and the rights of other human beings. From a professional viewpoint, he knew how completely unjustified the prejudice which produced that situation actually was.

Genetic slaves might have been tailored—designed—for specific ends, but they were just as human as anyone else, and the bigotry which denied that simple fact was not simply morally wrong but based entirely on ignorance and stupidity.

And from a philosophical perspective, he was firmly convinced that MGC's public proselytization in favor of genetic uplift (and the Alignment's covert enhancement of Mesan citizens) had been held back for T-centuries by Mesa's association with genetic slavery. For that matter, much of the continuing galactic prejudice against the entire concept of planned genetic uplift was fueled by the existence of genetic slavery—and the public's attitude towards it—in Jackson Chicherin's opinion.

And now it had brought them *this*. It made him want to weep. He had no burning sympathy for the Audubon Ballroom—genetic slavery's moral corruption couldn't simply grant carte blanche to its opponents where the commission of equally ugly atrocities was concerned—but he found it difficult to *blame* the Ballroom for its hatred and the tactics that hatred spawned. At the moment, it was easier to blame the terrorists than usual, given the number of personal friends and colleagues he'd lost in the nuclear attacks like the one on Saracen Tower, yet how could shedding even deeper rivers of blood make the situation *better*? It was hardly likely to deter any future attacks which had already been planned, and it *was* likely to produce even more terrorist recruits among the seccies McGillicuddy and Snyder wanted to terrify.

None of which even considered Pearson's point about the propaganda advantages Mesa's enemies would wring out of any *government-sponsored* atrocities!

Despite all of which, he could already see which way this was going to end. Snyder was far and away the single most powerful member of the General Board. Manpower had spent too many T-years cementing its alliances with the other megacorporations who named the Board's members, and its thirty percent interest in Noroguchi Nanotech and Cybercom of Mesa (not to mention its never officially acknowledged outright ownership of the Jessyk Combine) gave it plenty of raw political power of its own. With McGillicuddy backing her play, she was going to carry the day eventually.

Unfortunately, he was right.

❖   ❖   ❖

"All right." François McGillicuddy's eyes were hard as he sat behind his desk, facing the holographic images of Commissioner Bentley Howell and Commissioner Fran Selig. "The Board's greenlighted Rat Catcher. What do we need to make it work and how soon can we implement?"

"That depends on how hard we intend to hit them, Sir," Howell replied.

The handsome, dark-haired, dark-complexioned Howell was the commanding officer of the Mesan Internal Security Directorate. MISD—its critics normally pronounced the acronym "missed," especially since its . . . overly enthusiastic reaction to Green Pines—was technically a mere division of the Office of Public Safety. Of course, OPS had a lot of divisions, and more total manpower than any other agency of the Mesa System government. It needed the warm bodies because, despite its relatively innocuous name, it was the primary suppressive arm of the Mesan government and it answered only to the Procurator of Public Safety and, beyond the

Procurator's Office, to the Director of Security. The Procurator, unfortunately, had been attending a soccer match at a stadium in Dobzhansky when a nuclear device exploded directly above it. For the present, McGillicuddy had taken over the Procurator's duties in addition to his own, which was how he came to be speaking directly to Howell and Selig, who—as CO of the Office of Public Safety—was Howell's superior. Nominally, at least; MISD had a reputation for creatively misconstruing directives with which it disagreed.

Selig was a small woman, barely a hundred and fifty-seven centimeters in her bare feet, with dark blue hair and intense green eyes. There were other, more subtle genetic mods in her family background, however, and she was far stronger and tougher than she looked. She was also a savvy, skilled bureaucratic infighter, although that hadn't helped her rein in Howell. MISD was a separate fiefdom within OPS, and the gauntleted fist gripping the drawn dagger of Public Safety on the MISD shoulder patch reflected that status only too accurately. When push came to shove, when it was time to put away the neural whips and the water cannon and the tear gas dispensers and send in Public Safety's true hard men and women, that was when MISD came into its own.

"How hard to do you think I *want* you to hit them, Bentley?" McGillicuddy replied to Howell's question. "I want those seccy bastards *hammered*. I went them hammered so flat they won't even *think* about getting back up."

"So you're not talking about just breaking a few more heads, Sir?" Selig asked, and McGillicuddy snorted.

"I'm talking about putting pulser darts through a

few heads," he said flatly, and Selig nodded. If she was surprised, it didn't show. And, in fact, she'd been anticipating that decision for some time. Her uniformed OPS troopers had already broken quite a few heads over the past day or so, and she was entirely in favor of taking things to the next level.

"Do you want to put my people in immediately, Sir?" Howell asked.

"Not immediately." McGillicuddy shook his head and pointed at Selig. "First, I want *your* people to push the rabble back into its kennels, Commissioner Selig. I want them holed up so Commissioner Howell's people will know right where to find them in large enough numbers to make sure the survivors hear our message loud and clear. Understood?"

"Understood, Sir." Selig smiled coldly. "We'll get right on that."

⋄   ⋄   ⋄

"What's going on?" asked Lajos Irvine. "I heard— well, more like felt—what seemed like explosions nearby."

Victor Cachat shook his head. "They weren't nearby. The reason you felt them is because they were nuclear detonations. Half a dozen of them, all told. The news media are reporting casualties—most of them fatalities—in the tens of thousands."

He paused for a moment and gave Lajos that frightening level stare. "They're saying the detonations are being done by Ballroom terrorists. But that's ridiculous—and you know it as well as I do. What I think is happening is that your Alignment is pulling everyone off the planet and covering their tracks. And if that requires mass murder, so be it."

Lajos felt an urge to protest against the accusation, but he said nothing. He was pretty sure Cachat was right. And if he was...

Then why hadn't anyone told Lajos himself about an evacuation? The only answer he could think of that made any sense—

And it *did* make sense. He rose to his feet. "It's an onion," he said. "It's always an onion. And it seems I'm not—"

The sensation was a curious one. Disorienting more than frightening. But he wouldn't have had more than a few seconds to be frightened anyway.

✧   ✧   ✧

Cachat caught him as he slumped, and was able to keep his head from being injured. But it didn't matter. The man was unconscious within seconds and died not long thereafter. A massive stroke; perhaps; but it was more likely to have been a pulmonary embolism—or something that mimicked it, anyway. The prisoner's mouth was coated in foam and he'd suffered massive and complete incontinence. If Victor remembered correctly, those were often symptoms of the condition.

Even if a medical regeneration unit had been immediately available he probably couldn't have saved the prisoner. But the few such units in their possession had already been moved to more secure locations underground. He could never have gotten the man into one in time.

Callie Patwary and her former gang partner Teddy came into the cell. They must have heard something.

Victor straightened up from his examination of the corpse lying on the floor. "When was the last time you saw him alive?"

Callie nodded her head in the direction of her former gang partner. "Teddy checked in on him about two hours ago."

"He seemed fine," Teddy insisted. "We didn't speak to each other when I brought him breakfast, but he looked at me and didn't seem sick or anything." He sounded nervous, as if he were worried that Victor would blame him for the prisoner's death and...

Do...something.

Victor found the reaction irritating, but he was used to it. He didn't quite understand why, but he knew from experience that a lot of people found him frightening. As if he might kill or injure someone for no reason. A notion which he found ridiculous, but...there it was.

"Not your fault, Teddy," he said. "If it's anyone's, it's mine. I was being circumspect in my questioning of him because I was pretty sure he had a built-in suicide program that would be triggered off by anything too overt. Apparently, I wasn't circumspect enough. Or he just got too excited and triggered it himself."

"Could you have done anything to prevent it?" asked Callie.

"Not if it was well-designed—which I'm sure it was. The people he worked for are ruthless."

He spotted the expressions on both Callie and Teddy's faces and had to fight down a smile. They were looking at him the way people might look at a shark who accused a crocodile of being excessively carnivorous.

"Have we got an easy way to freeze him?"

Teddy pointed over his shoulder with a thumb. "Dusek's people have a bunch of military-grade body-bags. Must have bought 'em from somebody they knew in the Peaceforce."

"All right. Put him in one and find a secure place to store his corpse somewhere underground—not too close to here, either. Hopefully, the corpse will survive what's coming. An examination by a really good medtech pathology unit might tell us something. It's not likely, but it's worth taking the chance."

He didn't bother to add the hope that they might survive what was coming also. Callie and Teddy were hardly what you'd call intellectual heavyweights, but they weren't dimwitted. They knew perfectly well they were all in for a desperate struggle.

He looked back down at the corpse. Victor had never asked the man his name, out of worry that might also trigger a suicide program. Now that it was all a moot point, he found himself regretting the fact. There was something indecent about a man dying nameless in the hands of enemies. Just one more thing to chalk up against the Alignment in his black book. A very small entry, admittedly, in what was by now a massive tome.

Still, he wouldn't forget. When it came to remembering the misdeeds of his enemies, Victor Cachat's memory was flawless.

CHAPTER 57

"That's right—kick the bastards in the balls and stomp on their throats when they go down!" Sergeant Amos Barkley shouted. "Show this shit what happens when they start throwing nukes *our* way!"

The troopers of his OPS section had their neural whips dialed to their highest setting. Technically, that was against regulations, just as it was against their official orders. But any Office of Public Safety noncom was well accustomed to reading between the official lines to what the orders really were, and in Amos Barkley's opinion, it was long past time the seccies were put firmly in their place. He didn't care what the official story was; he knew damned well those Ballroom bastards couldn't have gotten the Green Pines bomb into place without active seccy support. He'd known that from the beginning, even before he'd seen the bootleg copies of the classified transcripts of post-Green Pines seccy interrogations, and now, with this latest series of explosions...

The drably dressed seccies in front of him had just suddenly appeared out of an alley mouth. There were a half-dozen adults, most of them women, and closer to two dozen children, all of them obviously running from someone else. Sergeant Surekha's section was supposed to be clearing out the rats nest of apartments in the cellars of Sukharov Tower, and Barkley wasn't a bit surprised Surekha had flushed these seccies into his lap. Sukharov wasn't supposed to be a residential tower, at all. In fact, it wasn't even a tower, really— barely more than fifty stories tall and crammed full of mostly automated light manufacturing equipment. The owners had winked at the seccy squatters in their cellars for years, in no small part because many of those seccies were off-the-books maintenance techs, fully capable of overseeing Sukharov's maintenance remotes and even making repairs themselves in return for a roof over their heads. OPS had known about it all along, of course, but they, too, had turned a blind eye...in return for a suitable subsidy from Sukharov's owners. And, of course, a suitable "residence tax" extorted from the seccies themselves.

Barkley always accepted his own share of the rake-offs, but it had griped him. Once you started making accommodations with scum like the seccies, it could only get worse in his opinion. Respect and fear started to erode under those circumstances, and it was damned well time to put that fear back into Mendel's seccies.

Those of them who survived, at least.

The high, shrill whine of the neural whips sang suddenly louder, only to be buried an instant later under the even shriller sound of human screams. Very *young* human screams. At their present settings, a neural whip would have been lethal to four out of five fully adult humans in good physical condition.

Even the one in five who might have survived would
have suffered massive damage to his nervous system.
He would almost certainly have been paralyzed for
life below the point at which the whip contacted his
body, and it was entirely probable that he would have
suffered catastrophic brain damage, as well.

A child under fifteen T-years old stood no chance
at all against that agonizing form of death.

Some deeply buried core of decency, even in an
Amos Barkley, cringed as the first three kids went
down. But it was very deeply buried, that ragged,
shopworn decency—deeply enough he had no difficulty
ignoring it. Besides, plenty of his fellow troopers' kids
had been incinerated in the Dobzhansky explosion and
the Blue Lagoon Park attack. And in the words of an
old, old cliché of which Barkley had always been fond,
nits made lice. Besides, there'd always be more where
they'd come from. The damned seccies bred like flies!

Another fleeing child stumbled, almost falling. Her
mother snatched at her arm, yanking her up, but the
two of them had been delayed just long enough. Toby
Qorolas, Barkley's section corporal, brought his neural
whip around and almost casually clubbed both of them
to the pavement. The little girl didn't even scream,
but her mother certainly did.

❖   ❖   ❖

Shasta McGuire had never thought of himself as
a particularly good man, which was reasonable—he
wasn't one. What he was, was just over two meters in
height, with an ugly, scarred face, knuckles that were
even more heavily scarred, and a twenty-T-year history
as one of Maysayuki Franconi's enforcers. Franconi
probably wouldn't have qualified for sainthood in most

people's eyes, either, but she'd always done her best to run her territory with a minimum of unnecessary bloodshed. By and large, she'd succeeded in doing just that. And when bloodshed *had* been necessary, there'd always been McGuire.

The Sukharov Territory had never been large—gangs which operated in the industrial "fire breaks" between the seccy residential towers had to be careful about emerging too far into the light—but it had been well organized. Franconi had headed that organization for the better part of forty T-years, and she'd reached a mutually profitable understanding with Sukharov Light Industries long ago. And with OPS, for that matter. Her territory had been largely spared after the Green Pines bombing, although enough people who lived in it had lost relatives—or had them beaten and crippled—for the lesson in terror to be fully absorbed. The instant they'd heard about the new, devastating chain of attacks, they'd known who'd be blamed and gone to ground.

Unfortunately, this time the Sukharov Territory's immunity had shattered.

McGuire stood at Franconi's shoulder, gazing down from her office window at the group of Public Safety troopers clubbing down women and children with their neural whips, and something deep inside him snarled. Franconi was scarcely half his height, a slender woman with silver-streaked dark hair, and he could see entirely too clearly over her head.

"Bastards!"

The single word rumbled up from his thick throat like the first pumice cloud from an active volcano, and his hand clenched around the butt of his holstered pulser. Neither he nor his boss could hear the shrieks through the sealed window, but they didn't need to.

Franconi stood motionless, gazing down with basilisk eyes for a dozen slow breaths. Then she turned from the window, lifting those stony eyes to her chief enforcer's face.

"Break out the heavy stuff, Shasta," she said, her voice cold and even harder than her eyes.

He stared at her for a moment, stunned by the order. Like most of Mendel's gangs, Franconi's had assembled a potent arsenal over the years. Mostly small arms: pulsers, flechette guns, the occasional civilian-grade pulse rifle. But along with that was her small cache of military-grade weapons. Heavy pulse rifles, light tribarrels, even a handful of antitank weapons and man portable surface-to-air missiles. She'd never really expected to need them, but—again, like most of Mendel's gangs—she'd believed in rainy days and making preparation against them. Yet McGuire knew she'd never been insane enough to even consider using them against any of the planetary security forces.

Until now, at least.

"You sure about that, boss?" he rumbled, yet there was surprisingly little surprise in his voice.

"Damned right I am," Franconi said. "That's how they're *starting out*, Shasta—you think it's not going to get one hell of a lot worse before they're done?" Her lips worked as if she wanted to spit, but she only shook her head sharply. "There's not going to be enough left of our territory to sweep up in an old-fashioned dustpan, and if those bastards think they can come in here and just slaughter *my* people and walk right back out again, they're fucking wrong! Break out the heavy stuff," she repeated, crossing to her desk and yanking open a drawer. She reached into it for the heavy military-grade pulser which had once been her father's and checked the magazine and the power level expertly.

"*Now*, Shasta," she said, turning to face him with the weapon in her hand. "I want every one of our people here in the tower armed and downstairs to meet me in five frigging minutes! Is that clear?"

"Yes, Ma'am!" McGuire said.

It was insane, of course. He knew that as well as she did. They weren't even one of the middle-sized gangs, far less one of the big outfits like Dusek's or Bachue the Nose's. They'd be like spit on a griddle in one of the seccy greasy spoons when OPS or MISD came calling. It couldn't end any other way; Shasta McGuire had seen too much of life in Mendel's seccy district to have any illusions on that score.

And it didn't matter.

"We'll be there, boss," he promised her, and headed for the office door, already reaching for his personal com.

✧　　✧　　✧

Sergeant Barkley's section turned the corner at the eastern edge of Sukharov Tower. A few of the seccies behind them were still twitching. One of them was even trying to crawl across the body-littered pavement, but he and his troopers couldn't be bothered to go back and clean up. They were too many fresh prey waiting ahead of them, and the sweet, hot taste of blood was in their mouths. They'd find—

Barkley straightened suddenly, wheeling around as a crimson caret flashed at the corner of his helmet visor HUD. Someone was lasing him!

He just had time to see Shasta McGuire lying prone behind an overturned garbage can with the military tribarrel braced across it. The sighting dot was directly in the center of his chest, and his light, unpowered armor—fully adequate to resist knives, clubs, improvised weapons, possibly even light pulser fire, if he was lucky—was no use at all against the tribarrel's hypersonic five-millimeter darts.

None of the rest of Amos Barkley's section—or Gunther Surekha's—survived him by more than twenty-seven seconds.

❖ ❖ ❖

"You're not serious!"

Lieutenant General Gillian Drescher gazed across her desk at Colonel Byrum Bartel, her chief of staff, her almond-shaped eyes narrowed in something that wasn't so much disbelief as a desire to disbelieve. After Green Pines, she'd thought she'd seen just about anything that could happen during her three years as the commander of the Capital District of the Mesan Planetary Peaceforce.

Apparently, she'd been wrong.

"The Safeties got their asses kicked, Ma'am," Bartel said flatly. The colonel was a tall, beefy man, half again his diminutive superior's height and as fair-haired and complected as she was dark-haired. "They thought this was going to be just another Green Pines sweep, and they were wrong. According to the preliminary reports, they took something like five hundred casualties, most of them fatal." He grimaced. "We've got surveillance video of most of the firefights, and what happened to any of the Safeties the mob got its hands on wasn't pretty."

Bartel had a gift for understatement, Drescher thought. She didn't need to see the video he'd mentioned to be able to picture what must have happened to any OPS trooper who'd fallen into seccy hands. She wasn't going to shed any tears for the bastards, either. While she had a certain grudging respect for the Security Directorate, the Safeties had never been anything remotely approaching soldiers. They hadn't even been very effective policemen, for that matter. What they *had* been was a blunt instrument used to bloody the seccies' heads whenever they seemed to be getting uppity. From the moment she'd been briefed on Operation Rat Catcher, she'd been unhappy about the notion of allowing Public Safety off its leash this way.

From the sound of it, she hadn't been unhappy enough.

"How did even Selig's idiots put their foot in it that badly?" she demanded.

"It looks like nobody counted on the seccy crime bosses." Bartel shook his head with a disgusted expression. "When they realized the Safeties were deliberately running up the body count—that it wasn't just a case of collateral damage this time around—some of the gang members started shooting back. Mostly with nothing heavier than pulsers, at first. Just whatever carry weapons they had with them when the ball dropped. But within the first half hour or so, they started breaking out heavier weapons. Military-grade tribarrels, grenade launchers—even a couple of plasma rifles."

His eyes met Drescher's, and the general nodded ever so slightly, acknowledging what he hadn't said. Military-grade weapons, especially plasma weapons, had almost certainly come from the Peaceforce's own stocks. It was common knowledge, if never discussed, that armory clerks and ordnance officers occasionally disposed of surplus weapons—and, in some cases, *non*surplus weapons—in black market transactions. A lot of those weapons went to various system-based and transstellar corporations' covert operations units, but at least some of them had been falling into the hands of seccy criminal organizations for decades. In fact, Drescher and Bartel had been warning people for T-years, and especially since Green Pines, that the seccies had almost certainly gotten their hands on a lot more—and a lot more *potent*—weaponry than anyone had ever acknowledged.

They'd also cracked down on the Peaceforce. Several of those armory clerks and two field grade officers had been court-martialed and severely punished for selling arms under their control, but the crackdown had been all too much like locking the barn door after the horse had been stolen. For that matter, far more weapons had certainly been quietly transferred to seccy ownership by corrupt members of the OPS and the Internal Security Directorate than by the Peaceforce. Which offered its own painful irony just at the moment, she supposed.

"It looks like the first organized seccy response was around the Sukharov manufacturing center," Bartel continued. "That one took out two complete sections of Safeties before any of them even got out a mayday. It's gotten worse since then, of course."

"How much worse? And what's happening now?" Drescher asked.

"A *lot* worse, Ma'am. And they're sending in the

Misties," Bartel told her. "Howell's got blood in his eye, too. They'll be going in hot, with shoot on sight orders."

"Wonderful." Drescher pinched the bridge of her nose. "And just what are his objectives?"

"He's planning to sweep the central arc of the northern seccy ring and drive as many of them as possible towards Neue Rostock and Hancock, then punch out both towers. Dusek's got one of the biggest—and almost certainly the best trained and disciplined—gangs, and a lot of seccies have already refugeed towards Neue Rostock. Bachue the Nose has even more warm bodies in her organization in Hancock than he does in Neue Rostock. They're not as cohesive and probably not as well armed, but they've got a reputation as tough, hardnosed bastards, and most of the seccies who didn't make for Neue Rostock seem to have headed her way."

"He's planning to *assault* residential towers?"

"Yes, Ma'am." Bartel's expression showed his opinion of that particular notion. "The idea, as I understand it, is to pen the seccies up in one convenient spot, then kick in the doors and clean them out once and for all."

"Wonderful. Just frigging wonderful!"

Drescher suppressed a sudden urge to break something, but she wasn't really surprised. Bentley Howell was good-looking and projected an aura of command—to the easily impressed, at least—but she sometimes wondered if he had two brain cells to rub together. Oh, he was reasonably intelligent in a lot of ways, but his contempt for seccies was bottomless, and it had led him into seriously underestimating them on several occasions she could think of right offhand. Once his prejudices engaged, his brain *dis*engaged, and she had a sinking sensation it was going to be up to her to clean up one of his more spectacular messes.

The idiot probably thinks it's going to be a routine corridor-clearing exercise, she thought disgustedly. *From what Byrum's saying, he and his people are going to be in for one hell of a painful surprise if that is what he thinks, though. It's one thing to break up riots, or to sweep a single neighborhood in one of the towers to pick up a specific suspect, but this is going to be an entirely different animal.*

She thought about that for another moment or two. She really didn't like Howell, and he didn't like her very much, either. But the Peaceforce was specifically tasked to stand behind OPS and MISD operations in case heavier support was needed. For that matter, the Mesan Planetary Peaceforce's entire reason for being, really, was to respond to threats of seccy or slave unrest before they turned into genuine rebellion.

And, of course, to watch MISD like a hawk...and vice versa, she reminded herself.

The system government deliberately encouraged a certain degree of mutual antagonism between the Internal Security Directorate and the Peaceforce. OPS and MISD had significantly more combined manpower than the MPP, but the MPP had one hell of a lot more *firepower* than either—or both—of François McGillicuddy's agencies, and it answered to General Caspar Alpina. Alpina was the Planetary Peaceforce's senior uniformed officer, and under the Mesan constitution, *he* answered directly to CEO Ward, not McGillicuddy. The regular police forces, the ones that dealt with criminal investigations and peacekeeping among Mesa's full citizens, stood completely outside the organizations specifically tasked with suppressing any seccy or slave unrest, of course. As such, even their SWAT teams had precious little in the way of heavy weapons. But the various security agencies had *lots* of weapons, ranging upward from OPS' neural whips and flechette guns through MISD's armored air cars, tribarrels, and plasma rifles to the MPP's armored fighting vehicles, plasma *cannon*, and assault shuttles. Modern armies tended to be quite small, since there was no real point trying to defend a planetary surface if someone else controlled that planet's orbital space, and technically—*technically*—not even the Planetary Peaceforce was actually an "army," at all. But when roughly a third of the planetary population had to worry about mass uprisings from the other *two* thirds, the people responsible for preventing those uprisings needed plenty of firepower.

And their civilian masters needed to be confident that the people who commanded all that firepower weren't going to be tempted to get together and use it to get rid of the aforesaid civilian masters. Actively fostering the tension between MISD and the MPP was one way to help prevent that from happening.

Unfortunately, that tension could also produce unhappy consequences when McGillicuddy's security agencies and Alpina's Peaceforce needed to cooperate.

Crap, Drescher thought. *I don't have a choice. I have to com the bastard.*

She punched a dedicated button on her desk com and sat back. A few seconds later, a young man in MISD uniform appeared on her display.

"Internal Security Directorate, office of Commissioner Howell," he said crisply. It was like Howell to use a live human to run his switchboard rather than letting the automated systems get on with it, the general thought disgustedly.

"This is Lieutenant General Drescher," she told him. "I need to speak to the Commissioner. Immediately."

"Hold, please," the lieutenant replied. His image disappeared, replaced by MISD's wallpaper, but the mailed fist and dagger of the Security Directorate's insignia disappeared quickly.

"General Drescher." Bentley Howell nodded his head in acknowledgment as his image replaced the wallpaper's. "What can I do for you?"

"I understand you're preparing to launch a sweep of Neue Rostock and Hancock," Drescher said, coming straight to the point, although calling what he intended to do a "sweep" was clearly an enormous understatement.

"That's right." Howell nodded again. "I'm sending in two regiments—the Fourth and the Nineteenth."

"I see." Drescher looked at him for a moment, then cocked her head. "Under the circumstances, don't you think it would be a good idea for us to liaise with each other? Make sure we're all on the same screen if things turn ugly."

Turn ugly again, *you ass*, she added mentally.

"Liaise?" Howell looked at her as if she were speaking an unknown tongue. "I'm sending my people in loaded for bear, General. Things are going to turn 'ugly,' all right, but not for them!"

"Commissioner, you're talking about regiment-sized attacks on residential towers," she pointed out as calmly as she could. "We've never done anything like that before, even after Green Pines. And the seccies have already demonstrated they're in possession of heavier weapons than anything they've ever shown us before. This is *not* going to be a cakewalk."

"Nobody thinks it is, General." Howell's tone was much cooler than it had been, and his eyes were even colder. "They're still seccies, though. They'll break quickly enough if they see us coming in hard and fast."

"These aren't 'just' seccies, Commissioner," Drescher said. "They're organized groups with weapons heavier than anything we've ever faced before, and they're going to be fighting on their own ground inside those damned towers."

"Your 'organized groups' are packs of common criminals and seccy street scum, General. Are you suggesting that their discipline's going to be able to match *my* people's?" His upper lip curled. "They'll run for their kennels as soon as they figure out what's happening!"

"I wouldn't count too heavily on that, if I were you," Drescher said. "And tower assaults—especially on towers like Neue Rostock and Hancock—are one of the nightmare scenarios we've spent a lot of time thinking about over here. Those aren't like Rasmussen or Tyler Tower, Commissioner. You can't envelop them vertically using the atriums and air shafts, and the way their interiors lay out, they're even more damage resistant than one of the citizen towers. Trust me, if it turns into a serious firefight inside one of those towers, you're going to lose a *lot* of people. Frankly, the best way to take one of them would be to seal it off and wait it out. Sooner or later the people inside it are going to run out of food, at which point they either come out and surrender or starve. Unfortunately, that takes time, and I'm fully aware that the General Board wants this concluded as quickly as possible. But if we want to do it quickly, and if everybody's committed to assaulting them, then you need to open them up with kinetic weapons before you go poking your head into the dragon's mouth."

"You want to use *KEWs* inside Mendel?" Howell shook his head incredulously. "You really think you're going to get authorization for that?"

"I'm aware that the General Board's already discussed the option," Drescher replied in a much cooler tone of her own. "I believe, however, that at that point the discussion centered around using KEWs to completely take out the towers. There are smaller sledgehammers available, Commissioner, and enough blows from a *little* hammer will do the job of a great *big* one."

"I've got all the hammers I'm going to need," Howell said flatly.

Drescher gazed at his com image for a moment. He probably really believed that, she thought. And it was even remotely possible—*remotely* possible—he could be right...assuming Jurgen Dusek and Bachue Emmett and their people broke a hell of a lot faster than Maysayuki Franconi's had.

She wasn't very fond of the MISD, and she didn't really much like Howell, but this time she found herself hoping he was right and she was wrong. Because she obviously wasn't going to change his mind, and if he wasn't right—and if she was—he was going to discover that a seccy slum's residential tower was one of the toughest, most intricately subdivided fortresses the human race had ever built.

CHAPTER 58

"—and sweep northeast, towards Hancock," Colonel Teodosio MacKane, CO, 4th Regiment, Mesan Internal Security Directorate said, jabbing his index finger at the holographic display in his lightly armored Cyclops command vehicle. "And while the Nineteenth's doing that, we're going to sweep north*west*, towards Neue Rostock. Randy," he looked up to dart a ferocious look at Major Randall Myers, commanding officer of his 2nd Battalion, "your people are going to take point. Brockie"—those angry eyes moved to Major Camelia Brockmann, 1st Battalion's CO—"you'll be watching Randy's back, and I want you to peel off two companies as our reserve."

Both majors nodded their understanding. Brockmann seemed a little less enthusiastic than Myers did, MacKane thought. It wasn't that she looked hesitant, or afraid. She just didn't seem as fired up and ready to go as Myers obviously was. That was the main reason he picked 2nd Battalion to lead and 1st Battalion as its supporting element. Myers and his company commanders were clearly eager to get to grips with the seccies who'd mauled the Public Safety troopers so badly, and MacKane wanted someone who was ready to kick ass leading the way. It wasn't that anyone in the MISD felt all warm and fuzzy where OPS was concerned, but it was a really bad idea to let seccies get the mistaken notion that they could kill *any* security troops without paying the sort of price that would give any survivors, their children, their grandchildren, and their *great*-grandchildren nightmares.

"All right, then. Get back to your units. We kick off in twenty minutes."

❖   ❖   ❖

"What now, Ferguson?"

Captain Gavin Shultz sounded more than a little exasperated as he glared at Bravo Company's problem child. Schultz had commanded Bravo for almost three T-years, and Lieutenant Connor Ferguson had commanded Bravo's 2nd Platoon—and been a pain in Shultz's ass—for just over one of those years. To be honest, Shultz had never been able to figure out why Ferguson had joined the Security Directorate in the first place. The man's mind—or heart, at least—simply wasn't in the job, and he was a stickler for following rules and procedures, the sort who didn't seem to grasp that sometimes you just had to ignore The Book and get the fucking job *done*. Schultz had known a few others like Ferguson, people who prided themselves on their "professionalism" but didn't have the guts when the dirty work came along. Who thought they could keep the fucking seccies in their place without breaking a lot of heads and an occasional neck in the process.

Schultz hadn't heard Regan Snyder talking about the "seccy problem" at the Directors' conference, but if he had, he would have endorsed her sentiments strongly. He knew exactly why *he'd* joined the MISD eighteen years ago. Whatever people like Ferguson might think, *he* knew—like Snyder—that the mere existence of the seccies owed itself to a centuries-old blunder which had gifted later generations of Mesans with a problem that could only get worse. And it had. Anyone with eyes to see had known that even before Green Pines. Seccies were scum, genetically indistinguishable from the slaves who'd spawned them, and they bred like flies. Everyone knew they routinely evaded the birth licenses citizens abode by, and they packed into their filthy warrens like rats, scurrying around in their own filth. And they were always *there*, always turning up on the news, reminding people that the galaxy wasn't perfect. There was always some stupid damn intellectual to whine about how *terribly* the seccies were treated, how restricting them to second-class citizenship was a blight on the honor of Mesa's full citizens. But worse—worst of all—their mere existence was a constant, standing threat to Mesa's fundamental security. They'd come from slaves, been manumitted, granted their freedom, and if it could happen to *their* ancestors, then why shouldn't the *current* generation of slaves aspire to the same thing? And it was that kind of aspiration that led to things like Green Pines or Dobzhansky.

That was what people like Ferguson never seemed to grasp, and it was why Gavin Shultz had joined the Champions of Safety and Order when he was only twenty-three years old. The CoSO wasn't quite legal, but it wasn't really *ill*egal, either. Its members understood that seccies had to be kept in their place, and Shultz, who'd risen to the rank of Champion First, had done his bit—after hours and purely on his own time, of course—to teach quite a few seccies their places over the years. Of course, he also used his official contacts to figure out which of the seccies needed tutoring, as well. That was one reason he *loved* his job.

And the stupidity of people who couldn't see the truth when it stared them straight in the face was one of the reasons he had very little patience with people like Connor Ferguson.

"I just wanted to be clear on the rules of engagement, Sir," Ferguson said now.

At only a hundred and seventy-seven centimeters, Ferguson looked like a teenager beside the taller, much more powerfully built Shultz, even in his utility armor. The MISD's UA wasn't quite the equal of battle armor, for a lot of reasons, starting with cost. Battle armor was expensive, and not even an affluent star system like Mesa had an unlimited budget. Worse, the corporate interests who managed Mesa had no desire to pay any more taxes than they absolutely had to, which meant that the Mesa System government's budget got a substantially smaller slice of the Gross System Product than was the case for most other wealthy systems. Besides, MISD troopers didn't really need all-up battle armor. They weren't going to be fighting in a vacuum; a lot of their combat missions *were* going to be inside structures, where battle armor's bulk could be a distinct disadvantage in close quarters combat; and they weren't likely to need to carry full-scale plasma cannon around with them. Even more to the point, battle armor was an energy hog; utility armor got over three times the endurance off of little more than two thirds the power, which meant its wearer could remain on station and in action for five times as long off a single set of power packs. "Dwell time" was a major consideration in peacekeeping missions, and any MISD trooper would agree that more time out at the sharp edge was worth the sacrifice of a few bells and whistles. But if UA was more compact than battle armor, it was certainly bulky enough to project an aura of brute, threatening power, especially in the eyes of someone who had no armor at all, and MISD's designers had deliberately enhanced that aspect of it. It was inky black, trimmed in scarlet, with exaggerated, spiky pauldrons, spike-knuckled gauntlets, and one-way mirrored visors marked with the MSID's gauntlet and dagger insignia.

At the moment, Ferguson's visor was raised, and Shultz saw the unhappiness in his brown eyes.

"I believe the colonel was perfectly clear about the rules of engagement," the captain said coldly. "If you failed to understand him, however, I'll clarify for you. We're operating under Rules of Engagement Omega, Lieutenant Ferguson."

"I understood that, Sir," Ferguson said stubbornly. "I just want to be perfectly clear about taking prisoners and about minors."

Shultz glared at him. ROE Omega called for the immediate application of lethal force; allowed the use of all available and necessary supports—including airstrikes, armor, and indirect fire up to but not including KEW strikes—all released to frontline commanders on an on-call basis; and authorized the engagement of any potential threat without regard to possible collateral damage. The keywords, as Shultz and Ferguson both understood perfectly well, were "*potential* threat." Officially, that simply freed an officer's hands to deal with enemies who hadn't already clearly resolved whether or not they were "potential" dangers by direct hostile action. In fact, it could readily be construed to cover *any* situation, because in an operation like Rat Catcher—especially after it had already gone so spectacularly wrong earlier in the day—a unit commander could construe just about anything as a "potential threat."

The universe was an imperfect place, however, and even MISD had been forced to cave to public opinion—and appearances—in some respects. The bleeding hearts could always be expected to whine about the rigor reality required, and there was always somebody to point to the "interstellar public relations" consequences of being *too* forthright in anything that was committed to writing and available as part of the public record. That was why even under ROE Omega, someone attempting to surrender was supposed to be allowed to do so and why MISD personnel were supposed to minimize casualties, especially among minor children. And unless Shultz was sadly mistaken, Ferguson had his armor's tac systems online, which meant he was almost certainly recording this entire conversation. It would be just like the sanctimonious SOB, and there was no telling how a court of inquiry might...misconstrue anything that wasn't by The Book.

"All right, all right," the captain said testily. "If the fucking bastards want to surrender—and if they get their goddamn hands up quick enough—let 'em. And if you can tell it's a kid, and if it's not carrying a grenade around with it, you can secure it and hand it over to the consolidation teams. Is that clear enough?"

"Yes, Sir. Thank you, Sir."

Connor saluted, closed his UA's visor, and headed back to his platoon with Gavin Shultz's glare boring holes in his back the entire way.

◇   ◇   ◇

Section Sergeant Kayla Barrett watched Lieutenant Ferguson from behind the protective concealment of her visor with smoldering eyes as he walked back toward her. Most of the time, Barrett found Ferguson tolerable enough. Too much of a goody-goody two-shoes for a MISD combat officer, maybe, but fair-minded and firm about discipline and training without descending into martinet territory. But today wasn't "most of the time," and *today* Kayla Barrett had very little patience for anyone who wasn't as eager to get it stuck in as she was.

She stood very still, hazel eyes hard, and felt herself quivering with rage. Before the Blue Lagoon Park atrocity, she'd had a brother, a sister, a sister-in-law, two nieces, and a nephew. Today, she had none of them, and nothing in heaven or hell was going to stop her from avenging those deaths. She didn't know if anyone in front of her had personally had anything at all to do with that attack, and it didn't matter. If they hadn't done it themselves, they'd still produced whoever had. Those murderers had come out of the seccies, they were hiding *among* the seccies, and that meant they were being hidden *by* the seccies. The evidence was clear enough on that . . . and that was all she had to know.

Barrett had never joined the Champions of Safety and Order like Captain Shultz, but she knew *he* had, and she'd been tempted a time or two herself. Today, she wished she had. In fact, that was something she intended to look into when they pulled back to barracks.

But for now—

"Get them saddled up, Section Sergeant," Lieutenant Ferguson said. "We move in in five minutes."

"Yes, *Sir!*"

❖   ❖   ❖

"Shit—those're Misties!" Nine-Finger Jake exclaimed.

He and Jenney the Hand crouched in the mouth of a drainage culvert on the edge of Trondheim Park. Trondheim wasn't that much of a park compared to the facilities available to the children of full citizens, but it was normally kept neat and clean and it offered a wide green space, dotted with only moderately run-down playground equipment, around a small pond suitable for toy boats or wading, and it was usually well populated by kids.

Today it was deserted, aside from the dozen or so bodies scattered across it. Most of those bodies belonged to seccies, but two of them had been OPS troopers. The Safeties had been stripped of their equipment, and Nine-Finger had liberated their secure coms in the process. He'd sent one of them farther up the line to Jurgen Dusek, but he'd kept the other, and he'd been listening to it for the last couple of hours. He'd rather enjoyed the panic he'd heard in the voices of the Safeties once they realized they weren't going to have things their own way for a change, and he'd taken a savage delight in the steadily mounting casualty totals they'd been announcing. But Nine-Finger had been around for almost seventy years. He'd known how Security was going to respond to the Safeties' heavy losses. Still, he hadn't expected to see MISD troopers this soon.

"Shit," Jenney muttered beside him.

Technically, neither she nor the considerably older

Nine-Finger were formally associated with the Dusek Organization. They were independents, but any independent knew enough to stay on good terms with the local boss, and Dusek was more reasonable than most. As long as they paid the turf fees he charged—and they weren't exorbitant—independents were welcome to fill any of the niches between his organization's main areas of operation. In fact, he often had odds and ends of jobs he was willing to farm out to the independents who kept their noses clean and followed the rules . . . the very first one of which was that they never, *ever* made any grief for the "civilians" living in his district. Nobody got robbed, beaten up, or raped in the Neu Rostock District unless they'd crossed the line themselves first. Dusek took that sort of thing seriously—violence and casual thievery weren't just bad for business; they were also things the people in his district expected him to hold to a minimum—and it looked like he felt even more strongly about it than Jenney had realized.

He'd already put out the word that Neue Rostock Tower was buckling down for heavy action, and she knew she and Nine-Finger could find a place there. But the western boundary of Trondheim was Eaker Boulevard, one of the underground pedestrian ways—a seccy pedestrian way, of course, which meant its powered slidewalks worked no more than half the time—and an awful lot of seccies were fleeing towards whatever refuge they could find on foot, now that public transportation outside the towers themselves had been shut down by the Mendel authorities. Working slidewalks or not, Eaker Boulevard was one of the primary accesses to Neue Rostock; if it was blocked, a lot of people trying to find safety for themselves and their families would be caught in the open or trapped in its underground portions. As independents, she and Nine-Finger had no formally assigned role in the Dusek Organization's defensive plans, so they'd appointed themselves as lookouts for the crowds of civilians following the boulevard towards the hoped-for safety of the boss's tower.

"What the fuck do we do now?" she asked, watching the UA-clad figures step into the open and begin moving methodically across the park.

"Damned if I know," Nine-Finger replied, rubbing his depilated scalp with the maimed left hand which had earned him his nickname. "I was hoping it'd be more Safeties, but these pop guns—" a twitch of his head indicated the civilian pulse rifles he and Jenney had been issued "—aren't going to do much against UA suits."

"What're those bastards in front carrying?" Jenney asked nervously. "Don't look like pulse rifles or flechette guns to me!"

"That's because they aren't," Nine-Finger said grimly. "Those're neural disruptors, girl."

Jenney shuddered. She'd never actually seen a disruptor used, not in person, but she'd seen them on HD, and one of her cousins had lost the use of her right arm after a Safety casually lashed out with a neural whip in a "crowd clearing" operation. Disruptors used exactly the same tech, but they were a lot more powerful than any neural whip, and a whip was no more than a meter or so in length. That was all the range it had, whereas disruptors could kill someone at as much as a hundred and fifty meters. They were shorter ranged than pulse rifles and far less efficient at simply killing people than flechette guns, but the Misties didn't use them because they were *efficient*; they used them because they were terror weapons. Even someone who might face a pulser dart with a snarl of defiance might think twice—or even three times—about facing a disruptor.

"What—" She stopped and swallowed hard. "What do we—?"

She swallowed again, and Nine-Finger turned his head to give her a grim, humorless smile. Then he handed her the com he'd looted from the Safeties' bodies.

"What *you* do is shag ass back to Eaker Boulevard," he told her. "Take this with you. Dusek'll have some of his people out trying to manage traffic. Find one of them and give it to him. Then head for Neue Rostock yourself. They're going to need every shooter they can find before this is over."

"*Me?* What about *you?*"

"Me, I'm thinking I've let the fucking Safeties and Misties hammer enough people I cared about." Nine-Finger's eyes were back on the approaching MISD troops. "Time I did a little hammering of my own."

"Are you fucking *crazy?* They'll *kill* you, Nine-Finger!"

"A man's got to die doing something," he replied. "Might's well be something I *enjoy* doing and not just sleepin' in bed. 'Sides, I've got a surprise'r two for those bastards. Now *get*, girl!"

Jenney darted one more agonized look at his face, torn by terror, fear, hope, and shame at the thought of leaving him behind, but he only quirked one corner of his mouth and jerked his head towards Eaker Boulevard.

She gave his shoulder one quick, fierce squeeze, then disappeared down the culvert at a run.

❖   ❖   ❖

Trooper 1/c Jubair Azocar watched his HUD with one eye but kept the other peeled for things the HUD might overlook. He'd found out the hard way that his UA's sensors were biased in favor of threats its onboard computer recognized and tended to ignore things that didn't fall neatly into its threat hierarchies. It looked for power sources, infrared signatures associated with vehicles or opponents in powered armor, and large numbers of individual IR signatures that its analysis indicated were moving—or positioned—to act cooperatively. Within those parameters, it was very, very good. *Outside* those parameters, it was dumb as a rock. Of course, anything it missed spotting was unlikely to be dangerous enough to actually get through Azocar's armor, but he and the rest of Bravo Company had passed at least twenty or thirty dead Safeties already. He had no desire to suffer the same fate they had.

He paused suddenly, raising his right hand in the ancient visual command to stop for the benefit of the riflemen covering his flanks.

"Central, Bravo-Two-Niner," he said. "Patch Bravo-Zero-Three." He waited a single heartbeat as the communications net's AI connected him to Sergeant Barrett. Then—

"Bravo-Two-Niner, Zero-Three," Kayla Barrett's voice said in his ear bud. "Go."

"I've got what looks like one Tango about six hundred

meters west of r

lighting the ice

displayed it

quartet of

for som

the d

on A

"Wha

"Just sitti

real likely he'd

something, though.

"Well, we're under t

almost hear her shrug in

"Gotcha, Sarge," he replie

cautiously towards the motionles

Normally, Azocar would have be

of his section's heavy tribarrels. Or he

been carrying the plasma rifle which was his

alternate armament. But today, he'd been issu

of the neural disruptors, and after the thousan

civilians these terrorist bastards had killed—an

the dead Safeties he'd passed on the way here—

was ready to use it. In fact, he was looking *forwa*

to using it...a lot.

He wasn't stupid, however, and he made sure his

flanking teammates were covering his ass with their

pulse rifles. The only real drawback of the disrup-

tor, aside from its weight, which was a bitch, was its

relatively short range. On the other hand, his sensors

had pretty clearly identified the Tango's weapon as a

light civilian-model pulse rifle. That had been plenty

to slaughter the Safeties, in their lighter, unpowered

body armor, but it wasn't going to do squat against

meant the short range of
atter at all.

adows of the picnic shelters.
ustic looking, the tough plas-
on disguised—imperfectly—to
e bark still on them, and his
he heart shape and interlocking
eccy had laboriously carved into
l. It had clearly been done with
ade, not a lasergraver, and doing
ave taken hours.

way, *stupid way to spend your time*, he
at ptuously, but his eyes never stopped
ught roundings, alert for any threat. There
eepi helters were empty with a solid ceram-
wasn't offered no place to leave booby traps
acre ers, and there wasn't anywhere anyone
or den under the picnic tables, either.

⬦   ⬦   ⬦

er Jake watched the trio of Misties head-
towards his position in the culvert. He'd
they'd come his way—the culvert was
st, best protected route from this side of
m Park to Eaker Boulevard, and unlike cer-
ther aspects of the area around Neue Rostock,
as probably on the city maps they'd uploaded for
he operation. On the other hand, the probability
that they'd come this way was the entire reason he'd
chosen this particular position.

He smiled at the thought. It was the sort of smile
a wolverine might smile, or perhaps a wounded tiger
as it watched the hunting party come within its reach.
There were a few things he knew about Trondheim

meters west of my present position," he said, high-lighting the icon on his HUD, which simultaneously displayed it on Barrett's. It was on the far side of a quartet of picnic shelters, in exactly the right place for someone to be hunkered down in the mouth of the drainage culvert showing on the terrain overlay on Azocar's HUD.

"What's he doing?" Barrett asked.

"Just sitting there, near's I can tell. Doesn't seem real likely he'd be hanging around if he wasn't up to *something*, though."

"Well, we're under the Omega rules." Azocar could almost hear her shrug in her voice. "Waste his ass."

"Gotcha, Sarge," he replied, and started moving cautiously towards the motionless icon.

Normally, Azocar would have been carrying one of his section's heavy tribarrels. Or he might have been carrying the plasma rifle which was his standard alternate armament. But today, he'd been issued one of the neural disruptors, and after the thousands of civilians these terrorist bastards had killed—and all the dead Safeties he'd passed on the way here—he was ready to use it. In fact, he was looking *forward* to using it . . . a lot.

He wasn't stupid, however, and he made sure his flanking teammates were covering his ass with their pulse rifles. The only real drawback of the disruptor, aside from its weight, which was a bitch, was its relatively short range. On the other hand, his sensors had pretty clearly identified the Tango's weapon as a light civilian-model pulse rifle. That had been plenty to slaughter the Safeties, in their lighter, unpowered body armor, but it wasn't going to do squat against utility armor. And that meant the short range of Azocar's weapon didn't matter at all.

He stepped into the shadows of the picnic shelters. They were deliberately rustic looking, the tough plastics of their construction disguised—imperfectly—to look like logs with the bark still on them, and his lip curled as he saw the heart shape and interlocking initials some stupid seccy had laboriously carved into the rocklike material. It had clearly been done with an old-fashioned blade, not a lasergraver, and doing it that way must have taken hours.

What a fucking stupid way to spend your time, he thought contemptuously, but his eyes never stopped sweeping his surroundings, alert for any threat. There wasn't one. The shelters were empty, with a solid ceramacrete floor that offered no place to leave booby traps or hide ambushers, and there wasn't anywhere anyone could have hidden under the picnic tables, either.

❖   ❖   ❖

Nine-Finger Jake watched the trio of Misties heading directly towards his position in the culvert. He'd been afraid they'd come his way—the culvert was the shortest, best protected route from this side of Trondheim Park to Eaker Boulevard, and unlike certain other aspects of the area around Neue Rostock, it was probably on the city maps they'd uploaded for the operation. On the other hand, the probability that they'd come this way was the entire reason he'd chosen this particular position.

He smiled at the thought. It was the sort of smile a wolverine might smile, or perhaps a wounded tiger as it watched the hunting party come within its reach. There were a few things he knew about Trondheim

Park that the Misties didn't, and he waited patiently, his eyes on the one with the disruptor. Another three meters, he thought, and then—

❖ ❖ ❖

Jubair Azocar's computer's estimate of the threat potential of Nine-Finger Jake's pulse rifle had been completely accurate. However, it had failed to notice a few other minor items. Probably because they were so primitive that they didn't register as threats at all. After all, what could be particularly dangerous about a couple of abandoned, old-fashioned gas grills?

As Azocar stepped between them, his computer and he found out.

❖ ❖ ❖

Nine-Finger pressed the button.

Gas grills for recreational cooking had been around for more than two thousand years, and they hadn't changed a great deal over that long, long period. Most of them still used butane, and most of their storage bottles stored the gas at about the same fourteen bars of pressure which had been the norm since well before humankind ever left the Sol System. These grills, however, were no longer quite standard. Nine-Finger had been an off-the-books employee in Sukharov for almost thirty years, and he'd made a few selections from Sukharov Tower after the initial OPS advance had been driven back. Among other things, he'd helped himself to, a pair of air car hydrogen tanks. They were only about twenty percent bigger than the gas grills' normal bottles, which meant they could just be squeezed into the same space under the burners, but the gas inside them was stored in liquid form... at *eight hundred* bars of pressure.

When Nine-Finger pressed the button, the catalyst cutting heads he'd installed around each hydrogen tank's feed valves activated. It was like closing the blades of a hedge trimmer on a green branch; the cutting heads sliced through the tanks' tough synthetics without fuss or bother . . . and without striking a single spark.

Fortunately, Nine-Finger had thoughtfully positioned the tanks valve-up. Instead of heading for the sky like rockets, the sudden twin hurricanes of erupting hydrogen shrieked up through the grills like cryogenic cyclones, blasting their covers several meters into the air with a sound like dying banshees.

❖   ❖   ❖

Azocar froze, stunned by the sudden eruption, as the world around him disappeared into a cryogenic fog. For an instant, until his UA's sensors adjusted and dialed the volume back, the scream of escaping gas was like being hit in the head. There was a moment of heart-stopping panic, but a huge tide of relief followed almost instantly. The sight of the grill covers lifting into the heavens on the columns of vaporizing hydrogen had been startling, but it would take more than that to damage utility armor, and—

❖   ❖   ❖

Nine-Finger pressed another button, and Jubair Azocar discovered—briefly—that he'd been wrong as the cloud of hydrogen gas erupted in an improvised fuel-air bomb that was fully capable of shredding, and incinerating, even utility armor.

CHAPTER 59

"*Down!* Get the fuck down right fucking *now!*"

"All right! *All right!*" The young seccy woman went to her knees on the parking garage's ceramacrete, hands already clasped behind her head, her face tight with fear as she looked into the emitter of Kimmo Ludvigsen's neural disruptor. "I'm down," she said. "See? I'm down!"

"Shut the fuck up!" the MISD trooper's UA's external speakers turned what was already a shout into a deafening bellow. "How many others are back there?!" he demanded. "And don't fuck around with me, seccy!"

"A dozen, maybe." The seccy tried to keep her voice as level and submissive as she possibly could, but the words came out cracked and shaky, as frightened as her face. "They're just kids, Sir. Only kids and a couple of teachers. We're . . . we're just trying to get them somewhere safe."

"I told you to shut the fuck up!" Ludvigsen screamed, and the seccy clamped her mouth shut, her eyes—more terrified than ever in the face of his contradictory commands—cutting to where Section Sergeant Barrett stood watching.

Barrett saw the fear in those eyes, and a part of her

almost sympathized with the seccy. Almost. Maybe she really would have sympathized a few T-centuries ago— when she'd still had siblings and nieces and a nephew... and before Bravo Company had taken so many losses.

Jubair Azocar and Trooper Irena Gnoughy had been 2nd Platoon's first deaths, and Márton Neveu, the second of the two riflemen who'd been supporting Azocar, was going to be a long time regenerating. Nor had they been the platoon's only casualties. Despite their armor and the limitations of the seccy's improvised weapons, the seccy had cost 2nd Platoon three more troopers when they went after him, and 2nd Platoon's casualties were actually light compared to some of the other units. Colonel Dothan Perelló's 19th Regiment had been hit even harder as it headed towards Hancock, but at least the combat chatter suggested the 19th had gotten more of its own back. The bastard who'd killed Azocar and Gnoughy—and who'd also killed Matheson, van Noort, and Sugase—had gotten away clean in the confusion.

Barrett felt her jaw muscles clenching as she remembered that. The incredible thermobaric explosion which had taken out Azocar's entire fire team had stunned her just as completely as anyone else in her section. She still didn't know exactly how the goddamned seccy had pulled it off, or how he could've gotten something that powerful close enough without Azocar's armor sensors picking it up. She'd been back over the sensor data herself three times, and there was nothing—*nothing*— aside from the standard igniter power cell in either of the booby-trapped grills. Nothing else, not even trace emissions from old-fashioned chemical explosives!

They'd gotten a firm position fix on the seccy who had to have detonated the trap, though. Her own section had halted in place, prepared to cover Brad Kempthorne's 2nd Section as it leapfrogged towards the seccy's position. That was standard operating procedure, and this time around SOP had been a real lifesaver . . . for *1st Section*, anyway.

The seccy might not have had utility armor or its sensors, but he obviously hadn't been blind. He'd seen what was coming and hightailed it down the drainage culvert before Kempthorne's section could nail him, and 2nd Section had gone in pursuit. That was how they'd discovered the *next* booby trap. Whatever he'd used the first time around had worked even better underground. The thermal pulse had virtually vaporized Kirsten van Noort. There hadn't been a lot more left of Matheson or Sugase, and the pressure front erupting from either end of the culvert had sent two more of Kempthorne's section to the hospital. If not for their utility armor's protection and their helmets' self-contained air supply, the casualties would have been still worse.

Even *with* the armor, 2nd Section was down five of its twelve troopers, and the survivors' morale was badly shaken. The deaths had hit all the rest of 2nd Platoon almost equally hard, for that matter. They hadn't been Barrett's troopers. For that matter, she and van Noort had cordially hated one another. But they'd still been part of the same platoon, part of the same unit, and all the death and injuries had only intensified 2nd Platoon's hatred and fury. The platoon wanted revenge, and the fear of similar booby traps, of similar attacks from the hated and despised seccies who were supposed to be fleeing from them in panic, only fanned that hunger's ferocity.

Just as it fanned Barrett's own ferocity.

"Get the rest of them out here, seccy!" the section sergeant snapped. The kneeling woman stared at her, then collapsed with a wailing cry of pain as the butt of Ludvigsen's disruptor smashed into the pit of her stomach.

"That's enough, Kimmo!" Barrett snapped as the trooper raised the disruptor high, obviously preparing to bring the buttplate down on the seccy's skull. His mirrored visor—featureless, but for the MISD emblem—turned to look at the section sergeant for a heartbeat before he stepped back slowly, obviously unwillingly, in obedience to her command.

The seccy writhed, fighting to get her breath back, and Barrett stepped closer to her. She prodded the prostrate woman with the toe of an armored boot.

"I *said*, get the rest of them out here," she said in a cold, flat tone.

The seccy managed to struggle back to her knees, staring up at her imploringly, and the section sergeant let the muzzle of her own pulse rifle line up with the other woman's forehead.

"If we have to go in there after them, it'll be even worse," she said. "And you won't be here to see it."

The seccy swallowed hard, then nodded.

"Please don't hurt them," she half whispered. "They're kids—only *kids!*"

"*Now*, seccy," Barrett replied.

The seccy stared at her for a moment longer, then licked her lips and raised her voice.

"Come on out, kids!" she called, her eyes locked with Barrett's. "It'll be okay. Promise."

Nothing happened for a few seconds, then, slowly— one by one—another young woman and eleven children, all of them probably between ten and eleven T-years old, crept out of the shadows where they'd hidden behind the derelict, obviously abandoned air lorry. Twelve more faces, each as terrified as the first seccy Ludvigsen had caught, stared imploringly in the section sergeant's direction as they, too, went to their knees.

"All right," Barrett said. "Now we're all going back to—"

The sudden, evil whine of a neural disruptor cut her off, and her head snapped around as Ludvigsen and Brock Sanchez fired into the kneeling prisoners.

Very few ways to die were more agonizing than a bolt from a neural disruptor. It literally tore the central nervous system of its victim apart, and unless the brain itself was hit directly, the victim was denied even the threadbare mercy of unconsciousness.

Ludvigsen and Sanchez swept their fire over the children and the other seccy woman, and the convulsing, shrieking reflections of their victims danced across their mirrored visors like demons. Despite her own fury, her own hatred, Barrett's felt her gorge rising, tasted the acrid bite of vomit at the back of her throat, but there was nothing she could do about it. From the instant those firing studs were depressed, all the seccies—all the *children*—were dead. All that remained were the long, horrifying seconds it took for every organ in their bodies to stop functioning and their brains to gutter down into the merciful dark.

Barrett stared at the twisted, still twitching bodies. Then, against her own will, her eyes returned to the young woman still kneeling in front of her. A young woman whose expression was absolutely blank, blank with something that went beyond horror and shock into the pure, unadulterated inability to believe what she'd just seen. And then, slowly, like images appearing on an antique negative in the developing bath, understanding, knowledge—and *hate*—seeped back into her face. She looked up the length of Barrett's pulse rifle, her eyes filled with soul-searing hatred and the knowledge of what had to happen next, and for an instant, Barrett saw what she saw. Saw the hulking, black-armored shape, picked out with scarlet, blazoned with MISD's gauntlet and dagger, faceless behind its mirrored visor. And in that instant, the section sergeant realized exactly how Mendel's seccies must see her and her troopers.

Her finger squeezed without any conscious thought on her part, the seccy's head exploded under the pulser dart's hypersonic impact, and as the body pitched backward, spraying brain tissue and finely divided fragments of skull across the ceramacrete, Kayla Barrett didn't know whether she'd pulled the trigger out of hatred, to silence a possible witness . . . or simply to escape the bottomless hate radiating from those eyes like a curse.

❖   ❖   ❖

"What the *hell* do you people think you're *doing?!*"

Barrett's head snapped around and her face paled as Lieutenant Connor Ferguson appeared. Second Platoon's commander had been moving with its third section, where he and his platoon sergeant could keep an eye on his reserve force. For a moment, Barrett had no idea how he could suddenly be *here*, instead of there, but only for a moment. He must have been monitoring the take from her own armor's sensors—as the platoon commander, he could plug into any of his noncoms' sensor feeds at will. And, knowing the lieutenant, he'd been headed her way at a run to try to get a handle on the situation.

Why the fuck *didn't you get here thirty seconds sooner?* a bitter voice demanded in the back of her brain. The memory of her brother's face floated before her, but it was no longer an icon demanding vengeance. He'd been a good man, her brother—a *gentle* man— and all she saw in his eyes now was horror.

"I'm—" she began, with absolutely no idea of what she was going to say, but Ferguson cut her off.

"I don't want to hear it." The words were carved out of frozen helium, but they came over the dedicated command channel, excluding the rest of her section. "I expected better out of you, Section Sergeant," he continued in that same ice-crusted tone. "I *depended* on better out of you. You're relieved. Report to Platoon Sergeant Frasch. Tell her I want her out here to take personal charge of this cluster fuck you've created."

"I—" she began again, then swallowed. "Yes, Sir," she said.

Her voice sounded dead in her own ears, but she saluted—out of ingrained habit and muscle memory more than volition—slung her pulser, and started towards the rear.

Ferguson watched her for a moment, then turned to the rest of the section.

"I know all of you—all of *us*—are keyed up, pissed off, and confused as hell," he said over the section-wide circuit. "But there's no excuse for this kind of thing. The Omega rules don't mean we can just slaughter *children* out of hand, for God's sake! How do you think Command's going to react when they review the tac recordings from your armor? Or were you *thinking* at all?!"

Barrett stepped out of the parking garage and trudged towards Platoon Sergeant Loretta Frasch's icon on her HUD. Her utility armor's exoskeletal muscles didn't seem to be working very well. Each of her feet weighed at least a ton, and the slung pulse rifle on her shoulder weighed at least ten times that much. The memory of those screams, the bone-breaking contortions as the disruptors hit, and the *look*—the hatred and knowledge—in the kneeling seccy's eyes . . . all of that went with her, curses from beyond the grave which she knew she would never—*could* never—be free of that dragged at her soul like an anchor. It was just—

"Sarge! Sergeant Barrett!"

She froze, then whirled. It was Ludvigsen, waving frantically for her to come back. She didn't want to. More than she'd ever not wanted to do something in her entire life, she wanted never to enter that parking garage again. But Ludvigsen only waved harder, and she drew a deep breath, squared her shoulders, and went back the way she'd come.

Every step seemed even harder than the ones she'd taken away from the garage, and as she turned the corner back into it, she saw what she'd somehow known she was going to see.

"The bastard must've been hiding over there in the back corner, Sarge." Ludvigsen was talking fast, so quickly the words blurred into one another, as he jabbed an index finger at the patch of sunlight admitted by the break in the garage's back wall. "We were all listening to the lieutenant, and nobody even noticed the son of a bitch until he'd fired! Took us all by surprise. By the time we realized, he'd ducked back through that opening. Sanchez and Timmons are after him now, but I don't think they're going to catch him."

Barrett gazed down at the armored corpse lying half across one of the dead seccies. A seccy sniper—*that* was what they wanted her to believe? And a seccy sniper who'd somehow magically squeezed himself— and his weapon—through a half-meter hole to escape pursuit before anyone could even open fire on him?

The entry point was only a tiny hole in almost the center of Ferguson's visor. She was confident that if she'd measured it, it would have been precisely five millimeters in diameter... exactly the same as the Mark 9 pulse rifle's darts. Judging by the wreckage and the blood spatter, it had been a Mark 3 explosive round, not the solid Mark 1. There was just... nothing left of the back of the lieutenant's helmet.

Or of his skull.

Someone wanted to make damned sure, didn't they? The thought flowed through her brain as she looked down at the body. *Idiots. Do you think he turned off his tac recorder while he reamed you a new one? The court-martial'll never buy that shit about seccy snipers! Where the hell would they get—*

And then it hit her. Ferguson probably *had* killed the "record" function on his armor systems. He'd probably done it even before he chewed *her* out. It was the sort of thing he *would* have done, trying to nip the situation in the bud before it got even worse. Trying to get his people back under control before someone farther up the military food chain had to take cognizance of it and hammered them, made an example out of them. And that meant...

She looked up from the body, saw Ludvigsen and the others in a half-circle on the other side of the corpse, standing among the seccy bodies. She couldn't see their faces any more than they could see hers, but if she could have, she knew exactly what expressions she would have seen. It was odd. Her life hung in the balance, depended on the next words she said, and all she felt was ... empty.

She never really knew how long they stood there, each looking at the others' blank visors. It couldn't possibly have been as long as it felt. But then, finally, Sanchez and Timmons reappeared, joining the others, and she drew a deep breath.

"Any sign of the shooter?" she heard her own voice ask, never looking away from Ludvigsen.

"Not a trace, Sarge." Sanchez sounded a lot calmer than Ludvigsen had, she noted, and Timmons carried his pulse rifle like a hunter, its forestock resting on his left forearm and the muzzle not—quite—aimed in her direction.

"Too bad," she said. Then shook herself. "Central, Bravo-Zero-Three," she said. "Patch Bravo-Zero-One."

"Bravo-Zero-One," Loretta Frasch's voice said in her earbug. "Talk to me, Barrett. What the *hell* is going on in there?!"

"Sorry, Sarge," her voice said. She didn't seem to be consciously choosing the words; they just came, as if she were listening to a stranger. "Been a little confusion here. We flushed a nest of seccies, and while the lieutenant was starting to interrogate them, somebody sniped him through a break in the back wall. He's dead."

The silence on the command circuit was absolute.

It lingered for what seemed like a very, very long time. Then Frasch cleared her throat.

"And the seccies?"

"Killed in the crossfire when we returned fire," that voice which sounded so much like her own replied steadily while she looked at Ludvigsen and the others.

"The sniper?" Frasch sounded resigned, and Barrett shook her head inside her helmet.

"Got away. The hole he fired through's no more than half a meter. By the time we sorted out what the hell had happened and Sanchez and Timmons managed to squirm through it after him, he'd disappeared down some damned rathole or another."

"Understood. There's likely to be some hell to pay over this," Frasch continued. "Regiment's going to want to talk to all of you later. Near as I can tell, the LT'd dropped out of the tac net when he headed into the garage, so I've got damn all *I* can give them. Maybe you and the others can put together some kind of accurate picture of what happened for them."

"We'll certainly try to," Barrett said, hearing the buried message in the platoon sergeant's words and sensing the relaxation of the troopers around her.

"You'd better," Frasch said flatly. "Trigger the LT's retrieval beacon, then get your asses back out here. We're falling behind the other platoons."

CHAPTER 60

"I can't believe these idiots," Thandi Palane muttered, looking up from the HD and the imagery of MISD troops sweeping the green belts, industrial spokes, and the parking and support facilities that serve them. "What the hell do they think they're *doing?*"

"They think they've got a free hunting license," Jurgen Dusek said coldly. He stood beside her, watching the same imagery, and his expression was even grimmer than hers. "I don't know who really set those nukes off, and I'm still not convinced Captain Zilwicki and Mr. Cachat are right about who was behind it, but they were damned well right about the consequences. Whoever it was gave people like that bitch Snyder the excuse they've been looking for. This—" his chin jutted at the HD "—is the early stages of Snyder's 'final solution to the seccy problem.' Besides, after what happened to the Safeties, they don't have any real choice. They've *got* to take out at least a couple of seccy towers—and do it pretty damned spectacularly—if they don't want what's happening here in Mendel to spread. And, trust me, Snyder and McGillicuddy *definitely* don't want that!"

Thandi glanced at him thoughtfully for a moment, then nodded. She was no longer surprised by Dusek's obvious familiarity with the innermost workings of the Mesa System government. He was a seccy, which automatically precluded him from participation in that government, but he watched it the way any predator watched its environment. He had to know what was going on inside it, because whether seccies were permitted a voice in it or not, it controlled everything about their lives. Indeed, the fact that they had no voice made it even more vital for him to know what its objectives were, who the major players within it were, and how all of that was going to impact his own district and his own organization.

And after the weeks she'd spent on Mesa, she'd come to regard Dusek himself in rather a different light. Victor had been right about the role the various crime bosses played in the seccy community. No one would ever confuse Jurgen Dusek with a white knight, and he certainly typified the old cliché about doing well by doing good. In terms of both personal wealth and personal power, he was quite probably one of the most powerful individuals in the entire city of Mendel, not simply in the seccy communities. Since he and Victor had become ... associates, she'd realized Dusek's contacts went far beyond the seccy districts. The "gray economy" of Mesa was grayer than most, even among the system's full citizens, and Dusek had formed alliances in some very peculiar places where no seccy would ever have dared to go openly.

Those alliances had been shattered by the wave of "terrorist" attacks, however. It wasn't so much that any of his allies thought he'd had anything to do with them. It was simply that the hammer which was about to come down on Mesa's seccies—especially here in Mendel, where so much of the total seccy population was concentrated—was big enough no one wanted to get caught under it with him.

He knew it, too. Yet that was purely secondary to him at the moment. Well, maybe not *purely* secondary; if there was a tomorrow for Mendel's seccies, Dusek clearly intended to stay right at the top of the pile. But at the moment, he was operating not as a crime lord skimming profit from troubled seas but as exactly what Victor had said he was—the closest thing to a government the thousands of seccies living in Neue Rostock Tower had ever known.

"—security forces have regained control of most of the districts where Office of Public Safety personnel were ambushed in yesterday's fighting," the commentator was saying in the background. "Faced with an organized, resolute response, the rioters who instigated the violence are retreating everywhere. Director of Security McGillicuddy's office issued a statement just a few hours ago in which the Director said, I quote, 'The perpetrators of these cowardly, vile attacks on OPS personnel attempting to apprehend several suspects believed to have been complicit in the Dobzhansky and Blue Lagoon Park attacks will be brought to account. It is regrettable that the decision of the terrorists and their sympathizers to seek concealment in the seccy districts has already led to so much loss of life, and will, unfortunately, lead to still more. In the face of the atrocities which have been committed by the Audubon Ballroom terrorists operating from those districts, however, the Office of Public Safety has no option but to continue its operations until such time as those responsible for the terrorist incidents *and* those seeking to aid and abet them after the fact have been taken into custody to face the full legal penalty assigned to their actions.'

"In light of the Director's statement, and the ongoing operations we've seen today, it seems likely that—"

"It seems likely that a lot of people are going to get killed," Thandi finished harshly, killing the sound.

"They don't mind that at all, as long as it's the right people," Dusek told her. "And what they think they're doing right now is driving every seccy they can into their killing zones. Of course, that might not be *exactly* the way things are going to work out for them."

He smiled thinly. The evacuation of Neue Rostock's inhabitants had begun days before, within twenty-four hours of Victor's presenting Anton's analysis of where the mounting tide of "terrorist attacks" was going to lead. It helped that he'd organized an evacuation plan for the entire tower years before, more as an exercise in "what if" than because he'd ever really expected to need it. Now he was glad he had, and he'd been getting his people out from under that looming hammer well before the string of nuclear strikes drove the security forces mad. The tunnels and passages under Neue Rostock Tower were hardly broad thoroughfares, and distributing the evacuees discreetly enough elsewhere to prevent OPS from noticing a sudden influx of seccies had been a nontrivial challenge. Fortunately, they'd begun early enough that virtually all of Neue Rostock's residents—aside from a surprisingly high percentage of bloody-minded individuals who'd chosen to stand and fight along with the members of Dusek's organization—had already filtered to safety before OPS and MISD had even started casting their net about it. Now, as refugees fled in front of the MISD hunter-killer teams, his people were guiding them down and out through the tunnels as soon as they reached the tower.

From the messages still getting through to Neue Rostock—and from the news broadcasts—it sounded as if Bachue the Nose's preparations had been less effective, though. She'd never been as tightly organized as Dusek, never tried to integrate all of the inhabitants of Hancock Tower into a single evacuation plan, and her people were less familiar with the tunnels and service ways spiderwebbing away from Hancock.

"They're frigging idiots." Thandi's voice was harsher than ever. "Look at them! They can't have more than a couple of regiments out there. That's a lot of manpower for hunting down and killing people in the open—especially people that can't fight back. It's not nearly enough to crack a tower like Neue Rostock."

"Unless they've decided to go with what your friend Captain Zilwicki so charmingly dubbed the 'Damocles Option,'" Dusek pointed out. "If they just go ahead and drop a big enough KEW on us, they won't need to use up manpower taking us out!"

"That's true," Thandi acknowledged. "The problem they've got is that the kind of KEW they'd need to really crack open a tower like this one is going to inflict a *lot* of collateral damage. Like I told you in the beginning, they can *do* it, but it's going to be even tougher than I'd estimated then. Whoever designed this place wasn't concerned with the sort of minimal amenities that go into full citizens' housing. They just wanted something they could pack people into, and atriums and air shafts use valuable space. They didn't feel like wasting any of that on you people, and that means your tower here is really one solid gridwork of ceramacrete walls and floors. Taking it down with a single KEW would require them to write off a lot of other real estate in the process. I don't think they're going to want to do that. Of course, I doubt they're going to like what happens when they try to *storm* a tower like this one, either. And I can *guarantee* that the bastards at the sharp end aren't going to like it one little bit."

Dusek nodded. She wasn't certain he really believed her, although neither Victor nor Anton had been at all hesitant in passing her off as the greatest military commander since Achilles. Given the already legendary status Torch had achieved among the seccy and slave populations of Mesa, despite all the authorities could do to suppress any news reports about the kingdom, they hadn't even had to work very hard at it. She still wasn't remotely comfortable at having her true identity known, but Victor had a point. If Neue Rostock ultimately fell, she and all the other off-worlders were as good as dead, anyway, so maintaining their secret identities would no longer be real high on their list of priorities.

"Besides," he'd said with typical, rather appalling Victor matter-of-factness, "think about what a major shot in the arm it would be for Torch when all those seccies we got out spread the word about Palane's Last Stand. I mean, I'd much rather live through it, and I think we've got at least a fair chance of making it. But if we don't, you'll give Torch its own combination of the Alamo and Horatius at the Bridge in one, single package. A good looking one, too, now that I think about it. The statue'll make even that thing of Duchess Harrington's on Grayson look positively bland."

There were times she wondered about Victor, she really did. Not that he didn't have a point, she supposed. Whether she liked it or not, she was no longer a Solarian Marine junior officer, and she'd changed even more than she'd thought she had along the way, because a part of her actually understood what he was saying. She had absolutely no desire to become a legend, but sometimes you got caught in what one pre-space history she'd read had called the Birkenhead Drill. If this was *her* Birkenhead Drill, she intended to take as many of these Mesan bastards with her as she could, and if the Kingdom of Torch needed a legend, she wouldn't be around to object, anyway.

"The thing is," she continued, turning from the HD and crossing the spacious room to the bank of consoles at its center, "a tower like this is just full of nasty accidents waiting to happen. With a little help, you can arrange for them to happen to the right people."

Dusek nodded again, more enthusiastically, as she seated herself in one of the comfortable chairs. He took the chair beside hers, and she looked around.

The room in which she sat was buried in the Neue Rostock cellars, five floors below ground level. Up until a very few days ago, it had been the control center for the incredible, complex entity that was Neue Rostock. Tenement tower or no, a structure eight hundred meters tall and a hundred meters on a side was an enormous edifice, and the environmental systems needed to keep it functioning were as complex as anything one might find in an orbital habitat or a starship. The technicians who'd overseen those systems had done so from this room, just as they'd monitored the tower's lift shafts, sewerage systems, water supply, security systems, and the fusion plant which provided the tower's stand-alone power supply.

The truth was that Neue Rostock was a small city, home to over thirty thousand seccies, with all of the support services a city that size needed. And because it was standard practice to make such towers as self-sufficient as possible, it was not simply a city but a citadel well suited to withstand both assaults and sieges. Oh, they couldn't hold out indefinitely. Feeding the defenders would become a problem after the first few weeks, although she'd been pleasantly surprised by just how much food was actually available. Power couldn't be cut off from outside the tower, however; the fusion plant's deeply buried storage tanks held almost a full T-year of reactor mass. Nor could their water supply be cut, since the builders had even driven wells down into the aquifer under Mendel—why not? it had been cheap enough with modern technology—to provide a standalone water supply, as well.

Sloppy thinking on someone's part, she reflected. *Obviously whoever authorized the plans wasn't thinking about what a copperplated bitch it would be to assault something like this. I'd've thought a bunch of paranoid slave masters would have given something like that some thought. Guess not even genetic supermen can think of everything. Pity about that.*

What was even sloppier was that they hadn't already taken steps to seal off Neue Rostock's subsurface accessways. In their defense, they'd probably anticipated taking the seccies by surprise, and realistically speaking, the possibility of evacuating that many people through the tunnels and cellars with little or no warning while actually under attack wouldn't have existed. For that matter, they might even have *wanted* a few of them to get out, spreading their tales of the terror of Neue Rostock's fall among the rest of the seccy population. Then again, it was equally possible they hadn't been stupid enough—initially—to contemplate actually attacking the towers. It was at least remotely possible that the original Office of Public Safety sweeps hadn't been intended as the first step in a major bloodletting. The initial reports certainly seemed to indicate the Safeties had never anticipated what had happened to them, never expected the seccies to fight back. Which was only going to make it even uglier in the end, she thought grimly. The hatred and thirst for vengeance which had animated the OPS troopers in the beginning could only have been reinforced and strengthened by the casualties they'd taken.

"Do you really think we can hold out until your friends can get someone in here to help us?" Dusek asked very quietly, his voice low enough none of the other technicians in what had become Thandi's command post could hear him.

"Realistically?" Thandi regarded him levelly, then twitched her head back in the direction of the HD they'd been watching. "If what we've seen so far is typical, I'd say the odds are probably at least eighty-twenty in our favor, always assuming they don't just haul off and drop one of those big assed KEWs on us after all. If they find somebody who doesn't have her head thoroughly up her ass to take over from that idiot Howell, the odds go down. In fact, depending on how good Howell's replacement is, they could go down a lot."

"I see."

Dusek took it well, she thought. On the other hand, she was none too sure he'd ever really believed the entire Grand Alliance would drop everything and send a rescue fleet just because Victor Cachat and Anton Zilwicki asked it to. As she'd gotten to know him better, she'd come to the conclusion that he probably would have done exactly what he was doing even if he'd *known* there would be no rescue in the offing. There was an unexpected streak of the berserker in Jurgen Dusek. If the Mesan government had finally decided to slaughter the seccy population down to a manageable size, then he was going to kill as many Safeties and Misties as he possibly could first. And if it turned out that there really was a fleet coming to save him, that was only icing on the cake.

She nodded to him and turned back to the displays. Yana and Victor were both occupied preparing fighting positions under Andrew Artlett's guidance. Andrew and Nolan Olsen, the man who'd been Neue Rostock Tower's Building Supervisor, were in the process of doing some profoundly unnatural things to the tower's internal systems. Olsen's family had already departed through the escape tunnels, but no one else knew Neue Rostock the way he did. On the other hand, Andrew had grown to adulthood surviving on a steadily disintegrating orbital habitat, and he'd learned to do some . . . highly inventive things with environmental systems along the way. Between them, they'd come up with several surprises for anyone foolish enough to walk into their parlor, and Andrew had the tower's schematic—the *real* schematic, the one that showed Dusek's alterations, not the one any invaders would have—on his display. At the moment, he was directing Yana in the placement of shaped charges in some of the corridor walls.

Victor had his own copy of the schematic, and he and Triêu Chuanli had their people building firing positions, cutting loopholes, and laying out routes to move from one position to another under cover. They didn't have anything like the MISD's utility armor, but the weapons Dusek had stockpiled over the years were almost as good as anything the security forces had—especially given the short range at which any combat would occur—and their knowledge of the building's layout would be a huge advantage.

Thandi would really have preferred to be out there herself. At heart, when she came down to it, she was still really a company grade Marine officer, whatever other hats she'd had to take on since meeting Berry Zilwicki and Victor Cachat. But if they were going to have a chance of winning this thing, it was going to depend on her ability to exercise tight tactical control over fighters who'd never received the training and experience she had. Yana and Victor had plenty of combat experience, although most of it had tended to be . . . idiosyncratic, to say the least. Many of the others had been in gunfights, knife fights, brawls in plenty, but that was a far cry from the sort of concentrated mayhem they were about to encounter. When the time came, they were going to need a voice—a calm voice—telling them what to do, when to do it, and where. And for her to be that voice, she needed to be exactly where she was at this moment, tapped into all of the tower's internal surveillance equipment.

She smiled thinly, fingers moving briskly as she scrolled through view after view of corridors, apartments, shopping malls, cafeterias, gymnasiums, freight passages, grav shafts, stairs, ventilation ducts. The entire tower was there at her fingertips, which meant she was going to have a degree of situational awareness better than anything even the finest utility armor's sensors could provide to the other side.

You just come right on in, you bastards, she thought, glancing sideways again after the exterior views of the approaching MISD troops. *We'll be sure you get a warm reception.*

CHAPTER 61

Gavin Shultz scowled as he raised his helmet's visor. The stink of smoke was everywhere—he wouldn't have thought there were enough flammable materials even in a seccy district to produce that much of it—but it still smelled better than the inside of his utility armor after an entire day of combat.

He didn't like the losses Bravo Company had taken, especially in 2nd Platoon, and there wasn't much of an excuse for them, in his opinion. They were only fucking seccies, after all, and he'd gotten enough hands-on experience of his own during the day to confirm his opinion of them. He'd tried conscientiously to bear in mind that his own experiences might not be representative of what had happened elsewhere, but still...

He lowered his visor again—not all the way; he still wanted the fresh air, smoky though it was—far enough to bring up the map display on his HUD as an armored air car settled on the far side of the jury rigged command post. The swaths of green indicating pacified areas in the approaches to Neue Rostock and

Hancock were smaller than they ought to have been, and Colonel MacKane wasn't delighted about it. Well, neither was Gavin Shultz, but—

"Where's Colonel MacKane, Trooper?" a voice demanded, and Shultz turned towards it in amazement.

"Commissioner Howell!" he blurted, then snapped to attention as Bentley Howell turned from the corporal who'd been unfortunate enough to be standing there when he climbed out of the air car. The commissioner wasn't in armor, but he wore a vehicle crewman's helmet with the visor down. Unlike the utility armor's visors, it was only lightly tinted from the outside. It was enough to project the necessary HUD for its wearer, but Shultz could see through it more than clearly enough to recognize the MISD's commanding officer.

"I didn't expect to see you here, Sir!" the captain added as Howell scowled.

"Well, Captain . . . Shultz, isn't it?" Shultz nodded, impressed by the commissioner's memory for faces, without even thinking about the possibility that Howell's helmet systems had pinged his UA transponder's ID code. "I didn't expect to be here," Howell continued. "I *expected* to hear that my advanced elements had already closed up to Neue Rostock and Hancock."

Schultz swallowed. The commissioner's tone was not happy, and it seemed prudent to keep his own mouth shut.

Howell regarded him for a moment, then smiled unpleasantly.

"Don't worry, Captain. I'm not going to rip *you* a new asshole. But I do need Colonel MacKane, so where is he?"

"Sir, I'm not really certain, but Major Myers is about two hundred meters in that direction." He raised his hand, pointing in the proper direction. "Can I escort you to him?"

"No. I've got his icon now," Howell said, manipulating the data pad on the side of his helmet. "And it looks like Colonel MacKane's with him. Good. Thank you, Captain."

He nodded curtly to Shultz, then jerked his head at the two utility armored troopers who'd unloaded from the air car behind him, and headed off in the indicated direction.

Shultz watched him go, bodyguards at his heels, then turned his attention back to the map display.

❖   ❖   ❖

"Well, Colonel," Howell said. "Would you care to explain why you're no further forward than this?"

"Resistance is being a lot stiffer than our intelligence estimates predicted it would be, Sir."

Teodosio MacKane's tone was perhaps a bit more pointed than it should have been for a mere colonel addressing a commissioner who carried the equivalent of lieutenant general's rank. There wasn't much give in his eyes, though, and Howell reminded himself not to rip out the man's lungs.

"I am aware of that, Colonel," he said instead. "What I want to know is why we haven't done something about that."

"Commissioner, we've cleared this area here, and this one, this one, and *this* one," McCain said, jabbing his finger at the indicated points on the map as he spoke. "That's basically all the ground level approaches to Neue Rostock from the east. We haven't been able to get around the far side of the tower yet, but we're making progress. And, Sir, I have to point out that I've taken over two hundred casualties so far, twenty-three of them fatal."

Those hard eyes met Howell's, and the commissioner grimaced. That was a casualty rate of over ten percent. How the hell could a mob of *seccies* be inflicting that kind of loss rate on armored MISD troopers?

He scowled down at the map, thinking about all the other reports he'd received during the day. Much as he hated to admit it, MacKane had a point about the intensity of the resistance. His original plan to sweep the areas around each of the seccy towers, driving them into neatly confined centers that could be dealt with one at a time was working, but it was costing more than he'd anticipated. The two regiments he'd committed to the Neue Rostock and Hancock areas were spread over too great an area, and the losses they'd taken were undercutting their fighting spirit. On the other hand, it was obvious that the seccies in and around Neue Rostock and Hancock were putting up the toughest resistance. Or inflicting the most casualties, at least. The question was whether that was because the seccies were better organized and better equipped or because 4th Regiment and 19th Regiment were more ineptly led?

"All right," he said finally. "I want you to leave one battalion to secure the approaches to Neue Rostock. But I want your and your other battalion to support Colonel Perelló. Colonel Metz and the Seventeenth Regiment will be joining you and Colonel Perelló. We're going to knock Hancock out first, and then we're going to take Neue Rostock down, understood?"

"Understood, Sir." MacKane didn't sound as if he were filled with enthusiasm, and Howell smiled thinly.

"I know it sounds like a tough assignment, Colonel. And I know you've been out here all day already. But they're only seccies, and now that we've driven them to ground, they have to stand and fight—they can't fade away the way they've been doing out here in the open. It may seem that I'm asking a lot of you and your people after everything you've already been through, but I'm not going to ask any of you to do anything I'm not willing to do myself."

"Sir?" MacKane's eyebrows rose, and Howell's smile grew still thinner.

"I've got my UA in the air car, Colonel MacKane. I'll personally be leading this attack."

❖   ❖   ❖

"Captain Shultz?"

Gavin Shultz turned and found himself facing Section Sergeant Kayla Barrett. She had her helmet under her left arm, and her dirty face looked drawn and anxious.

"Yes, Section Sergeant?" he acknowledged a bit impatiently.

He couldn't believe Commissioner Howell planned to lead the assault on Hancock in person, and he wasn't at all sure it sounded like a good idea. Howell was a great man, someone who obviously understood the nature of the seccy problem, but he hadn't held a field command in at least fifteen or twenty T-years. On the other hand, it sounded as if he was going to be going in with Colonel MacKane at his elbow. That should preclude any *serious* mistakes... Shultz hoped. And in the meantime, he had things to do that were a hell of a lot more important than taking some kind of report from a section sergeant.

"Sir, it's about Lieutenant Ferguson," Barrett said, and Shultz's jaw tightened.

"What about him?"

"Sir, I'm not sure exactly how it was reported, but—"

"Section Sergeant Barrett, we're about to kick off an assault on an entire tower full of seccies," Shultz said. "I'm sure there will be plenty of time to sort out exactly what happened to Lieutenant Ferguson—and any of the other people we've lost today—after it's over. Just this minute, though, I've got about a dozen other things I need to be doing. Can this wait?"

It had damned well better *wait,* he thought grimly. He had a pretty good idea of what had happened to Ferguson. There wasn't any evidence to support his theory, but the fact that there wasn't *any* evidence, of any sort, of what had actually happened strongly suggested that he was correct. *And if I am, this isn't a can of worms I need to be opening right now, especially with Commissioner Howell himself right here on top of us. Besides, Ferguson was a whining, holier-than-thou pain in the ass when he was alive; I'll be* damned *if he screws up my career now that he's dead. The son of a bitch probably had it coming, anyway.*

He held the section sergeant's eye, his expression less than encouraging, and silence hovered for a half-dozen heartbeats. Then—

"Yes, Sir," Kayla Barrett said softly. "Yes, Sir. I guess it can wait."

❖ ❖ ❖

"How stupid do you think I am, Kyle?" Audrey O'Hanrahan demanded.

Kyle Fraenzl clamped his teeth tightly on what he *wanted* to say in response to that acid question. The problem was that the one thing O'Hanrahan most definitely *wasn't* was stupid. It would've been so much simpler if she was as clueless as the journalists covering the *Magellan* sinking, he reflected.

"No one thinks you're 'stupid,' Audrey," he said in his most soothing tones. "It's just that you seem to have gotten hold of some garbled information, and you're really too well known for any of us in Culture and Information to feel . . . comfortable letting you get too close to the shooting." He shook his head, expression grave. "The truth is, we can't afford the bad PR if we let you get killed on our planet, and it's really, really bad out there, Audrey. The seccies are shooting at anything that moves."

"Oh, for God's sake!" O'Hanrahan glared at him in searing, disgusted contempt. "The *seccies* are shooting at anything that moves? That has to be the biggest piece of bullshit anyone's ever tried to hand me, even here on Mesa!"

Fraenzl's lips thinned and his face darkened, and she shook her head.

"I have not gotten hold of any 'garbled information,' Kyle." There was less searing disdain in her voice this time, but the slow, patient tone she'd adopted—as if she were speaking to a five-year-old—wasn't much of an improvement. "I've gotten hold of perfectly *accurate* information, quite a bit of it from your own security forces' electronic chatter." She smiled sweetly, holding up a Solarian made security band scanner which should have been confiscated from her coming through Customs, and Fraenzl felt his teeth grate on one another. "And I do have other sources, even here. That's why I know it's not the *seccies* shooting people out there. Or, at least, if they *are* shooting anyone at the moment, it's almost certainly in self-defense!"

"Now you wait one damned minute!" Fraenzl snapped, abandoning his effort to stay focused and professional as fury flashed through him. "Whatever's happening out there 'at the moment,' as you put it, don't you forget for one instant who was setting off nuclear explosions here on *my* planet! It's not Public Safety or the Security Directorate running amok out there in the streets—it's the fucking seccies and their Ballroom friends!"

"The hell it is," O'Hanrahan shot back, and this time her voice was lower, almost soft. "I don't know for sure who was responsible for those terrorist attacks, Kyle. I'm inclined to take them at face value, as genuine Ballroom attacks, even if it isn't really their usual style, but I don't *know* that, and before you get all fired up again, don't you pretend to me that the Mesa System government is a staunch champion of freedom of the press. We both know differently, Kyle. And we both know it's your job to tell me exactly what your superiors *tell* you to tell me, no matter how little resemblance to the truth it may bear. So why don't you save yourself a lot of trouble and effort and simply admit what we both know is true. Your security personnel took casualties when they set out on a general punitive sweep of the seccy districts, and they got out of hand as a result. *They're* the ones committing atrocities out there. *You* know it, *I* know it, and your superiors know it."

Fraenzl drew a deep, deep breath, held it for a ten-count, then exhaled hard.

"I apologize for losing my temper with you." His tone was utterly sincere; his eyes were not. "In my defense, I can plead only exhaustion, stress, and grief. I lost several close personal friends in the Dedrick Tower attack, and one of my wife's cousins is—was—a Security Directorate lieutenant who was killed today. So, yes, I'm just a little personally invested in this story, and my professional detachment is a bit lacking. I'm even prepared to admit—off the record and not for attribution—that there have been *some* instances in which some of our troopers, reacting in the middle of a combat situation, probably *have* used excessive force. You've covered enough military actions in your career to know that sort of thing happens, even with the best troops, sometimes. But there is not a general pattern of 'atrocities' on the part of our troops, and there *certainly* is no truth to the rumors that any Public Safety or Security Directorate officer has ordered, authorized, or turned a blind eye to those excesses. I assure you that any provable instance of the use of excessive force will be thoroughly investigated and prosecuted in the fullness of time."

"You actually managed to make it sound like you believe that," O'Hanrahan said in a tone of mocking admiration, then snorted harshly. "Kyle, I've covered Frontier Security operations. I've seen the Gendarmerie at its worst, and I know damned well what I'm seeing when I look at that HD or when I go out on my balcony and look at the smoke rising from the seccy districts. You can deny me access to the scene where all of this is happening if you want. If you do, however, please be sure that Director Lackland and the rest of your superiors understand that I'll be reporting to all of my viewers that despite repeated requests on my part, the Mesa System government refused to allow me to cover this story. They might want to think about how that report from me is going to impact the amount of credence the public in general will extend to *their* account of what's happened here."

"Audrey, I don't think—"

"I think we're through here, Kyle," she said, not unkindly, and shook her head. "I know I've got a temper, and I also know you're doing your job the way you understand what has to be done. I understand that. But you'd better understand that *I* have a job to do, too, and that I'm *going* to do it. So before you say anything else, and before we start screaming at each other again, I suggest you go and pass my message along to your bosses. Tell them that either they grant me access starting tomorrow morning, or I'm on the first ship out of here to tell the Solarian League at large that you and they are obviously covering up *something*—something so big and so ugly that you didn't dare risk my getting even a whiff of the truth."

CHAPTER 62

"Well, I suppose it's about time...not that I'm looking forward to this," Gillian Drescher said sourly. She shook her head. "This is going to be a cluster fuck, however we go about it, you know."

"Be a worse one if we left it all up to Howell and his idiots," Colonel Bartel pointed out even more sourly. "They've managed to lose almost five hundred people, and they aren't even up to the damned towers yet!"

"Fair's fair, Byrum." Drescher shook her head, her expression worried. "The truth is, our people didn't project this kind of seccy resistance, either. And so far, it's been mainly small arms and improvised booby traps. You think it isn't going to get worse—for our people, not just theirs—before it's over?"

"I'm damned sure it is, Ma'am. That's one reason I'm so pissed at Howell—and McGillicuddy, for that matter—for handing this shit sandwich off to us."

"Well, it's not ours yet." Drescher looked at the orders on her terminal again, then shrugged. "At least we've already stood up our people. How long till we have them on the ground?"

"It'll still take at least another six hours, Ma'am." Bartel shrugged irritably. "Just moving them's going to be a problem, since the Misties 'borrowed' so much of Fifth Brigade's transport."

Drescher grunted unhappily. Howell's troop movements had been on a much larger scale than he'd ever anticipated, and, just to make things worse, he'd managed to lose something on the order of three dozen air lorries and a dozen APCs in a single seccy raid. Fortunately, he'd lost them parked on the ground, without anyone aboard them to be killed when their hydrogen tanks exploded, but what kind of idiot established a major vehicle park without at least securing the access points to the utility tunnels *underneath* it?

Actually, I know exactly what kind of idiot does something like that, don't I? she reflected.

"In that case, we'd better get started," she said out loud.

❖   ❖   ❖

"Yes, Sir. Of course. I understand, Sir."

Bentley Howell managed somehow to keep his searing anger out of his voice and expression as he gazed at François McGillicuddy's com image. To McGillicuddy's credit, the Director of Security didn't look a lot happier than Howell felt, and he damned well shouldn't have.

"Until General Drescher arrives on-site, you're still in command, Commissioner," McGillicuddy said. "I expect you to exercise good judgment in the interim."

"Yes, Sir."

"Good. In that case, I'll speak with you later. Good luck, Bentley."

"Thank you, Sir."

The com image disappeared, and Howell allowed himself a snarl. So, they were going to take Rat Catcher away from him and hand it over to that oh-so-superior sanctimonious bitch Drescher to take the credit after *his* people had bled to get to this point? It was probably Pearson's doing. Or Alpina's. The Peaceforce's CO was always on the lookout for ways to improve the MPP's position at the Office of Public Safety's expense!

He glowered down at the map display.

Fourth Regiment's 1st Battalion had a cordon around the Neue Rostock approaches. Howell was positive no more seccies were getting into the tower at ground level, and Major Brockmann would keep it that way. In the meantime, he'd moved MacKane's 2nd Battalion, and all of Perelló's 19th Regiment and Sergio Metz's 17th Regiment up to invest the approaches to Hancock Tower. They were perfectly positioned to assault the place, and now he was expected to stand here with his thumb up his ass while Drescher's Peaceforce strolled through his lines, took *his* prize, and walked off with all the fucking credit, was he?

McGillicuddy said you're still in command until Drescher drags her sorry ass to the front, he reminded himself. He caught his lower lip between his teeth, his mind racing as he considered the possibilities. Then he drew a deep breath, nodded once, hard, and looked up at the man on the other side of the Cyclops' map display.

"Colonel MacKane."

"Yes, Commissioner?"

"The assault elements are in position?"

"Yes, Sir."

MacKane's tone was difficult to parse. On the one hand, he'd heard Director McGillicuddy's conversation with Howell, and it was obvious to the commissioner that the colonel was less than fully confident in his own plan of attack. On the other hand, MacKane was MISD, and it was his people who'd already paid cash to get this far.

"In that case, Colonel, let's get to it," Commissioner Bentley Howell said flatly.

◇   ◇   ◇

"Oh, shit," Kayla Barrett said with quiet, intense sincerity as the order came over the com net.

She and her understrength section were on Hancock Tower's eastern side, hunkered down along the bank of what had been intended—once upon a time—as a scenic canal or river (she wasn't sure exactly which; the dry bed was studded with too many artistically spaced rocks for a canal, but it seemed awfully damned straight for a river) flanked by a scenic hiking trail. Since this was a seccy district, the canal (or river) had never been properly finished and the hiking trail's landscaping was less than scenic. Worse, there'd been some fighting before the MISD secured control of the canal cut. The seccies had used it as a fighting trench—there were still a half dozen of their bodies in it—which was exactly what Barrett's section and the rest of 2nd Platoon was using it for at the moment.

And what she really, really didn't want to do was to climb out of that trench's protection and advance into that hulking, mountainous tower. Unfortunately, no one seemed especially interested in what *she* wanted just at the moment.

"Saddle up," Lieutenant Marilyn Kalanadhabhatla

said sharply over the net. Kalanadhabhatla had transferred in from 17th Regiment to replace Connor Ferguson as 2nd Platoon's CO, and that was another thing Barrett didn't like. Kalanadhabhatla was a complete unknown. The one good thing about that from Barrett's perspective was that she'd apparently come in cold, without any prior knowledge of what had happened to Ferguson...or how. The really, really bad thing about it was that no one in the platoon had ever worked with her before, and that was not a good state of affairs for one of the units picked to lead the assault into a seccy-held tower.

"You heard the LT!" Platoon Sergeant Frasch said sharply. "Off your asses and on your feet, people!"

At least the seccies who'd been sniping from Hancock's outer windows had been driven mostly to ground, Barrett reflected, and the hissing, whickering crack-crack-crack-crack of the tribarrels' covering fire was one of the most welcome sounds she'd ever heard. Every twelfth dart was a tracer round; at the tribarrels' incredible rate of fire, those tracers looked like a death ray, reaching out to the tower and lacing its surface with a hurricane of explosions. Dust, splinters, and chunks of debris blew back—not even ceramacrete could take that kind of punishment without its surface shattering—and five battalions of MISD troopers moved forward under the protection of those thunderbolts.

Despite the covering fire, here and there a seccy popped up in one of the windows not currently under fire—there were far too many windows in the tower's outer walls for *all* of them to be taken under fire continuously—and ripped off a burst from the military-grade pulsers Bachue the Nose's people seemed to have in unpleasant numbers. Every time one of them did, the covering tribarrels immediately turned their attention to the window in question, ripping it apart and undoubtedly filling the room behind it with explosions and lethal shrapnel.

Barrett felt confident that many of those seccies were dead shortly after squeezing their own triggers, but she had a nagging suspicion the death toll was a lot lower than she could have liked. The long-standing contempt she'd cherished where seccies—and especially seccies' toughness and willingness to fight—were concerned had taken a beating right along with the rest of 2nd Platoon. Whatever else they might be, *these* seccies had learned a lot of lessons the hard way since Rat Catcher had kicked off. The stupid ones were probably already dead. Certainly the ones that were left didn't appear especially afflicted by stupidity, and that meant that most of the seccies popping up to fire knew what was going to happen to their firing positions as soon as they did. And that, in turn, meant they'd almost certainly planned on being somewhere else by the time the tribarrel gunners spotted them and shifted aim.

And the bastards are probably doing just fine at it, Barrett reflected.

The advancing troopers went forward at a run, each unit directed at a specific entry point—freight delivery doors, for the most part, because they were larger, but a handful of pedestrian entrances for Hancock's residents, as well. Those entry points had been subjected to special attention from the MISD heavy weapons teams to demolish any barricades the seccies had attempted to erect. Dust and chunks of debris, cascading down the tower's outer face in stony avalanches from the covering tribarrels' fire, bombarded 2nd Platoon as Barrett's section closed with its own entry point. Something large and heavy—or falling from far enough up to *feel* large and heavy—rebounded from her utility armor's helmet with force enough to half-stagger her, but she stayed on her feet and followed Ludvigsen's fire team through the shattered pedestrian entrance and into the tower interior.

She wasn't certain exactly what she'd expected. At the very least, she'd counted on running into a lookout or a sentry. But there was nothing.

The corridor leading away from them was typical of the passageways in a seccy residential tower—much narrower than in the full citizens' towers, dingy, and poorly lit at the best of times, which this wasn't. The main lights were out, but the emergency lighting was still up, dimly illuminating the layers of dust drifting in from outside through their entry point like fog. The dust floated around Barrett's knees as she consulted the schematic on her HUD.

This was far from the first time she and her section had invaded one of the seccy towers, but it was the first time she'd ever seen the corridors completely deserted, and something with lots of tiny feet scuttled up and down her spine as she gazed down that long, poorly lit bore. The passageway ran arrow-straight towards the bank of grav shafts serving this quadrant of the tower, but there was none of the openness, the airiness, she would have seen somewhere else—like her own tower, for example. The quarters were tight, the walls lined with closed doors on either side, interrupted every ten or fifteen meters by a cross corridor, and her heart sank. It was one thing to advance confidently and arrogantly up a narrow gut like that as part of a routine sweep, or on her way towards a specific apartment number to drag out a specific seccy while all his friends and neighbors froze in their burrows like mice when the cat was a-prowl. It was quite another to contemplate it in the dusty darkness, with a quarter of her section already dead behind her, knowing an ambush might lurk at any point.

"By the numbers, people," she said flatly. "Ludvigsen, you've got point."

"Right, Sarge."

There was a lot of anger in Ludvigsen's acknowledgment, Barrett observed. Maybe the SOB thought she was trying to get him killed to eliminate him as a witness to what had happened to Lieutenant Ferguson . . . and to those massacred seccy children. Which, now that she thought about it, might not be that bad an idea.

"Malden, stay on your toes," she continued.

"Gotcha, Sarge," Corporal Denise Malden, the leader of Barrett's second fire team, acknowledged. The rest of 2nd Platoon was flowing into the tower behind them, and Barrett waved into the dimness.

"Let's go," she said.

❖   ❖   ❖

Kayla Barrett's mouth was unpleasantly dry. It didn't matter how much water she sucked from her helmet's nipple, either. She supposed that what she ought to have been feeling was relief, but what she was actually feeling was something very different.

Second Platoon had advanced to and beyond the first bank of grav shafts. Not surprisingly—this *was* a seccy tower, after all—the shafts were down. That was scarcely unusual, although she couldn't help wondering if this time around it was genuinely lack of maintenance or if some overly clever seccy hadn't simply switched them off. If they had been turned off, however, whoever'd done it had also managed to block the Emergency Services override codes to turn them back on, and that suggested some things she really didn't want to contemplate about what *else* might have been done to the tower's internal systems.

The advance had gone well, though. The rest of 4th Regiment's 2nd Battalion had made entrance behind Bravo Company successfully, as well. Like 2nd Platoon, Bravo's other platoons had moved inward, providing point teams for the rest of the battalion. Those point teams swept the dimness before them with their sensor systems, weapons ready to engage anything they encountered, while the covering teams following on their heels systematically kicked in doors and sensor-swept the apartments behind them. So far, 2nd Platoon had encountered no resistance, although 1st Platoon and Bravo's HQ section had walked into a nasty little firefight. First Platoon had lost three people, but Captain Shultz and the HQ section had come in on the flank of the seccy firing position through a cross corridor.

The fighting had been brutal, if brief, and none of the eight seccies in the position had survived.

That had been about it, though, and Barrett sensed a growing confidence in the men and women of her section. A *dangerous* confidence.

"Stay *sharp*, damn it!" she snapped over the section net. "There're thousands of the bastards in here somewhere! You think they're going to let us waltz all the way through and out the other side just like *that*?"

No one answered her, but Malden's covering team moved a little more briskly, a little more alertly, as they kicked open more doors and scanned cross passages.

Even a miserable rats nest like Hancock had to have some open spaces in it. The squat, eight hundred-meter high cube did have a single central access well, but it was only about twenty meters across. Aside from that, it was a squared off, monotonously repetitive grid. The sort of maze laboratory rats had been sent to negotiate for millennia... and which had dominated the design of government housing warehouses for almost as long. But according to her HUD schematic, they were coming up on one of the tower's commercial sections. It wouldn't be anything like the spacious malls in the citizens' towers, but it offered a fairly broad central arcade, surrounded by shops, stores, and restaurants.

The arcade was Bravo Company's designated objective point. When the company's troopers reached it, they would have secured a roughly pie-shaped section sixty meters wide at its base and eighty meters deep. Adding the arcade's grav shafts to the banks the MISD had already secured and bypassed, they'd have at least a dozen potential points of access to the floors above, and Howell's other two regiments each had a pair of battalions driving in on separate axes. Their joint objective was a sports complex—a large gymnasium with adjoining tennis courts and a large swimming pool. They had less distance to cover, but they were also moving a lot more slowly. When they took the sport complex, however, they would have secured almost half of the rest of the ground floor and all of the grav shafts and stairs which served it. Even with the shafts powered down—and there was no question in Barrett's mind now that they *had* been powered down, deliberately—counter-grav equipped troopers would be able to ascend them, and the defenders were going to find it difficult to cover all of those points of vulnerability.

"Sarge, I've got eyes on the objective," Ludvigsen reported.

Most of the anger had faded from his voice as they moved steadily deeper, and Barrett was glad to hear it. It was still going to be there between them afterward, and she had no idea how that was going to work out, but for right now they all depended on one another to survive long enough for there to be an "afterward" to worry about.

"Don't get carried away," she replied. "I don't want anyone rushing out into the open just because we haven't run into anybody yet."

"Don't worry about *me* getting carried away!" Ludvigsen snorted, and continued cautiously forward.

❖   ❖   ❖

"The bastards coming up Gladstone are almost in the zone, Bachue," Fred Trujillo said tautly.

"What about Merriwell and Patterson?" the tall, rawboned woman with the beaky nose asked harshly.

"Not yet. They're still about two cross corridors out," Trujillo replied.

"Shit."

Bachue the Nose rested her right palm on the butt of the pulser at her hip, fingers drumming on the holster's plastic. Her gang was less tightly organized—less *disciplined*, much as she hated to admit that—than

Jurgen Dusek's, and she hadn't spent as much time as he had worrying about planning for a possible situation like this. Why the hell should she have? The notion of *seccies* actually being able to defend a residential tower against a frontal assault was ludicrous.

Yet, as the warning signs had accumulated, she'd realized Dusek was right about what was coming down this time. Personally, if she'd been able to get her hands on the Ballroom bastards behind the nuclear strikes, she'd *gladly* have handed them over to the Safeties. It wasn't like the lunatics were actually going to *change* anything here on Mesa, and the security agencies' reaction had been as predictable as sunrise. For that matter, she was none too fond of anyone prepared to kill that many people just to make a point herself.

But she *couldn't* get her hands on them, because she had no idea where to find them—not that she expected the Misties to believe that for a moment—which had left her with only one option. Even a cornered rat would fight savagely when it had no option, and Bachue the Nose was a hell of a lot more dangerous than any *rat*.

"Any sign the Gladstone bunch is planning on pushing past Brookner?"

"Not yet." Trujillo shook his head. "Looks like you called it, boss. They're planning to link up at Brookner."

Bachue grunted. The Brookner Plaza—although she'd always thought calling it a "plaza" was pretty damned high-flown and fancy for a down-at-the-heels, threadbare shopping arcade—at the intersection of the Gladstone, Merriwell, and Patterson trunk corridors had been an obvious weak spot in Hancock's defenses.

Of course, as Dusek's advisor Palane had pointed out, *obvious* weak spots could be very useful things from a defender's perspective. But to make it work, she wanted as many of the Misties in her sights as possible.

"What about the ones coming in from the west, Levi?" she asked.

"They're still about ten minutes out from Crawford, maybe fifteen at the rate they're moving," Levi Andrade, Hancock Tower's building supervisor, replied from his central console.

Bachue nodded. There were twice as many Misties in the four-pronged advance moving in from the west, and they were more widely separated. It looked like they were heading for the Crawford Sports Complex, located right off the tower's central air shaft opening, but their approach routes made it difficult to be certain. Even if they were, though, they'd never reach it by the time the first bunch reached Brookner. Still, she'd made preparations on that front, as well.

"Get Pablo and his people over to the west side," she said. She turned her head, looking at the crimson lines advancing across the building manager's schematic. "Tell him they'll be coming up Whitman, Seversky, Ibanez, and Chasnikov. They're not going to be far enough in for the Crawford charges, so tell him to make for the secondary trunk positions."

"On it, boss," Andrade told her, and she turned back to Trujillo, moving closer and resting her left hand on his right shoulder as she looked over his head at his display.

"We wait a bit longer," she told him. "I want Pablo in position, and I'd really rather have as many of these other bastards as deep as as we can get them before we pull the plug. Keep a close eye on the Gladstone bunch, though. Let me know if they get antsy."

"Gotcha."

❖   ❖   ❖

"Malden, secure the entrance," Barrett directed. "Ludvigsen, I want you and your team about as far out there as that first kiosk. Don't think about wandering any farther until Captain Shultz and the rest of the Company gets here!"

"Wouldn't dream of it, Sarge," Kimmo Ludvigsen said fervently.

❖   ❖   ❖

Captain Gavin Shultz smacked his left hand on his armored leg in satisfaction. His HUD showed 2nd Platoon already on the objective. He still didn't like to think about how . . . messy accounting for Ferguson's death might turn out to be, and he hadn't been delighted to get a brand-new replacement for the dead lieutenant on such short notice. But damned if Kalanadhabhatla hadn't turned his frigging problem platoon around!

His other platoons were making good progress, as well, and aside from that little firefight where he'd managed to get his HQ people stuck in, there'd been no resistance at all to speak of. He always known seccies were cowards, and they were damned well proving it now.

"All right, people," he said, striding along just behind 1st Platoon's point team, "let's close it up and get a move on. We've got us some seccies to kill!"

❖   ❖   ❖

"They're all into the zone now." Trujillo's voice was tighter and a little higher-pitched than it had been, and Bachue looked over his shoulder at the display.

The Misties were so self-confident that they hadn't even tried to knock out her corridor surveillance cameras. Or perhaps they simply hadn't realized they were there. They were completely separate from the *official* surveillance system even seccy towers were required by law to provide, and their pickups were far better maintained—and concealed—than the official ones.

"How's Pablo doing, Levi?" Bachue asked over her shoulder, never turning away from Trujillo's display.

"About there, boss. He says two minutes."

"Are the Misties into the secondary zone?"

"Just about. My cameras aren't as good as Fred's on this side. Looks like we've got maybe . . . seventy-five, eighty percent into the zone. Probably got a few already past it, though."

Bachue frowned thoughtfully, then nodded.

"Let those bastards moving up on Brookner get a little deeper into the zone, Fred," she said, squeezing Trujillo's shoulder. "Another fifteen or twenty meters."

"You got it, boss."

❖   ❖   ❖

Bentley Howell gazed down at the Cyclops' map in satisfaction as his battalions penetrated deeper and deeper into Hancock Tower. The green lines indicating their progress crawled across the display steadily, and he smiled triumphantly. He'd told that idiot Drescher the seccies would break and run when they realized the situation was hopeless. He had them bottled up in their holes now, and they were probably pissing themselves just thinking about what was headed towards them. He'd have all of the first five floors of that damned tower secured by the time Drescher ever even got here! He wouldn't be able to keep her from claiming credit for the occupation of the *rest* of Hancock, but the record would clearly show who'd executed the initial breaching operation and damned well *handed* her the tower! In fact, he was looking forward to—

❖   ❖   ❖

"Now," Bachue the Nose said softly.

❖   ❖   ❖

Hancock Tower lacked the spaciously laid out cellular structure of a tower like Saracen or Rasmussen, but the loadbearing walls and floor plates of its relentlessly square grid work were just as tough, just as strong, as those other towers' structures. Ceramacrete was ceramacrete. There was no point in anyone's trying to provide substandard materials, because the basic materials were so cheap to begin with. And there was no point skimping on the fusing, because either it fused completely or—for all intents and purposes—not at all.

That meant that despite its smaller size, the much more tightly divided Hancock was actually structurally stronger than Saracen or Rasmussen. And, of course, "smaller" was a purely relative term. Bachue the Nose's organization had been unable to evacuate as many of Hancock's residents as Dusek had managed to get out of Neue Rostock. They hadn't planned for it, and—as Thandi Palane had suspected—they hadn't explored the subsurface passages and networks as diligently as Dusek had. Bachue had managed to get five or six thousand of Hancock's people evacuated through Neue Rostock, using the tunnels Dusek had mapped, before the Safeties and Misties cut the two towers off from one another, but she still had well over twenty thousand "civilians" to look out for.

A surprising—or perhaps not so surprising, under the

circumstances—number of those people had volunteered to assist the gang members in preparing Hancock for what was to come. Again, Bachue had started later, with less warning from Victor Cachat, but her people had pitched in enthusiastically once she did start. And, strong as ceramacrete was, it wasn't battle steel. A little judicious work with rock drills and the odd kilo of blasting compound—civilian, construction-grade compound would do just fine—tucked into the drilled holes could accomplish wonders.

Fred Trujillo pressed a button, and the distributed charges—*some* of the distributed charges—exploded thunderously.

❖   ❖   ❖

"Shit! *Shit!* They've—!"

Lieutenant Meryl Rodman's voice cut off with a knifelike sharpness as a twenty-meter stretch of the Patterson trunk corridor descended like a vengeful giant's boot. A cubic meter of ceramacrete weighed roughly three thousand kilograms, and Patterson's roof—which was also the floor of the corridor above it—was a ceramacrete slab thirty-five centimeters thick. There were seventy-five cubic meters in that plunging juggernaut, and the two hundred and twenty-five-ton sledgehammer turned Lieutenant Rodman, her platoon sergeant, and twenty-one of 3rd Platoon's thirty-eight troopers into bloody gruel.

Behind her, two more twenty-meter piledrivers came down on most of Alpha Company, as well.

❖   ❖   ❖

Kayla Barrett was far enough forward to escape the avalanche that descended on Lieutenant Kalanadhabhatla and a quarter of 2nd Platoon's remaining troopers. A dusty hurricane howled past her, but before she could really react to that, a ten-meter square of Brookner Plaza's ceiling blasted loose in *front* of her, as well. It crashed down in ruin, but there was no one under it. So why had the seccies—?

"They're coming through the fucking roof!" someone screamed.

It sounded like Ludvigsen, and Barrett flung herself prone as dozens of unarmored seccies on counter-grav belts plummeted through the sudden, gaping holes, weapons blazing.

❖   ❖   ❖

"Motherf—!"

Lieutenant Leandro Wallace's voice broke off in mid-word, and his icon disappeared from Gavin Shultz's HUD with sickening suddenness as the Gladstone roof plummeted down onto 1st Platoon's heads. More of Wallace's people survived than 2nd Platoon or 3rd Platoon could claim, but more than half of them still died, and 4th Platoon, Shultz's reserve, was on the far side of the plunging ceramacrete. Only six of its people were killed, but Charlie Company, following behind it, was less fortunate when the roof above *it* came plunging down, as well.

Schultz stood frozen, stunned by the sudden, massive carnage. A flood of loss-of-signal codes exploded over the 4th Regiment's com net as the transponders in crushed and flattened utility armor went abruptly off the air. And, as he stood there, his HUD suddenly flashed and flared as dozens—hundreds—of other LOS codes came roaring in when still more tons of ceramacrete hammered down on 1st Battalion, 19th Regiment, and 2nd Battalion, 17th Regiment.

Eighty-three percent of the troopers in the three battalions Bentley Howell had ordered into Hancock Tower—just under seventeen hundred men and women—were killed or incapacitated in less than two minutes. The survivors, like Gavin Shultz and Kayla Barrett, were stunned by the sudden, catastrophic carnage, and two hundred and thirty seccies—most members of Bachue's organization, but with a sizable reinforcement of volunteers—swarmed down through the newly blasted breaches upon them.

❖   ❖   ❖

The attackers were armed with pulse rifles and grenade launchers, and Section Sergeant Barrett heard her own voice cursing in a flat, staccato monotone as they opened fire. Her armor's sensors were a huge advantage in the sudden darkness and swirling dust produced by the explosions. Or they should have been, anyway. But there was too much confusion for them to sort out, and there were too damned many *bodies* coming at her.

The passageway behind her was blocked by the ceiling which had crushed the rest of the platoon. From the confusion on the com net, it sounded as if at least some of Delta Company, which had been following 2nd Platoon's advance, was still fighting, but the information was useless. She couldn't retreat that way, and even if she'd tried, a torrent of seccies was pouring down across the rubble. Besides, it didn't sound like Delta was going to last much longer than her own section. The members of Malden's fire team flung themselves around, hammering disruptor and pulser fire back the way they'd come, and Ludvigsen, Timmons, and Sanchez sprayed more fire in all directions as the baying seccies closed in.

Some of the attackers were going down—Barrett could tell that much—but not enough of them, and a sudden sense of something almost like calm flowed through her, despite the terror and adrenaline lashing her system. She settled herself into the prone firing position she'd learned on the MISD's rifle range so long ago, looked for a target, found it, and squeezed the trigger. The seccy went down, and she swung her electronic sight to the right, looking for another target, knowing it wasn't going to make one bit of difference in the end.

"Follow me!" she heard Captain Shultz shouting over the com, and wondered vaguely where he was headed. Forward, probably, knowing him. It didn't matter anyway.

"*Follow me!* Fol—"

The captain's voice died abruptly, and it didn't matter. She heard someone else screaming endlessly over the com, and that didn't matter either.

Nothing mattered, and as Kayla Barrett squeezed her trigger again and again, a small, distant corner of her mind realized she wasn't going to have to worry about a court-martial after all.

CHAPTER 63

"—understand that, Sir," Gillian Drescher tried to keep her voice as calmly reasonable as possible, "but what happened to Commissioner Howell's troops is an indication that if we don't—"

"And I understand your position, General," General Caspar Alpina interrupted from the com display of her Minotaur command vehicle. It was bigger and more heavily armored than OPS' Cyclops, and both its computer support and its communications facilities were better. Not that Drescher was especially thankful for the latter, just at the moment. "I'm afraid the decision's been made—made at the highest level—and there's no point in our continuing this discussion at this time."

Alpina was a trim, muscular, quick-moving man with a depilated scalp, a thin mustache, and dark eyes. Under normal circumstances, he radiated an aura of decisiveness, and Drescher had always found him a reasonable man to work for. Unfortunately, she was coming to the conclusion that however excellent he might be as a peacetime administrative, even as a trainer of combat troops, that decisiveness of his was sadly lacking once he came up against the hard edges of reality.

You're probably being too hard on him, she told herself. *He's standing between you and the General Board, and you know perfectly well what kind of shit has to be coming down all around him after Howell's fucking stroke of genius. You should be damned grateful he's there to weather the shit storm instead of you! But if the Board really insists on this . . .*

"I understand my orders, Sir," she said, locking eyes with him on the com. "And I will, of course, carry them out to the very best of my ability. For the record, however, if my requests for supporting fires are . . . disallowed, both the cost in lives and in lost time will go up, possibly dramatically."

"I'll take your comments under advisement, General Drescher," Alpina replied. "I'll go further and say I fully understand your reservations and that I'll pass them on to CEO Ward with my own endorsement. But we're both soldiers. We don't always have to like our orders. We don't even always have to agree with our orders. We do have to *follow* them, however."

"Understood, Sir." Drescher smiled grimly. "One way or the other, we'll get it done."

"Good, Gillian," Alpina said in a markedly less formal tone. "I know you will. Now I'll get out of your way and let you get to it."

"Thank you, Sir," Drescher said, and then snorted as the display went blank. Both she and Alpina knew "thank you" was the last thing she'd wanted to say. Unhappily for a serving officer, there were times when what one *wanted* to say was . . . unacceptable. And, she acknowledged sourly, when saying it damned well wouldn't do any good, anyway.

She climbed out of the comfortable crash chair and crossed the Minotaur's cramped compartment to the open rear hatch. She stood at the top of the ramp formed by the lowered hatch door, feeling the night wind ruffle her short-cropped black hair, and looked out into the wreckage Bentley Howell had left her.

It was remotely possible that Howell's patrons on the General Board would manage to save his hide in the end. Whether or not they could save his *career* was a much more doubtful matter, and if there was any justice in the world, he'd end up stripped of his rank and spending at least a decade or two behind bars. It was even remotely possible the Board would offer him up as the sacrificial victim—and deservedly so, in this case—when they had to face the rest of the galaxy and explain just what the *fuck* they thought they'd been doing.

She looked to the east, where the thick column of smoke still rose above the shattered ruins of Hancock Tower, black and silver in the light of Mesa's larger moon, like the plume streaming from a volcano's caldera after the eruption.

There was plenty of other smoke to join it, and more than enough fine ash and dust for any self-respecting eruption. Only this was no volcano.

"Did the general change his mind, Ma'am?" Colonel Bartel asked, and she turned her head to where he stood beside the Minotaur.

"I'm afraid it's not General Alpina's mind we have to change," she said. "You were right about how the Board was going to respond."

"*We* were right, Ma'am," he corrected, and she shrugged. He was right, of course, although she'd been at least a little more optimistic about getting the civilians to understand simple, self-evident military truths. Probably, she conceded, because as the commander upon whom this disaster had been dumped, she'd *had* to be more optimistic about that. On the other hand, optimism was something in increasingly short supply.

She had no idea what might have been going through Bentley Howell's mind. In fact, she rather doubted that *he* did at this point, either. Whatever might have passed for thought on his part, however, had probably been about equally compounded of fury, panic, and—most important ingredient of all—sheer fucking stupidity. And all of it had undoubtedly been made worse by his sudden discovery that his lifelong contempt for seccies had been . . . misplaced.

The defenders of Hancock Tower had butchered three of his battalions. Barely eight percent of the men and women he'd sent into the tower had stumbled back out again, and a third of those had been wounded. Officially, the remaining eighteen hundred-plus MISD personnel were currently listed as "missing in action." Since their bodies hadn't been recovered, there was no official confirmation of the armor telemetry reporting their deaths. That was a mighty thin fig leaf for the Culture and Information people to be waving about, however, and Drescher—and anyone else with an IQ above five—knew perfectly well that every single one of those people was dead.

The lucky ones got killed in the fighting, she reflected grimly. *Given the way seccies feel about all nonseccies, but especially about the Safeties and the Misties, whoever didn't die fighting died* hard. *I wonder if that was a factor in Howell's thinking? After the way he screwed the pooch by the numbers, did he think he could at least give them quick deaths?*

Well, whether that was what he'd been thinking or not, he'd certainly succeeded in providing them. Along the way, he'd killed at least another twenty or thirty thousand people by Drescher's most conservative estimate, and not all of that other twenty or thirty thousand people had been seccies or slaves.

The KEW he'd called down on Hancock hadn't been any of the low-kiloton range strikes Drescher had had in mind. Oh, no. He'd wanted something more *decisive* than that. Something of *Jovian* dimensions. And he'd gotten it, too. No one was giving Drescher any hard yield numbers on the strike, probably because the people who had those numbers were pissing themselves trying to figure out how to convincingly understate them to the media and no one wanted the real ones leaking.

Culture and Information was already beginning to suggest that the devastation had been solely the result of cornered Ballroom terrorists detonating yet another of their nuclear devices in order to avoid capture, interrogation, and trial. According to that imaginative exercise in creative writing, Howell's attack had actually been *succeeding*, when the heinous terrorists—whose presence in Hancock, incidentally, proved the attack had been totally justified in the first place—chose to end their lives in spectacular fashion. And, of course, in their fanatic determination, they'd used the biggest device they had in order to inflict whatever damage they could on the rest of Mendel's infrastructure. That was, equally of course, yet more evidence of just how ruthless and bloodthirsty their mindless fanaticism truly was, since in the process they had slaughtered every inhabitant of Hancock Tower, as well. Those thousands upon thousands of *seccy* deaths were ample proof of the Ballroom's fundamental insanity.

It was possible—*remotely* possible—that a particularly credulous ten-year-old might actually believe that, Drescher thought. No military analyst or trained physicist who examined the site was going to buy it for a moment. And neither were the non-Mesan newsies who were either already on-planet or undoubtedly swarming towards it by way of the Visigoth Wormhole at this very moment.

And that was the very reason—*one* of the very reasons—the General Board wanted her to wrap up the fighting in Mendel before that incoming tsunami of journalist outrage crashed ashore.

The idiots.

If this goes as badly as I expect it to go, newsies are going to be the least *of our problems,* she reflected grimly. *No way in hell am I going to "wrap this up" quickly if they won't release the tactical KEWs to me, and what happens when the seccy districts of our other cities figure out how long it's taking—and how big a percentage of the Peaceforce's total firepower it's tying down—while I try to "wrap it up" here in Mendel? Especially with what happened to Hancock as an indication of how far we're prepared to go?*

She stood looking at that rising smoke for another few moments, then shook herself and inhaled deeply.

"All right," she said. "I suppose it's time we got down to it. I want a face-to-face meeting with all the brigade commanders in thirty minutes."

"Yes, Ma'am." Bartel's tone suggested that he'd understood the reason she'd specified a *face-to-face* conference. A commander could say things to her subordinates in a conversation like that without putting anything out over the airwaves or recording it for posterity.

Or for use by the prosecution at any subsequent courts-martial.

"Thirty minutes," she repeated, and turned back to the *Minotaur's* map table.

✧ ✧ ✧

"I told you this would be a disaster," Brianna Pearson said flatly. Regan Snyder glared at her across the conference table, but François McGillicuddy seemed rather more shaken. "My God, this is even worse than I expected, and I didn't think that was *possible!*"

"I don't know that pointing fingers is going to do us any good, Brianna," Brandon Ward said from his place at the head of the table. "For the record, I, for one, am perfectly prepared to stipulate that you warned us about the public relations aspect of something like this. I don't think any of us really considered the other potential consequences, however."

Pearson bit her tongue rather firmly against the burning temptation to point out that someone—like, oh, François McGillicuddy, for example—damned well *should* have given at least a smidgen of thought to what a megaton-range kinetic energy weapon was likely to do.

It had taken out Hancock Tower, all right. Of course, the blast wave had completely flattened and destroyed the industrial spokes on either side of the Hancock District, and the nearest towers beyond those spokes had been severely damaged, as well. That property damage alone was probably in the range of hundreds of millions of Solarian credits. Then there was the damage to the subsurface infrastructure serving the *entire* city, and not just the seccies. Damage there was going to be in the *billions* of credits, and so far the confirmed death toll among first-class citizens—mostly of people who'd been flying in the vicinity in personal air cars, taxis, or buses, or the ones who'd been unfortunate enough to find themselves in subway tubes when the shockwave raced outward through them from Hancock—was over eight thousand. Another four to six thousand were unaccounted for, although most of them would probably be found safe and sound—or relatively so, at least—once the disrupted city services were restored and rescue crews could start picking through the wreckage.

Probably.

There was going to be hell to pay. In fact, there was *already* hell to pay, and Pearson suspected that one reason for McGillicuddy's subdued manner and shaken expression was that he was the one who'd cleared Howell's request for a KEW powerful enough to take out the entire tower. This one was bad enough that they weren't going to be able to settle for hanging responsibility on a disposable underling. This time somebody at the top of the tree, somebody at Director's level, was going to the wall as well, and it would be fittingly ironic if the person who took the fall truly was the one who'd authorized the strike.

"So what are we doing now?" she asked, looking directly at Ward.

"General Alpina has ordered Lieutenant General Drescher to secure control of the Neue Rostock tower as quickly as possible," the chief executive officer replied. "We're moving five brigades into position to support the three she already has on the ground."

Pearson's eyes narrowed. That certainly sounded impressive, but it also sounded ominous. The Mesan Planetary Peaceforce wasn't an enormous organization. In fact, its total strength was only about twelve brigades, little more than thirty-two thousand men and women plus support arms. Given the amount of firepower it deployed and the fire support it could call in from orbit, its combat footprint was far, far larger than most people might have thought just from the numbers, but it still had only so many warm bodies. If they were sending eight brigades, two thirds of the MPP's total combat formations, to *Mendel*, what was going to be left for the *rest* of the planet's seccy districts? And why in God's name did anyone expect to need twenty thousand fully armed and armored soldiers to take a single tower? Oh, obviously the MISD's initial attack on Hancock had been made in too little strength, with too little knowledge of the terrain it was going to confront and far too little forethought, but still...

"That sounds...like a lot of combat power," she said, carefully skirting the word *excessive*. "Does General Drescher feel she's going to need all eight of those brigades?"

"We have to get in and clean this up as quickly as we can," Snyder snapped. "If that takes a bigger hammer, then a bigger hammer's what we're going to use."

"I understand the time pressure, Regan," Pearson said coolly. "Especially after what happened at Hancock." Her thin smile could have frozen a nova's heart and Snyder flushed angrily. "I'm just trying to understand how the Peaceforce intends to employ all those personnel."

"We don't know that Drescher is going to need all of them," Ward said pacifically before Snyder could bark back at Pearson. He watched the Director of Commerce from the corner of one eye, and Pearson suddenly understood. "We simply felt—that is, *General Alpina* simply felt—that it would be prudent to ensure that any combat power she might find herself needing was already deployed and ready to respond."

"I see." Pearson sat back in her chair, gazing at Snyder and Ward, and wondered how many of her other colleagues had been involved in the decision. McGillicuddy, for certain, she thought. And probably Gannon at Industry and Suchein at Foreign Affairs. Maybe Anson Cenáculo at Treasury? It didn't really matter. The fix was in, and the same idiots who'd let Howell get away with using the massive kinetic weapon which had wreaked so much havoc weren't about to let Drescher use *any* KEWs.

And Pearson knew why, too. It was suddenly blindingly obvious to her, and she didn't know which she wanted more, to laugh hysterically or to curse.

The frigging idiots, she thought. *The* idiots! *They really think they're going to be able to sell that Ballroom nuclear suicide to the rest of the galaxy. Surely even they aren't that stupid! Or maybe they are. Or maybe they figure they can sell it right here on Mesa, at least, after this whole wave of bombings, and they're not even worrying about selling it to anyone else, since "anyone else" is going to be skeptical as hell whatever we say. Either way, they aren't going to let any more KEWs come zooming down from the heavens. Why, that might give credence to the vicious, traitorous, groundless rumors that it was our own fearless and dedicated security forces who blew the hell out of Hancock Tower and the rest of the capital!*

She might, she forced herself to concede, be doing them at least a little bit of a disservice. Some of it was quite possibly the result of genuine shock and dismay on the part of people who'd never really visualized what a kinetic strike was actually like. Maybe some of them—Barbara Suchein came to mind—were operating in that special sort of panic mode which rejected even the tiniest possibility of a second Hancock-level strike. Maybe they were even sufficiently panicked they couldn't—or wouldn't—differentiate between the massive overkill Howell had inflicted and the smaller, lighter tactical strikes someone with a working brain, like Gillian Drescher, might call in. But however much of the decision was rooted in that sort of shock and apprehension, the real string-pullers behind it were undoubtedly Snyder and McGillicuddy, and those were the two who were most likely to think they really could convince at least *someone* that all the devastation was the doing of suicidal Ballroom terrorists.

No way, she thought now. *No way in hell. And just what the hell do they plan to do when the seccies in Detweiler City or New Athens decide they don't have anything to lose, either? Or, worse, that the fight Neue Rostock's putting up proves they could fight—and win—as well?*

She had no idea how to answer her own questions, but as she looked at the fortress of Regan Snyder's face, she had the sinking suspicion they might all be going to discover those answers.

❖   ❖   ❖

"And I say we just go ahead and cut her fucking throat right fucking now!"

Kayla Barrett didn't know who the hate-thickened voice belonged to, but she knew exactly whose throat it was talking about. And as she sat on the cold, damp floor, leaning back against an equally damp wall with her arms tied behind her, she wished they'd all just get themselves together and take the voice's advice.

She couldn't see anything, thanks to the bag tied over her head. It smelled like onions, and it was made of some sort of fabric—*textile* fabric, not plastics; she felt it fluttering as she breathed. A faint smear of light penetrated its weave, but that was about it. It was a simple expedient, yet an effective one, although she wasn't any too sure she'd really be able to *see* anything even without it. She was pretty sure she had a concussion, at the very least, and she doubted her eyes would have focused very well in her present state.

Then there was the damage to her right leg. She was just as happy she *couldn't* see that. The pain was bad enough, and even if they'd had them, seccies were . . . unlikely to waste painkillers on a Misty. Fair enough. In their place, she wouldn't have either. In fact, in their place she would've already cut the Misty's throat.

"No," another voice replied, firm and flat. "Bachue said take her to Dusek, and that's what we're going to do."

"In case you hadn't noticed, Bachue's frigging *dead*, Alvin. And so's everybody else in the organization, and everybody *else* in the goddammed tower, and this bitch's friends're the ones who did that!"

"Don't know I'd call them such great 'friends'

of hers, Geerard," Alvin—whoever he was—replied sardonically. "If Bachue hadn't ordered us to drag her ass over to Neue Rostock, they'd've dropped the damned thing right on *her* head, too! Not exactly a friendly thing to do."

"Bullshit!" Geerard snapped, his voice even uglier with raw, burning hatred. "Don't you try'n kid me along, goddamn it! Molly and the kids're gone, too!"

"I know," Alvin said more gently. "I know they are. And so's everybody else. And if killing her slow and painful'd bring a single one of them back, I'd hand you my knife an' step back and cheer." There was, Barrett thought from the dizzy darkness which enfolded her, nothing but total sincerity in that last sentence. "But it won't bring any of them back, an' getting her to Neue Rostock, someplace where someone like Palane can get information out of her, might just keep someone else alive. Might even make the difference in what happens to all of us who're still left."

"Difference," Geerard half-sneered. "You saw what they did to Hancock. What kind of fucking 'difference' is anything she may know gonna make if they're ready t' do *that* kind of shit?! We're screwed, Alvin. Bachue should never've listened to Dusek and Palane—if it's *really* Palane, at all!—in the first damned place."

Someone else muttered what sounded like agreement.

"Wasn't going to make any difference whether we fought or not," Alvin said heavily. "Not this time. They were moving in to kill everybody in sight, and you guys all know it. Sure, if we'd all hunted hidey holes, some of our friends—hell, some of our families!—might still be alive. But they probably wouldn't be, and how many other people's friends and families'd be dead instead?"

"And what exactly's gonna be different in the end doing it *this* way?" Geerard demanded. "They busted Hancock wide open with one frigging KEW, and those damned things're *cheap*, Alvin. They can send 'em down all day, and sooner or later, that's exactly what they're gonna do to Neue Rostock. And then they're gonna send the Misties in, prob'ly this time with Peacie tanks backing them, and they're gonna sweep right through all the other districts just like they did to Hancock and just like they're gonna do to Neue Rostock."

"Maybe you're right," Alvin conceded. "Maybe we're all going to die, and maybe Dusek and Palane were frigging lunatics to think fighting back could make any difference. But I'll tell you one thing, Geerard. If I'm going to die, and if all my friends're going to die, then before I do, I'm going to kill every fucking Misty and Peacie I can! And if we get her to Dusek, it may help us kill a few more of the bastards."

There was silence for a moment, and Barrett wondered almost idly what the rest of her captors were thinking. Then another voice—this one female—spoke.

"Alvin's got a point, Geerard. Course, odds are we're all gonna get killed trying to take her to Dusek. But if we *don't*, it might actually let him and Palane kill another stack of Misties, maybe this time with a few Peacies thrown in. And if we don't make it, we can always cut her throat then. Or maybe the Peacies'll do it *for* us when they take us out!"

Several people chuckled wolfishly at the woman's last sentence. Then there was another lengthy silence until, finally—

"All right," Geerard agreed at last, his tone sullen.

"All right, I'm in. But if it looks like we aren't gonna make it, then I'm personally cutting her throat."

"Not a problem," Alvin said mildly. Then he went on, "Milla, you and Scott get to carry her for the first leg. Geerard, I want you and Luke scouting ahead for us. I got so turned around when the big one hit that I'm not sure where the hell we are, so if any of you think you see anything that looks familiar, sing out."

CHAPTER 64

"*Down!* Down, Jackie!"

The warning shout came a lifetime too late. The Peaceforcer at the point of the three-man fire team feeling its way along the rubble strewn corridor went down in an explosion of blood and rupturing power packs. His utility armor was—or had been, anyway—considerably stronger and more capable than the equipment issued to the MISD, but it had never been designed to stop an Auger anti-armor missile.

The Auger was the Mesan Planetary Peaceforce's standard light anti-armor weapon, capable of knocking out any armored personnel carrier. Of course, no one was trying to use any APCs inside Neue Rostock tower, but the Auger was capable of killing utility armor, or even the full battle armor of the Peaceforce heavy assault companies, all day long.

Or as long as the defenders' supply of them held out, anyway.

The Peaceforcer behind the point man went down as well, screaming, the right leg of her utility armor shattered by blast and shrapnel. The last member of the fire team grabbed her by her equipment harness, dragging her frantically towards safety, but a heavy tribarrel fired a short, deadly burst down the passage.

His armor's backplate was thinner than its breastplate. It was unlikely that it made a lot of difference, however. The tribarrel would have had a better than even chance of taking out *battle armor*, even with a frontal hit. Hit from behind, the UA never had a chance.

The rest of the squad poured answering fire up the passage. Their armor's sensors could pick up the energy signature of the tribarrel, now that it had been brought online, and their fire was deadly accurate. But the seccies behind that tribarrel had been instructed by Thandi Palane, Victor Cachat, and Yana Tretiakovna. The barricade of piled sandbags and slabs of ceramacrete—provided by demolishing some of the tower's internal loadbearing walls—was impervious to pulser fire and shrugged off even heavy tribarrel darts, at least for a while. And the Peaceforcers were far more exposed than the seccy gunners.

A grenade bounced off of the corridor roof, spinning crazily to land on the far side of the strong point. It armed when it hit the roof, but one of the seccies pounced on it, snatched it up, and spun to drop it into the grenade sump they'd built behind the barricade.

He didn't make it. The grenade exploded in his right hand, killing him instantly, but his body absorbed most of the blast. One of the tribarrel gunner's assistants was badly wounded; no one else was even scratched, and the Peaceforcer who'd fired the grenade went down an instant later, shredded by the tribarrel's fire.

"Back to the cross passage!" the Peaceforce section sergeant who'd tried to warn Jackie ordered, and the survivors retreated hastily. They dove into the cross passage on either side of the main corridor, scuttling out of the tribarrel's field of fire, and the section sergeant counted the icons on his HUD and swore with silent venom. Then he gave himself a shake.

"Central, Delta-Zero-Six," he said. "Patch Delta-Zero-Two."

"Delta-Zero-Six, Delta-Zero-Two," the platoon sergeant's voice came back.

"Sarge, we're stuck at—" the section sergeant consulted his HUD "—Fox-Seven-One. The seccies have a tribarrel dug in at Fox-Seven-Three. We're not gonna budge it without a hell of a lot of support. I'm down four—three dead, and one wounded I can't recover. We need some help in here."

"Delta-Zero-Six, hold on," the platoon sergeant replied. The link went silent for perhaps two minutes, then, "Zero-Six, hold what you've got. Delta-Zero-Eight's going to punch across to Fox from Golf-One-Niner. I say again, from Golf-One-Niner. That should let him come in behind your tribarrel. He'll contact you direct when he's ready to move. Be ready to put some covering and distraction fire down. Understood?"

"Roger, Zero-Two. Zero-Eight will be coming in behind the tribarrel. Standing by to provide cover fire."

"Confirm," the platoon sergeant said. "Estimate fifteen minutes."

"Delta-Zero-Six copies fifteen minutes," the section sergeant said, then looked around at his troopers in their filthy, battle stained armor.

"Fifteen minutes, Sergeant Carla says. Then it's our turn."

❖   ❖   ❖

"I know there's no justice in the world, Byrum," Gillian Drescher said mildly. "If there were, though— if there *were*, I say—then after this is all over the Board would give me about a half hour—no, forty-five minutes—alone with Bentley Howell and a very, very dull knife."

"Never going to happen, Ma'am," Colonel Bartel replied. "But if it did, I could get rich selling tickets."

Drescher snorted. It was a harsh sound, made harsher by the two solid weeks that had passed as her Peaceforcers clawed their way one bloody centimeter at a time into the bowels of Neue Rostock Tower. The body count was atrocious, and she strongly suspected that she'd lost more people than the seccies had, so far at least. Of course, ultimately, once the seccy defense finally broke—and it had to break soon, one way or the other, if only because they must be running out of ammo—it would be a bloodbath. That was what happened when one side decided to fight to the bitter end, and that certainly appeared to be what the seccies had decided to do.

They should've cut and run, she thought grimly, standing beside her Minotaur and glaring at the battered, crumbling ceramacrete cube that was her objective. *They should've cut and run at least a week ago. God knows* we *couldn't've stopped them!*

After she got done gelding Bentley Howell with a dull—a dull and *rusty*—knife, she intended to have a few constructive moments alone with the city engineer and his staff. It was sadly apparent that the maps of the underground service ways and access routes were badly out of date. Her troopers had run into ceramacrete walls where there weren't supposed to be any, and discovered dozens of tunnels that weren't supposed to be there but were. It was bad enough fighting a way through terrain like that when the bits and pieces of it were where you thought they were; it was infinitely worse when your maps lied to you.

Of course, the city plans of the inside *of the frigging tower're even* more *useless,* she reflected grimly. *But that still doesn't explain why they didn't pull out days ago. I know damned well they've still got underground access we're not even close to finding yet, so why the hell haven't they used it already?*

The truth was that she was afraid she knew the answer to her own questions. The seccies hadn't run because they didn't *want* to. Or, perhaps more accurately, because they'd *chosen* not to, whatever any putatively sane person might have wanted to do.

They were making a *statement,* as well as a stand. They were telling the Peaceforce and all the rest of the Mesan government that they were willing to die where they stood, and that they could kill a hell of a lot of Peaceforcers first. But their true audience wasn't the government; it was every other seccy on the planet.

There were already signs, she thought grimly. There'd been incidents in Detweiler City. Nothing like Hancock or Neue Rostock—not yet. But there'd been no OPS or MISD sweeps in Detweiler, either. That meant the incidents had all come from the *seccies'* side, and that was scary as hell. So far, the Safeties had managed to keep a lid on the situation, although Drescher wasn't optimistic about how much longer they could continue to do that. It went against the Safeties' training and inclinations to practice "crowd control" without corpses, but thank God McGillicuddy—or someone—had hammered them hard enough about the need to do just that. The last thing anyone needed was for Detweiler to go the way Mendel had.

Besides Neue Rostock, OPS and MISD troopers had four more towers—Stamford, Kovaleski, Hadar, and Lindbergh—surrounded in the capital's seccy districts. So far, none of the seccies in any of those towers had attempted to test the security forces' cordons, but the whole reason they'd been surrounded was the potential for additional violence from them which OPS' surveillance systems were picking up. The situation was tense as hell, and with so much of the MPP committed to Neue Rostock or being held ready for instant deployment to Detweiler or any of the other cities, there was damned little available to support those cordons.

The wheels could come off of this thing at any moment, she thought grimly. *And if they do...*

At least her warnings seemed to have finally started getting through to the civilians, she reflected even more grimly. They hadn't wanted to listen to her. In fact, they'd fought tooth and nail against it, but they'd finally released the use of tactical-level KEWs to her. Of course, they'd hedged it around with all sorts of asinine restrictions, but the truth was that even if they'd let her use heavier strikes, by now her own people were too deep into Neue Rostock for her to really hammer the tower. Still, she was steadily reducing its upper stories to rubble at the same time her people fought their way deeper and deeper into it along the two or three floors above ground level. Eventually, they were going to start losing enough of their noncombatants that they'd have to either pull out, counterattack, or try some sort of negotiations. Or they might be crazy enough to stand and fight until their families were slaughtered behind them, as well.

Please, God, she thought. *I know you probably aren't even on speaking terms with us at the moment, and we probably deserve it. But* please, *help me find a way to not kill every single person in that tower.*

✧   ✧   ✧

"We lost Aaronson and his tribarrel when they punched out the Proctor and Sangamon junction hardpoint," Triêu Chuanli said wearily. He scrubbed one hand across his face and shook himself. "We got Serengeti and his crew out first, though."

Thandi Palane nodded. She sat tipped back in the central control chair, her expression calm, but the awareness of approaching defeat swept through her. Frankly, she was surprised they'd held this long, once the Peaceforce took over from OPS and its stooges.

She knew who was in command on the other side now. Despite the savagery and close quarters nature of the combat, they'd taken a handful of prisoners—and captured quite a lot of highly useful weapons—over the last terrible weeks, and most of those prisoners had a tendency to spill their guts once they realized they'd truly fallen into seccy hands. Others had been more defiant, even though she knew Dusek's people had been less than gentle with them. She supposed they probably ought to be observing all the niceties of the Deneb Accords, since the Peaceforce was, after all, a uniformed, regular arm of a legally recognized government. On the other hand, Dusek's people and the volunteers who joined them had never ratified the

Accords, and they could all be fairly confident that the MPP wasn't going to be observing them where *they* were concerned, either.

Actually, the most interesting of the prisoners was the MISD section sergeant who'd been delivered—eventually—to Dusek. The handful of survivors from Bachue the Nose's organization had endured several narrow escapes evading security forces in the labyrinth of underground passages between what had once been Hancock Tower and Neue Rostock, but they'd made it in the end. Thandi was glad they had, although she was far from sure what to make of Kayla Barrett.

The woman's right leg had been beyond salvage by the time her captors dragged her into Neue Rostock, and Rudrani Nimbakar, who'd received quite good bootleg medical training despite her seccy origins by way of some of Dusek's "gray economy" contacts, had amputated it just below the hip. If the woman lived—which seemed unlikely—regenerating the lost limb wouldn't be particularly difficult. Aside from that and a moderate concussion, she'd been in pretty good shape, all things considered, when she finally arrived in Nimbakar's infirmary, but there was something about her...

Thandi supposed any Misty who found herself in seccy hands, especially after what had already happened, was bound to be at least a little off. But Barrett seemed remarkably calm. She did what she was told to do, she was actually courteous—courteous, not fawning or subservient, and there definitely was a difference—to her captors, and she readily answered any question put to her. She hadn't had an enormous amount of information to offer about the Peaceforcers, but she'd readily provided all she did have. And yet there was that sense of something broken inside her. Something even worse than the sorts of sights and sounds so many others were enduring. It was as if she was merely waiting for something only she knew was coming, but whatever it was, it had stamped out any interest she might ever have had in her own future.

Thandi gave herself a mental shake. She doubted she'd ever find out what was actually going on inside Section Sergeant Barrett's head, and that was probably just as well. She doubted she really *wanted* to know. But the way her mind kept wandering back to Barrett was probably a sign of her own growing mental fatigue.

"We're not going to make it, are we?" Jurgen Dusek sounded as weary as Chuanli looked, and she glanced across to where the gang boss sat at another console. "They're going to take Neue Rostock away from us way before your friends could possibly get here, aren't they?"

"Probably," Victor Cachat said. He'd arrived in the control room with Chuanli, and even his improbably handsome disguise looked worn and battered. He was as dirty as Chuanli, a bulky bandage swelled the bloodstained shirt covering his upper right arm, and a hand-sized bruise discolored the left side of his face. He had to be just as exhausted as the seccy, but no one would have guessed it to look at him. In fact, he looked as calm and collected as he'd been at the start of the siege. It took someone who knew him really well—someone like Thandi Palane—to realize just how desperate even he must be beginning to feel. Of course, Victor's desperation wasn't quite like anyone else's, she reflected.

"Victor's right," she said. It didn't occur to her to

offer Dusek any comforting half-truths. Even if it might once have, it didn't now; she and the gangster had been through too much by now. "I'll be honest, this Drescher who's calling the shots for the other side's a lot better than I'd estimated she'd be. And the Peaceforce is better, too." She shrugged. "Maybe I let myself be persuaded to underestimate them because of what miserable excuses for troops the Safeties and Misties are." She snorted. "Hard to believe, but most of *them* were actually *worse* than I'd expected! Probably only fair that the Peacies turned out to be better."

"Well, there aren't as many Misties left as there used to be," Chuanli put in grimly. "Not after the way Bachue cut them to pieces in Hancock."

Thandi looked at him and nodded. She'd distrusted Bachue's gleefully triumphant estimate of how many MISD troopers the initial Hancock ambush had killed, but only until she'd had an opportunity to talk to Barrett. Until the section sergeant had confirmed it, Thandi wouldn't have believed anyone would be stupid enough to send three battalions of the MISD into that kind of opposition without *any* intelligence on what the other side had or how it was deployed.

Unfortunately, by the time Barrett arrived in Neue Rostock to do any confirming, Bachue and all of her people—including all of the "civilians" still trapped in Hancock—had been dead, which had deprived Thandi of any opportunity to apologize for her original skepticism.

"No, there aren't," she agreed out loud. "And I think our Peaceforce prisoners are probably right about who called in the tower buster on Hancock. They're probably even right about why Drescher didn't use *any* KEWs on us for so long."

She smiled thinly, and despite their grim situation, Dusek and Chuanli actually laughed. It was part of the bizarre nature of the fighting that here in Neue Rostock's central control room the air was still cool and dust free and they still had access to the Mesan information net. But the same could not be said for certain other places, both inside the tower and out. And it would have been just a bit pointless for even Culture and Information to try to hide the nature of what had happened to Hancock, since three quarters of Mendel had been blanketed in a snowlike covering of dust and ash. Thandi doubted very much that anybody actually believed a single word about the "nuclear suicide bombers" story Bryce Lackland and his minions were spouting to explain that ash fall, but it had suggested one reason for Drescher's restraint where kinetic weapons were concerned. Probably not *Drescher's,* really; it had the stink of a political decision to Thandi's nostrils. Either way, she was grateful for it. Once the KEWs had started falling again, she'd known their time was growing short.

"I think it's time we started thinking about withdrawing as many of your people as we can," she said, looking back at Dusek.

The gangster frowned, and she grimaced.

"Look," she said, "you and Triêu are right, Jurgen. They *are* going to take Neue Rostock away from us, probably in less than a week. The one thing that's actually worked out better than I'd projected, though, is that we still hold the grav shafts and *they* still haven't managed to seal off the tunnels. That means we can still get your people—or a lot of them, anyway—out, and it's time we started thinking in those terms."

Dusek continued frowning, and she glanced at Victor.

"Thandi's right, Jurgen," Victor said. "I know I'm the one who got you into this, so you might not think I'm the best person to be giving advice now, but she's right. You need to get as many of your people out as you can...and *you* need to go with them."

Dusek looked up sharply, his frown deeper than ever, and Victor smiled wolfishly at him.

"Culture and Information's mouthpieces wouldn't be spending so much time trying to blame this all on you—specifically on *you*—if they weren't scared as hell of you," the Havenite said. "The last thing a genuinely repressive regime wants is a folk hero on the other side, and that's exactly what you've become."

"I'm not going." Dusek's voice was flat, and Thandi felt one eyebrow quirk. "Maybe it is time to start getting some of our people out, but I'm not going to be one of them."

"This isn't the best time to start turning all noble," Victor said mildly.

"Fuck noble," Dusek replied even more flatly. "I'm not going."

Thandi started to argue, then stopped herself and glanced at Victor and shook her head ever so slightly, instead. He regarded her quizzically for a moment, then gave a patented, minimal Victor shrug.

"Have it your own way," he said, and Dusek grunted in obvious satisfaction.

Thandi was positive the gangster would never put it into words, but she knew exactly what was going through his head. Before she'd met him—and before he'd allied himself with her and Victor—she might not have believed it was possible. Now she knew better, and she felt a deep and abiding sense of warmth as she looked at him.

Victor had been right from the beginning; Dusek always had been more than "just" a gangster, whether he would ever have admitted it or not. But he'd still been *mostly* a gangster, and now he'd become something else. The crime lord was still in there, and not very far from the surface, yet it wasn't the crime lord who'd announced that he wasn't leaving Neue Rostock. No, the Jurgen Dusek who'd announced that had made the transition from gangster to patriot.

She glanced at Chuanli and saw the same hardness in his eyes. Both of them knew the equation on Mesa had been changed forever, whether or not the Grand Alliance ever responded to their desperate call for help. The seccies would never again simply lie down and die for the Office of Public Safety. They'd seen where that led . . . and they'd discovered that they could fight back. That they could *hurt* their oppressors, punish them in return . . . even *defeat* them. What had happened to the Security Directorate in Hancock, what was happening even now to the Peaceforce in Neue Rostock, proved that, and all of the Culture and Information propaganda in the universe couldn't hide that truth.

More than that, Neue Rostock's stand had already bought time for other seccy communities to begin organizing, begin stockpiling weapons and preparing their own defenses. The forces Mesa had been forced to commit to reducing Neue Rostock alone had prevented the Office of Public Safety from breaking up those defenses, and the longer Neue Rostock *continued* to stand, the higher the blood price the Safeties and Misties would pay if they attempted to break them up afterward. None of the other seccy communities by themselves could hope to stand off the massed might of OPS and the Peaceforce, but neither could` the security establishment possibly hope to suppress *all* of them. The only way they could do that would be to call in the KEWs from the very beginning . . . and the seccy communities were inside their own cities. To rain kinetic weapons on them would be to devastate their own communities, their own infrastructure . . . their own *families*.

My God, she thought. *Victor was right again— probably more right than even he realized. We've started a genuine revolution, and if the seccies go up in flames, the slaves aren't going to be far behind.*

She remembered the comment Victor had made about providing Torch with the equivalent of its own Alamo if they all died here in Neue Rostock. Jurgen Dusek had probably never thought in terms of a glorious last stand in his entire life, but now he'd grasped the reality—the larger-than-life reality, but still reality—that draped itself around those sorts of stands. The reality of Thermopylae and Masada, of Fort Saint Elmo and Khartoum. Of the Alamo, Verdun, and Stalingrad. Of the Battle of Carson and the Second Battle of Yeltsin and a thousand other places where men and women had stood their ground. Stood to die. "They shall not pass!" All too often the defenders who'd shouted that warcry had failed. They'd fallen, and the enemy had marched forward across their bodies. But for every Thermopylae there was a Battle of Salamis, and for every Alamo there was a Battle of San Jacinto. For every Stalingrad there was a Battle of Kursk . . . and ultimately, there was a Battle of Berlin, as well.

That was what Jurgen Dusek and Triêu Chuanli had decided to give the seccies of Mesa—give their *people*, with an awareness that they *were* their people—their own Leonidas, their own Travis...their own Spartacus. And if they died in the giving, so be it.

"I think we should at least start evacuating the wounded," she said.

CHAPTER 65

"—and then," Gillian Drescher said using her pointer to drop an icon into the holographic terrain display, "Brigadier Hanratty's people will attack *here*. Essentially, First Brigade and Third Brigade are diversions. If either of them has an opportunity to convert a diversionary attack into an actual attack with a chance of success, I expect the opportunity to be taken, but there's no prize here for running unnecessary risks and getting your people chopped up."

She looked up from the display to meet her regained commanders' eyes levelly.

"We're grinding them away, but they've proven repeatedly how badly they can hurt us if we get ahead of ourselves. So we're doing this methodically, carefully, by The Book." She forbore to mention that the *old* Book had proven itself woefully inadequate. All of them understood that she was talking about the *new* Book. *Her* book, rewritten and annotated on the fly. "Sixth Brigade is the key here. If they can reach this objective, we'll be positioned to squeeze out this entire portion of the tower—" her pointer's icon shifted, circling a crimson-coded portion of Neue Rostock's interior "—and *that* will flank their position on the gamma group of grav shafts."

She stood for a moment, gazing at them, then deactivated her pointer and shrugged.

"This operation isn't going to give us Neue Rostock," she told them. "But what it is going to do is to make it even harder for them to get in and out of the damned tunnels. And it's going to put us in a better position to drive for the central residential sections. If we cut off the tunnels, we cut off the flow of reinforcements, and once we do that, we can finally start rolling them up one section at a time. Is that understood?"

Her subordinates nodded, their expressions grim, but confidence glittered in the backs of their eyes, and she nodded back. None of them expected it to be easy, and all of them expected to lose a lot more people, but like her, they realized the end was in sight for the seccies.

"All right. Let's look at some of the details. Byrum?"

"Yes, Ma'am." Colonel Bartel stepped forward and activated his own pointer. "Brigadier Edson, to make this work, your Second Regiment will have to advance to at least *this* point. Once you've reached it, we'll be able to—"

❖   ❖   ❖

"Shit!"

The shouted expletive was all the warning the seccy strong point had. The Peaceforce didn't have a great deal of all-up battle armor, and battle armor wasn't really that well suited to fighting in the close confines of a seccy residential tower. That was the main reason Gillian Drescher had been holding it in reserve. The other reason was that she'd been waiting for the proper moment to commit it.

That moment had come.

The Mesan Planetary Peaceforce's assault companies weren't as well trained as Solarian League Marines or the Royal Manticoran Marines. Very few military organizations matched the capabilities of those elite forces. But they were well trained enough and there was nothing at all wrong with their courage, and they bulled forward, heavy tribarrels blasting. None of them carried plasma rifles—there were limits to the amount of destruction they could inflict without effectively blocking their own advance—but the hurricane of heavy tribarrel darts was almost as bad.

The strong point was a solid wall across the corridor, built out of slabs of ceramacrete and sandbags. The only opening in it was the firing slit which had been left for the tripod-mounted tribarrel—in this case, one of the several Peaceforce tribarrels which had been captured by the defenders. It wasn't a very large opening, but there were thousands of darts screaming towards it. Ceramacrete dust erupted, the incredible, deafening thunder of the exploding darts filled the corridor, and a few of those darts actually slashed through the firing slit and exploded against the tribarrel's battle steel splinter shield.

The seccy gunner stood her ground, holding down the firing stud, hosing the Peaceforcers with her own explosive darts, and even battle armor had its limits. She killed five of them and wounded two more before their companions' fire punched through the splinter shield and blew her apart. Her assistants dragged her body frantically aside, trying to get the tribarrel back into action, but the battle-armored Peaceforcers had gotten close enough to launch a fusillade of grenades through the slit. Fresh thunder rolled, punctuated by screams—*brief* screams—and then the Peaceforce combat engineers swarmed forward, setting the charges to blow the barricade.

They were almost done when Nolan Olsen pressed a button in the command center and the shaped charges on either side of the passage blew. Blast and fragments swept the engineers, whose utility armor was far less resistant than battle armor, and their screams disappeared abruptly as a massive chunk of ceramacrete smashed down onto them. But the blast did little harm to the battle-armored troopers who'd been waiting impatiently behind the engineers, and the explosions effectively breached the barricade the engineers had been trying to remove in the first place.

"*Go!*" the Peaceforce sergeant bellowed, and his troopers charged forward once more, over the bodies of the seccy defenders and their own engineers, alike.

❖　　❖　　❖

"They're punching through at Atwater and Chester."

Thandi Palane's voice was almost maddeningly calm in Triêu Chuanli's earbud as he stood at the intersection of Chester and Agostino. They were using standard civilian coms, tied into Neue Rostock's hardwired internal com system, and even though the surveillance systems had taken heavy damage, Chuanli knew they still gave Thandi a far better picture of what was happening than anyone else had.

"What do we have between there and here?" Chuanli asked.

"Nothing," Thandi replied flatly, and he swallowed a curse.

"More battle armor?" he asked.

"Some. Looks like they're down to about seven or eight suits, though. Our people have been costing them all the way in."

Once upon a time, Triêu Chuanli might have sneered at Thandi's use of the words "our people," but not anymore. Yana Tretiakovna was in Doc Nimbakar's infirmary, minus her left arm and unconscious while Nimbakar and Steph Turner worked on a sucking chest wound, but the Amazon's counter attack had retaken the critical strongpoint she'd gone in to restore, pulser in one hand and vibro blade in the other, and she'd littered the corridor with Peaceforcer dead before she went down herself. Andrew Artlett's right eye was covered by a thick dressing—it was going to take regeneration to restore his sight—but he was still on his feet, toolkit still slung over his shoulder, moving through the chaos and the confusion to somehow keep the tower's internal systems running. And Victor Cachat had led more forlorn hopes—and somehow gotten back alive each time—than anyone else in Neue Rostock. By now, the tough, cynical seccies of Jurgen Dusek's gang would have followed him in an attack on Lucifer's own palace, and every man and woman in Neue Rostock knew how much they owed to Thandi's icewater control of their desperate defense.

"Okay," he said, vaguely surprised that his own voice sounded almost as calm as Thandi's. "We've got it. How soon can you get someone else to back us up here?"

"Eight minutes. Diasall's on his way with a heavy tribarrel and a couple of grenade launchers, but they're still on the fifteenth floor," she replied, and he nodded.

That much firepower should—*should*—let this position hold, assuming it got here first. Unfortunately, one thing he'd learned was that when Thandi Palane gave a time estimate, it was accurate, and if the Peacies were punching through at the Atwater and Chester strongpoint, he didn't *have* eight minutes. He had to slow them up somehow, stall them long enough for the promised support to get there.

He looked at the dirty-faced teenager equipped with one of their few, precious remaining Auger launchers.

"Sammy, you and Luca hold here." He jabbed his index finger at the barricade behind which they stood. It was only half finished, neither as thick nor as tall as many of the others had been. But it would offer good fighting positions for Diasall and the others when they arrived, and it could be improved quickly, if they managed to hold it against the initial attack. "Jenney and I will try to buy you some time. If we can't, hold your fire till you're sure you can take out at least one of the heavies on point."

Sammy nodded tautly, and Chuanli glanced at Jenney the Hand. The young woman's face was pale and frightened, but she met his gaze steadily as the scooped up the knapsack.

"Come on," he said.

❖   ❖   ❖

Corporal Thomas Crunn moved forward down the corridor his HUD labeled "CHESTER AV," wishing fervently that these damned corridors were wider. Not that he would even have considered trading his battle armor for the smaller, more maneuverable utility armor. On the other hand, his power cells were getting low, and the seccies had done a better job of slowing 1st Platoon's advance than the ops plan had allowed for. Of course, the bastards always did.

Crunn had never really thought too much about what seccies might think or feel. He hadn't known any of them personally growing up, and the only ones he'd had contact with since joining the Peaceforce had been problems to solve, not people to know. Hell, they hadn't really been *people* at all, as far as he'd been concerned. Over the last several weeks, though, he'd been forced to think about them quite a lot. No one would ever confuse him with a philosopher, but combat had a way of sharpening a man's concentration, and he'd come to several unpleasant conclusions.

One thing he'd learned was that whatever anyone else might say, seccies were tough bastards when they decided to dig in and fight. He hadn't observed a whole lot of cowardice on their part, either. And for people who weren't trained soldiers—who would've been subject to lengthy prison sentences, or even execution, if they'd ever tried to *become* trained soldiers—they were entirely too damned good at killing people who *were* trained soldiers. They were also far too proficient at booby-trapping the damned hallways, and they were obviously using the tower's surveillance systems to keep track of the attackers. The Peaceforce had discovered the hard way that absence of resistance usually meant something extra nasty was waiting up ahead and that the fools who rushed to meet it seldom survived. Those who'd lived through one such experience had learned that caution and a certain methodical, deliberate rate of advance was the best way to go right on living, and that meant—

❖   ❖   ❖

"Talk to me, Palane!" Triêu Chuanli whispered over the com.

"Forty-five meters and closing," Thandi replied. Her

voice was level, almost conversational, but her eyes were dark, because she realized exactly what Chuanli intended to do.

"Get back," he said to Jenney the Hand, and jerked his head at the cross corridor they'd passed ten meters before. Their eyes met, and he smiled tautly. "You should have an opening any time now."

"Yeah." She swallowed hard. "Triêu—"

"No time, kid." He clapped at her on the shoulder. "Tell Jurgen I said he should sign you on permanent."

"I will," she whispered, although both of them realized how little chance she'd ever have to do anything of the sort.

"One minute," Thandi said over his earbug.

"Go!" he snapped to Jenney, and she dashed towards the position he'd indicated.

"Thirty seconds."

"Got it."

Triêu Chuanli watched Jenney go, then squared his shoulders under the straps of the knapsack suspended across his chest. He really wished they'd gotten the roof of this section booby trapped, but the speed of this advance had taken them by surprise, and the Peacies had broken through to areas where they hadn't been expected yet.

Wish we had more of these handy, too, he thought harshly, stroking the knapsack with the fingers of his left hand. *Not that anybody ever expected to be able to use the ones we do have.*

Even more than he wished they had more of them, he wished there'd been time to use *this* one some other way, but there wasn't. Not if he was going to slow down the fucking battle armor.

"Fifteen seconds."

"Been a pleasure, Thandi," he said softly. "Look after yourself."

"Not so shabby yourself," she replied. "Five seconds."

Chuanli drew a deep breath, rested the ball of his thumb on the detonator in his right hand, and stepped out of the recessed doorway in which he'd been waiting into the center of the corridor.

⋄　　⋄　　⋄

A warning ping sounded in Thomas Crunn's earbug and an icon flashed sudden crimson on his HUD. His eyes flicked in the indicated direction, his tribarrel started to swing, but there wasn't enough time.

Jurgen Dusek had acquired less than a dozen of the Black Widows, otherwise known as the Mark 3, Mod 2 EEP Antitank Mine (Heavy). First, because he really hadn't been able to imagine any circumstances under which a mine capable of destroying a hundred and thirty-ton main battle tank would be of much use to a gangster. Second, because Black Widows were the sort of ordnance the Peaceforce got antsy about when it disappeared from one of its warehouses. In fact, they'd ended up in his possession more or less accidentally when the ordnance clerk who'd been supposed to send him three crates of pulse rifles bobbled the paperwork. Under the circumstances, however, it had seemed...unwise to try to return them to sender, so he'd kept them.

So far, Neue Rostock's defenders had used six of them. Now they used a seventh.

Triêu Chuanli pressed the button, the Black Widow strapped to his chest detonated, and three self-forging penetrators, each more than capable of penetrating the belly armor of a Mandrake-class heavy tank, screamed down the corridor. One of them struck Corporal Crunn just above waist level, punched through his battle armor, through his body, through the armor's back plate, and then seared its way equally effortlessly through Trooper 1/c Claire Shwang, immediately behind him.

A second penetrator killed Trooper 1/c Andries Benkô, casually ripped off Corporal Aldokim de Castilho's right arm, and then obliterated three of the combat engineers who'd been following behind them.

The third penetrator went straight down the center of the corridor, killing two more engineers and four utility-armored troopers coming on behind the battle-armored point team.

Chuanli was dead well before any of his victims, of course. The detonation hurled his shredded body all the way back beyond the cross passage where Jenney the Hand had taken shelter. Even aimed away from her, the directional blast half-stunned her in the corridor's confines, but unlike the Peaceforcers she'd been expecting it, and she threw herself back out into the main passage on her belly.

The military-grade pulse rifle she'd been issued was a far cry from the light civilian-grade weapons she'd had when she and Nine-Finger Jake first saw the Misties advancing across Trondheim Park towards Eaker Boulevard. The sophisticated electronic sighting system penetrated the billowing smoke and dust easily, and she squeezed the stud, hosing explosive darts into her enemies.

There was no one left in battle armor to get in her way, and her fire slammed into the more lightly armed troopers who'd survived Chuanli's blast. Three of them went down. Then two more. A sixth.

Jenney the Hand killed a total of twelve more Peaceforcers before the launcher-fired grenade exploded sixty-four centimeters from her head.

It took the attackers almost fifteen minutes to get themselves reorganized and resume the advance.

Twelve minutes later, that advance ran into Athanasios Diasall's tribarrel and missile team, well dug in behind the barricade at Chester and Agostino, and disintegrated in bodies and blood.

❖   ❖   ❖

"So, do you think the rumors are accurate, Byrum?" Gillian Drescher asked.

"Which ones, Ma'am?" Colonel Bartel asked wryly. "I've heard so damned many of them over the last couple of weeks it's kind of hard to keep track."

"I suppose it is." Drescher twitched a smile, then looked back down at the holograph on the map table. "In this instance, though, I meant the ones about Thandi Palane."

"Oh, *those* rumors." Bartel grimaced. "I don't know. I'm inclined to think they could well be, though, Ma'am." He shrugged. "Before this whole disaster started, I'd've argued that it would have taken someone like a Palane to get seccies to stand up and fight this way. Now, though." He shook his head. "I've had to...reexamine certain of my fundamental core beliefs where seccies are concerned, you might say."

"There's been a lot of that going around," Drescher agreed in a desert-dry tone.

Actually, she was two-thirds convinced—maybe even three-quarters convinced—that it truly was the infamous Thandi Palane who'd planned and commanded Neue Rostock's defense. On the face of it, it was preposterous. Only it was no more "preposter-ous" than everything else which had been happening since the Dobzhansky strike. And the rumor that the commander in chief of the Royal Torch military was here—right *here*, on Mesa—personally leading the seccy defiance of the planetary security forces had raced through the seccy communities at light speed. There was no stopping it now, and as the assault on Neue Rostock had dragged on and on and on, that rumor had become ever more credible in the seccies' eyes.

It was a name being whispered whenever three or four seccies gathered to discuss the battle. That name and the name of Jurgen Dusek, and of Bachue the Nose. It was hard to imagine a more unlikely trium-virate of legendary heroes, yet that was precisely what Palane, Dusek, and Bachue had become, and Gillian Drescher was too much of a realist to pretend that that legend could ever be killed. Easy enough to kill a woman named Thandi Palane, a man named Jurgen Dusek, but the *legend?* There weren't enough silver pulser darts in the galaxy to slay that.

But it's my job to kill the people behind it, she reminded herself, *and it's a job I swore an oath to do. Maybe I wish now that I hadn't. Maybe I wish I'd found something else to do with my life. But I didn't, and if I break faith with that oath, what else do I have?*

It was a question she'd asked herself more and more often of late, and one she couldn't answer. But she knew exactly what was going to happen sometime in the next forty-eight hours.

And that however great a success it might be tacti-cally, *strategically* it would be a disaster.

She understood now why Dusek and Palane—if that

really was Palane in there—hadn't evacuated. Despite her own earlier estimates, she was now certain that they'd managed to get virtually all of Neue Rostock's regular residents out through the tunnels well before the tower had come under actual attack. Everything she'd seen, everything her people had discovered—and fought their way through—only confirmed that they'd started fortifying the tower days, maybe even weeks, before the first OPS sweeps had run into disaster, and they must have evacuated everyone but their fighters along the way. Yet her people had finally cut those tunnels. No one else was getting out of Neue Rostock now, and her assault elements were poised for the final attack.

It was going to be ugly, and it was going to be brutal, but it was also going to be *over.* She'd gutted four brigades getting to this point, and she was about to reduce a fifth to wreckage. Altogether, she'd lost in excess of nine thousand men and women since she'd taken over from Howell. By her most optimistic estimate, that total would rise to at least eleven thousand—close to a third of the Peaceforce's total peacetime strength—before it was done, but she wasn't foolish enough to think anyone inside that tower would surrender before she'd paid every bloody gram of the price.

And ultimately, her people would pay that price in vain.

Snyder and McGillicuddy and their allies on the General Board might see Thandi Palane's presence here as a godsend—as "proof" Torch and, by extension, Manticore truly were in bed with the Audubon Ballroom. That they'd facilitated and enabled—probably even planned—the present wave of terrorist attacks, just as they had the strike on Green Pines. In Drescher's opinion, based on prisoner interrogation and every intelligence source available to her, that was nonsense. In fact, despite all the evidence, she was no longer fully convinced the Ballroom truly had been responsible for all of the atrocities credited to it. It was probably insane of her, possibly a symptom of combat fatigue, yet she couldn't quite shake the suspicion. And even if it was true, even if Torch had been complicit in every single one of those attacks, it didn't matter. It wouldn't change what Palane and Dusek had already set in motion.

It was too late for any clever propaganda tricks to change what was going to happen. It was no longer a matter of *if* the regime was doomed, but of *when* the regime would fall. In the end, the ship of state was going down, as surely as ever the *Magellan* had, with its keel ripped apart on the reef of Neue Rostock and the general seccy resistance which was bound to arise from the tower's ashes.

Yet she had no choice but to burn that tower to the ground. To turn it into the lifeless wreckage from which a dozen—a hundred—other Neue Rostocks would spring up like dragon's teeth.

It was her job.

"I think we're about ready, then, Byrum," she heard her voice say. "Pass the word. I want all brigade and regimental commanders in the com briefing at nineteen hundred hours."

❖   ❖   ❖

"Well, I certainly hope we have some *good* news for a change," Regan Snyder said sourly as the General Board gathered around the conference table.

Brianna Pearson didn't bother even to glare at her. There was no point anymore. Instead, she looked at Brandon Ward as the CEO settled into his chair at the head of the table.

"Actually, there is," Ward said. "According to General Alpina, General Drescher will be launching her final assault in approximately twelve hours. He tells me that she's confident this *will* be the final assault, and that she estimates the core of resistance in Neue Rostock will be broken within thirty or forty hours from the time she attacks. Mopping up may take some days longer, but she should be able to hand that back over to MISD and pull the Peaceforce brigades back to refit and reequip within two days."

"Well, it's certainly *taken* her long enough!" Snyder snapped pettishly. "After all the money we've plowed into the Peaceforce, you'd think they'd have been able to take a single tower away from a pack of ragged-assed seccies in less than a T-month!"

"It hasn't been a T-month," Pearson said coldly. "It's been about three T-weeks from the moment the first shot was fired. And considering the opposition and the nature of the mission—*and* the fact that she was denied the fire support she needed for *two* of those T-weeks—General Drescher's done one hell of a job with very little support from this Board."

"Oh, bullshit!" Snyder snarled. "It's all her fault—well, the *Peaceforce's* fault—we're in the mess we are right now. You've heard about the incidents happening all over the other seccy districts by now. You think that would've happened if she'd done her damned job in the first place and nipped this whole thing in the bud?!"

"So now you're going to blame the Peaceforce for *your* mess, is that it?" Pearson snapped back, too furious to worry about how dangerous an enemy Regan Snyder had proven herself countless times in the past. "You know, Regan, there comes a point at which self-delusion becomes genuinely dangerous, and you're so far past that point that I doubt you could even see it in your rearview camera!"

"Is that so?" Snyder asked in suddenly silky tones. "Well, we'll just have to see about that, won't we? And now that Drescher's *finally* going to take Neue Rostock down, it's time for us to decide which seccy district Public Safety is going to clean up next."

"Are you really *that* far out of your frigging mind?" Pearson demanded. "You want to kick off *another* Neue Rostock, is that it?!"

"There won't be any more 'Neue Rostocks,'" Snyder sneered. "The only reason—aside from Drescher's incompetence—that this entire disaster's stretched out this way is this bitch Palane! *Thandi Palane!*" Her lip curled in contempt. "A mongrel from Ndebele who *deserted* from the Solly Marines to throw her lot in with a passel of escaped slaves! Just the sort of scum who'd come here, to Mesa, trying to foment rebellion. Hell, she probably brought the Ballroom bombs in *with* her, and you know it, Brianna! Well, she won't be around to command any more 'gallant defenses,' now will she? And without *her*, the seccies will go back to being exactly what they've always been!"

My God, Pearson thought. *I think she actually* believes *that. But she* can't *really be that stupid, can she? Or is it that she's that* desperate? *That she* has *to believe this line of bullshit she's handing out, because the only alternative would be to face the truth? God knows that's the last thing anyone associated with Manpower wants to do right now, but if we let her go on this way, drag all the rest of us down with her, then what happens to us? For that matter, what happens to Mesa? What's going to stop the seccies and the slaves from taking exactly the kind of revenge anyone else would take in their place and turning this entire planet into one huge graveyard?*

Brianna Pearson had never thought of herself as a religious woman, but in that moment, she found herself wishing she did believe in God. Or did she? Because if there truly had been a God, the people whose prayers he'd be listening to were probably the ones inside Neue Rostock Tower, not the ones sitting around this conference table.

"I don't think that's a very good idea," she began. "As a matter of fact—"

The conference room door flew open, and heads snapped around at the unceremonious, unexpected, and unacceptable interruption.

"What's the mean—" Brandon Ward began thunderously.

"I'm sorry, Sir!" his senior aide cut him off. "I'm sorry, but . . . but this is—"

She slithered to a stop, as if groping for words, and Ward's frown turned even darker.

"What the hell are you talking about, Andrea?!" he snapped.

"Sir, Perimeter Tracking just reported a hyper footprint. A *big* hyper footprint—at least a dozen ships-of-the-wall!"

CHAPTER 66

Thandi Palane checked the pulse rifle magazine, then locked it in place, cycled a round into the chamber, and set the safety. She'd already checked the vibro blade at her left hip and the pulser at her right.

She looked up and saw Victor gazing at her.

"I hate legends," she said, with an off-center smile.

"I admit they can be unpleasant things," he acknowledged. "Messy, even. Useful, though. And you have to keep your eye on the final prize."

"Have I ever mentioned to you that you're a very strange person, Victor Cachat?"

"Yes, you have." The handsome face and blue eyes met hers levelly, and he shook his head. "And for what it matters," he said, his voice unaccustomedly soft, "I'm sorry. I'd really rather not have turned *you* into a legend, Thandi."

"Don't be," she replied. "Sometimes you just draw the short straw, and I can think of a lot worse things to be fighting for—or against, for that matter."

"At least we gave the bastards a hell of a hard time," Dusek said from where he sat in one corner, counting hand grenades. He looked up with a crooked smile of his own. "You really think the rest of them will finish it up for us?"

"One way or the other," Victor said. "We may not have kept them busy long enough for Duchess Harrington to get here from Manticore, but we sure as hell kept them busy long enough for the other seccies to get organized."

Thandi nodded. They could still pull in Culture and Information's so-called newscasts, and it didn't take a huge amount of skill at reading between the lines to know the Mesan government was sweating bullets over the pressure building in the other seccy districts. None of those other districts were as well organized—or armed—as Neue Rostock had been, but she had no doubt at all that they were a lot better organized—and armed—than they'd been three T-weeks ago, and there were a lot of them. She remembered a certain Old Earth legend, and snorted.

"Something funny?" Dusek asked.

"Just that I never realized I should have been named Pandora Palane, not Thandi."

"Pandora?" Dusek raised both eyebrows.

"A Solly legend," Victor said, "and she's mixing it up." Thandi stuck out her tongue at him, and he smiled. "You're not inflicting all the world's evils on your *own* people like that silly twit, Thandi. You're inflicting them on the *bad* people." He paused for a moment, scratching the lobe of one ear, then shrugged. "Um. Now that I think about it, you might have more of a point than I thought, though. What was the last thing to come out of the box?"

"Hope, I think." She shrugged. "It was in the version of it I heard, anyway."

"Well, I think you could probably make a case that *hope* is exactly what we're delivering to the seccies and slaves here on Mesa. And even though I rather doubt *Duchess Harrington's* ever been called 'hope' before, that's damned well what the seccies are going to call her when she rolls into the Mesa System with blood in her eye in another few T-weeks. Of course," he smiled unpleasantly, "I tend to doubt that's how the system government and the Mesan Alignment're going to see her."

"Probably not," Thandi agreed, and looked down at her handful of still live monitors.

It wouldn't be long now. Two days before, Drescher's troops had finally driven a twin pronged assault entirely through the tower on the twenty-third floor. They'd taken the central grav shafts at that level, and they were working their way methodically both up and down from that point. It was still costing them people, but the defenders were critically low on ammunition for the heavy tribarrels, and they were essentially out of missiles. They still had sizable stocks of satchel charges manufactured out of commercial blasting compound—several tons of which had been smuggled into the tower before the underground accessways were cut—and plenty of ammunition for pulsers, but those were of limited effect even against utility armor, far less against the battle-armored troopers Drescher was increasingly using as her point elements.

In addition to the stranglehold Drescher had locked on the twenty-third floor, her troops were working their way up from the sub cellars, and the Peaceforcers advancing from that direction were going to reach the control room well before the ones fighting their way down from the twenty-third. There weren't as many booby traps and strong points between them and their objective, and it was pretty clear they'd figured out where Thandi's command post was, despite any false information their maps of Neue Rostock Tower might contain. It didn't really matter, though, because they'd taken the fusion plant nine hours ago. The tower was operating on battery power now, and that would last little more than another eleven or twelve hours, at which point the remaining environmental systems would shut down. Most of her surveillance systems were gone by now, anyway; judging by the methodical way the Peaceforcers had been taking them out, Drescher had clearly realized how valuable they'd been to her.

At least Yana, Steph, and Andrew should be okay until Admiral Harrington gets here, she thought.

They'd gotten Doctor Nimbakar's infirmary out before the Peaceforcers finally cut the last escape tunnel, and Thandi had ordered Steph and Andrew to go with them. She'd tried ordering Nimbakar to go, as well, but she might as well have saved her effort on that one. Stupid, really. Anybody Nimbakar patched up was going to die anyway, in the end. But that was the way human beings were, she supposed. Sometimes it was really hard to judge where stupid ended and gallant began, and one thing Nimbakar had plenty of was guts. Who was Thandi Palane to tell her she couldn't die caring for the wounded?

She looked back up at Victor, and for just a moment, he wavered through a sudden prickle of tears. There weren't many of them, those tears—certainly not enough for anyone else to notice—but in that trembling heartbeat of time, she found herself wishing passionately that she could see his face—his *real* face—one last time.

Don't be any stupider than you have to be, she told herself. *You can see his "real" face anytime you want to.*

She closed her eyes for a moment, summoning the memory, treasuring the remembered smile in those dark brown eyes. Not many people had ever seen that smile, she reflected. A lot of people would have flatly denied it could exist. But *she'd* seen it, and she knew exactly who it was for. And that was enough, even here at the end.

She reopened her eyes, looking once again at the outward stranger disguising the inward man, and her lips twitched in an unwilling smile.

"What?" he asked.

"Nothing," she said. "Just a passing thought."

He cocked an eyebrow at her, but she only shook her head. It wasn't really all that funny, she supposed, but it *was* inevitable. The vote had been unanimous, in fact, and her gaze rested for just an instant on the detonator hanging against his chest like a necklace pendant. They didn't have anywhere near the mountain of blasting compound they would have required to bring Neue Rostock down, even placing the charges internally, but they had enough to implode a *lot* of the tower. They ought to be able to take at least another thousand—more likely two thousand—Peaceforcers with them when they went. And no one had doubted whose hand they wanted on that trigger . . . or whose brain they wanted calculating the exact moment to press it home.

Spiteful of us, I guess, she thought with another of

those half-imagined smiles. *But if I'm going to wind up becoming a damned legend, I want it to be a practical, bloody-minded, stubborn, vindictive* bitch *of a legend, by God!*

"Thandi?"

She looked up as Nolan Olsen called her name. The Neue Rostock building superintendent's refusal to leave had been just as adamant as Rudrani Nimbakar's, and Thandi had wasted less effort arguing with him. Partly that was because she'd gotten to know him better and realized more quickly how futile it would have been, but mostly it was because he'd been much more useful for the grim grinding out of the defense. He'd done wonders keeping the internal systems online—or limping along, anyway—and he was at least as exhausted as anyone else in the control room. Yet there was something peculiar about his tone.

"What, Nolan?"

"We've got a com call coming in." He sounded almost bemused, although there was something else— something tauter, even darker—under the bemusement. "It's for you."

"What?" Thandi straightened. The Peaceforcers hadn't been able to shut down their internal communications net, but they'd managed to cut any external links. "For me?" Olsen nodded. "From who?"

"She says she's Lieutenant General Drescher," Olsen replied.

Thandi blinked, then looked at Victor and Dusek.

"Little late for any surrender demands, don't you think?" Dusek asked wryly.

"Won't cost her anything to try," Victor pointed out. "And she probably has at least a pretty good idea of how much it's going to cost her to finish things up the hard way, too." He shrugged. "Hard to blame her for giving it a shot."

"I suppose you want me to say something deathless and noble to her?" Thandi said, looking at him sourly, and he chuckled.

"Deathless, maybe. Noble?" This time he actually laughed. "Neither of us is a Manty aristocrat, Thandi! I vote for something pungent and to the point."

"Such as?"

"'Go fuck yourself?'" Dusek suggested helpfully.

"Too many syllables," Victor said, shaking his head. "She's only a general, you know. She'd get confused."

"And which one of the two generals involved were you referring to?" Thandi inquired.

"The other one, of course. Wouldn't be safe to talk about *you* that way."

Thandi snorted, but she also looked back at Olsen.

"Can you switch it to my station, Nolan?"

"Yeah, I can still manage that much."

He punched in a command and one of Thandi's dead monitors flickered to life with the image of a petite, dark-haired woman in the uniform of the Mesan Planetary Peaceforce with a lieutenant general's insignia. She was a few centimeters taller than Jacques Benton-Ramirez y Chou, yet she strongly reminded Thandi of the Beowulfer. That was irritating, given how much she'd liked Benton-Ramirez y Chou.

"Yes?" she said, more than a bit brusquely.

"I'd asked to speak to Thandi Palane," the woman on the monitor responded stiffly.

"I'm Palane," Thandi said even more brusquely, and the other woman's eyes narrowed.

"Not according to the imagery of Captain Palane from the Solarian Marines you aren't," she replied, and Thandi felt her eyebrows rise.

It certainly wouldn't have been impossible for Mesan intelligence to get its hands on a copy of her official Marine file, but it wouldn't have been easy, either. On the other hand, once Torch declared war on Mesa, it would have made a lot of sense for the Mesan intelligence agencies to look for all the information it could find on one Thandi Palane. Although, now that she thought about it, it was questionable just how much good that would do them, given the various unnatural things Admiral Rozsak had done to her *official* file when she went to work on his personal staff.

"Surely not even a Mesan would have expected me to come waltzing in wearing my own face, General Drescher?" she pointed out acidly.

"I guess not," Drescher conceded after a moment, her eyes still intensely focused on Thandi's face. "Good disguise, though. Beowulf?"

"Given the fact that your government—such as it is and what there is of it—is already trying to blame *Torch* for those 'Ballroom terrorist attacks,' do you really expect me to say anything you could cut and edit to accuse anyone else of the same sorts of things?"

"I guess not," Drescher said again, this time with a snort that sounded like genuine amusement. Then she shook herself. "I'm going to take you at your word that you really are Thandi Palane, though."

"You have no idea how deeply flattered I am by your concession. And would it happen that that means you're about to get around to telling me why you commed?"

"It would." Drescher's expression sobered. "The

reason I screened was to propose an immediate cease-fire in place, followed by the phased withdrawal of all of my personnel from Neue Rostock Tower."

Despite herself, Thandi blinked, then shot a sudden, incredulous glance at Victor and Dusek. Dusek looked as stunned as she felt. Victor . . . not so much. He did look suddenly and intensely interested, however, which was about as close to "stunned and incredulous" as Victor Cachat ever came.

Thandi looked back down at Drescher's image, trying to imagine what could be behind the other woman's last, preposterous sentence. Surely she didn't think she could dupe them into lowering their guard, letting her surprise them with a sudden attack in the midst of "negotiating" this cease-fire of hers! But if not that, then—?

"Why?" she asked bluntly, and Gillian Drescher smiled very strangely at her.

"Well, General Palane, it seems something new has been added to the balance of forces here in the Mesa System. Thirty-five minutes ago—"

CHAPTER 67

"Your Grace, Captain Lewandoski is here."

Honor Alexander-Harrington rose behind her desk as Lieutenant Commander Waldemar Tümmel, her flag lieutenant, escorted her visitor into her day cabin aboard HMS *Imperator*.

Captain Spencer Hawke, her personal armsman, followed both men, his eyes narrow and his gunhand hovering near the pulser at his hip. Hawke's uneasiness would have been obvious to anyone, far less someone with Honor's ability to taste the emotions of those around her, and she didn't blame him. But she wasn't really focused on her armsman's emotions at the moment, either, because her visitor's had hit her over the head like a club the instant he came in range.

She heard a soft sound behind her as Nimitz vaulted from his bulkhead perch to land on the corner of her desk. The treecat's ears stood straight up, his tail rising behind him, and the sharpness of his own concern flowed to her over their link as he, too, sampled that storm of emotion.

"Captain Zilwicki," she said, holding out her hand,

and saw—and tasted—Hawke's astonishment at the greeting. She didn't blame the young Grayson for that any more than she'd blamed him for his uneasiness. The last time either of them had seen Anton Zilwicki, he'd still looked like Anton Zilwicki. This man had the same basic physique, but that was the only real point of physical resemblance between him and the Zilwicki they'd both met.

Honor was less surprised than Hawke—or Tümmel, for that matter—but that was because she'd recognized the codeword "Lewandoski" had transmitted as soon as the yacht *Brixton's Comet* emerged from the Manticoran Wormhole Junction by way of its Beowulf Terminus. Lieutenant Commander Harper Brantley, her staff communications officer, had patched the incoming transmission through to her somewhat against his own better judgment. He probably wouldn't have put through a transmission from a completely unknown foreign civilian under normal circumstances, but he'd been with Honor for a long time now. Along the way, he'd discovered that she knew quite a lot of unlikely—many would have said disreputable—individuals, and Captain Lewandoski had been . . . insistent.

Honor hadn't recognized him any more than Brantley had, yet she'd recognized the codeword "Pygmalion" which had been chosen (inevitably) by her Uncle Jacques. And since the man on her com display had been using that codeword and obviously wasn't Thandi Palane, Yana Tretiakovna, or Victor Cachat, there was only one person he could have been. And so she'd authorized the yacht's luxurious shuttle to dock aboard *Imperator* and cleared Lewandoski—Zilwicki—to be escorted to her day cabin.

The mere fact that Zilwicki had returned so unexpectedly and so much ahead of schedule had filled her with disquiet. She'd never been familiar with all of the details of his mission. There'd been no reason she should know, and she'd been rather preoccupied with her own duties—the ongoing process of fusing two navies which had been mortal enemies for the better part of seven T-decades into a smoothly integrated fleet undoubtedly qualified as one of the trickiest bits of cat-herding ever to come her way—when he actually departed. But she'd known its general parameters and that he shouldn't have returned home this precipitously.

Now, as she coped with the hurricane of worry, tension, and fear behind the impassive façade of Zilwicki's disguise, she was sinkingly certain her disquiet had been amply justified.

"Your Grace." Zilwicki's deep, rumbling voice was flattened around a burr of tension someone without her sensitivity might have missed as he took her proffered hand. "Thank you for seeing me under these... conditions." His free hand gestured at his physical appearance, and despite that stormfront of emotions, his lips quirked in a wry smile. "I'm afraid I'm not quite myself at the moment."

"So I see."

She released his hand, waving him towards one of the chairs on the other side of her desk, then sank back into her own chair. Nimitz hopped from her desk into her lap, and she wrapped her arms around him, bending her neck just enough to rest her chin on top of his head while both of them regarded Zilwicki with matching intensity.

She considered buzzing James MacGuiness, but

the last thing Zilwicki needed at this moment was something to drink. Instead, she looked up at Tümmel and Hawke.

"I think the captain and I need a few moments alone, Waldemar. Spencer, I'll buzz if I need you."

Tümmel, despite his own raging curiosity, simply nodded and started for the hatch. Hawke hesitated, his expression rebellious as professional paranoia warred with deeply ingrained obedience . . . and his trust in his steadholder. Honor held his gaze firmly.

"I'll buzz if I need you." There was just a hint of steel in her tone as she repeated the words, and Hawke braced briefly to attention.

"Of course, My Lady."

He withdrew . . . not without one last darkling glance at the transformed Zilwicki. The hatch closed behind him and Tümmel, and Honor returned her gaze to her visitor.

"Tell me," she said quietly.

"I know you didn't expect to see me this soon, if at all, Your Grace." Zilwicki's tone was clipped, calm but burnished with a patina of the fear bottled up inside him. It wasn't for himself, that fear, Honor realized, yet the iron control he'd fastened on it only made it even more intense. "The real reason I came straight to you," he continued, "is that you're probably the only person who knows—or would believe—who I am and also has the clout I need. The problem is—"

The words spilled out of him—still clipped, still calm—as he laid out his report with all the clarity and organization Honor had come to associate with him. She listened intently, not just to his words but to the emotions behind them, and she felt Nimitz listening with her, felt the sub-audible vibration of his purr as Zilwicki's emotions poured through him, as well.

"—so even after Victor explained who we were to Dusek, and even after Dusek agreed to fortify Neue Rostock, we knew we wouldn't be able to hold out indefinitely. That was when—"

"When you all decided someone had to go for help," Honor interrupted, straightening in her chair. "And that the best person to send for it was you. And that because I've met all of you *and* I'm Grand Fleet's CO, I was the logical person for you to approach here in Manticore."

"Exactly." Zilwicki nodded hard, his relief at her comprehension obvious, then frowned as she shook her head with one of her slightly off-center smiles. That was the *last* reaction he'd anticipated out of her!

"I apologize, Captain," she said as she tasted his consternation. "I really do understand the tension you've been under, and I'm not trying to make light of it. However, there's something you should see."

Consternation gave way to simple confusion as his mind tried to catch up with what she might mean, but she only gave him another smile, then reached out a long right arm, still cradling Nimitz with the left, and punched a complex password into her desktop terminal.

"This is a message Queen Elizabeth recently received," she said. "So far, only seventeen other people in Manticore have seen it. You'll be number eighteen."

Zilwicki's eyes narrowed, but before he could ask for any additional clarification, Honor tapped one final key and the com display on her desk came

to life with the face of an ebon-skinned woman in
the uniform of a Manticoran admiral. She had the
unmistakable features of the House of Winton, and
Zilwicki recognized her instantly.

"By the time you view this, Beth," Admiral Gloria
Michelle Samantha Evelyn Henke, Countess Gold
Peak and commanding officer, Tenth Fleet, said from
the display, "I'm sure at least some of my professional
colleagues are going to have cast a certain degree
of doubt upon my alleged mental processes. In this
instance, they may even have a point. But I think
this is important—well, obviously I think that, or I
wouldn't be doing it." She shook her head with a slight
smile. "Trust me, I'm aware of the risks involved. I'm
also aware that when you've already got a shooting
war with the League on your hands, having someone
dash off on her own and open yet another front may
not be incredibly high on the list of your priorities.
On the other hand—"

He watched it all the way through, and when it
ended, Anton Zilwicki's eyes were wet. He wasn't actually weeping, but he hovered on the edge, and Honor
tasted those tears as clearly as he did. It wouldn't have
required her empathic sensitivity to know that this was
a man who more or less defined the term *stoic*, but
under that stoicism was a man. A very warm, *caring*
man who felt far more deeply than anyone without
her sensitivity might ever have believed.

"Only Her Majesty and her closest advisers have
seen this before you, Captain," she said quietly.

She didn't bother with any admonitions binding
the captain to solemn vows of secrecy. With Zilwicki,
there was no need to.

He pinched his eyes with his thumb and middle finger, stemming the tears. When he spoke, his voice was soft and husky. "I once had to watch, completely helpless, when my wife Helen went to her death."

Honor nodded. She knew the story. Every officer in the Manticoran navy knew the story of Helen Zilwicki's defense of Convoy MGX-1403. Ambushed at minimum range inside a hyper-space gravity wave by five *Scimitar*-class heavy cruisers, her two *light* cruisers and three destroyers had fought to their own destruction in the finest traditions of Edward Saganami's navy. None of them—and none of the men and women aboard them—had survived, but the damage they'd inflicted before they died saved the entire convoy . . . including the transport *Carnarvon*, in which her husband and four-year-old daughter had been embarked.

Helen Zilwicki had been awarded the Parliamentary Medal of Valor for her actions. Posthumously, as was so often true with that decoration. And Anton Zilwicki had watched on the transport's main display, with his sobbing daughter sitting on his lap, as she earned that medal with her life.

"I thought—the whole way here from Mesa—that I was on another death watch," he said now, and Honor drew a deep breath.

Whatever had happened in Mendel was already over, of course, and nothing she or Zilwicki could do would change that. But if Thandi Palane had put up the kind of fight Honor was certain she had, and if Mike Henke had met her own schedule . . .

"You may have been anyway, Captain," she said now, her voice gentle, and he looked at her mutely.

"You *may* have been," she repeated, and her tone had hardened. "But from what I know of General Palane, I don't think you were. And either way, Captain Zilwicki—Anton—" she met his eyes very levelly, "from what I know of Admiral Gold Peak, by this time, I guarantee you those people on Mesa have a much better understanding of the phrase *the wrath of God is upon you.*"

CAST OF CHARACTERS

Alexander-Harrington, Admiral Hamish: RMN (ret); Earl White Haven, First Lord of Admiralty.

Alexander-Harrington, Lady Dame Honor Stephanie: Duchess Harrington; Steadholder Harrington; Admiral, RMN; Fleet Admiral, Grayson Space Navy.

Alexander, William: Baron Grantville, Alexander-Harrington's brother, Prime Minister of the Star Kingdom of Manticore.

Anderson, Janet: Colonel, Beowulf's Biological Survey Corps (BSC).

Arai, Hugh: Consort of Queen Berry of Torch.

Arpino, S.: Agent of the Mesan Alignment's Genetic Advancement and Uplift League (GAUL).

Ariel: Treecat companion of Queen Elizabeth III.

Artlett, Andrew: Great-nephew of Ganny Butry; tech specialist; lover of Steph Turner.

Barrett, Kayla: Section Sergeant, Mesan Internal Security Directorate (MISD).

Benton-Ramirez y Chou, Jacques: Third Director at Large of the Planetary Board of Directors of Beowulf.

Bogunov, Caroline: Captain of the slave ship *Prince Sundjata*.

Brandt, Roldão: Captain of the slave ship *Luigi Pirandello*.

Butry, Elfriede Margarete: Also known as "Ganny" or "Ganny El"; captain of the *Hali Sowle*.

Cachat, Victor: Special Officer of the Republic of Haven's Federal Intelligence Service.

Caldwell, Harriet: Mesan security analyst.

Caparelli, Admiral Sir Thomas: First Space Lord, RMN.

Charteris, Lisa: Mesan Alignment scientist; Zachariah McBryde's boss.

Chicherin, Jackson: Vice President of Research and Development for the Mesan Genetic Consultancy.

Chuanli, Triêu: Jurgen Dusek's chief lieutenant.

Conde, Xavier: Solarian League newscaster.

Condor, Cary: Mesan seccy revolutionary.

Damewood, Loren: Commander, Beowulf's Biological Survey Corps (BSC).

Daramy, Vittoria: Solarian League news producer.

Detweiler, Albrecht: Head of the Detweiler family and Chief Executive Officer of the Mesan Alignment.

Drescher, Gillian: Lieutenant General, Mesan Planetary Peaceforce.

Du Havel, W.E.B. ("Web"): Prime Minister of the Kingdom of Torch.

Dusek, Jurgen: Criminal boss of Neue Rostock seccy district.

Emmett, Bachue "the Nose": Criminal boss of Hancock seccy district.

Ferenc, Csilla: Traffic controller, Balcescu Station.

Ferguson, Connor: Lieutenant, Mesan Internal Security Directorate (MISD).

Fraenzl, Kyle: Mesan government public relations officer.

Goosens, Hasrul: Mesan seccy street kid.

Henke, Michelle: Rear Admiral, RMN; Countess Gold Peak.

Howell, Bentley: Commissioner, Mesan Internal Security Directorate (MISD).

Imbesi, Walter: Head of the Imbesi family; unofficially, one of the four people in the quadrumvirate that effectively rules Erewhon.

Irvine, Lajos: Undercover agent for Mesan Alignment.

Jeremy X: Secretary of War of the Kingdom of Torch; formerly head of the Audubon Ballroom, the ex-slave guerrilla force considered by some people to be a terrorist organization.

Juarez, Stefka: Mesan Alignment task force director.

Justice, Sharon: Havenite FIS agent assigned to Erewhon and Torch; Yuri Radamacher's lover.

Kabweza, Ayibongwinkosi: Lt. Colonel, Royal Torch Army.

Lackland, Bryce: Mesa's Director of Culture and Information.

Ludvigsen, Kimmo: Trooper, Mesan Internal Security Directorate (MISD).

MacKane, Teodosio: Colonel, MISD; CO, 4th Regiment.

Marinescu, Janice: Member of Mesan Alignment; senior "wet work" specialist.

Mayhew, Benjamin Bernard Jason: Benjamin IX, Protector of Grayson.

McBryde, Zachariah: Brother of Jack McBryde; scientist for the Mesan Alignment.

McGillicuddy, François: Mesa's Director of Security.

McGuire, Shasta: Mesan seccy gang member.

Montaigne, Catherine: Leading figure in the Liberal Party of Manticore; common-law wife of Anton Zilwicki; longtime and close friend of Web Du Havel and Jeremy X.

Moriarty, Stephanie: Mesan seccy revolutionary.

Nimitz: Honor Harrington's treecat companion; mate of Samantha.

O'Hanrahan, Audrey: Agent for the Mesan Alignment; Solarian League news reporter and analyst.

Palane, Thandi: Commanding officer of the armed forces of the Kingdom of Torch.

Pearson, Brianna: Vice President of Operations (Mesa) for Technodyne Industries; also a member of Mesa's General Board.

Petersen, Anton: Captain, RMN; adviser to Thandi Palane.

Pritchart, Eloise: President of the Republic of Haven.

Radamacher, Yuri: Haven envoy to Erewhon; lover of Sharon Justice.

Rozsak, Luiz: Rear Admiral, Solarian League Navy; Governor Barregos' top military officer.

Saburo X: Former member of Audubon Ballroom; later head of Queen Berry's security force.

Samantha: Hamish Alexander-Harrington's treecat companion; mate of Nimitz.

Schultz, Gavin: Captain, Mesan Internal Security Directorate (MISD).

Selig, Fran: Commissioner, Mesa's Office of Public Safety (OPS).

Simões, Herlander: Mesan Alignment scientist in exile at Manticore.

Somogyi, Zoltan: Balcescu Station's CO.

Snyder, Regan: Mesa's Director of Commerce and Manpower Incorporated's representative on the General Board.

Summers, Grace: Assistant to Mesa's Director of Security McGillicuddy.

Supakrit X: Sergeant, Royal Torch Army.

Sydorenko, Anichka: Former Scrag, now a major in Torch's navy.

Takahashi, Ayako: Freed genetic slave.

Theisman, Admiral Thomas: RHN; Havenite CNO and Secretary of War.

Toussaint, Donald: Formerly Donald X, Audubon Ballroom; now a colonel in Torch's military.

Trajan, Wilhelm: Director, Foreign Intelligence Service, Republic of Haven.

Tretiakovna, Yana: Former Scrag, now one of Palane's "Amazons"; detached to work with Victor Cachat and Anton Zilwicki in the mission to Mesa.

Turner, Steph: Mesan seccy working with Victor Cachat and Anton Zilwicki; lover of Andrew Artlett.

Usher, Kevin: Director, Federal Investigation Agency, Republic of Haven.

Vickers, George: Member of the Mesan Alignment; Assistant Director, Central Security Agency; Lajos Irvine's immediate supervisor.

Ward, Brandon: CEO, General Board of Mesa.

Watanapongse, Jiri: Lieutenant Commander, Solarian League Navy; Rozsak's staff intelligence officer.

Weiss, Gail: Analyst for the Mesan Alignment.

Williams, Karen Steve: Mesan seccy revolutionary.

Winton, Elizabeth Adrienne Samantha Annette: Queen Elizabeth III and Empress Elizabeth I, Queen of the Star Kingdom of Manticore and

Empress of the Star Empire of Manticore.
Adopted by treecat Ariel.

Winton, Ruth: Manticoran princess; close friend
of Berry Zilwicki; assistant director of Torch
intelligence service.

Zhilov, A.: Agent of the Mesan Alignment's
Genetic Advancement and Uplift League (GAUL).

Zilwicki, Anton: Head of Torch intelligence,
although he is still a citizen of the Star
Kingdom of Manticore; formerly an officer in the
Manticoran armed forces; common-law husband
of Catherine Montaigne; father of Helen Zilwicki
and adoptive father of Berry and Lars Zilwicki.

Zilwicki, Berry: Queen of Torch; adopted daughter
of Anton Zilwicki.

Zilwicki, Lars: Brother of Berry.

Snorrason, Hjálmar: Lieutenant Commander,
Solarian League Navy; CO, DD SLNS *Napoleon*.
Also CO DD Division 3029.1.

Spangen, Vegar: Barregos' personal bodyguard;
commander of the governor's security detail.

Stahlin, Jim: Lieutenant Commander, Solarian
League Navy; CO, DD SLNS *Gustavus Adolphus*.
Also CO DD Division 3029.2.

Stensrud, Melanie: Commander, Solarian League
Navy; CO, arsenal ship SLNS *Charade*.

Stravinsky, Pierre: Citizen Commander, People's
Navy in Exile; operations officer, PNES *Leon
Trotsky*.

Szklenski, Ted: Lieutenant Commander, Solarian League Navy; XO, SLNS *Marksman*.

Takano, Haruka: Intelligence officer, BSCS *Ouroboros;* also a member of Arai's commando team and later a member of the Biological Survey Corps team detached to serve as security detail for Queen Berry.

Taub, Andrew (Andy): Cousin of Brice Miller.

Trajan, Osiris: Admiral, Mannerheim System-Defense Force (Mannerheim System-Defense Force); commanding officer, Task Force Four.

Trimm, E.D.: Officer, Mesan System Guard; senior inspector, customs operations.

Underwood, Charles-Henri: Citizen Commander, People's Navy in Exile; XO, PNES *Chao Kung Ming*.

Vergnier, Olivier: Citizen Captain, People's Navy in Exile; CO, PNES *Leon Trotsky*.

Watanapongse, Jiri: Lieutenant Commander, Solarian League Navy; Rozsak's staff intelligence officer.

Winton, Ruth: Manticoran princess; close friend of Berry Zilwicki; assistant director of Torch intelligence service.

Wise, Richard: Barregos' senior civilian spy.

Wix, Richard: Manticoran hyper-physicist assigned to Congo Wormhole survey expedition.

Womack, Robert: Lieutenant, Solarian League Navy; TO, SLNS *Marksman*.

Wu, Richard: Lieutenant, Solarian League Navy—astrogator, SLNS *Marksman*.

Yana: Former Scrag, now one of Palane's "Amazons;" detached to work with Victor Cachat in the mission to Mesa.

Zachary, Josepha: Captain, Royal Manticoran Navy; CO of the survey vessel HMS *Harvest Joy*.

Zilwicki, Anton: Head of Torch intelligence, although he is still a citizen of the Star Kingdom of Manticore; formerly an officer in the Manticoran armed forces; common-law husband of Catherine Montaigne; father of Helen Zilwicki and adoptive father of Berry and Lars Zilwicki.

Zilwicki, Berry: Queen of Torch; adopted daughter of Anton Zilwicki.

Zilwicki, Lars: Brother of Berry.

Mission of Honor
hc • 978-1-4391-3361-3 • $27.00
pb • 978-1-4391-3451-1 • $7.99

The unstoppable juggernaut of the mighty Solarian League is on a collision course with Manticore. But if everything Honor Harrington loves is going down to destruction, it won't be going alone.

A Rising Thunder
hc • 978-1-4516-3806-6 • $26.00
trade pb • 978-1-4516-3871-4 • $15.00
pb • 978-1-4767-3612-9 • $7.99

Shadow of Freedom
hc • 978-1-4516-3869-1 • $25.00
trade pb • 978-1-4767-3628-0 • $15.00
pb • 978-1-4767-8048-1 • $7.99

The survival of Manticore is at stake as Honor must battle not only the powerful Solarian League, but also the secret puppetmasters who plan to pick up all the pieces after galactic civilization is shattered.

HONORVERSE VOLUMES:

Crown of Slaves (with Eric Flint)
pb • 0-7434-9899-2 • $7.99

Torch of Freedom (with Eric Flint)
hc • 1-4391-3305-0 • $26.00
pb • 978-1-4391-3408-5 • $8.99

Cauldron of Ghosts (with Eric Flint)
hc • 978-1-4767-3633-4 • $25.00

Sent on a mission to keep Erewhon from breaking with Manticore, the Star Kingdom's most able agent and the Queen's niece may not even be able to escape with their lives. . .

House of Steel (with Bu9)
hc • 978-1-4516-3875-2 • $25.00
trade pb • 978-1-4516-3893-6 • $15.00
pb • 978-1-4767-3643-3 • $7.99

The Shadow of Saganami
hc • 0-7434-8852-0 • $26.00
pb • 1-4165-0929-1 • $7.99

1633 (with Eric Flint) hc • 0-7434-3542-7 • $26.00
  pb • 0-7434-7155-5 • $7.99
  1634: The Baltic War (with Eric Flint) pb • 1-4165-5588-9 • $7.99
American freedom and justice versus the tyrannies of the 17th century. Set in Flint's *1632* universe.

THE STARFIRE SERIES
WITH STEVE WHITE:

The Stars at War I hc • 0-7434-8841-5 • $25.00
Rewritten *Insurrection* and *In Death Ground* in one massive volume.
The Stars at War II hc • 0-7434-9912-3 • $27.00
The Shiva Option and *Crusade* in one massive volume.

PRINCE ROGER NOVELS
WITH JOHN RINGO:

"This is as good as military sf gets." —*Booklist*

March Upcountry pb • 0-7434-3538-9 • $7.99

March to the Sea pb • 0-7434-3580-X • $7.99

March to the Stars pb • 0-7434-8818-0 • $7.99

We Few pb • 1-4165-2084-8 • $7.99

Empire of Men omni tpb • 978-1-4767-3624-2 • $14.00
March Upcountry and *March to the Sea* in one massive volume.

Throne of Stars omni tpb • 978-1-4767-3666-2 • $14.00
March to the Stars and *We Few* in one massive volume.